THE GRASS MEMORIAL

THE GRASS MEMORIAL

Sarah Harrison

THOMAS DUNNE BOOKS
St. Martin's Press ☆ New York

THOMAS DUNNE BOOKS.
An imprint of St. Martin's Press.

www.stmartins.com

Library of Congress Cataloging-in-Publication Data

Harrison, Sarah.
    The grass memorial / Sarah Harrison.—1st U.S. ed.
        p. cm.
    ISBN 0-312-29086-1
    1. White Horse, Vale of (England)—Fiction. 2. World War, 1939–1945—Veterans—
Fiction. 3. Americans—England—Fiction. 4. Women singers—Fiction. 5. Young men—
Fiction. I. Title.

PR6058.A69426 G73 2002
823'.914—dc21   2002023785

First published in Great Britain by Mackays of Chatham plc, Chatham, Kent

First U.S. Edition: August 2002

10 9 8 7 6 5 4 3 2 1

For Patrick, and the many hearts of a various world

'All flesh is as grass, and the goodliness thereof is as the flower of the field: The grass withereth, the flower fadeth, because the spirit of the Lord bloweth upon it: Surely the people is grass'
—The Book of Isaiah

SLEEPING

Harry 1854

Long before he opened his eyes he believed that it was morning – early morning in England, fragile and fair.

The sun on his bare head, the pungent scent of the grass, and the cross-hatching of its stems under his cheek painted a picture of his surroundings as clear as any that hung on the walls of Bells. He could see, like dawn coming up in the dark of his mind's eye, the soft, booming curves of the hills with their coarse pelt of pale grass, and stamped on their flank the sharper white of the primitive horse, millennia old. He saw the watercolour wastes of sky which in summer seemed to quiver with the song of invisible larks, and the tumbled roofs of the village houses that clustered tenderly around their patronal church. And now he could hear the bells of that and other churches, tumbling and tolling, catching randomly on harmony and dissonance, sometimes together, sometimes in counterpoint like the hooves of trotting horses. The very smell of those horses flooded into his head, warm and branny, with an edge of leather and sweat, a smell that rose poignantly off the past and caused tears to ooze from beneath his lids.

The picture intensified, became close and particular, encompassing himself as he was now, lying prone in the four-acre field as the sun climbed, the idle cropping of the horses just reaching him as a rustling and uneven heartbeat through the grass . . .

Past and present fused. With great difficulty, and without lifting his head, he opened his eyes.

★   ★   ★

What he saw was strange: the same but subtly and disturbingly altered as if the reality had been in his head, and this was some kind of mocking dream. His vision was blurred not by tears so much as a stinging veil of sweat. All other sensations were brutally enhanced. The light, not mellow gold but pallid and glaring, hammered at the side of his head. The stench of the ground and of his own body was rancid. He seemed to be in a pocket of silence, far beyond which a distant, animal clamour was just audible. The sound made his stomach churn. He was damp beneath his heavy clothes, and not just with sweat. He knew his shell of calm was vulnerable, that the calm itself was an illusion, that he should move. His body felt heavy and inert, a dragging burden that would not – perhaps could not – respond. With a huge effort he pulled his left arm beneath him and used it to raise his torso from the ground.

A sickening gush of hot fluid rushed from him. Shocked, he clutched at himself and fell forward once more, thinking to staunch the flow against the ground. The past was returning to him – the recent past, shrieking and buffeting like an angry wind. Inescapably terrible, and real.

With a moan of fear he tilted his head back, grazing his cheek on some small prickly plant as he did so. This was the only pain he felt, though he knew now that there were gaping holes in him through which his life was trickling away, seeping into the foreign ground. At the farthest edge of his vision he could see what he was looking for – the mare's angular, rough-coated brown bulk. She seemed to be lying on her side and turned away from him, it was the top of her rear quarters he could see, and the hintel of the saddle, still miraculously in place and glossy with elbow grease.

'Clemmie . . .' He made hardly a sound. He tried to swallow but his throat was parched. 'Clemmie—'

She was quite motionless. He remembered going down to the four-acre paddock as a boy and finding the horses still asleep, lying on their sides in the long summer grass, and his childish fear that they might be not sleeping, but dead. He saw that she was breathing, but his relief was shortlived. With each exhalation she was wracked by a long shudder.

'Clemmie—' He forced the word out, but still it was scarcely more than a rasping whisper. His agitation caused another squirt of blood and with it the small, threatening stab of returning pain.

The mare did not respond to his voice, but as he strained to look a great blowfly settled on her rump and her hide twitched violently, shaking it off. The fly was gone for only seconds before returning. It became suddenly of overriding importance to him, upon whose face and neck the flies were also settling, to rid Clemmie of their greedy attentions.

He began to inch, on his side, towards her, his left arm clamped to his midriff. He tried to keep each minute movement as smooth as possible, to avoid any further pain or loss of blood, but with his agonisingly slow, slithering progress he could feel the long tear opening him from breastbone to stomach. He told himself that if he could only reach the mare, rest against her and protect her from the flies, he would achieve some sort of peace, and the achievement of it would protect them both from the horror carried on the breath of that far-off shouting.

He reached her and rested, exhausted, his cheek against her withers. His sudden touch startled her and she convulsed, snorting with fear, her legs flailing the air helplessly. Slipping his arm over her neck he said her name again and she quietened, though she still trembled with every breath. Gently, no longer aware of his own pain, he stroked her neck, running his hand along the strong swell of muscle beneath her mane. Her ears moved slightly forward in recognition. He thought that was how he would remember her, neck arched, ears pricked – ready, in her animal innocence, for anything.

Now he could see the marks of what she had been through. The scummy lather of sweat around the girth and pommel and where the reins lay on her neck; the bulging scarlet seam of a sabre slash on her haunch, on which the flies feasted, out of his reach; and the smaller and even more dismaying scars of his own spurs, employed in a feverish excess of panic and bravado, to goad on a mare who had not a mean or timid bone

3

in her body and who had only ever served him with her whole strength and trust.

Worse still was to imagine the damage he could not see. For Clemmie was clearly unable to stand. She was as helpless and vulnerable as a starfish left by the tide, and he could do nothing to protect her. He had not even the strength nor the means to despatch her cleanly himself. She had done all that was asked of her and now could only lie here in this dry valley far from home, waiting, like him, for the end. Life was leaking out of both of them as the sun climbed high in the sky. His eyes closed again in despair.

Feverish now, he saw other pictures. Pictures of Hugo on Piper, furiously alive, riding bareback like a savage through the edge of the trees at Bells, whooping and waving, ducking to avoid branches, the scarcely broken yearling all fiery and sweated-up with excitement, nostrils blooming like two crimson roses, a tell-tale paring of white in the corner of each eye . . . Images of youth in all its reckless glory.

These he saw in vivid colour and movement, as if they were happening before him. But the next picture was still, and in black and white, sombrely framed: Hugo and Rachel on their wedding day, he uncharacteristically solemn, scarcely able to believe his luck, glaring out at the world and defying allcomers to find him wanting as a husband; the bride slender, composed in mind and heart, gazing calmly into her future. And then there was Rachel alone and all in black, clothed in the desolate dignity of young widowhood, her terrible thinness guarding Hugo's precious legacy.

He heard once more the sound of the cart in which he and the men had taken Hugo to church – no working horses that day, they'd lined up along the shafts and pulled the cart themselves. Rachel had walked with them, her gloved hand resting on the side, and Colin Bartlemas leading Piper, unsaddled and with only a head collar, behind them. The colt, unaware of the solemnity of the occasion and spooked by the blundering rattle of the wheels, had skittered and danced, tossing his head wildly up and down, his mane like black flames. To him, and he was sure to Rachel, Piper had

4

been the keeper of Hugo's spirit, the reminder of the life now gone.

Now he was certain he could really hear those wheels, the creak of the weathered wood, lumbering close. Pain and a terrible lassitude weighed him down; he could no longer distinguish between what was here and now, and the pictures in his head. But Clemmie also sensed something, and jerked feebly. He didn't want to see what it was that loomed over them. Friend or foe it could only mean some sort of release. He wanted to pray but could think of no words.

The wheels had halted and he heard footsteps crunching on the dry grass. There was a sharp, alien, chemical smell that cut across his dulled senses. The coolness of a shadow fell on him for a second, he could have sworn he caught the sound of breathing, soft and concentrated. He held his own breath, the mare's trembling had ceased, as if they both knew it was the end.

There were more sounds, a little distance away and unidentifiable, but which he took to be those of preparation. His flesh, along with the slow coursing of his blood, seemed to be sinking into the earth, losing with every second its personal and particular detail, and becoming only matter. The pain was no longer sharp but a muffled drumbeat, in time with his failing heart.

A hiatus. Not even the rustle of grass. The far-off shouting faded, with his consciousness.

The last sound that he heard was the distant pealing of bells, ended by a dull, truncated explosion. Clemmie did not move, for she had already gone.

CHAPTER ONE

———◦◦◦———

'Before the gods that made the gods
Had seen their sunrise pass,
The White Horse of the White Horse Vale
Was cut out of the grass'
  —G.K. Chesterton, 'Ballad of the White Horse'

1997

Spencer, getting dressed, could see the White Horse from his window. What a logo, he thought. Thousands of years old and good as new, unfurled like a banner up the face of the hill, proclaiming not just the Bronze Age fort but the brazen confidence of its occupants. You had to hand it to them.

This morning, Spencer's last in England, was the finest since he'd arrived two weeks ago. Not that he was complaining, he'd had a fondness for the English weather ever since the war. Soft, capricious, teasing – female weather, as against the blustering machismo of the elements back home. The sunshine, even when it came along, had a tremulous quality. And as for the winters, only a nation accustomed to that special brand of grey, icy wetness could have invented the sturdy delights of bread and dripping, bread sauce, crumpets, and that treacle-coloured beer (now less common, he found) the temperature of body fluids in which the hops seemed still to be growing . . . God knows the Brits back then had had little enough to enjoy. It was no wonder he and his like had been greeted as saviours. You could forget the air war

6

over Europe, it was get out the goodies when the Yanks came to call.

With a small grunt of effort he placed his right foot on the edge of a chair to tie his laces. Coming back as an old man on the eve of a new age, he appreciated for the first time just how bad things had been then. The small country hotel he was staying in wasn't materially different in period and design from the Seven Stars in Church Norton, or the Scratching Cat, or the Pipe and Bowl, or any of a score of other pubs he could remember, but it had wised up and got itself three stars in the guide by creating a beefed-up version of a fantasy English inn, the sort which had probably never existed outside Americans' imaginations. He changed feet laboriously, conceding that they'd done a good job. Now, the quaint freestanding tubs were spanking new, with jacuzzi ducts, and the brass mixer faucet delivered water soundlessly at the right temperature and roughly the right pressure not only into the tub itself but from the shower. The double bedstead was oak repro, the mattress posture-sprung, the kingsize duvet a riot of tea roses. Breakfast was fine, dinner was better, but the great British afternoon tea (he sighed fondly as he buttoned his shirt) appeared to have gone by the board. There were phones with voice-mail in the rooms and you could receive faxes and e-mails at reception. Old world, hi-tec: a Britain at peace, and in clover.

He brushed his hair, bending his knees slightly to look in the mirror. Something had been lost, he reflected, but it was almost certainly he, and not the British people, who had lost it. You couldn't go back, you couldn't relive the past, nor retrieve the special cocktail of experiences which had made your pulse race at twenty-one . . . He picked up his room key.

Just the same, there was a teenage waitress down in the dining room he found himself watching. He did so now, after he'd given her his order and was eating the fruit compôte which salved his conscience about bangers and eggs to come. She wasn't from the usual run of waitresses, a student probably. One of those aloof English girls, cool and clever and shy, her shiny mouse-brown hair pulled back into a pony tail, her long thin legs in unseasonal black tights. Not a beauty exactly, but oh, my!

7

Like Rosie, in fact.

And probably not much older than she had been – what, eighteen, nineteen? Hard to tell. Girls these days were more knowing, it seemed to him, but had an extended youth. They went on playing and choosing and scooting around for as long as they wanted, leaving home, going back, living with guys and living alone. There was no pattern.

He finished the fruit and glanced at his folded newspaper, his eye running up and down the same column of print until she came back. When she did return she hesitated, not wanting to disturb his reading by reaching across with the plate. He looked up and smiled, rescuing her.

'Is that my breakfast?'

'Yes.'

'Come on then –' he tapped his place mat '– I can hardly wait.'

Colouring up a little, she put the plate in front of him. She blushed easy, but her whole manner warned him, if he were thinking of such a thing, not to make anything of it. Which he would never have dreamed of doing.

'Thank you. I'm going to miss this.'

'Oh? You're leaving?'

'Later on today.'

'And don't you have nice breakfasts in America?' A tiny glint of irony.

'We have great breakfasts, but when it comes to sausages, you win.'

'Really? I'll take your word for it. I'm a vegetarian.'

'You don't know what you're missing.'

'Oh, I do, that's just the point.'

Definitely not a full-time waitress. He watched as she walked away again. She had that gait characteristic of a certain kind of English girl, a long, loping stride which attempted to deny any hint of sexiness, but which was in consequence as sexy as hell.

As he left the dining room, she said: 'Safe journey.'

In the hallway the receptionist hailed him. 'Mr McColl, e-mail for you.'

'Thanks.'

It was from Hannah.

Just to let you know I can hardly wait to see you day after tomorrow — has it really only been a week? I suddenly got this sick fancy you might not want to come home, all those old memories, all that quaint old charm . . . remember I've got quaint old charms too. Hurry back, honey, love you. XXX Your old lady.

'Can I reply right away?'

'Of course. Office is round the corner.'

His message was brief.

Relax, old lady. Get the pipe and slippers out, I'm on my way. XXX Spence.

Back in his room as he put the last couple of items in his bag and prepared to leave he secretly conceded that Hannah's fancy had not been as sick as all that. There might have been no particular moment when he considered staying, but neither had he especially looked forward to returning as he should have done.

Downstairs, he settled up, ordered a cab for later, left his bags at reception and set out on foot for the White Horse.

For the last few days, the past had become his magnetic north.

It had been easy to fall asleep: it was hell waking up.

This disproved at a stroke Stella's mother's oft-repeated maxim that things would look better in the morning. As a child it had certainly been true. Stella had lost count of the number of agonising anxieties, fears and looming horrors which had resumed their correct proportions over porridge and brown sugar, against the burble of the news on her father's wireless and the chugging of the early-morning water pipes. Night was black and eternal, a featureless abyss in which separate problems had merged to become the single great insuperable problem of Being Oneself (another of her mother's maxims). But back then, good old day made light work of the dark stuff.

Not this time. Jesus wept . . . The back seat of the car, so cosy five hours ago, felt like some kind of mediaeval torture device, a way of chilling, twisting and compressing the human frame till it cried uncle.

She'd left the northern town at eleven last night, still on a roll from the show, her system fizzing with adrenalin. Even the heartache – who was she kidding? The heart–rip, heart–haemorrhage – which had been her constant companion for months was subsumed in the sheer simplicity of the decision: she was going home.

All she had to do was climb into her car, switch on the engine and point south. To get from A to B that was all it took.

They – the management, the producer, even Derek – thought she was off her trolley, that she wouldn't come back. She saw it in their pale, startled faces as they wished her a safe journey. There was always this faint sense that they didn't trust her – not that they thought she'd deliberately deceive them, but that she was a loose cannon, not quite in control. This in spite of twenty years in the business with never a cancelled performance (not counting the great schism) or, she flattered herself, a duff one. But of course they were right without knowing how right they were. Only Stella knew how many small victories went into the delivery of one great song. Her onstage persona was not an escape, but her means of survival.

Anyway, to hell with them. It had been Saturday night, she had thirty-six hours, she needed to be home. She'd driven on auto-pilot with first Missa Luba, then Billie Holliday, finally Brahms, to keep her company. She hadn't had a drink since leaving the stage, her head was clear and the white line stayed single, but just the same she knew her reactions weren't a hundred per cent. Once, on the M6 near Wolverhampton, she came *that* close to ploughing into a juggernaut as it moved into the middle lane in front of her. The driver had signalled with time to spare, she could comfortably have pulled out to accommodate him, but her brain had failed to register the winking light until she heard the hysterical whine of the lorry's horn, and was flooded by the livid glare of its full-on lights in her rear windscreen.

Then the shock-sweat had broken out all over her. For half

an hour after that she'd pushed a hundred, putting time and space between her and the incident, scared that the vengeful (and she was sure misogynistic) juggernaut might pursue her like the one in the Spielberg film.

At around two-thirty a.m. with only a few miles left, she was suddenly poleaxed by exhaustion. She was off the motorway and on the A-road, deserted in the small hours, when her head nodded and for a nanosecond she slept. The car swerved crazily, she was disorientated, it careered back and forth across the road three times before she regained control of it. Had there been anyone else coming, in either direction, she and they would have been killed. No great loss for herself, she was tempted to think, but that was wicked – what about the other people?

Shaken and shamed she'd turned into a lane which crept from the snug fold of the valley round the flank of a hill until suddenly the White Horse had appeared in front of her, huge and strange, a creature of earth and air, leaping towards the heavens like the magic rocking horse of children's fiction. She'd stopped exactly where she was, knowing this place and confident she was alone on this narrow thread of road. It had once been a track up to the fort; people had trudged, and run, and ridden and toiled up this same road for two thousand years. All that lay between their way and hers was a thin skin of tarmac.

She'd switched off the lights and the engine, and got out of the car. She walked a little way up the grassy slope, trusting to instinct until her eyes adjusted to the darkness. Then she stood quite still, breathing in the secret deeps of the hillside, the wild, arrested flight of the White Horse, and the glitter of the endless stars.

For the first time in weeks – months – she felt the jagged corners of her spirit soften and extend like the fronds of a sea anemone in the incoming tide. Minute muscles in her neck and face yielded just a little, releasing some of the tears that she'd so far been unable to shed.

After a few minutes she returned to the car, shuffling and stumbling like a drunk, scarcely able to walk for tiredness. She took her tissues out of the glove compartment and blew her nose, shattering the spell with a loud, prosaic honk. Then she climbed into the back seat, unlaced her boots and curled up, her arms wrapped around her face. She had nothing to cover herself with, because it was summer, and she had brought nothing with her. She was relaxed. She sank into sleep like a child.

But this morning her body at least was grown-up. A bloody Methuselah, thirty-nine years old, with aching joints, cold hands and feet, an empty stomach and eyes itchy with last night's stage make-up. A mouth like a fell-runner's crotch and breath – she tested it warily in her cupped palm – like a car crash. She unwrapped a wrinkled stick of chewing gum, put it in her mouth, and kneeled up to inspect herself in the driving mirror. Her reflection made her flinch. The only time she looked in a mirror was before and after a show when her face, uncompromisingly lit, was just a commodity – a blank canvas on to which she painted Stella Carlyle, entertainer. Be yourself? And what, in God's name, was that? Her raspberry-red hair stood up in wild stooks above her poor, pasty complexion, legacy of two decades of slap. Last night's healing tears had left snail-tracks of dried mascara down her cheeks. She found a fresh tissue, spat on it and scrubbed at her face and eye sockets. Who the fuck that mattered, or cared, was going to see her anyway?

There was a half-full bottle of tepid Evian water rolling around on the floor by the front passenger seat, along with the usual drift of old newspapers, burger cartons, road maps and dead flowers. She got out, retrieved it, took the gum out of her mouth and gulped down the water as she took in her surroundings.

It was ten o'clock, and now that daylight had restored detail and scale to her surroundings the White Horse seemed farther away. Even at this time on a Sunday morning there was a walker up there, moving at a snail's pace uphill, along the horse's back. Looking away, about three miles down the valley to her right, she could see the line of trees of the Mayden watercourse and make out the conical church tower of Fort Mayden. Above and beyond it the hill with its cape of ancient woodland, that protected the old manor house. To her left, the west, the smooth moon-coloured contours of the downs rolled towards Salisbury, forty miles away.

Between where she was now and the main road was a broad, shallow sweep of coarse hill grass, thinly fenced with posts and wire. There were three horses inside the fence, two big alert-looking chaps and a third lying on its side asleep. When she began to walk towards them the two lively ones began to trot and then canter about, arching their necks, kicking, strutting their stuff – horsing around, she supposed. Stella had a lifelong fear of horses, but this artless *braggadocio* was bewitching. At one point they seemed to charge the fence and be about to leap over it, and she took a couple of steps backwards in alarm, but at the last minute they turned and galloped westward along the inside of the fragile wire, tails streaming, necks snaked forward, ears flat, in mock competition.

As they stormed away Stella's eye was drawn back to the third horse which still lay motionless in the grass. Its head was towards her, and it had not moved by so much as a muscle. Knowing nothing about horses she was nonetheless struck by something fixed and unnatural in its position – something about the way the legs were held. She squinted shortsightedly – could the poor thing be dead?

She returned to the Ka and took her glasses off the dashboard. When she looked again, the two show-off horses had come to a halt and were cropping the grass, tails still switching skittishly, some hundreds of yards away at the north-western corner of the field in the lee of the smooth barrow known as Knights Hill. The third horse still lay in that odd, rigid attitude. Stella's heart sank. She'd barely slept, she was knackered and famished, her eyes felt as though they'd been sandblasted and she was scared of horses. But her wretched conscience pricked her. To drive away now, in the cosy expectation of tender hugs and home comforts, not knowing whether the animal was dead or alive . . . was that the action of a decent human being?

Praying with an atheist's bad grace that the fence was not electrified, she bent and very gingerly slipped between the top strands of wire. She took a few steps and paused. The two frisky horses had picked her up on their radar and raised their heads to look at her. One movement in my direction, she told herself, just one, and I'm out of here. But having made their long-distance assessment they began once more peaceably grazing.

Moving very slowly, not wanting to attract their attention again, she advanced. The notion entered her head, unbidden, that Vitelio would have been proud of her.

Last night Robert had embarked on a precipitate white-water ride of furious, focused energy for which he knew he'd pay heavily. He would allow nothing to blur his brutal clarity of purpose. This was a small country, nothing was far away in terms of distance or time, and he had at his command a performance car the full rampaging glory of which he rarely indulged. For once he was going to put his foot to the floor and let her go. He hadn't had a drink, and if he was caught for speeding it hardly mattered. For once, success would be surrender, and it would be cheap at any price.

The arterial roads out of London were virtually empty, dark and hollow as drains. On littered wastes of pavement occasional war parties of teenagers moved from club to club chi-iking, spilling off the pavement, grimacing, gesturing, seething with sex and substances. In the unsmart northern suburbs quiet ranks of semi-timbered respectable homes stood patiently, stoically awaiting the teenagers' return. Further out in provincial laybys, lorries and their drivers slumbered, with coyly curtained cabs. Others thundered on, winking indicator lights confidingly to let him by – no competition at this hour, they were all knights of the road.

It took him only three hours to reach Manchester, twenty minutes to locate the hotel. The night porter was initially the very soul of discreet intransigence, but mellowed under the influence of a fifty-pound note.

The party in question had returned from the theatre, but he couldn't recall Miss (no chance of a Ms here) Carlyle being with them. Then could you, Robert had asked with unusual politeness, possibly, as an enormous favour, call Mr Jackman's room, say it's Mr Vitelio, an old friend of Miss Carlyle's?

The porter pointed out that it was one in the morning. Robert's turn to be intransigent. This was absolutely crucial.

Jackman came on the line, sounding surprisingly alert considering the hour.

'Mr Vitelio? Are you who I think you are?'

Robert thought, How the hell should I know? 'Possibly.'

'Stay there, I'll come down.'

Robert replaced the receiver and addressed the porter. 'He's on his way.'

Unlike most performers seen off stage, Derek Jackman was bigger and taller than Robert had expected. He was tousled, but wore black trousers and a denim open-necked shirt. He held out a hand the size of a teatray.

'How do you do. What can I do for you?'

'I want to contact Stella.'

'Shall we sit down?' Jackman led the way to an enclave of sofas in the corner of the lobby. 'Do you want anything, the porter'll get it?'

'No, thanks.' Robert perched on the edge of the sofa. 'I want to contact Stella.'

'She's gone home.'

'What?' He was rocked back. 'London?'

Jackman shook his head. 'Don't think so. Down south to see her mother, her sister . . . Barmy thing to do after the week we've had, but she wasn't about to listen to us – off she went about – what? – a couple of hours ago.'

'Jesus!' Robert pressed his hands over his eyes, trying to hold himself together.

'Sure you wouldn't like a drink?'

He shook his head. Lowered his hands and placed them, fingers spread, on his knees.

'What a stupid bugger I was not to ring first.'

'It wouldn't have done any good, she made up her mind on the spur of the moment and that was that. Typical Stella.'

'Yes.'

'Tell you what though.' Jackman looked into his face, man

to man. 'You *will* be a stupid bugger if you let her get away this time.'

In any other circumstances Robert would have resented this presumption of understanding, but now he was too unmanned by tiredness to object.

'I know that.'

'Her sister lives in a barn conversion at a house called Bells – near a village called Fort Mayden, not too far from Oxford. There's a White Horse there, if that means anything to you. That's as much as I know.'

'Thanks.'

'So what are you waiting for?' They rose, shook hands. 'Good luck.'

He hit the road again at once, not lingering for so much as a sandwich or a cigarette. He wanted swiftly and seamlessly to rewind the long tape of motorway, to kid his system into believing that the previous three hundred miles had been not a fruitless diversion but a means to an end.

At the first all-night services he came to he stopped for petrol. He also bought two large bars of plain chocolate, one of which he opened and broke into chunks. He spread these out on their foil wrapper on the passenger seat – a drip-feed of artificial energy.

By the time he was passing through the western outskirts of London the everyday world was beginning to wake up. He resented the lightening sky, the first trickle of domestic cars dithering along at a conscientious seventy. It was business as usual with the lorries too – any small-hours camaraderie was a thing of the past, it was every man for himself and the devil take the middle lane. Once he'd passed the city he was going against the prevailing tide of traffic heading for work, so there was at least a grim *schadenfreude* to be enjoyed in watching the poor devils crawl into town.

He remembered Stella mentioning the White Horse, and he knew which one it was. He'd have to get there and then ask. Beyond Oxford, there were roadworks – winding columns of cones, narrow lanes, innumerable contraflows and a bloody diversion. All this, with the chocolate and the sleepless night, initiated a pounding headache over his right eye. Once the open road spun out again in front of him and he was closing on his objective he experienced a rush, though whether for fight or flight he couldn't say. His sole aim had been to get to where she was, and now that he was within a few miles of the place he realised that he had no idea what he intended to do. He had not mentally rehearsed a single word or gesture, was rashly trusting to instinct to see him through.

For barely a second he considered stopping and getting his head together, before telling himself that since the whole enterprise was impulsive, to lay the dead hand of planning on it at this stage might be to render it dead in the water. He was astonished to realise that he was actually afraid – afraid of reflection and hesitation, afraid of weakening – painfully afraid of failure.

There was no problem finding the house, the first farmworker he asked knew exactly where it was. He arrived there at half-past nine, and approached the converted stable block. A heavily pregnant woman in baggy joggers and a sweatshirt bearing the legend 'Ski Colorado' opened the door.

'Good morning!'

'You don't know me—'

'Thank God for that, I thought I might be having a senior moment.'

He detected a familiar note in this remark – he had come to the right place.

'I'm sorry to turn up on your doorstep like this. I'm actually trying to get in touch with Stella Carlyle and someone indicated that she might be here.'

'They did?' A small girl appeared and the woman pressed the child's head absentmindedly against her thigh. 'Well, I'm her devoted sister – Georgina Travis, by the way – so there is always that likelihood, but it's the first I've heard of it.'

His face must have been an open book, for on hers he saw first sympathy, then dawning realisation.

'You're not by any chance Robert Vitelio?'

'I'm afraid so.' He had no idea what effect this information would have. How did he stand with Stella's family? Was he the one that got away? Or a bounder, a bastard, an untouchable?

'Put it there—' she held out her hand '—you are the only man ever to have got under my sister's skin.'

'It's mutual.'

'Look, what am I doing keeping you hanging about on the doorstep? Come in.' She stood aside, but he didn't move. 'My husband's gone to collect the children from school for the day. This is Zoe.'

'Hallo.'

'When we get the baby,' Zoe informed him, 'I'm getting a pony.'

'Not from the same place, I trust.'

The child stared suspiciously at him, but Georgina laughed and said again: 'Come on in, do.'

He shook his head. 'I won't, thanks.'

'Whatever. Who told you she'd be here?'

'Derek Jackman.'

'Well, he's a fairly reliable source. But aren't they in Manchester? I remember her saying what a pig it was that they had to go straight from the Parade up north without a break.'

'They are up there, but Jackman told me she'd driven down here last night.'

'So we're no further forward.' Georgina folded her arms, frowning. 'Have you tried her London number?'

He shook his head. 'Jackman seemed sure she was coming here.'

'Okay . . . So what would you like to do?'

'He mentioned your parents – might she have gone to them?'

'I doubt it, not first anyway. Dad's not well, they're not up to receiving company before ten at the earliest. Do you want me to ring and ask?'

'No, no, don't disturb them. Perhaps if I—' he wracked his brains while she stood there smiling encouragingly '—if I go and stretch my legs, it's a fine morning – and then I could call back a bit later.'

18

'Sure, if that's what you'd like. You know where we are.'

'Thank you.'

'Pleasure. If she turns up I'll tell her you were here, and that you'll come back.'

'Thanks.'

He turned, and as he began walking away, she called after him: 'Stella will be so pleased!'

He started the car and gunned the engine noisily out of the drive, fighting down his feelings: corralling them for when they would be needed. Nonetheless his eyes smarted and the outline of the White Horse shimmered on the other side of the valley.

That's what he'd do, he'd go for a walk. Fresh air and exercise were restoratives he frequently commended to his post-operative patients but rarely employed himself. Get some space around him, and into his head. He took the road back down into the valley and turned westward, away from the village. After about half a mile he came to a green footpath sign pointing south, towards the hill fort. He parked and got out of the car. The path could be seen wriggling through the first field, beyond the gate, but there was no sign of a stile, or of the right of way having been maintained beyond that.

Still, if he was allowed to do it . . .

He was a city animal, used to the heady anonymity of busy streets. Setting off along the bumpy track he felt watched, conspicuous in his black shoes and fashionably baggy suit. As a concession to the countryside he removed his tie and stuffed it in his pocket.

In spite of himself he had to concede it was a glorious morning, with that shiny, new-minted quality to the sunshine which you only got in England where such days were rare. The field he crossed was empty, but there were signs (he circumnavigated them fastidiously) that it had been used for cattle. The low, tangled hedge to his right was laced with dog roses, and heraldic-looking thistles sprouted between the cowpats.

At the far side of the field the path petered out uncertainly –

bolder ramblers than he had obviously passed this way and thought better of it – but he was determined not to be deflected. A walk needed an objective, and he wanted to climb the hill to a point which commanded a view. Allied to this was the barely acknowledged idea that to overlook his surroundings might be to gain a calmer perspective on his problems. In the corner of the field he discovered a place where the hedge had been breached, and he went through, the blackthorn spikes catching at his sleeves, and began trudging up the slope.

He breathed heavily, keeping his eyes on his feet. He wasn't fit, and what with no sleep either, the ascent took it out of him. For the umpteenth time he told himself it was time to get his act together. Practise what he preached: give up the weed and the whisky. Sex could stay. If he was spared – Christ!

Starting to sweat, he took off his jacket and rolled up his shirt sleeves. His sinewy arms looked alarmingly white – townie's arms – but his blunt, short-nailed hands were more like those of a navvy than an eye doctor. Working hands, there wasn't that much difference in it. He might not win any prizes for temperance and clean living but he could, he reminded himself, restore sighted life to other people for them to fuck up as they wished.

As usual this thought invigorated him as he plodded on. His job was always the weight he placed on the other side of the scales, balancing all the shit and shambles. Good work was what he believed he did, in both senses, well done and worthwhile; and handsomely paid which didn't hurt. The thought of losing it was intolerable to him. He permitted himself a look up the hill and was pleased to find he'd made reasonable progress, and that there was only one more field, with a strange tumulus to the right, before he'd be on the open slope of the White Horse.

He stopped. For a split second his whole system seemed to cut out in a micro-death, like a silent sneeze. In the watercolour wash of these surroundings the pink car was as conspicuous as an alien spacecraft. Hot pink, the in-your-face colour of Brighton rock and candy floss and tarty lipstick.

The second after, his system went from pause to fast forward. His heart pattered dangerously and his lungs heaved, gulping in air. A few metres in front of him was a wire fence. He lurched towards it and grabbed one of the posts, leaning both hands on the top of it to steady himself.

It had to be her. But where? At his approach a couple of horses which had been grazing near the barrow began trotting about with heads lifted and tails like flags, prompted by some atavistic herding and defending impulse.

He scanned to the left.

There she was.

He was so attuned to her, he knew her so well. Even from several hundred yards away he could tell the expression on her face by the angle of her head. She was worried, and cross about being worried. Her arms were folded over her thin diaphragm, hands tucked into her armpits. As he watched she pulled off her glasses and with the inside of the same wrist rubbed her face and the top of her head, making her hair stick up even more. From this distance and in these surroundings she looked like a rather radical scarecrow. The beloved scarecrow of his most secret heart.

There was a large object lying at her feet. He thought perhaps she had been carrying something up the hill and been forced to put it down, which would account for the air of dejected frustration – she hated to be beaten.

But now she sank to her knees, as though praying, and as she did so he recognised with astonishment what it was in the grass.

Spencer had reached the top of the White Horse. He wasn't in such bad shape for his age after all – not too puffed and the hip was holding up well.

By the horse's poll he sat down and rested his arms on his knees. Lord, but it was pretty. God's little acre. Or rather man's – all history, artefact and modification, not much left of what the Bronze Age warriors, let alone the Almighty, would have looked out on from this point. He could see some landmarks he recognised – the village of Fort Mayden, the big house on the opposite hill – but the horizon in any direction seemed no more than a few miles away. From the mountain road behind his house in Moose Draw, Wyoming, he could see, on a clear day, for fifty, sixty miles. Still, this place had a magic of its own, and he was susceptible to it. He shortened his focus and looked down at the white stuff near his feet. He'd read about it. It wasn't, as was commonly supposed, a design created by simply removing the turf, but a deep pit filled with chalk rubble. Those Ancient Brits hadn't been scared of hard work – this place, Stonehenge, weird circles, more darn great forts and castles than you could shake a stick at . . . And I'll be . . . There was a cigarette end lying right there on the surface of the chalk. Incensed, he stretched out one leg and scraped it towards him with the toe of his shoe. Then he scrabbled a small hole with the fingers of one hand and buried it, patting the ground tidy and flat on top like a grave.

There was a little pink car parked beside the road about half a mile below where he was sitting, he'd noticed it earlier as he began his climb. Someone – he thought a young man – had got out of it, to take a leak probably. Now he could see whoever it was down in the field beyond the road where the horses were. The figure had gone over to the one that was on the ground asleep and was studying it. Then looked up, casting around. Actually he could see now it was a skinny woman – something in the angle of the head – which would explain the pink car. Her attitude was one of anxiety, concern. She probably knew nothing about horses, he could remember as a kid thinking they looked dead when they lay like that. She could see him up here, could even holler if she wanted help, so he didn't wave. On the other hand it was time he began the descent. He rose laboriously – knees, feet, backside, *eeeasy* does it – and that wiped the silly grin off his face. It wasn't the walking, it was the seizing up got you every time.

The head was already emerging – slick with fluid, webbed with membranes, steaming from the hot secrecy of the womb. Stella watched with a kind of awe this process which all her life she had striven to avoid both as participant and helper. Here was the real meaning of travail. The mare's body surging and convulsing, subject to this ferocious physical imperative, her head stretched in a concentrated agony, eyes staring but unseeing, focused on the birth.

Should she do something to help? Leave well alone? Stay, go, tell someone else? If so, who? Her fear and ignorance were humiliatingly complete.

At that moment the foal's head moved a little further out, and twisted slightly. The movement made Stella think of its flailing legs, still inside the mare. She winced. Was all this normal? Some dim memory of a film seen in childhood suggested that a foal came out feet first, what in humans would be called a breech birth . . . or had the film got it wrong? The mare snorted violently, struggling for breath. Instinct overrode revulsion and with a groan of anxiety Stella knelt down, pushed up her sleeves, and prepared to engage with matters of life and death.

Robert had to pause again. He was too short of breath to call and she seemed too preoccupied to have noticed anyone else. Besides which he reminded himself that he was the last person she would be expecting to see, so she would be unlikely to identify him. In the middle distance another lone walker was making his way down the slope with short, careful steps, following the back of the White Horse. An elderly chap, Robert surmised, chary of his joints. But at least the old bugger had got up there without having a seizure.

Spencer shielded his eyes and took another long look at the woman in the field. She was on her knees by the horse. Something was wrong. He went so far as to cup his hands round his mouth to holler, but thought better of it. There was a guy a bit closer to her than he was who she could ask for help if help were needed. Spencer was old, with quite a way still to walk and a plane to catch. If he reached the road and an offer of help seemed appropriate, he'd make it. Otherwise – when in Rome – he'd mind his own business.

★   ★   ★

Stella knew that she had to overcome her squeamishness and apply brute strength. The other option was to run back – uphill, she reminded herself – to the car, and put the mobile phone to use. But the signal had been weak when she'd tried to ring George en route, and even if she were able to locate a vet through directory enquiries, what was rural protocol *vis à vis* unilaterally summoning help for someone else's horse? She entertained visions of a man in a cap and gaiters carrying a gun and asking what in blue blazes gave her the right to interfere?

She was giddy and nauseous with apprehension as she took hold of the foal's head. But it felt surprisingly solid, a proper horse in miniature and not the slimy unformed thing she'd feared. Also to her surprise it didn't fight her touch, though with her peripheral vision she saw the mare's head lift in consternation before sinking back submissively.

Instinctively Stella knew that her own strength must be used with that of the mare – it was like singing, taking a deep breath and letting your voice ride out on it. What she must not do was to work against nature, she must go with the flow. When the mare next went into a contraction Stella heaved at the foal's head, trying to ease it a little further out, feeling the angle at which the rest of the body lay. On the first occasion nothing happened. On the second there was a slither, a rush of fluid and the folded knees appeared, followed by one leg. Stella experienced a release of pressure in her own body.

I've done it, she thought. Together, we're doing it.

'Well done.'

That voice – so familiar, so longed for, so often imagined that she thought she must have imagined it now.

'Not bad for an amateur.'

'Bastard.' Beloved.

'Here we go. All hands to the pump.'

She hadn't so much as glanced at his face, she hadn't needed to. His hands came down to join hers and, hand over hand, shoulder to shoulder, they worked together.

CHAPTER TWO

'Back to the front,
Back to the old campaign
Out to the bad old fight once more
Off to the war again . . .'
                    —Stella Carlyle, 'Back to the Front'

Stella 1990

Gordon Fellowes was patient, generous, undemanding and infatuated. In other words he was a thoroughly nice man, and Stella was starting to despise him.

For almost a decade Gordon had attended her shows, anywhere south of Birmingham being his catchment area. She'd arrive on the first night and there would be the note, the flowers, the mildly worded invitation to dinner, all perfectly polite and proper, the lace cloth draped over his bulging, burning need to have sex with her.

He was never importunate. She had never, over the eight years of their intermittent association, felt in the least threatened by his attentions. His was a pathetically selfless devotion. When he caressed her it was with hands which, though no longer moist with awe, were cautious and beseeching. She found this gentleness both touching and infuriating, a tension which prevented her from being totally indifferent to his lovemaking, so that she never got round to telling him to push off. On a day-to-day level he was acquiescent to a fault, never raising a murmur of complaint when she refused him, nor failing to

25

rise to the occasion when she was demanding. Timorous as a schoolboy, priapic as a satyr, Gordon's combination of servility and ardour preserved his place in Stella's life – just.

The club he belonged to was far from exclusive, though he had senior-member status. Stella's admirers were legion, and most took her stage persona at its face value. Alone in the spotlight, eyes closed, barefoot and wasted, the fabric of her skirt scrunched in her thin hand, swaying to the beat, keening into the microphone her songs of squandered passion and squalid betrayal, she was every halfway-feeling chap's shot at redemption She was the little bad girl with the big broken heart just waiting for the good guy from Esher to come along and wrap her up safe in his arms. It was the persona that denied the spirited, conscientious working wives of the fans the conjugal attention they deserved after the show, as their husbands lay wide-eyed and spellbound in the dark.

Most of the chaps recovered pretty soon. They never even got as far as the stage door, and after a couple of days they returned to reality and saw once again how attractive and admirable – not to say faithful – were the women they'd married. Those who did continue to carry a torch tried to do so casually. 'Ever see Stella Carlyle live on stage?' they'd ask in the Fish and Ferret over lager and *fajitas* with their colleagues. 'If you get the chance, sell the house for a ticket, she's absolutely – well, I won't spoil it for you, just see for yourself, it's an experience . . .'

A very few were braver or, like Gordon, simply more starstruck. They told themselves that she might be a noted chanteuse but she was only human, and it was a bloody lonely life on the road if the documentaries were to be believed. No woman could possibly take offence at being offered a nice dinner by a respectable bloke who admired and fancied her half to death. The worst that could happen was that she'd turn him down. Nothing ventured, nothing gained.

These bold individuals were astonished and gratified to discover they gained a great deal more than they'd bargained for. They came upon Stella all wired and skittery after the show, libido in overdrive, judgement (though they didn't appreciate this) suspended. She ate their dinner, smoked in their faces, drank prodigiously, fucked their brains out and finally sank into an exhausted deathlike sleep, curled skinny and hot against their still-heaving chests. It was impossible not to believe that they'd made a difference. In fact they were generally so shellshocked by the whole episode that like those sworn to honourable secrecy about encounters with royalty they never even boasted about it. They had been used, chewed up and spat out – and felt privileged. Thenceforth they submitted to her use whenever she was performing within easy reach of where they lived. Each of them knew he wasn't the only one, but knew too that he was special.

Gordon's claim to uniqueness, apart from his persistence, was that he thought no such thing. Humbly and realistically he acknowledged that the only special one was Stella, and that he was just a stupid, bumbling, bedazzled moth. It was one of the few songs she sang that she hadn't written herself – the old Dietrich number 'Falling in Love Again'. Her audience could have wept for pity. They wanted only to save her from the terrible fate of being desired too much, a butterfly bruised but as yet unbroken on the wheel of adulation.

So Gordon, to his credit, knew his place, and Stella kept him in it.

On the occasion in question, though, he was treated more cruelly than he deserved or could possibly have anticipated. He had no way of knowing, on this freezing pre-Christmas night, that he had walked into a viper's nest.

The showdown had been coming for some time. It had stalked the band like a stealthy predator, haunting even their moments of elation. If they celebrated, their celebrations had a feverish edge. When they laughed, their laughter seemed a cover for something else. If they told each other how great they'd been it was as if they were saying goodbye. If there was a confrontation it was brief and savage and swiftly stifled, like the flash of a flicknife. The women were afraid of their own potential to wound, and they were right to be.

The performance that proved to be their last was the third and final one in a converted Victorian settlement off the Kilburn High Road. The Curfew was one of their regular haunts, a venue where there was never any doubt they were playing for a home crowd, the people who'd liked Sorority when they were nothing, and who presided over their current success benignly and with a certain satisfaction in having been on side first. The audience profile had scarcely changed over the ten years of their association. Apart from a decade's worth of marginally altered style and well-managed ageing they were the same civilised, liberal, silk-and-denim people they always had been, mostly couples linked by commitment if not by marriage, with children now at the exam stage. They laughed readily and with a sense of ownership. Sorority was their band.

Stella had always taken the view that this cosiness was to be fought.

'Fuck the warm fuzzies,' was her line. 'We rang their bell because we were different, so that's how we need to be now.'

She insisted on trying new material at the Curfew, and no matter what the pressure of foot-stamping would only do one encore which she ruled should be something off-beat rather than an old favourite. There was generally a certain amount of half-hearted wrangling on the subject before her view prevailed, but it had never before been a serious bone of contention. The audience always responded positively, perhaps flattered by the notion of being used as a sounding-board: they were being accorded the respect they deserved, and they reciprocated.

Sorority were four, of whom Stella was the leader. She it was whose fierce, hungry talent and vision had attracted the others and kept them together through the initial two years of attrition. It was Stella who'd driven the battered camper-van from hall to hall, criss-crossing the country like a gnat in a paper bag, singing, swearing, begging and bullshitting, getting them there somehow and setting them on their feet for the performance. She created for herself a role that was part slave-driver, part den-mother, part mad-eyed general, an over-the-top leader for whom anyone would go over the top. A historic drinker herself, she banned booze before any performance, and had no truck with hangovers. Even genuine illness had to be of disabling severity before she gave it any credence. She herself led from the front. A dose of the 'flu that would have sent strong men whimpering beneath the duvet she set to work for her, giving a performance of 'Bloody but Unbowed' and other torch ballads that those who were there still talked about, and working up a fever-busting sweat that flew in fine arcs over the front row.

In those days she'd quite simply been the band – its instigator and inspiration, its star, its manager, its roadie and its self-belief. On one occasion when their spirits and finances were at an all-time low she'd walked into a supermarket and emerged with a bottle of Jack Daniel's and a sack of corn chips. Sitting in a layby off the A1 half an hour later the others reacted with horrified admiration to the revelation that the goods were stolen.

'What if they catch you?' asked Mimi.

'If they catch me,' said Stella, 'I'm buggered.'

'And so will the rest of us be.'

Stella cast her a sidelong, red-eyed look. 'Better hope I'm not caught then, eh?'

You could never get Stella to apologise for anything. If it was the eating of humble pie, crow or just plain shit you were after, you were dealing with the wrong woman. It was Mimi who had the greatest difficulty with this. She was the oldest member of the band by ten years, a curvy crooner who had hovered in the ranks of the almost-theres for just too long and had opportunistically – somewhat desperately – hitched her waggon to Sorority's uncertain star. While only admitting to forty, Mimi was an old-style trouper, heart of gold and copper-bottomed tonsils, hardworking and philosophical. To her, Sorority represented not so much a new and exciting concept as her best shot at a meal ticket in the shark-infested waters of what she referred to, without irony, as showbiz. She admired Stella's *chutzpah* and energy, but was profoundly wary of her excesses. Mimi had learned singing from her mother and professionalism from her father, a saxophonist with a dance band: in her book you turned up, looked good, went through the dots, did your set and cleared off. No temperament, tears or tantrums and certainly no ego. Talent would out, that was what you believed – what you had to believe. When this hadn't proved to be the case she'd been prepared to throw in her lot with Sorority, but she couldn't quite come to terms with their leaderene's modus operandi.

Faith, on the other hand, lived up to her name. This was due partly to age, partly to temperament. She was in her mid-twenties, not so very much older than the oldest children of Sorority's audience, a product of public school and Cambridge, tall and patrician with a voice like a tenor sax and the confidence to match. After the departure of one of the founder-members to the cast of a long-running musical, Stella had picked Faith up at a post-production party, vamping it up to 'Ain't Misbehavin'' round the piano. It was the sort of apparently flighty but actually calculated gesture at which Stella excelled, guaranteed to make a couple of paragraphs in the diary columns because of Faith's beauty and socio-economic status, and to pull in a fresh audience for the band. Only once did Faith make the mistake of flaunting that status by suggesting that her father, an entrepreneurial baronet, might be persuaded to invest in the band, and had been almost wiped out in the thermo-nuclear blast of Stella's contempt.

'Don't go waggling your silver spoon at me, sweetheart. We'll do this on merit or not at all, okay?'

'Of course, I wasn't implying—'

· 'Glad to hear it.'

From that moment Faith was ensnared. She adored Stella with a passion that was too hot not to cool down. In her she saw the *sine qua non* of credibility, a person smart, abrasive, principled and altogether wicked.

Helen, the fourth member, kept her own counsel, as well she might. Along with a head for figures and a vicarage near Cheltenham she had a perfectly nice husband who occasionally helped out on the technical side. She was a gifted amateur singer who'd obtained an Equity card by sheer hard graft and was not about to rock the boat with open disagreement. It followed as the night the day that Stella did not trust her an inch.

By the time of the ill-fated performance at the Curfew

Sorority also had a manager, Teresa, who had realised a little late in the day that her job was something of a poisoned chalice. She didn't so much manage as mediate – between Stella and other managements, between Stella and the agency, between Stella and her co-performers. She was sensible enough to know that this mediation was a necessary part of the job, but sufficiently experienced to realise that it should not have been the whole of it. A worm of professional discontent was beginning to uncurl in Teresa's bosom and was long overdue to turn.

Stella herself looked on the Curfew performances as a necessary evil. She disliked the slightly smug air of patronage exuded by the audience, the idea that she in some strange way owed them something – when frankly she owed them shit. These smiling punters were just fortunate to have been in the house when Sorority had hit their stride. She'd never pandered to them then and was even less inclined to do so now when the band was an established force on the circuit.

Unfortunately this was the moment that Teresa decided that some concessions were not only desirable but commercially advisable. Over drinks in the Curfew's unlovely local she posited this idea.

'I think we should give them a little more of what they want.'

'They want what we're good at,' Stella replied, ominously reasonable, not meeting her eye.

'Of course, but they'd like to hear some of their favourites.'

'Stuff that, I'm not Max Bygraves.'

'And thank God for it, but you have written songs which have won a place in the public's consciousness, in *your* public's consciousness—'

'Teresa. Gimme a break.'

'No, I mean it. There are a few numbers which people relate to in a big way—'

'Only a few?'

Teresa took a deep breath. 'Many, but a few which they remember and which it flatters them to hear.'

'I don't see why I should be interested in flattering them.'

'Let me put it another—'

'Surely the most flattering thing I can do is to treat them like discriminating adults.'

'And you do,' persisted Teresa, 'you do that. All the time. But let me put it another way—'

'Must you?'

Teresa closed her eyes briefly. 'To reprise a few hugely successful songs is to acknowledge that you're famous, right? It's like you and they have shared memories. It doesn't detract from the new material, it enhances it.'

Stella stirred the ice in her glass with her forefinger. 'Crap. Sorry but it's unmitigated crap.'

This juncture, with the exchange at its most sensitive and potentially explosive, was when Teresa, stung, chose to make her crucial mistake.

'I think you'll find a couple of the others agree with me.'

'Do they really?'

Slowly, almost dreamily, Stella placed the back of her hand against her glass and swept it over the edge of the table. It didn't even break on the carpeted floor but lay in its small puddle of ice and liquor, an empty gesture in every sense, but no less shocking for that.

'Sorry,' said Teresa reflexively, as though she had done it.

'Think nothing of it.'

'I just believe it's something we should consider, that's all.'

'And you've already been considering it with the others.'

'Only in the most general way.'

'Ah.'

Teresa stooped to pick up the glass, shovelling ice cubes with her other hand. 'There's no plot or anything.'

'You're telling me. You've lost it.'

Teresa, again ill-advisedly, treated this as a joke. 'You may be right! Let me get you another?'

Stella shrugged and Teresa took this as an acceptance and went to the bar. When she returned, Stella had left.

Stella walked back to her flat, three miles through the London streets, crossing roads without looking, impervious to blaring horns, shrieking brakes and the imprecations of outraged drivers. It was late November, wet and raw, and she had the wrong shoes on for this sort of undertaking but there was no way she was going to hail a taxi. This was what she'd always told herself would be likely to happen, but now that it was happening her sense of outrage surprised and overwhelmed her.

At home she stepped out of her pathetic sodden pumps, yanked off her clothes, taking a delight in the snap of fastenings and crack of tearing seams, and got under a shower. She didn't wash but stood there with the hot water hammering down on her head. When she stepped out and caught sight of herself in the mirror there was something satisfying about her ugliness: the wet ratstails of thin hair, the exaggerated eye make-up snailing down her cheeks, the skeletal jut of her collarbones. Serves you right, you scrawny witch, she thought, you had it coming.

She'd always known this was the only possible outcome. No one could mind so much, carry so much, make so much of an investment, without eventually being resented. It went with the territory. There had been treachery in the air since the beginning of this tour, but what got to her – what made her blood boil and her spirit writhe – was the mealy-mouthed way in which it had manifested herself. That they should have agreed with Teresa behind her back . . . and what was Teresa doing raising it with them anyway? Sorority was the closest Stella was ever likely to come to having children and now she felt just how much sharper than a serpent's tooth was a child's ingratitude. Had Faith, she wondered, gone over to the other side as well? Of course she had. Turn all that bright hero-worship inside out and you found jealousy, soft and rotten . . .

She scrubbed at her face with a tissue, and applied a towel with the same vigour to her hair. Then she put on her plaid dressing gown and whiskery walking socks, poured herself a glass of bourbon and lay down on her bed to watch the dark descend.

All sweet reason, she asked them which numbers they thought would be appropriate. Startled and cautious, they made their suggestions. She slotted them in through the last days' rehearsals; they watched her warily. She didn't put a foot wrong. Teresa stayed out of the way.

The audience reaction at the first performance was ecstatic – warm, wild, adoring. She could see how mutually gratifying the whole thing was. The others said nothing, but they didn't have to. They thought they'd been proved right, whereas Stella knew she had been.

Right on cue, Gordon was there at the end of the show. She invited him into the cramped green room with the other guests: Helen's husband, Faith's chinless cousin and his fiancée, some gamey old girlfriends of Mimi's, Teresa, the black-t-shirted stagehands, the obligatory group of gay women.

Gordon wore a three-piece suit and a striped shirt. He parted his hair a touch too low so that the long side tended to flop – a characteristic, Stella thought, of upper-middle-class men of his generation.

'Absolutely brilliant,' he said, kissing her on either cheek and pressing freesias into her hand. Their stalks felt thin and stiff like plastic wires. Once, ages ago, she'd said she liked freesias, so that's what he always got her. She wondered if she now said she was mad about Christmas-flowering cactus whether he'd start bringing her those.

'Thank you.' She gave them a peremptory sniff before Teresa took them off her to stick in one of the Curfew's lager glasses.

'You were different tonight,' declared Gordon, colouring up in a way which she had once thought quite sweet, but more frequently these days found irritating.

'Oh? In what way.'

'A little – softer. Bit less combative. You did one or two of the old songs. When I saw you in Watford you didn't do that.'

'No.'

'Was that – some sort of policy decision?'

'I suppose so.' Stella felt Mimi arrive, beaming and glowing at her elbow. 'Gordon, would you like to go?'

'Of course!' He was flustered, mortified, all consternation, painful to behold. 'At once, I do apologise, I thought—'

'No, Gordon.' She laid her hand on his shoulder. 'I mean, shall we go? Us, together.'

'Oh!' So *bouleversé* was he by this suggestion that he went even redder. 'Where would you like to – what would you like to do?'

'We're all going to the Sixth Happiness,' said Faith, sparkling and eager – disgustingly relieved.

Gordon gazed wildly at Stella, no longer able to second-guess her. She looked at no one as she picked up her dilapidated leather coat and headed for the door.

'So we won't be,' she said.

She took Gordon to the smarter of the two French café-bars near her flat. He had his car, but they went by cab: she was in charge.

Over dinner he recovered. He was always better on his own with her. Apparently oblivious now to her uncertain mood he rattled on, accepted her invitation to choose the wine and make suggestions about the menu. Because Stella was a feather in the restaurant's cap Gordon benefited by association. She drank and smoked steadily, watching him, letting him get on with it. Using him.

'I particularly like that "Return to the Front" one,' he said enthusiastically, as he tucked into onion soup. 'I play that in the car all the time.'

Stella, who had no starter, sat with her elbows on the table, her glass resting against her upper lip. It was odd, even after their long, interrupted association, to think of having such an intimate place in this man's life – to think of her voice accompanying him as he went to work, to the dentist, home at the end of the day.

'. . . although of course when you did it tonight there were certain key differences. It was interesting to hear how you varied it in a live performance.'

She made some non-committal sound, agreement, a comment on his perceptiveness, something to keep him going. The wine was slipping easefully through her veins, warming her, getting her head straight.

Gordon finished his soup, dabbed fussily at his mouth. 'So how do you feel the tour's going?'

'Pretty good.'

'I was at Watford and Guildford, as you know. Couldn't make Brighton, which I regretted.'

'Brighton's always fun.'

'All those gay men?' he suggested.

Sometimes Stella took exception to an implied gay-icon status, sometimes not. Tonight she couldn't be bothered. She blew smoke over her shoulder.

'Possibly.'

Gordon leaned forward and chinked his glass against hers. 'You were especially wonderful this evening though.'

'Thanks.'

His brow furrowed. 'Are you all right?'

'I'm fine.'

'Only you're usually so fizzy after the performance. You seem . . . a bit flat.'

'Don't worry,' she said drily, 'I'm fizzing away inside.'

'Good!' He seemed perfectly satisfied with this. 'As long as you're okay. It's easy for a mere paying customer like myself to forget how exhausting a tour must be. What have you still got left?'

'Umm . . .' She paused, stubbing out her cigarette as their *foie de veau* arrived. 'Glasgow, Wolverhampton, Sheffield, Belfast—about another half a dozen.'

'And then what? A well-deserved rest? A holiday?'

'I haven't arranged anything.'

His hands hovered over his knife and fork like those of a conductor readying an orchestra. Stella saw with dismay that his colour had deepened again.

'I wonder if I—' he began. She shook her head at him. 'If I – sorry?'

'No, Gordon.'

'You don't know what I was going to say.'

'I've a fair idea of the ballpark.'

He'd started, so he was going to finish. 'I was about to ask if you'd allow me to take you away for a relaxing weekend somewhere.'

'No.'

'You could choose. Expense no object.'

'Forget it.'

'I can't,' he said, crestfallen. 'Couldn't you – indulge me?'

She shook her head. 'Take your wife.'

It was below the belt, but she considered that she was being cruel to be kind.

'That's not the point,' he mumbled miserably.

'The point is,' she said, 'that I don't want to go away for a weekend with you, but she probably would.'

Wounded, Gordon protested: 'I do take her away . . . of course I do.'

The ludicrousness of his position suddenly struck Stella – that this adoring, adulterous married man, her casual, ever-ready fuck, should be so anxious to present his credentials as a caring and dutiful husband.

The laughter was already blooming in her chest as she said: 'I'm glad to hear that Gordon, I really am—' And then it burst out of her in a series of wheezy, explosive arpeggios that had the other diners glancing her way and smiling timidly as Gordon sat with downcast eyes, on fire with embarrassment.

'Well, what did you want me to say?' he asked when her laughter had subsided and they'd broached a second bottle of wine. 'I don't understand you sometimes, Stella.'

He never understood her, she thought. Thank God. The day Gordon understood her would be the day she packed it in.

She let him pay. When the young waiter, dark of chin and scrubby of hair, came back with the credit-card chit he handed Stella a rose.

'It's an honour. You're brilliant.'

'Thank you. You've seen the show?'

'Not this time, couldn't get in. A year ago.'

'We're at the Curfew in Kilburn for three nights. I'll

leave a ticket on the door for you tomorrow night, if you're free.'

'Don't worry!' He beamed, at ease with her favours. 'I shall be, even if I have to hand my notice in!'

'You're so kind to everyone,' said Gordon as they stepped out into the street. 'Too kind.'

'One ticket doesn't exactly qualify me for canonisation.'

'You know what I mean.'

'It's called PR and God knows I don't do much of it. Shall we walk?'

As she asked she had already begun walking, and he had to take a couple of long, bounding strides to keep up with her, almost stumbling into the path of the oncoming traffic as he took up his position on the outside.

'Sorry! Got to keep my sword arm free.'

She took no notice of either the stumble or the apology but kept moving briskly, quite near the edge of the pavement so that Gordon had to keep putting one foot in the gutter, bobbing up and down like a latterday Long John Silver.

After a few hundred yards they came to the junction of Alma Road, the turn off for Victoria Mansions. She put her hand on his sleeve.

'Hang on.'

'What?'

She didn't reply, but looked up, so that he did the same. The late-evening crowd flowed round them impatiently on the littered pavement, the traffic surged and fretted, and lighted shopfronts, pubs and restaurants pulsed with irritable energy. But above them the rooftops dreamed, forming Disneyesque black silhouettes against the sulphurous urban night sky, with beyond them a pale sprinkle of stars, distanced by light pollution, and the steady wink of a plane on its descent to Heathrow.

'Nice,' said Gordon.

And so is he, thought Stella. More's the pity.

Even had it been his intention, or if Stella would have allowed it, Gordon's regular and infrequent visits left no trace in the flat in

38

Victoria Mansions. His briefcase contained, among other things, his toothbrush and electric shaver, and a spare pair of boxer shorts. In the beginning it had also held a packet of Featherlites but Stella had an aversion to condoms as too calculating.

'But what about safe sex?' Gordon had enquired cautiously.

'We're much too old to worry about that. And the last thing sex should be is safe,' she told him.

On this, as on most things, Gordon deferred to her. He considered her somewhat unwise, but his desire for her far outweighed his inclination to be sensible.

Tonight she instructed him to make himself at home while she had a bath. It was an instruction with which he couldn't possibly comply. He had never felt at home in 21 Victoria Mansions except for those times when he was clasped by Stella's thin legs, being gulped down by her insatiable, energetic body . . .

He put down his briefcase and sought out the Jack Daniel's bottle in the kitchen. He wasn't a spirits man but it was the only kind of booze she kept so he'd adapted. With a glass in his hand he returned to the living room and sat down on the sill of the uncurtained bay window.

You couldn't have described Stella's flat minimalist because its emptiness was not due to design. She had got as far as getting it painted white and having beautiful beechwood floors laid throughout, and then lost interest. So her small store of studenty possessions, enlivened by a few impulse-bought pieces, lay about in the vast mid-nineteenth century space like vagrants in a cathedral. Books stood in staggering uneven piles. Music and magazines lay in scattered drifts. In the Japanese kitchen were two mighty cast-iron saucepans, a milkpan and a microwave; in the bedroom a brass bedstead and a pine chest of drawers with a copy of *Spotlight* replacing one missing ball-foot. The room where Gordon now sat was cavernous, with a twelve-foot ceiling, a fireplace (Stella had filled it with pine cones but ruined the effect with sweet papers) and twin bay windows looking south towards Lord's and the cheery beacon of the Post Office Tower. You couldn't have called it a drawing room, or a living room. The flat was a place to work, with other basic functions permitted space round the edges. The only furniture in here was a sagging sofa with William Morris loose covers, a white oval table surrounded by odd chairs and, in pride of place, a piano. There were dozens of pictures – paintings, photographs, prints, posters and programmes – but only a few of them had found their way on to the walls. This was not a place to sink into, unlike Gordon's own home in Hatfield which had a soft, squashy texture, sound muted by fitted carpets, outlines padded by cushions, walls enlivened by sconces, fitted bookcases and family photographs.

But the difference satisfied him in that it was a metaphor – he could no sooner become part of this than he could own even a part of Stella. He was an outsider, and content to be so. On very rare occasions he had a dream in which Stella suddenly declared herself his, and his alone, ready to live a shared life – and it shook him to the core. Gordon knew his limitations. In the wholly unlikely event that this avenue were to be opened up, he feared he would turn and walk away, though every step were agony.

Stella returned in her Black Watch dressing gown. It was the sort of dressing gown Gordon used to have in prep school, right down to the cord with tassels (there were cords like that on the curtains back home), and he sometimes wondered if part of Stella's ferocious attraction for him was her boyishness – her knuckly hands, the nape of her neck, her narrow hips and the fragile rib cage on which her shallow breasts sat like a couple of fleshy raindrops trembling on a window pane.

'You got a drink.' It was a statement, as she crossed into the kitchen. She came out carrying a tumbler half full of bourbon, no water, no ice. In the middle of the pale pond of polished beechwood she stopped and undid the tie of the dressing gown.

From out of nowhere, against the flow of the evening, she had the urge to cherish him. A sweet tenderness overcame her, a usually hidden part of herself that bloomed in the half-light of the bedroom like the brilliant, long-withheld flower of a desert cactus. She stroked and whispered, licked and kissed with petal-lightness, she moved over and about him with silken fluency, so that he scarcely knew where she was nor which part of her he touched. She tuned him and strung him out until he was all hers to do with as she liked, and then she in turn became all his, lifted and carried by the volcanic overflow of his desire.

Afterwards he was tearful with gratitude.

'God, Stella, that was astonishing . . . you have no idea how much . . . how much . . .'

She pushed back his damp hair from his forehead. 'Yes, I do.'

'I wish I could give you more.'

She hated this kind of exchange, and removed her hand impatiently. 'It's not a trade-off, Gordon.'

'Just as well.'

Yes, she reflected, pulling the quilt up to her armpits and staring at the ceiling, just as well. Because he was about to get the shitty end of the bargain.

Gordon left at one a.m. He never stayed the night, it wasn't part of the deal. He cleaned his teeth, changed his underwear, freshened up and bade goodnight to the comatose Stella before closing the door behind him. But his heart was fabulously light as the lift sank to the ground floor, and it was no surprise to him that a cab with its flag up manifested itself in Alma Road almost immediately.

Once he was back in his own car and on the Finchley Road going north, in the direction of tomorrow's appointment in Luton, he put a Sorority tape on — it was an old one, before the advent of CDs — and listened to Stella as he thought about her.

For the first time he dared allow himself to think that she cared about him. Perhaps, in her prickly combative way, she even loved him. In all the years of their liaison he had asked nothing of her, allowed her to call the tune, been only positive and passionate, never whinged. He had kept and defended his secret with tigerish intensity – his wife knew nothing. And Stella was an unusual person, her love would not take the form of other women's love – would not envelop or enmesh him (though he would willingly have been both enmeshed and enveloped), nor want anything in return. All of that he could cope with. Tonight she had been unimaginably different, they had both been transported. If sex were the conversation of souls, the sweetest and most meaningful of words had been spoken tonight. He felt light, drained, as though the tired old molecules which made up his body had been mysteriously reordered. The drive north was like a flight, his reactions were diamond-sharp, he seemed to have a heightened sensory field through three hundred and sixty degrees. He slipped past other cars but never broke the speed limit, made it through lights without ever crashing a red, threaded between lanes and on to roundabouts with a charmed facility.

Nothing would change, he told himself, except that now she loved him.

'"Back to the front",' she sang, with that courageous throb in her voice that brought her face instantly to mind. '"Back to the old campaign . . . cover the scars, and back to the war again".'

At four a.m. Stella woke up. She often did this when a man had left, when the beautiful stillness of her flat lapped gently around her, all hers once more.

It was odd to think that this had been her last time with Gordon. She searched her heart and mind for some other feeling, a more emotional reaction. But there was none. She wished him only well, but she was about to make a leap into the unknown and to carry even the smallest burden might cause her to drop like a stone.

The second night at the Curfew, the Friday, was if anything even more warmly received. The Friday-nighters were gen- erally a responsive bunch, brains still sufficiently in gear from

42

the working week to pick up on the detail, and hearts lifted by the prospect of the weekend to come, a sensation dulled by domestic reality by the time Saturday night came round. Sorority performed the same programme and were taken to their audience's hearts.

No one would have dreamed of saying 'I told you so' but Helen approached Stella with a level look and thanked her for the concession she had made to honest, old-fashioned sentiment.

'It's scarcely a concession,' Stella pointed out sweetly. 'I write the songs that make the couples cry, remember?'

'Thanks anyway,' said Helen, who was much too sensible to argue the point.

On Saturday Stella took her soon-to-be-eighteen-year-old godson Jamie out to lunch at the Six Bells near Regent's Park. Her relationship with him was one in which she took a keen, though entirely secular, interest.

'I'm looking forward to the party,' she said. 'What do I wear?'

'Just come as you are,' said Jamie.

Stella watched him fondly as he wolfed garlic bread. 'Are you sure?'

'Yeah. Anything goes.'

He was massively built – a natural for the rugby front row at school – and dark, with brown eyes; non-designer stubble, slept-in clothes; a black elephant-hair bracelet on his left wrist, above his watch. Sweet.

'How's the love life?' she asked.

'All right, yeah.'

'Anyone special?'

'I try to spread it around.' He gave her a hot look beneath flue-brush lashes. 'You know, present a moving target. But I met this woman in a club in Manchester . . .'

'Nice?'

'Really nice. But we're taking it easy.'

He began on the lasagne. It was one of the great delights of taking him out to lunch, the steady voraciousness of his appetite, the sense of fuelling a mighty engine. Stella's involvement extended only to raids on the double portion of chips.

'Mind if I smoke?'

He shook his head. 'I'll join you in a mo'. How's yours then?'

'Love life? Non-existent.'

'I always thought famous people could send out for hot and cold running sex whenever they felt like it.'

'Even if that were true it wouldn't constitute a love life, would it?'

He pulled a rueful face. 'I keep forgetting you're a romantic.'

'It's the only way to be.'

'You reckon?'

She tapped ash. 'What's this woman's name then?'

'Ingrid.'

'Is she Scandinavian?'

'No, but she looks it. Tall, blonde – and the rest. Like Ulrika's sexier younger sister.'

'No wonder you like her. And she lives in Manchester?'

'Roehampton.'

'At school?'

'She's a beautician.'

'Right.' Stella nodded, considering this.

Jamie gave her a look tinged with quiet pride. 'Yeah, she's twenty-three.'

'An older woman!' Stella tipped her head back and gave her rasping laugh. 'That's my boy, Jamie baby. Does she know she's a cradle-snatcher?'

He began to laugh too. 'She likes it.'

'And will she be at the party? I want to meet her.'

'It's a tough one. Haven't decided yet.'

'You have your reputation to consider.'

'Sod that. It's her feelings I'm considering. I'm not sure what she'd make of my relations.'

Stella leaned forward, prodding the air with a chip. 'That's quite enough of that.'

'You're not a relation. She's heard of you, by the way.'

'I'm delighted to hear it.'

She realised she'd walked on to his punch as the grin sneaked across his face. 'Her parents went to one of your gigs.'

After lunch Jamie declared a laddish assignation with his flatmate and the latest blockbuster in Leicester Square, and Stella walked to the top of Primrose Hill. The sky was blue but the wind was icy and she swathed her Dr Who scarf several times round her head and across the lower part of her face. At the top of the hill she sat down on a seat, huddled inside her wrappings, the still centre of a weekend web of couples, kids, buggies, rollerbladers, kites and dogs.

She had warned Jamie's parents that her role in their son's life would be that of the Scary Godmother. Her acceptance had carried one condition: that there should be a full complement of appropriately religious godparents so that she was effectively a spare, able to write her own job description. It was a simple one – she'd never pretend to be other than she was, nor ask her godson to be other than he was, and from this accept-ance they would forge a mutually educational and rewarding relationship.

In this spirit of openness, Stella only knew what she thought when she heard what she said. Like her affirmation of being a romantic. No one privy to her behaviour over the last couple of days would have believed this, and yet saying it had made her realise it was true. Romanticism was not an excuse for her conduct, but it was a reason. A fierce desire for the band to accord perfectly with her original vision of it was the cause of her fury over its present shortcomings. And her occasionally cavalier treatment of the men in her life was because she had yet to find the man who could make her pulses race by simply appearing. There were a few – even Gordon, last night, though for all the wrong reasons – with whom she could achieve that state largely by her own efforts, but none as yet who could accelerate the pulse without effort on either side.

She was thirty-two – no age, she knew, at a time when fifty

was being hailed as the new thirty, and thirty-somethings ruled the world with their brilliant careers and their fat incomes and their brittle sexual consumerism – but much of the time she felt old as the hills. And was she perhaps old-fashioned as well? She wanted no truck with a white fence, a cake in the tin, a baby at the breast and one on the way, but she did aspire, passionately, to a free, equal and all-consuming love.

That was all, she told herself wryly. But that wasn't such a bad example to pass on to one's godson, as long as he didn't begin to see her as sad and thwarted, and there was no fear of that at the moment. Quixotic, perhaps, but not sad. She liked the idea of Jamie with his older woman, and approved his attitude that it was her he was protecting and not either himself or his friends and relations. It might not be true, but it showed the right spirit.

After about half an hour the afternoon began to cloud over and she grew cold. But her lunch with Jamie and her analysis of herself made her feel calmer, as she walked back down the hill, than she had done for some days.

Saturday night abounded with the warm fuzzies that Stella so stringently disparaged. The slightly less perceptive audience were more sentimental, they even attempted to join in a couple of choruses. Stella could feel the glow of gratification rising off the other women, they were revelling in it. If one of them had even for a fraction of second encouraged the joining in, she would have walked off the stage, but they knew when they'd achieved a famous victory, and were generous.

They assembled behind the table in the lobby to sell tapes and sign programmes, an activity for which they traditionally remained in their stage clothes and full slap, a farrago of feathers, rhinestones and exposed flesh. Stella scrubbed her face and changed into her antique market mufti – a rag, a bone and a hank of hair among the glitz.

The burbles were soupy, the fans were out in force. 'It sounds soppy,' said one woman, 'but I'm going to say it – you made me cry tonight.'

'Good.'

'That is the idea, I assume,' said the woman's denim-shirted husband, smiling collusively at Stella to show how unsoppy he was, and how he understood the mind of the professional entertainer. The pillock – she could always see the join.

'Pretty much,' she agreed. 'Would you like a dedication on this?'

'Please – Roger and Pat.' The woman tilted her head to watch her write, as if she might get the spelling wrong. 'We've been with you from the beginning.'

'Really?'

'Yes!' said Roger. 'We can honestly say we knew you when you were nobody.'

I was never nobody, sweetheart, she thought, looking over his shoulder at the next person. But you always will be.

Afterwards she felt detached from the celebrations, but if anyone noticed they certainly didn't comment, they were used to her moods. They were however avoiding her eye. They seemed to look at her as they whooped and kissed and chattered and drank, but their great silly smiles slipped over her as though she were invisible, leaving only the faintest snail-trail of pity. Pity! Poor bitches, she thought – save your pity for yourselves.

The Curfew's manager, Rupert, came up to her. She liked him, he reminded her of Jamie, and she slipped her arm wantonly around his waist.

'What can I do for you, young man?'

'Ask not what you can do for me, darling – your friend's outside.'

'Friend? What friend? I don't have any.'

'Your friend Gordon.'

She squinted into Rupert's face. 'You're joking.'

'Anticipating your reaction I kept him in the holding bay till I'd spoken to you.'

'But he was only here on Thursday.'

'I know. What can you have said to encourage him?'

Stella went out into the corridor. Gordon stood some yards away, facing in the opposite direction, briefcase in hand, his other hand in his pocket. If he had change to jingle, he was jingling it. She took a deep breath.

'Gordon?'

'Oh – Stella!' She could tell from his startled expression the sort of thoughts that had been in his head. 'I hope you don't mind – after the last time – I had to see you again.'

'Not a good idea, Gordon.'

The first cut, but the blade was so fine and quick he scarcely noticed it. 'I realise you'll want to be with other people tonight, but perhaps, I don't know . . .'

'No.'

'Very well.' They were still standing six yards apart but now he came up to her, opening his briefcase as he did so like a door-to-door salesman preparing to make a pitch. One of the strapping young female stage hands came bouncing down the corridor, carrying a bottled beer, and ricocheted off him so that he staggered.

'Oops, easy!' said the stage hand. 'Nice one, Stella.'

'Thanks.'

'Here.' Gordon handed Stella an envelope. 'I really only came to give you this.'

She looked at it without taking it. 'What is it?'

'All the things I'm not good at saying.'

'There's no need.'

'Oh, but there is. Last time—'

'Forget it.'

'I can't.' His face was incandescent. 'It was so different. You were so different.'

No, I wasn't, she thought, but I am now.

'You're right, Gordon,' she said. 'Everything's changed. I don't want to see you any more.' The brutal simplicity of the words was so childlike she half-wanted to expound, explain, wrap the whole thing up in a few platitudes, just for the sake of how it sounded and how he would remember it. But she managed not to.

He looked worse than stricken – wiped out. So pale that she feared he might be about to faint.

'I don't believe you.'

48

'I can't help that.'

'What were you doing then?'

It was said without aggression – he hadn't a mean bone in his body – and she understood him perfectly.

'Saying goodbye.'

As the words formed in her mouth she knew they were true, and that he recognised their truth.

'At least,' he said, proffering the note, 'take this.'

'No.'

'To remember me by if nothing else?'

'I shall remember you, Gordon.' Until I forget.

She left him standing there, note in hand, went back into the green room and closed the door behind her. The seethe of smiles and bodies and the babel of euphoria in a blur of cigarette smoke was bizarre – could all this be going on as before when she'd just ripped a man's heart open?

'Poor old Gordon,' said Rupert, wrapping her fingers round a glass. 'Who'd be a stage door johnnie?'

'Piss off, Rupert.'

He laid a sympathetic hand on her shoulder. 'Never under-estimate the recuperative powers of the male ego. He'll be re-jigging the whole episode to his own advantage as we speak.'

She flashed him a hot, vexed look in acknowledgement of the sympathy. 'Maybe.'

'Don't flatter yourself, lady.'

He left her, to be replaced in short order by Teresa.

'Well! A triumph, I think.'

'It was all right.'

'All right?' said Teresa. 'All right? They were orgasmic out there.' She tipped her head quizzically. 'You know, Stella, you are allowed to be pleased.'

'You what?' Stella thrust her head forward, eyes narrowed in disbelief.

'It's okay to be chuffed. Pleased with yourself. You blew them away. You played a blinder.'

'It was nothing to do with me.'

Teresa laughed uproariously. 'Spare me the false modesty, Stella, it doesn't suit you.'

49

'That's right, it doesn't. And neither does associating myself with self-regarding, self-referential, meretricious crap.'

'I beg—'

'Which is why I don't intend to do so for one second longer.'

'I'm afraid—'

'Be afraid,' said Stella, flying now, with the whole room listening. 'Be very afraid, my darling. Because as of now you're on your own.'

They all gaped at her. It was very heaven.

'What do you mean?' asked Teresa.

'I mean I'm going.' She put down her glass and scanned their faces, giving the performance of her life. 'Read my lips. Going.'

'You can't!' said Faith in a high, breathy, girlish voice.

'Watch me.'

'But for heaven's sake, why?' This was Mimi, in the tone of someone who genuinely could not fathom it out. What planet did these women live on?

'Because we no longer see eye to eye,' she said. 'And there are more of you, so I'm getting out.'

Teresa snorted. 'That's so unreasonable.'

Stella opened the door. 'Goodbye, good luck, God rot you.'

'But what are you going to do?'

'I'm not aware that it's any of your business.'

'And us?' Helen came over and squared up to her. 'There are legal and financial implications, what about us?'

'Umm, let's see . . .' Stella smiled, the embodiment of sweet reason. 'You could try fucking yourselves.'

She closed the door with a clean, dry snap, heard the brief lull followed by the hubbub and then the door reopening. But she didn't stop. She didn't even return to her dressing room. Stuff would be returned to her and if it wasn't she'd replace it. More important now to make the exit of a lifetime. Someone was calling her name, someone else said, 'Let her go, she'll get over it,' and a third ran behind her and caught at her arm, but she shook the hand off and kept moving.

When she reached the main door of the Curfew it was pouring with rain. Not a regular autumnal English drizzle but a cloudburst of operatic proportions, coming down in such volume and with such intensity that it exploded back up from the ground in a hissing microstorm. A heavy bead curtain of water rattled down in thick liquid strands from the cornice above the door. The pavement was covered in a sheet of water and the gutter was a black torrent, bearing a spinning flotsam of rubbish. The traffic up on the main drag was scarcely moving, the massed headlights blurred and seemed to melt under the onslaught of the rain. Some cars had simply given up and pulled over.

Stella paused, but only for a second. Hesitation might not be fatal, but neither was it in keeping with her headlong mood. She stepped out into the downpour.

Within seconds she was soaked, her skin numb and her hair directing a secondary rivulet down her neck. It was perfect. She whooped and threw up her arms as she ran with long splashing strides through the maelstrom towards the main road, drunk with abandonment and reckless with freedom.

The Rolls must have been the only car travelling at more than ten miles an hour, and in the bus lane at that. It slewed round violently to avoid her, sending up a leaping fan of spray that slapped down on her a split second later. She saw the driver's furious face, teeth bared, and heard the massive bass heartbeat of music turned up full on the stereo. She didn't move a muscle, but stood there, drenched and vengeful as, with the other traffic patiently circumnavigating them, he got out and slammed the door.

'Madam,' he said in a thin, Scots snarl, approaching until his streaming face was six inches from hers, 'enlighten me. Are you mad, or am I?'

The woman was crazy, he hadn't the slightest doubt of it. On something, or several things, undernourished, poorly dressed, not even a handbag, eyes starting out of her head, apparently laughing in his face as she shouted back at him: 'What sort of question is that?'

'I beg your pardon?'

She put her cold lips to his ear. 'If I was mad, how would I know?'

'Are you all right?' He forced the question through gritted teeth. All around them in the dull roar of the rain was a clamour of conflicting horns like an orchestra tuning up. In reply she lifted her arms high in the air and danced round on the spot, knees going up and down like pistons, feet splashing, a wild female Fagin.

'I've got to move the car!' he bellowed, losing patience.

She yelled something back and before he could stop her had run to the passenger door and let herself in.

'What the hell are you doing?' he asked, turning on the engine and wrenching the wheel round.

She covered her face with her hands – long thin hands on which the bones stood out, but strong-looking. She seemed to be shaking – with laughter? Tears? Rage? Sickness? The car surged ahead, the arcing tyres sending up more water, and she jolted forward like a rag doll.

'Put your bloody seat belt on, woman!'

She still sat there with her face covered so he reached across, steering the car with one hand, and yanked the strap across her, round her arms, everything, and snapped it into the socket. What in God's name, he asked himself, am I doing? I didn't invite her, I don't want her, she's patently barking and she's making a mess on my upholstery.

'Right!'

He drove another hundred yards and turned off the main road at the next reasonable turning, pulling up under a street lamp, keeping the engine and the heater running. The rain had eased a bit. He got out his cigarettes.

'You okay?'

She flopped back now, her head on the neckrest, and to his considerable relief he saw that she wore an expression of almost exalted happiness. This was what those poor sods who tried Joan of Arc must have had to put up with, this infuriating confusion. He offered the cigarettes.

'Want one?'

She felt for the packet, took a cigarette, and placed it between her lips so that it stuck up at a jaunty angle. He lit it and she inhaled deeply and expertly a couple of times before removing it between two fingers, middle and third, that trembled slightly, though whether from cold, emotion, or some drug-related state he couldn't begin to speculate.

He lit his own. 'So where were you going? Where can I drop you off?'

She shrugged, and the shrug turned into a silent, shoulder-shaking laugh. Mad as a snake.

'We were both of us extremely fortunate not to be killed back there,' he pointed out.

He'd deliberately left the remark open-ended. Don't admit fault, don't antagonise, keep things even. So he was surprised when she said in a perfectly strong, normal voice: 'Yes, sorry about that.'

He allowed a beat before conceding carefully: 'Six of one, I dare say.'

She rolled her head and gazed at him, grinning round the cigarette. Alarmingly, considering that she was on the face of it one of the least alluring women he'd ever encountered, he experienced a strong glandular thump in the pit of his stomach. An appeal straight to the vitals.

'Oh, no,' she said, 'I don't think so.'

'Well, allow me to apologise for my part in the incident anyway – for not being the most gentlemanly near-miss you ever had.'

'Fine.' Back in profile. She couldn't have cared less

A long moment passed. The rain was now a gentle patter beyond the warm breath of the car heater.

'You must be frozen,' he commented. 'I ought to take you home.'

'Thanks. And I ought to make it up to you.'

'No need, really.' He laid hold of the handbrake and as he did so felt her hand, cool and damp, over his. When he looked at her it was to meet her eyes again, which flicked back and forth across his face, scanning him.

'Okay, big boy,' she said, in a voice that seemed to stroke his cock. 'Fancy the fuck of a lifetime?'

CHAPTER THREE

*'A wall-eyed stallion – vicious – is held solitary in a paddock
   at the back,
Not tamed nor saddlebroke, a wilderness horse stripped of all
   his mares,
With scars from other horses' hooves and cougar-claw stripes
   from a vicious cat attack,
Crook-footed when he sleeps, he shudders as dreams relive
   each scar'*

—Elizabeth Read, 'The Captive'

Spencer 1933–6

The first of three incidents that shaped Spencer McColl's future life took place on his eleventh birthday, on 25 May 1931, in Moose Draw, Wyoming.

Even though it was spring vacation Mack had given him a day off from the store, so he'd woken up early. It was like something in your head told you when the whole twenty-four hours was yours to do as you liked with, and that something roused you so you wouldn't go missing any of it.

Spencer was no momma's boy, but one of the best things about the early start and the lack of chores was the company of his mother, Caroline. Mack called her 'Cairlahn', but she had never lost her English accent and Spencer copied her pronunciation, giving each syllable its full, round value like three chimes of a bell.

There were a lot of English people in the area, mostly rich

or aristocratic or both, occupying the big spreads and choice fancy houses around Moose Draw. Caroline said they were mainly just money, and was at pains to point out that she herself came from a 'very ordinary' family (as if that were far more honourable) from a small town north of somewhere called Oxford. In spite of this Spencer liked to think that in some unspecified way his mother was set apart from the lump of Moose Draw society. She certainly looked and spoke as though she should be: not high and mighty and stuck up, but just the opposite – always polite and elegant and soft-spoken and more fastidious in her person and dress than any storekeeper's wife had a right to be. Spencer once heard a customer refer to her as a 'gracious lady' and he considered this a very apt description. An illustration in the children's Bible at school depicted the Virgin Mary, pale-skinned and draped in pastel blue, listening with grave attention to the words of the Angel Gabriel and looking the spit of Caroline when serving a difficult customer. Mary was also described in various readings as 'spotless' which all seemed to fit.

Mack was Caroline's second husband. Though Spencer had been brought up to call him by his name out of deference to the dead, the word might as well have been 'Pa' or 'Dad' because that's what it meant for both of them. Mack was tall and sinewy with a melancholy Buster Keatonish face. From the moment he was able to receive such impressions Spencer intuited that Mack adored Caroline in a way that none of his friends' fathers adored their wives. It was as if the taciturn, hardworking Mack, having inherited this precious legacy from another man, couldn't believe his luck and was quite stunned by his good fortune and the responsibilities that came with it. Sometimes Spencer caught Mack watching his mother in a manner so painfully raw and unguarded it felt shameful to have noticed at all, like catching a grown man crying.

As for his real father, Jack Royle, the man who'd plucked the English rose and transplanted her to cowboy country, Spencer knew next to nothing about him. He'd been told of his existence very early on, and shown a photograph which his mother kept beneath an agglomeration of old keys and broken pencils in a tin with a king on the lid. If the photograph was to be believed Jack had been high, wide and handsome, with wavy dark hair, a piratical moustache, and an air of swaggering confidence. All that Caroline would say about him was that he died in a tragic accident, 'in the midst of life' as she put it.

From all this Spencer had assembled a picture of a dashing adventurer, and a great love story cut down at its fullest flowering. At school he was the only kid with a step-parent, let alone who called that step-parent by his Christian name, and Spencer was in the habit of taking one or two innocent liberties with his family history. He didn't think of it as telling lies – since he didn't know the truth that would have been impossible. But he did extemporise imaginatively on the facts. In assorted versions the deceased Jack had been an English earl, a rodeo rider, a racing car driver and a war hero, sometimes a combination of any two. Once the junior teacher, Mrs Horowitz, had come upon him in full flow in a corner of the schoolyard and put a brisk stop to his monologue.

'Now, Spencer, that'll do, no one wants to hear all that.'

'Oh, but, ma'am, we do!' chorused Spencer's audience, both from genuine interest and a well-developed sense of where the more immediate drama might lie. 'Please, ma'am!'

Mrs Horowitz was young and pretty, but a disciplinarian nonetheless. When she held up her hands for silence she got it. 'You want to be running around,' she declared in the face of the evidence, 'not sitting listening to stories. That's for class,' she added, with a flash of inspiration.

'But, ma'am, it isn't a story,' protested Judy Phelan. 'It's about Spencer's folks.'

'I dare say, now off you go.' Mrs Horowitz placed one firm hand on Judy's back, and made a shepherding gesture with the other. 'And, Spencer, will you come with me, please?'

He followed the teacher into the wooden schoolhouse. The soft pad of their footsteps on the packed earth took on the more official slap and tap of indoors. She closed the door behind them, folded her arms and looked down at him reprovingly.

'Now, Spencer, what *was* all that about?'

'Like Judy said, ma'am. About my folks.'

'That is certainly what Judy said, but I'm asking you.'

'About my folks . . .' His voice faded uncertainly.

Mrs Horowitz raised her eyebrows. 'I dare say, but we both know it wasn't true.'

'Do we, ma'am?'

He meant this literally, did she know something he didn't? He was baffled, but Mrs Horowitz was quick to pounce.

'Don't get fresh now, Spencer.'

'I wasn't. Sorry, ma'am.'

Mrs Horowitz sighed. She was expecting a child of her own in six months' time and was full of warm hormonal turmoil and good intentions. Spencer was a bright, sensitive boy and she wanted to do the right thing.

She bent over and looked kindly into his face, which was pink. 'It's okay, Spencer, I'm not mad at you. But try and keep that vivid imagination—' here she tapped the side of his head with her finger '—for when you write in class.'

Spencer sensed imminent escape. 'I will, ma'am.'

'Very well. Your mother would be sad if she could hear you making things up about her, and I know you don't want that.'

'No, ma'am.'

'Good!' She opened the door. 'Now go find your friends, bell in five minutes.'

He needed no second bidding, and the exchange ceased to trouble him the instant it finished. Adults inhabited a different world, they had a different way of looking at things and one made allowances for that. Since he was by no means sure for what he had been reprimanded – he spoke only good of his mother and father after all, and his version was as likely to be true as anyone else's – he didn't stop telling the stories. But he made sure Mrs Horowitz didn't find out. He liked school and didn't want to rock the boat.

Spencer's boyhood was safe, stable and grounded. Its day-to-day texture was made up of the small details and events, the worries and understandings and standoffs which were the stuff

58

of most childhoods and which children assume will never change.

As a boy, no matter how much Mrs Horowitz ran the end of her pencil round the stateline on the map, Spencer thought of living 'in Wyoming' as one might of living 'in comfort' or 'in ignorance' or more like 'in seventh heaven' – it was not so much a state as a state of mind. This notion was underlined by his mother's habit of customising British folksongs to fit. One was: 'Wyoming, Wyoming, Wyoming's been my ru-i-in . . .' and another, 'Roaming in Wyoming with my lassie by my side'. No, Wyoming was a condition for which there was no cure.

Like all good things he didn't appreciate it till he was out of it. Till then it was just home. Parted from it, his head was full of its streaming heights and spaces, his heart ached for its gigantic and uncompromising beauty which made you and your family and your little town and tiny house feel like a fly on the hide of a grizzly.

Even Moose Draw, flanked as it was by soaring peaks, was six thousand feet up. In summer let alone winter your breath smoked before dawn. And summer was short, but gorgeous, heady with scent, the thick grasses topped with a waving surf of seedheads and aromatic with sagebrush and lavender, bright with indian paintbrush and huge flathead daisies, more wildflowers than even Caroline could identify. In spring and in summer the lower slopes were hung with trembling silver-green curtains of aspen and larch, changeable as water. In winter they gave way to the opaque stands of lodgepole, fir and pine. Everywhere huge boulders like the corners of giant skeletons burst through the ground, scabbed with lichen red, yellow and black.

Winter was bitterly hard, brutally cold, by turns dazzling with ice and opaque with driving snow, always seeming interminable. At the end of each winter everyone always said it was the longest they could remember, but only because they chose not to remember the last.

Whatever, Spencer McColl was brought up in Wyoming and it could never be got out of him.

★   ★   ★

As a sideline to McColl's Mercantile Mack ran a highly informal machinery repair business. No job too big or too small. At any given time the earth lot at the side of the store would accommodate, as well as crates of goods beneath tarpaulins and on wooden pallets, and Mack's beat-up Dodge, a collection of jobs in progress ranging from tractors to lawn mowers, and there was generally a sewing machine or some such in the kitchen as well. Mack could fix things, and he fixed them well and cheaply, but it was best not to be in a hurry. Like the farm machines, he was strong and sound but slow-moving. It was plain that Mack was a good man in every sense, but Spencer cherished the notion of his birth father as a far more exotic bird, someone of wide horizons and boundless possibilities urgently embraced – a fantasy which Caroline's reserve on the subject did nothing to dispel.

On the birthday in question Spencer hung around the kitchen, watching his mother wash the dishes. She did this as as she did everything, with a swift precision, her pretty hands with their slightly upturned fingertips darting like a couple of birds over their task. She glanced over her shoulder, smiled, and tweaked a checked cloth off the wooden rail, tossing it gently to him so that it landed on his head.

'There you are, birthday boy – if you like it so much you can join in.'

He pulled the cloth off his head with a sheepish grin and began drying. His mother started to sing. Not to herself, but openly, in her thin, true voice that reminded him of spring water. An English song: '"Early one morning, just as the sun was rising, I heard a maiden sing in the valley below . . ."'

It was Spencer's cue to join in, and he did so. His voice was just on the cusp, it gave a yodelling quality to his singing which would have embarrassed him in any other context, but here and now not at all. They were like a flute and a bagpipe together.

'" . . . how could you use a poor maiden so?"'

By the time they'd done two verses and choruses the washing up was finished. It was eight o'clock and the store was already open. They could hear Mack talking to a customer, and that reminded them that they too must have been heard, and they giggled together. No matter how busy the store was, every transaction was accompanied by measured conversation. In a town where a regular customer could live a hundred miles away these exchanges reaffirmed and informed, and were as much part of the currency as the cash changing hands.

Caroline dried her hands. 'So what are you going to do today?'

'I dunno.' He said it not dismissively, but with a sense of many choices.

'Fishing?' She smiled. She and Mack had given him a new rod, a proper one.

'I will do soon,' he promised. He was a little nervous of the rod.

'Don't worry, we shan't be offended. It's there for you to use when you feel like it. When you're in the mood.'

'Thanks, Mom. It's great.'

'We're glad you like it. Anyway, your time's your own, isn't that nice?'

It was nice, but he still didn't rush. This was a strange time of year in Moose Draw: like his voice, betwixt and between. Oftentimes they got their worst weather now, with heavy snowfalls, and this morning though sun glinted off Phelan's trailer in the side lot there was plenty of white stuff on the shoulder of the mountains six miles away. The little streams were gurgling and swollen but shards and crusts of ice clung to the ragged banks. In the day it could be seventy degrees, but Caroline kept the range and the fires lit. She told Spencer that in England the spring was earlier, but then the winters weren't so cold nor the summers so hot. There were even flowers that sprouted right through the snow. Sometimes Spencer thought he detected something wistful in her look or voice when she said these things, but she always concluded with: 'But this is a great country,' or something like it.

At a quarter after eight Caroline went through into the store to help Mack and Spencer put on his jacket and went out to the shed to fetch his bike. They'd understand about the rod – he'd go another time with Joel and the others, or Mack would take him on a Sunday – but for now he wanted to get up the canyon to his lookout place and dream a few dreams.

He set off down Main Street at a leisurely pace, savouring his freedom. Past Mad Molly's bar with its 'Molly welcomes hunters' sign in the window; past the gas station with its single pump where Aubrey Rankin, the proprietor's father, sat in the window watching out for customers; past the saddlery and farrier's; round the corner by the doctor's house, the drugstore and the funeral parlour, conveniently grouped together; a discreet distance to the church, whose clockwork bell chimed the half hour with a snatch of '*Frère Jacques*' as he pedalled past.

Then he was on the open road, humming along on the new tarmacadam. He speeded up, making the most of it until the good surface ran out. On either side were a scattering of small farmhouses with their attendant clutter of sheds and trailers and animals – most had a dog or two, on guard but too well trained to bark or run into the road. He passed the 'Moose Draw, Population 623' sign: it had a friendly moose outlined above the words, but from this direction it was just a weird wooden shape, the antlers like a big bow perched on top.

The road began gradually to climb – gently at first but enough to make Spencer find another rhythm – and as it did so the character of the land on either side rose with it. You couldn't see any of the really big properties – the Firth place, or the Buttroses', or Kenwright the Coal King's palace with its fancy tower – they were still miles away, and protected from public view by majestic drives as long as highways, and processions of great gates. Spencer only knew they were there because Mack had pointed them out to him when they were driving down the mountain road, each one like a private kingdom. But here and there you could make out a flash of smart white fencing in the distance that marked the perimeter of some fancy spread or other.

And it was where the horses began. Spencer himself had never been on a horse, but this was horse country and they were as much a part of the landscape as the longhorn cows, the cottonwoods and the prairie dogs. And these were some horses – pampered beauties, bred to make money and for the kind of riding that the residents of Moose Draw never saw, and could scarcely imagine: polo, racing, drag hunting. Caroline had told Spencer that many of these horses were thoroughbreds from England or Ireland, or their descendants, and changed hands for more money than the Mercantile made in a year. Spencer slowed down slightly to admire a bunch that were close enough to see. They treated his interest with the disdain it deserved – only one looked up, briefly, and then continued with its unhurried grazing, a process by which they idled across their thousands of acres of lush grass like expensive yachts on the open sea.

Another mile and he turned off down the dirt road for Bucks Creek Canyon. He was sweating but this was the good part now, a bone-shaking couple of miles through ruts and potholes and across two shallow streams to reach his objective.

By comparison with the great clefts and gulleys that thrust fingers of darkness into the base of the Gannon mountain range, Bucks Creek was a tame, baby canyon hardly worthy of the name, but it was a natural playground for the kids of the area and the mouth of the canyon was the site of a dude ranch, the eponymous Buck's, of unparalleled size and splendour. Spencer had been there with Mack to make deliveries, and considered that everything about it – the gate, the sign, the fencing, the thirty cabins 'with every modern convenience', the outbuildings converted into rooms for dining and dancing and the large white two-storey house from which Buck Jameson ran the operation – was the height of glamour. Caroline had pointed out with a hint of coolness that he must remember that Buck's was a sort of toy ranch, a pretend place for rich people to come and play at being cowboys, and that therefore it wasn't to be taken too seriously – though of course McColl's Mercantile was glad to have the business. Business notwithstanding, Mack was even less approving, hinting darkly at play which extended beyond what was decent and respectable. Spencer sensed another adult undertow which he couldn't begin to understand.

The bridlepath to the canyon had a right of way across the corner of Buck's land in back of the cabins. There wasn't much to see at this time of the year, the season hadn't started properly and there were no guests except presumably for the famous but hard-drinking writer who overwintered here every year: Spencer had never seen this mysterious figure, and there was no sign of him now, but a couple of hired hands were fixing guttering and they gave Spencer a nod as he bumped past.

On the far side of Buck's ground he got off his bike, pushed through the small gate at the side of the five-bar and propped the bike on the fence. As soon as he began to walk he heard a solitary deep 'woof' of greeting and waited for Tallulah to catch up to him.

'Hi, Lula, good girl, come on then!'

Their mutual greeting was ecstatic. Tallulah was a black labrador who lived up at the house and although Spencer knew she was free with her favours and welcomed every hiker with the same exuberance it was still good to receive this warm, buffeting, slobbering embrace and to see her running ahead, tail waving, his dog for the next few hours. Mack had a collie called Kite, a wall-eyed one-man bitch who guarded the side lot and rode around in the back of the Dodge, but she wasn't what you'd call fun. Tallulah was the indulged pet not just of the Jameson house but of the ranch guests and all the hikers who came this way. Tallulah's role in life was to enjoy herself and (though she didn't know it) to help other people do the same. From her slippery black nose to the tip of her springy tail she was a canine good-time girl.

She trotted along some fifteen yards ahead of Spencer, turning now and then to check on his progress. At this point the track was still broad, and the river burbling alongside at a steady pace, but after a while the path began to climb and the river gulch to narrow and deepen, squeezing the water between its walls. Its fluctuating rushing sound was what Spencer liked, it cut him off from everything else, he became a silent boy with a silent dog, in a separate world.

That was the second stage. After that you reached a kind of natural platform overlooking the creek, the precipitous forested slope on the far side, and the no less steep but more welcoming prospect further up where the path parted company with the creek to cut across a broad meadow scattered with smooth, bedded-down boulders.

Tallulah waited on the outlook, standing with her forepaws on the rocky outcrop like a heroic dog in a movie. She didn't fool Spencer. The minute he caught up and sat down by her she stopped being heroic and began nudging and jostling – this was where hikers stopped for a bite. All Spencer had in his coat pocket was the remains of a packet of hard gums, but he shared them with the dog, who swallowed them whole.

Five minutes later he got up and trudged on. You sometimes came across other kids up here, and ranch guests and hunters in their due season, but he was glad it was deserted today. He began to sing, somehat disjointedly because of his heavy breathing, another of his mother's English songs: '"The water is wide, I cannot get o'er, And neither have I wings to fly ..."' The song made him think of a vast expanse like the Mississippi, which he'd learned about, or the Atlantic Ocean, but Caroline had said it was about a regular English river, scarcely more than a stream or a little lake, and that it was really more about the difficulties of loving someone you couldn't reach. He believed her, though he didn't quite get it.

Up on the meadow he continued to climb towards his special place, saving it up, not looking back till he got there, while Tallulah described a series of elliptical circles across the path in front of him.

He stopped when he reached the stone beneath the lone pine. He'd first come across it one hot afternoon when he'd flopped down in the shade of the only tree on this high meadow. Otherwise he might always have missed it, for it wasn't conspicuous, just a slab of rock, twelve inches high, smooth on either side, its top edge left rough and unworked, bedded in the ground. But the writing on it was engraved clear and true, the work of a craftsman: 'To Lottie, 1900–1921, who loved this place best'. He'd sprung up in alarm, spooked at the idea he'd been lying on a grave. But when he'd mentioned it to his parents Caroline told him that it was only a memorial, a stone to remember someone by, and that there were lots of them around Buck's because of all those rich people who came to escape from the city.

'So they didn't die there?' he asked.

Mack shook his head. 'No, but they sure would have liked to have done.'

Spencer couldn't imagine liking to die anywhere, let alone at the age of twenty-one, but it was a relief to know that Lottie's bones weren't lying beneath the turf on the high meadow. Since then he'd formed a kind of friendship with the stone, and made a point of going to look at it when he passed. After all, if Lottie wanted to be remembered it was right that somebody should.

It was while he was standing by the stone, reflecting on Lottie and chewing a hard gum, that Tallulah's ears went up and she stood very still, indicating that they weren't alone.

'What's up, girl?'

It was a riderless chestnut horse, standing about twenty yards to his left, clearly as surprised as they were, and in the same attitude as Tallulah – motionless but alert, ready for flight. Spencer could feel the thread of nervous tension between the two animals. The horse snorted and Tallulah sat, with a small whine, shifting her front feet.

'Hey . . .' Spencer turned slowly. 'Where did you come from?'

The horse nodded its head, kind of mock fierce, and its fancy bit rattled. The rein was slewed way over its neck, threatening to catch its leg if it moved suddenly. Also, there was the question of the rider. Spencer's free morning was suddenly clouded by a whole pile of scary decisions.

The first thing would seem to be to catch the horse. Though Spencer had no direct experience with horses he was used to seeing them around, and the way other people handled them. This wasn't a big horse like the thoroughbreds he saw from the road, but it was pretty, with a long pointy mane like a shawl, and a tail that almost brushed the ground.

He took a single careful step and it was like trying to catch a grasshopper – the horse shied as if stung, Tallulah jumped up and barked, the horse skittered a few yards further away and stood with its back to them, blowing nervously.

Without taking another step Spencer turned his head and said with a firmness he did not feel: 'Lula – sit! Sit!'

She did so, her haunches just a squeak off the ground. She was trembling all over with wanting to play.

'Sit!' Very gently he raised an admonishing finger and scowled, as Mack did with Kite. 'Stay!'

The haunches lowered a fraction. A long string of saliva hung quivering from her muzzle – she was drooling with excitement.

Spencer began to move forward at less than a snail's pace. The horse's rear off hoof was cocked, so that the horseshoe faced him – not lucky but slightly threatening. Tallulah gave a muted yelp and he growled 'Stay!' without turning round. The horse's ears were like a couple of prairie dogs sticking up, turning this way and that, flicking back and forth like they were watching him.

Not wanting to get too close without warning and startle her – he felt somehow that this was a mare – he said: 'Hey, girl, good girl . . . easy does it.' Though why she would know that he was talking to her and not the dog he couldn't say. The ears went back.

'Steady, girl . . .'

That hoof was still cocked warningly. He'd seen the damage one of those could do. Instinct told him that he should move out to the side, so that she could see him before he reached her. Though that might scare her away – it was a calculated risk.

Still murmuring under his breath he began to edge out to the left. From here he could see the 'B' on her rump, engraved on her hide as neat and clear as the writing on the stone. She didn't turn her head but he could tell she'd seen him because she began that nodding again, tossing her mane as if to say, 'Just you try it!'

But still he was getting closer. She was sweated up, her neck was dark on this side where it wasn't covered by her mane, and there was a dirty grey lather around the girth. She was real spooked – that was when you had to be careful.

His plan was to try and get the rein, about a foot from where it linked up with the bit, so that he had enough to pull on, and if – when – she started she wouldn't get tangled in it. He didn't think beyond that, the objective was to grab a hold.

He kept murmuring and inching forward. He'd managed to get within a couple of yards of her when it all went wrong.

There was a sudden shout, a man's voice from somewhere down in the creek, Tallulah leapt forward, the horse whickered and jumped like a cat, Spencer lunged, tripped, fell – and looked up to see the horse trotting down the hill, tossing her head and picking up her feet in a sassy way that said: Screw you!

'Bad dog!'

It was hardly fair, but Tallulah cringed with guilt and rolled over, averting her head like a sheepish kid. He put his own head in his hands.

'All right.' He patted her to show there was no ill will. It hadn't been her fault – no, it *hadn't* been her fault. He remembered the shout. He wasn't alone.

Scrambling to his feet, he started down the slope in the direction the horse had gone. Tallulah, her mood instantly restored, cantered ahead, tail waving, nose to the ground which was falling away more steeply all the time. They could hear the rushing of the river again now, from deep below the tree line. Spencer was suddenly afraid of what he might find – a man desperately injured? the horse stuck on some awkward and unreachable ledge? – and how he was going to handle it.

He hesitated, and at the same time Tallulah also stopped, her head lifted, sensing or seeing something that he couldn't.

'Lula?' His voice, small and anxious, came back at him off the canyon walls. The dog barked, and the sound was still ringing round when horse and man emerged from the trees.

It was the same horse, and the man was leading it. The animal's whole demeanour, its very physiology, was altered. She was no longer bunched and sweating, ready for flight. Now her head swung comfortably, her walk was weary and relaxed. Even at this distance Spencer could have sworn her eyes were half-closed.

The man on the other hand seemed angry and energetic, stalking up the hill with long, punishing strides. He had some sort of knapsack on his back, and in his free hand he carried a wide-brimmed felt hat – not a stetson, but something more like the hats worn by George Raft and Edward G. Robinson in the movies. He took no notice whatever of Tallulah who fell in behind him in her easy, fickle way for all the world as though this was the guy she'd come with.

Spencer didn't know whether to walk on and pretend he'd been going down there anyway, or to retrace his steps and risk the awkwardness of the man following him. So he remained where he was, and the stranger, drawing level, said: 'You from Buck's?'

He was big and broad-shouldered but his chest was heaving and his face was a bad colour like someone who didn't walk up many hills.

'No – well, kinda,' replied Spencer. 'I just came up from Moose Draw.'

'See Moose Draw and die,' was the man's impenetrable comment. He flapped his hat at Tallulah. 'So she came with you?'

'Yeah, she always does.'

'She whores around. Must've still been in the house when I left this morning.'

'You're from the ranch?' Spencer recalled the 'B'.

'That's right, I'm working there.'

'Oh.' For the life of him Spencer couldn't fit this stranger with the two men fixing the guttering this morning. He said: 'Glad your horse is okay.'

'She's dandy, I nearly wasn't though . . .' The man gave the animal's neck a slap and then turned a penetrating glare on Spencer. 'Where d'you find her?'

'She sort of found us. We were up there—' he pointed '—and when I turned round she'd snuck up on us. I tried to catch her but Lula—'

'That's where I was heading,' said the man, having apparently lost interest in this line of enquiry. He began trudging on and up towards the lone pine. Spencer, in response to a kind of complicity in his remark, walked alongside. The adventure had ceased to be a worry and had gotten interesting. Out of the corner of his eye he inspected his new companion. He was oldish – Mack's sort of age – but even now that he wasn't cross he was surrounded by a forcefield of fierce energy. And the way he spoke was different from local folks, clipped and sharp.

Spencer made conversation, the way Caroline said it was polite to do. 'She throw you?'

The stranger shook his head. 'I wish I could say she did, but nothing so dashing. I just came off.'

'Do you ride a lot?'

'I do not, and now I know why. A wise man once told me that the horse is a wild animal at heart, and many times as heavy as a man, and it'll kill you if it gets the chance. Or if you make a mistake. I did the latter.'

The writer! He was the writer.

'Are you the writer?'

The man gave a sniffing, voiceless laugh. 'Maybe. Which one?'

Spencer coloured. 'I don't remember his name.'

'Then it's bound to be me, isn't it?' They were up under the pine tree now and Spencer waited for further information, but none was forthcoming. To give his own name uninvited seemed too bold, and anyway his companion didn't seem interested.

'Did you see this?' The man asked, indicating Lottie's memorial.

'Yes, sir, I found that a while back. I always come and take a look.'

'You do? Why?'

'I dunno.'

'Sure you do.' The man was looking at the stone, not at Spencer, but he sounded impatient. 'Think about it.'

Spencer thought. 'Well, my mom said the stone was to remember her by—'

'Your mom's seen it?'

'No, but she—'

'Fine, go on.'

'She said it was to remember her by, but it's a long ways out of town and I thought, who's going to remember if they don't see it? So when I'm up this way, I stop by.'

The man's fierce expression hadn't changed. He was still

70

staring at the stone, half in the here and now, half far away. 'You know who she was?'

Spencer shook his head, realised he wouldn't be seen and added: 'No, sir.'

'She was very pretty, very wild, very smart. Much too pretty and smart to die, too wild to live.'

Spencer gazed at the stone, chastened.

'You knew her?'

'I did. She broke my heart . . .' For the first time the man's voice slowed and softened, and then he slapped his leg with his hat and rounded on Spencer with a kind of mad-dog grin. 'So maybe it serves her right!'

Spencer was shocked, and glad that no reply seemed to be required.

'Well, young man!' Another alarming change of gear had taken place. 'Thanks for trying to catch my horse.'

Spencer shrugged. 'Sorry I couldn't do it.'

'You made her run right back to me so it came to the same thing.'

'She didn't give you any trouble?'

'No.' The man fondled the mare's forelock – she seemed tranced, nearly asleep. 'You know why?'

Spencer shook his head.

'Because she's just a big chicken. She wanted to run away and leave me looking like an idiot. But she wanted even more to be caught.'

It was true, Spencer could see that. It was the horse's fear which had made him wary – it had been an unstable substance, liable to do anything. Now she was just a dude ranch ride again – pretty, but not smart and certainly not wild.

'Never wish for freedom,' said the man, putting his hat on his head and his foot in the stirrup. 'You might get it.'

Up in the saddle he looked enormous. 'Good day, friend,' he said, and wheeled the mare away, her head pointing back down the canyon. Tallulah, without hesitating, trotted after him. The man glanced down and Spencer heard him say, 'Faithless hussy,' and assumed he meant the dog, though it was by no means certain.

71

Spencer plodded on up to a big outcrop of flat rocks like a lookout point that you could climb and perch on top of. The glitter had gone from the day, but only because it had been outshone by this odd meeting. From his vantage point he could just make out horse and rider, with the dog at their heels, winding down the last visible bend in the path until the trees swallowed them up.

Everything around Spencer, even here, seemed smaller, paler, flatter. Whatever had been inside the stranger's head was a hundred times more interesting than little old Bucks Creek. The encounter had raised far more questions than it answered and the questions hovered at the top of his mind like great wide-winged birds too mysterious and distant to identify, too thrilling to ignore. Even Tallulah's defection seemed in order. Why would she stay with Spencer McColl when she could choose that powerful and seductive strangeness?

See Moose Draw and die! He was dazzled.

Only hunger drove him back, later in the afternoon. Mack was in the side lot, picking bits out of Phelan's tractor. He said 'Hi there' when Spencer dropped his bike to the ground next to him.

'Hi.'

'Where'd you go?'

'Up Bucks Creek Canyon.'

'Your mother wondered where you got to, but I told her not to go fussing.'

Mack was still working away, his greasy black fingers handling the nuggets of machinery with the delicate dexterity of a surgeon. He never stopped when he talked to you, but that was just his way.

'I met someone.'

'So who was that?'

'I dunno, he didn't say his name.' An instinct concerning Mack prevented Spencer from saying who he thought it was.

'What doing – fishing?'

'His horse threw him.' Here again Spencer, out of deference to the stranger's magical qualities, forbore to tell the whole truth.

'He hurt?'

'No.'

'You able to help?'

'I tried to catch the horse, but she ran off. But she ran to him and he caught her.'

'He was lucky then.'

'I guess so.'

There didn't seem much to add, at least as far as Mack was concerned. He was a person who dealt with the basics, the simple, broad strokes of life, and Spencer's mind was stretched to bursting with wild imaginings and suppositions.

Fortunately the store was quiet and his mother was sitting behind the counter with a book.

'So there you are!' She smiled at him. 'Mack said not to worry.'

'Sorry. The time just kind of went by.'

'That's what happens.' She closed the book to pay attention to him. By that one action she told him what he already knew: that she would understand about his strange meeting. 'Did you have a good time?'

'I think I met that writer – the one who stays at Buck's in the winter?'

'You mean, you think you met him, or you think it was the writer?' She was teasing but she was also a stickler for this sort of thing.

'I did meet him and I think it was him.'

'What made you think that?'

This was a good question and his brow furrowed. 'Well . . . The way he spoke, for one thing. And he was staying at the ranch when there was no one else there . . .'

'How did he speak?' Her tone had changed from one of simple maternal questioning to one of real curiosity, and Spencer felt proud to have been the cause of this.

'Real quick and sharp, not like from round here. And he said crazy things.'

She laughed. 'Like what, for heaven's sake?'

'Like "See Moose Draw and die".' Spencer glowed with pleasure as Caroline laughed some more.

'So he doesn't come to Buck's to research small-town life!'

Warmed by his success Spencer remembered something else. 'I know – he said he worked down there.'

'But he wasn't a ranch-hand.'

'Uh-uh!' He shook his head emphatically, and she didn't ask him to explain why he was so sure.

'What did he look like?' This was easy. 'Real tall with a huge nose, hair going at the front – he looked like a big old buzzard.'

'That's him all right. So what was he up to in the canyon, just mooching around like you?'

'He came off his horse and I found her, and then after he caught her we got talking.'

'You do realise,' said Caroline, 'that you succeeded where a hundred highly paid journalists have failed?'

'How d'you mean?'

'He's very reclusive – he keeps himself to himself. That's why he likes to be at the ranch when no one else is there, so he can write undisturbed. And he doesn't like talking to the press. What else did he say?'

This was Spencer's trump card, he'd been husbanding it because after this there wouldn't be much more to say.

'He said that this girl Lottie – the one with the stone – that she broke his heart.'

'Did he now?' Caroline's eyebrows lifted.

'He said she was . . .' Spencer paused, wanting to get it right ' . . . too pretty to die, too wild to live.'

Now Caroline leaned right over the counter, laughing her head off, and cupped his face in her hand. 'Spencer McColl, you do see life!'

In bed that night, bathed in the afterglow of the day's events and his mother's delight, Spencer reflected that it had been a great birthday. And the effect of his long, solitary hike was that much of it remained to be enjoyed: the fishing rod, the mouth organ (which Mack had been teaching him, but now Spencer had one of his own), almost all of the frosted cake which, after two helpings of fried chicken and mashed potatoes, he hadn't had room for. Tomorrow after he was done helping in the store he'd call for Aaron and Joel – maybe Judy, she was all right – and they could take some of the cake and try out the rod while he told them about meeting the writer.

From downstairs he could hear the radio, one of those comedy and music programmes that they liked to listen to, with the advertising jingles. This one was sponsored by breakfast cereal. There was a group of girls who sang the jingle and it was maddeningly catchy – sun and fun, day and gay, strong and song, all day long . . . When the jingle ended it was voices talking again; the cheery familiarity ebbed away and the strangeness and glamour seeped back into his head.

'*The water is wide, I cannot get o'er, and neither have I wings to fly . . .*'

Something else his mother had told him about that song. As a little girl she'd lived in a tall town house where she wasn't particularly happy. Her parents weren't interested in her and there weren't any other kids to play with. But she told him she had a special friend who lived on the top floor of the house, who she wasn't really supposed to spend time with but she did anyway. And they used to look out of the top-floor window to where there was a wood with a pond, and Caroline's friend used to tell her about her own home in the country . . . Spencer liked that story, and the way it tied in with the sad, wistful quality of the song.

As he floated in the strange third dimension between waking and sleeping he entertained a fleeting fantasy that his father hadn't died at all, but had become a famous yet reclusive writer, haunting the hills around Moose Draw.

It wasn't till three summers later when he was fourteen that he found out the truth, and everything changed.

A lot had changed already. Spencer was at high school, his

voice was deep and his body was different and wayward. He had gotten big and tall for his age. His friend Joel looked like a kid next to him, but he'd rather have been with Joel than with Judy and the other girls who giggled and cut their eyes his way. The truth was he didn't belong anywhere − not with the kids, not with the older guys and the men, certainly not with the girls.

And increasingly these days not in Moose Draw. It was home, but he no longer felt at home in it. He was discontented, which he didn't like, but there was nothing he could do − there were years before he could escape and even then how was it to be managed? He wasn't too smart in school, not a high-flier and a goer-places. He was average, but dreamy. Sometimes he wrote something in class which got read out because it was unusual, but that didn't happen all the time, and anyway he didn't want to stand out. What he wanted most of all, and knew was hopeless, was to recapture the sense of belonging.

Quite often he thought about the famous writer. One of his novels had been taught in class, they'd had to read it chapter by chapter, talk about it, analyse what he meant. The author's picture was on the back of the teacher's copy, so there was no doubt about it. Spencer kept quiet about having met him. In fact he kept quiet altogether. He could not manage any startling insights or neat observations. He just heard the writer's voice and saw his fierce eyes and his mad grin, and knew, well, of course, that's exactly how he *would* write.

The novel told the story of a man who couldn't handle happiness. The teacher referred them to a quotation from an Irish playwright called Wilde: 'For each man kills the thing he loves'. The man in the book didn't exactly kill the thing he loved, he killed the love itself so that he could move on. It managed not to be dull and depressing because it was full of action: the hero − if you could call him that − was an adventurer, always hungry for new experiences and horizons. The most important strand in the book was a romantic love story which made most of the boys squirm and snigger, but Spencer found it thrilling and faintly sinister. Was this about Lottie? The novel (he checked) was first published in 1920, so it was quite possible. But the woman in the story, a married woman

76

whom the hero couldn't have and so continued contrarily to love, wasn't young, wild or pretty. Only smart.

The summer that he turned fourteen time meandered along like an amiable drunk, stumbling now and again, seeming occasionally to stop altogether or bend back on itself, pointless and unfocused. The pleasing balance of school, chores, the store and free time had gone; these things now formed a clunking chain that dragged him unwillingly through the days and weeks. In some ways free time was the worst. It lay there, inert, with boredom buzzing over it like a cloud of midges. And out of the boredom there occasionally grew the terrifyingly pleasurable sensations which made him still more wary of girls.

Spencer's dullness affected Mack and his mother as well. There were no fights, he didn't rebel against them, but they'd have had to be superhuman to remain unaffected by his state of mind. He knew they were no longer comfortable with him – he wasn't even comfortable with himself, so how could they be? He intuited that it was Mack who got rattled and Caroline who stood up for him. There were many occasions when he was aware of Mack buttoning his lip, so there was bound to be some sort of explosion, if only because of the pressure-cooker effect of the summer heat, and the tension, and the Mercantile not doing so well.

He was sitting by the back door at about three o'clock one afternoon, reading a comic – well, looking at the pictures. His mother was behind the counter in the store. Mack was stripping down the minister's wife's bicycle. Kite lay on the ground between them and at right angles, like the hand of a clock, nose on paws, slightly inclined towards Mack. Spencer wanted to move and was thinking of doing so, but he sensed a mood in his stepfather and had a kind of animal sense that it would be better not to attract attention. So like Kite he stayed put and bided his time.

After a while Mack stood up and said, still looking down at the bike, 'You want to give me a hand?'

The answer was no, but such a simple refusal was unthinkable.

'I was going over to Joel's.'

'Looks to me like you were sitting reading the funnies.'

For Mack to venture anything like a joke, let alone a sarcastic one, was sufficiently unusual to warn Spencer that he was on thin ice.

He got up slowly, like someone who was going to do so anyway. 'He had to straighten his room. He reckoned he'd be through by three.'

Spencer hadn't wanted to look at his watch and give himself away, so this was a guess. It was a good one, but not good enough.

'It's half-past three,' said Mack, without looking at his watch either. This was also ominous, it meant he'd been keeping a check on how long Spencer had been sitting there.

'Better go then.'

He turned. The comic was rolled up so tight in his hand it felt like a stick.

'Hey.'

He looked over his shoulder. Mack was standing with his fists on his hips.

'Over here.' He motioned with his head.

'But I gotta go.'

'No, you don't. He'll still be there when you're done helping me with this inner tube.'

'But—'

'Hey!' Another jerk of the head.

Seething, Spencer dropped the comic and trailed over, with as much visible resentment as he dared show.

Mack was a gentle man, getting tough for what he believed were good reasons. The moment Spencer complied he was mollified, but Spencer could have been forgiven for not know-ing this as he was handed the inner tube.

'Go get a pail of water and check for punctures.'

Spencer took the tube and started back towards the house still boiling with the injustice of it. Even so all might have been well had not Kite, who was still lying there like a hairy arrow, growled at him.

It was only a small growl. It might have been something to do with the swinging inner tube, or with the tone of the

78

exchange, or it might even have been because she was getting old and had a bellyache, but whatever the reason growl she did, and that caught Spencer on the raw.

Without thinking he raised the inner tube like a weapon and made a feint at Kite.

'Get out of it, damn' mutt!'

Kite never moved, apart from pulling her lips back in a long red and black snarl, revealing teeth gappy with age but still terrifyingly sharp.

It was Mack who was on to Spencer, gripping his upraised wrist and pulling it down hard, behind his back. Spencer's eyes watered with fear. There was no pain right now, but the tiniest movement would cause it. He was humiliatingly helpless.

Mack's voice, when it came, was completely normal. 'Listen to me, son. Don't you ever – *ever* – do a thing like that. Not to the dog, not to anyone. You understand?'

Spencer nodded.

'I want to hear you.'

'I won't,' muttered Spencer, and was released. Humbled and mortified he was prompted to add: 'And don't call me son.'

Mack had returned to the bicycle, maddeningly unperturbed. 'You are my son.'

'I am not. You're not my father.'

There was the tiniest pause: 'I been a father to you.'

'I'm not your son.'

Mack got on with replacing the chain. 'Maybe. And you look like him. I'm no movie star but you'll do better to take after me.'

'What do you mean?'

'Your father . . .' Mack angled his head, intent on his task ' . . . he was a man used to get his own way with his fists. When I see you act like that—' he jerked his head in Spencer's direction without looking '—I see him.'

Spencer was dumbstruck. These few short sentences were the most mention there had been of Jack Royle in fourteen years and they'd blown everything apart.

'No,' he said. 'No.'

'Right enough. He was a bad apple. Drank, beat your mother—'

'No!'

'—your mother and anyone else he didn't like the look of. Got run down blind drunk in the street, and good riddance.' Mack did look at him now. 'You love your mother?'

Spencer nodded, speechless with shock.

'Don't go being like him. I done you a favour. Now go and check that tyre.'

Spencer went into the house, dropped the tube on the kitchen table and went upstairs to his room. His mother was serving someone and as he passed the shop entrance he felt her look at him, but he didn't stop. He closed the bedroom door and lay down on the bed on his side, his arms crossed over his chest.

So there it was. No bold dashing adventurer, heroic horseman or army officer. Certainly no brilliant, famous writer. Just a violent drunk who hit a woman and who got run over in the street. A man whose tainted blood ran in his own veins and whom he must strive at all times not to resemble.

He didn't cry, but he wished he could have done. The agonising disappointment of it mocked his earlier boredom. For as long as he could remember there had been in the corner of his mind's eye this distant, brilliant light – his father – a reminder that life could be more exciting. And now that was snuffed out. Not only snuffed out but removed altogether and replaced with something dark and shameful.

The door opened a chink. His mother asked: 'Spencer, may I come in?'

'I guess so . . .'

She entered and closed the door after her softly, discreetly, with two hands, showing him how private this was to be. Then she sat on the edge of the bed.

'I've been with Mack. He shouldn't have told you.'

Spencer shrugged.

'He didn't like to see you going to hit Kite. I know you wouldn't have done, but it bothered him to see you do that.

It wasn't for him to tell you those things, but he did it because he thinks the world of you.'

'Sure,' muttered Spencer bitterly.

'He does.' Caroline touched his cheek with the back of her hand like she did when she was checking for fever, and then she stroked his hair and went on: 'Of course he does. Perhaps I should tell you something too.'

He didn't reply, and she withdrew her hand and sat leaning forward with her arms resting on her knees, gazing in the same direction as Spencer, as though Jack were standing on the far side of the room and they were both looking at him.

'He made a bad end, but when we fell in love, in England, he rescued me. He was so handsome and he spoiled me – I'd never been spoiled before. I was never so happy in my life, before or since. I've been more content, safer, calmer – we both owe our whole lives to Mack, though he'd never say so and he doesn't see it that way – but your father and I had joy, can you understand?'

Spencer couldn't really, and so remained silent.

'Joy is another thing altogether,' she continued. 'Your father wasn't wicked, he didn't mean to bring me out here and then treat me badly, but he was disappointed. That doesn't excuse what he did, but it was the reason. When he died I thought I'd never stop crying because it was so sad, the waste, the suffering . . . but I had to get on because you were on the way.'

Picturing the accident, so different from the one he'd always imagined, Spencer found his voice.

'What happened to him?'

'He'd had too much to drink, he fell over in the street. There were scarcely any cars around then, but some people had them. He fell under the wheels but it probably wasn't that that killed him. He broke his neck.'

Spencer closed his eyes, tight, and asked: 'Does everyone know?'

His mother made a little sibilant sound that might have been laughter or crying. 'A few. People were understanding, they didn't judge. They let me mourn the man I fell in love

81

with . . .' She touched his hand. 'And we must let you do that too.'

'That's stupid,' said Spencer. 'I hate him.'

'You do now, but all these years he's meant a lot to you, I've seen it. And it's right that he should. He had big ideas and when they didn't work out it crushed him and he crushed other people to get even. But that doesn't mean that big ideas aren't good.' She tapped his nose with her finger. 'You hang on to them. That's a good way to be like your father.'

She stood up and he opened his eyes.

'Is Mack mad at me?' he asked.

'No. He's mad at himself, and sorry about the whole thing.'

'Me too.'

'He said you were going round to Joel's and he stopped you.'

It seemed only right to Spencer to repay this magnanimity with some of his own. 'I only thought of it when he asked me.'

'Well then, why don't you finish the job, and then go?'

'I will,' he said, 'in a minute.'

'Spencer . . .'

'Yeah?'

'You two are the people I love most in the world. I really need you to be friends.'

She left the room, closing the door in the same careful way. Five minutes later he went downstairs, filled a bucket of water and took that and the inner tube out to the side lot. Mack had turned the bike right way up again and was straightening the front mudguard. Kite watched Spencer as he put the bucket down and crouched next to it.

A reflective silence reigned as they worked. The dog relaxed, and slept.

Not long after that, in mid-July, it was the annual rodeo in Salutation. The three of them went, as they used to do but hadn't in the last couple of years. Though nobody said so it was a kind of ritual, an affirmation of their having weathered the storm.

Salutation was a hundred miles to the north, on the edge of the Sioux reservation. The drive took them across the reservation at one point and Mack would comment grumpily on the unkempt farms with their stripped-down motors and poorly managed land. But every so often they'd pass one painted in bright colours – orange, aquamarine, cobalt and yellow – with tepee poles standing against the side wall, and a couple of paint ponies in the paddock, and Spencer would experience a thrill of recognition. Indians.

Salutation City, Population 2000 as the sign proclaimed, was heaving. Because of the nearby coal mines it had a sassy, self-assured feel, and when the rodeo came to town it got all gussied up and laid out the welcome mat. The rodeo lasted three days, but they always went on the first, to take in the parade and also because that was when the most people and animals were there. There was plenty to see even away from the main arenas.

Spencer had always loved the rodeo, but this time it lacked something. Or he did. The rough, tough glamour, the brassy music, the edgy crowds, and most of all the competitors, filled him with melancholy. This band of swaggering mercenaries, who risked life and limb for money the length and breadth of the country, epitomised what he could never be. He felt himself to be a dull, bloodless creature next to them.

The heat was intense, and the air was a stew of smells – sweat and leather and liquor, and cheap perfume and hot dogs and horse shit. Once, he'd found the smells intoxicating, but today they made his gorge rise. The reddened grinning faces offended him. As they stood in the crush watching the parade go by he wondered if the famous writer was out there somewhere. This was the kind of event he liked, and he'd even tried some bronco-busting in his time if his book jacket was to be believed. But it must have been one of his less successful adventures if he could come off a dude-ranch pony . . .

'Penny for them,' said his mother into his ear.

'Nothing,' Spencer mouthed back. She gave his hand a squeeze which he hoped everyone round them didn't see.

After the parade they made their way to the edge of town to the main site. Mack was a systematic spectator – he liked to get into his seat and watch the events through the day, following form and swapping opinions with the people round him. He was at his most animated in such circumstances – this, the ball game, fights on the radio – as though the emotions he was careful not to show most of the time were permitted safe expression when it came to sporting events.

But the thought of joining his parents on the hard benches in the central arena didn't appeal to Spencer. Even if their attention was elsewhere he couldn't think his gloomy thoughts properly when he was beside them. He flattered himself that the thoughts were worth a great deal more than Caroline's English penny, and even she wouldn't understand.

They were almost at the ticket booth when he said: 'I'm not going in.'

'Sure you are,' said Mack, 'come on.'

'No – I want to take a look around.'

'Do you feel all right?' asked his mother.

'Fine. I just want to take a look.'

Mack shrugged. 'We'll get you a seat, give you the ticket.'

'All right.'

While Mack bought the tickets Caroline gazed thoughtfully at Spencer. 'You will come and join us, won't you?'

He promised he would, pocketed his ticket and escaped. Guiltily, he realised that his spirits lifted and he walked taller the instant he was away from them. He looked older than fourteen, and no one here knew who he was. He had a couple of dollars of his own money on him and, greatly daring, bought a beer. Just holding the bottle was as intoxicating as drinking the stuff. At least now he seemed part of the crowd, even if he was a sham.

Cleaned out by the beer, he couldn't spend on any of the other attractions, and there were plenty. He watched strutting local pretenders at the rifle range and the bell-hammer, shrieking girls on the spider-ride, couples cosying up as they waited to have their fortunes read by Moonwater, the Red Indian mystic . . .

With about half the beer gone, he fetched up next to the stock paddocks a bit queasy and light-headed. Nonchalantly he threw the bottle in a trash can, hoping no one would see it wasn't empty.

A whole collection of rough corrals, stabling and pens were erected each year by the city fathers of Salutation, an investment in the financial milch-cow that was the rodeo. Spencer liked this part of the site because it was like an armoury or a munitions dump, full of the rodeo's potentially lethal raw material. Alongside the stock paddocks was the competitors' camp, a sprawl of trailers and tents for the old troupers, young pretenders and no-hopers who didn't qualify for star treatment in the town's hotels. Even if they weren't top of the bill Spencer still thought they were great, the embodiment of laconic toughness, untroubled by the small domestic stuff of other people's lives. Their days were taken up with travelling, waiting, husbanding their energies for those explosive seconds of tumultuous calculated risk, the slug of neat danger that could mean big bucks, broken bones – even death. These god-like beings smoked cigarettes they rolled themselves, and drank strong liquor and had eye-popping women in tow: it was hard to imagine them doing anything as mundane as eating, or going to the bathroom, or posting a letter.

He walked self-consciously past the encampment, unaware that his painful desire not to attract attention was the most obvious thing about him. At the stock enclosures he moved swiftly past the young steers brought in for the roping compe-tition all jostling and honking like a traffic jam, their panicky white-rimmed eyes rolling in the haze of dust; then there were the bulls, huge and weirdly shaped – a bull didn't move quite as fast as a horse, but its frame was packed with so much muscle power it was like riding a rubber Buick, so Judy Phelan's brother said, whose friend's uncle had once tried it.

But it was the horses which drew Spencer. There was something magical about their beauty – though it was a word he'd have been embarrassed to use, even in his head – and their fierce, expectant fear. They seemed to know in their bellies that humans, the creatures they were there to fight and discard, were the same people who'd get them in the end, and with whom they'd form an alliance based on the cleverness of one and the speed and strength of the other. He recalled the words of the writer: 'She wanted to be caught . . . Don't wish for freedom, you might get it . . .' For the purposes of the rodeo these horses were kept in a state of suspended development, unbroken but always in the company of the old enemy. Even Spencer, who posed no threat whatever, was greeted by a spreading ripple of consternation, as if he'd thrown a pebble into a pond. Some of the younger horses were corralled together in groups, but the champions, the guys to beat, were kept separate. Spencer walked slowly along the pens, inspecting these awesome creatures. He felt for their lack of dignity, cooped up here waiting to entertain the crowds, and kept his distance out of respect. At the last pen however his curiosity was piqued and he went closer.

This, he suspected, must be one of the veterans who had won so many encounters he was wheeled out as a kind of mascot at the end of the show, his bucking bronco days long over, left high and dry in an involuntary truce.

He was small, and dun–coloured, and seemed to be dozing, with his head held low. His coat was rough, and his darker mane and tail grew thick and tufty like scrub. On his hocks were the faint greyish stripes that marked him out as a wild horse. Mack had shown Spencer wild horses over on the lower slopes of the Prior Mountains, and now he wondered if this guy had ever had mares and foals of his own. These plain, mule–headed stallions turned into something different if they got wind of any danger to their family, and the fights that broke out between leaders and contenders left scars on winner and loser alike.

Spencer leaned on the side of the pen to look more closely, and then it all happened at once. There was a sudden explosion of noise and movement so violent that the wooden bars banged against his ribs. The sound was a feral scream more like the cry of a big raptor than a horse, and the stallion seemed to double in size and to launch itself vertically into the air, landing with its legs straddled like a cat coming down off a roof. As it stood there vibrating with its own furious energy its head was towards him and he saw its eye glaring, a pale eye barred with black, edged with a yellowish white, and lit by an uncompromising hatred.

This, reflected Spencer, as he beat a hasty and shaken retreat, was one horse who had never wished to be caught.

CHAPTER FOUR

Harry 1853–4

In a properly ordered world it would all have been otherwise, Harry thought. Certainly the patterns of everyday life in this sparkling early spring of 1853 seemed regular enough, but the deeper currents were beyond the control of even the Latimer family with its solid, yeoman traditions.

There had been no black sheep among the Latimers. Their boast, had they been given to boasting, would have been that an unbroken line of industrious and benign landowners stretched back for nearly a hundred and fifty years, two-thirds of that time at Bells. Large, strong sons had served their country in war and peace, and pleasant, open-faced daughters had married well, borne children of their own and raised them in the same way. But Harry never knew, as he returned with interest the steady gaze of the portraits on the stairs and around the walls of drawing and dining rooms, what private price had been paid by those who had been different. There must surely have been young men who defied tradition and expectation, and girls who kicked against the traces. What of them?

Did the rebels, if rebels there were, flee the nest as quickly as possible, never to be heard of again? Did they pale and pine as they did their duty? Or did they, like his elder brother Hugo, reach an accommodation with their natures and their lot, and make the best of it?

Harry thought about these things as he rode home in the trap alongside Colin Bartlemas. He rode as an equal, on the driving board, but the short journey from the station was not without its tensions, where once there had been none. Not all that long ago it would have been 'Harry' and 'Colin', at least in private, but now it was 'Captain Latimer', and though he could not bring himself to say 'Bartlemas', for him to use the more familiar form of address would have sounded insulting, so he managed, somewhat awkwardly, with neither.

The afternoon was clear and cold. The breath came out of their mouths in a fine vapour, and the briskly trotting horse trailed a pulsing cloud of it, like the smoke of the London train – the outward and visible sign of an inner, harnessed strength.

'So is life in the cavalry everything they say then?' Colin ended the question with a little slap of the reins, to show he was aware of his position.

'I'm not sure . . . I don't know what's being said.' Harry did know, but he wished to hear it at first hand from an old and trusted friend who wouldn't mince his words.

'They say the officers know nothing about fighting, and the men spend all their time on spit and polish and parading.'

'That's partly true,' conceded Harry, 'but the people who say that should remember that we have no war at present to cut our fighting teeth on. And it would hardly be Christian to wish for one.'

'An army's for fighting,' declared Colin incontrovertibly.

'And we're ready if the need arises.'

'Soldiers get bored.'

'That's why we keep them busy. Being smart on parade brings discipline in battle.'

'Maybe.' Colin sounded sceptical, with some justification Harry allowed, since he himself was only spouting what had been dinned into him and which he took on trust. 'How's Clemmie?'

The question referred to Harry's mare, born at Bells, saddle-broken by Colin and presented to Harry six years ago on his sixteenth birthday.

'She's flourishing. Army life suits her.'

Colin's just-civil grunt indicated his incredulity. But Bells was now in sight, its red brick rosy in the afternoon sun, a perfect exemplar, Harry considered, of everything English that was good, gracious and immutable.

Except that here was he, who would have liked nothing more than to stay as its custodian, returning from the army only briefly this Christmas. And there was Hugo, with enough flash, dash and fire for an entire company, preparing for the life of a country squire. That was the inconsistency in the pattern.

'If there were to be a war,' he asked, 'would you want to be in it?'

Colin jerked his head. 'I would. Because if a war's won you'd want to have helped with the winning, and if it's lost you don't want to have been the cause of it. Not that one man can make the difference, but you understand me Captain Latimer.' As they came within the aura of the house the habits of man and master reasserted themselves.

'I do. It's how I feel myself. Would you mind stopping? I'll walk from here.'

Colin reined in the horse, from whom the steam now rose slow and vertical like an engine in a siding, and Harry jumped down.

'Thank you—' he wanted to add something, some suggestion or pleasantry, but there was no longer anything that was appropriate. 'Thanks.'

The trap rattled away and he set off towards the house. Probably someone would have seen it in the distance and would come out to meet them and wonder where he'd got to. He liked to approach the house quietly like this, not as a visitor down the long formal curve of the drive, but as a boy again, between the trees and over the grass. Though Bells in its present form had been built by the Latimers just over a hundred years ago, there had been other houses and other settlements on this hill, right back to the time of the

White Horse. He liked to think that in spite of the war-like nature of the fort, the horse and its makers had protected the people of this lesser hill, so that they had gone about their peaceful business not in its shadow, but in its keeping.

The trap was outside the front door now and Colin was unloading his bags. He saw Jeavons and Little emerge, and the exchange between the three men, Colin explaining where he was before the cases were taken in. As the trap drew away again in the direction of the stables he saw Maria appear on the step with her arms lifted high, her shawl hanging from them like dark wings.

Harry raised his own arm, waved, and began to run.

Fully as tall as her son, she held his face between both her hands, gazed at him, kissed him fiercely on either cheek, turned his head from side to side for a closer inspection. Said in her rich, throaty voice that could never be entirely English: 'What shall I do with you, Harry . . . scampering over the grass like a great puppy?'

'It's so wonderful to be home.'

Maria stroked his face with her thumbs. 'Are you well?'

'Very well.'

'And happy?'

'Content.'

She pinched his cheeks. 'And you won't tell me any more, I know. No!' She raised an imperious finger before his face. 'Not another word. Come and see your father.'

Maria had greeted him with arms wide and lifted. In the drawing room Percy waited for his son with his hands behind his back. And yet it was Percy with whom Harry felt a deep, unexpressed bond of kinship – not of greater love but of greater likeness.

'Harry, welcome.'

'Father.'

They shook hands, Maria still with her arm about Harry's waist.

'Where is Hugo?' She made the enquiry sound like a demand.

Percy said drily: 'About his business.'

'He should be here when his brother returns!'

'All in good time.'

Maria gave a shrug which employed shoulders, hands, eyebrows, head – everything. 'Ah, listen, Harry – the motto of the Latimers!'

It was after sunset when Hugo returned. He came into the house like a manifestation of the April night, dark and brilliant, shining with cold, still in his stockinged feet having left his boots in the kitchen. Percy looked discreetly away as his sons greeted one another. Maria beamed and applauded with hands held high.

'Hal, you dog!'

Hugo was like his mother, given to extravagant displays of affection. His arms went round Harry like a vice, and his fist beat on his back. Harry could never have initiated such an embrace, but to be subjected to it was to be ignited by happiness.

'Hugo . . . Good to see you.'

His brother pushed him away, still gripping him by the shoulders. 'Captain Latimer . . . extraordinary! Not too smart for us then?'

'Scarcely.'

'You never know. I live in expectation of being spurned as the provincial clod I undoubtedly am.'

Now they all laughed because the mere idea of Hugo's being any kind of clod, or of anyone being themselves so cloddish as to spurn him, was unthinkable.

Now he backed towards the door, holding up his hands to warn Harry not to go.

'Little's drawing me a bath, but I shan't linger.' He paused. 'Unless you want to come and talk to me, that is?'

Had his father not been in the room, Harry would have gone. As it was he shook his head. 'I'll wait.'

'Don't blame you. But don't go to war before I get back,' said Hugo.

For as long as Harry could remember his brother had been an inspiring figure, part heroic part demonic, wholly delightful. Hugo was a mere two years older, but even when they had been three and five respectively Hugo embodied a ferocious appetite for life that propelled him down banisters, up trees, across streams and into proscribed places and situations, while Harry followed trepidatiously or hung back but was never mocked for either. Because he took Hugo for granted he did not, until they were both at public school, realise there was anything unusual about him. Older brothers, he assumed, came like this.

But at Eton it was clear that this was not the case. In fact in a great many instances it was plain to see that most older brothers were at least as fallible, inept and unprepossessing as the smaller fry. They might be bigger and therefore able to row or play cricket more competently, but they lacked the quality which Hugo possessed in abundance: charm. Charm in its easy outward form which, allied to the hot, dark good looks inherited from Maria, could bring birds from trees, have haughty prefects eating out of his hand, and hoodwink apoplectic schoolmasters into magnanimity. And charm too in its more mystical sense of a spell. Harry had witnessed it all his life, but only now been able to observe its effects and see that it was a rare and powerful thing. Everyone, from the most timid fag to the most bumptious member of Pop and feared Latin master, was slightly less themselves in Hugo's presence: he cast a strong, warm light on those around him so that they seemed better than they were, but were also hopelessly outshone. It was not a weapon that he wielded for his own ends but a gift from the gods.

Harry's own less expansive nature was caught between hero-worship and envy, though as the years went by both were tempered by the realisation that his brother's charm did not always work to his advantage. Hugo was no cleverer in the classroom nor talented on the playing field than his contemporaries, and Harry at the same age was a more promising scholar. Hugo was simply more audacious and likeable, and there were those who found something untrustworthy in these characteristics. Where there was so much popularity, jealousy and suspicion could be fellow travellers.

Now, when their respective paths seemed set, each in a quite different direction from that which had once seemed likely, their relationship had settled into something a shade more guarded on both sides. With adulthood had grown a respect for each other's strengths and a careful regard for each other's weaknesses. The perfect fit of inspirational leader and awestruck follower was gone, to be replaced by something more complex and watchful.

There were times when Harry mourned its passing, and others when, as now, it seemed scarcely to have gone at all. For a while he was subject again, willy-nilly, to the extraordinary and irresistible force of his brother's personality. But when Hugo had spoken jokingly of being taken for a clod, Harry had thought he detected a wistfulness which moved him.

Just the same, over dinner Hugo kept them entertained.

' . . . I came on the boy redhanded rigging up some sort of make-do trap, and do you know what he said? "But I wasn't setting it, I found it and I was taking it down for you." Can you believe it?'

'Sadly,' said Percy, 'I can.'

'Well, naturally I let it pass, one has to reward inventiveness wherever one finds it.'

Maria gave a hoot of laughter, tipping her head back and clasping her hands. 'Splendid! Quite right!'

Percy's reaction was less enchanted. 'You mustn't encourage these scamps to imagine there's something clever in thieving.'

'No, no, he'd never have caught anything in the contraption except his own fingers, it was a positive farrago of wire and string.'

Percy smiled a small, dry smile. 'That's scarcely the point. It was the boy's intention to take what didn't belong to him.'

'He was no hardened criminal, believe me.' Hugo looked across at Harry. 'Any more than we were, and we scrumped apples, didn't we, Hal?'

'I'm afraid so.'

94

'And great sport it was. That old fellow . . .' He narrowed his eyes, trying to remember the name.

'Seth Prothero,' supplied Harry.

'Prothero, that's it – he used to come haring after us brandishing whatever he could lay his hands on, a ladle once as I recall' (here Maria burst out laughing once more), 'and calling down a murrain on all boys and us in particular.'

'Quite right too,' said Percy. 'Since you were robbing him hand over fist.'

'We didn't want his apples, though, did we, Hal?'

'I'm afraid not,' admitted Harry. 'We simply enjoyed provoking his rage.'

'We did! It was sublimely comical, you never saw anything like it.'

'You were *very* naughty boys,' declared Maria indulgently.

Percy laid his knife and fork together precisely. 'If I had ever got to hear about it, I'd have tanned your breeches for you.'

'Of course,' said Hugo disarmingly, 'and we'd have borne it manfully, but as it was old Prothero lost very few of his wretched wormy apples, we had great larks, and your conscience, Father, remained untroubled. So everyone was happy.'

Hugo liked everyone to be happy. He shared the running of Bells now, but his *modus operandi* could not have been more different from their father's. Percy Latimer had been a tough but fair innovator who had kept the farms safe and habitable, improved the quality of the herd, applied sensible modern techniques to the land, looked after the woodland and the hunt, and maintained good relations with his tenants and employees by gaining their respect. He was a reserved, ascetic man whose choice of wife was the only thing that saved him from the accusation of being cold.

Maria, though she had been brought up in London, embodied the ice and fire of her Spanish mother – a proud and splendid bearing imperfectly concealing a stormily passionate nature. She had been an exotic beauty as a young bride, and was still, at fifty, a striking woman – tall, square-shouldered and statuesque, with black hair untouched by grey, dark eyes beneath winged brows, and a broad mouth of uncompromising sensuality beneath a short, deeply grooved upper lip. It was a mouth so perfectly suited to the pleasures of the flesh that usually self-possessed and intelligent men quite lost their train of thought when sitting near her at social occasions.

Her effect on the natives of Bells and the surrounding area had been profound and lasting. She had first shocked, then bewitched them. At the harvest celebrations in the first year of her marriage, halfway through the St Bernard's Waltz, she had broken into a tarantella-like dance which was only barely respectable and that only because she could claim Latin blood. But she had then silenced the whispering by persuading several other ladies of the village, of varying ages and stations in life, to join in, clapping and twirling like dervishes. When Hugo was born she was often to be seen out walking with the baby tied in a fringed shawl on her back, and when Harry arrived she did the same with him, while Hugo rushed about and swung from her hand. The locals had not exactly designated her one of them, she was a little too strange and foreign for that, but they regarded her as they might have done a unicorn that had suddenly appeared on the hillside – with wonder, delight and a sense of privilege. Besides which her presence proved beyond doubt that Mr Latimer was no dry stick.

Hugo, his mother's son through and through, certainly was not. He discharged his responsibilities at Bells as though they were child's play. And in fact games of various sorts were the hallmark of his stewardship. He wasted no time in reinstating the Mickelmas Charge, a neglected tradition whose origins were lost to memory and which involved the young men of the neighbourhood competing in a race around the perimeter of the village. The unique characteristic of the race was that the competitors should overcome rather than avoid all obstacles on the prescribed route – ditches, hedges and streams must be gone through, walls and fences climbed over, and irate bulls outpaced, egged on by a shrieking crowd of girls and children, and accompanied by a scampering pack of overexcited dogs. It was hectic and dangerous, and for both these reasons hugely popular. Hugo took part in the race himself, never winning, but always courageous and enterprising. At the end he was invariably the muddiest, the bloodiest and the most elated in the field.

Apart from the charge there was the annual cricket match between a Bells team and the locals, an event which Percy had instigated but in which he had never taken part. Hugo was a fast bowler and lower-order batsman of unorthodox power. Bells rarely distinguished themselves, but they did keep the onlookers amused. Maria's summer party for the younger children was another occasion suited to Hugo's talents – as soon as he was old enough he organised all kinds of races and games which though boisterous were also diplomatically engineered to take account of the children's varying strength and abilities and so ensure that honours would be evenly divided.

In other words Harry had come to realise that his elder brother was like a child himself. There was a simplicity in his nature, a lack of guile and an unguarded enthusiasm, which was both a strength and a weakness. Boyishness in a grown man and an employer won over even the most sceptical hearts, but it was perceived by some as a quality of incompleteness – of growing up yet to be done. Latterly, Harry had often felt sad for Hugo, and when he examined this sadness concluded that it was because fate dictated that such happiness and popularity could not last. They were the attributes of a certain kind of carefree youthfulness, which could not itself continue for ever. And yet it was hard to imagine Hugo changing.

Tonight he was on his most sparkling form. His manner took no account of the complications and imponderables of life. All for him was fun and frolics, sunshine and light, in which the rest of them were content to bask.

'This is so utterly delightful!' exclaimed Maria, holding out her arms to encompass the the four of them. 'We are such a fine family!'

It was inevitable that at this moment Harry should catch his father's eye. They both looked away again at once, dis-comfited by a complicity which amounted to a small betrayal of the others.

As they left the table, Hugo said: 'Come on out to the stables and I'll show you Piper.'

97

'At this time of night!' exclaimed Maria, not wanting to lose them. 'Are you mad?'

'No, my dear,' observed Percy, taking her arm. 'They are young.'

Maria's eyes narrowed at this reversal of the usual roles. She was a squeak taller than her husband and could if she wanted give the impression of looking down at him from a great Castilian height.

'It's just as well, Percy,' she said, 'that I am not a lady of fragile sensibilities, or I should construe that remark as most ungallant.'

The crystalline sunshine of the day had transmuted into a diamond-sharp night of glacial moonlight, the sky glittering with frozen stars. At ten o'clock a frost had already breathed on the grass at the front of the house, and there was a sheen of ice on the water trough in the stable yard which Hugo broke with his hand in passing.

'Here's my fine fellow,' he said quietly, opening the door of the stall. 'Move gently now.'

If this was a warning, Harry took it seriously. He had enough experience of his brother's predilections to know that they leaned towards excitement rather than ease.

The two-year-old Piper was dark and restless, as much Hugo's familiar as any witch's cat. Harry stood obediently at the side of the loosebox as the two greeted one another, and Hugo slipped a headcollar on to the horse and turned him to be admired. Even in this confined space Piper swished his tail and arched his neck in a pretty display of youthful high spirits.

Hugo kissed his head tenderly, just below the eye.

Harry shivered at the thought, quite unbidden, of how short a shrift his fellow officers would have granted this gesture. The officers' mess of the 8th Hussars was a place of fierce regimentation in all its forms, home to proud and privileged men – some admirable, many best left alone – with no sympathy or understanding for those not blessed with their own set of certainties. For this reason Harry kept his head down and his private opinions to himself, and was treated in turn with the lofty tolerance generally extended to those who were different but who had the sense nonetheless to behave themselves. Whereas Hugo, in that one unwary moment, would have placed himself beyond the pale.

' . . . heart of a lion, speed of a jack rabbit,' he enthused. 'And lives of a cat, though he may have used up one or two of those – did I tell you he tried to kick down the box when the farrier came, and sliced his back leg almost to the tendon?'

'You described it in one of your letters.'

Hugo smiled ruefully. 'That's the trouble with being stuck in the country, there isn't enough news to prevent one repeating oneself. Here, make friends.'

He handed the headcollar to Harry, who could have sworn he felt a warning vibration pass along the rope. He ran one finger gently up and down the horse's nose until the tremor subsided. Hugo looked on benignly, a philanthropist observing the fruits of his labours.

'That's good . . . excellent . . . the two of you will be firm friends in time.'

'Is he good to ride out?'

'To ride out, to hunt, to jump – I tell you, Harry, this is the horse I dreamed of owning when we were boys. Like that one of Sir Lancelot's in the King Arthur book.'

'You'll remember,' said Harry, 'that the artist was mistaken, or fanciful, because the Knights of the Round Table would have ridden palfreys – great lumbering beasts like carthorses. This chap's knees would have buckled under the weight of a knight in full armour.'

'Don't be such a pedant, little Hal! You do remember the picture?'

'Of course.'

'And you remember me saying that I'd own a horse like that?'

'I do. And here he is.'

Hugo's beam of gratification was such that in spite of having been recently referred to as 'little' Harry felt like some beneficent elderly uncle who had just parted with half a crown.

'And now,' declared Hugo, taking the rope and slipping off the headcollar, 'I have something still more astonishing to tell you. And you will be among the first to know.'

'I'm honoured – or should I be appalled? I think you owe it to me to prepare me.'

'It's nothing you need be prepared for.' Hugo opened the door. 'Come, come on and walk.'

They left the stables and Hugo struck out along the side of the hill to the north, at the back of the house. A darker mass, glowing here and there like the rubble of a domestic fire, showed where the village lay in the valley to their right. The pale chalky cart track wound away before them.

'I'm going to be married,' said Hugo.

He spun round and walked backwards in front of Harry, grinning exultantly. 'I'm going to be married! What do you make of that?'

Astonishment was too weak a word for what Harry felt.

'Hugo! Married?'

'Yes!'

'But who . . .'

Hugo let out a great 'Ha!' of laughter. 'You can't believe any girl would have me, can you?'

'It isn't that—'

'And you don't believe I have it in me to be a husband!'

'Not in the least, I—'

'But out there—' Hugo pointed a wagging finger towards the village, and then changed direction '—or to be precise out *there*, is the woman who could make a devoted and uxorious husband out of the worst *roué* imaginable.'

'Really?'

Harry had stopped in his tracks, stunned, but now Hugo put an arm round his shoulders and propelled him onwards. 'Truly!'

'Tell me about her.'

'Oh . . . I *want* to say she is beautiful and good, except that you might infer from that that she's dull.'

'I might,' conceded Harry, 'if the person who made the observation was anyone but you. I can't conceive of your taking up with a woman who was dull.'

'Thank you.' Hugo gave his shoulders a squeeze. 'I'll take that as a compliment. Though naturally I wouldn't want to be thought intolerant, either.'

'And do I already know this paragon?'

'I believe not, she wasn't one of those whinnying girls we used to have to dance with. Her name's Rachel Howard.'

Harry shook his head. 'I don't remember.'

'She's wise, and clever, and quiet.'

The first two adjectives Harry might have expected, the third was more surprising.

'In what way is she quiet?'

Hugo released him with a push. 'Are there so many different ways? No, she is quiet, you won't hear her across the room, or know her opinions on everything, or know what her laugh sounds like — not until you know her well. She keeps her own counsel. She's — serene. I adore her.'

Impressed by his brother's ardour and sincerity, Harry realised there was something important that he had so far omitted to say.

'Hugo — congratulations! Many, many of them. It's wonderful that you're happy, that she — Rachel — makes you so happy.'

'And even more wonderful perhaps, certainly more to be wondered at, is that she loves me.'

'That isn't so surprising.'

'When you meet her, Harry, you'll see that it is.'

'I want to.' Something occurred to him. 'I'm surprised that Mother and Father made no mention of all this.'

'They aren't sure what to make of it.'

'You mean they aren't pleased? But that's extraordinary.'

Hugo's pace quickened. 'They're suspicious.'

'Of what?'

'Oh — nothing! Rachel is older than me, and a widow, she simply doesn't accord with their picture of a blushing bride. In spite of the fact that their own match was scarcely conventional. Or perhaps because of that.' He shrugged. 'Perhaps they see in me some sort of discomfiting echo of their own past, and consider that they and they alone have the strength of character to succeed against the odds.'

'But—' Harry shook his head. There were simply too many new and startling revelations to absorb all at once. 'But they're surely not raising any serious objections?'

'Not objections – reservations. And neither would make the slightest difference.'

The track now began to descend towards the village and Harry said: 'Shall we go back?'

'I'd rather go on.'

Hugo raced ahead, abandoning himself to the steep incline. Harry followed, watching his step.

When they had reached the village, and were walking westbound along the valley road, Harry asked, 'So Rachel is a widow?'

'Her husband died four years ago. She's almost thirty.'

'Are there children?'

'No. And he left her provided for. He was an engineer on the railways. She lives alone in Vayle Place. It's that house with the turrets. The one we used to think of as haunted.'

Harry remembered the house. They'd used to ride past it simply in order to scare themselves. It was generally supposed to be a folly, built no more than a few decades ago by an eccentric with a penchant for Gothic novels. But this didn't alter its strangeness, and it was stranger still to think of a solitary woman living there.

'You've been to the house?' he asked.

'Naturally.'

'And do you still think it's haunted?'

'Of course,' said Hugo. 'But not in the way we meant as boys. It has an atmosphere all of its own. It casts a spell.'

Not wholly frivolously, Harry suggested: 'Your Rachel is a sorceress.'

'Oh, yes,' replied Hugo. 'She is.'

'She is a witch!' hissed Maria as she and Harry went up the stairs that night. 'There can be no doubt of it. What other reason can there possibly be for Hugo's infatuation with her?'

'I believe they're in love,' Harry reminded her gently.

'Love?' Maria snorted scornfully. 'I think not. It isn't in her. She is a cold, pale, provincial adventuress who has ensnared Hugo because she is able to do so.'

His mother's jealousy was so raw that Harry thought it better not to respond.

Only two days later he had the opportunity to form his own opinion of Rachel Howard, when Percy and Maria held a dinner party in his honour to which their eldest son's fiancée had naturally to be invited.

The moment that she entered the drawing room – the last to do so – Harry realised what Hugo had meant by her 'quiet'. Here was a stillness so complete that it demanded attention. It struck a chord which resonated beneath the social chatter, and which caused him to look round as if someone had called his name. There was Hugo at her side, talking, laughing, putting her arm through his, quite disarrayed with pride and passion, and there the object of his love – calm, barely smiling, unreadable. Her hair was a silvery mouse, her complexion lily-pale, her eyes light as water. She was small and slight, and wore a dark blue dress not in the height of fashion. And yet her presence was such that Harry's was not the only glance she drew that was more than simply curious. He watched as Percy greeted her with perfect, amiable correctness, Maria with more flourish and less warmth. If Rachel was aware of any reservations on their part she did not show it. Her composure amounted to a kind of passive power. He could not take his eyes off her.

When Hugo at last introduced her Harry was sharply aware of her hand lying coolly in his. Her grey eyes surveyed him unblinkingly: he felt transparent. When she said that she was delighted to meet him, had been told so much about him, he heard not the social platitudes but the soft, intense timbre of her voice.

At dinner he was seated next to her. She was polite and asked him questions about himself, accepted his congratulations gracefully, spoke charmingly of her hopes for the future. At no point was there anything either effusive or disobliging in her outward behaviour, and yet he felt himself to be constantly at a disadvantage, as if she had some special knowledge or understanding of him which he himself did not possess.

'And so,' she enquired, 'shall you make the Army your career?'

'I believe so. Until I no longer have the stomach for it.'

'"Let him that have no stomach for this fight, let him depart, His passport shall be made and crowns for convoy put into his purse".'

'You like the history plays?'

She raised her eyebrows and gave him a slight quizzical smile. 'I don't think that *liking* is quite apposite in Shakespeare's case.'

'No?'

'He is a part of our lives and our language. Inescapable. Wouldn't you say?'

'Of course.'

At this point the gentleman on Rachel's other side conscientiously turned towards her and Harry did the same with the lady on his left, aware that in the past few seconds he had caught a glimpse of the enquiring intelligence which she chose most of the time to conceal.

A glimpse which, a little later in the course of dinner, prompted him to touch on the matters which interested him most, though he had seen enough not to begin by eliciting personal information. Instead he remarked lightheartedly: 'You know, I am quite jealous.'

'Of whom?'

'You, of course.'

'Surely not. Why should you be?'

'All my life,' he explained, 'I've looked up to Hugo, not simply as my elder brother who has led and protected me, but as someone with qualities completely different from and greater than my own.'

She consulted her plate. 'And what do you perceive those qualities to be?'

At this moment there was a burst of laughter from the end of the table where Hugo sat, keeping the company around him amused. Hary nodded in his direction.

'I rest my case . . . What everyone sees in him. Openness, humour, courage, generosity. A great embracing of all that life has to offer.'

'And yet,' she said tranquilly, 'Hugo is here, and you are in London. He is looking forward to a life of blameless domesticity and filial duty in the country whilst you will probably at some time face danger and death in battle.'

'If by blameless domesticity you mean marriage to yourself, then I don't believe that is quite the unadventurous choice you imply.'

He had been bold, but was rewarded with a hint of a smile. 'Nor a universally popular one.'

It would have been insulting to her to deny this, so he simply said: 'You are unexpected. You concede that. Give them time.'

She gazed steadily at him. His skin prickled. 'I hope you will understand that I mean no disrespect to your mother and father when I say that their good opinion is not a consideration to me. Except insofar as the lack of it might trouble Hugo. I am no longer a young girl. I have money. And I love Hugo in a way that I never could have believed possible.'

If he had been bold, then Rachel had repaid him in kind, and with interest.

'He's extremely lucky.' Harry meant it, but regretted the platitude, and his slight embarassment may have prompted him to add: 'But then, he's been the catch of the county for some time.'

'He could have had any lovely young thing for the taking, and look what he chose . . .'

Harry was appalled. 'That is not what I meant.'

'Oh, but it is. You said that you were jealous, which I don't believe. But if there is even a hint of jealousy it is because, like your parents and everyone else—' here her eyes flickered for a split second around the table '—you are utterly baffled by Hugo's choice.'

Before he could stop himself, Harry said: 'And yours also.'

'What a mystery it all is.' Even on such a brief acquaintance he should have known better than to expect her to be offended.

Maria rose, and as Rachel prepared to follow her hostess's lead she gave him a look that was like a slow, sensual shrug.

'Mine was not a choice.' From that moment on Harry, too, had no choice. No choice but to think of Rachel Howard.

Next day the brothers rode out, on a grey blustery morning spiked with the threat of sleet – Hugo on Piper and Harry on Percy's cob, Darby.

'So what do you think?'

Harry had prepared himself for this question. 'She's a remarkable woman.'

'Isn't she, though?'

'You are embarking on an adventure.' There it was, the echo of last night's conversation with Rachel.

Hugo flourished one fist. 'I am! And how many men can say that as they contemplate marriage, Hal? Most would say that on the contrary their adventures were over.'

'Hugo—'

'Ah. Here it comes.'

'What?'

'The word of warning, the hint of caution, the voice of common sense.'

'That isn't fair. Or correct. I was about to make an observation.'

'I'm sorry, then do.'

They were moving along the flank of the valley, heading west, with the White Horse to their left and the site of the old settlement protruding like a jetty from the hillside to their right. Abruptly, Hugo drove Piper up the steep side of the promontory, the horse striving and struggling beneath him until they reached the flat top. He shouted over his shoulder: 'Come on!'

Harry and Darby joined them by a less challenging route, zig-zagging up the main hillside until they reached level ground. On the edge of the manmade plateau the wind boomed round them and the grass raced like fast-flowing water beneath the horses' hooves.

'What were you going to say?' yelled Hugo above the wind.

'Be careful you don't love too much!'

Hugo tipped his head back and roared with laughter. 'I have been warned!' He turned Piper's head and began moving away. 'But don't worry, there's no such thing!'

They passed a couple of farms, at the second of which Hugo had some tenants' business to attend to. A mile after that the incongruous Gothic turrets of Vayle Place came into view.

'Shall we pay our respects to my betrothed?' asked Hugo, whose plan it had clearly been all along.

'If you'd like.'

'I like!'

In the event they encountered Rachel before they reached the house. She was walking, wrapped in a cloak, and accompanied by a huge, broad-headed dog, along the path towards them. On seeing them the dog gave a booming bark and she caught it by the collar as Piper shied.

'Cato! I am sorry, I wasn't expecting to meet anyone.'

Hugo slipped off Piper and Harry, hanging back, held out his hand to take the reins. Rachel put the dog on its lead, but it was quiet now and laid its ears down subserviently when Hugo patted its head. Here the wind was a distant presence, churning and whistling beyond the lee of the hill.

Harry could not hear what was being said between Hugo and Rachel, nor did their hands so much as touch, and yet he felt like the grossest intruder. To see that still face and those pale, all-seeing eyes turned towards his brother, the air of concentrated containment which promised so much, all for Hugo ... He felt the ugly twist of a most unfraternal jealousy.

'Good morning, Harry,' she said, walking towards him with the great dog padding beside her. 'How rude of us. And how patient you are.'

★   ★   ★

At the end of May (almost indecent haste, Maria called it) they were married. At the bride's request, the wedding took place not in the parish church of St Catherine's but in the tiny, windswept church on the hill which marked the spot of some long-ago pilgrims' shrine. Of necessity the congregation was small, comprising the Latimers and a few select friends, but then Rachel brought no one except the saturnine elderly lawyer who gave her away.

'Has she no family?' asked Maria before they took their places. 'No friends? It is extraordinary.'

It seemed odd to Harry, too, but he wished to defend her. 'Perhaps she has decided not to invite them – or has none that she wishes to invite.'

'But why would she decide such a thing? Is she ashamed of them? Or—' Maria's nostrils flared at the outrageousness of this possibility '—of us?'

'Neither, I'm sure. She is simply someone who does not like a fuss.'

'But this is her wedding!' His mother's voice rose emphatically. 'It's supposed to be a celebration!'

'The most important people are here,' he pointed out. 'You look wonderful, by the way.'

'Hmm. Percy thinks my hat is *de trop*.'

'For once Father's wrong.'

With a toss of her head to show off the hat, Maria, only slightly mollified, turned towards her seat. The swish of her skirts gave off a thick, warm scent. There was no organ in the little church, but Hugo had secured the services of Paget, a fiddle-player from the village. His robust, untutored talent was more usually employed at dances, and even during the sweet meandering of his playing before the bride's arrival one had the sense that a foot-tapping jig was waiting in the wings.

'Can this fellow play hymns?' asked Percy, leaning across.

'I've no idea, but I should think he can turn his hand to anything.'

'Yes, but generally with help from the brewer.'

'We can always sing unaccompanied.'

Percy grimaced. 'Surely I'm not the only person here who needs a note?'

Hugo came in from the porch, combing his hair back off his face distractedly. 'Where is she? I want this to be over.'

'You are about to be married, my darling,' said Maria, 'not have a tooth extracted.' She cast a sidelong what–did–I–tell–you? look at Harry.

As they went to their places, Hugo muttered: 'That's it, I want to *be* married and for all this to be over and done with.'

When the bride did arrive Paget rose to the occasion, giving the 'Wedding March' certain stirring *glisssandos* and vibratos of his own devising. His long face, reddened by beer, the weather and an unaccustomed cold shave, twitched with effort.

The lawyer, a shy elderly gentleman not used to the limelight, relinquished his charge and his responsibilites and retreated to the pew behind Hugo and Harry. As Rachel took her place next to his brother Harry saw that she wore a plain ivory high-necked dress, without a veil — a combination of restraint and candour which he already considered characteristic of her. She carried no flowers and the prayer book in her hand had a worn, brown leather cover. The face she turned to Hugo was as composed as ever, though Hugo's own hand shook as he took hers. She has such power, thought Harry, does she know how much?

Throughout the short service he watched her, but if she knew she was watched she betrayed no sign of it. She followed the hymns in her prayer book, but though she did not sing, nor say 'amen' after the prayers, she spoke the responses in a low, clear voice that carried through the church. When they went to sign the register she proffered her cheek to Maria, to Percy. To him. And as they walked down the aisle she seemed still entirely her own person, attached to Hugo by only the lightest pressure of her hand on his arm; there was none of the triumph, demonstrativeness and dependence of most young brides.

Later that day, when the champagne and cake had been consumed, some carefully worded speeches delivered, and Rachel was changing into her travelling clothes, Percy questioned Harry man to man.

'Shall they be happy, do you think?'

'I'm certain that they will. I rarely saw such strength of feeling between a couple.'

Percy surveyed his son narrowly. 'Equal strength of feeling, in your opinion?'

'Equal, I'm sure, but different.' Harry chose his words carefully. 'As you would expect in two such different people.'

The pointedness of this second observation was not lost on his father, who let the subject lie there.

They left in the trap for the London train, with Colin Bartlemas at the reins. The sun came out. Rachel was neat in brown velvet and a bonnet with a broad apricot ribbon, Hugo exuberant, standing and waving, clasping his wife and kissing her on the lips, to cheers. She was neither blushing and awkward, nor apparently in the same extravagant mood as her husband. But when Hugo kissed her Harry detected in her attitude the merest trace of something less than maidenly – the angle of the head, the lowered lids, the gloved hand that half-rose – that spoke of many such kisses, perhaps more, in the past.

He was scalded, again, by jealousy.

Some two weeks later at the London garrison he received a letter from Hugo in Italy. The large, racing black hand-writing, scattered with dashes, exclamation marks, underlinings and crossings-out, was so typical of Hugo that it was almost like hearing his voice, and indeed his epistolary style owed little to grammatical construction and everything to the boisterous informality of his speech.

> . . . *life with Rachel – I will not call it married life because that sounds so dull – is more than I ever dreamed of – she is DEFINITELY A SORCERESS as you said, and I hope the spell may never be broken. Every day is sun, and simple food and wine, and the pleasure of each other's company which grows greater not less, and every night is even more . . . My little brother, I only wish that you will find*

in the woman you may one day marry but one half of this –
what can I call it? – bliss! ecstasy! that I enjoy. My
only terrible fear is that nothing so passionately perfect, so
diabolically divine, can last, but if that means we are going
to die of delight, then what better way to be consumed? You
will gather from all this that I have become the very uxorious
husband we talked about – didn't I tell you? Only then it
was my belief and hope, while now it is the astonishing and
wonderful truth . . .

It is hard to imagine life at Bells, with Rachel as the
lady of the house, and all the usual day-to-day nonsense to
be attended to, but while we have each other nothing can be
dull . . . And now we are going to swim in a river – in our
skin, Harry, with the sun on our shoulders! And then who
knows what? And supper on our vine-draped verandah under
the stars . . . I shan't ask you to think of us, it would be too
cruel, and you gone for a soldier and all! To think I envied
you – I never want to die, especially not young, no matter how
gloriously.

Your ever-loving brother,
Hugo

One year later, he was dead, with his first child no more than
a pulsing, translucent comma of flesh in Rachel's womb.

Poor Hugo, his honeymoon wish confounded on both
counts. His death was both premature and, in its own
quixotic way, glorious. So like him, everyone said, to
lose his life on the crest of a wave, on the very morning
that he learned Rachel was expecting their child. A mood
of wild, joyful celebration had killed Hugo, a mood to
which he was physiologically disposed as others were to
consumption or fits. All agreed that it was a tragedy, but
a poetic one.

Harry was at Bells that day, and saw it happen. With war
in the offing, he had come down primarily to visit Percy and
Maria, who were somewhat fractious in the dower house. He

had been pleased to find that Rachel was managing Bells more than competently and had had the good sense to change little. At the same time she was every inch the chatelaine, and it was clear that she managed in every sense for in what had been Percy's study it was now her fine, small handwriting on every document. Cato lay watchfully beneath the window. Rachel had made the house her territory.

'He's out riding,' she told Harry when he asked about Hugo. 'But he knows you're coming. I'm sure he won't be long.'

'Which way did he go?'

'Not far.' She smiled warmly. 'Only in the park itself.'

The smile was so unusual, and therefore so unsettling, that Harry absented himself on the pretext of meeting his brother.

He walked fast away from the house and across the open ground towards the trees, with the spaniel Merlin running beside him. Here and there on the grass were drifts of the small, wild, sweet-smelling narcissi that Maria had set, and the branches were just beginning to be beaded with sharp green. On this fine, still morning he heard the hoofbeats long before he saw horse and rider, and stopped, wanting to savour the moment. Merlin, perfectly trained, halted also, standing with one paw raised, anticipation made flesh.

Hugo, when he came into view, was riding Piper bareback. They were cantering steadily, but when he saw Harry he gave a war-whoop and lifted his arm. Piper sprang forward, lengthening his stride. The sleeve of Hugo's raised arm caught on a branch, and his 'Halloo!' sharpened into a scream of pain as his body was whipped round and came crashing to the ground, bringing part of the branch with it. Piper thundered past Harry too fast for him to catch but stopped, blowing in terror, flanks heaving, between him and the house.

There was a sudden, shocking silence. Even the birdsong was stilled. Hugo lay exactly as he'd fallen, in a fixed, puppetlike attitude, one leg bent up, his near shoulder raised slightly from the ground as if he was about to sit up. The fingers of his left hand trembled slightly.

Merlin was first to move, trotting forward with his ears

down to investigate. He sniffed, backed off slightly, sniffed again. Whined.

Hugo was dead, his neck broken and his eyes wide open. Harry was to see a great many deaths, but none that would strike him with such brutal force as this. The instant that he looked down into the staring, mocking emptiness that had been Hugo was the instant everything changed.

He thought he heard someone call his name, and saw Rachel standing by Piper. The horse was quiet now, and her hand was on his mane, but her eyes were fixed on Hugo. Harry took a step back from the body, and as he did so she walked forward, erect and unflinching, armoured already in her widow's dignity.

If she wept at all, no one ever saw her. Pale and practical, head held high, her condition closely covered up, she went about her business. That she won the respect of all and the affection of few was not surprising. It would have taken a woman of altogether different character to achieve that – a woman of less competence and more tears, a woman prepared to expose her grief.

Rachel allowed people to think what they liked. They could assume she was cold and unfeeling, or that her feelings were held deep inside her. In either case they would not warm to her and she would not court their sympathy.

Apart from Harry only Maria – curiously enough – understood this iron control and the pride from which it drew strength. She never admitted as much, but her actions spoke louder than words, and the two women formed an intuitive alliance, based not on intimacy and the exchange of confidences, but on a guarded and unspoken understanding.

Harry himself knew now, if he had ever been in doubt, that he was lost. In dying, Hugo had left him with a double burden of grief and hopeless love.

CHAPTER FIVE

'Are you there?
I've been expecting you;
Please answer if you're anywhere
Out there.'
—Stella Carlyle, 'Are You There?'

Stella 1990

The next morning she woke up alone, and eerily calm. Serene – she felt serene. A cold, uncompromising sun was shining. She'd made him (they hadn't exchanged names) drive her home via the Curfew and ask the stage doorman to get her bag, so she was solvent and mobile. Also it was Sunday, which happily precluded making sensible moves such as phoning her solicitor and accountant, not to mention Teresa. She could do as she liked.

'Oh, what a *treat*,' said her mother. 'But don't hurry, we'll hold lunch.'

After the excesses of the previous night she wanted only to be comfortably androgyne. She put on baggy jeans, desert boots shiny-toed with age and a man's frayed sweater whose provenance was lost to memory. She wore her glasses and no make-up. Her hair, flat and fine without attention, she scraped back into an elastic band.

The prep school of which her father was headmaster was on the Oxfordshire-Wiltshire border, but the van could almost have done the two-hour drive without her. Unusually for her she was perfectly content to observe speed limits and let other motorists whizz past. As the female driver of a battered white Bedford she was used to being treated with a certain wariness by other road users. To be law-abiding made her feel honourable, as though she were repaying a debt. The awful thought occurred to her that perhaps this was the beginning of being grown up, but was soon sent packing by the recollection of recent events.

There was no question of lunch having to be held. It was a case as her father would have said of more haste, less speed. In this benign and accommodating mood she was within ten miles of her destination by eleven-thirty, and pulled off the main road to stretch her legs. Her choice of a stopping place was not arbitrary – from here on a clear day like this you could make out the White Horse in the middle distance, cavorting on its hillside in an attitude which might have been one of aggression, fear, sex, or sheer high spirits. Like a primitive mask it absorbed and reflected back Stella's buoyant mood on this first icy, sunlit morning of her new life.

On those rare occasions when Stella felt a pang of unease over her promiscuity she usually wound up by reminding herself, as Jamie had reminded her, that she was a romantic at heart. And that if she was, it was all her parents' fault. The marriage of Andrew and Mary Carlyle was living proof not only that Cupid was a knavish lad, but that given his well-placed dart the most unlikely and unpromising alliances could stand, triumphantly, the test of time.

Arriving at midday at Vayle Place Preparatory School, Upton Magna, its whimsical Gothic towers dwarfing the sixties science block and new hall, Stella could see soccer practice in progress on the front playing field. She had no difficulty in picking out her father on the touchline because he had belatedly embraced the long-defunct fashion for highly coloured shellsuits with all the fervour of a convert and was this morning tricked out in a vehement shade of electric blue with a high shine, and a red baseball cap. She stopped the car and switched off Bob Marley because it amused her to watch.

The boys were being put through their paces by Mr Hanniford, his muscular black arms shown to advantage by a sleeveless fleece. The boys were very small, and at the age when the concept of occupying a strategic space was an alien one. Their instinct – one which Mr Hanniford was battling to combat – was to follow the ball in a herd wherever it went, wearing themselves out and leaving the goals and their diminutive defenders horribly exposed. As she looked on, one rather bigger boy suddenly broke away from the herd and tore down the field unopposed. Only the goalie's frantic waving and pogo-ing reminded him that he was going in the wrong direction, and he executed a wide U-turn to find himself facing a phalanx of players into the midst of whom he kicked the ball, in a desperate bid perhaps to get them fighting amongst themselves. Mr Hanniford, tooting on his whistle, waded in to sort things out and Stella saw her father clasp his hands theatrically to his head and turn round on the spot in mock despair. A bit rich, she considered, when he himself had no aptitude whatever for sports.

After retrieving the ball and delivering what looked like a colourful team-talk, Hanniford shepherded his charges off the field, and Stella got out of the car and scissored her arms above her head.

'Dad!'

Spotting her, her father waved his ridiculous hat in reply, put it back on and executed a few purposeful jogging steps in her direction before slowing to a walk and then standing still until she reached him. Andrew Carlyle was sixty-two, young for his age in most of the ways that mattered, but not of a generation or a disposition that set much store by personal fitness. His corporation was still heaving slightly as he clasped her to it, and she could smell the whiff of his medicinal hipflask on his breath.

'My darling old girl! Mary said, but it's still absolutely . . . Good God, you're a skeleton.'

'No more than last time.' She pushed him away. 'And you're too fat.'

He slapped his belly with a kind of rueful satisfaction. 'You wouldn't say that if we were Tongans.'

To this, as to so many of her father's pronouncements, there was no answer and she didn't attempt one but asked, as they headed for School House: 'Any Shearers in the making, then?'

He kissed her cheek once more impulsively. 'Lovely! Oh, Dennis Hanniford seems to think there are one or two and I've no option but to take his word for it. You know me, as a sportsman I make a first-class upholsterer.'

'He was looking as toothsome as ever.'

'Now, now, you leave him alone.'

'*Moi?*'

'Anyway he's going to Japan in the summer so we'll have to find someone else with the correct brain-muscle ratio. At least Dennis is tolerably cultured unlike most of the public-school brick privvies we get applying for that job.'

The Carlyles' home, School House, was part of the old Vayle Place, with communicating doors into the main building, which was rumoured to have a suitably colourful history peopled by the weak, the wicked and the generally unsound. 'So no change there,' as Andrew was wont to say. But today the hall smelt so sweetly and evocatively of gravy being made in the roasting tin that Stella could almost fancy she heard Desert Island Discs with Roy Plomley . . . Instead, from the drawing-room came the chitter of the computer.

Three boys of about eleven dressed in mufti scrambled to their feet as Andrew put his head round the door.

'Right, who's staying, who's going?'

'Sir, Mrs Carlyle said we could all stay.'

'Is she out of her mind?'

'No, sir.'

Andrew squinted at the screen. 'Is this Super Mario?'

'No, sir, it's—'

'Turn it off anyway, that'll do. You know my daughter Stella.'

'Yes, sir,' they said.

'Hallo.'

They mumbled something back, gazing warily at Stella and she at them. What, she wondered, did their parents say about her, and what nasty little opinions had they formed? These were not the self-absorbed babies of the soccer pitch, but senior boys of eleven and twelve, subject to the sniggering kick of hormones. With her own nephew and niece, her godson and the kids of friends, she swept aside any difficulties by shamelessly aligning herself with them, a subversive fugitive from the adult world. But at Vayle Place, with her parents' position to think of, that was not possible.

'Get yourselves smartened up,' said her father, 'and we'll give you a shout.'

'Cool tracksuit, sir.'

'I'm glad you approve.'

The beef was resting on the side, and Mary, sipping a gin and tonic, was turning roast potatoes with a pair of barbecue tongs. She was what men of any age meant by a pretty woman, a man's woman of the sort that women warmed to, and was as usual a picture of unforced elegance in stone cord trousers and a cream knitted cotton jumper over a white shirt: Stella detected Gap. Her hair, with imaginative assistance, had arrived at that flattering shade between blonde and grey and was soft and feathery. She had made the wise decision not to lose too much weight, and the strategic one to be happy in her lot, with the result that she looked almost her age, which was the same as her husband's, but beautifully.

'Mum . . .'

'Hallo, you star, you.' Mother and daughter kissed. Mary smelt of Penhaligon's Bluebell, her only big indulgence. 'We've got boys, do you mind?'

'Of course not, I'm the interloper.'

'They won't stay once they've got pudding down their necks,' said Andrew. 'Hard stuff or wine?'

'Wine, thanks.'

'So we'll be able to talk properly then.' Mary held out her glass. 'I'll have another of those so I can seem suitably abstemious at lunch.'

Conversation around the table turned to films and plays, and which was better.

'I'd much rather see a good film any day,' observed Mary. 'It's cheaper and the seats are more comfortable.'

Andrew raised his eyebrows for the boys' benefit. 'I'm not sure that's the right criterion by which to arrive at a decision.'

'My sister took me to see *Miss Saigon*,' said a boy. 'And it was mega-boring.'

'I bet she liked it,' suggested Stella.

The boy agreed. 'That's why she took me.' She could see him weighing up his next remark. 'She liked your show.'

'Good. Did you go?'

The boy shook his head. 'I wasn't allowed.'

'The other thing about the cinema,' interjected Mary smoothly, 'is that it's actually magical.'

'What about the magic of live performance?' asked Andrew. The boys' eyes were bright, they couldn't know that this hint of domestic disagreement had been part of their hosts' double act for decades. 'That's far more impressive.'

'I suppose,' said Mary. 'But then in a long run the poor wretched actors are doing the same thing over and over and over again, they must get stale.'

The first boy looked back at Stella. 'Do you ever find you get tired – I mean, when you're on tour and stuff?'

'Yes,' she said. 'But not of the material.'

'She has to say that,' said Andrew in a stage whisper. 'She wrote it.'

This got a laugh with which Stella joined in, relieved to have established her weight and role in the conversation.

Over lemon meringue the garrulous boy returned to his theme. 'My sister wants to know when you'll next be in Bristol.'

'I don't actually know.'

'It's a tour every couple of years, isn't it?' enquired Mary, keeping the ball in play.

'Yes, but we may take more of a break this time. Tell your sister sorry I can't be more help.' Something occurred to her. 'How old is she by the way?'

'Fern?' The boy pulled a doing-sums face. 'Thirty-two.'

'Right. Nothing personal, just doing market research.'

When the boys had, with permission, put their plates

in the dishwasher and withdrawn once more to the computer, Andrew jerked his head in their direction as he refilled the glasses.

'That's pretty typical. Father's been married three times, Fern's the stepsister by number two, number three's younger than Fern . . . I think I've got that right.'

'Jesus wept!'

'Ask him another!' suggested Mary. 'It's his specialist subject, "The ins and outs of the new extended family".'

Stella spoke from the heart: 'I am so bloody glad I'm not part of one. I mean that I spawned. In my adult life.'

'And how is your adult life?' asked Andrew. They were never less than direct, but never pressed her, either, for more than she was prepared to divulge. Consequently she was reasonably open with them.

'Mixed,' she replied. 'I've walked out on Sorority.'

'Good heavens!' exclaimed Mary, reaction as always perfectly tuned and timed. 'Was that wise?'

'Time will tell. It was certainly satisfying.'

She described the atmosphere and events of recent weeks and their eventual outcome.

Andrew summed up: 'So you couldn't go back even if you wanted to?'

Stella shook her head. 'No. I boat-burned for Britain.' She grinned. 'As a matter of fact I was sensational. You'd have been proud of me.'

Mary caught her hand. 'We always are.'

It was true, and Stella was glad of it, though she refused to feel grateful. Lurking in the wings (though not through their agency) was the sense that she was a cross her parents had to bear.

'What are you going to do?' asked Andrew. 'Is everything secure financially?'

'Don't worry, I'll have a roof over my head, but the one thing I won't do is wrangle with them about money. I walked out, they can keep the name, the goodwill, the bookings, the lot. Clean break time.'

'But they won't have *you*,' Mary reminded her, 'so those

things won't be worth as much. Even the publicity will follow you – I hope you're ready for that darling.'

'Ready and willing.'

'But they're bound to feel entitled to some sort of compensation.'

Stella tossed a hand. 'Then they can have it, within reason. I was right to walk out but I know it carries implications.'

Andrew got his cigarettes out of the kitchen drawer and offered them to Stella before lighting one himself.

'She's a businesswoman,' he said to Mary. 'We can't teach her anything about the shark-infested waters of showbusiness. Anyway—' he coughed '—it's only money. Your mother and I are far more interested in whether you're going to marry a nice young man.'

This was a perennial joke between them which she was content to join in. 'Who knows? New chapter, new perspective, penniless and indigent. I might surprise you.'

'You'd do a good bit more than that, you'd finish us!'

Mary asked, in a less facetious tone: 'What about that man who joined us for supper after the show last time we came?'

'Gordon.'

'He seemed rather more than an admirer . . .'

'He was a bit wet,' commented Andrew.

'That's what I think,' agreed Stella. 'So I've given him the bum's rush.'

Mary bit her lip. 'I do *hope* you were kind.'

'I think so. In the sense that I gave him the time of his life and then pulled the plug on him. Happy to the end, you know?'

'Poor man.'

'His wife will be delighted.'

This sally, though it silenced Mary, Stella did regret. It was true, but in this context it was an unforgivable error of judgement.

'Sorry,' she muttered. 'Uncalled for.'

'No, no,' said Andrew, stubbing out his cigarette, 'it's lamentable but it's a fact of modern life. And the responsibility must rest squarely with the man.'

She bit down hard on the perverse urge to take issue

with this, and instead asked: 'How are George and the family?'

'They're very well,' said Mary. 'In fact she may bring the children over this afternoon, Brian's away on exercise and she'd love to see you.'

'That'd be nice.'

Stella's younger sister Georgina and her army officer husband were currently stationed at a sprawling camp fifteen miles away. The mud-encrusted Ford Sierra estate turned up a couple of hours later, and Kirsty and Mark stormed into School House ahead of their mother with the aggressively expectant air of police officers conducting a raid. Stella was the result they'd been looking for, and they fell on her like dogs.

'Watch out!' cried George in their wake. 'Steady on! She doesn't want to be fought over! Hallo, Mum, hallo, Dad, my God how many people did you have here at lunchtime?'

'Boys,' explained Andrew.

'You poor cow.' George hauled her children off Stella and bestowed a smacking kiss on her cheek. 'I really would have thought that the one Sunday you had a bona fide daughter of your own coming you could have let the little blighters eat with their own kind.'

'I only invited myself this morning,' explained Stella. She turned to Kirsty. 'If you want the bunce it's in my rucksack thing in the hall.'

Both children disappeared. George said not very convincingly, 'You shouldn't give them cash every time. It's bribery.'

'No, it's not, I don't ask for anything in return.'

'The proper term is currying favour,' said Andrew. 'Which is still bribery but of a more generalised kind.'

Kirsty appeared in the doorway carrying Stella's purse. 'You've got a fiver and some quids.'

'How many quids?'

'Quite a few.'

'Count them. You see,' she told the others, 'this is all quite educational.'

'Seven,' said Kirsty. 'And some other stuff.'

'You can have two each.'

'Cool.' She disappeared.

'You're a damn' sight more trusting than I would be,' said George.

'What the hell?'

Andrew leaned forward in his chair in the manner of someone putting a stop to all this. 'Shall we take the small fry for a health-giving constitutional, my darling, so these two can talk?'

'Daddikins!' George rolled her eyes imploringly. 'Now that *would* be beyond the call of duty. Are you sure? I mean, we aren't intending to stay all that long, it's school tomorrow . . .'

'Just let them do it, George.' Stella adopted a mock-confidential tone. 'Before they change their minds. Another couple of years and they'll be too infirm to be of any use.'

'That's true.' Mary slapped her knees as she got up. 'Keep moving, that's the thing.'

Five minutes later they left.

'"Forth they went together",' intoned George comfortably, '"through the wild wind's rude lament . . ." Rather them than me. Don't let me fall asleep before you've told me everything.'

It always struck Stella how exactly like their father George was. She had his stocky physique and broad, humorous features, though what was amiably troll-like in him was transformed in her into the sort of warm domestic sexiness that was only enhanced by ten years' propitiation of an ambitious career soldier husband and the rearing of his mouthy children. Nor was she anyone's fool. A good upper second in modern languages (Bristol) had been subsumed in following the regiment, though unlike many of her kind George made a good fist of learning the lingo in overseas postings.

Stella counted herself lucky. To have as a sister anyone remotely like herself would have been complete and absolute hell. And open-mindedness on both sides made virtues of their differences.

'Can I bum a fag?' asked George. 'I've given up again but this doesn't count.' She leaned to Stella's match, then back, exhaling extravagantly. 'Shit! Okay, go on, yours is always better than mine.'

The news about the band was greeted with typical worldly equanimity. 'Oh, well, I suppose you know what you're doing. But do take care of yourself. You know where we are if you want us. I know Brian can seem a bit blimpy *de temps en temps* but he's always fancied the knickers off you so his Scotch is your Scotch.'

'Put like that . . .'

'How about the sex life?'

Stella decided not to disappoint. 'I ditched one faithful fan, and picked up a total stranger two hours later.'

George cackled with delight. 'Plucked from among the groundlings, was he, for this honour?'

'No. Never seen or heard of me before he nearly ran me over outside the theatre, then went and had the gall to go on the offensive, like you do—'

'Like *they* do.'

'Right, so I offered him my body as compensation.'

'Which he accepted, I hope, with gentlemanly alacrity?'

'Mm . . .' Stella narrowed her eyes. 'With alacrity, any-way.'

She allowed a lengthening pause to develop which George would be compelled to interrupt: 'And?'

'It was a disaster.'

'What, you mean him?'

She shook her head. 'He did his stuff, I did mine. But no fireworks. I promised him the fuck of a lifetime, but it was not to be.'

'He may have thought it was.'

'No, I'm pretty sure we were of one mind on the matter.'

'God,' George sucked her teeth, 'you were right, he was no gentleman. He nearly ran you over, you'd think the least he could do was to fake a bit of earth-moving. I mean, we do it all the time.'

'To be fair I don't think he was one of nature's fakers.'

George widened her eyes. 'So who did he turn out to be?'

This was Stella's trump card. 'Search me.'

'Yesss!'

★   ★   ★

124

Homeward bound in the slow-moving army of red tail-lights Stella felt the itch of something she dimly recognised as conscience.

In the interests of not disappointing her sister, and of keeping her amused, she had not been wholly candid about the previous night. While it was true that on a one-to-ten of casual sexual encounters it registered pitifully near the bottom, it had been memorable on several other counts.

For one thing, she couldn't work out *why* – why it had been so lacklustre. The man had been attractive in a rough, rich-bastard sort of way – an unpolitically correct allure to which (her public would have been surprised to know) she had always been shamelessly susceptible. A decent body stretched and stressed by life. An acerbic manner. Sure, practised hands. Not only that, but there had been a disarming confidence in his ready acceptance of her offer. He'd taken it at its face value, without demur, asked no questions, neither given nor elicited any apology for its failure, and disappeared into the night with commendable promptness.

But – and this was what she remembered most clearly – not so promptly that he hadn't found time to kiss her cheek before leaving. She'd been foxing, pretending to be almost asleep, but she remembered the distinctive Corona-and-Boss smell of his suit as he leaned over her, and the way he put his hand on his tie so it wouldn't fall on her face. If he'd kissed her on the lips or – God forbid – on the forehead, she would have had his number instantly, and scrubbed it from the memory bank. But a kiss on the cheek was different: a token of equality and friendship. It left her wishing to God she'd asked his name. Or even that he had asked hers.

It all got messy, of course it did. Over the next few weeks she never actually regretted walking out on the band but she frequently cursed the day she created it.

'Talk about Frankenstein,' she complained to George over the phone. 'You cobble something together in your own image and what happens? It shafts you.'

'Do you want to come and stay? The offer still stands. Brian's quite put about at the thought of providing sanctuary for a star on the run.'

'Sorry to disappoint him but I wouldn't inflict all this on my worst enemy.'

'But you are all right?'

'Sort of. But it's tough being non-contentious. My agent, my lawyer, the others, the theatre managements . . . the more I hold my hands up and say "fine", the crosser they get. If they're not bloody careful I'll turn nasty and really give them something to get worked up about.'

'As long as you see yourself right,' said George. '*Vis à vis* finances.'

'Don't worry. Apart from anything else I have faith in my own modest talent. It got me where I was a couple of weeks ago, it can get me there again.'

On this score Stella sounded more confident than she felt. Starting all over again held no fears for her, but she had never been a solo performer. An aspect of her talent in which she took some pride was her ability to fire people up in the service of a common enterprise, provided of course that the said enterprise was her idea. For years, she'd done that, and stood tigerishly between Sorority and the horrors of the road – all those motorway miles, and mean-spirited managements, the disgusting dressing rooms and brain-dead punters – and she'd enjoyed it. Got off on it, even. She was better equipped to cope with the exigencies of graft than the fine-tuning of success. That was why she preferred to take the risk of new material – it reminded her of the struggle. She had no desire for the sort of success that meant safety.

But money, as everyone including George kept reminding her, was an issue. She had her flat, her van, her piano, and a few thousand in a building society. She had her modest talent. She wasn't lazy but she was unsystematic – it was part of the same thing really, she had to make things hard for herself in order for them to feel worthwhile. So she worked up against deadlines, in the middle of the night, omitted to eat, drank Red Bull and bourbon, chain-smoked, left final reminders unpaid and caring messages unanswered . . . And emerged wrecked but triumphant, to raise two fingers and a dozen new songs at her creditors.

She told herself that her life so far, both professional and private, had been an exercise in crisis management, and with a little tweaking this latest contingency could be viewed as more of the same. But she was going to have to reinvent herself.

Her svelte solicitor Apollonia had views on this, and gave her the benefit of them over tea in her office overlooking the Zoo.

'You should go all-out sexy.'

'I hoped that's what I already did.'

'Yes, but I mean—' Apollonia waggled her shoulders and pouted '—sexy!'

'Please. I don't have the chest or the inclination.'

'Forget the boobs, it's purely and simply a question of attitude.'

'The thought of it makes me heave. And I have just enough respect for the customers to think that it would make them heave too.'

'You're too modest,' said Apollonia, who definitely didn't get it.

'No, I'm not!' barked Stella in exasperation. 'I'm as vain as hell which is why I have no intention of tricking myself out like some poor-man's Madonna!'

'Okay,' said Apollonia, dunking a low-fat cookie, 'so what will you do?'

What she did was, go to Scotland. It was a happening rather than a decision. With her dues paid and the dust settling she went to Jamie's eighteenth and there met his Aunt Fran and Uncle Roger, in the first half of the evening before she got too pissed.

'You're a genius,' said Fran. 'We both think so.'

Stella, acutely sensitised to such things, thought she detected the spider-foot of patronage and was tart.

'You're easily pleased.'

'No,' said Roger. 'Far from it actually. But guilty as charged of hyperbole.'

'Did I gush?' asked his wife, rhetorically. 'I beg your pardon.'

By the time Jamie hove in view, doing the rounds, Stella had forgiven Fran, and learned that they were academics from Nottingham, not a true uncle and aunt but second cousins, and contentedly child-free (she was attuned to whether or not this was an elective condition). She explained her own connection, and the three of them agreed that the celebrations were a tribal rite which they felt privileged, as non-initiates, to attend.

Jamie was accompanied by a soignée blonde Valkyrie whom Stella took correctly to be Ingrid.

'Hi,' she said, 'I don't know a soul so you'll have to excuse me.'

Fran and Roger took her small clothes, stupendous curves and estuary vowels entirely in their stride, though whether through tact or because, unbriefed, they simply didn't notice, was hard to tell.

As they quizzed her like troupers about alternative beauty treatments Jamie put an arm round Stella's shoulders and a warm, winey mouth to her ear.

'Read about it in the papers.'

'About what?'

'Don't about-what me! You flouncing out.'

'I didn't flounce.' She caught his eye. 'Okay, I did. It was a bloody historic flounce, though. A class flounce.'

'Glad to hear it.' Unlike her, the birthday boy was already well ratted. 'What do you think of Ingrid then?'

'I've hardly spoken to her.'

'Neither have I . . .'

She had to laugh, he was a broth of a boy. 'She's a knock-out.'

'That's what I reckon.'

'And I like Fran and Roger, too.'

'Do you?' He looked at them as though seeing them for the first time. 'Yeah, they're okay. Right old hippies. They've got a house on one of those Scottish islands, you know? One of those shaggy sort of commune things in the sixties.'

'Sounds good to me,' said Stella. 'Do they still go there?'

'I dunno, I suppose so. Ask them. I say, Stella . . .'

'Go on.'

'Will you do a song?'

'No. I'm strictly a civilian tonight.'

'But it's my *birthday* and I'm asking you.'

'No.'

'I can always wait and ask you in front of everyone when I'm even more drunk than I am now.'

'It'll get you nowhere.'

'You're so horrible.' He kissed her moistly, leaning heavily on her shoulder for a second as his balance wavered. 'Sorry . . . Better circulate while I still can.'

Stella, seeing Ingrid link her arm through his as they moved on, considered that her godson could do a great deal worse.

Of course she sang one number, after dinner, in between the band's first two sets. It was 'Still the Same As Ever in My Head', about getting older. She substituted Jamie's name for one or two of the more general references to the young, so although the song was wistful in tone there was cheerful chi-iking from his friends. Given the pre-dinner champagne and subsequent well-chosen wines, and the band's alien keyboard, she was by no means certain how she'd performed, but Jamie's mother Helen was effusive.

'That was really, really kind of you, Stella. We'd never have dreamed of asking, I do hope he didn't put undue pressure on you.'

'Of course not, it was my pleasure.'

'You were fantastic,' said his father Bill, whom Stella had once slept with, many years ago. 'Not a dry seat in the house.'

Helen frowned proudly. 'Darling, that's disgusting!'

'I'm sorry, it was meant as a compliment.'

'And taken as such,' said Stella.

'See?' said Bill. 'Woman of the world.'

What, wondered Stella, all those years ago, had she been thinking of?

By two a.m. the party had, like good stock, reduced and concentrated. The younger element remained in the marquee with the band, the remaining older guests who were either staying or too lazy to go home were scattered about the house with their shoes off feeling no pain. In a more anonymous context Stella would have favoured the marquee, and indeed Jamie had implored her to stay, but the two brain cells still unaffected by drink warned her against placing herself in temptation's way. Tonight might officially mark the end of her godmotherly tour of duty but it would be unwise to be remembered as the woman who fondled sixth-formers.

Instead she sat on the sofa with Roger and Fran.

'Yes,' said Roger in reply to her question, 'we do, on Ailmay. Why, do you know the island?'

'I've heard of it.'

'Well, it's our proud boast that we bought our place there when nobody had heard of it,' said Fran. 'And since then we've seen it through the Ailmay Community, the pop stars' retreat, disgrace, decline and resurgence.'

'Disgrace?'

'Only by association, the pop stars got up to all sorts.'

'And what's it like now?'

'As beautiful as ever in its bleak way. If you like that sort of thing, which we do. Most of the commune houses are holiday cottages now and there's a couple of pubs that do food, and a perfectly good restaurant at the big house. Still only one shop but these days it stocks olives and pasta sauce. That sort of thing.'

'You have no idea how alluring you make it sound.'

'You know,' said Roger, 'if you ever want somewhere to escape your baying hordes of fans, or the press, or whatever, you'd be more than welcome to go there. It's nice for the house to be lived in.'

'Don't be daft, Rog,' said Fran, 'it's not Stella's cup of tea, she'd be chewing the carpet in two seconds.'

If Fran had not said this, Stella might have reached the same conclusion herself. But she was predisposed to be contrary. Chew the carpet, would she? She'd see about that.

Over the next couple of weeks the idea of a highland retreat took hold. She could almost feel the northbound motorways spinning beneath her wheels and unwinding behind her as she drove, the spray on her face as she stood on the pitching deck of the ferry, the cry of the curlews, the tangle of the isles . . . No one would know her, or care, or give a flying fart what she looked like. She could eat plain food and drink whisky and go for long walks. She might even (though she hedged her bets on this one) give up the weed. And write – she could be Ailmay's writer in residence, that eccentric woman from up the glen . . . There'd be no piano, but it wouldn't be the first time she'd managed without, and one of the pubs or the big house would surely have one . . . If she was going to recreate herself this would be the place to do it.

Once she had decided, and ascertained from Fran that the house would be empty and she was more than welcome, Stella made short work of arranging to go for a month. It was at moments such as these that she knew she had got everything right, that she could never for an instant have tolerated marriage, let alone a family. As it was she had no partner, no commitments, no pets, not even, at this moment, a job. Out of decency she dropped her mother a postcard telling her where she was going and why, but not giving the address.

As if to add wings to the enterprise there was a piece about Sorority in the newspaper. Stella didn't have a paper delivered, she bought one, if she bought at all, on impulse and according to mood. On this occasion it was a middle-of-the-road tabloid known to be popular with women. The entertainment section had a small paragraph about her walk-out due (as they described it) to 'a difference of opinion over the group's direction'. It went on to describe the remaining members' efforts to replace

131

her. It was shamelessly on their side, with a quote from Faith to the effect that 'literally hundreds' – dozens, Stella imagined – of talented hopefuls had turned up to audition for the group. Their choice, pictured left, was a punky girl called Gina who according to Faith had 'just seemed right from the moment she walked through the door, and it was a bonus that she had the voice of a fallen angel . . .' Jesus, thought Stella, had they no shame? What did it mean, for fuck's sake, to sound like a fallen angel? What did a fallen angel sound like? Had *she* sounded like one? And – shit! – was she jealous?

Later the same morning the phone rang and it was Faith, determined to be bold and straightforward.

'I just wanted to say that we miss you.'

'Nice of you to tell me, Faith, but I really couldn't care less.' A sarcasm that betrayed what it was supposed to conceal, but Faith was too self-obsessed to notice.

'Did you see the piece in the paper?'

'I don't take a paper.'

'We've taken on someone new.'

'Good.'

'But if you thought – I mean, if you do see the piece, don't think for a moment that she replaces you, because nobody could.'

Stella bit down hard on a silence. But the trouble with a silence was that it was subject to an infinite number of interpretations.

'Stella? Are you still there?' Oh, God, a creepy note of concern.

'Sorry, I missed that, I was getting a cigarette.'

'It doesn't matter. Anyway, I wanted to say thank you. For giving me the chance, and so on. Whatever I do from here on in it will be largely because of what you did for me and I shan't forget that.'

Stella heard it all – the bet-hedging, the self-serving, the good old-fashioned arse-licking. But worst of all was the assumption that she was someone to be remembered with gratitude while a younger, prettier woman soared into the showbusiness stratosphere.

'Of course you won't forget,' she said. 'Because you'll be contending not just with your grubby conscience but with me. And while you're wallowing in your sad, deluded star-is-born fantasy, I'll be out there cutting the mustard. Talent will out, sweetheart, and the brutal truth is that I have more of it than you.'

There was a tremulous sigh. 'I'm *so* sorry, Stella.'

Stella had forgotten more about psychological street-fighting than Faith would ever know, but as she hung up she had furiously to acknowledge the last word to her opponent. That perfectly timed and modulated 'so sorry', that was not so much an apology as an expression of sympathetic understanding . . . the little bitch! But then, she'd had a good teacher – in another time and place, Stella reflected, she could have been friends with Faith.

The morning she left for Scotland there was a letter from Gordon. She threw it unopened into the bin but sheer brute curiosity (she told herself) prompted her to turn back from the door at the last moment to retrieve it and stuff it in her coat pocket.

In the carpark of a Little Chef near Doncaster she lit a cigarette and read the letter.

'. . . *just want to say* . . .' Why did people always use the word 'just' when they were about to dump exponentially? And say 'sorry, but—' when they were the opposite of sorry? The germ of a song idea presented itself and she dug a biro out of her bag and put a circle round the 'just' before reading on.

'. . . *want to say that my feelings for you haven't changed. I have the greatest respect for whatever decision you have reached and your reasons for reaching it, though only you can know what those are. I shall of course continue to come to your shows whenever I can and "worship from afar". You cannot know what our association has meant to me though perhaps, being the creative person that you are, you can imagine* . . .'

Association? Stella shook her head, what sort of word was that? It summed up everything about Gordon that would

133

never do. His dogged timidity, his caution that amounted to emotional paralysis, his putting of politeness before passion. And yet . . . she frowned as she flicked her cigarette through the top of the window . . . here was the letter, in itself quite a bold move considering the short shrift given to his previous communication. She did him the favour of finishing it.

'. . . *can imagine. But it might surprise you to know that at long last my circumstances have changed . . .*' she supposed that by this he meant his wife '. . . *which is hard on everyone, but long overdue. I really don't know which way to turn at the moment, I suppose I've taken too much for granted for too long. Anyway, Stella, if you've read this far, which I doubt, please accept my good wishes for the wonderful future you deserve and if you should want me, for* anything, *you know where I am.*'

It was a poor stumbling thing, like Gordon himself, but for that reason alone it made her eyes prickle. Of course she didn't know where he was, she never had. She hadn't wanted or needed to, because he always came to her. And anyway, where would he be now that his 'circumstances' were different? Not, she fancied, in some cool and uncluttered bachelor flat. It was all too painfully easy to picture Gordon in a bedsit of the old *Rising Damp* variety, with a gas meter, a baby Belling, a candlewick bedspread and Y-fronts over the radiator . . . She grimaced with a sort of sorrowful irritation. Now the underlining popped off the page at her: '*anything*'. The awful truth was that he meant it. Anything that she needed and that was in his power to give, he would, from a bed (shared or otherwise) for the night, to his life savings or his internal organs, and no questions asked. It was pathetic in the true sense of the word.

On her way out of the carpark she drew up by a litter bin shaped like a Womble, and stuffed the letter down its throat. Ten miles later she realised she'd thrown away the song idea, and when she tried to remember it, she couldn't.

The weather, which had been bright and brisk on her departure from London, grew progressively more sullen as she got further north and the afternoon closed in. By the time she drove on to the *Countess of Ailmay* it had settled into a soft, muffling mist that left her coat and hair pearled with moisture and made the darkness opaque, so there was little point in spending the journey on deck. If there were any gulls wheeling they were keeping it to themselves, and the only sound was the churn of the ferry engine and the secretive tap and slither of the card game being played by two of her fellow passengers. The ferry was no more than a quarter full, and though the lower seating area abounded with facilities – a bar and self-service snack counter, fruit machines, a juke box – none was being used.

She went to the bar, perched on a stool and ordered a Scotch, with a pleasing sense of making the barman's day. 'I generally drink bourbon, but when in Rome . . . Plus whatever you're having.'

'Thanks, I'll have a beer.' He gave her a wry look along with her change. 'Don't fret about it, they all drink Chardonnay over there these days.'

'Too many people like me, huh?'

'They're no' so bad,' he said, admitting nothing. 'And the island would collapse without them.'

'Glad to hear it.' She raised her glass and gave him her foxiest smile. 'Here's to us.'

'*Santé.*'

Driving into the swirling unlit fastnesses of Ailmay at eight o'clock on a winter's evening, with only Fran's enthusiastically annotated map for company, Stella found herself wishing for rather more evidence of the Chardonnay-swigging incomers. But when she did eventually locate Glenfee there was only a couple of hundred yards of unmade road up not too hairy a gradient, and the house itself was reassuringly intact. It was possible to see that it had once been a simple, low croft clinging to the hillside, but however Fran and Roger had lived in the heyday of the Ailmay community, they'd since sold out to common sense and Glenfee was now to all intents and purposes a respectable re-cladded small house with a chalet roof, a garage, an outside light and double glazing. Stella was a little ashamed to feel comforted.

Inside it was spare but comfortable in the style of most holiday homes. Books ranged from Ruth Rendell to the local tourist guide, there were chess, Scrabble and Mid-life Crisis on the shelf, and a fridge-freezer and microwave in the kitchen. She had been warned about there being no television, that didn't bother her, but she was glad she'd brought her portable stereo and some CDs. The double bed was made up, and the radiators were not completely cold. A fire lay ready to light in the living-room grate. There was a note on the kitchen table.

'Dear Miss Carlyle, There are basics in fridge, pint of milk on order every other day. Heating is on timer, turn up in hall if wanted. Logs out the back. Payphone also in hall, my no. is 531206. Shop is Brundle's in the village, ten minutes by car, they have most things. Hope you enjoy your stay, Jean Sherlock.'

She unloaded the car, put her things away, lit the fire and made a bacon sandwich. Suddenly she was exhausted, poleaxed by the journey, the emotional and physical stresses of the past weeks and her own isolation. It was all she could do to drag herself away from the half-eaten sandwich, and the fire, and up to bed.

Later, when she thought of Ailmay and how events there changed her life, it was the memory of the view that first morning which brought it all back to her. The mist of the previous evening had cleared, to reveal the dark, secretive mass of Stone Fell overlooking the house to the north; the dour moors coloured like an alsatian dog – tan, brown, black, grey, scarcely a hint of green – rolling and stumbling towards the distant shine of pewter sand, beyond which fretted the Atlantic. And the sky, the extraordinary volatile sky, which on that morning was dramatic with thunderous galleons of cloud, their swollen sails seamed like black opals with fitful sunlight.

This was a mercurial landscape, charged with fluid energy,

continually changing character with the light and the weather. On those rare days where there were long periods of unbroken sunshine the island seemed to sleep, to be held in a spell of unnatural stillness before it could once again shake and stir and come to life.

Like a first real love-affair she was never to forget it, nor fail to acknowledge its influence. Nor did she ever go back.

She was utterly unprepared for the immediate effects of her self-imposed exile and the isolation she had so craved. Once she had located the whereabouts of the life-support systems – the shop, the post office, the garage, the pub – she fell into a routine that was almost completely solitary. She woke early and worked for a couple of hours, then walked down the unmade road to the point where it joined the tarmac, picking up her pint of milk every other day on the way back. She rediscovered the delights of a cooked breakfast and then worked all morning and had a bottle of beer and a sandwich at about two.

In the afternoon she walked. She had a map of the island and occasionally set herself objectives, but on the whole she walked on a time basis, being sure to turn back at a point from which she could reach Glenfee by dark. When she did check the distances covered in the first week they weren't that great – though mentally tough she was chronically unfit – but the space and air began to pump through her system and fill her head so that she felt as though the edges of her identity were blurring. Her sharp, intense sense of herself diffused under the onslaught of so much emptiness. The endless sky, the open sea, the mountains – especially Stone Fell, whose summit remained, for her, wrapped in mystery.

What she thought of as work here became a very different process from that which she undertook in London. As always when without a piano she had to find another place, a situation in which she felt secure so that her imagination could graze in its haphazard way. After a couple of days' trial and error she settled on a small folding card table which she set up in the picture window facing the sea, on the principle that there was no point in even attempting to recreate the familiar. She was dependent on what she herself could sing, and retain. This had the inevitable effect of making the music, like her surroundings, more fluid. She was by no means sure, when she hit on an emotive or witty sequence one day, that it would still be there in exactly the same form the next. The line or two of lyric with which, for Stella, every song began, became not just the genesis but an absolutely vital *aide memoire*.

And here was another thing. On Ailmay she thought differently. It was difficult here to find the smart, spoiled, fraught urban perception which informed the songs she wrote in London. Here she was subject to a wider, deeper emotional current which to begin with she resisted fiercely, terrified of letting sentimentality have its head. She was not immune to it, it was there in her and she'd been able to use it to good effect but always with that salutary touch of irony and world-weariness.

A song she had not heard or remembered for years haunted her.

'The water is wide, I cannot get o'er, And neither have I wings to fly . . .'

That was the kind of song she felt she might be able to write here – something timeless about yearning and separation. A song that relied not on specificity, but on something more visceral for its emotional pull. A song that would speak not just to individuals but to the common stream of which they were all part. And then she'd catch herself thinking these things and wince at her grand pretensions.

All things considered it was inevitable that on the fourth day she slid into a period of profound unhappiness. Not depression – she'd known the apathy and despair of depression in the past – but a helpless sadness. She who scarcely ever wept found herself trudging the sheep tracks with tears pouring down her cheeks. She couldn't eat . . . fell asleep in the day and was wakeful at night . . . longed for company but couldn't face people . . . The part of her that had always poured scorn on the counselling culture and its jargon fought the idea that all this was a necessary process of 'letting-go'. But the other and greater part, the analytical pragmatist and student of human nature, recognised that of course it was. Some years before, when George had claimed that the babies were driving her to the brink of insanity, Stella – herself in the wake of a termination –

had sent her sister a card which read: 'Don't tell me to relax – it's only my tension that's holding me together'.

Now that was QED, bigtime. Stella was a fully paid-up believer in the benefits of stress, but she was finding the effects of its sudden removal revelatory, and disturbing. Later she was able to pinpoint the moment when, in a spirit of who-the-hell-can-see-me-anyway, she gave way to the inevitable. It was about halfway up the west slope of the fell on a stormy afternoon, with a giant Atlantic wind banging around her head and her feet soaked. Above her the peak was obscured by a thick, rippling shawl of highland rain; below her the moor was smeared and flattened by the fierce hand of the weather. These were wild, hostile surroundings and she felt how utterly alone she was. Like a child she thought, If I die at this moment it could be weeks before anyone found me.

That was the first time she cried, loudly and messily, her sobs inaudible above the wind, her tears invisible in the rain, her famous toughness reduced to so much shattered storm damage.

For days thereafter she scarcely knew herself. But when she did emerge and begin to find her feet and her direction once more she felt better than she had in some time. Tired, but healthily so, as if her mind and spirit had caught up with her well-exercised body and been rid of longstanding toxins. She slowed down, slept longer, put on a little weight and rediscovered the pleasure – and usefulness – of doing nothing. She would sometimes sit at her table, or on a rock when she was out walking, and simply gaze for an hour or more. She became a sponge, soaking up impressions without feeling the need to process them.

The result, at the end of week two, was a song. A song that grew unforced, organically, out of this fertile new mulch. It began, unusually for her, with the music – three notes that she whistled on a dying fall, a wistful little phrase with a pleasingly celtic cadence. And three words to go with them. Three words that fell on to the notes from that mysterious place in her head which she acknowledged but could not identify.

Are you there?

* * *

She saw nobody, or nobody with whom contact wasn't dictated by necessity. She filled the car's tank with petrol and its boot with supplies on the first day, she kept Mrs Sherlock at bay with an appreciative call, and she didn't go near the pub. Her nearest neighbours were a quarter of a mile away and the man gave her the sort of offhand wave which denoted acceptance of Glenfee's shifting population. The notion of being a focus of local curiosity, the woman-in-dark-glasses fantasy which she had briefly entertained at home, was anathema to her now, as was the very idea of trying out new songs on some foreign piano. She drank at home and forced herself to regulate the drinking – a bottle of beer at lunchtime, a couple of Scotches followed by half a bottle of wine in the evening. A regime which, although far exceeding the recommended weekly number of units, was modest by comparison to her usual intake, and since she was currently celibate, smoking less and exercising more, she considered perfectly reasonable.

'Are You There?' pretty well wrote itself during the gentle melancholy of her recovery period, and she wrote another ballad on the back of it. 'All to Play For' mined the same seam of wistful optimism but to a sweet-sour ragtime tune. The contents of Gordon's letter came back to her and inspired 'Just to Say' and 'Sorry but I'm Happy'. She was pleased and surprised by the songs, and put them down on paper as best she could in her time-honoured shorthand of dots and scribbles.

Given her satisfaction with this initial output it was, predictably, music that lured her back into company. She'd been stocking up at Brundle's one lunchtime, and having put everything in the boot she went for a short walk around the harbour. It was a damp, fretful day with the sea combed by an onshore wind, slapping and surging around the legs of the wooden jetty and butting the fishing boats moored to the quay. The wake of the midday ferry to the mainland was still visible beyond the breakwater.

The Harbour Light was by some way the less attractive of the town's two pubs, a single-gabled grey Victorian building, scabbed and streaked by Atlantic weather, fronted by cracked hardstanding and with a flapping A-frame sign advertising Hot Food. But as she passed she picked up the unmistakable vibration of live music and the warm babel of a well-refreshed audience, a sound which exerted a magnetic pull over Stella. The excitable shudder of drums, the yelp of fiddles at full pelt and the trill of a tin whistle drew her into the public bar.

She need not have worried. The bar was packed and no one gave a stuff about one more squeezing in. She pushed her way to the front and ordered a Guinness just as the music stopped to an explosion of applause. The noise, the warmth, the crowd were overpowering after her fortnight's solitude and she edged her way to the corner of the bar where she could at least lean on the wall while she adjusted. From here she could observe the band as they put their glasses down and went into their next number. They were four, on fiddle, banjo, tin whistle and drum. The drummer was a red-faced boy of about sixteen, with an eyebrow-ring that sat uneasily with his bad, parted haircut. The banjo player was old, cool and black. The whistler was a stout, handsome woman of about Stella's own age in a long green skirt and a thick sweater. But it was the fiddler who caught and held her attention – an original folk wild man, tall, etiolated and hirsute, bending, weaving and stamping with the music, unseeing eyes either tight shut or bulging from his head, focused on God knows what. His face was webbed with angry red veins, his hands seamed, his thick nails black-edged and cracked. He wore plimsolls without socks, revealing skinny grey ankles. He played like the devil and his music was divine.

Gradually Stella unfurled and felt a part of her surroundings. It was good to be with people again, particularly this anonymous crush of genial, music-loving boozers. She ordered another Guinness, and one for the man next to her. By the time the band had done another three numbers he'd returned the compliment. There wasn't the slightest suggestion that either of them exchange a single word beyond these basic reciprocal transactions: no innuendo; no body language; no come-on, no standoff . . . No agenda. She had forgotten that such a situation –

unthinkable in London – could exist. It made nonsense of the woman-in-shades scenario. From the cosy outskirts of squiffiness, she thought: These are my people; I could live in this place.

The band reached the end of their first set, amid cheers and some token complaints. The woman waved her arms in the air.

'All right, all right, we love you too, we'll be back. Why doesn't someone else come up here for a few minutes, eh?'

This provoked some more barracking.

'Stuart!' She cast around the room, raised her voice over loud cheers: 'Stuart Macdonald, you drunken bastard, now's your chance!'

In the end Macdonald, a local hero with a snouty face that only a mother could love, was pushed to the front and the band retreated to the far end of the bar. Even allowing for the willing suspension of her own critical faculty Stella could appreciate that this was an amateur in name only. He played the mouth organ in the way the fiddler played the fiddle, with preternatural exuberance and flair, extemporising around various tunes – traditional, pop and even, cheekily, opera – and moving seamlessly between modes with the facility of a piano-bar pro.

When he'd played for five minutes without a break he simply stuck the mouth organ in his trouser pocket and walked off, apparently unmoved by the applause, blinking in acknow-ledgement as his back was slapped.

'Still drinking time!' called the woman from the back. 'Someone else do us a favour and get up there.'

Suddenly, it was irresistible. She didn't even have to think about it, but found herself standing in front of them all with her arms folded, in an attitude half patient, half threatening which she knew would make them shut up. They hadn't expected or noticed her, and she was neither recognisable nor very tall, so it took longer than it might otherwise have done, but in the end they fell silent. She could tell simply by the quality of the silence that they were a dream crowd – open-minded, appreciative, ready to empathise, honestly respectful of her wish to entertain, but discerning: her predecessors proved that.

In the absolute quiet, with her arms still folded, she drew a long breath and sang them 'Are You There?'

It was strange to hear the song that till now had existed only in the solitude of the house given its full value, the light and shade and feeling it deserved. As always with a good song she herself was moved by this first breathing of life into the words and melody. And it was a good song, it had both universality and particularity. It could live on its own. It sang her.

When she finished, she got off at once, as the others had; so promptly in fact that she did so in silence, and the warm wave of approbation didn't break over her till she was back in her corner with another half-pint being pushed in front of her. She was euphoric, but did not show it. She wanted only to be one of them.

It was as she stood there, saying that yes, she did write songs from time to time and, thanks, she was glad they liked it, but no, she wouldn't do another – as she stood there she felt, quite unmistakably, someone looking at her from across the room. Amid all the faces and the talk, the bonhomie and backslapping, she felt the touch of this one look like a butterfly's wing – the shadow of a butterfly's wing. She could not identify its source, but when the music started again and attention was once more focused on the band, she allowed herself to scan the room.

She saw him at once. His was the one face not turned to the front, but towards her, with furious attention. The shock of seeing that face, here, and being subject to its almost accusing output of energy, was intense. He'd been here all this time? Watching her? Yes, and he'd heard her sing, seen her stupid vanity, witnessed – Jesus! – her self-regarding emotion . . . But then why should she care at all about his good opinion?

Shaken, she began to make her way to the door, aware that he was doing the same thing. There was nothing for it but to tough it out.

She got out first, but he caught the bar door as it swung shut behind her.

'Not so fast.'

The first handfuls of rain rattled on the frosted glass at the top of the outside door. Behind them in the bar the music and the drinking continued. Between the two doors, in the small shabby hallway of the Harbour Light, that smelt of beer and old chip fat, they stood facing one another.

'Yes,' he said, as though she'd asked a question. 'I am.'

'What?'

'I am here.'

Maybe, she thought afterwards, *maybe*, in another place and in other circumstances she might have pissed from a great height on his arrogant assumption. But the experiences of the past couple of weeks had stripped a layer from her defences. She had set out her emotional stall in there, and been proud of it. Too late now to come the bitch from hell. Nor, she found, did she want to.

He spoke firmly into her hesitation.

'And I shall be for the next few days. But from tomorrow, I shan't be on my own.' So. Another married one, she thought as she drove back to Glenfee with one eye closed and his headlights in the rearview mirror. Married, rich, opportunistic, on holiday with his poor benighted bloody wife – the worst sort. Worse than basically honourable Gordon whom she'd kicked into touch. Far worse than any one of the three or four casual encounters she'd slept with since.

Worse still, because he'd been on her mind, and had stolen a march on her.

Three hours later he left. He did not, this time, kiss her on the cheek, but threw down his card, like a gauntlet, on the bedside table before leaving. She listened to his footsteps down the stairs; the brisk click of the front door; the sound of his car starting. The streaming, uncurtained window was illuminated briefly by his headlights, before the dark and rain closed in around the house like a hedge of thorns . . .

Stella closed her eyes.

Mad, bad – magic.

CHAPTER SIX

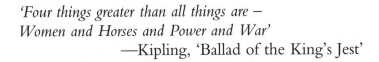

'Four things greater than all things are –
Women and Horses and Power and War'
        —Kipling, 'Ballad of the King's Jest'

Spencer 1942–3

1942, the year he turned eighteen, Spencer McColl ended his first real love affair and started unawares on the road that led to his second.

The first was Trudel 'Apples' Flaherty – Trudel for her German maternal grandmother, Flaherty from her father Seamus – who was one of those girls considered easy but, curiously, not despised for it. This was because with Trudel it was simply a matter of generosity, both of form and temperament. Five foot six, a hundred and forty-eight pounds and structured along Wagnerian lines – there was more than enough of Trudel to go round and it was her pleasure to share it.

The fact that there was a war going on on the other side of the pond between England and Germany lent a certain added piquancy to Trudel's attraction – it showed a good sound American independence of spirit to be fondling all that yielding Teutonic flesh, though Spencer felt he had to make a particular point of explaining to his mother that Trudel was only a quarter German, if that.

'Don't be silly, I know that,' Caroline had said, 'your friend's American. And besides it's the Nazis who are causing all the trouble, not the German people.'

It was only much later that Spencer fully appreciated his mother's fairmindedness. After all, it was her tiny offshore island that was under threat, her people who were fighting the war against what the press described as 'the most fearsome war machine ever conceived'. She scoured the papers for such paltry news items as were available and fiddled endlessly with the radio in the hope of picking up scraps of information. Her beauty faded a little and she looked harassed and tired. It wasn't too much fun being at home these days.

He'd known Trudel, or known of her, for some time, because everyone did. She was pretty unmissable with her big, creamy figure – another reason for the 'Apples' tag – and her halo of fuzzy blonde hair. All through the feverish whacking off years it was Trudel who saw you right, either vicariously or by giving you a helping hand.

She was a year older than Spencer and by the time she showed him what was what she'd already left high school and was working as a mother's help for Mrs Lowe, the doctor's wife. This mundane job only added to her charm. She seemed created for it. When she took the two little Lowes out in the afternoon, one in the stroller and one by the hand, she appeared much more like their mother, their ideal mother, than the squinny Mrs Lowe who lay on the sofa at home with another on the way. Calm, curvaceous, indulgent, nurturing, full of fecund promise, Trudel was the spirit of motherhood made flesh.

This was probably why it was impossible not to like her. Even the parents of Spencer's contemporaries, who must surely have known her reputation, tended to smile upon her as if they couldn't really believe what they'd heard. In spite of her undiscriminating sociability she was so clearly a nice girl. The Lowe children adored her. And as for their own sons, at an age when they wanted to feast their fill on the forbidden fruits of life, Trudel represented a table laden with an apparently inexhaustible supply of delectable goodies. Also, there was a kind of discretion in her general availability. You were safe with her because there was safety in numbers.

But Spencer fell in love with her for the oldest reason in the world: he thought he was different. He thought she understood him and saw something in him not present in her other admirers, and he in his turn took this as a sign that she was more complex and intuitive than she appeared to the herd. By definition this theory could never be tested, but once adopted it was only natural that he should make everything support it. So when in the extremity of passion she gasped his name, when she smiled and nodded as he talked (she was a good listener and not talkative herself), when she took his hand in both of her soft, cushiony ones, and told him in her confiding manner that she wanted nothing more than to marry a good man and have his babies – when she did these things they seemed unique and particular to him.

He was not so foolish as actually to propose marriage, but privately he considered himself to be marked for that preferment. Sometimes, in the summer after he too left high school and was working for Mack in the yard, he'd accompany Trudel on her afternoon constitutionals with the Lowe kids. There was no canoodling on these outings, both of them behaved impeccably though he'd usually wind up in a state of agonising tumescence that necessitated five minutes of solitary activity on the way home.

Another good thing about Trudel was that she came clued-up and fully equipped. She knew about rubbers, explained how and where to get them, and was able to put them on with delicious deftness. She kept a supply herself – a perk of working for the doctor – and in the rare situation of there being none available she was sufficiently practised to ensure that no risks were taken. She was in every sense a safe pair of hands.

To begin with Spencer didn't mind being one of the many, so long as he believed he was special. But after a while it got irksome, knowing that on evenings when he couldn't get away some other guy was having a good time, no matter how little it meant to Trudel, whose feelings he didn't for a moment doubt.

He put it to her one afternoon when they were with the Lowe kids. They were actually sitting in the Flahertys' back yard, where there was an old tin hip bath with water in, and the kids were running around in the buff having a terrific time.

Seamus was at work in the saddlery – he won county prizes for his leather-tooling – and fat amiable Mrs Flaherty was perspiring indoors with iced coffee and a magazine so there was no hint of impropriety in the arrangement.

'I can't get out tonight,' said Spencer. 'I've got to go out helping pick up and deliver jobs.'

'That's all right,' said Trudel placidly. 'You've got your work – I've got mine.' She nodded in the direction of her charges as they splashed and shrieked.

Spencer cracked his knuckles, and as he'd intended, she put her hand over his, wincing. 'Don't do that!'

'Sorry.'

'Cheer up. How about tomorrow?'

'Should be okay. Trudel—'

'Mmm?'

'Are you seeing anyone else tonight?'

'Not that I know of.' He knew she was telling the truth. She was such a free spirit, she wrote her own rules so completely, that it was a waste of time getting jealous or angry. But Spencer was struggling with both.

'Will you though – if someone asks you?'

She shrugged. 'I might do. No – I don't know. Why?'

He wanted to ask, Why would you want to? But instead he said: 'Because I don't want you to.'

'Oh!' She laughed in a motherly sort of way and patted his leg. 'Don't be silly. You're my number one. You know that.'

'I'd like to be your only one.'

'You are. Kind of.'

'I mean, really.'

She looked at him with a big grin and shining eyes. She seemed to find this whole conversation *fun*.

'Am I your only one, Spencer?'

'Yes.'

The moment he'd said it he wanted to take it back. Instead of the stirring declaration of singleminded passion that he'd intended, it came out sullen and pathetic.

'That's nice,' said Trudel equably. 'That's sweet.'

'It is not! It is not sweet.'

'Because you are sweet,' she went on as though he hadn't spoken. 'You're the sweetest boy in town. And the smartest.'

She looked at him as she said this and there was a warm lasciviousness in her tone and the way her lips moved around the words as though she were licking ice cream. He felt himself stir with desire and tried not to think of how close her body was, her billowing breasts in the cotton dress, her smooth thighs squashed down on the edge of the garden chair.

'I love you,' he said.

'I know,' she replied, as if it went without saying, 'and I love you.'

He didn't stop to ask himself why she thought him smart, it was enough for him that she did. Indeed the mere fact that he wasn't, on the face of it, the smartest, confirmed him in his opinion that theirs was a special relationship. He knew he was going to do something great with his life, he felt it in his bones, in his water, and Trudel with her woman's intuition knew it too.

Temporarily mollified, he let the matter rest there. But the worm of jealousy, having once stirred, waxed and grew fat. And the arrival of Bobby Forrest on the scene did nothing to dispel it.

As a matter of fact Bobby had been around for a while too, but unlike most of the other guys had shown no interest in Trudel. This, he let it be known in various subtle ways, was because he had no need of her. Bobby was one of those youths in whom the hormones struck even earlier and more impressively than in Spencer. He was very dark and by the time he was fourteen he was five-ten and a hundred and sixty pounds, sported a distinct moustache, his voice had broken, and he could do some pretty crazy tricks with his cock. Added to which he had a handsome confidence which proclaimed him ready for anything. Most of what the other boys learned about girls they learned from Bobby, or from stories about him. And at school he was a jock, which gave him still more of an advantage.

As if that weren't enough he was also a good-natured fellow who didn't in the least mind sharing the fruits of his experience with anyone who'd listen. In fact, had Spencer been able to he would have seen that Bobby was the male version of Trudel.

When he discovered that the two of them had been to the movies together he was shocked and outraged. Where had Bobby got the money to take her? And what had gone on during and after the show?

He asked her the very next time he saw her.

'You said you loved me.'

'That's right. And I do.'

'But you went out with Bobby.'

She laughed, 'Oh, Bobby!'

'What did you do?'

'We went to the Greta Garbo movie. She is the most beautiful woman in the world,' Trudel added a little wistfully, but Spencer wasn't bothered about that.

'Did you kiss him?'

'He kissed me,' she said.

'It's the same thing!'

'No, it's not.' She was calm as ever, not in the least defensive.

'You told him not to?'

'No.'

'You pushed him away?'

'Of course not!' She began to laugh again. 'Why would I do that? We were at the movies!'

'So what's the difference,' he insisted furiously, almost in tears, 'between him and me?'

She put her hand to his face and looked at him with a sweet, tender, silly-boy smile. 'You're *you*, Spencer, that's the difference, you know that.'

It wasn't much of an answer, but he was as always disarmed: willingly convinced for the moment that whoever else she allowed to kiss her he occupied some special and superior place in her heart.

But that was while he was with her. By the time he'd been one hour out of her company the terrible pangs had returned, chewing at his vitals.

'Aren't you hungry?' asked his mother as he pushed his supper around. 'This isn't like you.'

He shook his head. 'I'm sorry, I can't eat.'

'Oh, it doesn't matter, but do you feel all right? You're not sick?'

'I'm fine.'

'Do you want to leave the table?' Mack asked.

'Thanks.' He pushed his chair back and headed for the door, aware of the concerned look they exchanged behind his back as he did so.

Everything went on pretty much the same. Trudel never said no, seemed always to be available, but he knew – because others had told him with a hint of gloating – that she was still seeing Bobby. There weren't any others these days, it was a joke among the guys that Apples was turning into a nun, but that only made it worse. If there had once been safety in numbers there was now real danger in being one of only two, because that meant that sooner or later she was going to have to choose between them. At least that was what Spencer thought, even if Trudel didn't. With self-destructive persistence he urged her to make the choice and she mildly refused to be pushed around.

It did make him sick in the end. He lost weight, couldn't sleep, was cranky and miserable. Mack gave him a week off work and Caroline made him go to the doctor. He got to the surgery at the same time as Trudel was arriving for her day with the children.

'What's the matter with you?' she asked.

'Nothing.'

'Then why are you here?'

'I can't eat.' He was rather proud of himself for this obvious, physical sign of his consuming passion.

'Oh . . .' She stroked his hair back off his forehead. 'That's not right, Spence. You do look kind of thin, I noticed.'

He grabbed her hand and held it to his chest. 'You can make me better. You know how.'

She let her hand stay there, spreading her fingers under his, over his heart, so he thought he'd die of longing.

'Nonsense,' she said gently. 'You only have to eat. And be happy – don't get so mad at the world.'

If he was getting mad at the world, he thought, it was because the world was going mad round him.

And then Trudel disappeared. She just wasn't around, and Yolande Haynes started taking out the Lowe kids with the new baby in its baby carriage. All Mrs Flaherty would say when Spencer called was that she'd gone away for a while, but she looked tearful, and Mr Flaherty was grimly taciturn. Or at least he was until Spencer got to the gate, and then he called after him.

'Spencer McColl!'

Spencer stopped and turned. 'Yes, sir?'

There was some sort of hiatus, a muted exchange in the doorway: Mrs Flaherty appeared to be remonstrating with her husband but he shooed her firmly and gently back into the house and came down the path to Spencer.

'My wife's upset, as you can see.'

'I'm sorry. I guess she misses Trudel . . . we all do.' Mr Flaherty's eyes, narrowed and unblinking, focused mercilessly on Spencer, who felt acutely uncomfortable.

'Some more than others. Huh, young man?'

'How do you mean?'

Flaherty took a step closer, a whisker too close for comfort. Spencer could see a red fleck on his chin where he'd nicked himself with the razor, and see a couple of long wiry grey hairs curling in his nostrils. He gave off the sweet-sour smell of the saddlery.

'You wouldn't happen to know anything about all this, would you?'

'About what?'

'About my daughter being in the family way.'

'My daughter' – not 'our' daughter. Man to man. A challenge. Spencer had never been so scared.

'No, sir!'

Flaherty raised a callused finger between their faces. His eyes burned ice-cold. 'She wouldn't say anything about anyone. Said it was her fault. Went off to stay with her auntie in Chicago.

But it takes two to tango and you've been round here like a stray dog these last months. I'm not stupid, McColl—'

'I know that, sir—'

'Shut up. I'm not stupid and I'm not blind and I know my daughter liked male company. She's a fine looking girl.' He paused as if waiting for an endorsement which Spencer was by now far too terrified to give. 'But if – when – I find out who the little bastard was who did this to her, and who thinks he's got away with it because she's too darn' proud to sneak – when I find out who he is, his life won't be worth living. Understand?'

Spencer nodded. Flaherty held his gaze for a couple more interminable seconds and then went stumping back up the path and closed the door behind him.

Spencer only just reached the end of the fence before opening his pants and pissing a flood. His knees were trembling so much that he splashed himself. To give time for his pants to dry and to get his head straight he walked down to the creek and sat hunched over, shaken and miserable, on the bank. The resident muskrat plied back and forth about his business, trailing a spreading chevron of ripples in his wake. What the hell did he care? Spencer picked up a lump of earth and lobbed it at the rat, who submerged with a 'gloop'.

It wasn't him. It couldn't be him, they'd both been so careful about using the rubbers. Even when he'd been too excited to give a damn, Trudel had seen to it. She even made a point of testing the supply because she said it was well known there was always one with a hole for playing Russian roulette with . . .

He realised he didn't know whether Trudel was going to have the baby, or if she was ever coming back. He didn't even know her address, for God's sake, apart from Chicago, and that was an enormous city. But old man Flaherty had served notice – Spencer's life, if it was him, wouldn't be worth living.

And then a strange thing happened. As he sat there he began to feel the stirrings of something other than shame, bewilderment and terror. He started to feel a spark of pride, and with it, anger. Damn it, if he was the father he'd marry Trudel and show them he loved her and could look after her! Perhaps

153

after everything she'd said to him about being special she'd engineered the whole thing – perhaps she'd *wanted* his baby, and it was all meant to be, in which case he wasn't going to be made to feel it was some sort of crime, even by old man Flaherty. All of a sudden he could picture himself and Trudel, a young married couple, heads held high, wheeling their baby out on fine afternoons, just as they'd used to play at it with the Lowe kids. The picture was a pretty one, happy and strong and right.

But first he had to know. And to know he had to get in touch with her.

Spencer waited a couple of days till it was Monday and Trudel's father was at the saddlery. He took his own lunch break early, and even took a peek to make sure Mr Flaherty was where he should be, working away with his sharp, stubby little knife, before going round to their house.

Mrs Flaherty was just as direct as her husband, though the burden of her song could not have been more different. She was a big, rolling woman who seemed to be melting with melancholy.

'Oh, Spencer, what are we going to do? Come in, come in, you might as well . . .'

She seemed both to presuppose his involvement, and to invite his collusion. She was certainly not hostile, quite the opposite, as she escorted him into the parlour and plumped a cushion for him to lean on.

'Would you like coffee? A piece of cake?'

Since it was evident she'd been consuming both herself, he accepted the coffee, though not the cake, in the cause of solidarity.

'How is Trudel, Mrs Flaherty?' he asked carefully.

'She wrote me that she's well, but what should I think?' The vestigial German inflection in Mrs Flaherty's voice gave her plaints an operatic quality.

'You don't believe her?' asked Spencer.

'She's so far away. A daughter should be with her mother at this time!'

It was on the tip of Spencer's tongue to ask why, in that case, she wasn't. But he restrained himself.

'I'm sure she's telling the truth,' he said.

'You've heard from her?' enquired Mrs Flaherty with a sudden hint of sharpness.

'No.' He shook his head emphatically and thinking of Mr Flaherty gouging away with his knife, added: 'Why would she write to me?'

'Because you were her special friend. She thought the world of you . . .'

Spencer's heart swelled. 'I'm glad about that. And I'd like to send her a letter. Could you let me have her address?'

'Well . . . I don't know about . . . Mr Flaherty wouldn't like it. I mean he doesn't want anyone knowing about this, and he thinks you may have been responsible—'

Until he knew for sure, Spencer thought complete denial was the simplest thing. 'It wasn't me,' he said with all the firmness he could muster. 'It couldn't have been.'

Mrs Flaherty looked even more mournful. 'Sure it could have been, as much as anyone else.'

Spencer, mortified, drew a deep breath and declared himself. 'I loved her, I took care of her. That's what I want to do now – let me write to her Mrs Flaherty.'

'I don't know. My husband would be so mad. It doesn't bear thinking about!' She shook her head, closing her eyes and turning her mouth down in a tragi-comic expression like a clown's.

'Please.' He tried another tack. 'It would do her good to hear from a friend – to know we're thinking of her.'

'Maybe . . . Maybe you're right.'

'I'm sure I am.'

'Very well.' She got up and waddled massively to the bureau, coming back with a notepad and paper. Then she wrote down the address in her deliberate, florid hand, and passed it to him with a sigh. 'There you are, God forgive me.'

Fine sentiment was one thing, but to express it truthfully and well quite another, as Spencer was to discover. He threw away innumerable attempts at the letter because they appeared either cloying or sententious. There was also the simple fact that he, like everyone else, did not know the identity of the baby's father. To claim that it was his would be an arrogant and, given Mr Flaherty's attitude, possibly dangerous assumption; but to write as though it wasn't would seem cold and cowardly.

In the end he stuck to a sturdy message of love and concern, and a promise of support. It was a little drier in tone than he would have wished, but it was the best he could do given that he wanted to sound manly and mature. By the time he posted the letter, his brain was scrambled – he was unable to tell whether he'd struck the right note or not, and there was no one to whom he could turn for advice.

A couple of days after he'd sent it he met Bobby Forrest in the Diamond Diner. Or more accurately Bobby came up to Spencer when he was at the counter drinking a club soda with Aaron and Joel.

'Hey, Spencer McColl, howya doing?'

Spencer winced at the feel of Bobby's hand on his shoulder, like that of an arresting officer.

'Hi there.'

'Seen anything of Trudel lately?'

This casual enquiry surprised Spencer. For one thing Bobby seemed to take for granted that he 'saw' Trudel regularly; for another, he appeared to have no idea that she'd gone away.

'No.'

'Nor me. Where'd she get to?'

'She's gone to stay with her aunt in Chicago.'

'Lucky Chicago.'

'Yeah.'

'Funny she just upped and went, and never said nothing. She okay?'

Spencer deliberated for a split second before opting for the truth, if not the whole truth.

He shrugged, a man not overly concerned. 'Far as I know.'

When Bobby had gone, Aaron pulled a jokily admiring face.

'Well I'll be-! So you're like that with Apples, and Bobby Forrest doesn't care . . . ?'

'Ah,' said Spencer, 'he just knows when he's beat.' He might have acted casual, but there was no denying the strangeness of the exchange. In one way it had been flattering to be deferred to by Bobby. In another the whole incident seemed to confirm Trudel's status as a girl who didn't say no, and about whose movements there was consequently no shame in admitting ignorance. It also reminded him that the baby could be Bobby's.

Spencer was uneasy. Much, he felt, depended on the tenor of Trudel's reply to his letter. He allowed two days for it to get there, a further two – no, three – for her to absorb its message and compose her own, and two more for hers to reach him. Once that week had passed he started waiting in earnest.

No letter ever came.

The pain and frustration settled down into a dull anxiety. He didn't like to go round to the Flaherty place again, and no news was forthcoming. Bobby took up with another girl, red-haired Minna Goldie, and among Spencer's contemporaries it began to be generally accepted that Apples had finally got unlucky in some unspecified way that they could nonetheless guess at. No more suspicion fell on Spencer than anyone else and the matter was let lie there because of a tacit understanding that too many people had too much to lose. After two or three months Trudel as a subject for discussion was dropped altogether. Out of sight was out of mind.

She remained on Spencer's mind, but life went on. He was heartily sick of working for Mack, and they were starting to get on each other's nerves, so it was a good thing all round when he landed a job out at Buck's. The job itself was humble, no more than a handyman to begin with, but at least he had the satisfaction of belonging to an organisation whose associations reached well beyond Moose Draw and its small-town preoccupations. He lived in the bunkhouse and learned to fit in. In spite of his worry about Trudel, he enjoyed the work, and being with older men who treated him like one of the guys. He learned that the writer was in poor health these days and hadn't been at the ranch for a couple of years. Tallulah was still there, but old and fat, disinclined to do much of anything but lie on the front porch of the main house and snooze. A couple of crazy golden retrievers had taken her place. Spencer kept his eyes open for the little mare who hadn't really wanted to escape, but never saw her, and when he asked the foreman about her – mentioning the famous writer – he was told she'd most likely been helped on her way, they couldn't afford to keep horses past their best.

The horses were the motor of the whole place, its pulse and its heartbeat, and Spencer grew to love them in an inexpert, wholehearted kind of way. He'd never have made a cowboy, he was too squeamish and introspective for that, but he learned to ride and help out, and most of all to get to know the animals he'd admired from a safe distance for so long. In time he was to realise how wise and generous, in their stern way, were the Buck's cowboys. They may have engaged in a little gentle teasing – there was one incident with whisky, and another with chewing tobacco – but they never mocked his townie's view of the horses, nor his initial nervousness and ineptitude, and though they were tough and uncompromising they were not intolerant. These were men of deep and closely guarded feelings. The way they loved the horses wasn't so different from his – they were just as susceptible to the passion, but it was something that came to them second, that dawned on them after decades of riding and saddle-breaking, herding, branding and shoeing. The magic slipped in beneath their guard when they were doing this stuff, and took root. In spite, or because of, the necessary shooting. Spencer was respectful of the fact that you couldn't really say you knew horses until you'd had to put one down: something he was never obliged nor called upon to do – the cowboys knew his limitations as well as he did.

He didn't accompany guests on week-long treks, but watched wistfully, broom in hand as they set out loaded with packs and canvas tents and duffels. He did eventually get time off his usual chores to stand in for someone else on half-day and one-hour rides in the area around the creek. Occasionally for the same reason he was allowed to help turn the horses out at night, driving them two or three miles up from the ranch, proud of the show they put on for the guests who stood on their verandahs and porches, the kids in nightclothes, watching with shining eyes. It was even headier if they had to drive horses through town, with the shudder of hooves on tarmacadam, the bobbing, tossing mass of sorrel and roan and chestnut and black and grey and two-tone, and the dull old cars crawling behind because they had to. He never got over that, the thrill of being in charge of the horses in Wyoming where they had right of way . . .

In the morning, before six, they drove the horses back down, gathering up the different groups and their leaders. The leaders wore copper bells strapped close to their throats, and each bell was pitched a bit differently so they made a clangorous counterpoint to the bumpy rush of the horses' feet charging back down the valley.

In the autumn the horses' shoes came off and they were turned out on the high slopes to fend for themselves. They went feral, mixing with the wild horses and hearing the call of their ancestors. Rounding them up in the spring was a scary business, even the cowboys said so – the union between man and horse was stretched rag-thin, and the animals as they came back to Buck's were proud and flittery, and smelled brackish. Their manes and tails were burred and matted and the guard hairs stood out like metal wires over their long coats.

The horse Spencer rode stayed home. He was called Jim, generally recognised as a couch with hooves, perfect for kids and novices but Spencer was eternally grateful for Jim's plodding patience. It was through Jim's forbearance that he learned the hard, heavy work involved in cleaning tack and shoeing and grooming and feeding, the sheer weight of horses and everything that went with them, the way your sweat mixed with theirs and their smell became your smell, and your puny muscles ached in keeping up your end of the bargain. 'Tough love' was a phrase whose currency was decades away, but that was what it was, and Spencer thought he never wanted any other kind.

* * *

159

A long way second to the horses came the people who stayed at Buck's. It took him longer to get a handle on them. It was weird – these gilded beings with their sleek, grinning automobiles and smart clothes, expansive manners and confident voices, formed the shifting population of Buck's Creek for months every year, and yet their presence barely impinged on the rest of the community. They were like some rare, sparsely documented tribe who existed beyond the margins of Moose Draw, but occupied an important place in the town's collective imagination.

Still, the reality did not disappoint. Because of his youth and his lowly status he was most of the time amiably ignored as he went about his weeding, mowing, fetching, carrying and fixing, and so was able to observe unobserved. The most remarkable thing about the Buck's guests was their dedication to the idea of fun. In the experience of Spencer and most of the people he knew, there was work, and there was time off – even leisure would have been too strong a word. The time off was generally accompanied by mild boredom and discontent, occasioned by the knowledge that given the money and the opportunity, better things were to be had.

The Buck's guests had the cash, and all the time in the world. They were in no hurry. It fascinated Spencer the way they could lounge around for hours outside their cabins, endlessly smoking and drinking, talking vivaciously, breaking into great bursts of laughter. They came all this way and paid hundreds of dollars to pretend to be cowboys, but having done so they weren't going to be pushed around. They brought gramophones and played music, and on those occasions when Spencer stayed over to help with a barbecue he was astonished at the free and easiness of it all. There was no getting away from it: sex was in the air.

And not just in the air, but in the way these people talked and danced and laughed and dressed. It was in the way the women crossed their legs, and blew their cigarette smoke, in the way the men proffered lighters and poured drinks and told confiding, humorous stories. It was in the women's scent and the men's cigars. In the dark interiors of the long, parked cars, and in the twilit avenues of trees at the mouth of the canyon. Spencer kept his head down, his eyes and ears open, and his mouth shut.

There was one young woman there, not much more than a girl really, in her early twenties, whom he reckoned must be just like Lottie, whom the writer had loved and lost. This girl was not quite beautiful, nor even pretty, she was better than both – slim as a whippet, sharp as a tack, bright-eyed, fierce and quick. She came with a group of friends who seemed a little older than her, but she seemed not specially attached to any of them. Almost uniquely among the guests she'd throw a 'Hi' or 'Morning!' to Spencer when she passed. She drove fast in a white coupé, could ride and shoot, and entered into everything with concentration and energy. One evening, from the twilight sidelines of glass-clearing and ashtray-emptying, he saw her bebop like a dervish so that the floor cleared and everyone became a hollering audience for her and her partner. Sometimes, though, she just spent the day on the verandah, half-smoking endless cigarettes, with her feet on the rail and her nose in a book. He never knew her name, but years later when he heard the song 'That's Why the Lady is a Tramp' he was reminded of her. Only the rich could afford not to give a damn.

The ranch had an airstrip now, and as well as a little plane that took guests up for joyrides there were one or two guests who had light aircraft of their own, in which they arrived and departed.

One perfect morning when most of them were out trail-riding or sleeping off the effects of last night's party, Spencer was doing the rounds collecting trash and taking it to the gate for removal by the Moose Draw trash-waggon. There was a battered flat-bed truck for the purpose, and a strict speed limit of ten miles an hour. He trundled along the narrow paths in back of the cabins, stopping every twenty yards to pick up the next four cans, haul them to the truck and load them upright in neat, tightly packed ranks like gherkins in a jar. You could get sixteen on the truck, and that was it – he'd tried to be clever once by laying them flat and creating two layers, but the result had been disaster, with garbage spilt everywhere, a roasting from Buck Jameson and a cleaning-up operation which – undertaken singlehandedly – had taken most of the day. So there was nothing for it but to make the full six trips, quietly and tidily: it was his least favourite job.

This morning he'd just emptied the first batch into the container at the gate when a plane came over. The sky was an endless, pristine blue. The honeyed drone of the plane preceded it by a couple of seconds and then it appeared, like a solo dancer taking the stage. It was hard to believe the pilot couldn't see Spencer, that he didn't know he had this grounded, trash-stained audience of one. The plane swooped in a graceful curve, climbed steeply, rolled, looped, circled wide, repeated itself. Spencer stood there with his hand shielding his eyes, spellbound. The engine-song of the plane swirled with it, *crescendos* and *diminuendos*, upward and downward *glissandos* accompanying the fun.

The impromptu display must have lasted five minutes. Then the plane hummed away to the east. Spencer leaned back on the truck, rubbing his eyes. He felt bereft, possessed by the same grey recognition of his lot that overcame him after he'd met the writer, and when he came out of the movie theatre. That was the level on which the rich lived life – one of speed and glamour, drama and romance: life with the dull everyday detail airbrushed out.

Whereas this – he sniffed the sour smell on his hands and saw the stained butt ends on the ground around his feet – this was his level. For now.

He hankered after Trudel. It had to be love he reasoned because absence had not only made the heart grow fonder but winched up the physical longing to a quite unbearable degree. Her image remained clear in his mind, and (unlike Bobby, he reflected with grim pride) no one had replaced her in his affections. A couple of dates with other girls had proved as much. Six months went by and it was September, the end of the summer and of the season. From here on in he'd be doing basic maintenance at the ranch for another few weeks and then returning to help Mack – unless something else came up – through the winter. His heart sank at the prospect.

And then Trudel returned. With no baby.

He had no idea she was back until he saw her on Sunday morning coming out of church with her parents, and he was too shocked and astonished to go up to her or say anything. She didn't see him, which made his disappointing behaviour a little less shameful. She'd lost weight, and looked different in some other indefinable way as well. Her bushy blonde hair was rolled up neatly; she wore a black buttoned coat. But it was more than her appearance, a kind of air she had . . . Mr Flaherty walked in front, looking drawn and tired, Trudel and her mother followed, arms linked.

Something had happened. It was hard, confronted with this mysterious, united adult group, to recreate his spirited feelings of a few months ago. But he had to know. In the end he could stand the uncertainty no longer and on the Tuesday evening he plucked up the courage to go and call at her house.

She answered the door herself and greeted him as though she'd only seen him the day before.

'Spencer, it's so good to see you, come on in.'

With trepidation he stepped over the threshold. As soon as she'd closed the door she kissed him.

But delightful though the kiss was he knew at once that she'd changed, and so had things between them. With that kiss she acknowledged their former closeness but declared that this was the level at which they now were – that of affectionate and understanding friends.

'Are your parents in?' he asked warily.

'They're playing cards at the Driversons'.' She smiled. 'You mustn't worry, everything's fine – they aren't angry with you.'

She took him through into the parlour. The radio was tweedle-deeing away softly, playing dance music, and she turned it off. She made a deprecating gesture in the direction of the dining table on which stood a typewriter with paper sticking out of it and an open Pitman's book alongside.

'I'm teaching myself, but I'm all thumbs. Take a seat.'

'Thanks.'

'You want a beer?'

'Sure.'

He sat there as she went to fetch it. He rather wished she'd left the music on. He could hear the clock ticking in here, and Trudel moving around in the kitchen. He had to ask her when she came back in, and clear the air.

As soon as she handed him the glass, he blurted out: 'What happened to the baby?'

'What made you think there was a baby?'

He was stunned with embarrassment, but she remained solemn and enquiring. She seemed to have grown up immeasurably, to have left him far behind. He was going to have to shape up.

'Your father told me.'

'I hope he wasn't mean to you.'

'No – but he wasn't too pleased either.'

'There was a baby,' she said quietly, 'but it went away.'

'You mean—' He was floundering, way out of his depth, his brain teeming with dreadful half-formed possibilities. 'You mean, you—'

'It doesn't matter, Spencer. It's over now.'

'I'm so sorry.'

She tilted her head in the suggestion of a shrug. 'No need. No one's to blame.'

'Did you get my letter?'

'Yes. Thank you, that was lovely of you. No one else bothered, except Mom.'

'I meant what I said.'

'Of course you did.'

'So if there's anything you need, anything at all . . . Or if you just . . .' All his brave protestations of love died in his throat. 'You only have to ask.' He sounded like some half-assed, constipated character from an English novel. He could have wept, but she never wavered.

'I know. Don't worry, I shan't forget.'

He was in a chair, and she at one end of the couch. Boldly,

determined at least to try and bridge the gap between them, he went to sit next to her. But when he put his arm round her shoulders she was merely quiescent. There was none of the old, welcoming warmth, the open invitation, the delightful sense of mutual anticipation.

'How are you?' he asked. 'Are you all right?'

'Look at me.' She smiled, and made a little open-armed gesture which, without offering or inflicting the least offence, obliged him to withdraw his arm. 'What does it look like?'

He said: 'You've lost weight.'

'I sure needed to.'

Every word, every second, he felt sadder. It was like the fall from grace of Adam and Eve, the loss of innocence – whatever else had happened in Chicago, Trudel had tasted the fruit of the tree of self-awareness.

'So what are you going to do?' He jerked his head at the typewriter.

'I'm going to get a good job, and work hard at it, and make some money and move out east.'

He hadn't expected quite such a forthright and comprehensive answer. 'Is that all?'

'It may not work out,' she said, 'but you have to have a dream, don't you?'

'I guess so,' he agreed.

Crestfallen, in bed that night, with the cold of early autumn pressing on the windows and a skunk bumping around in the trash outside, Spencer realised he'd better get another dream and quick, because the one about his future, just like the one about his past, was dead as dead could be.

It was a long time coming, but in early December world events took a hand. The distant mutter of the war in Europe became a sudden thunderclap right overhead, and a simultaneous flash of sheet lightning as the torching of the fleet in Pearl Harbor woke America with a bang.

Even the small towns and the one-horse places stirred and shook their locks. Their young men swaggered and their maidens swooned and cheered. Mothers grew tight-lipped and fathers wished (at least in public) that they were younger. Even Moose Draw was going to war and that included Spencer McColl.

He'd always imagined that the expression 'a dream come true' meant the instant fulfilment of a wish – you woke up one day and whatever it was your heart desired had come to you, out of the blue. But in his case it came in stages – not easy ones, they were tough – in a process lasting nearly eighteen months. A long hard slog before he jumped down off the lorry into the liquid mud of the airfield at Church Norton, England, and saw his second great love standing there as if she'd been waiting for him all his life this far.

He wanted to fly. Since seeing the little plane spinning and swooping over Bucks Creek Canyon the idea had been in the back of his mind, but didn't take on any concrete form till the winter of '42 when war-fever hit. That was when he suddenly realised it was a possibility. Without being rich, he could be up there – in fact someone else might pay him to do it! Mack said there wasn't a hope in hell, you needed to be a straight-As guy for that. But Spencer found out that the Airforce was taking on men for flight training with only high-school level education, and with his parents' blessing he reported to the recruiting office in Salutation and sat the tests. There must have been a dozen of them there on the day he went, sat at individual square tables like grade school, chewing their pens and feeling like fools. But he was one of five who got through, and Mack ate his words and bought him a beer like a gentleman. When it came to the physical Spencer was more confident and his confidence proved justified. He was strong, fit and had twenty-twenty vision. They took him on and he reported for basic training at Montgomery, Alabama.

Each step of the way Spencer thought would be his last. Basic training wasn't so bad, it consisted pretty much of putting one foot in front of another, keeping your head and your spirits up and your eye on the objective. But the next step, college, was harder; he had to get back the studying habit, and struggled till his brain felt knotted with math, algebra and simple physics. His confidence took a knock and he was horribly homesick. The therapy for this was writing letters. Caroline wrote him most days – for the first time he was a little embarrassed by her open affection and tried unsuccessfully to pretend that the regular letters were from different people.

But this time Trudel replied to him too, and her immaculately typed letters made him walk twelve feet tall.

I'm so proud of you. I guess we're both trying to find a way out of Moose Draw, but the war's made it quicker for you. Dr Lowe's taken me back on as receptionist and I really like it – I even think I'm pretty good at it, is that terrible? I like dealing with all the people and trying to make them feel a bit better even before they see the doc. It's made me think I might do some kind of medical training one day, be a nurse or something, you never know. But that's a long way off. Pop's not well and Mom's unhappy so they need me around at the moment, I've caused them enough worry for a lifetime!

Spencer, I know we didn't see too much of each other after I got back but I still miss you, and just knowing you were around. Whatever we do and wherever we wind up in the future, let's hope we can stay good friends. Write when you feel like it but don't feel you have to, I can always pick up the news from your folks. Take care of yourself.

Love,
Trudel

He was touched by her letter. And another thing – his own separation, physical and emotional, from Moose Draw put him more on a par with her. He thought he understood now the change she'd undergone during that time in Chicago. Only for her it had been a hundred times worse because she'd lost the baby. He could see only too clearly now how impossible it would have been for her to accept his offers of love. She'd moved on and become someone different and that altered everything, created an irreversible shift in life's tectonic plates. Reading her letter he was sure, now, that they could be friends, and with that certainty came the private acknowledgement that he was no longer in love with her. He was free.

After the college course came Classification, in some ways the most agonising step of all because this would determine his role in the air: navigator, bombardier or pilot. Until he'd been accepted for flight training he hadn't, in his ignorance, even realised there was a choice. Now he was cast down by the thought that he might be condemned (as he saw it) to some job other than that of actually flying a warbird.

But a week later he was told he'd be a pilot, and he seemed to take off. Nothing after that, not the rigours of the physical training, the complexities of pre-flight, flying school and advanced flying, was too much for him. This – this – was the element for which he'd been born, where he felt at home and in command. In basic flying school he went solo in the lumbering BT13 Vultee Valiant (known as The Vibrator) after only eight hours of instruction. He was supremely confident. Navigation, night- and formation-flying, even the extreme disorientation of rolling 'blind', relying not on one's senses but on the instruments alone, he came through all of them with flying colours. And during the intensive aerobatics of advanced flying in the heavy snub-nosed AT6 Harvard, he shouted out once 'I'm here!' – confusing the control tower, his only bad mistake.

The day in February '43 when he received his silver wings was the proudest of his life. He returned to Moose Draw for two weeks' home embarkation leave already feeling like a hero. His first day back he went to call on Trudel at the surgery at lunchtime and they went over the road to the diner. She was smart and serious, doing a home study course in math and English, and helping look after her father, who could now scarcely breathe for the goop in his lungs. Spencer admired her for the honourable conscientiousness of that, and sensed a mutual affection and respect that was different from what they'd had before. It was more equal, deeper, it allowed for all kinds of possibilities. He was proud of the two of them and how far they'd come. He thought how strange it was that they, the overgrown loner and the easy girl – the very opposite of the prom queen and the sports star – should now be so conspicuously on their way. To be sure they weren't the only ones, Moose Draw's habitual torpor was riven with proud and fearful leave-takings and exhortations to do the job and hurry home . . . nonetheless their short shared history cast a reflective light over salt beef and coleslaw sandwiches in the Diamond Diner.

'He's going to die,' Trudel said of her father.

'I'm sorry.'

'I'm not.' She sighed. 'The sooner he goes the better for his sake. But I don't know what Mom will do, he's been her whole life.'

'And you,' Spencer reminded her. 'You've been her life as well.'

'Maybe. But I haven't done all the things she would have liked a daughter to do. When I was going with every boy in town – no,' she said, putting her hand on his, 'I was and we both know it. When I was doing that she was busy pretending I was just a nice friendly girl, and Pop toed the line so as not to worry her . . .' Trudel pushed her plate away. 'It's funny to be the same person, but not the same.'

'Yeah, I know. Me too, I was thinking that. I was pretty pathetic, wasn't I?' He asked this to cheer her up, he could sense her reflections turning a bit sad.

She rewarded him with a big soft smile, the old Apples shining through for a moment. 'No, you *weren't*, you were cute. And always so hot.'

'Weren't we all?'

'Pretty much.'

'Can I ask you something – I got my wings, I guess I'm just about brave enough.'

'Go ahead.'

'Was I different at all? I mean, to you?'

She looked down at his hand on the counter, and covered it with hers. 'Not really. No.'

It was a relief in a way to have her put the full-stop on

things, but a little bruising too, so he tried to turn it into a joke. 'I mean, don't feel you have to be kind or anything, just come on and tell me straight out.'

This time she didn't smile. 'You weren't different then, Spencer. But you are now.'

On the day he left for the posting to England, his mother didn't cry. It was Mack who looked all trussed up in unaccustomed, uncomfortable emotion, who crunched his hand and could find nothing to say nor any voice to say it with.

At this difficult moment Caroline protected all of them with what he'd always thought of as her Englishness – it was a quality she kept spotless and crisply folded in some mental bottom drawer, like a fancy tablecloth, to be brought out and used to put on a good show. She was upright, immaculate, sweet-smelling and self-possessed. If she wept and raged after he'd gone he never knew. What was more, she treated him like a man – there were no little maternal gestures, no fussing over packing, no patting of the cheek nor brushing of the shoulders – and he was more grateful than he could say for that.

The only thing, the only hint of a thing, that she did that day which recalled the past was not even intended for him. He heard it as he was upstairs changing into his uniform and she was down in the store, opening up. It was the song she was singing – or humming, for she wasn't using the words. *'The water is wide, I cannot get o'er . . .'*

By the time he was ready and down she'd stopped singing and he was composed.

'You look after England,' she said. 'For all of us.'

The journey was enough to take the wind out of anyone's sails, or in Spencer's case from beneath his wings. Their departure from the States had a certain febrile, farewell excitement, but from there on the uncertainty took a hold on their spirits. It invaded their minds like the Atlantic fog through which they crept at ten knots, for more than two weeks, part of a hundred-vessel British convoy: a huge formation of shipping floating, tiptoeing almost, above the prowling U-boats. Only now did they realise how unprepared they were for whatever lay ahead. Most of them had never been outside America before, had never crossed an ocean nor heard a foreign tongue spoken. They were a bunch of brash, callow youths off to defend strangers in a country of which they had only the sketchiest idea.

Spencer made two friends, one through coincidence and the other of necessity. The former was Flying Officer Frank Steyner, who was remarkable for his ability to cut himself off from his surroundings, either by sleeping or reading. Since boredom and apprehension made many of the men cranky and belligerent, and since the overcrowding aboard *Diligent* was chronic, the food poor, and the seas intermittently rough, this struck Spencer as an enviable talent. Unaffected by tedium, impervious to fighting and vomiting, Steyner inhabited his own little world in which order prevailed. He was a slim, pale, slightly prim-looking young man whose hair was already thinning at the front and sides, a physical type who at junior school might have wound up getting teased or bullied, but here there was something formidable in such innate composure. Spencer suspected he was way smarter than most of them. He was left respectfully alone.

But one bad day they wound up next to each other in the canteen. There weren't many in the queue because *Diligent* was pitching and wallowing like a stuck pig and that had robbed most of them of their appetite. But there was Steyner, neat as a new pin, feet braced apart, hanging out one hand for the swill of mince, gravy and mashed potato and holding in the other a novel by the famous writer.

'Mind if I join you?' Spencer asked boldly.

Steyner glanced around. 'Put two Americans in a large half-empty room and they wind up rubbing shoulders.'

Spencer wasn't sure whether this constituted a 'yes', so he added, indicating the book: 'I've met him.'

'You have?'

The note of interest persuaded Spencer to accompany

Steyner to a table. 'When I was a kid. He used to stay at the dude ranch outside my home town, in the early spring, to work.'

'Would that be Buck's?'

'That's right. How did you know?'

'I've read a lot about him.' Steyner put his bookmark in place and slotted the book between the middle two buttons of his shirt – you got in the habit in this weather of not just laying things down. He picked up his fork and began to eat, saying without rancour: 'This is the filthiest goddamn food it's ever been my misfortune to confront. So do you know about Lottie?'

'She's got a memorial stone halfway up the canyon. That's where I met him.'

'Mooning around?'

Spencer couldn't be sure whether Steyner approved of the writer or not. 'No, he'd come off his horse.'

This provoked an explosion of unexpectedly robust laughter. 'You don't say! The great outdoor hero himself thrown off by some old easy chair from a dude ranch!'

Spencer smiled modestly, pleased with the sucess of his story. 'Not even thrown as a matter of fact – I think she scraped him off on a branch.'

'Better and better!' Still laughing, Steyner held out his hand. 'Put it there. Frank Steyner, New York City.'

'Spencer McColl, Moose Draw, Wyoming.'

'A pleasure. Have you read any of his works?'

'At high school. We read one of them in class.'

'That's right, you would – so appropriate for growing boys, so muscular, so straight down the line . . .' Spencer was just beginning to appreciate Frank's conversational weight and to enjoy his style, but he didn't see why he should get away with too much.

'I liked his writing.'

'You and millions of others. He's certainly doing something right.'

Spencer pointed at his midriff. 'You're reading him.'

'I am. And he's the perfect travelling companion, that I will

172

say. A breath of good old fresh country air while cooped up on the ocean wave with our brave boys.'

Throughout this exchange Steyner had been eating, small, quick mouthfuls swallowed in a businesslike way without relish. Spencer had only managed a third of his, and was beaten. Steyner nodded at his plate.

'You want that?' He shook his head. 'May I?'

'Be my guest.'

'Thanks.'

'You bet . . .'

Spencer watched, respectfully, as the food disappeared. When he'd finished, Steyner rose.

'See you around, Spencer. We can talk life, love and literature.'

The second friendship, the one born of necessity, was with Brad Hanna from Moses, Utah, who was in the bunk above him and whose dangling arm, tattooed with a fanged serpent, and hand, holding a cigarette, became as familiar to him as his own. Brad was two years younger and a mechanic whose consuming passion was motorbikes. He was perhaps the only man left on board *Diligent* who still wholeheartedly believed the war to be nothing more nor less than a terrific adventure and (he was sure about this) an unrivalled opportunity for fraternising with grateful European girls. Brad's unrelenting ebullience was something of a mixed blessing. He read his stock of comics and film magazines in strict rotation, and seemed to regard it as his social duty to share the pleasures of both with Spencer.

His opening sally was to hang head-down over the edge of his bunk and waggle the journal of the moment in Spencer's face.

'Hey, cowboy, take a look at this.'

'What is it?'

Another waggle. 'You ever see a pair like that? I mean, ever? You got any of that up in frontier country 'cos we sure don't in Moses.'

'I believe you.'

'You know what I reckon?' At this point Brad would do a neat sideways vault down from the top bunk – a hard trick since the next pair of bunks was only eighteen inches away – and perch on the edge of Spencer's, flicking at the photograph with his middle finger. 'I reckon it's the clothes. You put a doll in duds like that, push some of it up and pull some of it in and get her to stand like she's begging for it – everything looks good, know what I mean?'

Spencer thought, I'm twenty-one years old but this guy makes me feel old and tired. At the same time there was something soothing in this superabundance of cheerful good nature which needed neither pretext, attention nor approval in order to flourish.

All he had to say was: 'You're right. She's no prettier than most of the girls back home,' which would in turn be the cue for Brad to throw the magazine on the floor and yelp 'Speak for yourself, buddy!' or something like it.

'In Moses a girl who looked like that'd be locked up, I'm tellin' yer. You got a girl at home, cowboy?'

'No.'

'Damn' right!' Brad treated any remark of this kind as though it were an article of faith rather than a simple, factual response. 'We got the whole of English womanhood waiting for us!'

If English womanhood was waiting, it was doing so discreetly and behind closed doors on the night the fighter group arrived in Church Norton, Cambridgeshire. Gazing exhaustedly from the lorry, one of a roaring, rattling convoy transporting them from the station in the local market town, Spencer could scarcely begin to imagine their effect on this dour little place. The RAF had been here until recently, but they were the home team, and in much smaller numbers. This was a full-scale invasion, albeit a friendly one. It had been raining hard and though it had stopped now it was still overcast, and the windows of the houses were blacked-out: what with the darkness and the age and appearance of the cottages down the high street it was as though they'd travelled not just across the ocean, but back in time.

The women may have been lying low, but not the kids. They saw mostly young boys who should have been in bed – it was past ten o'clock – hanging out of windows and standing by the side of the road, cheering and waving and shouting 'Hallo, mister!' Outside the door of the pub, whose sign Spencer couldn't read, there was a group of men who just watched them go by, though one of them did raise his glass slightly.

He could see the lorries in front heading to the left, and climbing slightly, and next thing they too had swung round a steep bend. There was a large building to their left, and Spencer could make out the silhouette of a stubby castellated tower with a rooster weathervane swivelling back and forth. He took this to be the church, and assumed that the proximity of this to the pub meant they were in the middle of the town. But at once they seemed to be out in open country again and after another half a mile they pulled over and clambered down from the lorries, their boots smacking down into what would come to be the familiar thin film of liquid mud, slurry and engine oil that coated the roads around the airfield.

The other thing Spencer always remembered was the wind. It was an overcast night in high summer but the base seemed to have its own micro-climate in which it was always blustery. There was a faint farm smell, as though the land from which the airfield had been carved refused to be dismissed. The McColls had not been great churchgoers, but Spencer remembered something about swords being made into ploughshares – he was itching to start flying and bomb the bejasus out of the enemy, but that underlying smell served as a reminder that the idea was for a guy to work himself out of a job.

They were taken to the airmen's quarters at Site 5, and Frank Steyner fell in next to him – Spencer hadn't seen Brad since disembarkation.

'Natives were reserving judgement,' commented Frank in his dry-stick way.

'Yeah . . . not exactly a tickertape welcome.'

'Who can blame them? Who wants to be under an obligation?'

'I guess.'

They entered a Nissen hut with two rows of narrow beds, lockers, a squat stove at the far end

'Honey,' chirruped Frank satirically, 'we're home!'

The next morning it was fine, and a pearly light was already breaking at four a.m. when Spencer woke. His bed was near the door. He pulled on his boots, and a sweater over his pyjamas, and went outside.

He drew a couple of deep breaths, stretching his arms above his head, and turning slowly through three hundred and sixty degrees. The airfield was like a stage set, primed and ready, half-lit, unpopulated, the far edges of it mysterious. To the north was the place through which they'd come last night; he could see the church tower like that of a miniature castle prodding through the surrounding trees. To east and west was open space, fanned by runways, some of them just pierced steel plating laid down over the farmland. Here and there clusters of Quonsett huts and low-rise buildings, the accommodation and amenities of the base – PX, stores, armoury, dormitories, latrines – enough for the several hundred airmen, officers, ground crew, cooks and clerks.

South was another small town, the church had a conical spire like a witch's hat; another pub, presumably, more urchins, more watchful local men, more retiring women . . . The brash sprawl of the base, with its long fingers reaching into the surrounding neighbourhood, must be twice the size of the sum of these two small, old places.

Something made him look over his shoulder. About fifty yards away, on the edge of the road they'd driven along last night, stood a small boy, straddling a pushbike. The MP in the guardhouse didn't seem bothered. The boy raised a hand, and Spencer tipped his forehead back. The kids at least were friendly.

He walked down the side of the dormitory hut and emerged on the far side of Site 5. From here he could see the hardstandings.

And there she was: 8′ 8″; 7,125 lb; 37′ by 32′. Built to slice the air like a whip at twenty-five thousand feet. So new she hurt the eyes, so lean and smart she grabbed you by the balls . . . So beautiful that she squeezed Spencer's heart.

'Good aeroplane, eh, mister?'

Spencer glanced round: it was the kid, without his bike. 'Yeah, looks that way.'

'She's a Mustang. You a flier?' Spencer nodded. 'You're lucky, she's yours.'

CHAPTER SEVEN

'Is my team ploughing,
That I was used to drive
And hear the harness jingle
When I was man alive?'
    —A.E. Housman, 'A Shropshire Lad'

Harry 1854

The last time Harry had seen Colin Bartlemas it was springtime at Bells, and his old friend's face had been round and pink as an English apple, a picture of rude health and optimism on the day he enlisted. Now, in the furious summer heat of the Black Sea coast, that same face was shrunken and aged beyond recognition by the agony which had killed him half an hour since.

Colin's body smelled, not just of the sickness, but of rotten flesh, so that Harry was obliged to put a handkerchief to his own face to prevent himself from gagging. Imperfectly cleaned through lack of time, a crusted delta of dried vomit spread from the corner of the dead man's mouth, attracting a gluttonous squadron of flies: death breeding life, nature at her most brutally logical. Harry slapped briefly at the flies with his handkerchief but they were far too numerous and persistent to drive off. The burial party were watching him with dull patience. He signalled them to get on with it, and walked away.

The French, who had been the bearers of the cholera from Marseilles, had suffered worst, but with allied encampments crushed together in the port's arid hinterland, the disease had swiftly and disinterestedly extended its empire and already the two armies had suffered tens of thousands of fatalities. Haughty, handsome young officers who, like Harry, had never smelt a whiff of gunshot outside ceremonial occasions; and indomitably cheerful fighting men, drunks, reprobates, petty criminals, the lionhearted salt of the earth – once cholera had taken hold all were reduced within hours to mere carrion, food for the humming hordes. Some poor fellows had arrived one day and died the next, barely aware of their surroundings. The practice of decent, dignified funeral parties, headed by trumpeters and accompanied by the playing of solemn music, had long since been abandoned, rendered impractical in the face of so much death. And besides, to hear the 'Dead March' continually throughout the day and night had a depressing effect on the spirits. In such pitiless conditions, swift and effective disposal of the bodies was of the essence.

And yet Harry found shocking the way each corpse – which only hours before had been a man of good heart and high hopes – was wrapped, removed and buried. The ground was baked to the consistency of rock; it took as many as a dozen men working flat out for two hours to dig a communal grave. It was not uncommon to see at least one of them collapse while at their task, a victim either of sheer exhaustion or the early stages of the disease they were struggling to contain. Many areas, like this, were now covered with rough mounds of earth like macabre giant molehills and Harry averted his eyes from the occasional protruding hand or leg of some wretched, inadequately covered cadaver.

Here he did what he could never have imagined doing and thanked God for the manner of Hugo's death and the peace, intimacy and dignity which had accompanied his funeral. And that led him to pray again as he so often did for Rachel, with tortured, passionate fervour.

Clemmie waited for him with head hanging. She did not acknowledge or welcome his arrival by so much as a twitch. When he put his foot in the stirrup to mount, and the saddle yielded and settled with his weight, she still did not stir. He looked back to where the burial party were already shovelling the desiccated soil back on top of the bodies. Even on the makeshift shrouds it made a rattling sound. His eyes smarted and he wiped away the sweat with his cuff. Tonight he would have to write to Colin's parents and tell them that their eldest child and only son, the apple of their eye, had died bravely in his country's cause without ever glimpsing the enemy. But not how. He would spare them the swift, convulsive horror of this death, the way it leeched the life from a man in his prime in no more than a few hours, leaving a husk that even a mother would scarcely recognise.

He turned Clemmie's head and rode back towards the camp. Nothing was as they had expected. In these terrible circumstances he could no longer say with certainty whether or not it was a mercy that they would never see a charge.

Looking back on all they'd been through, it troubled Harry that perhaps the euphoria of departure had been occasioned by no more than a spilling-over of strong feeling from a bored nation thirsty for excitement. And they had been susceptible to it themselves, only too ready to lap up the babel of adulation. They'd reached Varna without a shot fired except those mercifully expended on dying animals. It was almost forty years, a whole lifetime beyond the memory of the younger men, since a British Army had ridden out to war in Europe, sure as always of their greatness.

In the dead quiet – hideously apt expression – of this oppressive, flyblown, disease-ridden encampment, Harry was haunted by doubts. Stopped in their tracks, stranded and frustrated, doubt and depression settled on the army. Allied to the old enemy, France, and the courageous but untrustworthy Turks, and ranged against still-distant Russian forces of whose strength and precise location they were ignorant, for reasons that were unclear – although the pretext was the sinking of the Turkish fleet at Sinope – they sat here on the edge of the Black Sea, sickening and dying. Supplies were poor and sporadic, medical attention inadequate, and their future movements uncertain to say the least. He could not escape the impression that they had been sent here on a magnificent whim like roundshot from a gleaming cannon that had fallen dully, far short of its target.

Harry had so far escaped the cholera, but not the equally widespread and debilitating effects of worsening morale. Whatever they had been prepared for when they set sail from England almost three months ago, it had not been this. Pride, excitement, anticipation and (he admitted it) sheer ignorance had buoyed them up. There were some, both officers and men, who had seen battle in other theatres of war, but not many in the Light Cavalry. He had always considered himself able to stand aside from the more fatuous excesses of mess and parade-ground life, but now he realised, chastened, that he was no less spoilt and unthinking than his brother officers. He saw all too clearly that the Hussars had been for him a pleasant occupation in which the possibility of actually fighting a war had figured no more prominently than a distant flag, fluttering bravely in the sunlight. And when he had imagined battle it was the sound of the trumpet, the thunder of hooves, the much-vaunted élan of the Light Cavalry charge which he had envisaged. Instead there was this. This terrible inertia, sickness, hopelessness, uncertainty – and the heat. Both men and horses were entirely unprepared for it.

The exigencies of the voyage had been made bearable by the memory of their glorious send-off and the hope of more glory to come. For the first few days it was as though they could still hear the shouts and cheers of the huge crowd that had followed them to the docks, the boys hallooing and tossing their hats in the air, the old men with tears in their eyes, the women and girls blowing kisses and waving their handkerchiefs. Their ears rang with the music of the bands, 'Cheer, Boys, Cheer' and 'The Girl I Left Behind Me', stirring tunes for an expedition whose success, surely, was a foregone conclusion.

Later, when discomfort, seasickness and apprehension began to bite, they'd been able, borne on the strength of that public belief in their enterprise, to armour themselves in a sense of destiny. This after all was what they were if not exactly trained, then at least intended for. Even when in rough weather Harry went down to help calm the horses panicking in the hold, and saw in their rolling eyes the pure, violent terror of innocent victims, he had told himself that the weather would pass, and with it the animals' panic. Clemmie and Piper had no conception of what lay ahead. It wasn't dread they felt. The difference between their fear now and their fear of a storm at home was only a question of degree. But the extent of their suffering was still terrible.

The memory of the battened-down horse-holds during the ceaseless storms in the Bay of Biscay would remain with him for ever. It was nothing less than a vision of hell: dark and noisome, clamorous with the screams of the sick and terrified horses as the pitching of the ship sent them crashing into their mangers in the fitful semi-darkness, and the oaths and shouts of the officers and men, themselves already faint and nauseous, who had stood by their heads for more than twenty-four hours and were now in danger of being trampled to death in the panic of the animals they were there to save.

Except for a very few there had been no room for the horses to lie down, but in the battering fury of the high seas they fell anyway, thrashing and convulsing against their neighbours, were hauled to their feet and fell again, on boards which were slick with blood, excrement, and vomit. With the smell of the lurching oil lamps, of ammonia, and of the vinegar thrown on the decks and wiped around the nostrils of the horses, the stench was enough to make even a well man retch, and its effect, especially on raw recruits who had never been to sea before, was catastrophic. Harry had been humbled by the stubborn, selfless courage of men, themselves *in extremis*, who in these terrifying circumstances put the lives of the horses before their own, going down time and again amid the lethally flying hooves, yelling oaths and endearments, using every scrap of their waning strength to right the animal, tugging and coaxing, fighting and cajoling, like a strange sort of lovemaking.

Of his own horses, Piper had suffered worst, because he trusted least. Clemmie, more familiar with his voice and touch, had seemed to believe that he would see her through, but Piper felt only betrayal. From first to last he trembled with a seismic ague of fear and incomprehension, his nostrils gaped and sucked, his neck and shoulders were encrusted with a scummy lather of sweat. In the rough seas he did not simply fall but hurled himself back on to his hocks, or reared and crashed sideways, causing further mayhem among the horses next to him. All his incandescent youthful fire and energy, the pride of the parade ground, amounted to no more than a liability here.

After the storms, came the heat. In the Mediterranean the temperature in the horse-holds rose to a toxic one hundred degrees. The surviving animals, themselves more dead than alive, hung alongside those already perished in their canvas slings like sides of meat in an abattoir. Others went mad, something Harry hoped never to witness again, and had to be shot. There would then follow the regular punishing business of dragging the heavy corpses up the companionway on to the deck and throwing them overboard. This activity, though it created more space, disturbed the other horses, so the whole grim business was undertaken against a background of stamping and slithering and the uneasy feeling that a stampede might be about to take place.

Once as he had stood on deck watching the corpses bobbing in their wake, a man next to him had said: 'Sad sight, sir, isn't it?'

'One I never thought to see,' he agreed.

'Any of yours there, sir?'

'No, thank God.'

'Mine's gone.'

Harry refrained from saying what he secretly felt, that the horses now sinking to the bottom of the sea might prove the lucky ones, and confined himself to a safe platitude.

'At least his suffering's over.'

'Hers. My Lark.'

Whether this was the mare's name or a term of endearment Harry had no way of knowing, but it touched him.

'Poor old girl. I have a mare too.'

The man cast him a troubled look. 'Will you be able to get us more horses, sir, when we get there?'

'Of course. It will be an absolute priority.'

He was shocked, both by the question and by the glibness of his own lie. It was the first time that his own authority had been called directly into account. He was an officer in whom was invested not just rites and privileges but responsibility too. Of course they would need more horses – the bobbing wake of corpses testified to that – but how would that be achieved? And would it even be possible?

When they disembarked at Scutari the excitement of the horses at their new freedom was pathetic. As they led them, frisking and biting, through the shallow waves in blazing sunshine, the suffering they'd endured was all too plain to see. The pampered pets of Phoenix Park and Rotten Row were a sorry sight, and their released high spirits only emphasised their ribby flanks covered in galling and blisters, their scarred legs and staring coats.

On the sand ahead a pack of yapping, curly-tailed dogs raced excitedly among the new arrivals. When one pack horse stumbled and fell for the last time in the surf, not five yards from terra firma, the dogs fell on it in spite of the best efforts of the men round about and began tearing and shaking it when it was not yet dead, releasing a torrent of dark matter into the clear water, which the rest of them waded through, inured to disgust. Only Piper, darting and leaping like a kite on the end of his taut rein, would not pass through, and Colin was obliged to make a lengthy detour to get him ashore.

For the brief duration of their stay in Scutari, the conditions of men and horses were reversed, with the latter tolerably stabled, adequately if not satisfactorily fed, and at least content to be on dry land. The army on the other hand were billeted in an imposing but horrifically dilapidated Turkish barrack blocks, the dormitories alive with rats and the bedding so full of fleas that within twenty-four hours they were scratching themselves till the blood ran. The operation of the commissariat had largely failed, much of the supplies they had brought with them had not survived the journey in an edible condition, and very little had arrived here.

Harry and Hector Fyefield were among those deputed to round up more horses, but it was a dismal scraping-of-the-barrel exercise. Three days' exhaustive trawling of noisome back-street stables and outlying farms, struggling with the language problem and an apparently intractable reluctance on behalf of the locals to help their brave English allies, resulted in barely three dozen animals of which more than half were runtish and undernourished and fit only for pack-duty.

Hector was scandalised. 'These people are nothing but shiftless, filthy, cheating ruffians! Why the devil should we fight for them? I swear I'd rather be lined up with the Russians than with such a crowd of ne'er-do-wells.'

Harry was tempted to agree. It seemed they had travelled this far, and suffered so much, to meet with nothing but a grudging hostility. It was now that they were glad of the officers' wives who had accompanied their husbands, and of whom even the plainer and less spirited ones provided a reminder of a more normal life. Even Emmeline Roebridge's endless piping complaints about the vermin, the diet, the heat, the natives and the need for *any* of it, were a source of some wry amusement and helped them to put up with it all more stoically.

They were in Scutari no more than a month when, in early June, the order came through that they were to embark once again for the Bulgarian port of Varna. Though as a journey it did not compare in length to the one they'd recently endured it was still almost intolerable to have to go back on board ship, and especially to consign the horses, old and new, to the stifling torture of life below decks. True to form it was Piper who refused, with every quivering fibre, to do so, and since Harry would allow no one to resort to rough tactics it took half a dozen men exercising superhuman patience for more than an hour to get him up the gangplank and into the cauldron-like heat of the hold.

They lost no horses on that three-day voyage, but if they had thought that they were moving to more comfortable and better-managed conditions they were wrong. As they approached, the Bulgarian coast presented an aspect of dramatic beauty – the luxuriant green of the alluvial plain backed by purple mountains wearing plumes of dark thundercloud – but greater familiarity did nothing to gladden the heart. The hectic colour and chaos of their arrival in the heat of afternoon provided a temporary distraction from the horrors to come. The quayside was a feverish Tower of Babel, a jabbering confluence of east and west, north and south, packed with more different nationalities, styles of dress, uniforms, and languages than it was possible to count, horses fretting and shying, piles of arms and cannonballs, a motley traffic of waggons and *aribas*, and the ubiquitous sharp-nosed curly-tailed dogs looking for scraps and spoiling for trouble. But as the troops began to move off, the dismal reality of Varna was apparent. A more desolate, neglected and squalid place would have been hard to imagine, the streets no more than open sewers, littered with dead dogs and busy with fat rats, very much alive. The wretched infantry were obliged to camp close to the town in what had clearly been a graveyard for Russians who had died of disease during an earlier campaign and where the water came up thick and green.

So it was with mixed feelings of relief and trepidation that the cavalry set out to their own allotted position in Devna, fifteen miles to the north.

Once clear of Varna, they had at first been struck by the beauty of the countryside. Plump, peachy Emmeline Roebridge, her sturdy gelding unencumbered by any sort of baggage, had been in raptures during the eight-hour march to the site of the cavalry camp.

'Oh, but this is enchanting – look at the flowers! And this little path through the woods is exactly like Hampshire but even prettier, I think, and on a grander scale of course, and the birdsong – listen, George – I never imagined that going to war would be so delightful!'

The birds were certainly beautiful, from the jewel-like finches flittering among the branches to the storks, trailing their spindly legs behind great white canopies of wing. And far, far above the kites and hawks, motionless on the currents of scorching air. And above them, so high as to be mere specks in the white heat of the sky, the slowly turning black blades that they would in time learn to recognise as vultures.

Emmeline twittered away like a bird herself, the tribulations of recent weeks quite forgotten, and it would have taken an extremely churlish fellow to disagree with her opinion or dislike her for it. The wide undulating plains, soft hills bathed in sunshine and the dappled shade of the woods were certainly pleasant, and the situation of the cavalry camp itself around a fine lake and its attendant river infinitely more agreeable than the awful place they had just left.

The sense of respite and relief, however temporary, prevented them from sensing the damp fumes of infection that rose from every fold in the land and even from the shining lake itself. George Roebridge thought it quite a joke to report to the others one pellucid evening that he had been speaking to one of the exotic, brigandly *bashi-bazouks*, who had told him that the place was known to the Turks as The Valley of Death. Amid the facetious bravado that greeted this information, Harry alone was quiet, contemplating for the first time the possibility that he might not see Rachel again.

The Russian retreat from Silistria on the Danube in late June, following several months' ferocious besieging of the town and a spirited (but almost spent) defence by the Turks, had little effect except to induce a slightly greater respect in the British Army for their despised allies. As Hector Fyefield commented languidly after dinner one night not long afterwards: 'Thank God the ruffians are on our side . . . I heard they cut off Russian heads, ears, noses, whatever they could, and displayed them like damned hunting trophies on the walls of the city.'

'Before they ate them, I dare say,' said Harry drily, but the tenor of his remark was lost on Hector, and George.

'Shouldn't be in the least surprised!' agreed the latter. 'Plenty of fire but not a finer feeling between the lot of them!'

'So first blood to the infidel,' sighed Hector. 'And much help we were to them.'

'Perhaps,' said Harry, 'this means we'll get out of this wretched hole.'

George huffed. 'I should hope so, or the Ruskies will be starting to think we don't care to deal with them!'

Since then thousands more had succumbed to cholera, and there was still not the least sign that Lord Raglan and his staff intended to move them. Day in day out they drilled in the heat. Weakened men were hastened to their crowded graves by the perverse insistence on 'smartness', and horses already ill-fed and in poor condition were ridden to a standstill. In between times their brigade commander lay around in the shade outside his pleasantly situated requisitioned villa, conserving his energy, sipping champagne and endlessly devising new kinds of meaningless activity. The officers and men under Cardigan entertained mixed feelings for their commanding officer. They smarted under his lash – both literally, in the case of those flogged for failing to meet his exacting standards, and that of his cruel tongue – but they also felt a degree of pride in being who they were, the chosen ones, the swiftest and most skilful horsemen in the army, glittering in their matchless uniforms.

At the end of June Cardigan departed with nearly two hundred men – hussars and light dragoons – to make a reconnaissance along the banks of the Danube. The party made a splendid sight as they left, brisk and unencumbered, because their leader had decreed that food and forage be kept to a minimum and tents were unnecessary. All but the most sceptical felt a certain stirring of the heart to see them. And then they disappeared. What had been foreseen as mission lasting no more than a few days stretched to a week, and more, and there was still no sign of them.

It was nearly a fortnight later when Harry rode out with Emmeline Roebridge, he on Clemmie, she on the lighter and somewhat reduced Piper. In the wake of the epidemic military routine had relaxed, both of necessity and for the husbanding of men and resources. Even uniforms had been adapted and altered, in some cases discarded altogether in favour of more practical native clothing – loose cotton tunics and waistcoats, voluminous trousers, even, in the case of some of the more daring officers, turbans. Out of deference to Emmeline on this scalding afternoon Harry wore his uniform but it felt like a strait-jacket, and the innumerable insect bites all over his body were chafed raw by the rough material and smarted with sweat.

They rode out of the valley, and into the cool shade of the low trees that crowned the hill to the north. Here they paused and let the horses hang their heads for a moment. It might have been the rising ground, the smooth grassy hill, Piper next to him, but Harry was swept by the memory of the last ride he had taken with Hugo, when they had stood on the edge of the flat-topped hill in the clean English weather to gaze at the White Horse. When Hugo had said there was no such thing as loving too much, and when they had encountered Rachel walking in the secret woods . . .

'You're miles away, Captain Latimer,' said Emmeline.

'My apologies.'

'Were you in England?'

'Yes.'

Emmeline cocked her head flirtatiously. 'A penny for your thoughts.'

'They're not worth even that much, I assure you.'

'Then why not give them away?'

'I was remembering a ride I took with my brother. Just something about the aspect of this place, the way it falls away . . . It couldn't be more different in most respects but it put me in mind of that ride.'

'Your brother remained at home?'

'He's dead.'

There was no point in sparing her discomfort, since Harry knew she would only continue her dainty interrogation until she was satisfied. Her hand flew to her mouth, there was no doubting her mortification.

'No! Now I'm so ashamed.'

'There's no need. How could you know?'

'I do hope you didn't think that I was implying anything . . . that your brother . . . Oh, dear, I can be such a fool!'

Harry rebuked himself for having been too blunt, and was about to end the exchange by suggesting they move on when a man came round the shoulder of the hill below them and to their right, leading a horse at a snail's pace.

'Look!' exclaimed Emmeline, her sympathy directed as usual towards the animal. 'The poor thing – its leg – shall we go down?'

'Wait a moment.' He got out his spyglass and focused on the figures. Horse and man resembled an illustration from Cervantes – attenuated, spavined, barely able to remain upright, the animal limping so badly that its head nodded like that of a rocking horse. Though hatless, and coated with dust and grime, the man's uniform was just distinguishable as that of the Hussars.

'Shouldn't we go down?' asked Emmeline. 'The poor creature looks half dead, and what are they doing here on their own?'

'Stay with me.'

The same question concerned Harry as they rode slowly down the slope, and he kept one hand on Piper's rein as the black ears pricked forward so urgently that the points all but met.

'There's no need to hold on to me, Captain Latimer,' protested Emmeline, 'I'm quite capable of controlling him.' But he was adamant.

'He's a young horse, and nervous. We don't want two casualties.'

The man had seen them coming, and stopped. He appeared tranced, his arms hanging loose at his sides, his head sagging. Harry had the impression that he only remained on his feet out of an ingrained habit of respect for a lady and an officer.

'What's going on? Where have you come from?' he called. The man seemed to attempt to reply, but there was no sound that Harry could hear, and at that moment the horse collapsed like a pack of cards, front and back legs buckling in turn, head swaying, before crashing on to its side and lying with its saddle slewed to reveal weeping red sores. Piper shied, and Harry held him with difficulty and ordered Emmeline curtly to dismount, which she did this time without protest.

The man pointed in the direction he'd come, croaked a single word that sounded to Harry like 'finished', and sank to his knees.

Harry dismounted himself and went over to them. The man remained on his knees with his head sunk on his chest, as though too exhausted even to fall any further. His hair was caked with sweat and dust and round the inside of his collar was an angry suppurating crust of broken skin. The flesh of his face and neck was swollen red and covered in small cuts and abrasions and his hands were raw with broken blisters.

Harry addressed Emmeline. 'Mrs Roebridge, would you ride back to camp and tell them we have a casualty here? I suggest you ride the mare. And if you would first give this man a drink from your water bottle?'

For once she was shocked into silence, and while he exchanged the saddles, she advanced warily on the man and proffered the bottle which he snatched and gulped at, shaking his head like a dog.

'Hurry if you would. Leave the bottle. We'll make what progress we can if someone can be sent to meet us.'

'Yes, of course.'

Given a task of real urgency, Emmeline rose to the occasion, cantering away on Clemmie with as much well-bred determination and composure as if she'd been riding to hounds in the shires.

Having poured some of the water over his head the man seemed to be reviving to the extent that he sat back on his heels and watched dully as Harry inserted the neck of his own water bottle into the side of the horse's mouth. But it seemed too far gone to respond, and its throat palpitated with shallow irregular breaths.

'I don't like the look of him.'

'Nor I, sir, he's hurt hisself.'

'Where are you from?'

'With Lord Cardigan's party, sir. I was about the fittest—' he gave the ghost of a smile '—so they sent me on to report.'

'Whatever happened? Were you attacked?'

The man shook his head. 'No, sir. Worn out, sir. Worn

out, worn down, done in, man and beast. And nothing to report.'

Something in the man's voice, now that he was more animated, made Harry study him more closely. He was trying to get to his feet, using the horse's rutted flank as a lever, but he couldn't manage it.

'Stay where you are,' said Harry, putting a hand on his shoulder. 'I believe we know each other.'

'Believe we do, sir. On board ship.'

'That's right.'

'They got me another horse, sir.' The man grimaced. 'This one.'

The next morning the rest of the reconnaissance party returned, unrecognisable as the proud column that had left camp two weeks earlier. Even the most ardent of their brigade commander's admirers couldn't but feel that this had been a mission of profligate waste. The men were drawn and drained, carrying their saddles and almost dragging behind them their wrecks of horses, many of whom could scarcely put one foot before another and would not have looked out of place in a knacker's yard.

But Harry had seen enough weary and fruitless suffering in the space of the last few months to last him a lifetime. It was the face in profile of the commander as he rode rigidly and haughtily upright past the onlookers, that impressed him most. A face with a long, patrician nose netted with red veins, a sensual petulant mouth, fine curling hair and whiskers, and light blue eyes whose hooded lids and arched brows gave the whole a supercilious expression.

Above all, Harry saw the face of a man engorged with vanity, spoiled by pride, and impregnably certain of his own rightness.

The days toiled by. Harry ached with homesickness. Not only for his family and friends, and the familiar detail of the place where he had grown up, but for England itself, his homeland, in the soil of which his flesh and blood had its roots, and was buried. The smell, the light, the shape of England, its capricious but benign weather, the outline of its towns and villages that was like a secret language, the sound of its streets and the quiet pulse of its rivers. He had travelled before, been to Paris, Rome, and Vienna – it was almost unbelievable that he was now less than a hundred miles south of the Danube delta – yet he felt, but for the identity conferred by his constricting uniform, lost.

At night, heartsick for Rachel, he scarcely slept. But when the heat was less intense he attempted to banish her by sifting through his other memories as though they were entries in a commonplace book. He had a particular recollection of one morning in the spring of 1851, when he and a group of fellow officers had been out riding in Hyde Park. Their route had taken them down Rotten Row, alongside the enormous glass structure that had been erected to house the Great Exhibition. The Crystal Palace held no particular fascination for the Hussars, since they had watched it go up from its inception, but on this particular morning it was full of infantrymen, marching up and down the wooden floors like toy soldiers in a giant dolls' house. As Harry and the others rode by the front rank of soldiers kneeled, raised their firearms to their shoulders and fired a round of blanks into the huge space above them. Pigeons clattered in alarm from the roof and the less experienced horses danced sideways. The soldiers rose and continued with their pointless marching.

'What the deuce are they up to?' enquired George Roebridge of Harry over his shoulder.

'Polishing the floor?'

'No dusters.'

'No dancing either,' commented Fyefield, 'more's the pity. It's going to be packed to bursting with the British working man, his wife, children, dog and dog's dinner, gawping at the achievements of their betters.'

'Exactly!' exclaimed George, with the air of a man who had stumbled on an important scientific discovery. 'That's it – they're testing the building. Seeing if it can take the punishment. The perfect occupation for a standing army in peacetime.'

By this he meant, of course, the perfect occupation for infantrymen, and his observation was greeted with general laughter. Harry considered reminding Hector Fyefield that the working man of whom he was so dismissive had had a hand in the manufacture of some great achievements. But he did not do so, and the conversation turned to other things as they advanced on Kensington Gardens, the gloss and glitter of their turnout attracting general admiration in the spring sunshine.

It occurred to Harry now that Roebridge's facetious comments notwithstanding, the activities of the infantry in the Crystal Palace that morning were more purposeful and of greater use than their own, and possibly even than that of the British expeditionary force stranded at Varna. And the thousands from every walk of life who had flocked to the Great Exhibition had at least contributed to a general celebration of peace, prosperity and scientific advancement. But only three years later those same crowds had exulted in the departure of cavalry and infantry alike on this uncertain and ill-prepared errand. Harry was a younger son of no special ambition or talent, who like his brother officers had purchased his commission and become a member of the exotic tribe that was the Hussars. But unlike Hugo he was by nature a thinker, and here where there was unlimited time for thinking, that was not an easy or comfortable thing to be.

Least comfortable of all were his thoughts concerning Rachel, which would not be banished. The image of his brother's widow was with him always, retreating when duty drew his attention elsewhere, but always returning unbidden. That he was in love with her he could no longer doubt nor deny. At this distance he could with impunity admit what he had always known: that he had fallen in love with her on the day, at the very instant, that he met her. But distance had also served to turn his love into an obsession. He could not see her, nor talk to her, he could not demonstrate his feelings by the performance of even the smallest service. Worst of all was the possibility that he might not come back. It seemed increasingly likely that he might die here in Devna, unused and unsung, and join a pile of stinking corpses in a communal grave like poor Colin Bartlemas. And even if he were to survive this, the immediate future held only uncertainty and danger. In the meantime Hugo's child would be born in October, while Rachel was still in mourning. Loyalty, decency and every kind of social prohibition were ranged against him and served only to intensify his feelings. He was in turmoil.

He had written to her just before their departure, and again since arrival here. In his effort to convey only what was fraternally correct he feared both letters might have seemed cold and stilted, and the fact that he had received no reply appeared to bear out these misgivings. But then why would Rachel, whose heart and mind must be wholly preoccupied with the terrible loss of her adored young husband, be in the least affected by the tone of letters from her brother-in-law? He wished neither to appear cold nor to overstep the bounds of propriety, while all the time burning with fierce, unexpressed passion.

It coloured all that he did. When that evening he sat down at the entrance to his tent to write to the parents of Colin Bartlemas, it was with the shameful awareness that his letter, its style and content, might at some point reach Rachel's notice, and so it was doubly important that both should be apt, sensitive and well considered.

Naturally, he must spare them the squalid details of their son's death. But neither could he avoid the painful fact that Colin had died long before facing the challenge of battle he'd so welcomed. His personal effects – his cap badge, penknife, wallet, pipe and prayer book – looked a pitifully small legacy on the ground next to Harry as he laboured, scratching out half a dozen attempts before arriving at what he hoped was the right note.

My dear Mr and Mrs Bartlemas,
    It is with the greatest sorrow that I write to inform you of the death of your son Colin who was also my own true and lifelong friend. At a time when the so-called ordinary soldier is too often seen as a ne'er-do-well for whom no serious role in civilian life is possible, Colin was a recruit of whom the Army

could be justly proud, the more so because his true and honest heart was always in the countryside and the work that he knew – the horses, the dogs, the woods and the fields around Bells. After I had entered the Army he once told me that if there were to be a war he would join up to do his bit, and when the call to arms came the very qualities that were so much admired by those of us who knew him ensured that he enlisted.

I know that now, reading this letter, you can think only that he is gone, and of your own loss, which my own much humbler experience can help me in some small way to appreciate. But when in time the first pain of that loss is dulled, please remember that Colin's tragic and untimely death was caused by his good and stalwart character, a character loved by all who knew him . . .

Here Harry broke off and stared out over the sea of tents. Along with the ever-present flies, a dull, sour smell hung over this place. The bubbling chorus of lakeside frogs, which had so diverted them at first, now sounded like nothing so much as hollow laughter. Here and there men stunned by the heat lay on the ground as if already dead.

He returned with an effort to his writing.

He bore the pain of sickness courageously, and I know that you were in his thoughts when he died. (Harry did not in fact know this, nor even believe it, since the extremes of cholera did not allow for the luxury of reflection, but the spirit of it was true.) *I enclose some of his things, and hope that along with them you will accept my very deepest sympathy.*
    Yours,
    Henry Felix Latimer

Harry worked on the letter until there was no light left, and set it aside with a sense of relief.

The next day he read it through, despaired of its jejune, well-meaning sententiousness, and threw it away. The voice did not sound like his, nor the subject like his rough and ready friend. Those at home who knew them both would have to take his feelings on trust. He parcelled up Colin's possessions, wrote three simple sentences to accompany them, signed himself 'Harry Latimer' and left it at that.

He had the strong conviction that Rachel, above all, would know instinctively what lay behind the letter if she were to see it, and not think the less of him for it.

He had last seen her a week before they had embarked for the Crimea, when he had returned to Bells to make his farewells. He'd been shocked by his father's apparent frailty, and asked his mother if there were any physical cause, beyond those of old age and bereavement.

Maria responded with the slight show of temper that was, with her, a sure sign of anxiety.

'He will not eat! Whatever is put in front of him, no matter how much trouble has been taken, he turns his head away—' she demonstrated the turning of the head in a histrionic way that was all her own '—as if just to look at it makes him feel sick!'

'Perhaps it does. Has he been seen by a doctor?'

She made a small, impatient sound and flicked her hand. 'He refuses. And besides, neither of us has any faith in doctors.'

'But he looks so terribly thin and pale. I think you should send for Dr Jaynes whether or not Father wants it.'

'Dr Jaynes is a stupid old fool,' declared Maria. 'I shall look after my own husband myself.'

'But if Father won't allow you to look after him . . .' Harry allowed the comment to hang, but she turned away and her failure to answer confirmed him in his opinion that both parents were terribly afraid.

At dinner that night, he noticed that although – perhaps out of regard for his son's presence – his father did not spurn the food in the manner demonstrated by Maria, neither did he do more than stare at it, and push it around somewhat, so that soup, fish, meat and pudding were all removed uneaten.

Percy did however suggest that the two of them have a glass of port together at the table, and when Maria had gone, Harry spoke his mind.

'Father, you aren't well.'

'Out of sorts, merely.'

'Much more than that. You're too thin.'

'Nothing tempts me . . .' Percy held up his glass and peered into it. 'Except this.'

'But you're wasting away. You must eat.'

'I don't wish to.' The tone was almost petulant.

'Then you must make yourself, not just for your own sake but Mother's. And mine, too. The regiment embarks in a few days and I can't bear to think of leaving you like this.'

'Ah, blackmail now.' He smiled thinly, rubbing his face with a hand that was already skeletal, the bones standing out like twigs.

'Look on the food as medicine, force it down if you have to. But eat.'

Percy favoured Harry with the chilly look which in spite of his reduced condition retained much of the power that had always been able to quell offspring and employees alike. 'Am I to understand that you are —' he narrowed his eyes in a threatening imitation of disbelief '—ordering me to do so?'

'Yes.'

They stared at one another. Harry felt his father's gaze flicking back and forth across his own, as if trying to read it. Then the paper-fine eyelids lowered slowly, once, in a kind of acknowledgement.

'I'll do my best. But I promise nothing.'

There had been no news from his parents as yet. It added to Harry's sense of helplessness that while he was doing no good here, he could not help his father either.

The morning after his conversation with Percy he had ridden over to Bells to call on Rachel. It was cold and a light rain was beginning to fall but still, he was told, Mrs Latimer had walked up to the churchyard to Mr Latimer's grave.

'But that's a steep climb of two miles at least,' said Harry in disbelief.

'Two and a half, sir.' Jeavons assumed one of those expressions at which more senior servants quickly became expert, indicative of a host of personal opinions kept perfectly under control for propriety's sake.

As he rode up the hill on Darby with the rain spattering in his face, Harry reflected that he seemed surrounded by people with no concern for their own wellbeing. The thought of Rachel trudging up here in her condition was a worrying one. It occurred to him that Hugo had been so much loved, so vital a force in the lives of those around him, that his loss had robbed them of all judgement.

But when – long before she saw him – he'd found her, he understood. She was crouched by the grave, setting seedlings in the sodden earth with her bare hands. She wore a cloak but in spite of the rain had thrown it back off her shoulders so that her arms were free. Her pale hair was in an untidy, countrywoman's bun, and where it had come loose around her face he noticed that the damp had given it a slight curl. Or perhaps (and this thought thrilled him) this curliness was natural, but generally subdued into that quiet, perfectly controlled elegance.

She sat, too, in an attitude that was robustly practical rather than ladylike: crouching, but with one leg extended to the side to accommodate her thickening belly. The extended leg was visible almost to the knee, wearing a red and black patterned stocking and a heavy, mud-encrusted black boot. Harry had never seen such a thing outside the theatre and to encounter it here, in the drizzle of this hilltop churchyard, had a dizzying effect that made him catch his breath.

She worked away unselfconsciously, occasionally shifting to the side to get to a fresh patch of earth. She did this unceremoniously, putting one hand on the ground, gripping the folds of her skirt in the other and performing a little hitching motion, accompanied by a small but audible grunt of effort.

Darby nodded his head glumly at the rain and the sound of

the bridle made her look round. She seemed not in the least suprised to see him.

'Harry, it's you.'

'I'm sorry,' he said. 'I didn't mean to spy.'

He dismounted and dropped the rein over Darby's head. She rose heavily to her feet and rubbed her hands, first one against the other and then on her cloak. They were still muddy, there was no question of kissing either of them, so he gave what he felt to be a rather ridiculous little bow. 'I've only been here a matter of seconds.'

'I think you can be forgiven. I can see that I'm a spectacle.' This was said with no note of apology, and even the hint of a smile. 'How are you, Harry?'

'Well. I hope you don't mind – that I'm not intruding? Jeavons said you had walked here.'

'Yes, he did very politely try to dissuade me, but I like to walk.'

'You're in good health.' It was half statement, half polite enquiry.

'Perfect.' She indicated the grave. 'I'm trying to make Hugo's last resting place a little less austere. But that's really only an excuse. I like to come up here and grub about, and be with him. It's companionable.'

'Am I intruding?'

'Harry . . .' She tilted her head, gently admonishing. 'It's a great pleasure to see you, especially as I know you're leaving soon. Oh!' She wrapped her cloak around her as the rain intensified. 'Shall we seek sanctuary for a moment?'

Harry left Darby at the entrance to the porch and they went in. On this overcast morning it was dim inside the church, and the rain rattled like shot on the windows. She took off her cloak and spread it over the back of one pew, then went to sit in the pew in front, where he joined her. His senses were overwhelmed by her proximity, and the peculiar sense of intimacy conferred by these surroundings. Her dirty hands, her disordered hair, the moisture on her face and the mud on her boots and clothes, all these he found almost unbearably seductive. He had never before seen her other than armoured in her customary restrained and unshowy elegance, so that though she was wearing more and heavier clothes than usual it was something like seeing her without clothing at all.

But if Harry was unsettled, Rachel had never seemed more at ease.

'This is where we were married,' she said softly, gazing around as if reminding herself. 'Do you remember our wedding?'

'How could I forget? It was a great day. I'd never seen Hugo so happy.'

She looked at him. 'He was solemn. So very solemn, when I walked up here to stand next to him.'

'That was the measure of his happiness.'

'Yes, I believe that too. I never knew anyone as carefree as Hugo, but on our wedding day he was . . .' she sought the word '. . . careful.'

All the time she was speaking she had been rubbing her wedding ring with her thumb, so that now the gold stood out bright on her mud-stained hand. Harry would have liked more than anything to take the hand in his, but instead he said: 'He loved you more than he ever thought he was capable of loving. He was in awe of his own feelings.'

'I was fortunate,' she said, unaware that he was talking of himself, 'the most fortunate woman in the world. I often think of all the bright and beautiful young hearts that must have been broken when this thin, plain old widow came along and ensnared their Hugo with her witchlike wiles.'

She was only half joking, and now unthinkingly he laid his hand on hers. 'You are none of those things.'

She smiled. 'Certainly not thin . . .'

'And he was never in love until he met you. If there were girls who thought otherwise, then they were mistaken.'

'That's a comfort.' Her manner changed, became more lighthearted, so that although there was no suggestion that he do so, he removed his hand from hers. 'And what about you, Harry?' she asked. 'Is there some lovely creature in London who will be pining for you when you go to war?'

'No.' He tried to fall in with her manner. 'Not unless

there is someone who has successfully kept her feelings from me.'

'You must write to us if you can.'

'Of course!' He was eager. 'As often as it's possible.'

She stood up and he followed suit, stepping out of the pew to let her go first. It had stopped raining, but in the porch the flagstones were wet and littered with leaves and twigs blown in from the churchyard. Darby stood with his head and shoulders under cover and Rachel went over to him and patted his neck. She didn't look at Harry when she said: 'You're taking Piper with you.'

'If I may?'

'Of course. He should be ridden, whatever the circumstances, and who better to ride him than you?'

'It won't be easy on the horses.'

She stood back and gave him a direct look. 'Nor on the men, I imagine.'

He took Darby's reins. 'I wonder, would you like to ride?'

'I don't know how. It isn't one of my accomplishments.'

'I simply meant that I could lead you, to save you the walk back. This old gentleman's very quiet, you need do no more than sit on board and hold the pommel.'

She laughed, amused both by the idea and her own inexperience. 'But how shall I get on?'

He pointed to the wooden bench at the side of the porch. 'Can you stand on that? If you use my arm to lean on.'

'Even without the arm.' She put one hand on the back of the bench and hoisted herself up, strongly and with no loss of dignity. 'And now?'

He held the stirrup, and Darby stirred, his big hooves clopping on the stones. 'He's going to go without me,' Rachel exclaimed.

'On the contrary, he's looking forward to having a passenger. Put your right foot in the stirrup and sit sideways on the saddle. You couldn't ride this way on Piper, but this one has a back as broad as a table.'

'I shall take your word for it.' She followed his instructions. 'Well – here I am!'

'Are you comfortable? Do you feel secure?'

'At the moment, but then we're not moving.'

'Off we go.'

When Harry looked back on that journey down the hill from the church to Bells he saw that it was the closest he came to an expression of his own feelings for Rachel. Leading the horse carefully, pausing now and again to check that she was secure and comfortable, he took a quiet pride in being her protector, and in seeing her safely home. When they reached the house he led her to the stable yard and allowed her to dismount by herself, only offering her a steadying hand as she stepped down from the block.

'Thank you,' she said. 'I enjoyed my beginner's pleasure ride. Perhaps in the future you could teach me to ride properly.'

Ever since then he had cherished this small suggestion like a talisman, a hostage to fortune that would take him back to Bells to be of use.

By the second week in August the armies camped around Varna might have been forgiven for thinking they had endured the fires of hell and could not suffer much more. But if so they were punished for their complacency with the outbreak of a real fire that laid waste half the town and provided the pretext for troops of all nationalities to sack the other half. In spite of the enormous weight of manpower assembled in so small an area the generals issued no orders to control the excesses of the troops, though Harry and a handful of fellow officers were detailed to ride down to Varna and help enforce discipline and contain the worst of the looting.

Having rounded up fifty or so blackened miscreants from the streets and driven them stumbling back to camp it was clear that the British soldier had confined himself to drinking what was left of Varna dry.

'You would have thought,' drawled Fyefield as they saw to the horses, 'that they might have shown a little more imagination. They might as well have been in some provincial fair in England.'

'Thank God for it,' said Harry. 'What would you prefer – rape, pillage, wholesale plunder? A bit of drunkenness is almost excusable.'

'True,' Fyefield acknowledged. 'Just so long as it doesn't addle them completely before the real action starts.'

In the darkness, somebody laughed.

It was impossible that such an impasse could continue indefinitely. Some sort of movement had to take place, and two weeks after the fire the order for embarkation to the Crimea came through: on 5 September.

Men were still dying as they boarded the ships, but even the sickest were lugged aboard in the grim conviction that it would at least be preferable to die on the deck of an English frigate than the polluted soil of a Middle Eastern port.

In spite of everything, spirits rose. To be back on the move, to be closing on their objective, to be going, at long last, to confront the enemy – all this improved morale.

As Harry and the Light Brigade drew nearer to the embarkation point at Varna the evidence of cholera was still all around. The mass of hasty, shallow graves that disfigured the dry soil like a rash were many of them desecrated, dug up by scavenging dogs and by the Turks for blankets, the limbs of despoiled corpses jutting out like rotten tree roots. The dogs barked and snapped at them, to keep away. Once when Clemmie stumbled Harry looked down to see a human head beneath her hoof, half the face still clinging to the skull, an eyeball hanging from its socket. If they had thought Varna a squalid place on their arrival there, it was nothing to its condition now. There was only one thing to cheer Harry. Seeing in passing the French Post Office, pretty much dismantled, he called in with no very high expectations, to be handed no fewer than three letters – two of them from his parents and one from Rachel – which had got stranded there following the embarkation orders. These he kept, to read on the voyage.

But at this late stage Piper would not board. Harry's new groom, a wizened cockney sparrow named Betts, was at his wits' end. He was a genius with horses and had immediately seen in Piper a rare breeding and spirit, but his charge's furious terror was more than he could manage on his own. Grudgingly, barking instructions and abuse, Betts stood aside for the sailors to take over. But nothing that anyone could do in the way of ropes, chains and sheer brute manpower could move Piper without doing him an injury. Eventually he was so severely exercised, and his helpers so beside themselves with fury and impatience, that there was nothing left but for Harry himself to lead him back down to the quay and stand there, with Betts in attendance, attempting to comfort and quiet him.

The bustle and racket all around was no help to either of them. Sweated up and sensing treachery on every hand, Piper was uncontrollable, lunging, rearing, kicking and sidling, stretching his neck with his eyes starting from his head and his ears laid back flat so that his pretty head took on the mean, flattened look of a cobra.

Betts's eyes darted here and there. 'This is no place for 'im, sir.'

'I know that, Betts, but perhaps a few minutes here will persuade him that boarding ship is a better alternative.'

The little man shook his head. 'It's going to get him beside 'isself.'

He was right. When after some ten minutes on the quayside they attempted to lead him to the ship once more, even Betts was unprepared for the ferocity of Piper's resistance. He simply threw himself backwards with all his considerable force, as he had done on the ship from England, scattering assorted traders and hawkers, and sending for six several barrels of fish and vegetables over the slippery cobbles and into the water. Betts, who had a gammy leg, was sent flying. As Harry struggled to tighten his grip on the headcollar he lost his footing and let it go altogether. Piper, at full stretch already, sprang away from him like an arrow from a bow and was gone, careering through the crowds like a whirling dervish, snapping and kicking up his heels, creating a wake of Middle Eastern

205

pandemonium, screams and ululations and arms uplifted in supplication.

Betts's walnut-face was unreadable. 'That's a waste, sir,' he said. 'That's a wicked waste.'

When Harry sat on deck that night listening to the soft sounds of the pipe and mouth organ, and the croaking and rustling of the dying, he wept in the darkness for Hugo's beautiful horse, now food for vultures in a foreign land.

CHAPTER EIGHT

Just to say, I love you madly
To let you know I'm wild with lust.
Did I mention you're my hero?
Just to say it's shit or bust'

       —Stella Carlyle, 'Just to Say'

Stella 1990

The woman on the links, Stella thought, was an almost perfect example of her kind. There were another two women playing with her, but she was first to the sixth green and Stella, who was walking on the dunes, paused to watch her putt.

She herself had no interest whatever in golf, or indeed in any game except rugby with which she'd acquainted herself grudgingly for Jamie's sake, and if she was occasionally ambushed by it on television she switched off at once. She knew only that the object of the exercise at this stage was to get the ball into the small hole normally occupied by the flag.

This the woman did efficiently, from a distance of some three metres. Stella couldn't say whether this was particularly good, only that she couldn't have done it herself, which was no accolade.

The woman now stood to one side, holding the flag. With her short dark hair, Black Watch tartan trews and Lovat green jacket she cut a rather military figure, like some plucky, standard-bearing lad. While her two friends followed their own rather less distinguished putts back and forth across the green she suddenly seemed to realise they were being watched and looked round at Stella, giving a quick, friendly, aren't-we-all-duffers? sort of smile.

When they'd finished on the green amid a murmur of sporting self-deprecation their route of a few metres to the next tee ran parallel with Stella's on the beach, and she couldn't resist pausing again as the dark woman planted her tee, selected a driver and addressed the ball. When she struck it, even Stella from her position of complete ignorance could see that it was a mighty blow, so perfectly timed and angled that the head of the club made a faint whistle, like an admiring exhalation, as it arced downwards, and the merest restrained 'click' on contact. The ball simply disappeared. Her two friends made generous noises and took their turns. Stella dawdled and watched for another couple of minutes.

Though the dark woman's looks were not of a type that Stella herself would ever have aspired to, she drew the eye. The well-cut black hair, the strong, clear-skinned face and trim figure, even that well-judged smile, positively screamed class, confidence and composure. It was no surprise that she handled her clubs with such perfect control. And the clothes – tartan trews might be anathema in just about any other location one cared to mention, but on the Ailmay links they were stylish and even witty. If one had to be that sort of woman, thought Stella as she went on her way, then that was the sort of woman one would want to be.

She had never wished to be anyone but herself. She scarcely knew what it was to feel envy or jealousy, not because they were corrosive emotions best avoided by the sensible person, but because she regarded most other people's lives, and their partners, with a mixture of astonishment and dismay. The level of fudge, of compromise, of make-do-and-mend required by most ordered lives and so-called 'committed' relationships appalled her.

She walked for another half mile or so along the beach to where a promontory stuck out into the sea like a shaggy arm, shielding this bay from the next. Today's was classic Ailmay weather – dark sky one side, brilliant blue the other, high cloud in between, a changeable light that swept over the sleek sand and ruffled sea with an effect like a stately glitter ball. At this moment the Fell looked benign and approachable, bathed in sunshine, but after almost a month on the island Stella knew better than to take its kindly aspect at face value. She'd wandered soaked, frozen and disorientated in fog on its lower slopes on more than one occasion, an experience which raised the ignominious spectre of the sassenach saved by mountain rescue at vast cost to the taxpayer. These days when she walked on the Fell she stuck to the less adventurous paths.

This afternoon it was her plan to walk out to the end of the promontory to where the sea, even on a relatively calm day like this, fretted and fumed wonderfully over the rocks, and then to cut back along its far side to the coast road which provided the easy route home. The house was beginning to feel like home, and she to feel at home here. She even had the sense, possibly fanciful, that she was starting to be part of the scenery, that she was known as the tenant of Glenfee, the one with the strange clothes who had sung at the pub. She hadn't repeated the performance since, but she didn't rule it out. She'd been back several times and it was always suggested that she sing, but she'd declined and they'd left her alone. There was a natural discretion among the islanders, a taking of people at their face value, which she liked. No one had asked her about herself beyond where she was staying, but they'd liked her song and said so. When she was ready, they'd like to hear another. If that never happened, that was all right too.

She didn't know and couldn't tell whether this general discretion extended to more personal matters, but she hoped so. Her lover's car would have been conspicuous anywhere, and in a place where there was little traffic it stood out like a pig in a synagogue. It was one of his perverse charms that he seemed wholly without the caution gene. The Rolls arrived and departed with suicidal panache, not often it was true, but without warning and frequently in broad daylight

As she reached the headland it started to rain and she turned inland and slightly back on herself to cut her losses and join the road this side. As she trudged over the shallow dunes she could see the edge of the golf course, now veiled in fine, sifting drizzle, and the three women came into view, striding out briskly with heads down, hoods up and golf trolleys in tow. They conveyed the impression that nothing short of a full-scale blizzard would prevent them from finishing their game.

It was another half an hour's stiff walking, and coming up to four o'clock when she got back, to find the Rolls pulled up outside with its driver lying back in the reclined front seat, eyes closed, a cigar between his fingers and Rachmaninov pouring from the stereo.

She walked straight past him, unlocked the front door, and closed it after her. Two minutes later as she stuffed yesterday's *Daily Mirror* into her sodden boots, he knocked and came in. The thunderous knock and the entry were always synchronised, sounding as though he'd forced the door with his shoulder like some hotheaded television cop. The door banged shut. She didn't look up as he came into the kitchen, but stood her boots carefully upright on the boiler, their uppers resting against the flue pipe, her socks draped over the top.

'You look gorgeous doing that,' he said with a growly Glaswegian inflection, as if lodging a complaint.

Still without looking at him she went to the sink and ran her hands under the hot tap. Then dried them. 'You're easily pleased.'

'I am not.'

'Drink?'

'No, thanks, I don't have long.'

'Excuse me.' She went past him in the doorway. He was smoking the cigar, with his free hand in the pocket of his historically dilapidated waxed jacket, and he made no move to touch her, but she nonetheless sucked herself small as she went by so that there was a couple of inches between them. Still in her bare feet she went into the living room and knelt down to light the fire, conscious of him following and watching her from a distance.

'Where've you been?'

'Out for a walk.'

'You and your walks . . .'

'It's what people come here for.' She applied a match, shook it out. 'Most people.'

'Do I detect a note of censure?'

She cast him a sardonic look over her shoulder. '*Moi?*'

'*Toi*, my tatty. My stroppy little neep.'

She placed pieces of coal on the burning wigwam of sticks and paper. 'What do you do all day when you're here?'

'I rise late, drink and eat, smoke rather fewer of these—' he indicated the cigar '—but relish them more, admire the scenery through various windows, take the occasional boat trip, and cook simple but sensational meals.'

'While at all times preserving your self-esteem.' She dusted her hands and stood up.

'Naturally.' He moved to the fire and threw in his cigar butt. 'Stella, are we going to fuck? Because frankly I've got a bone like a dinosaur rib and I don't have all day.'

Afterwards she got herself a glass of wine which he declined on the grounds that it might incriminate him. He never referred to his wife, but instead made these unashamed, almost bullish references to the process of deception in which both he and Stella were implicated. In this he was better and worse than most of the other married men she'd slept with. Better because he was at least frank, and did not heap responsibility for his own behaviour on to his wife by listing her shortcomings; worse, because the effect of this was to reduce their meetings to the level of no more than a successful scam – an uncomfortably honest dishonesty.

Stella was used to being adored, and to not giving a shit. In Robert Vitelio's case there seemed a distinct likelihood that it was the other way about.

She didn't, of course, adore him, but there was the odd thing about him she adored. She liked – indeed found irresistible – his fierce, ugly, intelligent looks, his foxy pointed face with its high colour and sharp eyes, and his red hair (something she had always previously loathed), which was receding at the temples on either side of an already pronounced widow's peak. She was turned on by his voice – groiny but with the words enunciated diamond-sharp, a voice designed to cut the crap. She admired his cleverness, which he himself took for granted, and warmed to his complete lack of physical vanity. His unconcern about appearances extended to his lovemaking which was that of a far younger man – selflessly ardent and absorbed. She weakened at his touch, and at the sight of his touch – his large, corded hands, more like an artisan's than a doctor's, that moved over her own pale skin in a particular intense, focused way he had, as if he were reading her mind through her body.

And she was in danger of being read. For the first time she was a man's to command and she strove hard and constantly – she believed successfully – not to let him see it.

He looked at his watch, which he never removed. 'Ten minutes to pumpkin.'

'Why don't you go now?' The watch irritated her, it had become a symbol of his condition, as relentless as an electronic tag.

'Would you like me to?'

She shrugged.

'In that case, since it's a matter of indifference to you and I'd quite like a few more sticky moments, I'll hang on.'

Slightly nettled, she said: 'What are you doing here at this time anyway?'

'Making whoopee with you.'

'I mean, how come you're free?'

'I have my methods.' He turned his head on the pillow and she felt rather than saw him grin. 'Questions, questions.'

'I have my reasons.'

'Sex and backchat, what a woman . . .' He licked the side of her arm, a long lick like a lion washing. 'Have you decided how long you're staying yet?'

'No. I like it here, and I'm getting some work done, but real life will be camping out at my door when I get back.'

'Do you know,' he said, suddenly chatty, 'I can't imagine your real life. The life of a creative person. A life without imperatives. Doing a job that's only there once you've done it, because you put it there in the first place.'

'Is that what you think it is?'

'It's a way of looking at it for a non-creative person like me.'

'I do have imperatives.' She liked having this sort of discussion with him, found it sexy and combative. 'I have to make money and fulfil expectations just like anyone else.'

'Your song in the pub wasn't about money, though.'

'The impulse behind it wasn't money, but the song will have to pay its way in the end.'

'Poor little song.' He lurched upright so that her wine slopped. 'Sorry – got to go.'

She didn't answer but got out of bed before he did, pulled on her dressing gown and took her wine glass to the kitchen. Outside it was dusk.

He came down the stairs, flop, flop, flop, and picked up his waxed jacket from the chair in the hall. She felt messy and vulnerable in her old dressing gown, and folded her arms across her chest. When he'd put on the jacket he prised her arms apart and pushed his hands inside the gown to cover her breasts.

'Woman in a dressing gown. Sluttish . . . Great.'

She shut her eyes for a moment and hoped he didn't see. Then he closed the front of the gown, crossed her arms again as though she were a doll, said, 'Take care,' and was gone.

It was a new experience for her, this melancholy when left alone. She was more used to experiencing elation on a man's departure – no matter how great the sex, freedom was better. She felt it in her skin, which tightened as a defence against their neediness, and breathed again once they were gone. They might not ask anything specific from her, but that was because what they wanted was everything. They wanted her body and soul to make them feel wonderful again, to give them back something they'd lost. And whatever they thought had happened with her, she knew that it was something she did to them, before detaching herself and sending them on their way.

With Robert Vitelio her skin opened and bloomed, to let him in at every pore. Lying with him she was fluid and yielding.

In the tumultuous silence of sex he could have asked anything of her and got it. But he asked nothing. For the first time she was finding out what it was to be not the user, but the used.

It was five-thirty, no-man's-land. She poured herself a glass of whisky, lit a cigarette and sat on the floor by the fire which wasn't drawing properly this afternoon, sending up only a few sulky pale flames and a column of dank smoke. It occurred to her that one way of wresting back the initiative would be to leave the island before he did.

Halfway between Stella's house and his own, Robert pulled over and stopped. He passed his hand over his hair and sniffed it. Rubbed his sweater and did the same. Did he smell of her? She didn't seem to wear perfume, but every person had their particular scent, as singular and identifiable as a fingerprint. There were no marks on him, he was sure of that, even at her wildest she didn't bite or scratch. Remembering a little ruefully their first time, he was sure that she was the veteran of many such encounters, accustomed out of habit to leave no scars. He almost wished that she would – that he could make her lose it enough to break his skin, give him something to carry away and find excuses for. A reason to deny her.

He turned the stereo on and Rachmaninov once more flooded the car: a composer with a hotline to the emotions. He let the music swirl round and through him. It was a long time, years, since his own feelings had been so ferociously, intensely engaged, and he'd forgotten what it was that people did, or how they played it. Also, a long-ingrained habit of self-protection meant that he was waiting for signs from her which she might never give. He couldn't read her, didn't know what she was up to. Sometimes in bed there was something, he wasn't sure . . . But it was never articulated and he felt rebuffed, as though maybe she had been thinking of somebody else.

He brought nothing, he took nothing. If Sian were to say: 'Is there someone else?' he would of course say 'No' – and it wouldn't be entirely a lie.

★   ★   ★

When he got back Sian was sitting, still in her tartan golfing trousers, with her feet curled up on the sofa, reading her enormous, challenging, away-from-home novel. She wore her bifocals. As he entered she turned a page and then held out a hand to him without lifting her eyes from the book.

He took it: cool, trusting, familiar. She had what he had once heard described as a lucky palm, as smooth as an egg. In the early days of their relationship the feel of those hands, their satiny integrity, had driven him wild with desire. Now they were just her, like her little pinned-back lobeless ears, her 'pixie ears' he used to call them, and her long second toe, and the minute dusting of dark hairs along the line of her upper lip. Until relatively recently these hairs still had the power to move him; he was wounded when she went to some clinic or other and had them removed by electrolysis. But when she'd decided to do something she did it, and though she was teasingly sorry about thwarting his little fetish, the hairs had not been seen since.

She rubbed the back of his hand with her thumb. She did that. He always felt that she might be taking his emotional temperature by doing so. But when she eventually glanced up all she said was: 'Do you feel like making us a cup of tea?' And he went to the kitchen, glad of something to do.

Stella decided to stay for another fortnight. In that time she calculated that with a following wind she could compose another three or four good songs and some odds and ends that would reward further attention when she got back to London.

She also set herself some other targets: to sing again at the Harbour Light; to walk the whole perimeter of the island, not necessarily in one go; to treat herself to dinner at the restaurant in the big house; to be grown up and ring her agent, Alan Mercer; and to level with Robert Vitelio.

Alan was surprisingly bobbish about her prospects. 'There's someone I want you to meet.'

'What if I don't want to meet anyone?'

'Darling heart, you love meeting people.'

'So you keep telling me.'

'Lucky you. What it is to have at your disposal a man who knows you better than you know yourself!'

Stella took a beat. 'Who is it?'

'Wait and see.'

'Alan — I've been working up here. On my own. It's been bliss. It's reminded me how nice it is not to have to consult and confer.'

'Ah,' he said maddeningly, 'quite, but I'm talking yes-man.'

This remark had the twin effects, wholly intended, of making her vehemently deny that a yes-man was what she wanted, and piquing her interest as to the sort of yes-man Alan had found. They fixed on a date for the meeting.

Walking the perimeter of the island took her three days in fits and starts and on the third of these she got back to find a note from Robert. It was written in his rapid, raggedy black handwriting on the back of a ferry timetable.

'More bloody walking, I suppose. We go back in a couple of days. Any chance of seeing you before then? I'll call.'

He rang the following morning at six-thirty, from a phone box.

'What the hell do you mean ringing at this hour?' she complained, standing shivering in her pyjamas in the hall while every chink in the house's armour whined in a strafing nor'wester.

'I've been out in the fishing boat.'

'Are you off your trolley? It must be force ten out there!'

'Nothing like. But brisk enough to be interesting. I'll bring you a herring.'

'Keep your damn' herring, I should be in bed.'

'Exactly. Any chance of breakfast?'

'Not if you're after the full monty. You can get yourself tea and toast.'

'I'm on my way.'

She took the door off the latch, went back to bed and waited for him. Fifteen minutes later he burst in, ran up the stairs two at a time, pulled off layers of sodden, salt-smelling clothing and got in with her, wrapping her in his chilly limbs and pressing his cold wet nose into her neck till she bristled with goose-pimples, before growling 'Bugger breakfast' and falling asleep with his erection subsiding against her thigh.

She let him sleep for half an hour, then extricated herself and went downstairs where she made up a tray with tea and toast spread with peanut butter, though what the hell she was doing waiting on him she couldn't imagine.

'Hey.' She put the tray on the floor and shook his shoulder roughly. 'Wake up.'

He sat bolt upright immediately, and she could tell from his eyes that for a nanosecond he was disorientated and didn't know where he was.

'What time is it?' He looked at his watch. 'Christ, woman, you let me sleep!'

'Not for long.' She watched in amazement as he threw back the bedclothes and staggered to his feet on the far side of the bed. 'And I didn't "let" you do anything. You fell asleep on me. *I* got your damn' breakfast. *I* woke you up.'

'Too late now,' he snapped, as though sweeping aside a confession. He began blundering about the room, dragging on his clothes, cursing their wetness, overbalancing and catching himself on the end of the bed. Determined not to be drawn in she sat down on the chair by the dressing table. She hated him.

Hated him.

Hauling on his socks, he tottered and put one foot down on the edge of the tray, sending tea and milk all over the floor.

'Bugger!'

He gave the tray a kick and the stuff went everywhere. Stella darted forward, picked up one of the china mugs and threw it at his head. It missed, but caught him on the elbow with a hard, satisfying sound. She half expected it to be thrown back, but other than grunting with pain he ignored it.

A minute later he'd gone.

*　　*　　*

She told herself that she didn't expect to see him again, and didn't care. Only the first of these was true, but she was sufficiently battle-hardened to know that the second would become true, given time. If she had been granted one wish it would have been to turn back the clock, not make the tea and toast, and to have gone back to sleep herself. How she would have lain there, watching lazily as he acted out his little charade. How she would have yawned and stretched and told him to take it easy. How she would have burrowed tranquilly beneath the duvet as he thundered down the stairs. How she would have put the rude, self-dramatising bastard in his place.

The dinner out that she'd promised herself seemed itself something of a charade in the light of all this. What had been a feisty scheme for self-indulgence after weeks of jacket potatoes, baked beans and stoneground bread now looked like a sad and lonely stab at fun. But she rang and booked herself a table in a spirit of see-if-I-care.

Driving over the island on an unusually clear night with stars as big as lanterns she told herself that this jaunt was by any standards an aberration. In London she would no sooner have booked a table for one in the kind of restaurant this undoubtedly was, than flown. For some reason she found this a comfort. Normal rules did not apply.

But she was unprepared for the poshness of the place. A drive wound up between pines to a Jacobean house of glowing magnificence, tastefully floodlit, its golden windows like small stages filled with well-heeled actors.

She pulled up outside, peering crossly out of the car window. She wore one of her long velvet dresses, but it was not a long dress as the staff or patrons of this establishment – the establishment – would understand it. She had bought it in a flea market. It did not signify formality, rather the opposite, and the seam in the left armpit had opened as she was putting it on. She was overcome by a sudden powerful nostalgia for the mean streets of North London, their mess and mixture and teeming anonymity. A place where one belonged by not belonging. She felt not so much *déclassé* as rebellious. She almost wished that she had not put on the dress at all but stayed in her jeans or one of her ragged skirts so that some poxy hotel functionary would take issue with her. She could picture herself saying, 'That's quite all right, you've told me all I need to know,' or something like it, and steaming out into the night, absolved of the need to make any further effort . . . On the other hand she had come this far, she had money, so to speak, in her back pocket and her empty stomach was leaning on her backbone.

She got out, tied the belt of her big black coat more tightly around her and slammed the car door. At once her spirits lifted in response to the fresh, brackish night air, the heart-tripping starry beauty of the sky, the sough of the black pines and, yes – the sound of a piano rambling coolly and playfully over 'Love Is the Sweetest Thing'.

There was a flight of curved shallow steps at the front of the house, leading first to a broad, pillared portico, and then to stately wooden doors, standing open. Inside she could see a man resplendent in a kilt and a velvet jacket, a meeter and greeter of some kind, but she was spared his attentions because he was helping a couple with their coats.

In the portico Stella stood aside to let them come out. The woman wore a lilac pashmina over her head and shoulders. She was holding her husband's arm, not out of affection on her part nor chivalry on his but to support him. Robert Vitelio was drunk as a lord. Even had he not been unsteady on his feet, his face suffused and slack and his eyes blurry, his condition was proclaimed in the polite, icy relief on the face of the kilted man, and the loyal concentration on that of the woman.

Stella took another step back, but at the moment she did so Robert rocked sideways, in her direction. His wife said, 'Steady,' and Stella instinctively put out a hand and took his weight for a split second while the two of them regained control.

His wife looked across at her, and smiled her gratitude. The pashmina had slipped back from her dark hair and Stella recognised the woman from the golf course. In these horribly embarrassing circumstances her poise had not deserted her: the smile managed to convey a womanly appreciation, with no loss of dignity. There was no question of collusion, of her aligning herself with anyone other than her husband.

'Thank you.'

Stella nodded, shrinking, not trusting herself to speak. But Robert hadn't even seen her and was too pissed to identify her if he had. She watched in trepidation as they reached the top of the steps which, seen through their eyes, must appear awesome. She entertained a nightmare vision of the pram in *The Battleship Potemkin*, hurtling and bouncing down endless stone stairs, and was just about to step forward to help when a youth in a white shirt hurried past her and stepped into the breach, taking Robert's other arm with a well-trained, 'All right, sir?'

'Good evening madam, welcome to Loch Ailmay.' The kilted man's greeting indicated unequivocally that quite enough attention had been paid to those who had overindulged.

Stella had a drink while sitting in a deep rose velvet chair by a blazing fire, studied the handwritten menu, was shown to her table. Thick white tablecloths brushed the ground, candle lamps glowed, white vases overflowed with a profusion of bluebells and jonquils, the distant ceiling swirled with softly smiling nymphs, and the pianist gave his affectionately ironic take on 'Dancing Cheek to Cheek'. The service was of a cherishing perfection. She could have wept for the loveliness of it all.

She could have, had she not been in shock. As with hurting oneself when alone, reaction was both pointless and proscribed. Doctor Theatre saw her right. She got through three faultless courses and two glasses of champagne by thinking herself into the part of the curious and colourful metropolitan visitor. She made her surroundings her set. She had always been able to do this – alone and without saying a word she could make herself the centre of attention. It was a kind of sex appeal, a generalised allure, which she could switch on. It was the reason her audiences fell in love with her.

When she'd ordered her coffee she went outside for a cigarette. At the foot of the steps she took out her makings and rolled a smoke, knowing that the kilted man was watching her, interested but far too grand and polite to engage her in conversation.

Back at the table, her coffee arrived. The waiter said: 'Excuse me, madam, I have a message for you from our pianist, Mr Jackman. Here's his card.'

'Okay.' She took it warily.

'He recognises you, and wonders whether you might be prepared to sing one number with him. He's a fan of yours apparently.'

Stella noted the 'apparently' – the waiter was in his late-teens. A glance at Mr Jackman confirmed that he wouldn't see fifty again. Aware of the exchange, he caught her eye and tilted his head interrogatively as he segued into 'The Way You Look Tonight'. He'd perpetrated a breach of etiquette and they both knew it. He was chancing his arm, but it was quite comforting to meet a chancer in such unlikely surroundings.

'I'll go and have a word with him.'

'I think he'd be knocked out, madam.'

She poured herself a coffee and carried it over to the piano, only too aware of trailing a discreet Mexican wave of curiosity.

Jackman held out his right hand briefly. 'Charmed – it is Miss Carlyle, isn't it?' He was no Scot but a pouchy southerner with a dissipated pallor and estuarine vowels.

'That's right.'

He executed a choice flourish. 'Thought I wasn't wrong. Hope you don't mind my soliciting you.'

'I should but I don't.'

'I heard you at the Harbour Light. You were the business.'

'Thanks, that was a new song, first time I tried it out.'

'Want to try it again?'

'I don't have any music, I've been working without a piano.'

'Music?' He pulled his mouth down. 'You see any music? We're talking follow my leader here. I'll vamp, you sing darling, I'll cotton on.'

His hands pranced up the keyboard, flagging the end of the set. He smiled and bowed into the polite applause, pushed the microphone aside. She felt a fellow-entertainer's tribal sympathy with him.

'They like you.'

'They'd like anyone, they're a well brought up lot. I say that, but there was one here earlier that wasn't. Mouth like a toilet, thought he was at the Glasgow Empire.' He shook his head. 'Didn't bother me, it was like old times as a matter of fact.'

She made no comment, but he'd moved on to other things. 'Listen.'

With one hand he picked out the tune of 'Are you out there?' with only a couple of mistakes. 'How did I do?'

'I'm impressed.'

'Not perfect, I know that. I used to be able to hear a tune, play it from memory, harmonies, the lot. You're on your own in the middle eight, but other than that.'

'There's one or two bits . . .'

He put his hands on his knees. 'Show me.' She did so, singing a few of the words to make sense of it. He slapped his knees. 'All right. Shall we show them how it's done?'

'Why not.'

'You want an intro?'

'Just a chord.'

'You got it. Straight in.'

Having pushed his luck once he knew better than to do so again by introducing her. He simply adjusted the microphone and announced in his hammy old pro's way that they were about to hear a brand new song, and they were to remember they'd heard it here first . . .

She sang the song, but not well. Jackman's accompaniment was surprisingly sensitive, following her like a shadow, moving with her mood. And the diners stopped eating to listen, politely intrigued but unsure of themselves. The kilted major domo appeared in the high doorway. But the setting wasn't hers and these weren't her people. Her sadness and anger threatened to choke her, her voice lost its resonance, her style was cramped, she couldn't make her feelings theirs. She felt she was making a spectacle of herself.

When she'd finished they applauded heartily and returned to their dinners.

Jackman rescued her by saying it for her. 'Wasn't quite as good as the last time. Not your sort of venue.'

'That's no excuse.'

He began to play 'Yesterday'. 'Sorry if I hustled you, shouldn't have done that.'

'It did me good. I don't want to get precious.'

'Thanks anyway. I saw your show once in Bristol, it was great stuff.' He held out his hand briefly. 'Take it easy . . . You know what you needed, don't you?'

'What?'

'That mouthy bastard who was here earlier. He'd have made you feel right at home.'

Next day she received a card, posted in the town, with a picture of Ailmay harbour beneath improbably blue skies.

'*I was a pig,*' it said, '*and today I feel like shit, so there is some justice. And my elbow's giving me hell. I may never fix eyes again, and then you'll be sorry.*'

Not knowing whether to laugh or cry she did neither, and threw the postcard in the rubbish bin. As a medical man he made a great piss-artist.

She'd been away from home for six weeks but when she got back she was confronted by the evidence that time meant different things in different places. In Ailmay there seemed to be more time because there was more space, and its texture was different, the days and weeks seeping into one another, marked out by the land, the light and the weather.

She'd forgotten how here in London time operated in spurts – scurrying, stopping and starting, regulated not by natural rhythms but by activities like shopping and work and journeys, messages and meetings. For a day or so she was unable to recalibrate, felt like someone released from an institution, in whose absence everyday life has become almost too crowded and eventful to deal with.

But stuff needed doing. Among the drift of mail on her mat

were at least three red reminders, a cool note from Apollonia, a solicitor's bill, an invitation from Alan confirming the date of their meeting, a Welcome Home card from her parents and a letter from Jamie thanking her for her cheque and for singing at the party. She'd forgotten that, it was like another lifetime. But to be reminded of it was salutary – three times recently she'd been persuaded to sing on her own, a sure sign of being too easily flattered – she must be wary of getting soft. Besides, as Alan might have said, not only was a prophet without honour among his own, but people simply didn't value what they didn't pay for.

Robert, of course, had said: 'That song . . . that wasn't about money.' But then he knew shit about the business.

The person Alan had found for her was Jude Romilie, a witty, well-spoken, sexually ambiguous cabaret performer admitting to thirty; trailing clouds of Footlights glory, but well enough on his way to be a threat. But even had it been clearer who was giving who a leg up, he was unsuitable on just about every level Stella cared to name, mostly because he was too smooth for her. Smooth as silk, smooth as soap, Teflon-smooth, too smooth to get a purchase on, so together that there was no way in. Or not that she could see. Professionally speaking, as she told Alan over lunch, she preferred a bit of rough.

He was pained. 'Stella – you could hardly have called Sorority rough.'

'Maybe, but they were trailer trash compared with that prat.'

'He's very clever,' said Alan, 'and on the way up.'

She waited in vain for the other shoe to drop, before asking with heavy sarcasm: 'Meaning what exactly?'

'Nothing in the world except that it does no harm to pull in a younger audience.'

'I shan't pull in any audience at all without a congenial partnership.'

'That's true, but do think, angel-heart. The place is littered with the bleached bones of gifted performers who believed their mothers and thought it was enough simply to be them-selves.'

'Alan,' she smiled at him over her glass, 'I don't need this.'

He touched her arm, smiled back. 'I adore you. I want you to go stratospheric.'

She dropped her voice so that it was sibilant as the scrape of a razor. 'I don't need it, or him. Or you.'

He didn't believe her, of course, and she took an exquisite pleasure in listening to him laughing out loud, then, as he became less sure, trying to josh her out of it, doing tender and fatherly, then brisk and businesslike, unable to conceal the merest tremor of anxiety in case . . . He went through all these stages in the three minutes that it took her to finish her wine, and then she pushed her chair back and got up.

'Thanks for everything, Alan. Send on any mail, won't you?' Bye—' she kissed him briskly on either cheek '—angel-heart.'

'Stella . . .' He tried to rise, but was sitting on the banquette and the table was pushed (by her) a little too close, so he was trapped. 'Stella, I'll ring, yup?'

'If you must. But I'll write.' A waiter came with her coat and she thrust in her arms, flashing him an over the top, on-a-promise smile. 'Oh, and Alan . . .'

'What?'

'Tell Romilie from me to watch his back.'

To her intense delight he followed her, rushing out on to the pavement and calling her name. It was like a scene from a film. She didn't break stride nor so much as glance over her shoulder. She wished she had something of his, some small personal possession that she could have taken from her pocket or her bag and dropped, with withering insouciance, down a drain like the girl in the ad. But lacking that she simply waved one hand at shoulder height, the middle finger stiffly raised, and was rewarded with a cry of 'Bitch!' and a smattering of applause from the onlookers.

By the time she got back to her flat the elation had drained away, sucking every scrap of positive feeling down the plughole with it. What, she wondered, was the source of this pathological need to drive people away from her? What was she trying to prove? She did not, it was true, regret any of her actions, she simply did not understand them.

She rang Georgina, but her machine was on and Stella left no message. Sitting cross-legged on the window seat with a half bottle of Jack Daniel's she wondered what it was like to have a man in one's life, not one like Robert Vitelio but a man who cared, and listened, and said tender things like, 'Remember, darling, whatever happens I'll always be here,' while taking one in his arms with soft lips and a hard prick. For some reason these musings brought Gordon to mind and she realised that she did know more or less what that was like and it had driven her crazy with irritation

She consumed half a dozen JDs and smoked the same number of roll-ups before running out of both. She had no wine and there wasn't even any dope in the house. Drearily she went into the bedroom, opened the top right-hand drawer of the chest and found amongst her tangle of pants and socks the container with what remained of her happy pills. Years she'd been on them, but it was now eighteen months since she'd taken anything more mood-altering than a drink. She felt the weight and texture of the plastic tub in her hand, thoughtfully shook the pink and white capsules, dinky as children's sweets, that had the power to make every crisis seem like shouting in another street . . . But as she did she caught sight of herself in the mirror, forced herself not to move but to keep staring back. Look and remember. A modern morality tale captured by the camera. This is what the top of the slippery slope looks like. Skinny tart with pills. Woman on the brink. 'The decision'. Moment of truth. Crap like that.

She didn't throw the pills away – they were on prescription after all, she was entitled to have them – but she stuffed them back in the drawer and went out.

For Stella, afternoons were like a foreign country without language, map or currency, she wasn't at home in them and had no idea what the options were. Except to fuck, and that wasn't always available. In the build up to a show there were rehearsals. On tour or during a run afternoons were waiting time, two or three hours in which to taxi on to the runway and start revving up for take off.

She supposed that people had their routines. They returned, well-refreshed, to offices, they collected children from school, they shopped. They even 'went out shopping'. She herself had never to her knowledge 'been out shopping' in the approved, retail-therapy manner, but she resolved to do so now. She would get fags and booze, and then she would go in and out of shops until she found something else to buy. She wasn't acquisitive, she couldn't think of a single thing she hankered after, but if she exposed herself to enough stuff for long enough she would find the thing – 'item', shoppers called it – that she couldn't live without. And in acquiring it, life would become worth living. That, or so she understood, was how it worked.

Even in this mood of grimly determined frivolity a small internal voice warned against extravagance. She was out of work and pretty well out of friends, it would be wise to put checks and balances in place. She drew out a hundred pounds spending money, such a fat wad that she had to shuffle around the cards in her wallet to accommodate it. It astonished her to think that there were women – she'd read about them in the papers – who spent several times that on a dress, and yet she was relying on it to save her sanity.

It was surprisingly difficult at first, not because she was parsimonious, but because she simply had no cravings. But once she'd parted with some of the wad in the off licence and left her bottle of JD and tin of makings with Jamahl behind the counter she felt more in the mood. She bought some designer coffee in Must Have Beans, and a selection of highly coloured Indian sweetmeats, and then, telling herself that perishables didn't really count, went into Secondhand Rose and found a velvet shirt and a jet choker.

She had been out of the house three-quarters of an hour and had only spent forty pounds, but it was still more mindless spending than she normally did in a month. Over a double espresso in the café-bar, surrounded even at four p.m. by Jamie lookalikes and girls in combats, she told herself that she wasn't doing badly for a beginner.

Contrary to what many people thought, Robert Vitelio did not dislike his patients. He could not, under the grinding weight of the system and its manifest shortcomings, know them well enough to dislike them.

But most of them did irritate the hell out of him. He wanted only to make them better, to improve their lives, to apply his skill as accurately and cost-effectively as possible, but the sheer stupidity of the patients and their relatives silted up the process. They poured through his various clinics in their hundreds, enough human-interest stories to fill several tabloids, a great many of which they attempted to tell him in exhaustive and emotional detail when surely they could appreciate that while they were doing so dozens of others were waiting outside in the fearful, interior world of the partially sighted, unable even to resort to *Hello!* magazine.

He had long since given up on the notion that the eyes were the windows of the soul. Whatever their expression, or the mood, age, condition of their owner, when you looked right into them they were no more than a bundle of tissues, filaments and blood vessels in a poor state of repair. They could certainly be beautiful. The sunken and rheumy eyes of a sick old man with post-retinal occlusion when viewed through the microscope presented a picture like a glowing crimson eclipse, outlined with a fiery halo of trapped light and full of incandescent threads like an opal. He was frequently put in mind of the famous Bacon paintings based on infections of the mouth, full of luscious purple and scarlet, fierce yellow and tropical pink. In the same way that a weed was just a plant growing in a wrong place, so a disease was only repellent because we did not wish it to be there. The condition of blindness might be grey and blundering, but its causes were exquisite.

He knew what his staff said about him, often directly to the patients: 'He's the best there is, but no bedside manner.' The nurses, from the humblest student to the most formidable ward sister, regarded him as some kind of *enfant terrible*, an attitude he found both patronising and flirtatious and which in his view he did nothing to justify or encourage.

He could not be image-conscious, but he was practical. His patients were not terminally ill, and there were innumerable support systems outside the hospital offering counselling, therapy and material assistance. He considered that he was never less than civil but his task was to home in on the problem, and zap – or anyway relieve – it with the greatest possible despatch. When they rested their often quivering chins on the headrest preparatory to the examination he couldn't wait to escape their pleading and emotional expressions and address the clinical reality.

Though he had none of his own, he liked children, and was better with them, which was not in fact so surprising. Children, however difficult, were only interested (like him, but for different reasons) in getting out of the place. They were not self-indulgent and they had no desire to unburden themselves. Essentially unregenerate (also like him, some would have said) they operated on a simple, animal level of pleasure and punishment, pain and reward. He pandered to this, keeping a tin of funsize chocolate bars to hand and using them shamelessly and almost always successfully as bribes. It was a clean, brutal tradeoff. He was not unsympathetic. His own perfect eyesight was something he had not taken for granted since a rugby accident in his late-teens had left him with blurred vision for several weeks. The degree of disability, inhibition, even loss of brain and motor function that this had caused had terrified him, and he had never forgotten it.

He knew what the staff thought. They thought he was more tolerant at the beginning of a clinic, but tended to 'lose it', as the phrase went, as time went on. He wished he could have locked them in that small room with him and shown them that the process was not one of losing, but gaining. As the day wore on, the time pressures snowballed and the patients became more querulous, so his professional focus sharpened to a pinpoint, bright as a laser. By five o'clock he could see, diagnose, prescribe treatment and deliver prognosis with fearsome speed and accuracy. It wasn't temper, it was talent, running on adrenalin.

His colleagues' view was qualitatively different from that of the clinic's staff. What he got from them, even to some extent the men, especially the younger ones, was the sense that he was an old softie really, unable to deal with emotions and concealing a tender heart beneath a rough exterior. If anything he found this even more maddening. Christabel was one of these, a nice intelligent woman and a competent clinician who quite simply insisted on understanding him better than he did himself.

'Bo-ob,' she would say, with a teasing, motherly downward inflection, 'give yourself a break . . .' And when he told her bluntly that he had no idea what the fuck she was on about, she'd add something like: 'Okay, all right, we all handle stuff in our own ways . . .'

Sometimes Robert entertained the scary notion that Christabel might have a crush on him. She was unmarried and of an age and type that didn't play the field. There was probably some sort of dismally inadequate token male friend lurking on the edges of her life with whom she went to arthouse films and Max Boyce concerts, but she came across as essentially unawakened, and the thought of all that seething latency being unleashed on him was frankly terrifying.

One of the things he most liked about his wife was her independence of him. She had banged for Britain in the seventies, all in the best possible taste, and then she had met and married him and become a smart but devoted wife without ever losing one iota of her impregnable separateness and self-esteem. Like her china-smooth palms she seemed to be able to move through life without being marked by it. It had stopped being sexy but it remained admirable. And others admired it too, which was gratifying. They saw him as a lucky dog and a jammy bastard who did absolutely nothing to deserve such good fortune.

He had never until recently been unfaithful in any meaningful way, though there had been encounters. It was quite possible that Sian had known about these but if so she had never shown it. She was far too savvy not to keep her powder dry.

Besides, they got on perfectly, and unlike him she had nothing to reproach herself with. Though cool, she wasn't cold – she had never over the whole period of their relationship taken the sexual initiative but neither had she ever failed fully to respond to him. For the past couple of years when this had scarcely been an issue she had not complained nor even commented on the fact. If she pondered those things at all, she kept her counsel.

If his staff, his colleagues or his patients had had any idea of his state of mind today they would not have kept theirs.

His last patient was a Mrs Jowett, with her daughter. This was a combination he especially dreaded, the querulous elderly person with the combative offspring there to see that full measure was given. And these two were classic examples of the genre. Mrs Jowett was fat and fluttery and tearful; the fortyish daughter – who introduced herself as Carol Hopkins, but wore no wedding ring – was a smart-suited business person with the studiedly even manner which he recognised as the result of an hour and a half spent in the crowded waiting area with only Mrs Jowett, the lavatories, and the preliminary checks for diversion.

Beyond acknowledging them at the start, he made a point under these circumstances of ignoring the third party, taking the view that if they had something to add or explain they would do so all too readily without encouragement from him.

He stood back as Hopkins helped her mother lower her broad beam into the adjustable seat, which she did with a tremulous sigh as if this were the crowning indignity in a whole chain of indignities. He studied her notes.

'Oh, doctor, I do hope you're going to be able to do something for me . . .'

'That makes two of us, Mrs Jowett.'

'My life isn't worth living at the moment.'

'Is it not? We can't have that.'

'Where would you like me to sit?' asked Hopkins.

This was one of the more asinine regular questions. There were only two other chairs in the room and one was the one by his desk which they had just seen him get out of. Pulling

231

down the headrest and not looking at her he replied: 'Wherever you like.'

'Here?' She indicated the second chair. He didn't answer and she said more quietly but as if answering for him, 'Here,' and sat, putting her own bag and her mother's bag, coat and stick on the floor next to her.

'Right, could I ask you to rest your chin on here and look straight ahead?'

Mrs Jowett did so, her brow furrowed with anxiety. It was like having a soulful pleading dog rest its head on your knee.

'Off again if you would, it needs to be a tad higher.' Another unhappy sigh. 'Thank you, here we go.'

To make clear what the priorities were he always began with a brief examination, then asked questions, examined more fully a second time, and pronounced. In this way neither the patient nor the hanger-on was left in any doubt that this was a medical consultation and not a session in the psychiatrist's chair.

The condition of Mrs Jowett's eyes was poor, but straight-forward. The muscle at the back of the right eye was atrophying, the left would follow suit. Not much could be done with the right eye but the left was operable.

He pushed himself back. 'Good, up you go.' He waited, studying the notes again as she made heavy weather of righting herself.

'Need any help, Mum?' asked Hopkins pointedly.

'I'll manage.'

'Now then,' he said. 'Tell me, please, when you began to notice a deterioration in your sight?'

'Well, doctor,' said Mrs Jowett, with that hint of mawkish relish that presaged ill, 'I've been on my own for five years now and I have arthritis as you can probably tell, so life isn't easy—'

'When did your eyes start to get bad?' he repeated, pointedly flagging the single syllables. Hopkins uncrossed her legs and recrossed them in a movement less Sharon Stone than garden shears. 'Can you remember?' he asked.

'Not really,' replied Mrs Jowett, 'you don't at first, it sort of creeps up on you, doesn't it? And when you're all on your own there's a lot of things you find difficult to do. You just have to get on with it, don't you?'

'Let's narrow it down. Two years? One year? Six months?'

'It's so hard to say . . .'

'About nine months, wasn't it, Mum?' said Hopkins.

'Nine months?'

'If you say so, dear.'

'It was about nine months, because it was midsummer,' said Hopkins directly to him this time.

'Thank you.'

The daughter was equally irritated with the old dear as he was – fed up at having to take time off to do this, fed up with the long wait, dismayed no doubt by her mother's condition – but the irritation would naturally be directed at him, that was how it worked.

'And now,' he said to Mrs Jowett, 'I'd like you to describe to me the precise difficulties you have with your vision. In your own words.'

The moment the last sentence was out of his mouth he wanted to take it back. It wasn't something he usually said, he'd added it this time as a palliative to the stroppy Hopkins. But it was too late now, Mrs Jowett had been 'drawn out'.

'It's as though half my life's been taken away from me,' she intoned, 'and the trouble is, I'm so depressed I can't function properly. Carol came with me to the doctor at home and he gave me some pills for the depression but they didn't agree with me—'

'Would you excuse me for a moment?'

Without looking at either of them he left the room and closed the door behind him. There was only one patient left outside, a post-operative check for Tony Woong, and the nurses were clustered round the desk chatting. They didn't exactly scatter as he came out but they did stiffen perceptibly.

'Everything all right, Mr Vitelio?' asked the charge nurse.

'Yes, thank you.'

He went out into the reception area. The receptionist was tidying up her cubicle.

'Hallo, Mr Vitelio, all right?'

'Yes.'

He went to the filtered-water container and poured himself a drink, chugging it down quickly and pouring another. He was slightly breathless. He could feel the receptionist's eyes on him.

'Gets so airless, doesn't it?'

'It does, yes.'

'Still, day's nearly over now . . .' She glanced at her watch. 'Been a long one, too.'

This time he didn't reply, but threw the paper cup in the bin and returned to the clinic. Woong's patient had gone in, the nurses didn't look at him.

The moment he got back Mrs Jowett made it three in a row by asking: 'Are you all right, doctor?'

'Of course.'

'Only we thought when you rushed out like that without a word—'

'I believe I excused myself. Shall we continue?'

'I've forgotten what you were asking.'

'I think you came here today to tell me about your eyes.'

Hopkins got up. 'We did, but we're going now.'

'I beg your pardon?'

'Come along, Mum.'

'What are we doing?' asked Mrs Jowett as her daughter helped her out of the seat.

'Leaving.'

'Are we finished, is that it? What happens next?'

'Coat, here.'

'Do I have to come back?'

'You certainly do,' said Robert, 'since we haven't yet completed the consultation.'

'Don't worry, Mum, it's all organised,' said Hopkins firmly, handing Mrs Jowett her stick and taking her arm. And then added more quietly to him: 'It would be just dandy if it wasn't for the patients, wouldn't it?'

'I beg your pardon?'

She raised her voice to its normal level. 'I'll make another appointment outside then, Mr Vitelio. And you will be hearing from us, of course.'

'Good.'

He held the door open for them and Hopkins flashed him a look of pure bile as she passed.

'Goodbye, doctor,' said Mrs Jowett. 'And thank you so much.'

He closed the door and flopped down in the chair recently vacated by Hopkins. If Mrs Jowett hadn't thanked him he might have maintained his fine fury a bit longer. But the moment she'd left, her wholly undeserved kind words hung in the air like a reproach. She was a nice, polite, sweet-natured woman who was losing her sight and was pathetically grateful for the smallest morsels of comfort. But her daughter was one of the new consumer breed: demanding, uncowed and on the *qui vive*. When she said she'd be in touch he had no doubt what she meant: a strongly worded complaint would be in the post by the end of the week.

He slumped, eyes closed, over his folded arms. Running through the consultation he was pretty sure he'd said and done nothing that constituted a serious breach of professional behaviour. He'd been testy and unsympathetic, and left the room to have a glass of water – not Dr Kildare, certainly, but no hanging offence either. Still, if Hopkins did write it would mean the third such letter in the past year, which along with his reputation would add to a generally disobliging picture. There was little use in being a first-class clinician if the patients wanted nothing to do with you.

He was suddenly absolutely shattered. And the thought of going home to Sian, with whom he could never bring himself to discuss this, was a bleak one . . .

Stella. He wanted Stella. Craved her. Could picture with almost painful vividness the feel of her sinewy limbs wrapped tight around him, locked on, her fanny and her mouth like two big soft flowers on her twiggy body. Oh, God. He wanted to roger her rigid and then confess all in her arms. He had the feeling, right or wrong, that even if she wouldn't approve his behaviour she'd understand it, and find something droll and abrasive to say which would make him laugh at himself and stop him feeling like a total shit.

But he had fouled up with her as surely as he'd fouled up with Mrs Jowett. And she was in showbusiness, for Christ's sake, a planet he could scarcely imagine, teeming with colourful characters both creative and commercial who were hers to command and who probably worshipped her.

There was a knock, he said 'Come' and Tony Woong put his head round the door.

'I'm off then.'

'Me too.'

'You look shot at if I may say so.'

'Yes, well, they were firing real bullets today.'

'So long as you didn't shoot back. Drink?'

'No, thanks.'

'See you Thursday then.'

'If I'm spared.'

Tony laughed as he closed the door. Robert remained in the chair for another ten minutes without moving, in a state of self-inflicted shock.

When Stella got back to the flat she dropped most of her shopping inside the front door, retrieved the Indian sweets and carried them and another of the bags to the windowseat. With a sticky cube melting like liquid velvet on her tongue she took out the picture she'd bought and propped it up facing her. It was her prize purchase, the one that had as it were paid for the trip. She studied it closely for a couple of minutes and then remembered something else and went to get her purse.

The wad was almost gone but her cards were still disordered. A good thing, because there was the one she was after. She removed it and laid it on the windowseat in front of the picture, pleased with the symmetry of it all. Some benign force had been at work, because she'd gone out with sod all except an attack of the blues and returned with all these riches – and change, just, from a hundred pounds.

The business card read: '*Derek Jackman – Mr Piano. Your favourite music, pop, show tunes, classical, for that special occasion.*

236

Background, cabaret or dancer'. There followed phone and fax numbers and an e-mail address.

She looked at the picture again. It was a Victorian photograph, mounted on card. Because of its age she took it to be carefully posed, but this didn't detract from its simple emotional effect. A horse lay on the ground, its back to the camera, neck outstretched. A man in uniform lay with his head resting on the horse's flank, one arm stretched over the animal's neck. The setting was some kind of broad, grassy valley that reminded her a little of the countryside around her parents' home, near the White Horse.

In the manner of the day the photographer had supplied a title for his work. It was printed in elegant copperplate beneath the photograph.

'Only Sleeping'.

CHAPTER NINE

—◦○◦—

'Britain may look a little shop-worn and grimy
to you. The British people are anxious to have you
know that you are not seeing their country at its best'
                    —'Over There' – Instructions for
                    American servicemen in Britain

Spencer 1943

They called the birds 'she', and the P-51 was the Betty Grable
of them all. Spencer named his 'Crazy Horse' and engineer Mo
di Angeli, the nose artist, did him proud. Though not without
putting up a fight.

'You don't want a girl?' he asked incredulously, spreading
out his portfolio on the bed. 'I do girls like angels, 's how I got
my name, you understand. Looka this . . . and this . . . huh?
Make you wanna fire bullets with your prick, yeah? Howbout
a cowgirl, kinda get the two ideas together?'

The girls were certainly sensational, with gravity-defying
bosoms and buttocks, nipples that could poke your eye out,
occasionally but not always holding in place an exiguous
wisp of gauze, cascades of luxuriant hair and satiny legs of
improbable length, generally ending in peep-toe shoes with
seven-inch heels. It was a joke on the base that Mo had no
problem clambering over the planes to do his work because
he had an extra leg. Decades later when Hannah dragged
Spencer along to see the movie *Who Killed Roger Rabbit?* (he
hadn't cared for it, too much slick brutality), the film's only

redeeming feature had been Jessica Rabbit, with her hourglass figure and Veronica Lake hair, who would have looked right at home on the fuselage of a P-51.

Mo had done his best, he was nothing if not a salesman. 'These are American girls, right? You won't see these around Church Norton, I'm tellin' ya. No, sir, these are all-American broads.'

They weren't, of course, they were girls from no country that ever existed outside a man's imagination, though there was something in their cheery come-hither smiles that reminded Spencer of Trudel. A little. Or Trudel as she had been, before she went away. Very briefly he'd thought along the lines of something like 'Apple Pie', a big down-home sort of girl . . . But all that had been such a long time ago and they'd both of them changed.

No, he knew what he wanted and once Mo stopped trying to change his mind he did just about the greatest picture in the Group: a bucking wild horse, arched at the very apex of its wicked, whiplash jump. A horse, fantastic as the girls were fantastic, a horse that had never thundered over any real plain, anywhere in the world. This was a mustang of the mind, with muscles like a weightlifter, a coat of molten metal, a mane and tail that flew from its body like fire, crimson nostrils and mad cobalt blue eyes, in each of which was reflected, tiny and perfect in every detail, a naked girl.

'Okay, okay,' protested Mo, 'perks of the job. Indulge me. Who's gonna know it's there but you and me?'

Soon there were two crosses under the crazy horse, like kisses on the end of a letter. Two crosses for two kills, not that Spencer really knew what it was to kill. With some of the pilots their swagger was as phoney as a three-dollar bill, but his was for real. For the whole of that summer he was in heaven. Or paradise, maybe, because he was young and still waiting for something, though what he didn't know.

That plane got a hold on his senses that kept him on a permanent high. As an old man, when he couldn't remember why he'd come into the room or where he'd left his glasses, there were certain things he could always remember, that were imprinted on his senses. The smell of the store in Moose Draw . . . his mother's delicate English scent . . . the sound of the bronco exploding in its stall . . . the feel of being inside Trudel for the first time . . . And flying the Mustang.

He had never ridden a wild horse, but he guessed this was what it must feel like. Alone in the cockpit of the P-51 you were astride the thundering Merlin engine like a cowboy. The plane was the most manoeuvrable at altitude of any in the skies over Europe but its power made every flight an act of faith. A faith which in his case had never been tested. There was that hot stink of farmland and fuel, the smell of the earth and of the sky. The moment when after a ragged, thumping start all the cylinders fired and you and the ship shuddered with the distinctive snarl of the Merlin and the propellor went from whirling blades to a grey circular blur like a kid's fairground windmill. And then the bumpy, lurching taxi-ing out from the hardstands, around the perimeter road and on to the runway, zig-zagging to compensate for the obscured view. This was when it began to feel good. You could see people watching, not airforce personnel but locals lined up on the airfield road to see the show . . .

And then that moment that defied belief, the biggest act of faith of all, when the speed reached a point of no return, like sex, and the plane lifted off the ground to where speed meant something different again, and the Cadillac of the air was cruising, in its element. The landmarks that had streamed, shuddering, past as the plane accelerated on the ground now floated serenely below: the twin churches, the lattice of narrow streets, the posies of woodland, the small fields and child-size barns. On a combat mission the whole sky seemed full of planes, a flock of aircraft hanging over the English countryside like migrating birds.

Spencer and Frank Steyner and a hothead nineteen-year-old, Si Santucci from Albuquerque, were in the same flight. Their wingman was a guy named Eammon 'Amen' Ford. Mo was their crew chief. They were about as mixed a bag as you could imagine. In the no-man's-land of waiting – and there was a lot of it – they fell unfailingly into type. Spencer would have a book in his hand but couldn't concentrate enough to see the print; Frank also had one, but read it, turning pages with metronomic regularity; Si was antsy and fired up, wanting to talk, or go outside and play ball, something he occasionally prevailed upon Spencer to do – but it wasn't much of a deal, Si was a star sportsman and they were poorly matched. He had some crazy ideas, too, shouted one to Spencer one day as he shied the ball at him.

'You know, you could catch a ball with one of these birds!'

Spencer grunted as the ball smacked into his cupped palms. 'Sure, how?'

'Under the belly! In the exhaust – bet you could!'

'Thinking of trying it?'

'Will do one day. Will you be pitcher?'

'Thanks, but no thanks.'

Eammon Ford was religious, the only one who didn't chain smoke. He was more overtly godly even than the chaplain, who liked to be seen as one of the boys. Eammon was older than most of them too, mid-thirtyish and quiet, with a wife and daughter at home and another child on the way. He didn't ram the Lord down anyone's throat, though, and even if he wasn't someone you could tear up the town with they respected him. Before each mission he wrote in a little book. He had very small handwriting, all the letters distinct and separate like hieroglyphs.

Si had the biggest pin-up collection on the base. He was eaten up with curiosity about Eammon and his little book, so it was only a matter of time before he got right in there and asked.

'Say, Amen, you feel closer to God up there?'

'No.'

'C'mon, up there above the clouds . . . "Closer my God to thee"?'

'That's not where God is,' said Eammon patiently. Spencer felt for him, he was being put on the spot and there was no mistaking the fact that other guys' ears were pricking up. It may have looked like they were playing chess or reading the funnies or writing letters home, but they knew when a bit of entertainment was being laid on.

'God's in your heart,' Eamonn added, perhaps hoping that'd see to it. But Si was aware of his audience now.

'Not in mine he ain't.' There was a murmur of laughter.

'You don't think so, but he's there.'

'You telling me I gotta have faith?'

Eammon lowered his voice still further. 'I'm not saying you gotta do anything – say, shall we drop this?'

'Sure.' Eammon continued to write, and Si to watch. 'May I ask you something?'

Eammon looked up.

'What do you write in there?'

'Oh it's private.'

'Hell, no, I don't want to read it. I mean, what kind of thing? Is that a diary or what?'

'It's not a diary.'

'Okay.' Si nodded sagely. His mischievousness was bordering on cruelty, but this waiting before missions was so strange and separate a time that normal rules didn't apply.

'You writing a book?'

There was a split-second pause and Eammon coloured slightly before replying: 'I'm writing for my own satisfaction.'

Si turned to the room. 'Say, hear that? We got a real-life writer in our midst!'

In a way, the moment had passed, because Si had exacted the information. There were a few mumbles, some more polite than others, and that was that. Frank was the only one who hadn't looked up once. But of course the seed was sown – everyone now knew that Eammon Ford was writing a book, and he could never do so again without people wondering what went into it.

That was another act of faith. In the air you had to trust the other pilots – especially in your flight and especially the wingman – because they had to trust you. When you were in a steep dive with the altimeter needles spinning crazily and the flak popping all around, you wanted men around you who were halfway sane. Which was why Si's little exhibition hadn't endeared him to anyone much, even if they did laugh.

So that was the waiting. And then there was the war.

And then again there was England – what Frank called 'familiarisation with our culture and history', and Mo called 'getting friendly with the natives', and Si called 'chasing tail'. Every man on the base was issued with a pushbike to help in these leisure enterprises. As a matter of fact, Frank was genuinely more interested in old churches and picture galleries than in other kinds of fun. From time to time he'd come along to a dance in the mess and stand looking on with a slightly mocking smile, quite relaxed but not joining in.

Mo was the one with the systematic ladies'-man approach, the chin like a chemist's shop, the sweet talk and the little parcels of nylons and candy, and it did seem to work. For a man with all the svelte looks of a pug dog and the elegant conversation of a Damon Runyon sidekick, he had astonishing success with the opposite sex. They queued for him at the main gate, he had to work hard at being scrupulously fair, and the most astonishing thing of all was that in spite of the competition which he made no attempt to hide they all thought he was the sweetest thing. They brought him eggs, and tomatoes, and little fairings they'd made, and invitations – more than he could handle. Spencer had to ask him how in hell's name he did it.

'Tough one, huh? 'S like they can't all be after my godlike body, so what can it be?'

'I didn't mean—'

'Sure you didn't. Listen, Spence, I *like* women. I tell 'em all the time that I do, show an interest, know what I mean? Put them first is di Angeli's rule of ladykillin'.' He put his hand over his heart as if pledging the Oath of Allegiance. 'Ladies first, every time.'

It was a philosophy of such blinding simplicity there had to be a hitch. 'But, Mo, how do you keep them all happy, how come they're not jealous?'

'Of me?' Mo held his arms out to the side, wiggled the area

where had he been two stone lighter his hips would have been. 'Joking apart, they trust me. Trouble with you good-looking guys is the broads feel insecure. Me they feel they gotta be kind to. And like I say, I tell 'em they're beautiful, give 'em presents, make 'em feel like princesses . . .' He leaned forward. 'And another thing.'

'Tell me.'

'I don't push my luck, know what I mean?' He raised his eyebrows so high each one was crowned with a series of semicircular furrows. 'Don't make like the sack's the one thing on my mind.'

'Really?' Coming from the man with the infamous 'third leg', the man who'd sent literally hundreds of improbably curvy cuties to flash their charms in the the skies over Europe, Spencer found this pretty hard to take, and Mo read his expression.

'Okay, I confess, it *is* the one thing on my mind. Like you, like everyone – surprise, surprise – I admit it. But you let them see that, you scare 'em off. Soft and nice, every time, Spence, remember that.'

Spencer bore this advice in mind, and though he didn't stack up the same number of conquests as Mo, he had a terrific time in the local pubs, at the officers' club dances and village hall hops, in the bars and restaurants of Cambridge and (when he could afford it) the fleshpots of London where he got lucky a few times – most notably with a girl from the Windmill Theatre and (on a separate occasion) with an older woman who turned out to be married to a civil servant in the War Office. Both of these conquests were memorable, the first because she had the body of a goddess and got plenty of practice, and the second because she was smart, with a lively imagination, and had been getting no practice at all. What's more, London and war being what they were, it was easy to look either or both of them up when he happened to be in town, no strings, no problem.

Around the base at Church Norton it was mainly good clean fun. There was no shortage of girls and contrary to first impressions the natives were far from hostile. The men, though civil, were understandably wary, but the women and children thought the Yanks were just great. They worked at it, of course.

The regulation issue booklet was full of well-meant tips some of which were sound, most of which they ignored, all of which were designed to keep their hosts happy (in the case of the girls not so happy that it would all end in tears) and them out of the clap clinic.

The kid Spencer had met on his first morning was called David Ransom, Dave to his friends, Davey to the Americans – it made the kids proud to have a nickname from the Yanks and they were happy to oblige. He was up at the airfield every second he could be, cycling up in break during schooltime and spending most of the day hanging around there at weekends, watching and listening, running errands with his 'I'll go, mister!' It was like having a big friendly dog who worshipped you, who'd do anything you asked, who you knew would go to hell and back for you – heady stuff for a young man like Spencer who'd never experienced the charms of hero-worship before.

Davey was always on at Spencer to come and have tea at his house with his mother and auntie. They lived way down Church Norton's main drag, the last in a terraced row called Craft Cottages. Spencer was doubtful because he didn't know whether the oft-repeated invitation had any endorsement from Davey's mother – if not, she might not be too pleased with some flashy stranger that her son talked about non-stop turning up expecting hospitality. Cautiously, he asked Davey about his dad.

'He's a POW in Germany.'

'Poor guy. And that must be hard on your mother.'

'She's all right. She says chin up, chest out, shoulders back.'

From this and other remarks concerning Mrs Ransom's bulldog spirit Spencer formed a slightly intimidating picture of her and her sister, Davey's aunt, which more or less convinced him that it would be unwise to accept any invitations except those that came, as it were, from HQ.

And then one Sunday afternoon in early July when a group of them were cycling unsteadily back from a pub crawl he heard his name being yelled, and looked over his shoulder to see Davey about a hundred yards behind, standing up on his pedals. The others joshed him about it. Davey was a funny kid, nice enough and willing, but intense.

'You got company, Spence!'

'Set a good example now!'

'I'll catch you up.'

'I doubt it!'

Spencer pushed his bike on to the verge and sat down next to it as Davey toiled up the slope. It was hot. He lay back. Not hot like at home, but you felt the heat more here because it was less usual. The grass was uncut, warm and fragrant and full of spindly wild flowers and buzzing, hovering, creeping life. The sky was a sweet, soft blue, not a plane to be seen, but somewhere up there a lark was twittering its heart out. His eyelids drooped. This was it, he thought: peace. What they were fighting for.

The unoiled squeak of the bike and sterterous breathing announced Davey before he flopped down next to him.

'Hi, Spence!'

Spencer rolled his head, shielding his eyes from the sun. 'Hallo, yourself.'

'I got something for you. Here.' He thrust an envelope at Spencer. 'It's from my mum.'

'Okay, so what do we have here . . .' Spencer propped himself on his elbow and opened the envelope, aware of being watched, that an effect was expected. It was a note from Mrs Ransom, written on mauve notepaper with a picture of a violet at the top, and all properly headed with the address and date.

> *Dear Lt McColl,*
>
> *David has been asking for some time if you could come round, but I have not wanted to bother you with it, knowing that you have many more important matters on your mind. But it would mean a lot to him, I know, so this is to ask if you would come and have tea at the above address next Sunday at four o'clock? There is no need to reply formally, just let David know.*
>
> *Yours sincerely,*
>
> *Janet Ransom*

Something about the rather stiff tone of the note persuaded him that he'd been right not to put himself forward. Although Mrs

Ransom was polite enough to make it sound like an imposition on his precious time, this was obviously an invitation extended under pressure.

'That's real kind of your mom,' he said. 'Will you tell her yes, and I'll look forward to it.'

'Yup.' Davey was nearly speechless with delight, his face red and shiny from the pedalling uphill and his hair sticking up in spikes.

'So will I meet everyone?' asked Spencer. 'The whole family?'

'Yes. My mum and my auntie and my little sister.'

'Great. I'll bring along a few things as a present, naturally, but tell your mom if there's anything she specially wants that I can help out with . . .'

'No, there won't be nothing.'

Even without the triple negative Davey's tone was emphatic enough to suggest that his mother was wary of Yanks bearing gifts and that even kids like him had caught wind of an implied tradeoff that was in some incomprehensible way unacceptable.

Spencer told himself that whatever the war had in store for him during this week he was going to need every resource at his disposal to get through next Sunday's engagement unscathed.

The weather remained perfect and they flew four sorties over the next six days. The whole of northern Europe was spread out like a map under clear skies. The 'Little Friends' had a field day and Spencer added a ground kill to his score when they strafed an airfield near Bremen.

Blue Flight seemed to be untouchable, especially Si Santucci who was out to get his name in the record books. He didn't only love the flying, he loved the killing. It wasn't something he chose not to think about: he revelled in it, got off on it, took terrible risks in order to see the faces of the guys he shot down. He was a hotshot, but a liability too, mainly to himself. You could tell that if he hadn't been doing this he'd have been causing trouble somewhere. He'd already proved that it was possible to catch the damn' ball in the plane's under-belly exhaust, in a display of flying so arrogantly dangerous that men had been throwing themselves to the ground, and if the grass had been any longer he'd have blown the heads off the daisies. A roasting from the general was water off a duck's back to Santucci. Spencer reckoned that if there was one thing war was good for, apart from the P-51s, it was that it got the crazy men off the street to where they could do a bit of good.

Frank had got himself some kind of plug-ugly dog called Ajax, with muscles like a prizefighter, jaws like a crocodile, slitty eyes and all the fearsome belligerence of Shirley Temple. And, as Mo choicely put it, 'massive meat and potatoes'. Frank had heard in the pub that the dog's owner had died and it had nowhere to go. One look at the hideously cute Ajax had been enough for him. It was, as Si put it, love at first fright. As they all stood round outside the canteen staring at the new arrival, his pink tongue lolling sidways from a face-splitting canine grin, Mo gave Spencer a nudge.

'Spence, see? 'S a mutt after my own heart, 's got it figured. He don't have a pretty face, but he sure fixes to please. Parts like that, he should worry . . . Next thing you know he'll be flying the fuckin' plane!'

Spencer conceded that such a thing would certainly scare the shit out of the Nazis. But it was good to see how Frank and Ajax got along. They seemed made for one another, a sublime attraction of opposites. The sight of Frank's skinny, tight-assed figure and the dog's broad, waddling one going about together became a symbol of normality around the base. And when Frank was just laying around reading, up against the side of the hut in the sun, or at night on his bunk, Ajax would snuggle up close with his chunky butt to one side like a mermaid, and his cock peeping out, and lay his great shark's head on Frank's shoulder with such a look of blissful devotion it damn near brought tears to your eyes.

At the end of that week Spencer had a letter from Trudel, a neatly typed one but with the 'Love, Trudel' written in ink to make it personal.

I've been accepted for nursing training in Laramie, starting this September, and I feel I've had plenty of practice over the past year or so. Poor Dad died in May and I know Ma doesn't want me to go but I can't spend all my life in Moose Draw, you understand that. I'm going to see if I can find some nice body who'd like to live in the house with her, keep her company and help out. I think a lot about you, and hope you'll be able to write soon.

Your mom came in the other day and told me she's hoping you're going to be able to get to see where her folks lived, perhaps take a picture. She misses you, Spencer, like we all do, and when we pray for 'our boys' it's you I'm thinking of. I know you can't be safe, but you can be careful . . .

Spencer did feel guilty about his mother, and about his lack of letters to her and to Trudel. He wrote to both of them, rather hurriedly, on Saturday before the band concert, and assured Caroline that next time he had a thirty-six-hour he'd try and get down to the Oxford area to look up the ancestral place. He meant to do it, had done so ever since he got over here, but when he had time off there always seemed to be other attractions of a more immediate nature that commanded his attention.

Sunday went from hot to sultry. Jenny, the English WVS girl who came with the chuck wagon – tea, rolls and doughnuts – said she had a terrible headache which meant there was going to be thunder, and several wags suggested that the headache had more to do with rough weather last night at the dance hall. She replied a touch frostily that it was nothing to do with that, and could someone please get that brute of a dog away from the van or she wouldn't be responsible, which provoked a bit more good-natured jeering.

Whatever the truth of Jenny's forecast it was stifling when Spencer cycled into the village, and he was obliged to get off the bike up the road from the Ransoms' address in Craft Cottages to mop his brow and cool off for a bit under a tree by the recreation ground. He'd thought carefully about what to bring with him that would look neither high-handed nor like a bribe, and settled for a tin of cookies and another of ham – good plain offerings for the family. It bothered him that by comparison with the wretched Mr Ransom, on short commons in some distant *stalag*, the Americans at the base must look like a bunch of spoiled high-school kids, but there wasn't much he could do about that except be scrupulously polite and not show off.

The door of the cottage was open and the moment he propped his bike against the garden wall Davey came out with that pink-faced, pop-eyed, tongue-tied look he got when he was excited.

'Hi, there.'

'Hi, champ.'

'Come in.'

The cottage was tiny, and the door led right into the parlour where the rest of them were waiting for him. In the confined space a round table had been laid for tea with a yellow cloth and flowery china. In the middle of the table was a blue jug with a bunch of simple little flowers like butterflies, pink, mauve and white, that gave off the sweetest scent imaginable. The room felt cool, but the single small window made it rather dark, and the table didn't leave a heck of a lot of room for manoeuvre. Spencer edged his way in, his feet seemed to have gone up several sizes. The way the family stood grouped together in a kind of reception committee in front of the fireplace made his heart sink. But if the formality of this arrangement accorded with his worst expectations, it was the only thing that did.

'Lieutenant McColl, how do you do? I'm David's mother.'

'Nice to meet you, ma'am.'

He shook her hand, which was warm and dry and boneless-seeming, and looked into her sad face. She was slim and dark, the same height as him and about ten years older, the most beautiful woman he'd ever seen. Like an Indian woman with a European skin. In the crook of her arm, perched on her hip, was a black-haired little girl in a checked dress, with a bright tin slide in the shape of a ladybird in her hair.

'This is Ellen.'

'How you doing, Ellen?'

'And this is my sister Rosemary.'

'How do you do, ma'am?'

She laughed. 'How do you do, Lootenant?'

And *this* was the aunt? The battleaxe in a hairnet? Rosemary was an auburn-haired and more voluptuous version of her big sister, with a broad smile, a small waist and a voice that could melt butter. There was a resemblance between them, but it was a fleeting, indefinable thing; he couldn't have described it to anyone. And she might – at a pinch – have been sixteen years old.

He handed over his offerings which were received with exactly the right degree of gratitude, as the contribution of a polite guest and no more, and then Janet took them with her into the kitchen at the back of the cottage, leaving him sitting on the couch with Rosemary, and David amusing his baby sister on the floor. The three of them looked a lot more relaxed than he felt. He stretched his arm along the back of the couch, tapping his fingers to show that it was a casual rather than a suggestive gesture; he tweaked his trouser leg and rested his ankle on his knee, felt stupid and took it off again. For a moment it was so quiet you could hear a trapped butterfly bumbling about on the windowsill.

'So,' he said. 'It's good to meet Davey's family at last.'

'We've been looking forward to meeting you, too,' said Rosemary, giving him a sunny, open look. She wore a pink and white dress with a Peter Pan collar and short sleeves, and flat, brown, childish sandals. There was a peachy amber down on her arms and legs. 'He talks about you all the time.'

'No, I don't,' said Davey.

'I reckon the base would fall apart without him,' said Spencer, coming to the rescue. 'He makes himself so darn' useful he should be on the payroll.'

'I hope he doesn't make a nuisance of himself,' Rosemary said, with mock primness. 'Janet thinks he spends too much time up there.'

Spencer held up his hands. 'I'm staying out of this one. If there's other things he should be doing—'

'Like school,' said Rosemary.

'I don't—'

'You do!'

'Give over!' Davey lunged at Rosemary's knees in a kind of soccer tackle, and she wriggled and kicked. They were more like a couple of puppies than aunt and nephew. Ellen continued to play with her farm as though nothing was happening, but Spencer, who wasn't used to this sort of family horseplay, watched a shade nervously. Far from feeling like a showoff who must restrain himself for form's sake, he was more like a fish out of water.

Janet came back in with a tray and put it on the table. 'Whatever's going on?'

Davey sat up. Rosemary said, with a sly glance at Spencer: 'He was trying to kill me, wasn't he?'

'Looked that way to me.'

'Well,' Janet held out her hand to Ellen, 'tea's ready so he can put it off till after that.' She took the baby to wash her hands and the rest of them sat down. Before taking his place with (appropriately) his back to the wall, Spencer couldn't help noticing that he'd be sitting beneath a framed photograph of the Ransoms on their wedding day. Not a white wedding, Janet wore a hat like a fedora with a feather, but there was a little bridesmaid standing alongside whom he realised must be Rosemary.

Now that he was closer he could see that the sweetly scented flowers in the jug were even more like butterflies because there were fine, winding tendrils sprouting off their stalks and leaves like antennae.

'Tell me, what are those called?'

Janet came back into the room. 'Sweet peas.'

'They're pretty. And they smell wonderful.' As he said this he caught Rosemary looking at him askance, and decided not to mention the flowers again.

★   ★   ★

The tea was good, and substantial. Sandwiches, cake . . . Janet had put some of his cookies on a plate, but more out of politeness than because they were needed to swell the feast. Conversation took a more predictable turn, with Janet asking him about America, his parents and where he came from, and Rosemary about flying, and film stars. The baby ate the middle of her sandwiches and put the crusts in a circle beneath the rim of her plate from where Janet retrieved them, suggesting gently that she try to eat them if she wanted to get curly hair. Davey ate concentratedly, watching and listening as though he were at a show.

After the baby got down to play, Spencer felt sufficiently confident to ask: 'Does either of you ladies ever come up to the base – to the dances or the shows?'

'No,' said Janet, 'we never have.'

'Yes, we did once, we went to see that play the RAF did when they were up there,' said Rosemary. She pronounced it 'raff'. 'It was terrible. The characters all talked about themselves all the time and the scenery fell to pieces.'

'It did?' Spencer couldn't help feeling a touch gratified by this British disaster. 'What happened?'

'The door came off,' explained Janet. 'But they covered up for it very well.'

'No, they didn't, they got the giggles and forgot their lines.'

Janet pointed out that it was a comedy after all, and Rosemary repeated, in Spencer's direction: 'It was terrible.'

'Did you see it, Davey?' asked Spencer.

He shook his head, and shifted his cake to the side of his mouth. 'Too grown-up.'

'Not grown-up enough if you ask me,' said Rosemary.

'We had a band concert up there last night,' said Spencer, edging the conversation sideways to avoid the family quicksand. 'Maybe I shouldn't say this, but it was pretty good. Some of our guys can really play, they were pros before the war. No singer, but you can't have everything. When we have another one, maybe you'd like to come up, as my guests.' He indicated the table. 'It's the least I can do after your hospitality.'

'That's very kind of you, you never know,' said Janet.

Meaning get lost, he suspected. But all of a sudden Davey piped up for the first time uninvited.

'Auntie Rosie sings.'

Spencer thought he saw a reproving look flash across the cake crumbs from Janet's end of the table, but it was directed at Davey, not him, and this wasn't the sort of information you could ignore.

'You do? What kind of thing do you sing?'

Rosemary made a face. 'Hymns, worse luck.'

'She's in the church choir,' said Janet with a certain firmness. 'Our father had a nice voice but it was only Rosie who inherited it.'

'You have ambitions in that direction?' he asked her.

'I haven't thought about it.'

'She has,' said Davey, 'you should see her room, she's got pictures of singers and bandleaders all over the walls.'

Rosemary looked daggers at him. 'David,' said Janet, 'will you take the plates out?'

'You should come and sing with our band,' suggested Spencer.

'Do you think I could?'

'No, Rosie, of course not,' said Janet with one of those laughs which disguised a warning. 'You're not old enough.'

'I was only joking,' he said. 'Any way you want to look at it you'd be too good for them.'

The girl gave him a wary look, for the first time not sure of her ground, unaware that Spencer was even less sure of his.

When he left, the women came out to see him off, Janet holding Ellen on her hip as before. They stood there looking, as sisters often did, discernibly alike, but completely different and distinct. One dark, sophisticated, reserved; the other red-gold, daring, testing her wings. Both separately and together more fascinating than any women he'd ever met. Janet had picked some of the sweet peas. She didn't actually proffer them but said diffidently, 'I don't know whether flowers are silly, but if you like them . . .'

'I'd love them, thank you.'

He took the posy, and then Rosemary stepped forward and whipped one out, and stuck it in his buttonhole. Her face was inches from his as she fiddled with it.

'You're a marked man now, Lootenant.'

In spite of a sky the colour of a black eye that threatened to justify Jenny's headache, Davey cycled back up to the base with him.

'That was nice,' said Spencer. 'I really enjoyed meeting your family.'

'Swell, aren't they?' said Davey

Spencer smiled. 'They're *real* swell. You must all miss your dad.' He felt somehow obliged to mention the wretched, absent Mr Ransom, cut off from the houseful of female beauty which was rightfully his. So he was surprised when Davey answered matter-of-factly: 'I don't.'

Spencer matched his tone. 'It's been a long time. I guess you kind of get used to it.'

'It's nicer without him,' said Davey. 'I'd rather have you.'

There seemed nothing to do except laugh, but it was a hollow sound. 'I'm flattered!'

'Will you come again?'

'If I'm invited, of course.'

They pedalled on for a bit, Davey's wheels creaking round twice for each turn of Spencer's, like a stately dance beat.

'You know, she *can* sing. Auntie Rosie.'

'I bet she can.'

'She sounds like someone off the wireless. She's really loud, Mum and I have to tell her to put a sock in it.'

This made Spencer laugh. 'Well, that's important. No point singing and not being heard.' Quickly, before he had time to change his mind, he asked: 'How old is she?'

'Fifteen.'

Well. 'It must be kinda fun – having an auntie that's so young?'

'It's all right.'

255

The rain began to fall suddenly, a few slow, slapping drops and then a torrent.

'Go on,' said Spencer. 'Git!'

As he dragged on dry clothes in the hut, Frank said without looking at him: 'So how was afternoon tea with the good ladies?'

'Oh . . .' he mumbled through the sweater he was pulling over his head '. . . not bad.'

'Okay, okay,' said Frank. 'Keep them to yourself, see if I care.'

And that was pretty much what he did.

The next Sunday Spencer went to morning service in the village church. He snuck in and stood at the back, but in truth that made him no less conspicuous because there weren't that many people at the service and they were all in a block in the middle. Not at the front, of course, he was getting to appreciate that that wasn't the English way.

There weren't many in the choir, either. Four flitty-eyed little boys of about Davey's age, three elderly men, and four women, including Rosemary. They wore blue gowns which must all have been made in roughly the same size, so that the kids were swamped in theirs, the tallest man looked like he was visiting a barber's, and the largest of the ladies like a well-wrapped parcel. He thought Rosemary was like an angel in hers – a fallen angel maybe, there was something so delightfully, irredeemably carnal in her grown-up little girl's face and figure.

They sang a hymn as they walked in, not one he was familiar with, but then he hadn't gone to church in years outside the occasional obligatory Air Force event. He didn't really bother singing, his attention was elsewhere anyway, but she was concentrating, her eyes on her hymnbook or straight ahead, and didn't seem to notice him. He couldn't distinguish her voice from the others as they reached the junction of the aisles and turned away from him towards the altar, and the choir stalls.

The service was long and dull, the priest had a voice like a sheep, and there was a lot of mumbled archaic language that passed Spencer right by. Besides which he had difficulty following the proceedings – the kneeling and standing and intoning, and the arbitrary leaving out of some things, the interminable length of others. He joined in with the Lord's Prayer, but stood silently through the Creed, having just enough respect for the Almighty not to lie outright. They sang – or the choir did, the congregation stumbled along in their wake – a couple of things in the middle that had no tune, but simply went on and on. The organist was a little bent old lady who started off each piece slowly, and got slower, so the longer it was the slower they got. All in all it wasn't an uplifting experience. He found himself thinking that if this was God's house and He'd been at home to begin with, He'd probably long since gone out till it was over.

But then they were told to sit down while the choir sang the anthem. The choir rose, turning very slightly towards the body of the church. The anthem was old-sounding and quite pretty, and halfway through Rosemary sang a few lines on her own. He was spellbound. Freed from the constraints of unison she released a voice of such rich, earthy power that it filled the church. For the first time there was something happening that was worthy of God, but oh, boy, thought Spencer, awestruck, did it ever speak to man! There was a throaty, gutsy edge to her voice that was the opposite of spiritual. He knew now exactly what Davey had meant when he'd said his aunt's voice was loud. It was a big voice but under control, you could tell she probably had the same again in reserve. And when she brought it down soft – the words were something about peace – it made the hairs rise on the back of his neck.

Then her little solo was over, and the others joined in again until the end of the anthem, when the padre said 'Let us pray'. He came down and stood in the aisle for this part, droning on and on about the king, and war and forgiveness, and Spencer had to shuffle along a bit in order to see Rosemary. She was on the end of a row and to begin with she looked prettily devout, with her hands clasped and her eyes closed. But after a couple of minutes or so she rested her chin in her hand, and her eyes and her attention wandered. At one moment her dreamy look slipped right over him like gauze, but if she spotted him she gave no sign of it.

They sang 'O, God, Our Help in Ages Past' – he knew that one, but was embarrassed to be caught with no cash on him when the plate came round – and then the padre delivered a sermon which seemed to be part propaganda, part religion, about hating the sin and not the sinner, but it was so full of long, reflective pauses and holy-joe cadences that Spencer lost concentration and just gazed at Rosemary.

During the last hymn the choir processed back down the aisle, and this time there was no doubt she'd seen him. He saw it in her eyes, and the tightening of the corners of her mouth – the smile she'd have given him if she'd been able. And he caught, too, the sexy swell of her incredible voice among the other voices, like an underground river.

After the blessing he didn't wait, though. He was out of the church door and on his way before the padre even came back out to shake hands. As a spiritual experience the service had left Spencer unmoved. As a carnal one it had been an epiphany.

That same afternoon he went to tea again, and this time after the table was cleared they sat round and played a kids' card game called Old Maid. Ellen sat on her mother's knee and selected a card from Spencer's hand when it was her turn. It was tranquil, he felt as if he'd always been there. He remembered with pride Davey's observation that he'd rather have him than his own father. The cottage door was left open to the sunny street and he took this as a mark of acceptance, that they wanted him there and didn't mind who knew it.

Over the cards, he said to Rosemary: 'I heard you sing in church this morning.'

'From the base?' asked Davey cheekily. 'Told you she was loud.'

Janet told him not to be rude. Spencer ignored him. 'I was in church.'

'I know, I saw you.'

'That is an incredible voice you have there.'

'Thank you.'

'You should do something with it.' He feared he sounded pompous, and added: 'Not that my opinion's worth a hill of beans.' He turned to Janet. 'What do you think?'

'It would be wonderful if she could.'

Rosie put down another pair of cards. 'But I start at the stocking factory in two weeks, so unless I get my big break before then I'll never see my name in lights.'

When the card game was finished, he asked if there were any jobs he could do around the place, to make himself useful, repay their hospitality. To get asked back was what he hoped.

'I don't know,' said Janet, 'but I'm sure I can think of some.'

'He could fix the pushchair,' suggested Rosie.

'I sure could,' he agreed eagerly. 'I grew up doing that kind of thing. Tractors, bicycles . . . I'm a whizz with an oily rag.'

Janet smiled. 'And yet you're a pilot not an engineer.'

'I kept quiet about it. I guess we all want to do something more exciting than what we're cut out for.'

'Telling me,' said Rosie with feeling.

The cottage had a tiny strip of garden between the front wall and the pavement; and it was planted with vegetables so close together that they looked like rows of knitting. Because they were on the end of the terrace there was a similarly small patch at the side, and this was where they grew the sweet peas in a wayward, fragrant wigwam. At the back was a small fenced yard with some balding, scrubby grass, a lean-to containing bikes and a few tools, a scattering of Ellen's toys and the dilapidated grey stroller.

It looked worse than it was, the seat had come adrift and one of the side shafts was buckled so the screw had sheared off. Davey kept him company while Ellen made a bed for her shock-haired doll and Janet watched through the kitchen window. Rosie stayed in the front room with the wireless on. Spencer was as happy as he'd been in years.

He couldn't do much about the shaft, because they didn't have any screws in the house, but he said he'd be back to do it next week. Janet said, 'I hope so.' He was sure she meant that she hoped he'd come back, not just that he'd fix the stroller.

Along with the adrenalin and the exhilaration, there was beauty – the sights they believed then that no one else was ever going to see in quite the same way . . . Moments – fractions of a second, no more – when you could see the curvature of the earth, and the cloud formations sitting on it like distant hills, all shot through with light. And other times when it was as if all of them, friend and foe, ally and enemy, were part of some great aerial ballet, criss-crossing each other like swallows, executing feints and passes and hurtling leaps, of which death was not the point and sole product, but a mere accessory, another move in the dance.

And since Spencer had met the two women, the dance had changed. Its focus was altered, it moved to the rhythm of a different drum. Another element had entered his life. He remembered a story his mother used to tell him. It was called 'The Snow Queen', and in it the boy got a splinter of ice in his heart that made him see the world differently. Only in Spencer's case it was no splinter of ice but the warm, sweet scent of a country flower.

He was bewitched.

On the Tuesday following the church service they flew a daylight-combat mission escorting the bombers over a munitions site just south of Bremen. After a week of showers, wind and mud, that morning broke with a pristine brilliance which was peculiarly English – the kind of glistening perfection that you only got when the summer weather was, for protracted periods, shitty.

There was no waiting. Briefing, equipment room, jeep to the hardstands . . . it was like setting off for a church picnic. The gradual homing in on *Crazy Horse* was like seeing a glamorous woman's make-up secrets under a harsh light – the plane was still a thing of beauty, but up close you could make out the black fuel streaks, the scabs of new paint and the metallic abrasions of the old, the cross-hatching of fine scratches on the Plexiglass hood, the stigmata of shared experience which only made Spencer love her more . . . That sensitive, touchy exchange with the crew chief, handing over his beautiful baby like a father giving away his daughter to another man. He had done all this, created this perfect thing, knew every inch and working of her, had struggled with her difficulties and cured her complaints and sat up all night with her when times were hard for precious little reward. And now along comes this cocky young fellow out of left field who can make her do anything he wants, and gets the best out of her every time. Like father and bridegroom, they both loved the same thing: but unlike them, there pre-existed between engineer and pilot a solid bond of mutual respect.

They customarily gave the bombers a two-hour start, and in these perfect conditions allowed rather more, so that they could really give the P-51s their heads and pelt away over south-east England and the Channel to catch up with their Big Friends just before the Dutch coast. Once they were with the forts they had to rein in and perform a steady zig-zag weaving motion, similar to that en route to the runway before takeoff, to enable them to keep their own pace down to a level where they could maintain contact. It was like Rosie, he thought, with her voice: the sweet, hot power of the Mustang was so great that half the time you couldn't unleash it. It was hover, weave, watch, hold steady. And then every so often there was the opportunity to let her do what she was capable of and the sky was a different place. When they first joined the bombers their massive, droning bodies and brown-painted wings made them seen like great furry moths blundering along, while all around the ritzy little fighters hummed like hover-flies, ready to zoom in and sting at the first sign of trouble.

Today Spencer was a liability. He sort of knew it, but the knowledge made no difference because he felt so great he must be invincible, and that was the trouble. Oftentimes he'd cursed Si Santucci for arrogantly peeling off in *Fast 'n' Loose* on his own little seek–and–destroy missions instead of sticking with the task of looking out for the bombers; but if Santucci's problem was too much focus, then today Spencer's was not enough.

Swinging back and forth through the thin, blue sunshine, it was like that stage of a night out, after maybe two or three drinks, when you just knew you were the funniest, smartest, sexiest goddam' guy in town – while in fact you were tipping over into being an amiable drunk. Every dial, switch, knob and wire in the narrow cockpit of *Crazy Horse* was as familiar to him as his own features in the shaving mirror each morning. He knew what to do. His head was crammed with more information than he'd ever have thought it possible to retain before the war; and was constantly, automatically, reshuffling the data according to circumstances, bringing the right stuff to the top, highlighting the options, zooming in on the best one, listening out for Frank Steyner, maintaining a cat's-whisker awareness of the movements of the rest of Blue Flight and their charges. Sometimes he could scarcely believe that, oh, wow! it was him, Spencer McColl from Moose Draw, Wyoming, who was up here in charge of all this highly charged metal and machinery.

But it was, and Spencer was still only young. And this day he could have thrown the whole thing away, and his life and the lives of others, because of a grass widow and her kid sister in a shabby cottage in England.

Today the only hint of cloud in the universe was a whisper of cirrus, floating like a snowy feather on the blue distance. The bombers and their escort described a fabulous, complex castle of steel, air and sound, drifting massively far above the French coast. You could just make out the movement of the surf like a throbbing silver vein between the sea and the sand.

And then in the distance they could see the first white arcs of anti-aircraft fire, neatly stitched with flak. And as they got closer they were in amongst the puffs of exploding shells, blooming like big black flowers and releasing their deadly sharp seeds, then withering, leaving dark tendrils in the air like blood in water. A brilliant sliver hit on one of the bombers, and a second. Then stuttering broken lines of tracer fire. A jabber of voices in his ears, sharp with tension.

The MEs, when they came, were choice targets, bulky and slow by comparison with the P-51s, but huge as they closed, like great black bulls bearing down on the Mustangs. One passed so close to Spencer that he could see the two men in its cockpit. He went into a half-roll to dive on the row of three beneath him, and as he did so the one he'd just passed caught a row of bullets from Santucci on his wing, and he saw the many-paned canopy of the ME frost over, the bullet holes stark as black spiders in the web of white cracks.

And all the time the bombers were advancing on their target, rumbling stoically, trustingly, towards the Hades of the box barrage, the pilot of each one now no more than a chauffeur as the bombardier took charge. Another act of faith. The firestorm had to be gone through, and *Crazy Horse* and the other Little Friends were left to skirmish with the MEs like kids playing in the backyard as the adults got serious.

That day it was like play to Spencer. He hit nothing, didn't get hit. It was like he was invisible, or the bird was made of some pliable substance, not metal. On the homeward journey the MEs snapped at their heels and caught one of the forts, the leader in the Purple Heart position, fair and square. Smelling blood, they peppered it with fire, then took off. Once wounded, the big plane stood no chance. It sank with the slow, tragic inevitability of a bull in the *corrida*, listing, breaking up, rolling over with a massive, heartbreaking dignity. The crew baled out, first plummeting, then floating beneath their chutes like pods from a laburnum tree into the green-grey Channel. When the bomber hit the sea the water seemed to give under its weight, rise and fold around it, and then throw it back up for an instant, like a child bouncing on a feather bed before finally swallowing it up.

All the way back it was fine. England dreamed, snug in the afternoon sun. Mission accomplished, no losses to the fighter group. Church Norton basked in the heat, barely stirred as the P-51s came back, howling their triumph. Ajax just managed to raise his head from where he lay, slit-eyed and panting, sides palpitating, in the short grass near the hardstands. Mo was full of grudging admiration.

'Congratulations, not a mark on her. What is it with you, you trying to lose me my job?'

It was only the next day, over breakfast, that Spencer thought of the bomber's pilot plastered to his seat by centrifugal force, devoted to duty, dead as a doornail.

But for Spencer that summer was about life. He visited the cottage whenever he could, lived for those visits. The tiny interior filled his head; it was, to him, bigger and more vividly real than anything else – the base, his friends, his own home, the war itself – and he dreamed about Rosie.

He could not remember ever wanting anything so much as he wanted to have her. Her unsettling combination of youth and knowingness, of naive simplicity and cute sophistication, was a mixture that had gone straight to his head, and his loins. He had had little or no experience of the sweet toxicity of girls in their teens, having gone straight from fearful ignorance to the older and all-embracing Trudel. He seemed to be on a carousel, being carried round and round and up and down, the view changing every second. The smallness of the cottage meant he was always close to her. Janet had a way of closing the air around herself, she could come into the tiny front room and leave the space undisturbed. When Rosie was there she filled it, so completely that Spencer could scarcely breathe. One moment she was fooling around on the floor with her nephew, whooping and laughing and not caring if her underpants showed; the next she was lying on the couch like a surly young lioness, her arm resting on the upturned curve of her hip, fingers tapping to music, her red hair shielding her face as she read a movie magazine with get-lost concentration.

Sometimes she lay on a rug in the back yard with her skirt tucked up, sunbathing, and he had to stop himself from staring at her pale, rounded thighs and the freckles that were scattered like a treasure-trail down between the buttons of her cotton blouse.

Ten minutes later and she'd be lying on her stomach with the dirty soles of her feet waving in the air, making elephant noises for Ellen with a blade of couch grass between her thumbs.

She was dangerously flirtatious, with her 'lootenant', and her sardonic pretence that he and Janet were engaged in some sort of conspiracy against her. If she asked him anything at all about his job she did so with a slightly challenging air that told him he showed off at his peril. It was no surprise that she had no boyfriend, he thought she must have terrified boys of her own age half to death, and yet the idea that some sweaty old supervisor or manager at the stocking factory might get his hands on her filled Spencer with horror. She was already so savvy, so sensual, so playful and witty and animal – it set him jangling just to touch her hand (the most he had ever touched), and the thought of a kiss, let alone anything more, set his senses reeling.

But of course it was out of the question. Her youth, his friendship with Davey, his privileged position in the household, placed her completely out of reach. And then her own status was unclear. Because of the age difference between the sisters, Janet treated her sometimes as an equal, sometimes not, though she was never anything less than moderate. As he went about the business of mending latches and shelves, and fixing up the back yard, and putting a door on the lean-to and cleaning the bikes, he found himself in awe of Janet. She was a little like his mother, holding the household together but never seeming to break sweat. He told her of the resemblance – in more elegant terms – one evening when Davey and Ellen were in bed and Rosie at choir practice. She claimed to be flattered.

'You mother was English? Whereabouts is she from?'

'Near Oxford. She wants me to go visit, see if the house is still there.'

'You must go, it would mean such a lot to her. And it's part of your past, after all. You'd be said if—' she seemed about to say one thing and then to change her mind '—it would be such a pity if you missed the chance.'

He knew exactly what she'd been about to say, and was glad that she hadn't.

And then there was the long shadow of Mr Ransom — or Sergeant Edward Ransom of the REME as Spencer now knew he was — to fall across his friendship with the family, and like a black admonishing finger over his passion for Rosie. Until one day in early September something happened to change everything.

Autumn was on its way. The Americans at Church Norton, already crabby at the prospect of another Christmas away from home, were being pushed beyond endurance, and as well as losses in the air there had been two fatal accidents, on both occasions pilots crashing before takeoff. A big old yew tree whose gloomy black branches had hung over the churchyard for centuries was felled by the second of these, its enormous bulk flattening gravestones and leaving the stubby church tower looking bare and vulnerable.

Blue Flight lost Eammon Ford, and the mystery of his little black book was revealed. It might have stayed secret had not Si been first on the scene from Blue Flight when Ford's locker was opened, and offered to send on his personal effects. He knew better than to broadcast the book's contents, but Spencer found him reading it that night in the hut, turning the pages as if he couldn't believe what he was seeing.

'Should you be doing that?'

'Guy's dead, Spence, what does he care?'

Frank looked up and said gently: 'That's not the point. He didn't want anyone to see. Just send the stuff back where it belongs.'

Si raised an eyebrow, gave the two of them a sidelong grin. 'You wanna know what's in here?'

Frank shook his head, but Si took Spencer's silence as a 'yes' and read out loud from the first page.

'"A book of prayers for my children, Molly and—" He's left a space there. First one goes, "Dear Lord, teach me to see you in everything, even the things I do not like. Let me always try to see the other person's point of view. Teach me to hate wrongdoing, but not wrongdoers. Show me how to forgive others, and myself. Let me never be

266

smug . . ." Can you believe this guy – hey, what are you doing?'

Frank had come over and taken the book out of his hands. 'Enough. It's private.' His voice was kind of sad and regretful, as though he himself were a father talking to a child who'd let him down. He closed the book and held it up, like an official in court. 'Will you send this stuff home, or shall I?'

'Take it easy, Frank, I'll do it – I'll do it!'

Spencer thought that judging from the little he'd heard, Eammon Ford was nearer the mark than the padre at Church Norton. Two weeks later a letter arrived for Eammon informing him of the birth of his son, Amos John, weighing in at seven and a half pounds and the dead spit of his father.

It was raining when a few days after that Spencer cycled over to Craft Cottages. The airfield road was slippery with mud, and there were blackberries on the hedge. It was evening, and with the cloud cover and the nights drawing in it was dark by the time he got there. Janet answered the door with her finger to her lips.

'The children are asleep.'

'Is Rosie in?'

'No, she's at the pictures and staying with her friend afterwards.'

She wore a dark blue dress, buttoned up to the neck, not a smart dress but oddly formal-looking as if she were going out somewhere. He'd brought a bottle of bourbon with him, but something about the dress made him shy. And Rosie's absence on this dark evening left a gap he didn't know how to fill.

'I brought this along.'

'Thank you, that's kind.' She took the bottle. 'Would you like one?'

'Only if you would.'

'Oh, I'm going to.'

He sat down on the wooden armchair opposite the couch, but when she came back with the drinks she didn't sit, but took a couple of mouthfuls of hers before saying: 'We got some news today.'

'Yeah? Not bad, I hope?'

'My husband's dead.'

Shocked, Spencer put down his glass and stood up. 'Lord, Janet, I'm so sorry. What happened?'

She still held her glass in front of her, in both hands. 'He caught a cold and got bronchitis. It turned into pneumonia. He always got chesty with colds, and I suppose the conditions . . . He wasn't so young, either. Poor Eddie.'

Her voice was low and sad, but steady. He was glad that she didn't seem about to cry.

'Would you like me to go?'

'No. It's nice to have you here, Spencer.'

'Do the children know? And Rosie?'

'Yes.' And Rosie, he thought, had gone to the movies. Janet's glass was empty. 'Would you like another of those?'

She smiled briefly. 'Thanks. It's in the kitchen.'

He went through and poured her a generous shot. When he returned she was standing there, head bowed in concentration, unbuttoning the front of her dress delicately with her long, pale fingers.

Spencer caught his breath. He couldn't move, was spell-bound. When the buttons were all undone she looked up at him. Her face was set and still but her eyes pleaded.

'Spencer . . . ?' She held out her hand to him, her right to his left as she did with Ellen. Slowly he put down the glass, stepped forward, and laid his hand in hers. She drew him towards her and slipped his hand between the open buttons of her dress, looking down as she did so in a way that turned his stomach to water. He felt cool, slippery material, warm skin, the hard tip of her breast.

'Please . . .' she breathed. Her eyes closed as her lips parted and softened. 'Oh, please . . .'

CHAPTER TEN

'Hast thou given the horse his strength?
Hast thou clothed his neck with thunder?
. . . the glory of his nostrils is terrible.
He paweth in the valley and rejoiceth in his strength:
He goeth on to meet the armed men'

—The Book of Job

Harry 1854

Before it had been horses thrown into the sea. This time it was men.

Cholera followed them on to the transports at Varna and was their fellow traveller as they sailed south to join the fleet at Balchik Bay. Even had infection not been with them to begin with it would soon have taken hold, because the transports were so crowded that it was impossible on many of them even to sit or turn round. Thirteen hundred men were packed on to one ancient man o' war where no provision for such numbers had been made beyond the removal of the guns. Lack of space dictated that everything except men was dispensable. Piles of clothing, tents, arms and equipment were left. Over five thousand horses – officers' mounts and pack animals painstakingly rounded up in Scutari and Varna – were herded into a hastily built depot and abandoned to what Harry knew must be certain starvation, or a quicker but even more painful fate at the hands of the Turks. He could almost find it in his heart to be glad that Piper had escaped. Better to think of him galloping until his heart burst in the heat, than rotting to death in what was to all intents and purposes a prison camp.

Emmeline Roebridge was smuggled on board somehow, under cover of the general chaos and confusion, and against the strongly expressed wishes of the divisional commander, Lord Lucan. But no contingency plans had been made to accommodate the hundreds of soldiers' wives expressly forbidden to continue with the army to the Crimea. The wretched women formed a hysterical mob on the dock, and in the end there was nothing for it but to load them, too, on to the already-overcrowded transports, at the expense of yet more supplies.

Across the unstable makeshift lighters trooped the women, and those horses allocated space, while on the quay the haphazard stacks of summarily unloaded equipment grew, even including medicine chests and ambulance wagons, to the delight of the locals. Not twenty yards behind him, in a cabin where at least one brother officer lay dying behind a rigged-up screen, Fyefield and the rest popped champagne corks and flirted with Emmeline, congratulating themselves on having got her on board. Harry, not wanting to appear prudish but unable to join in the merriment, went out on deck. From the scummy sea water around the transports there protruded bobbing corpses, jettisoned hours before but returned, as they rotted, to the surface, tenacious of their old element, their yellow-green faces puffed up by putrefaction in a mockery of rude health.

The process of embarkation seemed interminable, the confusion and noise beyond anything Harry could have imagined. The smoky air was full of the rattle of drums and the strident blast of conflicting regimental bands, designed to raise spirits but resulting only in a discordant row. The horses, underfed, overtired and agitated by the din, were fretful and hard to manage. But however justifiable their nervousness, to the sailors they were just one more bulky cargo to be loaded, and an inconvenient and contrary one at that. The men had no experience in handling them, and precious little regard for their feelings. Ears, tails, and even flailing legs were grabbed without ceremony, sometimes by more than one burly, cursing seaman, and blows meted out without fear or favour. Betts was enraged by this behaviour and in spite of his fear of water went down amongst the sailors to remonstrate with them, but he was hopelessly outnumbered.

Due perhaps to Piper's disappearance, Harry was not obliged to leave Clemmie behind, but when he went down to her in the hold it wrenched his heart to see the way her legs were splayed and her head hung as if still dangling in the loading sling, in an attitude no longer of trust but of dull, cowed lassitude. It may have been fanciful, but in spite of Betts's oft-repeated 'We'll see 'er right, sir', Harry no longer felt that when he laid his hand on the mare she took comfort from it: rather that it was seen as a sign of impending treachery. Yet Clemmie was fortunate in being in the first consignment of horses to be embarked, for not long afterwards a swell got up, making the rickety lighters heave and toss, panicking the animals and sending many of them, with the men leading them, into the water, their yelling and thrashing dreadful to witness, as the impassive dead looked on, riding the waves.

As they pulled out of the harbour, the officer whose last hours had been spent listening to the clink of glasses and the tinkle of Emmeline's laughter, was slung overboard, wrapped in a horse blanket.

To Harry all this seemed so far removed from his long-nurtured ideal of heroic warfare, that even had he been able to do it justice in a letter he could not have sent it, nor expected those at home to believe what he'd written. Except, perhaps, for Rachel, whose face was becoming more clear to him as it became more distant.

The short voyage south was almost dead calm. Even the least observant and imaginative infantryman could not fail to notice that there was no life to be seen – not a bird, nor a fish, scarcely a cloud that wasn't caused by their own smoke. It was as if death's presence on the voyage created a territory around them which no living thing was prepared to enter.

At Balchik Bay it was no better. The stately grandeur of

the mountains encircled a scene every bit as harrowing as the one they'd just left. Cholera had also ravaged the fleet here and bodies bobbed like corks among the ships. Through the night, as the vessels rode at anchor waiting for all the transports to arrive, beneath the babel of men and animals the ears of all of them became attuned to the intermittent soft splash of the dead going into the deep.

Even when they sailed on, the tall masts and funnels and the great columns of steam more like a factory afloat than a fleet of ships, it was still not for the Crimea, but north once again to rendezvous with the French at the mouth of the Danube.

Finally, on the afternoon of 11 Sepember the combined fleets set sail eastward across the Black Sea, their leaders having finally decided that they should make landfall near Eupatoria, at a place named Calamita Bay.

Harry read his parents' letters first, setting Rachel's aside to be savoured. His mother had written the letters, although his father had added his signature, somewhat unsteadily, to the end of them. Maria's writing was like her, full of real feeling naturally expressed, but staccato and disjointed, flitting capriciously from subject to subject using half-sentences linked by dashes, or simply running into one another. Harry was poignantly reminded of the last letter he had received from Hugo, on honeymoon in Italy, how its appearance had conveyed his elation as much as the contents.

She was well, reported Maria, and his father was trying to eat more, but failing to get any stronger in spite of everyone's best efforts. She had been trying to cheer him up by having some amusing little parties at which there had been music and singing and one or two parlour games: 'the funniest, funniest thing imaginable when a person must act some everyday activity "in the manner of the word" – I had to play croquet "passionately"! And then Mrs Carmichael to do "riding a bicycle" in the same way – I am afraid she was comical unintentionally as well – I thought I should weep from laughing!'

In picturing this gathering, though he knew how well his

272

mother meant, Harry could only feel sorry for his father, sitting baffled and below par as the merriment unfolded. But Maria went on to say that Rachel had also been present, 'and was a marvel, surprisingly (!) full of fun but not much inclined in her condition to caper about like the rest of us so she sat beside your father and quite took him out of himself for a while, even making him laugh from time to time, though whether at our antics or her comments, who knows?' Harry could see this scene, too, in his mind's eye and it made him smile. Maria said that she had also discovered, from Mr Carmichael, that it was possible to have letters delivered by Queen's Messenger from Horseguards, and this she intended to organise if possible, because she had little or no faith in the postal service in a theatre of war. It appeared that this scheme had been effective, because her second letter, though dated six weeks after the first, had apparently arrived within three weeks of it.

It made worrying reading.

'*I cannot pretend*,' she wrote, '*that there is any smallest sign of improvement, so when you consider that he has been like this for so many months, what is there to say but that he is worse? It is not possible for a man – who has been so strong and vital as you know – to be like this for ever, it is* not a life *–*' she had underlined these words fiercely '*– and if he were a horse or a dog I should put him out of his misery. And so, Harry, would you, out of common kindness and love – I cannot bear it and do not know what to do – the doctor is kind but* useless*, it is not his fault . . .*' Here she went on to deliver a colourful litany of the kind doctor's manifold shortcomings, ending with, '*The trouble is that he and I both know there is nothing to be done, but he will not say so from pride in his profession, and I will not because I will* not*, because I cannot bear to . . .*'

All this brought tears to Harry's eyes. Surrounded daily as he was by the horrible consequences of mass official neglect and disorganisation – disease and privation on a scale he could never have imagined possible six months ago – he realised that he was becoming habituated to the horrors. But the thought of his father quietly burning out at home in England in spite of every care and attention, however 'useless', made him sick with unhappines.

He turned to Rachel's letter last. Its tone, as he might have expected, was as different as possible from his mother's: measured, thoughtful but – he was certain he did not imagine this – full of a real concern not just for his welfare but for his thoughts and feelings, both about the war and his father.

I am sure your mother will have told you that your father is very ill, and of course she becomes so angry and despairing. She is a person who likes to do, *and there is nothing to be done. I believe he is far more philosophical than her, and it is wonderful to see the way he does his best to seem cheerful, to please her, so that she will not fret too much. They are so very different, and yet theirs is a marriage of minds and hearts such as most people only dream of, but which I know Hugo and I might have had. Dear Harry, I think often of the happy and loving childhood enjoyed by you and Hugo, and that it must have been that, in part, which gave him his own gift for life. I hope you don't think me presumptuous for writing in this way about the family that you know and love and from whom you are presently separated. I do so only to express my own feelings for them, and perhaps to bring them in some small way closer to you.*

I wonder whether your mother has described to you the jolly soirées held, as she would have it, to divert your father – all sorts of unlikely locals were pressed into service and did valiantly all things considered. Not that they had much choice. Maria as you know is not a woman with whom to take issue, even over charades! I think the evenings may have been as much to divert her, which is no more than she deserves, but seeing her laughing and carefree did make Percy smile, and he and I sat together like Derby and Joan and exchanged some very wicked and, dare I say, witty observations on the other guests and the proceedings generally.

And now, dear Harry, I wonder how it is with you?

I read the reports in the newspapers but they only describe the movements of ships and men, and not the sights that you see, the sounds you hear, the smells, the experiences, the excitements and discomforts. Even the horrors, if there already are horrors. When next you write, try to tell me something of all this, because I wish to try to be there with you in spirit. That, I think, is what letters are for, don't you agree? Not simply for the listing of events, though I am hungry for those too, but for thoughts and impressions, so that it is more like having a conversation, seeing not just what the other person sees, but how he sees it.

But of course I am clamouring like a child for things which for dozens of excellent reasons you will probably not be able to give. Understand that I ask only for what it would be a relief, or a blessing, or simply a diversion, for you to write if you have any time at all. And only of course when you have written to your mother and father who deserve your letters so much more. Nothing is too inconsequential nor too terrible for you to tell me – I shall not be shocked, I long for it all. One thing that I wish to ask is about Piper. How is he?

I am perfectly patient and philosophical as a woman in my ever-enlarging state must be. Please remain as safe as orders and your own bravery will allow.

Your ever-loving sister-in-law,
Rachel

Harry read these letters on the first night of their crossing, but the comfort he derived especially from Rachel's was shortlived. On the following night he became ill, with vomiting, diarrhoea and a fever. Sanitary arrangements aboard the *Simla* were minimal and had not been improved or extended to accommodate the numbers on board. It was almost as well that he believed he had the cholera and would die, or his own condition of incontinent filth would have been too much to bear. He was largely ignored except, surprisingly, by George Roebridge who attended to most of his more shaming needs with a kind of bluff tenderness while fastidious Emmeline kept to the decks with a book and a lace handkerchief. In fact there were probably more dismayingly intimate acts of kindness to be grateful for than he knew, for he was delirious for over twenty-four hours.

When the fever broke and he was able to take in his surroundings he could scarcely believe he was still alive, and George was equally incredulous.

'If you fail to come through this little skirmish in one piece, there's no justice. You're a man of iron, sir!'

'Not as much as you are,' said Harry, with feeling. 'I have to thank you, George.'

'Glad to be of service. And naturally I believe you'd do the same for me.'

Harry, white and sweating and weak as a kitten, was not so lightheaded that he couldn't see, with relief, the twinkle in George's eye. He might not have felt so relieved had he known how prophetic a remark this would turn out to be.

Two days later, as dawn broke, the Crimean coast appeared, a thin, brown line between sun and sea.

Rachel had at first decided to paint a landscape with the White Horse as its focus and centrepiece, but was obliged, dissatisfied, to abandon it. This was because the quality she found fascinating about the horse – one of mutability and movement – was something that was impossible, or that she did not have the skill, to capture. There were times when the creature seemed only just to have landed on the hillside, or to be gathering itself to leap away the next second. On those days when the weather and light were changeable it seemed to move as she watched, its outline trembling with life. Sometimes it appeared proud and angry, a wild horse in defence of its territory; at others it looked playful as a young colt, and in that mood it reminded her of Piper – and so of Hugo.

Though disappointed at having to give up her first idea, she had too much respect for her subject to persist and fail. Instead

276

she determined to paint a view of the house (she planned it as a present for Hugo's parents) in which the horse could be glimpsed peripherally, like a flash of white light in the near distance.

Having decided on this she went with her materials each day to the west side of the park, near the edge of the wood, and spent two or three hours there if it was fine. She went in the early morning, breaking her habit of attending to domestic and estate business at that time, because that was when the late-summer sun fell across the house in a way she liked, and also on to her as she worked. Jeavons would follow her across the grass, carrying in one hand the basket chair and in the other two cushions, hovering like a mother hen until he was satisfied that she was comfortable and wouldn't attempt to move the chair on her own. If she remained there past midday, he would emerge from the house with a high-sided butler's tray on which would be whatever cook had decreed she must eat 'for the baby's sake'.

The whole household was solicitous, and even slightly proprietary, about her condition. She appreciated this, and accepted it as a mark not just of their growing regard for her but also of their affection for Hugo, yet it drove her almost to distraction. For the fact was that she had never felt better. So far from being ill, or delicate, or over-tired she was in vigorous health, with a hearty appetite and boundless energy. Every day she thanked God that against all the odds for a woman her age, she had fallen pregnant so soon, and so had this precious legacy of Hugo inside her. She did not concern herself with whether it was a boy or a girl, she wished only for their child to be healthy and to be like its father. It certainly had his restlessness, bumping about inside her like a kitten with a ball of string, though as it grew larger there was less room for manoeuvre and it seemed to be pushing at the walls of her womb with its arm and legs, bending and stretching, eager to be born. Then there were days when it lay low and heavy, its contented hiccups making her body tick like a clock.

The baby was a reminder of Hugo's love and its manifestation. She would have endured anything for it, so her exceptional wellbeing was an unlooked for blessing. The physical warmth and mental serenity that she enjoyed were his gift, and the solid, fruitful weight of her belly and breasts were like his embrace, making the big bed less empty at night.

Rachel had not known love before, and it had transformed her. Darius Howard had been a clever, distant, ambitious man, devoted to her but preoccupied with his work. Being herself someone who liked her own company and pursuits and did not crave attention, she had been completely content with him. Their marriage was a serene and mutually accepting partnership, and its physical aspect followed the same pattern of tactful understanding. There was no reason for their not to have children, and she had assumed that in due course they would, but when after several years there were none she accepted that, too, and the lack of a family was never discussed between them. Their life together at Vayle Place was characterised by its calm observance of the proprieties. Rachel liked and respected her husband and was content with him, if a little bored. But when Darius had taken his own life, the aspect of the tragedy that most horrified her was that he must have been tormented, and had kept the torment from her. In that moment the whole fabric of her marriage was torn apart and thrown in her face.

Whatever his private agonies his death was an ordered one. His personal papers were meticulously up to date, his finances secure, his developmental project with the Great Western Railway conscientiously completed. On the day of his death he had gone to London on the train, put in a full day's work at the company's head office, went (it was later discovered) to the barber's for a haircut and shave, caught the same train back and shot himself in the middle of a field not far from the station. He was careful to position himself so that he could be seen from the road, and some kindly fate had ensured that he fell with his head amongst a clump of long buttercups so that the puddle of brains and gore exuded by the bullet hole was not fully visible to the two children who found him.

In the long and reasoned letter that was found in his briefcase, addressed 'To my dear wife', he told Rachel how sorry he was to inflict this on her, but that he could not continue to inflict on her the far greater wrong of his dishonesty.

'. . . nor can I,' he went on, 'any longer tolerate the burden of my wickedness. Suffice it to say, my dearest Rachel, that though I have lived another life, far beneath the one we shared, my best and highest feelings have always been for you, and you alone.'

She was quite mad with rage. People thought her wonderfully brave but it was anger, not courage, that kept her eyes clear and her head high. Anger that her husband had kept his secrets close, even in death; anger that he had needed 'another life' without ever considering that the two of them might have found such a life together; anger that he should speak of his 'best and highest feelings' being reserved for her, as though such feelings could never include passion.

Darius's death left her high and dry – childless, still young, financially secure, and physically unawakened. For four years after it she had sleepwalked through her life until Hugo had burst through the hedge of thorns, fallen in love with her as she slept, and woken her with a kiss.

With him, the world which had been a muffled, shuffling, half-realised place burst over her in a wave of clamorous sensation. Sight, sound, smell and even taste were suddenly intensified. His ardour and openness were a revelation to her, and with her love for him came the healing of forgiveness for her husband. Opening and flowering in Hugo's warmth, she released the bitter resentment and it simply floated away, like thistledown. And after their marriage, over those sensual weeks in Umbria, she had realised that the act of love was not simply a consummation but an initiation, a beginning – for her, a rebirth.

So when she was widowed for the second time her composure was founded on peace, not fuelled by anger. Even in the depths of her misery, just after the accident, when she had felt cheated and half crazed with pain, she had not experienced the corrosive bitterness that had followed Darius's death. And now, with Hugo's child in her womb, the happy memories were coming gently back, like true friends, to comfort her.

She had, too, seemed to see Harry for the first time. Perhaps because Hugo had been such a bright light, his younger brother had been cast in shadow. If she was truthful she had barely noticed him to begin with. There had been a dinner party at which they were introduced, but beyond a pleasant, serious face and a civil manner, more like that of a young doctor or academic than a cavalry officer, he had made little impression. Since then, he had become a friend. Over the arrangements for Hugo's funeral he had not just agreed with her ideas, but put those ideas into practice in a way that suggested he understood their provenance – indeed, understood her. He never claimed precedence, as he might easily have done, nor questioned even by implication her right to make delicate decisions. She remembered every step of that long, quiet walk to the hilltop church with the men – Harry included – pulling the cart, and Piper prancing and sidestepping alongside. In the churchyard Maria had been heavily veiled, Percy pinched and thin-lipped, over a hundred mourners waiting there in silence, a mass of faces turned towards her like pale flowers, reflecting her sadness.

Harry had read in a clear, boyish voice, a few lines from the *Book of Job* beginning:. 'Hast thou given the horse strength, . . . ?' And she'd noticed as he closed the Bible that his officer's hands were red raw from the shafts of the cart.

On his final visit, to say farewell before leaving for the Crimea, she had been aware of something, some depth of feeling, that he was too honourable to express. And as he'd led her down the hillside on the horse's broad back there had been a humility in his manner which moved her. Here, she realised, was a truly good man

There had been an incident since his departure which had brought him suddenly closer in a way nothing else could have done. Mrs Bartlemas had come to the door, white-faced with shock, to tell Rachel of her son's death. It was no surprise that she came on her own; her husband Dan Bartlemas was a mild, tongue-tied giant of a man who worked in the yard and cellars of the Flying Horse – all delicate negotiations and family matters were seen by him as female work. The two women sat quietly together in the sunny drawing room. Rachel, keenly aware of their relative positions, she expecting her first child, Mrs Bartlemas robbed of hers, had said little but allowed her guest to talk. She had showed Rachel the letter sent to her by Captain Latimer.

My dear Mr and Mrs Bartlemas,

I write to tell you that your good and brave son, my dear childhood friend Colin, has died of the cholera here in Varna. He showed the greatest courage to the end, and had a dignified funeral which I witnessed myself. Please accept the deepest sympathy of one who also feels his loss keenly, though so much less than you yourselves must do.

Your servant always,

Harry Latimer

Rachel would have cried herself at this letter had Colin's mother not been so grimly dignified. Instead she read it through twice in order to memorise it, and then handed it back.

'You must both be proud of your son, Mrs Bartlemas, though I know that pride can be no consolation.'

'He never even fought . . .' Her voice trembled.

'He fought sickness, Captain Latimer says so. To bear pain courageously is a triumph.' She heard herself sounding like an embroidered sampler, and reached out to cover the other woman's hand. 'I am so sorry. I can't think of anything more dreadful than to lose a child.'

'No, mum . . . thank you.' Mrs Bartlemas sniffed. 'It's a nice letter.' She folded it carefully and put it in her pocket. 'My Mercy read it to us. Harry was a dear boy, and Captain Latimer would never tell us a lie, would he?'

'No,' Rachel had replied. 'He never would.'

The place where she now sat with her painting was not two hundred yards from where Hugo had died. She could recall it without undue pain, rehearse each detail as if reading a poem. She had been at her desk in the drawing room and seen, in the mirror on the wall to her left, the reflection of Piper careering riderless towards the house with his harness flying, as if he would simply plunge through glass and brick and gallop over her. She'd got up and rushed to the window as he stopped, and Colin had picked up his reins. She saw at once what had happened and had walked steadily from the room, across the hall and out of the main door. At the edge of the wood among the creamy splashes of early narcissus she saw the two brothers, one lying, one kneeling. But on seeing her Harry had got to his feet and backed away respectfully. And had remained there, standing a little way off with his head bowed, like a guard of honour protecting her grief.

The combined fleet sailed up the Crimean coast as if performing a march-past. There was a certain splendour in such hubris, thought Harry, but hubris it surely was, when the Russians clustered on the ramparts of Sevastopol to watch them go by, and at night they were a seaborne city of twinkling lights and lanterns.

They were to disembark on the morning of 14 September. Harry still felt weak and faint, his bowels like water and his stomach resistant to everything but the smallest amount of liquid. Still, officers were to disembark in full dress with sword, and all men with three days' ration of salt pork and biscuits and full canteens of water, though the general weakness of the troops had led to their being ordered to leave their packs behind and to take with them only what they could manage to wrap in their blankets.

At eight a.m. the weather was perfect, carrying the warning of fierce heat later on. The bay was wide and sandy, one of a series of similar bays that scalloped the coast in either direction. On the way they had passed areas of beach with huts, striped canvas tents, and bathing machines bearing brave little flags. Here too it was pleasant enough: the sand rose into dunes in some places, low cliffs in others, and beyond these were shallow grassy hills reminiscent of Norfolk, where as boys Harry and Hugo had once spent a holiday with their governess, the kind but whiskery Salter. The sea had been so shallow for so great a distance that although Harry had not then been able to swim he could run straight out for over a hundred yards, with the waves still only around his legs, and then splash and lunge about while Hugo swam back and forth a little further out where it was deeper. Salter, who was terrified of the water, would occasionally lurch up from her deck chair both arms windmilling wildly, her frantic warnings made tiny by distance . . . There was something sombre about today's inversion of that childhood scene – he standing smartly dressed and armed on the deck of the *Simla*, waiting to wade through the water to the empty beach and whatever lay beyond it.

It seemed he was not the only one sunk in reflection. After all that had happened in the past weeks, so many men and animals dead or lost, so many still sick, it was chastening at last to be so close to their destination. Waiting for the order to disembark, there was a momentary lull in the shipboard clamour as fears and memories passed over them like a shadow.

Hector Fyefield, scanning the land with his spyglass, said beneath his breath: 'We are not alone.' He handed the glass to Harry, pointing with his other hand. 'Take a look and tell me what you see.'

A row of horsemen was drawn up on the crest of one of the little hills. There might or might not have been several hundred more in the valley beyond. These appeared alert. Their leader was busily engaged in making notes in a book, and beneath his arm was a large document, possibly a map. As Harry looked, he raised the binoculars that were hanging round his neck and seemed to be looking straight back. Harry experienced the perverse and childish temptation to wave.

Fyefield held out his hand for the spyglass and Harry returned it.

'Cossacks . . . They appear to be leaving.' He snapped the glass shut and gave a supercilious laugh. 'One can scarcely imagine the effect of all this on the poor fellows.'

Harry refrained from making his own observation, which was that there was something in the Cossacks' calm scrutiny and their officer's unruffled note-taking which did not denote abject terror.

★   ★   ★

When the order came, the quiet at once exploded into seething bustle and noise as the bands struck up and disembarkation began. The sunshine, the activity, the inviting emptiness and accessibility of the Russian beach and, above all, the long-awaited sense of purpose, dispelled anxiety.

The Light Cavalry were to wait until the infantry divisions were on land. Emmeline availed herself of George's spyglass and gave a running commentary on what all could see anyway – the soldiers swarming down the sides of the ships like ants into the waiting boats, the sailors shouting coarse encouragement (which made her blush, especially where it was directed towards the Scotsmen in their kilts) and the proud sight of the troops eagerly jumping out of the boats and wading thigh-deep to shore.

'At last!' she cried, eyes shining, clasping her gloved hands. 'We're really here!' Exactly, Harry remembered, as he and Hugo had done when free at last of shoes, socks and jackets they ran on to the cool evening sand after the interminable journey north with Salter.

All morning the operation continued, with the broad beach and its hinterland filling up with men and equipment and the sky with clouds, until at three o'clock it began to rain. With the rain the temperature dropped abruptly, and Emmeline went back into her cabin. A wind got up, not a gale such as they'd endured on the voyage from England but enough to make the exercise considerably more hazardous. Nerves and tempers frayed. The bawling of the sailors which had been good-natured before became impatient and bullying. An activity which would have been all in a day's work to them – swarming down the sheer side of a steamer on swaying, sodden ropes into small boats which the waves were tugging and tossing in every direction – was a dismaying one for the wretched foot soldiers, many of them sick with colic, dysentery and worse. Fear and discomfort were heaped on indignity. The rain picked up, lashing their faces, and a great many of their kit bundles fell into the sea.

Harry went down at night after dinner to see the horses. Since leaving Varna he had been assigned another charger,

Derry, a heavier horse than Piper, beside whom Betts, a pasty little monkey of a man, was like a dwarf. Betts was only twenty-five, the same age as Harry, but could have been any age from twenty to forty. Until the war he'd earned a living at one of the famous London breweries. One of the great dray horses had gently but firmly stood on his foot a few years back, and he walked with a jerky limp which only added to his air of indomitable cockiness. As well it might for in spite of the limp, his rickety frame and his deathbed cough, he had already survived several bouts of sickness and come through unscathed.

Down in the hold Harry went first to Derry, a homely bay gelding with feathered heels and a mealy nose, not sufficiently handsome in the first place for the depredations of the voyage to have spoiled his looks. Harry made a fuss of him and he nodded and stretched out quivering, hopeful lips. Derry was sturdy and willing, a horse that a child could have ridden, but entirely unproved. In spite of his name, Harry suspected him of being one of the horses rounded up in Varna, and therefore not accustomed to luxury.

Betts was crouched down by Clemmie's legs, rubbing her pasterns with liniment. When Harry arrived he would have got up, but Harry motioned him not to.

'Captain Latimer, sir.'

'Carry on, Betts.'

'Sir.'

When Harry went to Clemmie's head she turned her face into his chest in an attitude it was impossible not to interpret as despair. Betts hauled himself up and propped himself with one hand on her flank. He swayed a little with the motion of the ship; blinked fast a few times in the punchdrunk way he had before speaking.

'When are they going to let us off, sir?'

'Tomorrow, I believe.'

'Weather's foul, sir. How they going to get the horses off in this?'

'I don't know.'

'I hope there's going to be some forage for 'em, sir.' He

slapped Clemmie's side. 'Otherwise you and the other gents'll find yourselves quicker running after the Russians than riding these poor things. Their saddles'll be too 'eavy for 'em.'

'Don't worry, Betts,' said Harry, more from duty than conviction, 'we'll be provided for.'

'Sir.' Betts hawked richly and spat a yellow gob with fearsome speed and accuracy into the gulley at the foot of the bulkhead. He blinked rapidly. 'Glad to 'ear it, sir.'

All night it rained and the next morning at first light it was still doing so, but in a slow drizzle. Seen through the spyglass, the aspect of the beaches could not have been more different than the previous day's hopeful bustle. There were only a few tents and on the upper reaches of the sand and among the dunes sleeping men lay in the open, wrapped in their soaking blankets, like corpses in winding sheets. Piles of supplies, still lying where they had been unloaded, looked no longer encouraging but paltry and neglected. Officers, who had waded so proudly through the surf in their splendid full dress, sat about on powder kegs with the water streaming off their rubber capes.

The wind had dropped, and disembarkation of the Light Brigade began. Betts and the other grooms remained behind to assist with the unloading of the horses. As the cavalry officers descended the ladders the sailors held their tongues, canny rather than respectful, though Harry had the impression that if he or a fellow officer had missed his footing it would not have upset them. The hand that met his as he stepped off the ladder was hard as leather and knotty with rope-calluses. The boat, with twenty of them on board, towed like a child's toy by a team of sailors in a lighter craft, bobbed away from the relative security of the *Simla* towards the dismal chaos and unknown dangers of Calamita Bay.

It was a trip of no more than a quarter of a mile to the shore, but George Roebridge's head was lolling and he was deathly pale. 'Thought I'd have got my sea legs by now,' he muttered wanly, before vomiting painfully over the side. They were to be his last coherent words.

286

When the boat grounded the others, including Fyefield, leapt out and waded ahead eagerly. It took Harry and one of the sailors a couple of minutes to help George into the water, and once in his progress was slow and weaving as a drunk's, his weakened legs barely able to cope with his own weight, let alone that of the shallow waves. After only a few yards he fell to his hands and knees, and with a terrible growling groan was sick once more. There was no mistaking the sound and smell nor, as Harry hoisted him to his feet, the blueish shadow of cholera around his mouth. Emmeline was still on board, the cavalry officers' wives were to disembark last. At this rate, Harry calculated, George would be dead before she reached the Crimea.

On land there was no cover, no organisation, no apparent chain of command. Harry manhandled his companion to the top of the beach and laid him in the lee of a dune, lying on his own cape and covered with Harry's. He was now retching with every other breath, his eyes full of the same animal terror that one saw in the eyes of the horses – a trapped panic in the face of the inevitable.

Stifling his own anxiety, Harry went in search of cover. Such tents as had been brought (and in the confusion of embarkation at Varna there had not been many) had been loaded on to the transports first without thought that they might also be needed first.

Harry approached a senior infantry officer who appeared at least to be acting constructively, organising teams of men with a couple of *arabas* to move supplies further inland. When they'd begun leading the brokendown horses along the crowded beach, moving the living and dead roughly out of the way by main force, he asked: 'Sir, is there any form of cover for the sick?'

The officer looked at him with a weary expression that said, Trust a cherrybum to ask a stupid question. 'The sick must go back to the ships.'

'If they can, but it's impossible while so many are still coming ashore.'

'Then I can only suggest you do what everyone else has done. Find existing cover of some sort and take the sick to it,' said the officer. The almost insulting obviousness of this advice masked a hard truth: there were to be no more tents.

Harry thanked him and made a brief sweep of the surrounding area. The beach was severely crowded and as full of noise as a marketplace – shouted orders, groans and coughing, the creak and clatter of the farmcarts, the yells of the sailors in the landing craft and of RSMs bawling at the top of their lungs in a vain attempt to assemble regiments. Some men had taken cover under carts, but as the morning drew on these were being brought into service and the men were flushed out from beneath them like partridges. He did however come across a couple of gun carriages drawn up shaft to shaft about a hundred yards to the north beneath a shoulder of rock and which, with a cape thrown over them, would provide some sort of shelter.

He had some difficulty in locating George and when he found the correct area there were so many dejected men sitting and lying about among the dunes that it took him another few minutes to identify his friend. If he had ever hoped against hope otherwise, it was now clear that whatever measures he took to ameliorate George's suffering they would have no effect on the outcome. The poor fellow had taken on the horribly familiar appearance of those dying of cholera – a look common to officer and man, high or low, irrespective of age or nationality. His face seemed to have shrunk and aged even in the half hour that Harry had been away, and his body trembled and convulsed as the life drained out of it. Harry would even have welcomed the fear that had been in his friend's eyes not long ago – fear was at least a sign of life, a human reaction, but even that had now been replaced by the veiled, inward look of the dying.

The various regiments were beginning to find one another, and he could see a bright swathe of cavalry officers, still splendid and recognisable having not spent a night in the open, only a few yards away. Fyefield and a pop-eyed young officer named Philip Gough agreed to help move George, the former with a poor grace.

'It's sad, of course, but we're wasting our time,' he drawled as they carried George down the beach.

'If he's not going to live he might as well die in whatever comfort can be found,' said Harry. 'And in privacy.'

Gough, breathing heavily, asked: 'When will the horses come ashore?'

'Soon now, I believe.'

'Good,' said Gough. 'Then we can ride inland and make a halfway decent camp.'

All three understood that it was not just the establishing of a camp that made the horses' arrival so desirable. The lack of them was a great leveller now the army was on land, reducing the proud centaurs of the Light Brigade to the status of ordinary foot soldiers.

They reached the gun carriages. Another man had crept beneath them in Harry's absence, but when they gave him a shake to move him over it turned out that he had done so like a sick dog, to die. They dragged the wretch out and laid George in his place, wrapping him close in his own cape and spreading Harry's over the shafts above him.

'No point whatever in staying,' commented Fyefield, dusting his hands. Gough, uncertain where the balance of power lay, glanced from one to the other.

Harry said: 'His wife must know as soon as possible. We must ensure that a message gets to her.'

'The poor lady,' said Gough. 'She's surely not still on board?'

'No, no, the ladies are with us,' said Fyefield. 'I saw them taken to the tents.'

With a heavy tread Harry approached the cluster of tents in a hollow of ground some few hundred yards inland. To his dismay Emmeline was standing outside, holding her hat with one hand and protecting the side of her face from the blowing rain with the other. For the great events of today she had affected an appropriately military look: a dark blue riding habit with gold buttons. When she saw him she gave a little wave and walked to meet him, watching her step on the rough ground, holding her skirt up daintily out of the muddy grass. All he could think of was her excitement of yesterday, the way she had clapped her hands like a child and cried, 'We're here, we're really here!' as if she were on holiday; and then of George's face as he had last seen it, in the dripping shadow of the gun carriage.

He could not assemble the words to say what he must. He could only pray that God, or instinct, would provide. But as she drew nearer he stopped and saluted, and she must have read something in his face because she too stopped and her hands went to her cheeks.

'You have something to tell me?'

'I do. I'm afraid that your husband is very ill.'

'So he is not dead!'

She was clutching at straws, and Harry knew he must be careful. 'When I last saw him he was still alive. We succeeded in finding shelter for him – I can take you to where he is.'

'Thank you.'

As she hurried down the beach beside him he could hear her quick shallow breathing and stifled sobs, but when he offered his arm to help her through the throng she declined, and her face was set and pinched. He hoped against hope that when they reached the gun carriage her husband would already be dead so that she would not have to see him in the worst extremity of suffering.

George Roebridge was certainly dead, but whether from sickness or the iron-clad wheel of the gun carriage which had been roughly dragged across him, it was difficult to tell. The story was plain enough to see – the artillerymen had taken him for a corpse and in moving the carriage by the shortest route had unknowingly put him out of his misery.

Emmeline sank down on her knees on the sand, weeping loudly. Harry saw that she did not touch George, but bent over him as if trying to reconcile what she saw before her with the husband she remembered. When she turned to Harry he was shocked by the look on her face.

'You said that he was alive!' she screamed. 'You told me you had found shelter!'

'We had done so, madam, but the gun carriage has been removed while I went to fetch you.'

'And look!' She gestured at the body with a grimace of revulsion. 'He has been injured.'

'I cannot account for that. Perhaps the carriage—'

'He is injured! I hardly know him . . .' Her voice was distorted by sobs. 'I would not have known him. He is all . . .' She shook her head like a hurt animal and Harry only just caught the last words: 'All . . . spoiled.'

Less than an hour later he saw Emmeline returning to the ship, the body of her husband no doubt beside her in the boat as a sailor rowed. Her head was turned as if in mortification away from the land which had let her down so badly. She would never see her husband take part in the famed élan of a Light Cavalry charge. No sooner had they arrived than they were going back, the great adventure over. All spoiled.

When Betts had asked Harry how the horses were to be unloaded he could never have foreseen the method that was eventually employed. Attempts to land them on insubstantial homemade rafts and float them ashore proved unsuccessful for the same reason they had failed at Varna – the animals were upset after the long voyage and simply too agitated to handle: their legs flailed about pathetically as they descended, and were unable to hold them steady on the rafts once they were there, even with the help of the grooms and the less careful assistance of the sailors. It didn't take long for the latter to settle on a more effective course of action: the horses were simply bundled overboard and made to strike out for the shore. They were accompanied by the men who could swim, but many, Betts included, could not do so and were too terrified to try. The result was that while the non-swimmers were transported to land, numbers of horses were running loose on the beach, wild, cold and frightened, and with no means of identification or capture beyond a slippery wet headcollar.

Betts when he did arrive was quite beside himself. 'I never seen such a thing, sir! They was bad enough aboard ship without all this, and them ruddy sailors is only making matters worse with their yelling and larking about!'

This last was nothing less than the truth. The attitude of the sailors seemed to be that the army could not have landed nor even have been here without them, and that this entitled them to claim certain bonuses, one of which was a free ride. As the quaking horses skittered out of the surf, whooping sailors chased them and scrambled on to their backs, hanging on round their necks like monkeys and fearlessly galloping them around in the edge of the water. Even allowing for the reduced state of the horses it was a bravura display of unorthodox horsemanship which did nothing to endear them to those trying to find their mounts.

Betts, already mortified by his own inability to swim, was outraged. Spotting an animal he took to be Derry, he ran down the beach and tried to intercept him. But a small man with a limp was no match for a large, nervous horse being ridden at speed, and it was lucky for Betts that this particular midshipman lost his balance as he swerved to avoid him and crashed into the water. Harry could easily imagine the stream of imaginative abuse that was hurled at him before Betts went to recover the horse who had come to a standstill with his flanks heaving like bellows. Luckily Clemmie was led ashore, and by the end of the afternoon the Light Cavalry and most of their horses had moved inland to camp for the night.

Their three-day sojourn at Calamita was a cheerless and dispiriting business, made worse by the obvious superiority of the French commissariat. In spite of even more seriously over-crowded transports the French had disembarked sooner and more quickly in a bay just to the north, flown a jaunty tricolour and established a flourishing, well-supplied camp a full day ahead of their allies. Consequently they had also been able to infiltrate the surrounding countryside and collect together what there was in the way of additional food, transport and forage for horses. The sight of rows of snug French tents, and the appetising smell of cooking fires tended by cheerful *vivandières*, did little to cheer the British troops, dispersed mostly in the open and with only their meagre three-day subsistence rations.

There were tents for the more senior officers, but Harry and his colleagues had to content themselves with a sulky fire made from damp brush, and a meal of pork, biscuit and rice boiled to a sludge, only made palatable by wine. Out on the austere grassy plain the horses were like a dark low forest, the steam rising from their coats in a mist. In the far distance beyond even the French camp could be heard the wild celebrations of the *bashi-bazouks* to whom nothing, apparently, was so bad that it couldn't be overcome with *raki*.

'Perfect country for cavalry at least,' commented Fyefield, lighting a cigar. 'I can't wait to get at them.'

Harry warmed his glass by the pale flames. 'We need one or two days' respite, though, if only for the horses.'

Fyefield made a dismissive gesture. 'The horses will recover when they're put to the use they were brought here for. Just like us.'

A little later they were presented with coffee, bitter and watery and full of gritty flotsam, but nonetheless a triumph on the part of the cooks who had had to grind beans between stones and fetch water a distance of some two miles to produce it. And it was at least warming – as the weather cleared and the night drew in the air became cold and they moved in closer to the fire,

As they sat there an extraordinary group emerged from the darkness. It consisted of three exhausted-looking men, one carrying a pitchfork and the other two lugging between them the head of a cow, not freshly killed but with one eye still, and enough flesh on it to give a thoroughly macabre appearance, its enormous flannelly tongue lolling almost to the ground as it bobbed along. Two of the men had blankets tied round their shoulders and the other one a piece of sacking, and a strip of the same stuff about his head like a gypsy bandanna, stained with blood. All three were filthy and wet, it was possible to hear the squelch of their boots as they passed by, and the smell given off by the men and their grisly burden. The effect of all this combined with the pitchfork was eerie. They ignored or were too tired to notice the officers around their fire, but when they'd disappeared into the night Fyefield gave a low whistle.

'What the deuce was that?'

Gough laughed nervously. 'Old Nick by the look of it, serving us a grim warning!' And then added, none too convincingly: 'Locals, I suppose.'

'Maybe,' suggested Harry lifting his glass, 'we should not drink on short commons.'

It was almost an hour later when it dawned on them what they'd seen, and he said softly, 'Poor fellows', to think what British soldiers were reduced to.

The following morning when the soft breeze wafted the smell of fresh coffee and bread from the French camp, two hundred and fifty men of the Lights, with two guns from the Horse Artillery, were ordered to saddle up and accompany the same number of infantrymen on a reconnaissance expedition to bring in supplies. There on the edge of the infantry camp, as the Lights rattled briskly past, was the cow's skull, picked clean and shining in the sun.

That day turned into one of scorching heat such as they hadn't known since leaving Varna. It seemed that they were constantly to be buffeted by extremes of temperature and conditions, and to find themselves equipped for neither. The men who had been obliged to swathe themselves in blankets and sacking for the previous night's foraging were this morning dragging at their collars, sweating and cursing. The gently rolling plain, the perfect cavalry country of which Fyefield had spoken, now shimmered like a desert, an impression confirmed by an occasional sighting of camels. These fantastic creatures at least broke the baking monotony, and had the effect of cheering the foot soldiers, who laughed and jeered when the animals broke into their comical, loping stride.

There were scarcely any farms, precious little food and forage and virtually no water. All through the middle of the day they were tortured by mirages which trembled and gleamed, always in the middle distance. They came across one substantial lake but the horses showed no interest in it, understandably, for when the men plunged their faces into it open-mouthed they found it to be thickly saline. To make matters worse those who failed to wipe the solution off their skin were badly burned. The cavalry did succeed in acquiring half a dozen *arabas* but the only thing they carried back to camp were infantrymen collapsed through dysentery, cholera or heat exhaustion, several of them dead on their return.

Neither did Fyefield's bullish predictions about the horses prove correct. They were disastrously out of condition and in need of shoeing, and Harry was not the only officer who walked back into camp that evening, his feet slick with blood inside his boots (causing him to wonder what on earth the surviving infantry must be suffering) and Derry nodding at the end of his rein like a seaside donkey. He was only glad that he had not ridden Clemmie, who would certainly not have survived the day, and whom he had left in the tender care of Betts. For the whole of the dismal trek back he was haunted by the memory of Hugo on Piper, thundering through the trees in the fresh green English spring . . . and of the words spoken at his funeral: 'He paweth in the valley and knoweth not fear . . . the glory of his nostrils is terrible . . .' Perhaps it was true that the poor chargers needed to 'smell the battle afar off', but at this most dispiriting juncture it was hard to imagine them being anything but cowed by the prospect.

Though the cavalry did not for some days come to hear of Lord Raglan's decree that they should be kept 'in a band-box', there could be no doubt that they would now have to be rested, and that consequently there could be no advance for at least another thirty-six hours. The time was spent tolerably profitably, with the saddlers and farriers working long hours, kit and arms brought up to scratch and inspected, convalescent men ditto, and the usual drill for those men and horses well enough to do it.

On each of the two nights in camp, aching and blistered after a day which began at five a.m., Harry wrote his reply to Rachel. Though he had determined not to tell her 'everything' as she had requested, the picture of her which the act of writing conjured up, and her own injunction that their correspondence should be like a conversation, persuaded him otherwise. He tried, though, to paint a picture of events as he saw them rather than a litany of largely depressing facts. So that when he told her about Piper bolting he did not conceal his own distress, but added what was also true, that in view of all that had happened since it was a glorious escape. He described the voyage, the illness, the death of so many good men including Bartelmas and Roebridge, the kindness of Roebridge when nursing him, the devotion of Betts and his gallows humour, the suffering of the horses and the chaos of camp life. He described the sailors galloping in the surf, the strange, diabolical group who had passed the fire on the previous night, the loping camels and the cruel mirages. It was a comfort to do so, and his writing became less careful as he progressed. But when he turned to more personal matters he paused, and chose each word with the utmost care.

'I have done as you said and spared you nothing,' he wrote. 'And I only hope that I have not said too much nor said it too baldly, but I believe you capable of all women of absorbing these things. I have found it a great solace to be able to write of them so freely, and perhaps you knew this when you urged me to do so. If this is so, I thank you from the bottom of my heart. In addition, I can scarcely tell you how much it means to me to know that you are near my parents at this time when I cannot be, and that you are so good to them. They are, as you say, both unusual people whom it is not always easy to understand, and that you have done so after what is a relatively short acquaintance, disfigured by tragedy, is a marvel to me. Again, dearest Rachel, my thanks.'

His pen hovered for a moment as he debated whether to cross out 'dearest', but he left it in place and ended: 'I have no way of knowing when this letter will reach you, but it is my dearest hope that I shall receive another from you very soon, whenever our trials and tribulations allow. I remain your affectionate brother-in-law and friend, Harry.'

The morning after he completed this letter, the allied armies struck camp. The French were ready two hours before the

British, whose preparations for departure were characterised by all the usual confusion.

At last, at nine a.m., sixty thousand men were massed and ready to move off. At this time in the morning the sunshine semed a blessing, the air was balmy and sweet with the scent of flowers, warm grass and wild thyme, the sweeping plain melted, softly inviting, into the haze. Thin and pure above the armies' boom, a lark was heard to sing.

And then they surged forward in a wave a mile long of brilliant scarlet, green and blue, shining flashes of white, glittering gold and silver . . . the swing of capes, the gallant bobbing of cockades, the jingle of harness and the creak of leather. A gorgeous, mighty force riding out in the hope of a terrible glory.

CHAPTER ELEVEN

'When first you start to tease and flirt
Nobody tells you it's going to hurt,
Nobody warns you 'cause nobody cares
You'll get yours the way they got theirs'
                    —Stella Carlyle, 'Nobody Tells You'

Stella 1996

Stella was surrounded by flowers – a wash of colour all around her feet. Yellow, red, blue and white, so many she couldn't count or identify them, too many to gather up. Short-sightedly amid the dazzle and the din she stooped and picked one up, a fluffy yellow carnation. Having done so she wasn't sure what to do with it, this was a new sensation for her. She turned and looked at Derek who sat at the piano, facing the audience, his big hands on his knees, his face wreathed in smiles. She held out her hand to him and he stepped forward amid a fresh surge of noise, took her hand and lifted it to his lips. Mouthed: '*Brava*, baby!'

The curtain swished shut, and he put his arms round her in a swamping hug that almost lifted her off her feet. They were both furnace-hot, sweating as though they'd been in a fight or having wild sex.

'Yes!' Derek found another gear on the hug, clamping her against his big drum of a stomach. 'What a lady, what a night!'

He released her and executed a mini *haka* of his own devising, hips swaying, fists punching up and down like valves on a trumpet. Over his shoulder she could just make out the crew in the wings, their clapping hands like fluttering birds in the dark. From the other side of the curtain came the thunder of stamping feet and a shouted cascade of 'Encore!'

She peered at the wings stage left; she could identify Miles, their producer, by his first-night affectation of a white tux. He lifted his arms and made 'More, more' gestures. There was no let-up in the audience's enthusiasm.

She turned back to Derek. 'So what shall we do?'

'Make 'em laugh, make 'em cry – make 'em wait.' His face was one enormous grin. 'You're the boss.'

'All right. Only one, though.'

'Suits me, we've all got drinks to go to.'

'"Are You There"?'

He jerked his head in acknowledgement. 'That was where I came in.'

'Start and finish on my own.'

'You got it, darling.'

He went back to the piano, she nodded to the wings, the tabs opened and the applause rolled over them. She was still holding the carnation, and now she tucked it in the front of her dress between the little cloth-covered buttons, knowing they'd love it out there because at this moment she could do no wrong.

Make 'em wait . . .

She stood stock still, feet a little apart, hands at her sides, creating her own pocket of concentrated stillness that spread like water under a door until it reached the audience and they became silent.

Make 'em wait . . .

She allowed the silence to extend to where they could hardly bear it, and then let the first words drift, on a sigh, into the hush.

'Darling, you were *wonderful!*'

That was where the luvvies had got it from, thought Stella, they got it from their mothers. There was no approval so warm, so adoring, so steeped in unqualified admiration as that which you got from your mother.

'Well done, dear girl, magnificent show . . .'

She embraced both her parents, then George and Brian, the latter looking – perhaps intentionally – a little out of place in the green room in his blazer and regimental tie.

George said: 'I want you to introduce me to Derek Jackman, who is quite the sexiest thing I've seen in ages, present company excepted.' She slapped her husband's midriff. 'I like men about me who are fat.'

'That's not awfully kind,' said Brian without rancour. 'Go on, you painted Jezebel, go and get introduced.'

The moment they were out of earshot, George grabbed Stella by the arm. 'Quick, I need to know – are you sleeping with him?'

'Sorry?'

'Jackman. Are you and he . . . ?'

'Good grief, no!'

'Don't say it like that, he's adorable!'

'Adorable, and married.'

George pulled a face. 'I want it minuted that I forbore . . .'

Stella wished her sister would get the message that she no longer found this funny.

'Is she here?' asked George.

Stella shook her head. 'They're not as married as all that. Derek – excuse me – this is my extremely shortsighted sister George, who thinks you're adorable. Treat her nicely and you're on a promise.'

'Charmed, and I mean that very sincerely . . .'

She left them to it. Besides herself, her family and Derek, there were only about a dozen people drinking the management's competitively priced champagne, but even that was a dozen too many. She didn't want to see any of them. Not Miles, not the bright-eyed and youthful stage crew, the handful of theatrical friends and the clutch of couples. She wished them no ill, but she didn't want them here. The cheerful clamour of celebration echoed with the absence of the one person who wasn't here – who hadn't rung, or sent a card, or flowers, or even a message. Who hadn't fucking showed.

She went back to her parents who had been joined by Brian.

Her mother had sat down, and the two men, flanking her like punka-wallahs, presented an interesting contrast to one another. Brian, in spite of the blazer and the tie, wore his wavy hair slightly more than regulation length at the back, in the manner of more doggy Army officers, and was also managing to flash navy braces decorated with pigs and a glint of red sock 'twixt twill and brothel creeper. The *tout ensemble* simply screamed, in a well-brought up way: Wolf.

On the other hand, retirement had done nothing to make Andrew Carlyle more clothes conscious. For the first night of his daughter's show he wore a suit that looked new, but which he had as usual bought hastily and cheaply, so that the trousers were a shade too long with a hint of concertina at the ankle. He had also indulged his preference for double-breasted jackets, to produce an overall effect like one of the comic gangsters in an amateur production of *Kiss Me Kate*.

'We were just talking,' he announced, putting his arm about her shoulders, 'about the charms of reflected glory. All the adulation and none of the sweat.'

'And excuse the expression but you were sweating like a pig out there!' said Brian. 'It was frightfully sexy.'

'Ah—' Andrew raised a finger '—horses sweat, men perspire, but ladies merely glow.'

'Who said anything about ladies?' Brian gave his snarfing, lecherous laugh.

'Just a minute . . .' Mary got to her feet. 'I think it's high time I took some part in this conversation.'

'Mary dearest, please,' said Brian, 'you're surely not going to pull rank at this late stage in our association?'

'It's never too late.' She tapped her son-in-law's lapel with her finger before turning to Stella. 'But, darling, *such* hard work, and all that new material – how long is the run for?'

'A month. We're sold out for three weeks, and with a bit of luck this should do it.'

'Won't you be exhausted?'

'It's her job, for goodness' sake!' exclaimed Brian quite tetchily. It irritated him to hear showbusiness characterised as tough. 'It's meat and drink to her, the roar of the greasepaint.

I mean, I'm not saying it's *not* hard work, and I couldn't do it if anyone were mad enough to ask me, but I'm sure even Stella wouldn't put it up there with germ warfare, would you? You're simply making a bloody good job of entertaining a bunch of people who've come out with the express intention of enjoying themselves.'

'Precisely.' Stella had long since given up rising to this particular bait. 'Money for old rope really.'

Andrew looked around at the room, his brow furrowing. 'Have we been here before?'

'I don't *think* so,' said his wife thoughtfully. 'Or is this where we came to see that musical about Al Jolson?'

'No,' said Stella, 'that was the Palladium.'

'It looks familiar,' insisted Andrew. 'Maybe I came here on my own.'

Brian gave the laugh both barrels. 'Talk about a dark horse! How many other performers are you on backstage drinking terms with?'

'You just meant the place generally, didn't you?' said Mary. 'I can never distinguish one theatre from another once I'm inside.'

Andrew turned to Stella. 'Where are the girls, are they here?'

'Which girls?'

'The ones you do your show with.'

'No, darling, they're not here.' Mary handed her glass to Brian. 'Would you be a dear and find some orange juice to put in that?' She watched him go before adding: 'I don't suppose Stella invites them now she doesn't work with them any more.'

Andrew looked quizzical. His manner was as lively as ever, that was what hurt. 'You don't? You're on your own then?'

'No,' said Stella, 'Derek plays the piano.' She bit off the word 'remember.' 'He's over there.'

Andrew looked. 'Ah, yes, of course, got it. He's rather a find, isn't he? You can tell he's done it before.'

'So how do you feel about the rest of the evening?' asked Stella, addressing both of them, desperate to break the circle of misunderstanding. 'Do you think you'll come to the restaurant?'

'Try and stop me!' Her mother's brightness could have shattered glass. 'The feet may be weak but the spirit's ready for anything. This is our big night out, and anyway I'm absolutely ravenous.'

'We'll have to hang on here for at least another half an hour, but if you want to go on I'll give you the name of the place.' Go, she thought, go. Please go.

Mary had always been able to read her mind. 'Perhaps that would be best. Why don't we do that, Drew? Hop in a cab and go to the restaurant, then Stella won't feel she has to fuss over us instead of circulating.'

'Whatever suits. Come on then but be gentle with me.' Andrew placed his hands on Stella's shoulders and leaned in for a kiss. ''Bye-bye, old thing, come and see us again soon.'

Far from circulating she was still standing there when Brian returned with the orange juice. 'Where did they beetle off to?'

'They've gone on to keep the table warm.'

'Fair enough. Want this? I never touch the filthy stuff myself.'

'Hand it over, it's time I diluted.'

'The old man's enjoying himself,' observed Brian. 'All this has done him no end of good. He's a bit vague these days, but the life and soul this evening. He needs to get out more.'

Stella thought: life and soul? Maybe − but where did mind fit in?

In the Ladies at the restaurant, side by side at the mirror, George said, 'Sorry.'

'That's okay.'

'You know me, I lead a very sheltered life so I get pissed at parties. Derek's a nice man.'

'He is.'

'And I bet he has a nice wife.'

'I wouldn't know, we haven't met as yet.'

'I see.' George peered at her own reflection and sighed gustily. 'God in heaven, I can do no more! Anyway, you and he are a hot ticket. I was all aglow with pride out front today, we both were.'

'Thanks.'

There was a silence while Stella scrunched and tweaked at her hair, and George watched. She thought: Don't. Please don't ask, or sympathise, or show how well you understand me . . . or say anything at all. But she could feel the question coming like the flurry of air that heralds an approaching train in the underground.

'Still seeing Robert?'

'I have been from time to time. Okay.' She turned from the mirror. 'Shall we?'

George didn't move. 'How is it with him?'

'The same. Look, George, I know—'

'Still married?'

'As far as I know.'

'Come *on*.'

'Yes.'

'So it's been, what, seven years? Nearly a decade—'

'Six years actually.'

'Okay, but too long. Too long for a drop-dead wonderful person like you to be hanging about on the end of a phone waiting for a call from some clichéd married creep who wants to have his cake and shag it.'

'Cut it out, George.' Stella's head began to hurt. 'It isn't like that.'

'It's *always* like that.'

'Really?' She smiled sourly, and opened the door as another woman walked in. 'And I should know, hmm?'

On the way up the stairs George tried to apologise discreetly, in a deafening hiss. 'Stella, I'm sorry. *Again* already. But I care about you.'

'Good!' She walked back into the restaurant with a big smile. 'Let's hope we never meet when you don't give a shit.'

She got through dinner on auto-pilot. Made a short, self-deprecating speech. Said she hoped they'd all tell their friends.

Told them she and Derek were available for barmitzvahs, eighteenths and silver weddings. Said success wouldn't change her, she'd stay tight-fisted as ever. Asked if they liked the frock and said just as well because at that price she wouldn't be getting another. Thanked Derek, Miles, God and her parents. Did her Stella Carlyle number, in fact, then and for three solid hours thereafter. Drank twice as much as anyone else at the table and failed to get even half as drunk. Wanted only to put her head down amid the crumbs, the ashtrays and the wine stains and weep with rage and loneliness.

Towards the end George pushed over her programme, a menu and a biro.

'Beg pardon but I'm entitled to do naff things, I'm your sister. Sign those, there's a pet. One and a spare.'

'For the kids?'

Brian hee-hawed. 'Stuff that, we're the ones who need the social cachet.'

On the menu George had written in eyeliner: 'Are you in love with the bastard? Please advise, X for yes, XX for no.'

She signed it 'Stella Carlyle, with love' and the programme 'To two top people, George and Brian, with lots of love, Stella', adding no kisses to either of them.

'Spoilsport,' said George. 'I shall take that as a no.'

Stella had ordered a cab for her parents to take them to their hotel, and when the waiter came to tell them it had arrived she went out with them on to the pavement. Her mother kissed her and held her face for a moment, brushing her cheeks gently with her thumbs as if wiping away tears.

'It was a triumph, darling. Well done.'

'Thanks, I'm glad you enjoyed it.' She sounded stiff but couldn't help it. 'And thanks for the flowers.'

Mary laughed. 'Coals to Newcastle as it turned out!'

'They meant a lot to me, I shall take them home. 'Bye, Dad.'

''Bye, old thing, take care of yourself. Love to the girls.' Stella avoided her mother's eye as Andrew turned to the taxi driver. 'Paddington, and don't spare the horses.'

'The Royal Lancaster, Drew.' Mary smiled at her daughter. 'You can tell how seldom we stay in town.'

Andrew shrugged extravagantly, hands lifted, eyes to the heavens. 'Royal Lancaster then, woman, it's all the same to me.'

'That's right, you do what she says, mate, best policy in my experience.' The driver chuckled matily as they got in, but only Andrew joined in.

When all the others had gone Stella and Derek had a chaser courtesy of the management. Single malt for him, Jack Daniel's for her.

'Satisfied?' he asked. 'You should be.'

'We haven't seen the crits. And we've got the whole run ahead of us yet.'

'Bloody hell!' he said cheerfully. 'If ever I heard a glass–half-empty remark that's got to be it.' He sang, waggling his hands like a riverboat minstrel, '"Live, love, laugh and be happy!" Suit yourself.'

'I'm pleased, I'm pleased, okay?' She fiddled about, lighting a cigarette. 'Derek . . .'

'Spit it out.'

'Would a shag be out of the question?'

'O-oh, no! You don't get to use me as a stand-in. Or a lay-down.'

'You wouldn't be.'

'Give me some credit, girl,' he said gently, 'your fella didn't show.'

'No.'

He put his hand over hers, a huge hand that covered it completely. 'He couldn't make it, but he will another time. He's a doctor, right? They have funny lives, I've seen it on the telly.'

She shot him a wry, bitter look. 'Any moment now you'll be telling me to trust him.'

'It's none of my business, darling.'

'That's true. No –' she shook her head '—I didn't mean

306

that. As a matter of fact I appreciate your taking his side. It leaves me free to say what a stinking, cheating, worthless fucking lowlife he is.'

'Go, Carlyle!' said Derek. 'Ain't love a bitch?'

When she'd left the flat at five she had been winding up for the performance. She was so wired that she could scarcely remember what she'd been doing, only anticipate what was ahead. But returning in the small hours the evidence of her preparations was all there. The clean white sheets and the drawn blinds, the extra towel and the Crabtree & Evelyn soap, the Courtney Pine CD in place, the chilled fizz and the fresh jar of Marmite . . . The church candles, God help her, on the mantelpiece.

The candles were an invitation to do something she'd always wanted to do, and sweep her arm the length of the mantelpiece, carrying them with it. The action was satisfying, the result less so, because though the candles split into chunks they were held together by their wicks and she found herself drunkenly trying to reassemble them. You sad, sad cow, she thought, you can't even break something properly any more.

There was no message on the machine, no e-mail, no hand-delivered note. Just a big nothing and the broken candles standing like uneven towers of children's bricks on the floor. She hated him. Swore to herself that if she hadn't always been too proud to ask for his number, this was when she'd have rung him and blown his poxy life apart before getting the hell out. She even got as far as picking up the telephone directory, but he wasn't in her area, and she didn't even have his home address to offer to directory enquiries. Humiliated by her desperation and her ignorance, she hurled the directory across the room.

She went to bed but couldn't sleep. This was it, she told herself, enough. George had been right, it was always like this. She'd slept with enough married men to know that they were the most chickenshit people on earth, which was why she didn't care how she treated them. Derek was right too. About love, she supposed. Maybe. Every-fucking-body was right! *She* was right, for Christ's sake, she wasn't stupid, she knew the score, she'd been round the block so many times she could have done the trip with her eyes shut.

It wasn't even as if she had cleaved exclusively unto Robert Vitelio. Now that *would* be sad. She'd taken a nip from what was available now and again, here and there, to remind herself that she was a free agent and it could still be done. But the high, the sense of power that the casual encounters used to give her, simply wasn't there any more. She was heading towards forty, it was beginning to feel wrong, as though she were trying (and failing) to prove something. With the exception of this evening's lapse with Derek, which in any case she had known he would turn down, she had kept herself to herself for the best part of a year now. To herself, and him.

It was as if a great heavy cog wheel were grinding round inside her, heaving painfully into another gear. The resistance was powerful, but the wheel would get to where it needed to be eventually. And then she would have to accept that she was in love with this man, and decide what, if anything, was to be done about it. The lack of Xs on George's menu was a cop-out, but like a cheating alcoholic she wasn't yet ready to stand up and be counted.

There had been perhaps a dozen occasions over the past few years when they'd had a few days together – never more than a long weekend – and Stella had nervously discovered what it might be like to be a couple: begun to find out where they fitted and where they rubbed, not just in bed but in the real world of supermarkets, roadmaps, bathrooms, cinemas and domestic gadgets; which foods each of them couldn't stand, who could cook what, who bathed and who showered and at what time of day, who preferred tea and who coffee, which papers they read, how quickly and when, how their respective body clocks were set. How (she could no longer avoid the word) to compromise.

Most of these weekends were spent in Britain, a few in Italy and France, one or two at her flat. She never, on principle, asked him how he managed the time for them, what lies he'd told, what risks he ran. She knew that if she once started making his problems her own she'd have handed over her precious independence on a plate. It was difficult enough spending even that limited time on her own with him – she had never shared such large chunks of her life with any man, it increased a thousandfold her baffled and grudging respect for those who voluntarily took on marriage. They didn't get much sleep when they were together, and he was an habitual early riser unused to napping during the day. The unsocial hours of her work meant that she habitually slept late. Consequently there was often only a window of a few hours in the middle of the day when their moods and energy levels meshed. She lost count of the number of films whose ending she had to supply for him, and mornings when he shook her awake impatiently at eleven o'clock, unable to put the day off any longer.

Their relationship, she often felt, was like a fruit machine, nearly always arbitrarily mismatching their moods and behaviour patterns but just occasionally, when all the strawberries were in a row, showering them with an emotional jackpot. And those glimpses of what they were capable of kept them going through the long-drawn-out attrition of deceit and impatience and competitiveness and remorse. And passion – she must never forget the passion, through which they could always communicate when words and gestures failed.

There had been a twenty-four-hour escape in a northern city where Stella and Derek were on tour and Robert was attending a conference. Such a coincidence, providing them with an unlooked-for opportunity to be together without lies, was in itself rare enough, but for some reason (perhaps the lack of lies was itself the reason) they were at their best. They'd met on the Sunday morning and driven out into the high, austere countryside and walked for miles in a thumping rainwashed wind and fitful sunshine. The openness, the sense of being allowed to be together, made them relax. Each had spent the previous days in their own element and was now ready to unwind, to listen and make space for the other. They had lunch in a pub, and then retraced their steps to the car in the cool gathering dark of the afternoon.

Back in the city they'd checked into a hotel, made love and slept. In the early evening, looking for somewhere to have dinner, they'd found themselves near the cathedral close and gone in to stand at the back of choral evensong. Susceptible unbelievers that they both were, they were moved by the soaring music, the immutable grandeur of the building, the rolling cadences of the spoken words.

'Does it mean anything?' she'd asked as they walked out into the wet-black night.

'Does it have to?'

'It would be handy if it did.'

They were walking close together, strides matched but not touching, hands in pockets. He never held her hand or put his arm round her in public, it wasn't his style. Far from resenting this outward coolness she found it almost unbearably sexy. Before they emerged from the dim secrecy of the close into the prosaic brightness of the street, Robert stopped and looked up at the sky.

'That depends,' he said, 'whether you're godless or God-free.'

'What's the difference?'

'Same as children. Plenty of people don't have them, but some want them and some don't.'

'And which are you?'

'About God? Less, not free. I'm like you, I wouldn't half like there to be one. But that said—' he began walking again '—I'll need a hell of a lot of persuading.'

Apart from this one brief exchange Stella could not remember what they'd talked about that evening. That was because for once they were so in tune, so receptive to one another, that she could scarcely tell where he began and she ended. For a moment as they sat over the second bottle and the wavering candle, she caught herself thinking: This must be happiness, and was shaken by the impertinence of the thought. The night that followed was different from other nights, too – a dreamlike, timeless slipping in and out of love, a profound sensual mutuality. The next morning there was none of that sense of angry torn edges and unfinished business that so often accompanied their partings. They were calmer, more sure, than they had ever been.

Holding open the car door for her, he'd lifted her hand and pressed the palm over his mouth, not so much kissing it as breathing it in.

Eyes closed, he whispered: 'I'm scared to say anything.'

'Me too. So let's not.'

'We're such cowards.'

'I don't care if you don't.'

He'd returned her hand to her, placing it over her heart, and walked away.

For days she had lived in the afterglow of that weekend, its seamless harmony and deep delight.

But it was to prove the exception. Everything was against them, or so she told herself. She tried to manage him as she'd managed other men, by remaining separate and asking no questions, but then she had never had a relationship of this length. Sooner or later you had to know more about the other person than was available through sex and observation and shared activity. So in time she found out that he was a consultant ophthalmologist at a London teaching hospital, that he had been married for twenty years (at the time, that would be twenty-three now) and that his wife was a GP. They had no children, but he had represented this without regret as an incidental circumstance, not the result of a decision. He was the son of second-generation Scottish Italians who used to run a café and sandwich bar in Glasgow, but his mother had died some years ago and his father had sold the business and now lived in sheltered accommodation, 'wowing the old ladies' as Robert put it.

He had been christened Roberto, and had three elder brothers whose names were Guido, Seppi, and Ricardo. Only Seppi was still called that, the other two had opted like him for anglicisation – Guy and Richard. Seppi was the one most like their father, a tough, careful grafter: he and his wife had a grown-up married daughter and grandchildren, and ran a successful baby-clothes shop in Edinburgh. Richard – smooth, smart and opportunistic – had married the scion of a fabulously rich furniture designer from Milan and returned to Italy where he'd since taken over the business. Guy was a twice-divorced professional musician, gifted but shambolic, a clarinettist with the Northern Symphony Orchestra.

It was these brothers, more than anything, that brought home to Stella the anomalies of her position in Robert's life. It wasn't too much to say that he adored them, it was the one area of his life where he seemed more Italian than Scot. She envied them their tribal closeness, their easy, undeserving claim on his love, and bitterly resented the fact that as far as they were concerned she herself did not exist. She was a whole part of their beloved brother's life, and his nature, of which they were kept in ignorance. She was sure they admired his success, which would of course include his sound marriage to an estimable wife, but what of her, his passion, his addiction, the person he said he could not live without? The performer in her felt starved of the attention she deserved.

Seppi was the only one Robert saw with any regularity, and that not often. Richard was in flight from his background and rarely made contact. As for Guy, Robert seemed to find him droll, especially his disorganised emotional life, an attitude which under the circumstances she found patronising.

It was this that prompted her to say, in bed late one night: 'I don't see why he's such a big disaster.'

'I never said he was a disaster, he just can't cut the mustard, romantically speaking.'

'And what exactly constitutes cutting the mustard?'

Her head was on his shoulder and she felt him look down at her before replying: 'Forming a relationship. I know what you're going to say.'

'We're hardly in a position to criticise.'

'You mean that I'm not.'

'It takes two . . .'

'If you only knew,' he said thinly, pulling his arm from

under her and reaching for his cigarettes, 'how unconvincing you sound.'

'All right.' She sat up. 'All right. Your brother's been divorced twice, which you see as some sort of failure. And yet –' she looked at him '—you're here with me. How do you rationalise that?'

He blew smoke over his shoulder. 'You want me to get divorced?'

'That's not the point.'

'Ha!'

She hung on to her temper. 'It's not. But if everything was perfect you wouldn't be here. Guy at least recognised the imperfections and got out. Both times.'

'He ran away. Couldn't cope.'

'And you do, is that it? This is what you call coping, is it? Managing the marriage and the mistress, keeping all the plates spinning?'

He seemed to think about this, before saying flatly: 'I suppose it must be.'

Now she couldn't conceal her anger. 'Listen to yourself! You make it sound as though it all just happens to you, as if free will hadn't been invented.'

'I was having a stab at truthfulness,' he said. 'Obviously, I'm out of practice—'

'Don't be so bloody condescending.'

'—whereas you, I know, are never less than transparently honest, and have been living the life of a nun.'

It wasn't the words themselves that hurt, it was the intention to wound. 'Fuck off.'

'Very well. Your flat, your call.' He stubbed out his cigarette. 'But let me ask you something, Stella. If, tomorrow say, I were by some divine intervention to be suddenly free, no baggage, no guilt, no debts financial or emotional – what difference would it make to us?'

'If you have to ask, I'm not going to tell you.'

'Girlie answer.'

Nettled, she snapped: 'A big difference.'

'Ah,' he raised a finger, 'but would it? Would we spend

313

more time together? Live together? Have babies together?' Suddenly he put up a hand and caught her by the chin, twisting her head round hard to look at him. 'Will you marry me, Stella?'

To buy time she prised his fingers away. 'Don't do that!'

He gave a pinched, sarcastic smile. 'Exactly.'

He'd left then. The clock had showed two in the morning, he was good at these dog-hour departures, the car (a BMW these days) zooming away into dark, empty streets, every rising gear change telling her to put that in her sodding pipe and smoke it. She hadn't had time to make her cutting, perceptive points about the precise difference that his freedom would make: that it would enable them to look at each other properly for the first time, unshadowed by the drama of his infidelity; to assess what each had to gain, and to lose; to decide, in all probability, that they'd be poison for one another, and to get out before it was too late.

And tonight was the same. Yet again she'd been robbed of the opportunity to tell him how greatly she despised him, how pathetic he was, and how little she cared whether he lived or died.

Stella was on the edge of sleep – had just had that abrupt sensation of falling that went with the body's finally giving up and giving in – when Victoria Mansions' fire alarm went off. The red numbers on the clock said 3:37. She wasn't prepared to believe it, and rolled over, but in less than a minute there were voices outside, and some community-minded person banged on the door of the flat and shouted, 'Fire alarm! Everybody out!'

She could only remember it happening twice before and on both occasions it had only been a practice, tactfully signalled a week or two in advance. But there was no doubt now that there were people in the hallway, and the alarm blared on and on until finally she lurched out of bed, pulled on a coat and boots and obeyed the summons.

Out in the street the Mansions' residents numbered about forty, including at least half a dozen elderly people she'd never seen before in her life, two families with toddlers and a crying baby, and an Indian couple with three teenagers. The teenagers were fully dressed in outsize trousers, baggy parkas and big shoes, having clearly not been to bed at all. A police car was parked at the kerb with its blue light flashing.

The chairman of the Residents' Association was all urbane efficiency, moving among his flock in a Burberry and Wellingtons, disseminating information.

'Stella!' he said as though they had bumped into one another over the food counter at Harrods. 'We were starting to worry about you.'

'Glad to hear it,' she said. 'Where's the fire?'

'No, not a fire, a bomb scare.' He held up his hand to stem the anticipated wave of panic. 'The Asian lads noticed a flight bag in the back hallway which they said had been there since they went out. The boys in blue are investigating as we speak, but they assure me that nine out of ten of these things turn out to be false alarms.'

'When will we know?'

He shrugged, loving it. 'Lap of the gods. If they haven't sorted things out to their satisfaction in a quarter of an hour or so they'll find us some accommodation elsewhere for the night.'

'It's a quarter to four. There won't be any night left.'

'Perhaps not. Got a show on at the moment?'

'The run started last night.'

'Ooh, dear . . .' He was a mite reproving, this was an emergency after all. 'Still, can't be helped. Maybe tonight's the night for your understudy.'

He had no idea, she didn't even pretend to laugh. She was absolutely twitching with tiredness, she could have lain down on the pavement and slept. The last thing she wanted was to be spoken to, but there was evidence among her fellow residents of bonding in adversity, of the spirit of the Blitz coming into play, little stories about their quixotic rescuing of rings and bears and cookery books . . . the men saying you had to take this sort of thing seriously, the women joking about eyeliner and clean underpants. She perched on the edge of the grubby brick wall, aloof and grumpy. There were only two things she wished she'd brought with her and one was her car keys. The other (and here she had some sympathy with the story-tellers) was 'Only Sleeping'. It would be a crime if the handsome soldier and his horse were to be wiped out completely after all this time, their uplifting message of comfort blown to smithereens by the IRA.

The BMW slid between her and her thoughts. 'I know it's not an original line,' said Robert, leaning across to talk through the passenger window, 'but can I interest you in the fuck of a lifetime?'

Her line was scarcely original either. 'What are you doing here?'

'Cruising for women, stupid. Get in.'

'I can't just disappear, we're in the middle of a bomb scare.'

'What were you planning to do, give them your rendition of "We'll Meet Again"?'

'I don't know what's going to happen, I haven't got my keys – what am I saying? The whole place could blow up!'

'They haven't cordoned you off – look, will you get in or the rozzers will be after both of us.' He pushed the door open.

'Don't drive off.'

'I won't. I was planning to be invited up for coffee. Get. In.'

She climbed in. The warmth of the car, the softness of the seats, the smell of cigars and peppermint, the plaintive blandishments of Miles Davis, were like an embrace. It was hard to remember how much she hated him.

'I've got to say . . .' he barked with laughter, and continued to laugh as he pulled her head towards his '. . . you look like absolute hell.'

She fell asleep in the car. An hour later the chairman tapped on the window to say they were allowed back in. The flight bag had turned out to be full of what he called 'dirty mags', which seemed to indicate that it might have been a hoax. No one would have dreamed of pointing the finger at the teenagers who had reported it, but they all had their suspicions. The caretaker went round with his skeleton key opening people's doors for them.

Robert came in with Stella, and then it all came back to her. The broken candles, the telephone directory slewed against the wall . . . She faced him, still wrapped in her big coat, arms folded

'Look, I'm not sure I want you here.'

'I can't say I blame you.'

'So where were you?'

'Seppi called, his daughter's not well.'

'Your niece.' She didn't quite know what point she was making, something about pecking orders and priorities. She sounded sour and crabby, even to herself.

'Yes,' he said, 'Natalie. She'd be about your age, has to have a radical mastectomy.'

'I'm sorry,' she muttered ungraciously, on fire with humiliation. But also thinking, The bitch – the bitch to make me seem such a bitch.

'Anyway,' he went on, 'the prognosis is statistically pretty fair. But Seppi was understandably exercised about it, how everyone was going to cope while she was in hospital, all that sort of thing – a way of not focusing on the worst-case scenario. I couldn't get away.'

'I can see that.' Something occurred to her, an unworthy impulse to catch him out. 'So how did you manage to get over here at this ungodly hour?'

'Sian's away. Women's health conference ironically. And yes, I did initially forget about your opening night but when the penny dropped I would have tracked you down hours ago if Seppi hadn't called so late.'

'Forget it, it doesn't matter.' She couldn't stand much more of this torrent of rational explanation. 'You can stay if you want to.'

He glanced at his watch. 'I fear the hoaxers have put paid to that. You must sleep and I must work.'

'Don't you need to sleep too? What about the patients?'

'I'll catch twenty winks or so when I get there. My

competence will not be compromised and my interpersonal skills bottomed out years ago. As you know.'

He moved to kiss her but she could not unbend. She kept her arms folded and her lips closed. Refusing to accept her rebuff, he put his arms round her and said gently, into her hair: 'How did it go?'

'Fine.' Come on, Stella. 'No, it went well.'

'That's tremendous. I'm going to come and see it, very soon.' His hand slid up and down her back, his voice became ragged. 'When I said you looked like hell . . . I didn't mean it.'

'You did and you were right. I was entitled to look hellish, it was four in the morning in the middle of a bomb scare.'

She felt him pulse with suppressed laughter before he released her. 'True.' This time he succeeded in snatching a quick kiss on the lips. 'Gotcha.'

He peered at himself in the mirror, mumbled 'Christ' and scrubbed his hands furiously over his face and hair. Next to the mirror was the Victorian photograph, and he flicked it with his finger. 'It's a mystery to me why you like this thing.'

She shrugged. 'It's peaceful.'

'It's pseudo-religious, meretricious, sentimental crap, my angel,' he said. 'Listen, I'll call before the end of the week. Sleep tight.'

And on this characteristically acerbic note, Robert Vitelio left.

But not for the last time that morning, as she discovered when she struggled out of bed. There was a note from the porter among the post on her mat, indicating that a package had been left outside her door. It was a bundle of newspapers in a plastic carrier bag with the name of an off-licence chain. With the papers was a greetings card with a picture of a cuddly hedgehog in a straw hat and dungarees and the legend: 'You are my sunshine'. Inside, Robert had written: 'Sorry about the execrable tat, best your 24-hour shop could do. Thought you might like to see these – congratulations. Stella by name, stellar by nature. XRX'

The reviews ranged from good to ecstatic, with nothing whatever to raise the blood pressure, and rich pickings for the show's publicist. There were several morning messages on the machine, and she listened to them as she brunched on black coffee and a bacon sandwich.

The first was from Miles saying that the booking line had been red hot and there was every chance they should consider extending the run. The second was from George, overhung but jubilant: '. . . reckon I could flog those autographs for a tidy sum on the strength of your reviews, you old son of a gun. I am so, so sorry by the way if I put foot in mouth last night. By the time we got to the restaurant I was honestly too motherless to know what I was doing. Your affairs are none of my affair! Brian sends his best and a big sloppy kiss – you can imagine *how* sloppy after what he put away . . . Give us a buzz when you've got a moment. 'Byee.'

The third was Derek, characteristically chipper. 'Looks like we did it, doll, but it's no surprise to me. I'm off to Porchester Baths for a Turkish and a cold plunge before tonight, and who knows – I might get lucky. See you later.'

Last of all was her mother. 'I don't suppose you've seen the *Telegraph*, so I'm going to read you what it calls you . . . here we are . . . "Stella Carlyle", blah blah, "looks like a street urchin, sings like a siren", blah, this is the bit, "exudes an extraordinary sex appeal full of power and pathos. Carlyle—" I wish they wouldn't do that, but anyway "—is one of the few performers around today who can make you laugh and cry at almost the same moment". And so it goes on, isn't it wonderful? I expect you're having a lie-in but do call if you feel like it. Your father's not top-hole today, it's probably anti-climax, I'm sure he'd love to hear your voice.'

Not wanting to think about it for too long, she rang there and then.

'It's me.'

'Stella, darling, we are such proud parents. Look, your father's right here, I'll put him on . . .' She heard her mother say quietly but clearly, 'Drew, it's Stella — Stella for you. Remember we went to the show last night?' And then, to her again, 'Here he is.'

'Stella?'

'Hallo, Dad, how are you today?'

'Pretty good. How was the show?'

Her heart sank. 'It went very well.'

'And the girls?'

'They're fine.'

'We're frightfully dull and quiet down here, when are you coming to see us?'

'I might manage next Sunday, but I'll ring and let you know.'

He said, 'She's coming next Sunday,' and then: 'My brain's going more than somewhat, old thing, I mislay my marbles from time to time, you'll have to excuse me.'

'I hadn't noticed,' she lied.

'Come, come,' he said, 'I'd be astonished if you hadn't.'

'Everyone has lapses of memory.'

There was a short silence, and then he said: 'They do, don't they?' And then, 'Cheerio, keep the aspidistra flying.'

Mary came back on. 'So we'll see you on Sunday?'

'I might manage it, I don't know yet. Can I give you a ring?'

'Of course! Darling—'

'Yes?'

'Don't ever feel you have to, will you? We know you love us, you and George, you don't have to keep visiting us to prove it.'

When she'd put the phone down she sat head in hands, shamed by her mother's love, her generosity, her shining and impregnable loyalty.

Stella didn't make it on Sunday. For one thing she was exhausted, this show seemed to be taking more out of her than others; and for another – the real reason – she couldn't face her parents, when the gulf between their situation and hers seemed more than ever unbridgeable. On the other hand, Robert had not yet rung, and she wanted to be out if he did.

She called Jamie and asked if he'd like to go out to lunch. Since his eighteenth birthday and consequent striking from what she thought of as the godparental payroll, there had been a subtle recalibration of their relationship.

'Nice one!'

'My treat,' she said, from habit.

'We'll see about that.'

'If there's anyone you'd like to bring . . .'

'No, thanks, I'm resting between engagements.'

'Prince of Jaipur at one o'clock then.'

Having obtained a 2:1 in English and media studies at Manchester, Jamie had found employment as a junior producer on an early-morning breakfast show of breathtaking loudness and vulgarity, a job he hugely enjoyed. It had cachet, cred, a high totty factor and no dress code. From time to time he rang Stella to inform her of some item of his that was going to be on. These usually involved waking up unsuspecting minor celebrities and demanding to come in and inspect their bedrooms, or doing much the same thing to members of the public. Stella had warned him that if he ever pulled such a stunt with her their relationship would be terminated on the spot, but he had set her mind at rest by pointing out that from an OB point of view Victoria Mansions was about as user-friendly as Sing-Sing, so she was perfectly safe.

He was waiting for her in the Prince of Jaipur, at a table near the buffet, wearing jeans, a frayed striped rugby top and distressed trainers.

'Shall we get some in before we talk? I was largeing it last night.'

This came as no surprise. He was built on a titanic scale, but these days there was a distinct roll above the waistband of the jeans.

As they carried their starters back to the table, he asked, 'Is that all you're having?'

'I can go back, that's the idea.'

They ordered drinks – a pint of orange juice and Evian for him, a glass of white wine for her – and Jamie fell on his food with gusto.

'This was such a good idea, thanks for thinking of it – I'm so bloody idle, I never call you.'

'Don't worry, it was selfish, I needed cheering up.'

'But the show's a blast, I read a review. As a matter of fact I couldn't even get tickets for me and Jonno.'

'Before we leave tell me when you'd like to come and I'll make sure there are some on the door.'

'It wasn't a hint.'

'I don't care if it was. You don't have to hint, darling, just ask, it's what ageing godmothers are for.'

'Ageing, you?' Jamie gave her a cod-flirtatious look. 'Mind if I reload?'

While he was gone she sipped her wine. It was lovely to see him but the curry no longer seemed such a good idea. She pushed the greasy chunks of samosa around her plate, her stomach rebelling. When he returned, his plate piled with pilau rice and sauces red, brown and green, she decided to pre-empt further comment.

'I'm sorry, you're going to have to put up with me watching you eat. I'm just not hungry.'

'It's a free country.' He speared a samosa. 'I'll have it. So why are you depressed?'

'I'm not, really.'

'You said you needed cheering up.'

'Sunday blues.'

He made circular movements in the air with his fork while he finished a mouthful. 'How's the love life?'

She laughed, remembering that she used to ask him that. 'Quiet.'

'I don't believe you. Or have I got the wrong end of the stick – is quiet good?'

Suddenly, she wanted to unburden herself to Jamie. Unlike others in whom she might have confided – her mother, George, even Derek – she knew that in spite of his casual affection for her, the natural self-centredness of youth would ensure both his disinterest and his discretion.

'May I be frank?' she asked.

'Go on.'

She told him everything, without using names. He listened and ate. When he'd cleared his plate he scraped the contents of hers on to his own, and ate that. The only time he interrupted her was to order more drinks, a Tiger beer for him this time. She'd talked for half an hour when she ran out of steam.

'So there you have it. It's been salutary to do this, it makes me realise what a cliché the whole thing is.'

'Yes, but a cliché's a cliché because it's true.'

She smiled weakly. 'I suppose so.'

'And anyway, the situation may be a cliché, but you're you and he's who he is, so the chemistry's unique. What are you going to do?'

'What would you do?'

'*Oh*, no—' he held up his hands '—no, no! I'm staying well out of it. You don't need my advice.'

'I'm not asking you for it. I'm asking out of purely scientific interest what you would do in my situation.'

'Ideal world, or truth?'

She pulled a come-on face. 'What do you think?'

'In his place or yours?'

'Either.' She shrugged. 'Both.'

'Okay,' he said. 'Well, he's easy. If I was him I wouldn't have a clue where I stood with you, probably be shit-scared of you – no, you asked, this is my turn – so I'd be hanging in there waiting for something to come along and change the situation for me. I probably really like my wife even if we're not shagging, and feel I owe her something – especially if we're not shagging – so I'm not going to just walk out on her without a good reason. He's probably hoping to get caught so she'll throw him out, or that she'll start something with the neighbour so he can walk with a clear conscience.'

'Hang on.' Stella raised her hand. 'No good reason? I thought I'd spent the last however long telling you the reason.'

'But does *he* know – did you tell him?'

'What?'

'Shit!' Jamie blushed and banged his forehead with a fist. 'I dunno – that you're in love with him, something like that?'

'Not in so many . . .' She cleared her throat. 'Not in so many words.'

'Don't get me wrong, I'm not advocating it, I don't even know if it's true, all I'm saying is that in his shoes, hey, I'd need a pretty big incentive to blow everything out of the water.'

'Right. And what about in mine?'

'I give up.'

'No, come on, you promised, you're doing fine.'

'Yes, but that was the easy bit, blokes I can do.'

'Look on it as a challenge.'

'Fine. Then I'd probably let things go on as they are.'

'Would you?' She was crestfallen. 'Well, that sounds really, really exciting.'

'Don't be like that.' He looked aggrieved. 'The way you told me it *is* pretty exciting. Everyone gets to act out, and then go home. Who doesn't like a bit of drama? Especially you. Nothing wrong in that.'

Oh, well, she thought as she walked home, talk about 'Out of the mouths . . .' She'd asked for it and she'd got it. Not advice, but the unlovely and unpalatable truth.

Robert called her from the hospital early on Wednesday and said he could get away at midday, could he come and see her?

The first thing he said as she let him in, was: 'You're looking skinny, let's go out to lunch.'

'I'd much rather not. There's food here, and anyway I'm not hungry.'

'I am.' He put his arms round her amorously. 'But food doesn't feature.'

He made love to her with great tenderness but briefly, not holding back, as if he were simply breathing his passion into her. These days, after so long, it was often like this when they first got together – a blind, wordless, mutual imprinting.

He gasped, fell back, then buried his face in her breasts. 'God help me . . .'

She stroked his head, kissed his hair. 'Why should he? You don't pay him no never mind.'

His shoulders jerked with laughter. 'I'm told he likes a challenge.'

They lay quietly for some minutes, safe and sound. These were the almost-perfect moments, when they had made love, and effortlessly understood one another, and everything else was still out there, too far away to trouble them. If the essence of these times could be bottled, thought Stella, a spoonful a day would have seen them through. She put her arm about his head, cradling him. His breathing was deep and steady, but he wasn't asleep. His hand was moving over her diaphragm, her hips, her back. After a moment he tilted his head back to look at her.

'You know, you really are too thin.'

'I like to be near the knuckle.'

He grunted, ran his thumb over her collarbone. 'You're that all right . . . I suppose it's the show.'

'Probably.' Not comfortable with this subject, she asked: 'How is Natalie?'

He pulled himself up next to her, kissed her cheek. 'She's had the operation, and it was a success as far as it went. Now it's a case of keeping a close eye on things. And of course the poor girl has to learn to live with the prosthesis.'

'Of course.'

In the pause that followed he played with her hair. She sensed an announcement, and was not surprised when he said: 'We're going up to Glasgow to see them the week after next, I've got a couple of days off.'

'She'll appreciate that.'

'What, a visit from Uncle Bob?' He affected a strong Glaswegian twang. 'I don't know about that, it's more for our consciences than their wellbeing, but these things must be done. Only trouble is, you're so damn' popular I haven't been able to get a ticket between now and then.'

'Just turn up when you can. They can always find the odd one, and I'll give them your name.'

'Would you? Thanks, I'd hate to miss it.' He rested his chin on her shoulder. 'Did you say there was food about?'

They lunched on brown bread, ham, tomatoes, a wedge of cracked and crusty strong Cheddar, and red wine. The picnicky nature of the meal meant that her lack of appetite went largely unremarked. Afterwards, they went back to bed, and as usual it was different the second time: more protracted; more tense and aware, less relaxed; more to say and less time to say it. She thought she would surely come, and when she didn't, was desolate.

'Don't fret,' he said, teasing her mortification. As so often, he thought she hadn't seen him glance at his watch. 'You have nothing to prove.'

This was so like what her mother, and Jamie, had said to her, that she thought: The world is full of people who claim to know what I'm feeling better than I do myself. And the thought stopped her from saying, as she might otherwise have done, what those feelings were.

On the Saturday night there was a note for her at the stage door.

Dear Stella,

This is just to say that I shall be out there this evening and rooting for you every step of the way (not that you need it, according to the papers!). I am living and working very contentedly in Colchester now, at the above address. I mention this because I want you to know that I'm always there if I can be of service. It has been several years since I saw you, except in the spotlight, of course, and it would be so nice if some time or other we could meet up for a drink, and talk, but I shall leave the ball entirely in your court.

Yours ever,
Gordon

As she changed and made up she reflected quite fondly that Gordon was the one man who could sign himself 'Yours ever' and be taken literally. That in itself was a comfort, when comfort was scarce and she needed it. Jamie and his flatmate Jonno were in the audience tonight as well, there need be no feeling of exclusivity . . . On an impulse she summoned the ASM and sent her round to the front with an invitation to Gordon to join Derek, herself and the others (she was careful to list them) for a drink after the show.

It was the purest coincidence that she saw him. The small window of her dressing room overlooked the side alley between this theatre and the next, where the right-hand stalls fire exit opened out. At the interval she felt so hot and lightheaded that she opened the window and stood there for a moment, breathing in the bracing West End fumes and watching the people below. And there he was, smoking a cigar. He stood, typically, right in the middle of the alley, one hand in his pocket, as if about to address a meeting. Occasional couples, taking a shortcut, had to part company to avoid him.

She was just about to give him a shout when he dropped the cigar and screwed it out beneath his foot. His wife came up to him, she carried a programme – not the two-pound one, but the souvenir version, with pictures, oh, God, of the show in rehearsal . . . Stella stared, peered, tried to read their body language as they stood there, their lips as they exchanged a few words, but it was like trying to read Hebrew – upside down, back to front, unrecognisable, a closed book. How could she ever understand them with all those years of marriage to their name? They might be out there, she in here, but it was she who was the outsider.

He glanced at his watch – that, at least, was a familiar gesture – and they walked back into the theatre.

Stella's head swam as she sat down; her hands were white

and cold, like dead hands. There was a sour taste in her mouth, she only just made the lavatory in time.

'You played a blinder tonight,' said Derek. 'I thought you'd done all you could with most of those songs. Goes to show how wrong you can be. There were tears in my eyes once or twice. Put it there, doll . . . Blimey, but that's a frigid digit!'

Later Stella was at her most glittering, out of her skull on drink, applause and misery. She took them all out to dinner – Derek, Jamie, Jonno and Gordon – to one of those big, grand old restaurants where it was still possible to make an entrance. She who never pulled rank asked for a table in the middle and got it. Waiters hovered, candles glowed, champagne popped, heads turned. Isn't that . . . ? Have you seen . . . they say it's terrrific. She likes to surround herself with men, doesn't she? Do you think those young ones are her nephews, hmm? Never thought I'd say this but that is *too* thin . . .

She knew she was astonishing, could see it written in their faces. Derek's pleased, proud, a little baffled; Jamie's absolutely chuffed to death, a quite unlooked-for triumph notched up; Jonno, if-my-friends-could-see-me-now; Gordon – dear Gordon – quite simply the happiest man in the room. She spoiled them, flirted with them, flattered, indulged and amused them.

She dazzled, for tomorrow she died.

Outside on the pavement she accepted their thanks and kisses, but linked her arm through Gordon's.

'Let me get you a taxi,' he said. 'I can drop you off and go on to Liverpool Street.'

She sat with her feet up on the seat, her head on his shoulder. It was all draining away now, and she was cold. Cold, and tired, and sick. When they got to Victoria Mansions he roused her gently.

'We're here.' He kept his arm round her waist as he said to the driver: 'I'll just see the lady to her door, if you wouldn't mind hanging on.'

He supported her in the lift, and out of it, and found her key for her. In the open doorway she put her arms round his neck.

'Gordon . . . don't go.'

'But, um, I think you need to get to sleep.'

'I will if you stay.'

'I've told the taxi to wait.'

'Then tell him to go away.'

'Stella, I . . . Do you think this is wise?'

'Don't be pompous, Gordon.' She kissed him on the mouth. 'Get down there and pay the man.'

She tottered away from him, her shoulders shaking. Gordon, always humble, thought she must be laughing at him, but he was entirely wrong.

CHAPTER TWELVE

'On a small, crowded island where forty-five million people live, each man learns to guard his privacy carefully – and is careful not to invade another man's privacy'

—'Over There',
Instructions for American Servicemen in Britain

Spencer 1944

Spencer was Janet Ransom's lover for six months, but he never felt he knew her. The reserve she displayed in everyday life transmuted into a deep secrecy in the bedroom. There was no lack of physical passion, but it was as though she was speaking in a different language, or that she was feeling him blindfold, interpreting his touch through her own, in ways he could never know or understand. This was as exciting as it was saddening. The desire to break through the invisible barrier, to hear her call his name, or even open her eyes and look at him, drove him wild. Then, when once again these things didn't happen, no matter how great it had been, he was cast down.

Nor was there any way of saying how he felt about this, or asking her what she thought, because the rest of their relationship continued to all intents and purposes exactly as before. The presence of Davey and Ellen, and less often that of Rosemary, placed constraints on it, but even without these there was little change. He went to the cottage on Sundays, and on one evening during the week if possible. On Sundays there would be afternoon tea; on a weekday something also called tea, and with the teapot in attendance, but served later and consisting of something more substantial. In return Spencer took goodies from the base, and did odd jobs. If they were on their own and likely to be undisturbed, they went up to bed. The signal for this was always the same. She would hold out her hand and say: 'It's all right,' as if comforting a child. And, childlike, he went along. He learned that she never took any risks, was always to be trusted.

Davey was in the room next door, and the baby's cot was in the same room, behind a folding screen: to begin with he was like a cat on hot bricks in case they woke up. But Janet assured him that the kids could sleep through anything – fighters, bombing raids, it would take more than doing this to disturb them – and eventually he got used to the idea.

When it was over she would kiss his cheek and say softly, 'Thank you.' The thanks made him feel uncomfortable, as though this was just one more job that he did around the place. Then after a very few minutes she'd get up and dressed and go downstairs. She never came back up, or called him, and after a while he'd go down as well and there she'd be in the parlour with a tray of tea, and the bourbon if there was some, with a glass for him.

One evening he caught her hand as she was about to get out of bed and said: 'Honey – don't thank me.'

'Why not?'

'You don't need to. It's the two of us here. I'm happy, you're happy—' He rocked his head on the pillow.

She looked down at him, her hand lying quietly in his. 'I know that.'

'So no more thank yous, huh? For me.'

She'd smiled as if to say yes, but it had made not a blind bit of difference. The thanks were as natural to her as breathing. It made him wonder even more what went on in her head when they were doing it, so quietly and fervently.

Another time they took Ellen out round the village in her 'pushchair'. This was another activity he'd learned not to be self-conscious about, even though he was sure there were a few looks. Janet said it would be all right, so it was. And it did seem like whatever they might say about him, she had some kind of aura around her that other people noticed, and a natural dignity that they respected.

It was the end of October and they'd walked quite briskly down the high street, and then down the hill to where the little old river trickled along, known as Norton Water. They called it a river, but it wasn't much more than a ditch, it made Moose Creek look like the Mississippi. Along here it was more sheltered and they slowed down. Ellen had fallen asleep, her shiny red cheeks bulging out of her blue knitted pixie hood. Spencer plucked up the courage to ask about Edward Ransom.

'Tell me something about your husband.'

'What do you want to know?'

Everything, he thought. How you met, what he was like, whether you loved him – why you got me into bed the moment you knew he'd died . . .

'I don't know,' he said. 'Whatever you want to tell me.'

'Let's see.' The way she said that pretty much told him that she wasn't going to spill any beans worth having. 'He was very handsome – you've seen the photograph of our wedding.'

'A good-looking guy. You made a great couple.'

She smiled her close-lipped smile. 'He was a garage mechanic, here, in Deller's garage. A whizz with an oily rag, like you.'

'So where did you and he meet?'

'We'd known each other for years. Not well, but to say hallo to.'

'And then, what happened? Your eyes met, your hands touched – what?'

'Nothing like that. He asked me out.'

'You started dating – where'd you go?'

'The first time we went to see *The Thirty-nine Steps*, with Robert Donat.'

Spencer shook his head. 'Can't say I've heard of it. You remember anything of it?'

'Every word, almost, it was wonderful.'

'So you went to the movies – to the pictures – and what else? Dancing? Sports?'

'He was a good dancer.'

They were coming up by the church now, there was only another half a mile till they were back, he'd better cut to the chase.

'And the two of you fell in love?'

'That's were we got married,' she said, nodding at the church. 'And Rosie was bridesmaid.'

'That's her in the picture?'

'I made that dress for her. Except for the smocking, Mother did that.'

'She looked cute.'

Janet shook her head indulgently. 'She was terribly naughty on the day, up to all sorts. She ran us all ragged!'

Spencer returned to the subject. 'Janet – you don't mind me being around?'

'No.'

He'd been fishing, hoping for self-excuse, a declaration, an explanation, something, but they were not forthcoming.

Back at the base his liaison with Janet was not treated with the respect accorded it by the locals. Everyone seemed to know when it became more than strictly social and they were on to him.

'Hey, Spence, how's the merry widow?'

'Babysitting again, huh?'

'How many shelves you fix last night, Spence?'

He tried to take it in good part. Most of the guys were sowing a few English oats, it was even rumoured that the Colonel was romancing the daughter of an aristocratic family and might wind up being a lord of the manor if he got through the war and played his cards right. Frank put his finger on what intrigued them all about Spencer and Janet.

'She's quite a bit older than you. She has all those children. You do jobs around the house. Spence – you're not exactly painting the town red with this lady.'

'No.'

'So are you in love with her?'

333

This was something Spencer had asked himself. 'I don't know.'

Frank supplied the answer in his dry way. 'You're not in love with her. So what goes on? No, don't tell me, stupid question, I know what goes on. But be careful, Spence, a woman like that might want a whole lot more than you want to part with.'

Though Spencer had the greatest respect for Frank's opinion, he didn't believe Janet was after anything more. The slight distance that existed between them even in their most intimate moments convinced him of this. And as to why he kept on coming back, there were two reasons, and only one of them had to do with Janet.

Rosemary was around less often, she was lodging with a friend's family in town near her work. When she did come by, she'd changed. She was a working girl now with cash in her pocket and a bit of independence. Singing in the choir was a thing of the past, though she said she did the odd number with the Debonnaires, a band made up of workers at the stocking factory. Her attitude to Spencer had altered as well, it had lost its flirtatious edge. She treated him casually, like part of the furniture, but gave nothing away. He sensed, though she had never said anything, that she knew about him and her sister. Sometimes she went to dances and shows at the base, but she had no regular boyfriend and that didn't seem to bother her. Spencer reckoned most guys were scared of her. There could be no other explanation because she looked sensational, like a young Katharine Hepburn. The sassy natural wit had been brought under control. She had perfected an expression which said she could cream you with a word, but would let you off this time.

Only once the carapace of new sophistication cracked. They went for a cycle ride with Davey, and she and the boy began fooling around, taking their feet off the pedals and sticking their legs out, yelling things like 'Scramble!' and 'Gerry at four o'clock!' On the way back as it got dark they dismounted, panting, to push their bikes up the gentle hill into the village. Davey recovered first and went on ahead. That was when she asked: 'Are you having a thing with Janet?'

334

The question was so simple, direct and unexpected that he answered simply, too: 'Yes,' and then qualified it: 'Sort of.'

'What's a "sort of" thing when it's at home?' It was typical of her not to comment on what he'd said, but to pick him up on his choice of words. He was suddenly keenly aware of how carefully he must select the next ones.

'I mean, I think a whole lot of her, I try to make her happy, but it's not so long since she lost her husband.'

'Oh!' Rosemary gave a small disparaging laugh. 'Him.'

'It's pretty obvious they loved each other.'

She was silent for a moment, breathing steadily as she pushed. 'But now that he's gone she makes do with you.'

'If you want to put it that way.'

'Spencer—' She stopped. 'What do you see in her?'

Shocked and discomfited, he laughed. 'What kind of question is that?'

For a moment she just looked at him. It was getting darker by the second, all he could see now was the outline of her curly hair, the gleam of her eyes, a glint of mouth with smoking breath, like a small cute dragon, sizing him up.

Then she said, 'You're right, a stupid one.' And climbed back on her bike.

If he lived to be a hundred, Spencer thought, he would never understand her. But the less he understood, the more he fell under her spell.

October '44, everything went quiet. There was a combat drought while the Luftwaffe lay low, licking its wounds. It was eerie as they flew mission after mission almost untroubled by EAs, sometimes strafing isolated, half-empty airfields unopposed, just for the hell of it. The presumption was that heavy losses over the previous couple of months had sent the Luftwaffe away to regroup, re-equip and retrain.

The skies lowered, the nights drew in. Still there was nothing doing. On Thanksgiving the brass-hats laid on the usual celebrations – turkey with all the trimmings, pumpkin pie, plenty of booze – it was an overpoweringly sentimental time when the Americans pined for home. To make them feel better the enemy returned to the fray with a vengeance, swarming into the skies above the northern European coast in their hundreds, new planes flown by boy pilots with a minimum of training and a near-suicidal desire to shoot the crap out of the Yankees. Spencer's flight was involved in three missions escorting B-17s on strategic bombing missions against synthetic oil refineries in central Germany. On each occasion they were set upon by hundreds of FWs and MEs as if by killer bees. There was a kind of desperation in these attacks, no guile or tutored skill, just an all-out feeding frenzy. It made a nonsense of their training in cool decision-making; these encounters were about gut reaction, dog eat dog, the survival of the maddest. The Mustangs were fighting for their lives, and there was a heavy reckoning.

In the epicentre of one of these, with the fire criss-crossing the sky like a spider's web of shooting lights, Spencer saw Errol Lovic of Blue Flight exploded from his cockpit. He knew it was Lovic because of *Good Time Girl* on the fuselage, winking lasciviously over her Manhattan. It had been a moment only, less than a moment, but he could remember the detail. The endless instant when Lovic seemed to hang in the air amongst the debris, turning slowly, his arms and legs waving like an infant in the womb, and then suddenly plunged like a stone down a well, with *Good Time Girl* living up to her name, hurtling on without him, shedding pieces like confetti as she described her own long, leaning arc to destruction. In his dreams for a while after that he swooped and spun at terrifying speed amid blades of broken metal and long daggers of glass, the smell of burning fuel in his nostrils until he'd awake with a shocking, silent impact, his body rigid, eyes staring into the darkness, thinking for one fearful moment that he was already dead.

Winter deepened, and with it came some of the worst weather that even the oldest of the locals could remember. Flying conditions were atrocious, with snow, freezing fog, and dark, sleety storms that howled across the airfield, closing them down. It was the dark that most affected Spencer. Church Norton might not be half as cold as Moose Draw, Wyoming, but it was twice as bleak. He missed the hard, bright glitter of winters at home, the shining expanses of wind-whipped snow, the distant edges of the frozen mountain peaks like flint axeheads against a sky thin and pure as blue glass. In England, whole weeks went by when the sun seemed never to break through at all.

Any trouble with the heating, and the cockpit of *Crazy Horse* became bitterly cold. He got a cold that was so heavy he had to plug his nose when he was flying, and it developed into an ear infection which gave him some pain and discharge and made him partially deaf. With numbers down there was no chance of any but the seriously sick being rested, so they knew to shout at him over the pilots' frequency. But the deafness still gave a kind of unreality to events beyond *Crazy Horse*. It affected his spatial awareness and his judgement of speed – the deadening of sound meant that an enemy fighter could be a dot one second, a hurtling behemoth the next. And like thunder and lightning there seemed to be a minute, dislocating interval between sound and vision, so that the heavy, reaching boom of a hit pressed painfully on his eardrums just after the splintering sunburst of explosive light had dazzled him. In a dive, the pressure in his ears was such agony that they bled and he almost blacked out. The juddering airframe and flapping wings of the stressed plane were like extensions of his own body, about to fall to pieces. Every sortie felt like a series of near-misses, so that he returned shaking and bathed in sweat, his nerves shot.

But the top brass weren't stupid. When in early December he asked for a thirty-six-hour pass he got it. He secured the use of an old black Austin – it was hired out by a guy on the base on a cheap rate, user's-risk basis – and intended to drive down to Kinnerton, near Oxford to look up his mother's family place. He'd asked Janet if she wanted to go with him but was glad in a way when she said no. He wanted to take things at his own speed in his own way, to get an angle that was entirely his own.

'You want to go to the local church,' she said, 'they're bound to have all sorts of records there. And the town hall, and the local paper.'

He was holding Ellen on his knee, helping her put a coat on a doll. 'You know a lot about this kind of thing.'

'No, no,' she'd said, blushing almost as if he'd caught her

337

out at something, 'I don't. But you pick these things up.'

'Anyhow, what I want to do most of all is find the house, number fourteen Waverley Road, if it's still there.'

'I'll keep my fingers crossed,' she said.

The journey from Church Norton to Oxford that Saturday took four hours. Spencer almost wished he hadn't declined all other offers of company – Frank had offered to come along, and pool gas coupons, but he'd held out. He didn't want to have to accommodate anyone else. But the old car was touchy, with a sharp clutch and a tendency to stall in a low gear. Also, the day was bitterly cold with a whining wind off the tundra, it felt like, full of small gritty flakes like ground glass, too minute to settle but enough to form a rime on the windscreen, and penetrate the ill-fitting doors. By the time he reached Oxford his hands and feet were frozen, and he was damn' near hallucinating about one of the Diamond Diner's hamburgers, the soft fragrant bun and the sizzling hot meat, inches thick with everything on it, oozing fried onions, ketchup, mayo, prime beef, gherkins . . .

The pallid corned beef sandwich he actually had was no substitute but he smothered it in mustard, and the pint with it was good. He was getting to like the blood-temperature English ale with its colour like stewed tea and its hoppy, nourishing flavour, more like soup than beer.

He went into a newsagent's, not to buy anything but to sound out the storekeeper who he guessed, from his own experience of the Mercantile, would be a mine of local information. The man was more than helpful, and gave him detailed instructions which he wrote down.

In a spirit of camaraderie, Spencer said: 'My mother's family used to come from there.'

'That right?' asked the man. 'My wife too. Whereabouts, do you know?'

'Waverley Road.'

'Yes, yes, Waverley Road,' said the man, as though the name conjured up a host of happy memories for him. 'It used to be nice along there.'

It wasn't nice now, Spencer discovered. Kinnerton was no longer the pleasant treelined suburb of his mother's memory because that part of town had become a great sprawl of factories – aircraft parts, car tyres, service boots, tinned foods – a big ugly snapshot of wartime life in Britain.

Because it formed the western perimeter of a two-mile-square complex of similar roads, Waverley must many years ago, as his mother had described, been the nicest of them. Now it was the least attractive, because what had once been the meadow that its gardens backed on to was a works sports ground, studded with desolate tattered football nets and a single rickety stand, with a storage depot at one end and the brutish blind brick walls and narrow chimneys of the factory beyond. At the southern end of the road, where Caroline had described picking bluebells with her friend in a wood, there was at least a small gritty park, grandiosely named Victory Gardens. Spencer left the car by the park gates, and began his pilgrimage by taking a turn round its cinder paths. On this bitter afternoon he was the only one there except for a uniformed park keeper raking leaves and twigs.

Spencer was looking for clues, something that would link this cheerless space with his mother's childhood memories. There were few features: an expanse of tussocky grass broken by round, banked-up flowerbeds which looked at this time of year like giant molehills; a pond full of circling goldfish; a wooden shelter with seats, of the kind found on station platforms; a kind of arch over the path, pointed at the top like a church window; and a monkey puzzle tree.

There being no chance of bluebells in December he crossed the grass to the edge of the park and studied the trees. Apart from the distorted black limbs of the monkey puzzle it was possible that some of these were original inhabitants, granted a stay of execution to provide shade and shelter for the users of the park. He'd identified oak, ash and larch when he heard a shout and turned to see the park keeper prodding the rake in his direction.

'Oy!'

'Excuse me?'

Now the rake prodded a small sign at the edge of the grass. 'Can't you read?'

'I'm sorry, sir, I didn't see that.'

'It says, "Keep Off the Grass".'

'Okay.'

He returned to the path, the park keeper watching him every step of the way as if he might at any moment break into a wild run, kicking up divots and scattering flowerbeds. It seemed a further flouting of the past that this paltry patch of green should be so meanly proscribed, but he was in uniform, and if he'd been in the wrong he'd better be civil.

'My apologies, must have missed it.'

The park keeper made a sound that indicated they all said that, but close up Spencer could see that he was elderly and frail-looking, with tears of cold running from the outer corners of his eyes.

'Do you know much about this park?' Spencer asked. 'I mean, how long it's been here?'

'Just after the first war.' The man jerked his head. 'Date's on the gate.'

'Something else I missed.' Spencer smiled but got no response. 'The reason I ask is that my mother was raised down this road – she can remember picking bluebells in a wood here.'

'That's right.' The park keeper's expression did not change but his voice unbent a little. 'Barton Wood.'

'It must have been pretty here in the spring.'

'Park looks nice, too, right time of year.'

'I bet it does.'

The old man linked his hands, in fingerless mittens, on the handle of his rake. 'Where's your mother now?'

'In America.'

'Married a Yank?'

There was no point in details. 'Yes.'

'Good job you're over here.' Whether this was a comment on Spencer's personal errand or the American war effort was hard to say.

'What's the arch made of?' he asked. 'Is that some kind of timber?'

'Go and take a look,' replied the park keeper with a hint of pride. 'There's a plaque tells you all about it.'

Conscious of being watched, Spencer walked round the path. The arch might have been twenty feet high at its tallest point, and was planted in the grass at a distance of some three feet to either side of the cinders. On the inside of the left upright was an engraved metal plaque.

'The jawbone of a large blue whale, caught in the southern ocean by Thomas Adolphus Peake, 21 April 1900, and kindly donated to these gardens by his widow Lucilla on her husband's death, 7 June 1928. "O hear us when we cry to thee, For those in peril on the sea".'

'Incredible . . .' Spencer walked around the arch, awed by the thought of a creature big enough to have a jaw this size. He looked across at the park keeper. 'It's incredible!'

'Big enough for you?' replied the old man. 'Got anything like that in America?'

'No, sir!'

Number fourteen was exactly like every other three-storey, semi-detached house in the street – narrow red brick, with a bit of garden at the front, a bay window on the ground floor and the number in black lead on the fanlight over the door. Except that it also had a name, 'Charlmont', and a sign propped in the window between the net curtain and the glass, with the word 'VACANCIES'.

So it was a rooming house these days. He stood on the pavement staring, absorbing this fact. As he did so the door opened and an elderly woman appeared.

'Can I help?'

'No, thank you, ma'am. I was just looking. My mother lived in this house a long time ago.'

'Really? Would you like to come in and have a look?'

It was cold and the woman, unlike the park keeper, was friendly and welcoming.

'If you're sure it's no trouble?'

'No trouble at all.'

She ushered him into a dark, high-ceilinged hall, and told him to put his coat, cap and scarf on a chair. There was a long mirror next to the chair. Its glass was slightly flawed, so that as he checked his reflection he seemed to waver and distort like a ghost.

She introduced herself as Mrs Brock, and when he returned the compliment, asked: 'Where are you from, Lieutenant? I mean, where are you stationed?' When he told her, she commented: 'That's a chilly part of the world, you must miss the sunshine.'

He decided against telling her about the annual five months of snow in Moose Draw, the way every little hair on your body froze when you went outdoors, including the ones in your nose so you could hardly breathe.

'It's kind of bleak,' he agreed. 'But airfields are pretty bleak places, whichever way you look at it.'

'My son's in the Merchant Navy,' she said with a note of pride in her voice. 'Those boys are out in all weathers.'

Spencer detected the usual very slight inter-service edge, sharpened by his being a Yank. 'They do a great job.'

'Well.' She took off her apron. 'Shall I give you the guided tour? The house won't have changed since your mother was here.'

The rooms were comfortable and homely, furnished with inexpensive, well-cared for things, and full of ornaments. Each wall had a picture or a mirror as a centrepiece, and the windows at the front of the house were all covered by immaculately laundered nets. The kitchen had a grey metal range and there was a comforting smell of gravy, and hot cloth.

'I do tea at five-thirty,' she said, partly explaining the smell and partly he suspected from the long ingrained habit of showing lodgers round.

'How many guests do you have?' he asked politely as she led the way up the stairs.

'Two at present. We can take three, so there's a spare at the moment.'

'I suppose there's no shortage of takers in a university town?'

'No, but we have mainly business people, single people, you know. I'll show you Mr Hebditch's room, it's the nicest. He's neat as a pin, he won't mind.'

Spencer felt slightly embarrassed at having this stranger's home displayed to him, but the room's spartan bareness gave nothing away. Only a hairbrush on the chest of drawers, a whiskery brown robe on the back of the door and the twin heels of plaid slippers protruding from under the bedside table betrayed Mr Hebditch's occupancy. A faded rose-red eiderdown provided the sole splash of colour. The window overlooked the back garden with its obligatory rows of winter 'veg' (rather more flourishing, Spencer noticed, than Janet's) and beyond that the sports field, where a group of men were now kicking a ball around.

'Yes,' said Mrs Brock as though he'd asked something, 'this used to be our son's room, and the other two on this floor are to let as well. I'll show you the vacancy.'

He gazed politely round another, smaller room, even more monastic than the last. He seemed to be seeing a house from which every trace of individuality and atmosphere had been assiduously drained. He mumbled something about her running a nice place.

'We do our best, and it's a few more pennies.'

'What does your husband do?'

'He's in public works at the Town Hall.' This was an answer which might have been in a foreign language for all the sense it made to Spencer, and she must have noticed, because she added: 'Drains and sewage and highways, and all those things that make the world go round. And he's the local ARP warden as well.'

'Sounds like the town would fall apart without him,' said Spencer and was rewarded with a laugh. She was a nice woman, slightly on her mettle.

'I shouldn't be surprised! This is the ablutions . . .' She opened a door on a surprisingly large black and white bathroom with an anaconda-like convolution of pipes just beneath the ceiling, a gas geyser, and a cork bathmat propped against the bath. 'This isn't quite what your mother would remember, and we've made the toilet separate as well.'

'Great.' He thought, This is a waste of time for both of us, none of this means anything to me. And felt a little claustrophobic. Mrs Brock clearly wished to fill her vacancy.

'We're up on the top floor these days, I'll show you, it's even less changed now I come to think of it.'

'Thanks, I'd like that. Then I should be hitting the road . . .'

'You're never going back tonight?'

'That's the general idea. It's not my car for one thing, and there are some friends I'd kind of like to see.' It sounded lame, but he wanted to get away.

'Good heavens,' she declared, 'you shouldn't do that, it's miles. You could spend the night here.' She started up the stairs ahead of him. This flight was steeper than the previous one and she made heavy weather of it, trudging, leading with the right foot each time and catching up with the left, one hand on her thigh. She couldn't be much older than his own mother, but had crossed the invisible line into stiff, sexless old age – then again, it was two years since he'd seen Caroline. Strange to think that while he was in the place where his mother had lived as a child, back in Moose Draw she might by now have become an old lady too.

The moment they reached the second floor, he was aware of a difference. The ceilings up here were low, and sloped away to the left, and the wood floor was not dark-stained. Probably because this was the one part of the house that the Brocks had to themselves, it had a less scrubbed-up air. The rugs on the floor were threadbare, their fringing wispy, and the parchment shade on the overhead bulb had a crack in it so that when Mrs Brock switched it on it shed an uneven light as if there were an invisible window some-where.

The Brocks' bedroom was the same shape as the landing, with two small windows, one overlooking the sports ground, the other – a low dormer window – facing south along the line of the terrace. There was a frilly nightdress cover on the pillow of the double bed, books on the bedside tables – a wireless on one of them – a dressing table with a surprising number of bottles and jars and a triptych mirror which showed the two of them as

344

they entered, flanked by queasily transposed and foreshortened views of the room.

'This was probably the maid's room when your mother was here,' said Mrs Brock, going over to the larger window, tweaking and smoothing the curtains in an absent-minded, houseproud way. 'Even ordinary houses like this had a maid before the last war.'

'She never mentioned it,' said Spencer. And then realised that, of course, she had. 'Actually,' he said, 'she used to come up here sometimes, I think it wasn't allowed.'

'Ooh, no, mixing with the servants? That would never have done!' Mrs Brock's tone implied that she was of a much more democratic turn of mind.

'I think they were good friends. She said the – the other girl used to talk about her home in the country.'

'So you'll have to go and see that as well.'

He smiled wryly. 'Next trip maybe.'

She went to the smaller window. 'There's still a bit of a view from here.' She stood aside for him to look.

Surprisingly, Mrs Brock was right. Number fourteen was sufficiently higher than its neighbour that you could see across the rooftops to the park. Only you couldn't see the park itself, just the tops of the trees like black wrought iron against the reddening afternoon sky, and beyond them a glint of flat silver water. In that instant, Spencer felt that he was looking into the past, was inside the head of that little girl who became his mother and her friend Cissy, the maid, the homesick country girl, who gazed out with her over the rooftops, the woods and the water . . . not so very wide, but still an unbridgeable space between this drab world and another.

He turned to Mrs Brock. 'What's the water that we can see from here?'

'Water?' She leaned her head alongside his, peering. 'I don't believe there is any now.'

'Surely . . .' He turned back, ready to make his point, but she was right. There was no water, only a glimpse of road shining in the setting sun. 'Son of a gun . . . my mistake.'

'Funny you should say that, though,' said Mrs Brock. 'Because I believe there used to be a big natural dewpond there, in the wood, when it was a wood. But of course when they began to build around here they filled it in. They had a real problem as I understand it draining that bit for the road.'

The sun went down moments after that, he watched it sink below the trees, and the soft cold darkness seep up like water over the roofs of Waverley Road. Mrs Brock caught his mood, touched his hand gently and said: 'You come on down when you're ready.'

When he went back downstairs she was in the kitchen, peeling potatoes.

'I wonder,' he said, 'since you have the vacancy . . . Maybe I could stay the night?'

She nodded. 'I think that would be a very good idea.' She had a comforting natural tact. 'Bed's all made up.'

'You don't need to feed me, Mrs Brock, I'll go out.'

'Tea's always for three,' she said, 'so it makes no difference.'

'Then thank you.'

At five-thirty Spencer sat in the dining room with Mr Hebditch – the other guest Miss Mawes was away – and ate a mutton stew that contained very little meat, and a pink cornflour mould scattered with coloured granules. Afterwards he went out to the movies and saw Cary Grant and Katharine Hepburn in 'Bringing Up Baby'. Mrs Brock had given him a key, but he was back well before her ten o'clock curfew, and went straight up to bed.

He and his toothbrush scarcely filled the vacancy. But he was glad to be spending the night in this house where his mother had lived. It was like a rite, a sacrament. The clean, cold emptiness of the room was calming. Once he'd turned the light out he drew back the curtains and the black outs, and lay between the chilly, fiercely laundered sheets watching his breath smoke slightly, and looking out at the night sky through the window opposite. Round about midnight the wind got up again, stirring the branches of the trees with a sound like water, surging round the walls.

★   ★   ★

346

Next day he left early, before breakfast, pleading a long drive and uncertain weather. As she saw him off, Mrs Brock asked: 'What was your mother's family name?'

'She was Caroline Wells.'

'It doesn't mean anything to me, but I'll keep my eyes and ears open.'

In the event the day was bright and clear, but there was black ice on the roads and he had to drive slowly. Once he was out of town he pulled up and consulted the map. It was only about ten miles to the village where Cissy had lived – crazy to be down in this neighbourhood and not take a look.

But he struck an obstacle in the form of a huge British Army training depot, even bigger than the base at Church Norton. Quonsett huts littered the fields on both sides of the road, and there was a barrier across it at which he had to present his identity and pass cards to the MP on duty.

'Where are you trying to go?'

He pointed to Fort Mayden on the map. 'Here?'

The MP shook his head and pointed back the way he'd come. 'Can't get through this way at the moment. You need to get back up where you were, head towards town, then come out along the south road.'

'Forget it, it was kind of a snap decision anyway.'

'Sorry, chum.'

He drove back to the main road and turned for home. In the distance to his left he could make out some sort of strange white markings on the side of a hill. He guessed they must be something to do with the depot, or perhaps an orientation point for fliers. Funny, because as the road curved round and he got a better view, the markings were like the outline of a huge animal leaping across the ground.

That evening in the Ramrod Club he joined Frank and Si at the bar. Frank asked him: 'So how was it? Did you find the family seat of the McColls?'

'The Wells – my mother's side. It's a rooming house these days. I spent the night there.'

'*A la récherche du temps perdu . . .*'

'If you say so.'

'And was it as your mother described?'

'Pretty much. It's nothing special – old, kinda dark, the same as all the other houses on the street. But there was a view from one of the windows, on the top floor, that my mother told me about – that was the same.'

'So you slept there as a salute to the past?'

This time Frank had put his finger on it. 'That's right.'

Si pulled a face. 'What a way to spend a thirty-six – sleeping alone in some half-assed boarding house.'

'It was the object of the exercise. And it was kind of interesting.'

'I'll take your word for it!'

'I did see one thing you don't see every day.'

Si whistled. 'Amaze us,' said Frank.

'There was a little park at the end of the road, where there used to be a wood. There was a whale's jawbone over one of the paths.'

'A what?' Si's face was already creasing with incredulous laughter.

'The jawbone of a blue whale. Given to the park by the man who killed it.'

'Well!' They were both laughing now. 'I bet the locals were just tickled to death.'

'The sheer size – it's astonishing.'

Si leaned towards him. 'This rooming house . . . run by a lonely lady of a certain age with a soft spot for Yanks?'

Spencer smiled good-naturedly. 'Married lady, with a son in the Merchant Navy.'

'Only we know you're one hell of a dog with those older women . . .'

Frank pushed his glass over. 'Leave the man alone, Si, and go get the next round.'

★   ★   ★

They were put on stand-by for the following day, but as was so often the case after a clear cold night the whole of southern England woke to a morning closed down by thick, dank fog which lasted into the afternoon. To the pilots sitting round in the ready room with greyness pressing on the windows and the lights on, it was as though dawn simply hadn't happened; the only event that broke the tedium and marked the time of day was lunch.

Morale remained fragile, too. A second winter away from home, the feeling that following the big push in June the war should be over and wasn't, the inevitable attrition of losses, all told on the nerves. Some people – Frank was one – had always seemed to be slightly outside the herd and therefore less subject to communal changes of mood. Others, Spencer among them, coped by means of a sort of mental hibernation, withdrawing into themselves, consciously lowering their emotional temperature and husbanding their resources. A mercurial few, those with more energy than judgement, the ones you wanted on your side in the air, became big trouble.

Si Santucci was typical of this group. During that long, dingy morning he got gradually more jumpy. He started up conversations with the express intention of needling the other guy, he whistled and fidgeted and swore, and bounced his ball on the ground until he was told to stop, when he immediately began rocking his chair on one leg, twisting back and forth so the leg made a rubbery sound on the lino. It was bad enough for the pilots but Ajax couldn't stand the sound either. It seemed to hurt his ears and he started to whine and howl, driving them all crazy.

When it got to three o'clock the sun finally broke through and the fog began rapidly to burn away in tatters like train smoke. But by that time it was clear there would be no mission that day. Si and a couple of the other rowdies ran outside like kids let out of school. Ajax came out from under Frank's chair and stood in front of him, grinning hopefully, tail wagging.

'You want a walk? All right, you got it.' Frank rose to his feet, and looked down at Spencer. 'Spence, you want to stretch your legs?'

There was nothing else to do, so they set off round the perimeter, the dog trotting along next to them with his jaunty, rolling gait. They were on the south side, a little below the level of the hardstands, when they heard the ragged roar of an engine revving for take-off. It was Si's *Fast 'n' Loose*. They could see the hourglass red-head spilling out of her little waitress outfit on the nose.

'Oh, no . . .' Frank shook his head. 'Idiot! What does he think he's doing?'

'He's been building up a head of steam all day.'

'Yes, but taking her up for a joyride? He'll get a roasting for this.' They watched as *Fast 'n' Loose* thundered along the runway and rose over the trees and the church tower into the pale blue winter sky. 'Doesn't he know a fellow can get killed pulling those stunts?'

The plane circled wide, banked to the north over Church Norton, executed a slow arrogant spiral and climbed higher before screaming down into a half roll and buzzing the main runway. There was no doubt that Si now had what he wanted: an audience. Men on buildings maintenance, and ground crew around the dispersals and hardstands, were gazing up at the impromptu aerobatics, and there were others outside the control tower, the mess huts and ready rooms doing the same thing. The last traces of fog were still hanging around the shallow depressions to north and south, glowing pink as the sun got low. It turned the base into a picturesque backdrop for whatever stunt Si intended to pull.

There were a couple of men, the two guys Si had gone outside with, capering around on the grass in the middle of the runways. From the air this area looked a little like a baseball diamond, and the men were throwing a ball around. One of them had a catcher's mitt. Suddenly Spencer knew what Si was going to do, right now while everyone was watching after the long boredom of the abortive stand-to.

Frank said it for him. 'He's going to try and catch the damn' thing again.'

Fast 'n' Loose was momentarily out of sight, they could just make out the engine noise somewhere beyond the mist, gathering itself. The two men in the centre were turning, looking up, shielding their eyes, waiting for the big entrance. Then suddenly there he was, coming down from the north, in over the church tower so low he almost clipped the flag, air ducts howling. The man wearing the mitt rocked back, took aim, pitched. The plane was coming straight for him, the thin winter grass streamed flat as it drew closer, and swallowed the ball as both men fell to the ground beneath it – it was that or be decapitated. Up to then it was as near perfect as such a thing could be – clean, controlled, and taken at such speed it made the hair rise on your neck. No matter how damn-fool you thought it was, you had to admire the sheer ballsy skill of the thing.

But something happened. The onlookers could feel it more than see it, especially the fliers. He'd gone just a touch too low, too steep, didn't pull back soon or hard enough, Spencer could feel his own muscles tighten in sympathy with the effort of controlling all that plunging, screaming power, and then feel the sweat on his face and palms as it didn't quite happen – there was another split second when it might have gone either way, you could sense the plane heaving against its own trajectory, the frame trembling with conflicting forces. It half-rolled, but the moment was already past, the wing-tip hit the ground, scoring the tarmac with a stench of burning, and then it rolled over, suddenly huge and cumbersome and ugly, a smoking broken engine of death instead of the swooping bird it had been seconds before.

There was a moment of stunned, deafened silence, through which not a car, not a bird, not a voice could be heard. They stared, transfixed, as the black smoke poured upward and shimmering shock waves of heat radiated out from the wreck.

There were two things that Spencer would always remember about the vicious waste of Si Santucci's death. One was that minute, post-impact pocket of silence. The other was seeing for the first time tears on a man's face, as Frank began to weep.

Then, pandemonium.

He wrote Caroline and Mack, and Trudel, about his visit to

Oxford, but did not mention Si's death. He could not himself have said why this self-inflicted accident seemed more brutal than death in combat, but that's how it was. That, he told himself, was why Frank took it so hard.

Si's death wasn't the only bombshell to hit Spencer in those days running up to Christmas '44. On 20 December Rosemary came home. He'd been helping out at a kids' party organised by the base at the village hall. Mo was Santa Claus, but they had to stop the older kids, like Davey, giving the game away. One or two guys who were members of the Stars 'n' Stripes big band at the Ramrod Club came along and played music for the games, and while the kids ate their tea. A few of the mothers, Janet included, were there in a crowd-control capacity, something the airmen did not take for granted.

At the end, as the children were collected and left with their balloons and candy, Mo sat in the kitchen with his Santa whiskers pushed down so that they hung beneath his chin like a great fluffy bib. There was snow falling outside, but his face was nearly as red as his robe and covered in a sheen of sweat which he dabbed at with a handkerchief. Ellen ran in and out of the hall, peek-a-booing him, but he was all out of the festive spirit. Janet, who was doing the dishes with a nice, churchy woman called Mrs Cornforth, handed him a cup of tea.

'Freshly made for Father Christmas.'

'Thank you, ma'am. You don't by any chance have a cold beer?'

'I'm afraid not.'

'In that case . . .' He took a noisy mouthful of tea, the steam making larger drops of condensation on his nose and brow. 'Not bad . . . not bad at all. Tell you sump'n – I'd rather face the whole damn' Hitler airforce than a bunch of kids.' As the women laughed and went back to their washing up, he leaned confidentially towards Spencer, eyes sliding in Janet's direction. 'Nice lady, Spence. She's real pretty. Classy. You done good there.'

'Hey!' Spencer scooped up Ellen, preventing any further

comment, and hung her upside down so that her face turned red and she cackled with laughter. 'Leave Santa alone, he's had a hard day.'

Davey came in, his hair and shoulders dusted with snow. 'Spence and Mo, driver said to tell you jeep's going.' Like all the kids, especially the boys who hung around the base every free moment, he'd picked up American ways of saying things but they sounded quaint in his English country accent.

'Boy, is that music to my ears!' Mo put his empty cup on the draining board. 'Thank you again, ladies, terrific cuppa. Spence, you comin'?'

'Tell them carry on, I'll help the ladies finish up here and walk back.'

Mo made a get-you face, then slapped his hand on Davey's shoulder. 'Say, you wanna ride up in the jeep instead?'

'Can I? Yes! Mum, can I ride in the jeep?'

Janet turned, wiping her hands on her apron. 'Is it all right if he does that, Sergeant?'

'I asked him, didn't I?'

'But you'll walk straight home when you get there, Davey?'

'Yes!'

'All right then.'

They watched them leave, hands reaching out to help Davey jump up, and Mo with his hood up and whiskers in place against the cold, hoisting his robe to follow suit, breaking into a run amid rowdy laughter as the jeep pulled away.

'That's something you don't see every day . . .' observed Mrs Cornforth. 'Lieutenant, you've all given the children a really wonderful time – a party to remember. Thank you so much.'

'It's been our pleasure.'

'Well now.' Mrs Cornforth looked at them with the perfect, noncommittal politeness Spencer had come to associate with certain kinds of English lady. 'Are we ready to lock up?'

They did so and walked together to the end of the path, where they parted company. Spencer crouched down and let Ellen climb on for a piggy-back. It was bitterly cold, the snow powder-fine, the tiniest stardust-flakes in the blackness.

'You know,' said Janet, 'I shall miss the dark when the lights go up again. Even the few we've got here. Once you're used to it, it's friendly. It's only when you push it away that it seems frightening.'

'I guess so . . . in the country. But towns and cities should be lit up. London must be pretty dazzling when the lights are on.'

'Yes, I'll look forward to seeing that. And to hearing the bells ring.' They walked for a couple of minutes in silence and were in sight of the cottage when she said: 'You must be homesick at this time of year.'

'We all are. But I'm lucky, I have compensations.' Ellen's head was flopping with sleep on his shoulder. He held out his hand to Janet, but she did a little trick of hers of just passing her fingers quickly over his palm, not giving up her hand to his. He couldn't see her expression but he could imagine it – a little close-lipped smile, eyes downcast or averted: an evasive Mona Lisa.

When they got back she drew the curtains and then he carried Ellen upstairs and they got her into bed without waking her. Then to his surprise, standing right next to Ellen's cot, she took his hand, and said: 'Spencer.'

'We can't. Davey will be back.'

'Not for ages if he's gone up there in the jeep, he'll have to walk home.'

'And I should go.'

'In a minute.'

She led him to the bed. It was odd that she always both invited and yet seemed passive. She chose the time, then as it were made herself available. He could never tell where the balance of their relationship lay, who set the pace, what was going on, and this strange formlessness was part of its magic.

Now they took their clothes off and lay together, their two bodies stretched out, face to face, toe to toe, her arms beneath his. They were the same height, and he gazed at her face, trying to read it. Her eyes were closed, she seemed warm and present in his arms, and yet she had withdrawn into that other place in her head, behind her eyelids. He could almost feel her private thoughts swimming softly between the two of them like fish in a darkened tank. He kissed her on the mouth, and wondered, as her lips parted, who she was thinking of. Her secrecy as always excited him, she fuelled his desire by retreating from him, it was Spencer now who whispered, 'Please . . . please . . .' But she never made a sound.

At the moment of no return, he heard the front door, and voices. Forever after, the memory of sex with Janet would be linked to the shock of that moment. And for the first time her eyes flew open, staring wide and direct into his, and her hand was placed over his mouth.

From downstairs, like an alarm bell 'Mum!'

She uttered a single word, in a fierce whisper: 'No!'

Then she was out of bed, wrapping herself in her robe, pulling at her hair in the mirror. He could hear her breathing shallow and fast, punctuated by little whimpers of anxiety.

'Janet?' It was Rosemary's voice. And then with quick understanding: 'Don't disturb her, she must be having a lie down after the party, David!'

Davey's footsteps on the stairs, Janet whisking the door open, then closed, but not quickly enough to prevent the boy from seeing him, or to protect Spencer from the expression of confusion and surprise on his face.

'What's Spencer doing?'

'Having a rest.'

'Spencer!'

'He'll be down in a minute. Hallo, Rosie, why don't you get the kettle on? Go on, darling . . .'

She came back in, wouldn't look at him, got dressed as if he wasn't there, left the room and pattered briskly down the stairs. He felt paralysed by his own guilt and hers, could not even get out of bed when every movement, every line of her body, so absolutely rejected him.

When she'd gone and he was putting his uniform on he thought grimly of Mo's remark and reflected that he, too, would rather face the Luftwaffe than what awaited him downstairs.

The women were in the kitchen at the back. Davey sat at the table, drawing. He looked up as Spencer came in.

'Hi.'

'Hi, Davey. Good ride?'

'Yes, but they wouldn't let me walk back.'

'So, what – you got a ride back as well?'

'Some of the way. Auntie Rosie was getting off at the bus stop so they dropped me off there.'

Throughout this short everyday exchange the boy's eyes were on Spencer's face, and he looked exactly like his mother. Spencer could sense those confused, uncomfortable thoughts, the half-formed questions that might not be answered for months, perhaps years, yet. But eventually they would find answers, and he didn't want to be around when that happened. Terrifying, that one second could turn a tide and change a life.

'Good,' he said. 'Well, better be going.'

'Okay.' Davey leaned over his drawing again.

Spencer went into the kitchen. Janet was slicing bread. Rosemary was beating up a single precious egg with milk in a bowl, to make French toast – what they called gypsy bread.

'Hallo there,' said Rosemary, 'staying for tea?' Like Davey her voice said one thing and her eyes another, but with her there was no confusion.

'No, I'm late, I have to go.'

'Davey said it was a good party.'

'They seemed to enjoy it. 'Bye, Janet.'

''Bye.' She turned her head a little in his direction, but her eyes didn't meet his.

'Be seeing you.'

'I expect so.'

'Night, Rosie.'

'I'll see you out.'

'Night, champ.' He ruffled Davey's hair and was shaken off. Both gestures were a habit with them, but this time he thought he could feel a difference.

Rosie came to the gate and stood there with her arms folded against the cold.

'Don't worry,' she said. 'It'll be all right.'

He seemed to breathe properly for the first time in half an hour. 'I'm sorry.'

'There's no need.'

'But Davey . . . his father . . . I feel terrible.'

'I'll look after him.' She shrugged, wounded and wordless, and the shrug reminded him of how young she herself was. 'It's not the end of the world.'

'No.' He kissed her cheek, which was warm, touched her arm, that was cold. 'Thank you for being so understanding, Rosie.'

Her eyes were unusually bright as she said, quietly: 'I don't understand. That's the trouble. But I wish I did.'

He fled.

That was the end of it, of course, by mutual consent. But there was a postscript. On Christmas Eve he took down some presents and found Janet on her own, dressing their little tree.

'Rosie took them into town on the bus,' she said. 'I thought I'd have this done by the time they get back.'

'Can I help?'

'There's no need, I'm nearly finished.'

He sat awkwardly as she put the finishing touches. The tree was wedged with stones into a galvanised iron bucket covered in Christmas paper. It looked secure enough but it wasn't quite straight – he could picture the two women doing this on their own, the sort of job that only a few days ago they'd have asked him to do. Some of the decorations were proper ones – coloured glass balls and icicle-drops and tinsel – others were homemade, perhaps by Davey, from silver cigarette papers and coloured cardboard with string or cotton threaded through. On the top was an angel made out of a big clothes peg, with bright yellow wool hair and scarlet crayon lips.

'There . . .' She sat back on her heels.

'It's pretty. I brought a couple of things to go underneath.'

'You shouldn't have done.'

'Least I could do.' He put his offerings round the tree-bucket and then quickly laid his hand on hers. 'Janet—'

'Don't.' She removed her hand and did something unnecessary to her hair. 'It wasn't your fault.'

'Is Davey all right?'

'He's fine. We haven't talked about it.' She perhaps meant this to be soothing, but Spencer found it the opposite.

'And Rosemary . . . I know she's your sister, it's not the same, but she's still young. I feel bad about this.'

Janet didn't answer. She rose, dusted her skirt, adjusted the brassy angel with her long, elegant fingers. When she turned to him he was reminded of that first time, after the death of her husband – a moment of truth, but of truth known only to her.

'Spencer, I want to tell you something.'

He nodded, feeling that even the sound of his voice might scare her off.

'You'll be the only living person I have told.'

'Are you sure you want to?'

'Yes, you ought to know. It might help to explain.'

She didn't say what it might help to explain, and he didn't ask. He waited.

'Rosie's not my sister. She's my daughter.'

Of *course*, was what he thought. Of course. That was it: the strangeness, the secrecy, the thing he had never been able to fathom or understand.

'Does she know?'

Janet shook her head. 'Like I said you're the only living person who does.'

'But your husband – Edward?'

'Yes. When we married he took Rosie on, she'd been living with my parents. She called my mother Mum.'

'Will you ever tell her?'

'What would be the point?'

'And her own father – where's he?'

'Gone. He never even knew. It was only the once . . . and I didn't want it.'

Those last few words, so typically restrained, horrified him. He put his arms round her and she stood still in his embrace, not responding except to lean her forehead on his shoulder. He thought she might be crying, but when he released her, her face was waxwork-calm.

'So now you know.'

'I shan't tell a soul.'

She nodded. He was awed by her trust. But he was to be middle-aged and married himself before he saw how in this English family, the secrets, lies and loyalties of his own childhood had been repeated.

The week after Christmas Jenny the chuck-wagon girl, arriving early on her rounds, found Ajax sitting outside a latrine hut, whining. Inside in one of the cubicles was Frank's body. He had cut his wrists and then leaned forward into the toilet bowl, so there was no mess.

Suicide was in itself un-American, and as little was made of it as possible. No one speculated as to why Frank had done it – war was a bitch. If one or two of them had their suspicions they kept them to themselves, and Spencer did the same with the contents of the letter that was left for him in Frank's locker.

Some things were best left undisturbed.

CHAPTER THIRTEEN

'So saying he breathed strength and courage into the horses. They shook the dust from their manes on to the ground, and quickly carried the fast-running chariot'

—Homer, The Iliad

Harry 1854

The terrain was not unlike the rolling, grassy uplands of southern England, but that there were no trees or bushes, nor anything green to be seen.

Far to the west, beyond the ranks of the French divisions, the stately allied fleet moved with them, the funnels of the steamers belching mighty banners of smoke into the blue air, its guns capable of giving cover on the right flank as far as two miles inland. It was impossible not to feel a swell of pride in the English Army, the dazzling wave of the infantry's scarlet and white and the matchless splendour of the cavalry, the dash of its mounted officers, conspicuous as fighting cocks in their nodding white plumes, making the workmanlike, well-supplied French appear drab by contrast.

They moved in an order of broad columns, capable in the event of attack from the left or rear of forming a hollow 'box' with the baggage at the centre. The Light Cavalry formed the advance guard and left flank. From this position they could appreciate the deceptive openness of the country, and also recall the humiliating disappointments that it had inflicted on their foraging expedition of a few days before. Beneath the thin, dry grass the ground was bone hard. The only evidence of cultivation was concentrated close to the scattered farms and deserted hamlets. There was a pale haze, like the dust of an approaching army on the horizon, which presaged fearsome heat. There was no breath of breeze: the only movement of air was that stirred by their march. Proudly borne regimental colours hung in heavy swathes.

Riding steadily on the inland edge of all this, Harry could not help but feel the contrast between the noisy, colourful tide of the armies to his right, reaching to the sea, and the hot, silent spaces of the Crimea, from which their progress might be secretly, balefully, watched.

Hares started up all over the place, and to begin with the men of the infantry considered this great sport, the more energetic ones breaking ranks to chase them. The impromptu hunts, weaving in and out of the lines to the accompaniment of whoops and jeers, and the jaunty marching music of the bands, created what was almost a fairground atmosphere.

Some of the hunters were successful. Harry saw one victorious trooper with more youthful energy than sense, race to the front of his comrades and charge the length of the rank, roaring with elation, his kill held aloft in one hand so that its blood ran down his arm and on to his face. The men cheered and laughed but the trooper's contorted blood-spattered face and wild shouts chilled Harry, and stirred a memory or expectation of something terrible.

As the sun rose, so their spirits sank.

Sickness and thirst marched with them still, and flourished as they tired. The proud glory of their setting out, when each man had felt a part of the grand endeavour, gave way to the grim trudge of reality. The stirring panoply of war dissolved before the squalid detail of individual suffering. Within half an hour of their departure the first victims of cholera and heat exhaustion were beginning to fall, and the marching armies trailed a dense wake of discarded equipment, and dead and dying men, contorted by pain, vomiting and diaorrhoea, too weak to carry on. As the 8th Hussars rode forward on the flank, so the *arabas* rumbled by in the opposite direction, loaded with a pitiful human cargo. One or two of the more enterprising officers' wives were seen to be carrying armfuls of rifles for the weakened men with barely the strength to carry themselves, so that these well-born ladies, riding on their ponies and mules, looked more like peasant women with loads of brushwood.

One by one, the bands fell silent. And now in their place could be heard not the liquid purity of larksong, but the dry, dull buzzing of flies.

After one hour's march, a halt was called. It was strange to see the whole great swathe of infantry, scarlet and blue, sink to the ground as if cut by a scythe. All were aware of that small, meaningless rise in morale that accompanied change: too long in one place and the collective mood grew sullen and restless; orders to advance and they were briefly inspired; too relentless a march and in their debilitated state they flagged and their spirits wearied. In what had so far been a war of stops and starts uncertainty was proving to be their greatest enemy.

Harry dismounted and let Clemmie put her head down. She blew with relief, stretched her neck; her lips pulled hungrily on the dry grass; she munched, content in the moment. Harry envied her her simple world. She had forgotten the fear and pain of the voyage, she did not anticipate the danger to come.

Next to him, Leonard Palliser's grey gelding had thrown a shoe.

'Dammit, this ground's like rock – he'll have to go back.'

Harry called to him: 'If you see my man Betts at the rear, ask him to come up this way, can you?'

'If I do. It's no grand levée back there,' said Palliser grumpily.

Harry loosened Clemmie's girth. The cavalry saddles were becoming too big for their thin mounts, there was a real danger of sores and chafing. Her hide twitched and she shook her head as flies settled on her rump and around her eyes; but her once beautiful long tail had become short and tattered and though it swung from side to side it was no longer any use as a switch.

The infantry sat or lay; the cavalry stood amongst their horses. At ground level Harry ran with sweat and could begin to appreciate what the footsoldiers had been suffering. The scene was like a great colourful picnic, with men talking and reading letters and raiding their rations, except that many of those who lay down did so because they were unlikely to get up again. The cheerful sound of voices and the thin, jaunty music of the tin whistle drowned out the buzzing of the flies. Fyefield removed his shako, revealing a sunburned stripe, and lit a cigar.

'I had no idea,' he said, running a finger between his tight stock and reddened skin, 'that it would be so infernally hot. I plead pig ignorance. But the devil of it is that the French seem comfortable.'

'They appear to have what they need,' agreed Harry.

'Including,' put in Philip Gough earnestly, 'those rather excellent and amenable camp followers.'

Hector snorted with laughter. 'If they were that amenable the French wouldn't march so damnably fast . . .'

'No, no,' said Gough, 'I believe they're no more than cooks and nurses.'

'I don't deny it for a moment! And some of our fellows have brought along the flower of English womanhood – but speaking as a bachelor I feel bound to say that most are neither use nor ornament.'

'They came for their husbands' sakes,' said Harry, 'which is only to be admired. And they help where they can.'

'Hmm.' Hector sucked glumly on his cigar. 'Not trained up like those French women though.'

Harry could hardly deny this, nor the obvious fact that their allies seemed in general to be more 'trained up' than they were. Preparedness and punctuality had been the hallmarks of the French performance so far; chaos, confusion and delay that of the British. The resplendent appearance of the British Army, which had stirred their hearts at the outset of the day, seemed now vainglorious next to the French who had without doubt withstood the rigours of the march better. In spite of large packs they had kept up a killing pace in their less arresting but looser and more comfortable uniforms. Élan, reflected Harry, was something the British Army – and especially its cavalry – aspired to, but here élan was proving to be dependent not on show, but on practicalities.

'Ah, here we have it.' Hector pointed with his cigar. 'A visit from on high.'

Lord Raglan, Marshal St Arnaud, and a bevy of staff officers of both nationalities were riding along the front of the columns. As they did so many of the seated men got to their tired feet, waved or threw their caps in the air and cheered them to the echo.

'I sometimes think,' remarked Hector, 'that the ordinary Britisher will cheer a leader in direct proportion to the level of hardship he inflicts. It seems that the worse time a chap's having, the better he thinks the overall plan must be.'

'Then let's hope he's right.'

Watching Raglan as he paused to address some grateful infantrymen, Harry knew that in this, as in all Hector's acid and unheroic comments, there was more than a grain of truth. This dignified, stone-faced old man, maimed in body and reserved in demeanour, had as yet done nothing to earn the admiration of those he led. His tenure as Commander-in-Chief had been marked by indecision, secrecy and slowness. He displayed neither dash nor the common touch. His heart might be good, but his hand was cold and his nature cautious. Still, he was a 'toff'. His attraction for the men rested entirely in his aristocratic bearing. He had the appearance, thought Harry, of a man vouchsafed greater wisdom and judgement than the hoi-polloi, as he looked down from his placid charger to disseminate terse, dry encouragement. Recalling the face of Lord Cardigan, returning unabashed from his disastrous reconnaissance of the Danube – the handsome, highly coloured voluptuary's profile with its loose, petulant mouth and pale eyes – Harry wondered how on earth the one could ever presume successfully to command the other. Not that this was the only clash involving Lord Cardigan. The animus that existed between the divisional and brigade commanders of the Lights was well known and even the subject of much humorous grumbling both in the ranks and the officers' mess. Lucan was a sound if choleric commander, who obeyed orders to the letter. But the perversity of human nature dictated that given the choice the men would have ridden into hellfire behind the arrogant Cardigan.

'How is she, sir?' It was Betts at his elbow.

'Betts – she's going well, but I wonder when to rest her. What's your opinion?'

He ran an expert eye over Clemmie, and a hand over her fetlocks and pasterns. 'No problems that I can see, sir. It's the blooming heat that's going to tire them.'

'And all of us. Let's hope we reach some water soon.'

'Sir. If we do it'd better not be sea water like the last lot.'

'Is Derry doing well?'

'You know that one, sir. That's no cavalry charger if you don't mind me saying, that's a work horse. Keep going till 'e drops.' Betts' gaze drifted to the commanders and staff who were now directly before them at a distance of some seventy yards. 'Seen any cossacks, sir?'

The question was asked expressionlessly, but Harry had a good deal of respect for his groom's sardonic intelligence. The entire allied invasion force was spread out on the grass with their commanders-in-chief parading before them, in what was generally acknowledged to be some of the most perfect cavalry country imaginable, a vast sedentary target.

Palliser returned, huffing and puffing, from the rear with his fresh horse. 'Latimer, may I borrow your man?'

'Of course. Carry on, Betts.'

Twenty minutes after that they received the order to march. The great concourse of men rose with a sound like wind through wheat. The armies moved forwards once more in wave after slow wave over the dry plain.

Rachel was going through the house, room by room. It was something she had scarcely had time to do before Hugo's death but now the process had assumed for her an almost sacramental significance. As his child grew inside her so she was slowly but surely growing to understand the place where he himself had been born, and to feel less like a stranger to it.

For this to happen it was necessary for her to discover Bells on her own. If she had a question to ask she would ask it, but otherwise the servants left her alone. Her relationship with the household was an informal one. She relied heavily on the competence of the farm manager, Collins, and that of Oliver in the stables, Morrish in the garden and Jeavons in the house. She liked the work done well, but she wanted it done well for its own sake, not under duress. It was clear that Maria's incumbency had been characterised by temperament and inconsistency. Her mother-in-law had been held in affection for the master's sake, but it was a wary affection. She could be expansive and indulgent one minute, haughty and demanding the next. Her employees had learned that it was her way, and meant nothing, but they were still on their guard. Rachel herself knew that while she could never be as open about her feelings as Maria, she could for that reason maintain an even keel. She strove not for popularity, only trust and respect.

She had taken on Mercy Bartlemas (at sixteen the eldest of the children now) as an under housemaid to replace the income lost with Colin, but when Mercy grew peaky and wilted Rachel asked Morrish if the girl might do odd jobs out of doors. Initially he was dumbstruck at the thought of this break with convention – a young female invading his precious territory! – but Rachel persuaded him that it was only for a trial period and once he'd grudgingly agreed, the arrangement was a success. Mercy was a country girl with no liking for indoors, a girl who liked to be out in the fresh air, not gazing at it through glass. Given a few simple tasks in a setting that suited her she blossomed as the rose, and being from a large family she was well able to cope with Morrish's grumpy demands and teasing from the two garden lads. She did as she was told energetically and showed an aptitude for the work: she had green thumbs, things grew for her. Her sturdy figure in a brown sacking apron and muddy boots, hair frizzy as a rag doll's, became a common and soon an unremarkable sight about the gardens and park. For Rachel there was real pleasure in knowing not just that her family was benefiting (more in kind than in cash) from Mercy's job, but that here was another small link with the past, a young and vital one, making the beans and cabbages and flowers grow while her poor brother lay dead in a communal grave by the Black Sea.

She wrote of these feelings to Harry, in the letter that she wrote each night, like a journal, and posted once a week or so. She had no way of knowing how long these letters took to reach him, or if they did at all, but there was a comfort in the mere act of writing them. And even though she had heard nothing from Harry for some time she followed the reports of W. H. Russell in *The Times* and had formed a picture of where he was and what the conditions were like. Even so, this aspect of the present was at one remove, and the future was at best uncertain. The past had a greater solidity. That was a place she could visit and explore and which would only change with her own understanding of it.

There was a painting which hung in the hall by which she often paused because it showed the whole Latimer family – Percy, Maria and their two sons – perhaps twenty years ago. It was in most respects a conventional, well-executed painting of the family standing on a grassy mound, improbably in their best clothes, with a somewhat idealised view of Bells in the background. Rachel liked it for the story it told. Rightly or wrongly she perceived in it certain idiosyncrasies which the painter had been unable or unwilling to ignore – things which in a wholly respectful representation would have been left out. There was, for instance, a chair in the centre foreground which must surely have been placed there for Maria, in order for the family to present a traditional tableau – mother seated, paterfamilias standing at her shoulder, one son at her side, the other on her knee or on the ground nearby. Maria, however, was standing tall and proud next to her slightly shorter husband. What made Rachel sure that her mother-in-law had declined to sit was that the chair – and consequently the painting's focal point – was occupied by a liver-and-white spaniel with its tongue hanging out. Maria wore a wine-red dress, its severe elegance offset by the red flower just visible in her hair. When it came to the boys it was Harry, the younger son, who stood next to the chair with his hand on the dog's collar (it did in fact look as if it might leap away at any moment) and Hugo who sat cross-legged on the ground at the front, his chin in his hands, grinning impishly. Whatever the actual setting for the sittings, the artist had made no attempt to conceal the mud on the soles of Hugo's shoes nor his slightly grubby fingers and disarrayed hair. His grin and Maria's dramatic stare were vividly characteristic of mother and son.

The expressions of Percy and Harry were harder to read. In the case of Percy, Rachel knew her father-in-law well enough by now to understand that his forbidding and even slightly bored look was a carapace, painstakingly developed over the years, to disguise his thoughts and feelings. Harry was more mysterious, a small person – he could have been no more than three or four – with matters of moment on his mind. Often, when Rachel looked at the painting, she found herself going closer to study the boys' faces as though sheer proximity might grant her an insight beyond the streaks and swirls of paint. It didn't, of course, but she always came away with the same impression: that Hugo never doubted for a moment that life held for him adventure, friendship, love; whereas Harry jumped to no such conclusions, but watched and waited thoughtfully for what might transpire.

This impression was reinforced by some books she found in what had been the boys' nursery and schoolroom before they had been sent away to Eton. Hugo's written work was expansive but untidy, characterised by a lack of regard for correct grammar and punctuation. Asked to describe 'My favourite animal', he had covered three scrawled and spattered pages on the subject of his spaniel, Rowley – Rachel thought it might be the one in the painting – omitting no detail of the dog's delinquent behaviour, from 'chasing the chickins and eating most of one' (a crime for which Rowley had apparently endured a dead hen tied to his collar for three days) to 'barking at Father until he was driven nearly mad' and 'steeling the cricket ball when Little hit it for six'.

Harry's composition on the same theme at an even more tender age was punctilious and painstaking, and took an entirely different interpretation. 'The tiger is my favourite animal becos it is very beatiful and very wild. It has strips and yelow eyes. It eats other beests becos it is hungry. I have never seen one but it is in my book. I wud like to see a tiger.'

This was accompanied by a lifelike drawing of a tiger crouched over a hapless and profusely bleeding antelope, probably copied from the book in question and captioned: 'The tiger gards his pray'.

Rachel found the contrast between these two pieces piquant. Hugo was a person for the here and now, that was his passionate, childlike quality. Harry, it seemed, was the dreamer: the boy who thought of tigers.

Thinking she might like them, she took the exercise books to Maria who exclaimed nostalgically before being reminded of other things.

'That governess – Salter! She did them no good.'

'I think they wrote well, considering how young they were.'

'Hmm . . . perhaps. But they did as they liked, always.' Maria may have caught something in Rachel's expression, for she added: 'I didn't employ a governess for the boys to be like me – I employed her to be different from me. That is the whole point of employing people.'

This, Rachel thought, was the attitude which the servants found confusing. But Maria's tone brooked no argument. Percy had scarcely the energy to read, but Rachel read aloud some of the essays to him and they produced the trace of a smile.

'I remember that dog . . . bad blood, couldn't be trained. Tigers, now . . . never saw a tiger take a cricket ball.'

When she went home that day she left the exercise books on the small table next to Percy's chair.

Throughout that late summer and early autumn Rachel had a sense of the mysteriousness of time – that it was impossible categorically to divide it into chapters and say that such and such was then, and over. Increasingly it felt to her as though the past bled into the present and illuminated it. More than anything she believed in free will, this belief even qualified her cautious religious faith, and yet there were aspects of people's lives and behaviour which seemed to set them on a course from which no escape or deviation was possible. Hugo's premature death was his means of grace. Harry's soldiering was for the hope of glory.

One soft morning in September, before the day had shown its colours, she set off to walk up to the White Horse. She was heavy and cumbersome now, the baby seemed to sleep inside her, hanging weightily in its fleshy cradle. At times like this it felt big – far too big ever to leave the womb without tearing her apart, and she had to suppress a primitive fear of that separation – how it would happen, and when, and what the pain would be like. She wished that Hugo were here to clasp her in his arms and dispel her miserable fears with his confident delight.

The incline was too steep for her and she didn't reach the horse but stopped and lowered herself to the grass well short of it, at a point where its huge body arched over her, like the cow jumping over the moon. Cato, equally exhausted, flopped down beside her, panting gustily. Still, this place and the view it afforded quietened her. Bells, the village, her own former house away to the west, were all recent arrivals to the landscape. People, homes and settlements without number had come and gone in the instant that the White Horse leaped. Cato laid his head down and she did the same, lying carefully on her side and closing her eyes. The morning was still, but with her ear to the ground she could hear a dense, murmuring pulse of secret sound, like the earth's heartbeat.

She slept for no more than half an hour, but when she woke a pale sun had broken through. Cato was ambling about, tracing rabbit-runs with his nose. Stiffly Rachel got to her feet and began the homeward journey. Going downhill was if anything more tiring; she had to tense every muscle to pull her weight back and keep her balance. By the time she'd climbed the less demanding slope to the gate into Bells Wood she was very tired, but calm.

Coming back between the trees opposite the house a sound made her look up, and she was startled to see a face looking back at her from among the branches. The other person was equally surprised, for the eyes widened, the mouth made a dark 'O', and the next thing she knew there was a crash and rustle of breaking twigs as a small boy fell out of the tree and landed with a thud on the path in front of her.

'Are you all right?' She leaned forward and held out her hand to help him up, but he scrambled to his feet unaided and apparently unhurt.

'Sorry, miss, I slipped.'

'I can see that. Are you sure there's no damage done?'

He shook his head, his eyes taking in her condition with fascinated interest, making a series of lightning calculations and putting two and two together. He was about eight years old, dark, bright-eyed and sallow, like an Italian boy.

'Are you Mrs Latimer?'

'I am.' She waited, smiling. 'I'm afraid you have the advantage of me.'

Understanding the tone rather than the words, he said: 'I'm Ben Bartlemas.'

'Ah, you're Mercy's brother.'

'That's right.'

'Shouldn't you be at school?' she asked.

'Teacher's ill.'

'I see.' This made perfect sense, since the village school teacher, Mr Prale, was stricken in years and a martyr to all manner of respiratory and rheumatic problems whose influence began each autumn and lasted until spring. 'Does your mother know you're here?'

'Yes'm. She did say to tell you, she told Mercy to tell you but you weren't there.'

'Well, now I know, so that's all right.'

'Sorry.' He scuffed at the broken twigs. 'About the tree.'

'It's been there a long time, it's far older than either of us. I'm sure it will survive.'

'Yes,' he agreed. He had a composed confidence that stopped just short of cheekiness. He reminded her of Hugo.

'Would you like some lemonade?'

'Yes, please.'

'Come along then.'

He accompanied her over the grass, exactly matching his stride to hers. 'Can I come and work here when I'm older?'

Since directness was the order of the day she made her answer direct. 'Yes, if there's a job that needs doing that you can do.'

'I like horses.'

'So do I,' she said briskly, 'but that doesn't mean I should know enough to look after them properly myself.'

'My brother Colin used to look after the horses,' declared Ben.

'I know.'

He fixed a candid gaze on her, gauging her possible reaction to his next remark. 'He got killed in the Russian war.'

'Yes, I know that too. I was so sorry.'

She knew exactly what he wanted to ask, and waited to see if he would.

'Did Mr Latimer get killed in the war?'

'No. He was killed in an accident.'

'He fell off his horse, didn't he?'

So he had known the answer to the first question before asking it. 'That's right.' They reached the house. 'Just about where you fell out of the tree. Come along.'

They went across the hall, through the door and down the back stairs. In the kitchen were Jeavons, Mrs Mundy the cook, Little, and Mercy Bartlemas, the latter with a red face and hair on end. Jeavons and Mrs Mundy wore slightly disapproving expressions and Little had a sniggering air. All the expressions changed as Rachel and Ben appeared in the doorway.

'Ben!' Mercy advanced on her brother, too put out even to acknowledge Rachel. 'Whatever have you been doing? I looked everywhere for you, you little so and so!'

'I was climbing trees,' replied Ben, against a background of head-shaking and clucking from the others. He looked up at Rachel. 'Wasn't I?'

'When you weren't falling out of them,' she agreed, and turned to Mercy. 'He descended on me like Newton's apple.'

'Oh, no, he didn't, did he, mum? Did you get hurt? You're

372

going to get such a hiding from me, Ben Bartlemas! Are you all right, mum? And your father . . . just you wait! I'm ever so sorry, mum!' The tone of Mercy's outburst veered quite comically from remorse to vengeful fury.

'We were both quite unhurt, Mercy. And I understand that you would have told me Ben was with you if I hadn't been out for a walk.'

Mercy's colour deepened. 'That's right, mum, I would have done . . .'

'He can come whenever he likes when he doesn't have to go to school. On condition that he makes himself useful.'

Mercy looked doubtful. 'He's not up to much, mum.'

'We'll let Oliver be the judge of that, shall we?'

'Oliver?' Mercy's voice rose to a squeak, Little smirked, and even Jeavons and Mrs Mundy, ostensibly setting out cleaned silver on a tray, betrayed a discreet ripple of surprise. 'Oliver – the horses?'

'Exactly,' said Rachel. 'Ben tells me he'd like to work with horses so he might as well learn something about it.' She looked down at him. 'Does that sound like a good idea?'

To her amusement he gave a brief show of considering the suggestion. 'Yes, thank you.'

Mercy snorted. 'He's got an awful lot to learn, mum, I hope you'll tell Oliver that.'

'Oh, I shall.' Rachel turned to leave. 'After all, Mercy, you've learned wonderfully well about gardening, haven't you?' She nodded dumbly. 'Now why don't you introduce Ben to Oliver on your way back to work? And, Little, don't you have something to do?'

Mercy caught her brother's wrist in a grip so tight her knuckles showed pale, but it was plain nothing could tarnish his delight. On the point of going Rachel caught Ben's eye, and was rewarded by a smile so broad and confiding, so full of a regard that owed nothing to status, age or gender and everything to real affection and gratitude, that it tripped her heart and she had to leave swiftly.

* * *

373

The heat increased; the landscape grew emptier. Of natural wildlife there was no sign – swaying camels, sprinting hares, fluttering birds and butterflies, all had disappeared into the trembling glare of the sun's furnace. Even the drone of flies had subsided. And if they'd hoped to find domestic livestock to supplement their supplies they were disappointed. The few small farms they came across were empty, burned-out shells with neither man nor beast to be seen. Only once or twice they came across the picked skeletons of cows and were reminded that from some unimaginable distance in the whitened sky the slow-wheeling vultures watched their progress. One or two had been sighted, the first ever seen, it was said, in this part of the world. The conclusion that they must have followed the fleet from Varna was not a comforting one.

With the first smell of smoke there was another tremor of renewed energy through the ranks. The men's heads came up, the horses' nostrils opened nervously. Whatever else it signified, smoke was the airborne signature of those who had been that way before – and recently – and the notice of conflict to come. The enemy was near, and expected them.

They came over the next rise in heavy silence, the front line of their columns steady and unbroken, snaking to the distant sea. And like the curtain rising on a theatrical performance they saw for the first time the scene set for war. Far to their left was the source of the smoke – a torched village, still burning. In the shallow valley before them they could clearly make out the greener, tree-fringed path of a stream, crossed half a mile to the east by the post-road bridge. Just this side of the bridge, between armies and stream, was a neat whitewashed house, unmarked itself but surrounded by a charred barn and outbuildings. The rising ground a mile or so beyond the stream was shadowed with broad bands of trees and scrub.

The advance party of cavalry, Harry among them, went forward under Cardigan to investigate what they were told was the Imperial Post-house. Leonard Palliser jerked his head in the direction of a rider in dark civilian clothes, the Irish journalist of *The Times*. His lip curled.

'As if we don't have enough to contend with without the fourth estate tagging along.'

From the slight contact he had had with Russell, Harry liked him. He was a downright, curious, disrespectful sort of fellow completely unconcerned for his own safety and with no regard for the conventions of war.

'He seems a sound enough fellow. And at least those at home are kept properly and truthfully informed.'

Palliser harumphed. 'Ignorance is bliss.'

'Until the worst happens.' Harry thought briefly of Colin Bartlemas, and Roebridge – of Piper, even. 'Then one might wish one had been better prepared.'

'Disagree,' said Palliser who was nothing if not predictable. 'People in England need to believe that we are entirely successful. Then if a man dies it's a glorious sacrifice and not a damned shame, wouldn't you think?'

'Perhaps.'

As they drew closer to the post-house the dark patches in the middle distance which they had taken for trees revealed themselves to be a Birnam Wood of massed cossack cavalry.

'Ah,' remarked Palliser as though passing a friend's carriage in Kensington Gardens. 'At last. Our friends the enemy.'

Orders were given for some of the troop to spread out in a line parallel to the stream (they heard it was called the River Bulganak). Cardigan himself sat motionless on horseback near the bridge, peering through his spyglass at the hills opposite. A dozen or so riders including Harry, Palliser, Fyefield and the journalist Russell, went down to the house and dismounted.

To their surprise after so much lifeless desolation, there was a peahen stalking and pecking near the open door. She screeched halfheartedly at their arrival and flapped her wings, lifting herself off the ground by no more than a few inches before returning to her pecking. Harry found something comforting in her fussy, domestic goings-on, her sweet, foolish, chickeny ignorance of the two mighty armies which confronted each other beyond the confines of the courtyard.

Russell clearly thought the same, for he picked up one of the long, drab feathers shed by the peahen and tucked it in his lapel, before taking aim with his revolver and shooting her. The single shot in this enclosed space made the horses start and sidle. As Russell picked up the still-flapping bird he caught Harry's eye and gave him a jaunty wink.

'Gone but not forgotten,' he said.

Respect for its Imperial status may have prevented the house from being torched, but there was little of any consequence left inside. A picture of a sad-eyed saint presided over one empty room and in another a single broken chair lay on its side, with next to it a ripped yellow cushion, surrounded by a drift of downy feathers.

In the kitchen there were some pots and pans still standing on the range and a pestle and mortar on the windowsill. Bunches of aromatic dried herbs hung from the ceiling, whose smell could still be detected over the stench of smoke. Harry reached up and snatched down a handful of one of the bunches. The grey-green leaves and small flowerheads broke into fine grains in his palm and flooded his head with their wonderful scent. He pushed what remained of it into the pocket of his overalls.

The cavalry officers were incongruous in this confined domestic space, their brilliant colours harsh, their shakos brushing the ceilings, their spurs jingling. Fyefield pushed the tip of his sabre into one of the hanging saucepans and rattled it like a schoolbell.

Outside an extraordinary sight greeted them. The poor overheated infantry on arrival at the river had been unable to contain themselves and having broken ranks were down on all fours on the bank alongside the thirsty horses, lapping the water and splashing it over their heads and shoulders. Bowing perhaps to the inevitable a halt was called, so that all ranks could drink and fill their water bottles. Harry saw Russell riding to the back, the peahen tied to his saddle, presumably to hand her over to the cooks. In the opposite direction, perhaps a mile and a half away, he could make out the glint of sunlight on the cossacks' lances.

After an interval of around fifteen minutes during which the cossacks remained motionless, the order was given to form ranks and advance, with the cavalry going ahead. While Cardigan and his staff – accompanied as ever by Russell, now without his burden – trotted smartly over the narrow post-road bridge, the rest of them splashed through the stream. The water was low and when the horses emerged on the south side they were coated to the shoulder, and their riders to halfway up their boots, in mud like melted chocolate.

The order came to spread out and they rode forward at a slow and disciplined pace. Now that they were moving across the bottom of the river valley the picture before them was no longer clear. What from some distance away had looked like the solid face of an escarpment, carved by narrow gulleys, was now identifiable as a series of ascending ridges, and as they advanced so the enemy cavalry seemed to melt away beyond the first of these. To Harry it was uncomfortably akin to being drawn on by the false hope of a mirage, except that this carried a real threat. What might be waiting over that first gentle, unassuming rise? The heat was intense: the mud on Clemmie's flanks and on his boots was already dry and cracked. The mare's ears flicked back and forth nervily and he spoke to her in a soft voice.

They continued forward, and now they could see a handful of cavalry vedettes looking down on them from the shoulder of the first rise. In a moment they too had gone. Now they were trotting collectedly through a melon field and as the horses' hooves bruised and crushed the ripe fruit the air filled with a delicious sweet smell that made Harry's dry mouth fill with saliva. It was strange to be advancing in battle order across this fertile farmland, treading the melons to wine.

The ground began to rise. They came out of the field and the horses were working harder now to maintain the same controlled and steady pace on the incline. Clemmie's neck darkened and glistened with sweat along its strong swell of muscle. As they approached the top of the rise they received the order to walk, and Harry permitted himself a look over his shoulder. The narrow river still teemed as far as the eye could see with troops drinking and cooling down, with beyond them more and still more coming. On this side of the Bulganak the lancers were coming through the melon field, the younger and more irrepressible ones spearing whole melons and brandishing

377

them in the air, catching the dripping juice in their mouths. Their horseplay was in sharp contrast to the awful quiet on the other side of the rise.

They reached the top, and with it a full appreciation of their position. Another, but slightly less wide valley of no more than a quarter of a mile, now separated them from the cossacks, who were massed on the steep slope opposite. A halt was called. Harry and the skirmishers held their position. At this closer range the cossack force, still, darkly dressed and densely packed on their stocky little horses, presented a formidable picture: an army on its home ground, accustomed to the conditions and the terrain. For the first time his stomach fluttered with fear and a childish pang of homesickness at the thought that the face of one of these fierce unyielding little horsemen might be the last thing he saw on earth.

The order 'Skirmishers – draw swords – trot!' had been given, but was instantly revoked as Lord Lucan was seen approaching Cardigan. They halted, men fuming, horses champing at the bit. Behind the skirmishers there was now drawn up the full might and panoply of the British cavalry, gorgeous in scarlet, blue and gold, stopped in their tracks like some epic version of the game of Grandmother's Footsteps that Harry could remember playing with Hugo and Salter.

The argument continued, and was joined by Lord Airey, the emissary of the Commander-in-Chief. Sweat trickled from men and horses as they sat in their imaginary bandbox.

When the first carbine shot rang out, it was a relief. With that small streak of white smoke the tension was dispelled. Now, surely, it had begun! In the ensuing volley none of the shot came close enough to do damage, but incredibly the order was given for the skirmishers to retreat and rejoin their squadrons. To have come so far, and waited so long, to turn back in the face of fire – it was insupportable! In that instant Harry understood how strong, once initiated, was the impulse to attack. The urge was overwhelming to release the power of the horse and to go forward with ever-increasing speed, to do or die. The fear had not gone, but it swirled in him like strong drink, creating an energy which now that it was thwarted, rose in the back of his throat like bile. Between the carbine fire they could hear the whoops of the cossacks, jeering at them, adding to the bitterness of retreat.

Added to this humiliation, the Lights now discovered how terrifying it was to be an easy target, as the blocks of enemy cavalry parted to allow space for cannon. A puff of white smoke heralded the first round shot, that whizzed and thundered past them, leaping and bounding at murderous speed over the uneven ground. Most failed to hit home, but not twenty yards from Harry a horse was struck from beneath its rider, its belly burst open from stem to stern by the ball, its innards bursting from it like exotic flowers, glossy crimson, purple and black. Still with perfect discipline they withdrew at a measured pace, turning every fifty yards or so in case a charge should be launched, and lifting their rifles to return fire. The Royal Artillery had now come up into the space vacated by the Lights and the first blast of their roundshot appeared to pitch into one of the enemy guns.

The light infantry had now reached the brow of the hill and were also giving fire. The cavalry had no orders and could do nothing. The roundshot on both sides continued to fly and here and there to hit home, inflicting terrible damage. One trooper near Harry lost his leg at the knee, yet turned to ride to the back with the composure of a colour-guard, his face greenish-white with shock.

They rejoined their squadrons. The exchange of fire had lasted fifteen minutes, but had felt like hours – hours in which they sat in formation, proud and unflinching but without purpose, able only to sustain the shocks while the infantry and artillery pounded away manfully. After that quarter of an hour the enemy withdrew to their original position. The order came for them to do likewise. It was hard to know what advantage if any had been gained. A handful of wounded men had been transported, or made their own way, to the rear of the column. Half a dozen mutilated horses lay along the crest of the hill. Passing one of these – the first he had seen fall – Clemmie sidestepped and laid her ears back. Harry could feel her tremble and see the nervous gleam around her eye. The dead horse was a dreadful sight, not only because of the great scale of the injury but the look of its head, frozen in a scream of pain and fear.

After the scorching heat of the day the night brought a damp, autumnal chill which was welcome at first and then began to bite into their dog-tiredness. In the gathering darkness the Russian position was defined by the four-mile line of watchfires to the south and east.

They piled arms and bivouacked by the Bulganak in battle order, in readiness for an attack they were sure would come. When rum and meat rations had been given out the casks were broken up and used to make fires along with weeds, dry grass and nettles and whatever other kindling they could find.

The cavalry – Palliser said it was a mere sop to their professional pride – were set once more as an advance guard in the area between the stream and the melon field. They piled their equipment and picketed the horses facing inward around it. It was rumoured that Lord Cardigan had been almost overcome with rage at the command and had bawled at one unfortunate group of officers, who had only been obeying orders, that they were a bunch of old women not fit to wear the Queen's uniform. In this respect they themselves had got off lightly, but had nonetheless been moved twice by order of their furious and frustrated brigade commander, only to end up where they had been in the first place, and in rather worse humour.

Harry, Leonard Palliser and Hector Fyefield sat next to their saddles, wrapped in their cloaks, supplementing the meat and biscuit issue with chunks of pulpy melon and some unidentifiable soup knocked up by their resourceful cook.

Harry smacked his lips. 'Not bad.'

'Really?' Hector sniffed his soup doubtfully. 'Well, I suppose we might as well risk everything, for tomorrow, God and our commanders willing, we shall be allowed to fight.'

'That is if we're not attacked tonight.'

'We should have pursued them!' exclaimed Leonard, who

was personally outraged at the cup of glory having been dashed from his lips. 'They gave way before our fire and we were obliged to watch.' He slapped the ground in his indignation and held up his palm to show the mud. 'God in heaven, we're more likely to catch a head cold than the enemy at this rate.'

Harry surveyed the line of fires in the middle distance. 'They have a good high position and unknown numbers. We're being led on.'

'All the more reason why we should have given it to them when we had the chance.' Fyefield lay down with his head on his saddle, adding sarcastically: 'Be good enough to wake me if anything happens.'

Nothing did. It was a strange night. The mood along the Bulganak was uncertain, held on a knife edge between sombre reflections on the day gone by and apprehension of the one to come. Harry could not sleep. Even had he been able to clear his mind and close his eyes, there was no peace, for all the time the wretched stragglers were coming up from the rear, in carts and on foot, calling out the names and numbers of their regiments like lost sheep, with the RSMs up and down the line bellowing like angry beldames in response.

As he sat there he was astonished to see a small group of soldiers' wives come to the edge of the field to pick fruit. Two of them crouched down to cut the melons off the vines, and the others held out their skirts as panniers. They should not have been there but they must have walked a considerable distance on top of the day's march just to reach the field, and Harry did not want to be the one to put a stop to their resourceful foraging. And besides, there was a comfort in seeing the women, the solid practical grace of their movements in the small light of the fires, and to hear the soft sound of their voices, murmuring together. One of them laughed: it was a daring escapade.

To advise them that they were seen he himself rose, carrying his saddle closer to the fire, and they walked quickly away. When he lay down once more it was to thoughts of Rachel, whose time was getting close.

★   ★   ★

Ben Bartlemas had become her shadow. When he was not at school he was at Bells, and when he was not in the stable he stayed close to his benefactor. When others saw Ben, they knew that Mrs Latimer could not be far away. He didn't so much fawn upon her as maintain a watchful distance like a young animal that is finding its feet but still feels the invisible link with its parent. The head groom Oliver, a genial, gentle young man, was satisfied with his new charge, though when Rachel had first enquired about him Oliver had broken off from blacking the hooves of the carriage horses, and shaken his head in bafflement.

'He's a strange one, madam.'

She accepted the stool he offered her. 'Don't let me interrupt your work, Oliver. Strange in what way?'

'Thank you, ma'am.' He crouched down again, spat and rubbed at the shining hoof. 'It's a hard thing for me to say exactly . . . he's not like a child, is he?'

'I don't know. I haven't much experience with children as yet, but when I first encountered him he was falling from a tree,' Rachel pointed out.

'Oh, he's got plenty of nonsense,' agreed Oliver, 'but it's as though he's lived here all his life. Sometimes I have to remind myself that I've worked here man and boy for fifteen years.'

'You started with Colin, I suppose.'

'I did, ma'am.' He shuffled sideways on his haunches to the remaining front hoof. The horse seemed tranced by his attentions, her eyes mild and vacant, head hanging. 'I weren't that much older than Ben when I started out, thirteen or so, and Colin Bartlemas not a lot more than me, but a wonder with horses.'

'And Ben? Does he have the same gift?'

Oliver smiled to himself and shook his head, not so much in denial as bafflement. 'Couldn't say, ma'am, that's the truth. He's got something about him, and I've got no complaints – but he's a changeling if you get my meaning. One that doesn't fit with the rest.'

Rachel thought she knew what he meant. Ben was in almost every respect a boy typical of his age and class, but that respect in

which he did differ was strange and remarkable. He had a composure and an awareness of other people that transcended the
differences between himself and others. Even the stolid Oliver
recognised this, but she intuited that it was a quality most evident
to her. He slipped into her consciousness and her everyday life as
if he had always been there, and when he was not, she missed
him. Still it was hard to define exactly why this should be: she
simply felt at ease with him. If she was out of doors, drawing
or walking, or in the village, he could be at a distance of twenty
yards, engrossed in some boy's activity involving string, sticks
or a penknife, but if she looked his way he seemed to know it
immediately and always met her eye steadily, sometimes smiling,
sometimes not. He ran errands, but didn't pester for them. If she
was sad and silent he bore her company at a respectful distance,
acknowledging her mood without presuming to change it, providing comfort by quietness. If she was cheerful and energetic
he'd come closer and run and cartwheel like a clown.

Not everyone understood or appreciated this odd friendship.
The one who took it hardest was Cato, her faithful companion
through so much, who suspected (wrongly, but with some
justification) that he had been usurped and cast aside. Every
muscle and hair advertised his gloom. He seemed inconsolable,
until Ben in his innately sophisticated way befriended him.
This seemed to Rachel to be further evidence of a sensible
and sympathetic nature. For a short while, a matter of days,
Ben and Cato formed an alliance that seemed not to include
her, and only when the dog greeted him with an almost
unparalleled ecstasy was the triumvirate gradually returned to
its former balance: Cato closest in body, Ben in mind.

'Thank you for bringing Cato back to me,' she said.

'That's all right. It wasn't 'cause of you he left, it was
'cause of me.'

'That's true, but you won him over.'

'He's a good dog. He's the biggest I ever seen.' He patted
Cato's broad, massive head. 'Does he like babies?'

The wording of this question was discreet, but the meaning
clear. 'He's never known any. But I certainly hope he will.'

'I'll look after him,' said Ben, as if that took care of the matter. It was by no means clear whether he meant the dog or the infant, but Rachel strongly suspected it might be both.

The other person who was less than enthusiastic about Ben's presence was, not surprisingly, his sister Mercy, who made representations to her in the late afternoon one day when Ben had not been there.

'Is he being a nuisance to you, mum?'

'Not at all, Mercy. Quite the opposite. I enjoy his company.'

Mercy looked frankly sceptical. 'If you say so, mum.'

'I do.'

'Mother said to tell you to send him home if he's naughty or tires you out.'

'Don't worry, I shall. Tell your mother Ben's extremely welcome here. And that Oliver's pleased with him. But of course if I hear that he hasn't been attending to his school work then the arrangement will have to end. He knows that.'

'Yes, mum.'

It was clear from this exchange that Ben's mother and sisters took a somewhat less rosy view of the boy than she did, which was perfectly natural. Oddly, it was Maria who seemed to understand and accept the nature of the relationship. Coming round one morning to admire the nursery, she asked as they went up the stairs: 'But, Rachel – where is your little page?'

'He's at school.'

'How dull for him when he adores you so.'

'It will be much duller for him later if he doesn't go.'

'Ah, you're so sensible.' Maria sighed. 'And he is so like Hugo at his age . . . But be careful.' They paused on the landing. Rain slanted on the long window.

'What is there to be careful of?'

'When the baby arrives, everything will change.'

'I should hope so,' said Rachel spiritedly

Her mother-in-law's comment seemed to Rachel to be very like that which Ben had made about Cato. Except that in Maria's case there was no suggestion that she would protect anyone from anything.

★   ★   ★

At two a.m. Harry slept briefly. When they were all roused an hour later by the brisk hand of the RSM (orders had gone out that there should be no trumpet reveille or drums) it was still dark, but the quality of the darkness had changed: this was morning on the day of battle.

Along the swathe of land between the small rivers Bulganak and Alma the hundreds of twinkling watchfires gradually faded, like the stars, into the opaque greyness of approaching dawn. The fires had shown them, as nothing else could, both the enormous strength of the Russian force and the commanding nature of its position on the ledges south of the Alma. But as one by one the fires were extinguished, the might of the enemy seemed to become a phantom host, numberless and mysterious, that melted away with the dawn.

Harry ate, washed, checked his weapons and equipment, and waited, conscious of the tens of thousands of other men of both sides doing these same everyday things on a day which was not like any other. Such small, inconsequential rituals were preparation for a great pitched battle as much as for a day spent sitting quietly at home. From the cavalry position the two sides could almost have called to one another or sprung a surprise attack and hacked each other to pieces – and yet they shaved, cooked, tended horses, mended carts, cleaned tack, and talked in low voices of unimportant things. What strange creatures they were, who could be so wonderfully civilised when slaughter was the order of the day.

Betts came up with Derry, because Clemmie needed resting, and the lie of the land was an unforgiving series of ascending inclines which would need a stronger horse. He was as usual cryptic in his assessment of the situation.

'Pity you was held back yesterday, sir.'

'We might have achieved something . . . But no doubt Lord Raglan had his reasons.'

'Looking after you, sir,' said Betts with his deadpan look. 'Looking after you so you can go charging up them hills today.'

'We'll have our orders in due course.'

'Yes, sir.'

Watching Betts lead Clemmie away with his distinctive bobbing gait, Harry reflected that in another time and place his groom would have made a good royal fool, with his sly, droll candour.

Dawn turned into full day, bright and clear, but still no order came to advance. Outside the post-house which served as *ad hoc* staff HQ they could make out Raglan conferring with a number of his staff officers, all in their cocked hats, which should have meant business, but the content and conclusion of their deliberations remained a mystery. The delay spread its usual unease, not least because the climbing sun revealed once more the formidable strength of the Russian position. The grim and focused discipline which had prevailed at dawn began to crumble somewhat at the edges. A number of the TGs – travelling gentlemen civilians who were accompanying the army at their own expense and for their own reasons – gew restless and began riding about as if they were on a pleasure outing. The pony of one of them was very excitable, tossing his head, whinnying and calling like a stallion with a mare in sight, and his performance affected some of the less experienced cavalry mounts who in turn started to fuss. Palliser rode over to remonstrate with the gentlemen but his red face and bristling air on his return indicated that it had been an acrimonious exchange.

'Fools and idiots!' he expostulated. 'Worse than the women and with fewer manners.'

For upwards of four hours after sun up they formed ranks, wheeled and re-formed, but for some time it was apparent that the two allied commands had lost touch with each other and so like horses being brought to the line for a steeplechase it took several unwieldy attempts before the whole combined force was assembled in battle order and ready to advance. A large part of the British force was facing east to protect the baggage train and reserve supplies against a possible flank attack, and wheeling such a huge number of men through ninety degrees was a cumbersome and time-consuming exercise. Even the phlegmatic Derry was sweated up and it seemed increasingly likely that the Russian artillery, snugly ensconced in fortifications on the Alma heights, would simply lose patience, and all sense of fair play, and blow them to smithereens as they paraded about on the plateau like toy soldiers. Even Betts's dry prediction that the the Lights would be made to 'charge up them hills' seemed preferable to the edgy purgatory of waiting.

But it appeared that a charge of any sort was not to be. After the humiliatingly aborted advance of the previous day Lord Raglan had clearly decided that the precious cavalry were to go back in their bandbox until further notice, and when the armies finally advanced at ten-thirty, they were placed, along with the 4th Division, in reserve. Though from time to time the Lights had felt some sympathy with Lucan's awkward position, caught between two fires, there was scarcely a man now who did not secretly or otherwise refer to their divisional commander as Lord Look-on. All the fire and pride and brilliant turn-out in the world could not compensate for being relegated to the rear as the Light Infantry deployed from column into line in great swags of brilliant colour, and went forward to meet the enemy with trumpets sounding and colours snapping.

'It's a sight to be proud of,' said Harry to Hector Fyefield. 'Such order and discipline, and yet those men are going forward under fire.'

'At least we can say that we have experienced some of it too,' said Hector. 'The discipline under fire, if not the going forward.'

We sat on our horses, Rachel, among fruit trees, and watched. It was the strangest thing imaginable to know that good brave men were going into battle in their hundreds and their tens of hundreds while we looked on. After all the miles we have journeyed and the hardships we have endured it was bitter to be held back once again. The enemy fired the village of Bulganak above our position so that the smoke drifted amongst the trees and between us and the fighting, but we could hear the terrible clamour of artillery, and glimpse the walking wounded as they came back, emerging like phantoms from the smoke, some of them so terribly wounded that only shock and the strange effects of war can have enabled them to walk at all. One man had been struck in the side of his face, and his cheek and almost all his lower jaw were gone. If he lives, I thought, what will his life be like? Is there a wife or sweetheart in England who must accustom herself to the horror he has become? Another we saw without his arm, and another holding his intestines which would otherwise have spilled out on to the ground.

I am sorry, dear Rachel, to tell you these things, and indeed I may never send this letter at all, but I believe it was our sense of our own uselessness and helplessness that made these terrible sights so hard to bear. And because we had only the day before experienced something of the effects of roundshot, we could scarcely begin to imagine the plight of still more seriously injured soldiers who lay where they fell, unable to move. We understood that the order had been given that on no account was a man's comrade to pause to lend comfort or assistance, this was the task of the hospital orderlies who followed after. It therefore followed that there must be still more horrible suffering which we were spared the sight of.

And here is a strange thing – one of the TGs on our side, the man whose pony was so over-excited earlier – told us that he had been forward to the point where he had been able to view Telegraph Hill through his spyglass and had been able to make out a kind of miniature improvised grandstand in which sat quite a crowd of smart people, ladies included, with picnics and parasols and champagne and opera glasses, invited we suppose to watch the presumed rout of the enemies of Russia – ourselves. It seems to me strange and almost unbelievable that people should regard as entertainment an activy in which occurs the kind of hurt and destruction which we have witnessed – from nearly as detached a viewpoint – today. I have struck no blow, nor been struck, nor even approached the thick of this day's fighting, and yet I am more depressed and exhausted than I can ever remember. And this after a victory!

For it has been a victory, and a famous one, did I tell you that? In spite of what seemed like the unassailable position of *our enemy (and in this strange game it's odd that the enemy becomes 'ours' as if we had some proprietary interest in him) our army carried the day. It must be allowed that were it not for the heroic French and their wild and courageous* zouaves *who scaled the cliffs to the west we should not have been able to take the redoubts, but take them we did, at a terrible cost (though not as great as that exacted from the Russians). Our commanders were at all times courageous, Lord Raglan in particular. The staff officers are fine and conspicuous in their plumed hats and smart uniforms, but he cuts anything but a warlike figure in his blue frock coat, and nearly always proceeding at a dignified pace and speaking with a low voice. If he is cautious we know that it is because, although stiff in manner, he cares for and respects the men in his command.*

And what men, Rachel! Not only brave as lions but honourable also. For when the smoke cleared and we saw the side of the hill it was littered with more Russians than British, but our fellows went among them with their water bottles, giving what comfort they could without favour. It is a dreadful irony that war and battle should have the effect of making men savages one minute and angels the next. But it is not something that I shall ever forget.

Our frustration today is a two-edged sword. For can any man honestly put his hand upon his heart and say that he wishes to stare death in the face? I wonder.

CHAPTER FOURTEEN

'You will hear the beat of a horse's feet . . .
. . . As though they perfectly knew
The old lost road through the woods –
But there is no road through the woods'
Kipling, 'The Way Through the Woods'

Stella – 1996

Stella arrived at the Elmhurst composed. She had after all done this before. Boldly, she presented herself as an old hand: they politely ignored her. While she knew they were only doing their job she found this misplaced discretion excruciating – like being delicately brushed by the nettle that she wanted to grasp.

'Good morning,' she said, in response to the greeting of the slender Asian beauty behind the reception desk. 'I do hope you've given me a room on the garden side this time?'

The receptionist smiled a faint, sweet smile: she was not to be drawn. She wore a snow-white belted dress, too chic to be called a uniform; minute diamond earrings like grains of sugar.

'Later on, Miss Carlyle,' she enquired, looking up at Stella with Parker poised, 'would you like us to call you a taxi? Or have you arranged a lift?'

'I'll look after myself, thank you.'

'Good . . . fine. Well now, let me show you your room and then you can make yourself comfortable.' She came out from behind the desk. 'May I take your bag?'

'No, thank you.'

'This way.' She led the way to the lift, trailing a wake of some fresh, sophisticated scent. Her perfect matte skin and slender figure seemed untouched by the messy business of life, let alone the rude hand of man. Which was why, thought Stella bitterly, she was employed here. But if such an appearance was intended to be soothing, it did not soothe her. Beside this paragon Stella felt grubby and spoiled.

They stood in the lift gazing slightly upwards as one did for some reason in lifts. The receptionist caught her eye and smiled again.

'It's chilly out there today.'

Not as chilly as in here, thought Stella. 'I didn't notice.'

'It's the awful greyness,' the girl went on. 'I think I must be one of these light-sensitive people you read about, it completely alters my mood . . . Here we are.'

They got out on the second floor and the receptionist walked ahead of her, with the merest susurration of elegant underpinnings, down a corridor carpeted in a pale ash green, the colour of new life. At intervals on the walls were hung unthreatening modern paintings in restful colours.

'This is you.' The receptionist pushed open a door and stood back for Stella to enter first. 'Bathroom, television, telephone . . . No tea tray or mini-bar, I'm afraid, for obvious reasons, but later on you can let us know what you'd like.'

Later on. When one life had been terminated and another, currently on hold, continued.

'Thank you.'

'Do make yourself comfortable. If you wouldn't mind getting into your nightdress.'

'I know the form.'

Not a flicker. 'Take your time. And when you're ready, if you'd like to push the button someone will come and run through a few dull but necessary questions.'

'I know.'

'So.' The receptionist withdrew to the doorway with another whisper of silk, a breath of fragrance. 'If there's nothing else you'd like to know, I'll leave you in peace.'

'Thank you.'

Stella hadn't meant this to sound rude, but there was no reaction, and the door closed soundlessly.

If there was nothing else she'd like to know ... Only everything: the answer to it all. She dropped her bag on the floor and went to the window. As it happened they had given her a garden view: a reward, she surmised bitterly, for loyal patronage down the years. For those false starts, those secret, stifled endings. Those dead babies.

There was a trim flowering plant on the windowsill: a carefully considered message of welcome without the tasteless transience of cut flowers. Bleakly, she undid her bag and got out her pyjamas. She knew they preferred a nightdress but she wasn't going to buy one specially for this. There was something sacrificial about the process which the receptionist had described as 'making herself comfortable': undressing in this blandly tasteful empty room, laying her ragbag of everyday clothing on the back of the chair, getting into the pyjamas and dressing gown and sitting selfconsciously on the bed. It took her less than two minutes. She fiddled with the remote control and found piano music, something rippling and contrapuntal, it might have been Bach.

She put her feet up on the counterpane and leaned back on the pillows. No one knew she was here. They would only find out if she died, when it would no longer concern her. For a short while, at least until they took her down, she would occupy a little pocket of time and space in parenthesis as it were to the rest of life. She had not even, on this occasion, brought a book, since experience showed that she would not open it, nor be able to concentrate if she did.

The music finished on a flourish, and the presenter began to speak. Stella switched the radio off. The ensuing silence was thick and dense. The double-glazed picture window admitted no sound from outside, and she could hear nothing beyond the heavy door. She might have been alone in the building.

Alone, except for the baby inside her.

It was the first time she had permitted herself a thought like this, and it shocked her. Looking down at her still painfully

392

concave stomach she seemed to see right through the material of her nightclothes to where that small cluster of cells lay in their warm watery chamber – pulsing and growing to the rhythm of her own heart. Not just her own cells, but those of another person. And added to them the mysterious, unknowable factor which would produce an individual unlike any other. Or, under other circumstances, would have made.

She had tried often over recent weeks to imagine what Robert's reaction would have been to her pregnancy. She had stood him up like a tailor's dummy in her mind's eye and tried different moods on him for size. It was possible to imagine rage, and jubilation, and a kind of furious mixture of the two which was characteristic of him: less easy to picture indifference or measured argument.

This was the third time she had undertaken a termination, a fact of which she was not proud, but neither could she pretend remorse. The first occasion had been the result of an early fling, scarcely more than a two-night stand, exhilarating but out of the question. Neither of them had taken any precautions. There was no question of a third night, let alone a shared future. The decision had been made for her.

The second time had been not long before she had left Sorority. She had come off the pill and was using the coil – she was one of the unlucky two per cent. She could not even have said with any certainty who the father was, since she was sleeping with two men regularly (one of them Gordon) and there had been a handful of other casual encounters in the relevant period. The prospect of bringing up a child on her own scared her half to death and the thought of handing it over for adoption made her queasy, so it was with a grim sense of inevitability that she'd come to the Elmhurst again.

This time was qualitatively different. She knew whose it was. She also knew that there had been a faint, scarcely realised possibility that she might have spoken of it to Robert, that some sea-change might have happened, and that whatever was said might have brought them closer. But that possibility had been stillborn: stifled in the womb by his smug treachery.

She had not spoken to him since that night at the theatre. He had called several times but she had filtered all calls through the machine. He had rung her doorbell twice when she had been in, but she had not admitted him, had lain curled like an ammonite on her bed with her hands over her ears . . . And he had written her a letter. The letter, lying in her hand like the hand of a child, passive and confiding, had tempted her most. She had even got as far as opening it, but something stern and challenging in the first sentences had stopped her in her tracks. 'Stella, what's going on? Why can't we at least speak to one another? What hope is there if—' She had thrown it away, burning with unshed tears. She had created this situation, allowed it to develop, suffered its vicissitudes – enough was enough. And he had the gall to speak of hope?

And yet lying here in the enclosed stillness of this impersonal room she felt for the first time a direct connection with the life inside her. She closed her eyes and seemed to feel the minute, insistent patter of its heartbeat, the drip-feed of life – from her – through the umbilicus, the curious separateness of this relentlessly growing stub of flesh . . .

She put up a hand and pressed the call button. It made no sound in the room but she supposed that in some distant official zone there was a discreet buzz. She laid her hand on her stomach. Incredible to think that her attenuated, part-worn body could be the source of life, wrapping it secretly and tenderly in fluid, nurturing it, protecting and preserving it without her conscious will according to some atavistic natural order.

There was a tap and the door opened.

'You buzzed, Miss Carlyle?'

'I was told to when I'd changed.'

'That's right.' The nurse was plump and fair with a french plait. 'I have to fill in this form if you wouldn't mind answering a few questions.'

'No.'

'Right.' The nurse gave a little sigh as if empathising with the tedium of it all, and pulled up a chair. 'Let's see.'

Between them they confirmed her name, age, address, nationality, marital status (a phrase whose opt-out implications

Stella had always found insulting), and – even more incredibly in this day and age – religion.

'None.'

'It's in the extremely unlikely event of an emergency,' explained the nurse. 'Shall I put C of E?' She pulled a face. 'Same thing, really.'

'I have just enough respect for it to think it's not.'

'Fair enough'

They covered next-of-kin, allergies and medical history. The nurse, well trained, betrayed not a flicker of interest in the answers, writing everything down in its appropriate space in her clear, round hand. She took Stella's blood pressure and temperature and checked that she had neither eaten nor drunk that day. She asked, with no perceptible change of tone, how Stella would like to pay.

When the form was completed she popped her pen back in her pocket. 'Good. Now let me explain the procedure to you, it's all very simple and straightforward . . .'

Did they have no idea, thought Stella, how bizarre that sounded? Was irony deficiency a prerequisite in employees of the Elmhurst?

'. . . about one hour after the premed we'll take you down to theatre, and next thing you know it'll all be over and you'll be able to have a nice cup of tea and whatever you want with it.'

'I can't wait.'

'We like you to stay in for at least an hour afterwards and then you can go. Did Sunita ask you about transport home?'

'She did. I'm going to get a taxi.'

'Would you like us to order that for you when the time comes?'

'It's all right, I'll call one myself.'

'Fine.' The nurse's tone implied that they wished all their patients could be as easy as Stella. 'So – you've got everything you want?'

'Yes, thank you.'

'I'll be back to give you your premed in—' she glanced at the watch on her left breast '—about half an hour. I'm afraid that's when we'll have to ask you to put on one of our horrible gowns . . . In the meantime I'll leave you to it. Don't hesitate to buzz again if there's anything.'

When she'd gone, Stella turned the radio on again. The music now was baroque – wind instruments soulful as voices, keening a lovely, plaintive tune. She lay on her side and gazed out of the window. From here she couldn't see the garden, only the slightly stirring treetops, the uneven line of some domestic roofs and the glint of a distant office block. against a sky bruised with unshed rain. She laid her hand once more on her stomach which in this position sagged and swelled slightly with the passing of the years. This, she thought, was how it would feel – later, when even the most meagre and unaccustomed frame stretched to accommodate its burden.

Soft, unwilled tears slid down her cheeks, the sweat of her secret heart.

Sunita had just checked in a scruffy, dull-eyed, nineteen-year-old model, barely recognisable without the aid of lighting, stylists and clever camerawork. The model's surgically enhanced breasts sat like the halves of a melon, hard and round on her bony torso. She was accompanied by her boyfriend, a bullishly confident young man in a black suit and open-necked shirt. When she showed them into their room he threw himself down on the bed with his shoes on and turned on the television while she talked to the girl: he was, thought Sunita, a complete pig.

Mr Parsloe had a full list, it was a busy day. Returning to her desk, Sunita scrolled down the screen and marked off the model. When she looked up Miss Carlyle was standing there. Sunita smiled.

'Is everything all right?'

'I'm checking out.'

'That is your right,' said Sunita coolly. It made her uncomfortable when people backed out. They had been doing too much thinking, they didn't want what was on offer. As long as the women kept moving through the system the Elmhurst was providing a much-needed service. When the occasional one withdrew, it exposed the nature of the business. Sunita, a vegetarian, compared her squeamishness to that of meat-eaters about factory farming. It gave her what she wanted, but she preferred not to know.

Miss Carlyle agreed that it was certainly her right.

'May I ask,' said Sunita, 'why you have taken this decision?'

'I've changed my mind.'

'Excuse me, I have to ask this – but are you sure?'

The other woman's expression said that this enquiry was beneath contempt.

Sunita persisted. 'Time is a factor, as you know, and you are, let's see, fifteen weeks.'

'I'm aware of that.'

'I'm afraid,' said Sunita, 'that we shall have to ask you to pay for the room, which cannot now be used.'

'I'll pay for everything.'

'You do understand.'

'Perfectly.' The credit card was already tapping and turning impatiently on the edge of the desk. 'Will this do?'

Stella took a taxi home. She made sure that she was several hundred yards from the Elmhurst before hailing one, but even then she felt that her rucksack, like a prisoner's brown paper parcel, must shriek her provenance aloud. The cabbie made a few attempts at conversation, looking chirpily at her in the driving mirror, but gave up when she didn't respond.

She asked to be set down at the corner of Alma Road, and went into the Coffee House. She sat at a table in the window and ordered a large cappuccino, inhaling the hot fragrance of freshly roasted and ground beans. The smell, and the accompanying hissing, bubbling frothing sounds, seemed stronger and louder than before, as though her nose and ears had been suddenly cleared. When the waiter in his long white apron brought her cup she seemed to see each slowly spinning creamy bubble, each grain of powdered chocolate and spiralling tendril of fragrant steam, in the sort of detail more usually provided by dope. The first sip – the dry nip of the chocolate, the fluffy kiss of foam, the scalding sweetness of the liquid – was a revelation. She wondered if the foetus was experiencing the same heightened sensations or whether it was sleeping tranquilly, oblivious to its narrow escape.

A young woman came in with a toddler in a buggy. She parked the buggy alongside the table next to Stella's while she went to order at the counter. The toddler sat huddled in its outdoor clothes like a guy. She had no idea what sex it was, but its bright brown eyes were fixed on her with unblinking intensity. The woman came back with a cup of tea and a chocolate muffin in cellophane. She unwrapped first the toddler, then the muffin, then broke off a piece and held it out.

'Jack . . . Jack? Wake up, here you are.'

Jack took the cake and pressed it to his open mouth as if snogging it. Lumps of sponge fell on to his quilted legs, crumbs clung in a brown halo round his lips. What went into his mouth he sucked with a faint, adenoidal sound. His eyes remained on Stella, though rather absentmindedly as if he couldn't quite remember why. He had glossy black hair worn in long curls, which he hadn't got from his mother who had straight mousy strands and red cheeks. No wedding ring. She sipped her tea and gazed out of the window, glad of the break. She didn't eat her half of the muffin and when Jack griped and fussed he got another chunk. She was eking it out, piece for peace.

After a couple of minutes she suddenly looked straight at Stella, raising her eyebrows with a 'know us next time?' expression.

'Sorry,' said Stella. 'I was admiring Jack.'

'You what?'

'He'll be a ladykiller once he's learned to eat cake nicely.'

'He's only twenty months,' declared the girl in an aggrieved tone. 'What d'you expect?'

Rebuffed and misunderstood, Stella went to the counter and paid for the cappuccino. Toting her rucksack she didn't go straight back to Victoria Mansions but along the high road to the baby shop. This was how she thought of it, as though it sold babies, which in a way it did. Up till now she had regarded it not just with indifference but with a kind of superstitious aversion, like the temple of some alien cult. Now, she told herself, she had better get over that.

She walked in feeling starkly conspicuous as if she'd just left jail. Her age, her clothes, her telltale rucksack, did they mark her out as an untouchable, a woman who had stepped back from the brink in the nick of time? In fact the other customers were in the main not the petal-skinned dewy-eyed lovelies of magazine advertisements and TV commercials, but females of every age, shape and kind, from scarily youthful teenagers to women older than herself, some looking as if they might give birth at any moment. No, she told herself, she was anonymous here. Whatever she might feel, no one could tell from looking at her that she was a pregnant woman. She could be an aunt, a friend, a sister – a grandmother, for God's sake, to judge by some of the extravagantly fecund schoolgirls.

It was the merchandise that awed and shocked her. So much *stuff* – could one tiny infant possibly need or want this amount of clobber, so many things, such a variety of clothes, toys, gadgets, transports? It was inconceivable, obscene. She could not imagine a future occasion on which she herself would come here and walk out with the huge plastic sacks of goods she saw being borne away. She stood transfixed by shelves full of feeding bottles, teats, sterilisers, heaters, thermos flasks, spouted cups, dummies, teethers and dishes, pushers, bibs with troughs and bibs with tapes, and innumerable cunning compartmentalised carriers to put it all in. And then stacks of bedding – sheets, duvets, pillows, rubber sheets, cot bumpers (whatever they might be), papooses, cocoons, cellular blankets and lacy shawls. Numberless nappies, hosts of tiny clothes and shoes, fleets of prams and buggies each more elaborate than the last . . . Did each item, she wonder, perform a different function? Was one therefore required to have one of each? Or to make a selection? And if a selection, on what basis? How did all these women *know* what to get? And – Jesus wept! – how did they afford it?

The simple, animal connection she had made with the baby was dwarfed by this clamorous multitude of objects. In the middle of it all and in rising panic she closed her eyes for a moment as she had done in the clinic, to recapture those tender, profound feelings which had stolen over her. The other shoppers flowed round and past her, there were no nudges or bumps, no signs of impatience. Her heartbeat steadied.

She felt a hand on her arm. 'Everything okay?'

A child of about sixteen stood next to her, hugely pregnant. Her round face was a work of art, elaborately painted, pierced and studded.

'You okay?' she repeated. 'Do you want to sit down?'

'No, thanks. I was – trying to remember something.'

'Right . . .' The girl gave a slow nod, her eyes on Stella's face. 'I'll let you get on with it then.'

In front of Stella was a branching display unit hung like a Christmas tree with bootees, socks, mittens and bonnets in cellophane packets. The items were tiny as doll's clothes. Stella selected a pair of minute white lacy boots threaded with gossamer-fine ribbon, and went to pay. At the next till a woman was unloading a trolly-load of purchases, the bip-bip of the items going through was like morse code. Stella stuffed the boots in her coat pocket and set off for home.

Back in the flat she left her coat and rucksack in the hall, took the boots out of their packet and laid them on top of the piano. She gazed at them: tiny and fragile as snowflakes resting lightly on the symbol of her splendid independence. The first concession to the awesome changes she had set in train.

In silence, without music, she walked slowly from room to room. In each one she stopped and gazed, trying to imagine what it would be like to share it with someone else – or no, not to share, for sharing implied equality. She was going to give it up. For her child this would not be a chosen, but a given place. Not Stella Carlyle's apartment, but home. Every second of every minute of every day her child would be here, looking to her and her alone for food, drink, warmth, entertainment and love. It would take her and her care for granted, not realising that without her it would not live. The brutal simplicity of the deal made her head spin.

Returning to the living room she saw afresh the undemanding space she had been so careful to preserve, the sense of comforting impermanence which had kept her here for fifteen years. This would change. There would be clutter – she thought with cold dismay of the baby shop and its contents. There would be noise and confusion not of her making. Instead of a retreat from the passionate discipline of work and the turmoil of people there would be demands and responsibilities.

She crossed to the windowseat and sat down. The baby boots trembled slightly as she passed as if they might be sensitive to the presence of their future owner, like one of those plastic desk-flowers that moved in response to voices.

Stella reminded herself that in her rush to embrace and smother her fears she had neglected to take into account the very thing that had prompted her momentous change of heart. There would also, surely, be unconditional love.

The hospital carpark had a ten-mile-per-hour speed limit which Robert had once found irksome. Now he had no trouble sticking to it. He had scarcely exceeded ten miles per hour since turning into the access road. The great concrete complex of the Health Trust which used to fill him with energy and excitement these days oppressed his soul. It was a measure of his state of mind that even he could not ignore. Playing for time, he parked in his usual place, switched off the engine and sat listening to 'The Ballad of Lucy Jordan' a lament both sympathetic and sardonic, for lost opportunities.

The song was by Leonard Cohen, whom Robert greatly admired, not least for being able to write so alluringly about pain. The singer on this recording was a former sixties rock-chick, more renowned for her star-fucking activities than her handful of breathy minor hits. Now however she had reappeared on the scene, ravaged but still ravishing, her cropped hair swept uncompromisingly back from a face on which was gouged every bad trip and lost weekend. The soft, babyish voice had been replaced by a world-weary rasp fit to break your heart. He could not these days bring himself to listen to Stella but this, he thought, was how she might sound in the future when he no longer knew her, and when her voice bore the scar tissue of all the years between.

When the song finished, Robert switched off the stereo and sat in silence for a few seconds out of respect, as well as apathy. Then he gathered himself, his briefcase and his coat and set off to do battle with blindness.

He knew what they said about him – that Mr Vitelio was the best in the business but had no bedside manner. In this he felt himself to be a victim of contemporary political correctness. In a touchy-feely world perversely driven by economic imperatives he was too quick, too focused, in fact too hellbent on curing people, for comfort. What people seemed to want was a ruthless weeding-out of cases according to some bizarre value-for-money criterion, and then a soft-soaping of the remaining ones so that they went softly into the good night of partial or complete blindness, equipped with kind words, social services and a range of useful gadgets. Robert's preference was for doing as much as was humanly possible in the time available, and moving on. He was a top-notch clinician but his stated view on, for instance, counselling was that it was meretricious bullshit that kept its victims mired in self-pity instead of pursuing busy and productive lives.

Others, he knew, thought he protested too much – that he himself liked to present a moving target. That the reason he did not wish to listen to other people's problems was an unwillingness to consider his own. He conceded that this was probably correct, and was not ashamed of it – one measure of successful functioning was not whether one had shortcomings but whether one turned those shortcomings to good effect.

He had weathered the complaints because he had made no mistakes. There were no points on his licence. Not one error of clinical judgement, no diagnostic fudges nor botched treatment. He was spot-on.

But at the moment he knew he was pushing his luck. Instead of being his whole focus, his work had become a sideshow, a lightning conductor for the feelings he so infamously chose to keep hidden. He had fouled up in one area of his life and seemed increasingly likely to foul up in another if he wasn't careful. Always a doer, a sublimator, a worker-through, he was not used to the paralysis which currently afflicted him.

Today he had a full programme of laser treatments, an area in which he was the acknowledged king, the fastest gun in the department. He quite simply saw each tiny ocular blood vessel with more clarity and zapped it with greater speed and accuracy than anyone else. It was close, concentrated, pinpoint-fine work with no margin of error. Also, he was aware how painful it was for the patients. It was policy to speak of 'discomfort', but that was bollocks – the treatment involved a persistent small agony that could make strong men whimper. To this end, in his view, speed was of the essence. It made his own eyes water to watch the slow, gentle, tortuous work of some of his younger colleagues, and he'd been known to step in and finish the task at whirlwind speed.

But today, as he consulted his list and asked for the first patient to be shown in, he had the unsettling premonition that they would not be getting his best.

In the end it did not take a sledgehammer to break the deadlock, and his paralysis, but a handful of featherlight words spoken in an almost inconsequential tone.

As he opened the front door that night, Sian was coming down the stairs. She had just got changed, and was pulling down the bottom of her sweater over her cord jeans. He could see the way her well cut hair was still settling back after bouncing free of the roll-neck.

'There you are,' she said.

'Hallo.' He hung up his coat and kissed her cheek, which felt cold. 'Don't ask.'

'I wasn't going to.' She went ahead of him into the kitchen. 'Or not that, anyway.'

'That sounds ominous.' He followed her, watched her take

a bottle of wine from the fridge, pour herself a glass, lift it enquiringly in his direction. 'No, thanks.'

'Something stronger?'

'In a moment perhaps.' He knew he didn't have to prompt her, she was no games-player. She sat at the table, composed, her long-stemmed glass emerging like a flower from her linked fingers. He waited.

'I am going to ask,' she said, 'whether you feel we should separate?'

'I don't know,' he replied, the shock bleeding slowly through him. 'Do you?'

'Well ...' She frowned slightly, considering. 'I'm not happy.'

He was awed by her simple truthfulness. 'I'm sorry.'

'Yes.' She sounded wistful. 'Me too.'

'Do you, as they say, want to talk about it?' Christ, he thought, listen to yourself. But she knew him well enough to let the cliché pass without comment.

'I think we should.'

'This is because of me.'

'Partly. You and another. But I wasn't happy anyway, before that.'

He let the first part go, perhaps hoping that she would, too. 'You never said.'

'I didn't think about it very much. We got on with our lives, didn't we?' He heard, like a bell tolling, her bleak use of the past tense. 'But now that there really is someone else – I mean someone who is really important – I realise that I wasn't. So maybe it's time we called it a day.'

Her weariness, her stoicism, her goddam' *patience,* made him suddenly angry. It was a relief to raise his voice.

'Don't you think, Sian, that we're worth a bit more than this saintly chucking-in of the towel?'

She picked up her glass, said briefly, before sipping: 'You didn't think so.'

'How did you find out?'

She gave him a cool look. 'You're completely transparent, Robert, it's one of your greatest charms.'

404

'Don't be so fucking patronising.'

She didn't reply. But as she lifted her glass again there was the merest tremor.

'I'm sorry,' he said. 'I've got no right to say that to you.'

'You have every right. It's called having a relationship.'

'So you concede we still have that?'

'Of course. But it's no longer so important to us as some others.'

'I see.' He'd lost his way, as she had intended. And while she sat, he remained standing, like a recalcitrant employee reporting to the boss. He said hotly: 'So since it seems we've established what my problem is, would you care to return the compliment?'

'There is no one else, in the way that's generally meant. Just the rest of my life – colleagues, patients, my friends, our friends . . . I no longer care for the feeling that we're deceiving them.'

He dragged out a chair and sat down, because towering over her with his temper rising was too uncomfortable. 'Is that what we've been doing?'

'Oh, yes. Surely.'

Her manner was smooth and hard. He wanted to get between the plates of her defence and make her admit to something, anything, which did not imply that she had simply tried for this long but had now given up.

'You must speak for yourself. Whatever other agendas there have been I've always had the greatest respect for our partnership.'

She eyed him mildly, shaking her head a fraction, spoke softly as though to an agitated child. 'You pompous prick.'

He wanted to kill her. 'I aim to please.'

'I know, obviously, that you've not been faithful for twelve months together for the last – what? – ten years of our marriage . . . But spare me your "respect".' The inverted commas were audible. 'Please.'

'So why didn't you say something before? Or did you simply enjoy the sense of superiority that virtue brings?'

'You're right, that is pleasurable. In its way. But curiously, feeling superior isn't quite enough – even for me. And when I realised that your emotions as well as – the rest, were engaged elsewhere, I thought it time to speak up.'

'I see.'

There followed a silence. To Robert, his wife's silence seemed tranquil, almost glacial, while his own was tumultuous with confused emotion. His turn now to feel superior. She was after all a cold bitch.

'Are you,' she asked, 'going to give her a mention?'

'I'm not sure what purpose that would serve.'

As he said it he seemed to hear a cock crow. How could he not speak Stella's name when it had been the pulsing base line of his mind, his heart, his time, for so many years? How could he leave Stella in the lonely darkness of the wings and not bring her into the spotlight that was her natural place?

'It would,' said Sian, 'since you ask, be kinder to her.'

'It is not a question of kindness.'

'No, that's certainly true.' She was sensitive as a hair-trigger, able to turn his every word woundingly against him. 'And anyway it's not as if I don't know who she is – she's Stella Carlyle.'

He felt an explosive thud of shock. 'Yes.'

'I found out when we went to see her at the theatre. One of those small, extraordinary coincidences waiting to happen. You remember I was late joining you because of the queue for the Ladies? I went to buy a bottle of water, and there was someone at the desk hoping for a return. I heard your name mentioned because a ticket had been kept for you but not been used. In the end it was agreed to give your ticket away. I believe I knew instantly, but from that moment I noticed all the signs about you. You couldn't possibly hide them. I know you very well, Robert. And I have a very long memory.' She paused, but he could think of nothing to say, and she went on. 'When you're roused your hackles rise, did you know that? Your hair ruffles just here—' she put her hand to the back of her neck '—and your voice changes. You actually smell different. The minute the curtain rose I felt it on you.'

'It wasn't . . .' His voice was thick and he cleared his

throat. 'It wasn't a situation I sought, or that I was happy with.'

'I'd seen her before, did you know that? I don't mean on stage. Years ago when we were holidaying on Ailmay. I had no idea who she was then, but hers isn't a face one forgets.'

'No.'

'My only comfort is that she is so different. Different from me. At least I've retained my – what shall we say? – my individuality.'

He was suddenly exhausted by her cleverness, her precision, the way she was laying his life out before him like tarot cards.

'Sian . . . please.'

'One thing I would be interested to know. How does she feel? She doesn't strike me as a woman likely to be satisfied with second best. Has she put you under pressure? If she meant so much to you, why didn't you tell me?'

He considered the answer to this last question. 'I don't know. She's extremely independent. And also . . .' He fumbled for the words, which she in the end supplied.

'You thought it best to hang on to what you'd got. It's all right, Robert, there isn't a single thing that's new in any of this. Extraordinary how the old cliché comes up fresh when it's we who are experiencing it, isn't it?' She turned her head and gazed out of the window for a moment. 'But given all that . . . we must decide what's best to do.'

He wanted, for his own sake more than hers, to tell her that it was over; that Stella had taken herself away from him. But keeping that to himself was his last shot at dignity, like a screen anti-hero concealing, honourably, a fatal wound.

'We obviously need to be apart. At least for a while.'

'No.' She shook her head as if getting rid of a fly. 'It should be one thing or the other.'

He had lived for so long with her calm detachment, it was shocking to realise what had been running beneath the surface like an underground stream.

'Shall I go now?'

Gradually, with this brief exchange of words, the ball that

407

had been thrown so high was returning to earth, bouncing lower and more swiftly, finding its eventual resting place.

'I think—' she closed her eyes momentarily, a slow blink '—I think that would be precipitate. I mean, you would need to pack. To think, and so on.'

He knew what she meant. To say goodbye.

They had supper, taking things from the fridge and the cupboards and assembling them with unconscious teamwork. Cheese on that plate, tomatoes in this, the small dish of black olives from last night, butter for him, low-fat spread for her, another glass, a can of beer, a bottle of water, a loaf of bread, apples . . . There was a sacramental air about the putting together of this, their last supper under the old dispensation. They were quiet, and Sian turned on the radio and allowed the harmonious conversation of chamber music to ease the silence.

Over supper they spoke of family matters – of Seppi and his wife Denise, and Natalie and the children, and about the house to which they had planned improvements. It was as if they had opened a long-closed box and were taking out the small objects that it contained one by one, gazing at them and turning them over in their hands to reacquaint themselves with the shape and texture before replacing them carefully. Robert thought, A shared life is so fragile and yet so durable, like human hair or spider's web. It can withstand so much, and then the merest touch breaks it.

Towards the end of their meal the telephone rang and Sian went into the drawing room to answer it. He had scruples about leaving his plate, glass and cutlery in the dishwasher for another day, and so washed up their few things by hand, and put them away before making coffee. He reflected on Sian's admission that she had seen Stella before, on Ailmay. That must have been the cold early spring that he had heard Stella sing in the pub and boldly said that, Yes, he was there. So the seeds of this day had been sown in all three lives at the same time, and now all three lives were separating again, one from another. It was impossible not to see it as a story, with a desolate completeness.

He took the coffee into the drawing room, where she was still on the phone. He poured each of them a cup, put hers down at her elbow and took his into the study. He had no paperwork to speak of, but the sudden fastidiousness that had prompted him to wash up meant that he did not wish to sit with the newspaper, waiting for her to finish her conversation.

The study was a big room at the side of the house, with a window overlooking the small front garden and the street. Sian's area was perfectly tidy and ordered: his was chaotic. On her table her computer waited tranquilly, a dove floating and turning in slow motion on the dark, sleeping screen. On his lay an ugly slew of open and unanswered mail, papers, brochures, prospectuses, his laptop sullenly shut, a half-eaten bar of chocolate, a pottery mug full of chewed biros and felt-tips. It looked like not so much the desk of an untidy worker, as of a transient one – the detritus of a person disinclined to settle. Now, he thought, I should sort this out.

He began tidying, at speed – throwing away sheaves of paper, moving others aside for closer inspection. The curtains weren't drawn and he caught sight of his reflection in the darkened window: a strange, frantic figure, a man in flight, at home nowhere. His longing to speak to Stella was so strong that he actually picked up the phone, only to hear the voice of Sian's senior partner, and her crisp: 'We shan't be long'. Quaking with unhappiness he banged the receiver back and clasped his hands behind his head, his face clamped between his arms. The pain swelled and heaved around in him, his temples throbbed with it, his stomach contracted. It was like a birth.

'So after the triumph,' said George, 'what now? Time off for good behaviour?'

'Something like that.'

Stella was reluctant to tell her secret. Not that she wished to broadcast it widely at such an early stage, but having decided, for moral support's sake, to let George into her confidence, she found it difficult to do so. The reason was that while she'd kept it to herself all things had seemed possible. She might tell Robert, he might find out, he might simply storm back into her life and demand to know what was going on. She was dismayed to have uncovered this streak of unreconstructed pre-feminism in herself: perhaps it was pregnancy and its associated hormone-rush that made her so long to be overtaken by events. Or maybe – and this was something she only allowed herself to regard fearfully, at dead of night, from the corner of her eye – maybe she wanted his unconditional, overwhelming love more than anything, ever, in her life before. She had thrown down the gauntlet of her decision in the hope that by some mysterious telepathic means he would know, and come forward to pick it up. Having distanced him so throughly, sheer stubborn pride prevented her from giving an inch.

She was spending the weekend with George and Brian. On Saturday Brian (having taken the golden bowler and a job in human resources) had a course in Cirencester and the older children were not due out from their respective boarding schools until Sunday, so the two sisters had a day to themselves with three-year-old Zoe. The family had moved a few months earlier to the converted stable block of a large, rundown country house. The stable block was nicely enough done by a smart local builder, but it was the house itself, with its faded and neglected English beauty, that spoke to Stella.

In the afternoon they went for a walk around the unsympathetic post-and-wire fence that marked its boundaries.

'It's had a chequered history, poor old thing,' said George in answer to Stella's question. 'In the dim and distant it was owned by a family called Latimer, there's scads of them memorialised in the local church. Then as I understand it it was a convalescent home in the first world war, some sort of lunatic fringe experimental school in the twenties and thirties, and requisitioned by the army in the second war. Since when it's fallen on hard times rather, as you can see.'

'So who lives there now?'

'It's actually owned by the council and they let it to the Prior Foundation. No, I'd never heard of them either, but they run arts courses. All nice people, what we see of them, but I don't know whether it's a long-term arrangement or whether some beady-eyed moneybags that we wot not of is waiting in the wings ready to turn it into a country club or worse.'

They were standing about a hundred yards from the house at a point at the junction of the old driveway and the tarmacked Bells Yard development access road. Stella gazed at the brick, amber and grey in this light as a winter sunrise, the ample leaded windows and rugged chimneys. And for an instant she, the quintessential townie, the woman to whom the countryside was a fearsome wilderness, entertained a picture of living in such a place. Zoe was hanging on to the top wire of the fence, legs bent, bobbing and bouncing, and Stella thought: In three years' time my child will be like that

'Tubs! Come on, let's show Stella the wild wood. Tubs—' George went and retrieved her daughter from the fence and plonked her down between them.

'Hold my hands!'

'Only if you promise not to swing, it does my back in.'

'I promise!'

They each took a hand. Zoe at once began to swing. 'No, said George, 'walk properly, we're not going far. Why don't you go and hide behind a tree and see if you can jump out and give us a surprise?'

'Okay!' Zoe ran away, George pulled a 'so-sue-me' face. Stella thought: Remember this.

'Our little ray of sunshine,' said George drily. 'Our adorable afterthought.'

'She's sweet.'

'But you're hellish glad she's not yours.'

'I didn't say that.'

'You don't have to. The further I travel along the great road of family life the less I seem to know.'

'You do wonderfully well. Your lot are a credit to you.'

George paused for a moment, eyes wide. 'Did I hear aright?'

Stella shrugged. 'These things need saying from time to time.'

'You're going soft in your old age . . . Hang on, there she is, prepare to act startled.'

Zoe leapt out from behind a treetrunk and they obliged with an outrageous pantomime of mock terror which was well received and sent her scurrying off to repeat the exercise. They followed her into the wood, along a footpath marked by a post with a yellow arrow.

'This is part of the grounds,' explained George, 'but the council have done the decent thing and preserved the footpath. You can walk all the way down into the village from here, but it's a steep climb back and I don't fancy piggy-backing Tubs up the hill.'

The path wound between the trees pleasingly, as if following the footsteps of people who had meandered that way over the years. They didn't hurry. Zoe darted, and hid, and was distracted by an enormous fungus which demanded that they stop and pay their respects. It stuck out from the side of a treetrunk like a spongy discus embedded in the bark, its pallid upper surface spotted with mould, underside dark and leprous, edges delicately crenellated.

'It's humungous!'

'The perfect word for it,' agreed Stella.

'Will it poison me?'

'Not necessarily.'

'Only if you take a bite out of it.' George gave Stella a look. 'Sorry, no room for discussion on that one.'

Remember this, thought Stella. They walked on.

'Why Bells?' she asked.

'That's rather nice. Apparently on a still Sunday if the calendar's right you can hear the bells of seven churches. Though whether that still applies in the age of the group parish and dwindling congregations I couldn't say. I must test the proposition some time.'

'We could do it tomorrow.'

'I suppose we could.'

Stella chose not to notice her sister's quizzical glance. After another ten minutes in the wood they emerged on the brow of the hill with the village below them to the left and the White Horse opposite.

Stella sat down on the short grass with her arms round her knees. 'May we gaze?'

'Good idea. Tubs will be happy, she can orbit the site.'

They sat side by side, facing the horse. It was true – once a halt had been called Zoe seemed to settle, as though their fixed position were a kind of anchor. She pottered about, examining insects and tweaking off flowerheads to make a bunch, talking to herself. Remember this.

George cocked her head on one side. 'Are we sure it *is* a horse? I'm no expert but it doesn't look like any horse I've seen. And from what I gather horses in those days would have been sort of squat, with bog-brush manes. Not elegantly prancing steeds.'

'Mmm . . .' Stella reflected. 'It's a horse of the mind. A fantasy horse.'

'I shall hold that thought.'

'This is a lovely place, George.'

'We like it. But it's a classic case of falling for the romantic, impractical option.'

'Is it so impractical?'

'Oh, you know . . .' George picked a plantain and attempted to fire the head off. 'Damn, I used to be brilliant at that. No, it's the position. The kids are approaching the age when I shall be running a non-stop taxi-service to farflung town centres.'

'But they like it?'

'She does.' George nodded at Zoe. 'The others don't really think about it. But believe me they will when their social life bites.'

Zoe rejoined them and sat down next to Stella, pressed confidingly against her leg.

'I'm getting a pony.'

'Are you?' Stella glanced at George for confirmation of this.

'Maybe.'

'You said!'

'Probably. It depends.'

'You always say that.'

'Because it's true. Everything depends.'

'On what?'

'Everything else.'

This philosophical assertion seemed to bring the exchange to an inevitable, if not a satisfactory, conclusion. She would remember. They sat a while longer, with Zoe affecting moodiness a little way off, and the shadows of high clouds making the horse look as if it lay beneath flowing water. The peacefulness of the moment, the ease between the three of them, the sense of being cradled in the landscape, created a kind of spell that stopped Stella from speaking.

No rush, she thought. No rush.

On Sunday morning, when Brian had gone to collect the children from school, taking Zoe with him, and George was preparing the fatted calf, Stella went to see her parents. George, in her downright way, had made it clear that while they would normally have been invited to lunch as well, this arrangement had the double advantage of pleasing the old while releasing the young from the embarrassment contingent upon dealing with their grandfather on one of their few days out from school.

Mary and Andrew were sitting in the conservatory that was their pride and joy, drinking coffee. The cafetière and milk jug were on a folding tray-table between them. This regular drinking of proper coffee, a commodity previously reserved for visitors and best, was one of several small recent changes instigated by Mary for reasons which Stella suspected had more to do with her own state of mind than her husband's.

Another of these changes was Andrew's appearance: George had mentioned it. Their father's interest in his toilette had been at best sporadic and whimsical, but until relatively recently Mary had allowed him to get himself up and dressed no matter what that entailed in the way of odd socks, inappropriate t-shirts, undone flies and wrongly buttoned cardigans. She who was never less than elegantly turned out herself had exerted iron control in adjusting (with the greatest possible tact) only what was dictated by the need for decency and dignity. Only when the process of dressing in an ordered way became a trial for him did she intervene, and now a happy hour or more each morning was spent on this joint enterprise to the perfect satisfaction of both.

She had not, however, Stella noticed, attempted to impose her taste on her husband. So today where Mary was immaculate in Scotch House chic – a pale blue polo-neck and grey straight skirt – her husband wore joggers, a white shirt and a maroon sleeveless jumper, all spotlessly washed and pressed.

Mary sprang up and embraced her. 'Stella – lovely! Look, I even brought an extra cup just in case.'

'What's with the just in case? I said I was coming.'

'Yes, but I never take anything for granted. Darling, it's Stella.'

'I can see that.'

'Hallo, Dad.' She stooped to kiss him, noticing with a pang that his hair had been cut too. Mary had always performed this task, but never been allowed to take much off. In this one area she had not been able to resist indulging herself. The shorter cut made him look younger.

'How's life?' he asked.

'Oh, fine.' She took her coffee. 'I'm down staying with George and Brian for the weekend.'

'Good show.'

'Speaking of which,' said Mary, 'the run's ended?'

'Yes.'

'So will you get a bit of a break now?'

'As long as I want, really, boredom and the bank manager permitting.'

'Shall you take a proper holiday? Can you take off somewhere nice with friends?' This was one of those questions which displayed a certain quixotic hopefulness in her mother's attitude. The 'with friends' reference was a tactful, if wistful, assumption that there was no one special. Mary had never been a parent who weighed her children down with force of expectation, but occasionally Stella was aware that what she most wished for them was to be happy, in the straightforward way of her own experience. In the case of George this might seem, on the face of it, to have been achieved, but in Stella's it was more complicated. And at this moment, more complicated than they could possibly imagine.

'I might,' she said. 'You never know.'

'And what about work, have the offers been flooding in after your triumph?'

'It's good, I can be as busy as I want to be.' She thought she had better proffer some unsolicited information to keep interrogation, so to speak, at bay. 'We've been invited to do a short season at the Parade on the Park, and if that's not smart I don't know what is.'

'What fun!'

Andrew, who had been gazing at his daughter throughout this conversation, leaned forward.

'Tell me,' he said, 'where are you these days?'

Stella's heart lurched. In that question she heard his uncertainty, his instinctive, fumbling feeling of the way, like the hands of a blind person on her face. He knew something, but could no longer recognise what it was.

Mary topped up the coffee, eyes lowered, not intervening.

'Well,' said Stella, 'I'm still living in London. Though I must say after seeing George's new place I'm tempted for the first time by the idea of moving out. We've finished the West End run, so I'm taking stock.'

'We're going to Shanghai,' said Andrew. 'I'm taking some of the boys.'

'Are you?' Stella kept her eyes on his face. 'When will you go?'

'At the end of term.'

'It's something we've always wanted to do,' said Mary carefully. 'But whether it will come off or not is anybody's guess.'

Stella was caught in the cobweb of their gentle conspiracy. 'It sounds like the trip of a lifetime. Can I come?'

'No children allowed,' said Andrew. 'Positively no children. Grown-ups only, I'm afraid.'

Even if she'd been tempted to take issue with this contradiction, her mouth was stopped by her mother's first direct, warning look.

'Dad, you're preaching to the converted,' she said, and left it at that.

'How do you find the brood over at Bells?' asked Mary.

'I've only seen Zoe so far. She's seems great, but what do I know? Brian's gone to spring the others from jankers for the day.'

'That reminds me, I've got some things for them to take back. I'll go and get them right now while I think of it.'

As she left the room, Andrew smiled at Stella. 'Are we having boys for lunch, then?'

It was an old joke, and her father in turn sounded so much like his old self that for a split second she was disorientated. But with her laugh, his smile faded, and he leaned forward once more with a frown.

'Tell me,' he said, 'where exactly are you these days?'

Driving back to Bells she thought that this was worse than a bereavement. Worse because her father was still alive but lost to them. Not gone, as the pious hoped, to a better place, but trapped in one that was just out of reach. The fact that his old self was still not quite obliterated, that from time to time it showed itself and pressed its hands, like a mime artist, to the invisible barrier, made it still harder to bear.

She thought: I am about to bring a child into the world who will know its grandfather as a mad old man. But children accepted such things, didn't they? And new life was hopeful, a stake in the future. It would make Mary happy.

Everything depended on everything else.

They spent a nice day. A day in which Stella strove, for once, to be passive and allow herself to be carried along, to achieve a sense of where she stood in this pattern of family life. She was glad, now, that she had said nothing to George the day before. She wasn't yet ready, nor fully at ease with her decision. There were other and more important considerations than telling her sister. She had first to talk to herself.

The roast pork and apple sauce, the fresh raspberry trifle and ice cream, and the wonderfully crusty Cheddar cheese, were consumed, washed down by two bottles of Brian's special-offer New World Shiraz. The two older children were at first hyper and loquacious, showing off for Stella's benefit and drinking (though not finishing) French lager straight from the stubby. Under the influence of good food and grown-up conversation they reverted to type and retreated, when coffee appeared, to sprawl on the sofa and watch *Beauty and the Beast* with Zoe.

Brian had a glass of port on the strength of not having to make the return trip at six o'clock.

'The other side's turn,' he explained. 'I've done my bit.'

It was half-past three when they left the table and Brian declared that they should all stir their stumps and take the kite out on to the hill. George said it was only him who wanted to fly the kite, Zoe was too young for it and Kirsty and Mark too old: Brian replied that okay, he would fly it and the rest of them could watch. Normally Stella would have resisted these overbearing tactics and persuaded George to stay in, with loose talk, more wine, the Sunday supplements and an old musical. Today she acquiesced, with the result that the others were less mutinous than they might otherwise have been.

They went out of Bells Yard in the opposite direction from the one she and George had taken the previous day, up a Tiggywinkle thread of footpath that wound diagonally across the hill overlooking the village, with Brian piggy-backing Zoe in the lead, she accompanying George who carried the seagull-kite, and Kirsty and Mark bringing up the rear.

Brian called a halt at a point where the hill shelved and the path levelled out for a few hundred yards with a broad shoulder of grass on either side. On the crest above them stood a small ruined building, like a tor.

Brian got the kite into the air and they took turns at flying it, feeling the thrilling tug of the wind, making the seagull climb, turn and swoop. Each of them felt they were doing it for someone else, making a present of their skill. Watching the kite bound them together, they ceased to be a slightly fractious and unwilling post-prandial rabble and became a group, a team, all eyes fixed on the sky.

Remember this, she thought.

Everything depends on everything else.

★   ★   ★

It was at about eight o'clock when she was only halfway home that Stella began to feel tired. Not pleasantly sleepy, but as though her blood had turned to lead. She pulled into a garage and bought a bar of chocolate which she ate there and then, and almost immediately afterwards fell asleep. When she woke she was startled by her surroundings – the lights, the other cars, a man in a leather jacket peering at her from beside the pumps – and also by the length of time she had slept: it felt like hours and had been only fifteen minutes.

The nap stopped her eyelids drooping but the aching exhaustion remained. Crawling into London in the slow stream of Sunday night red tail-lights she had to exert tremendous concentration to keep going, to co-ordinate the usually unconscious small motions of driving, to read signs and judge distances. When she finally reached the sanctuary of her flat she was trembling with fatigue and went to lie on the bed, with her coat still on. Being there in her own surroundings, safe at last, she reminded herself that she was, after all, pregnant, and that perhaps this was to be expected.

When she woke, it was to a dull pain in her lower stomach and back, which instinctively drove her to the lavatory. By now she was shivering convulsively, her teeth were chattering and her hands, clutching her coat round her as she sat there, were blue and white.

The baby, what there was of it, fell out of her with terrifying ease, like so much waste material voided. As it poured from her one pain ended and another began. She sat hunched with her fingers pressed to her eyes, waiting for it to be over, praying for it to end: the sound and the sensation of loss . . . of losing it.

It didn't take long, a couple of minutes. She rose slowly, with one hand braced on the wall, and wiped herself. She yearned for a bath but retained some long-ago warning about hot water, that she might faint, or haemorrhage. She tried not to look down as she lowered the lavatory lid, but could not avoid a glimpse of the dark matter, part liquid, part solid, that had only hours earlier been new life, the focus of so much. Fiercely, she pulled the plug and listened to it swirl and suck away. Sweating and freezing she sat on the floor for a couple of minutes until the cistern filled, and then flushed again.

She couldn't bear to check a second time. She had to do something normal. Unsteadily she walked into the living room, pressed 'Play' on the answering machine and lay down stiffly on the chaise longue, her eyes closed.

'Stella, it's me, Robert. Please let me see you. Please let's talk. Everything's changed. We may not have the right stuff for a sensible partnership, but I believe we could have love, and that's all you need, some say. Please listen to this. I love you. Don't ring me at home, I'll call again. 'Bye. Goodbye? Au revoir.'

Don't ring me at home. So not quite everything had changed, then. Not for him.

Everything depended on everything else.

No right stuff. No love. No baby. She'd lost it.

CHAPTER FIFTEEN

' . . . *rights inherent and inalienable,*
among which are the preservation of life, and liberty,
and the pursuit of happiness'
—President Thomas Jefferson, Declaration of
Independence

Spencer 1946

Afterwards, when people said 'during the war' Spencer got two images in his head, and they weren't exactly of combat but of two enclosed spaces. The narrow, pulsating metal cylinder of the P-51, in which his body fizzed with adrenalin and his mind was diamond-bright and clear; and the tranquil domestic interior of the Ransoms' cottage where every response was muffled by secrecy and even sensation itself was ambivalent. In the first he looked down on a physical world made simple by speed and distance. The stillness of the second had afforded an altogether different view – the dim, uncharted landscape of the mind.

When the war ended, the impression he retained of that time and those places was like the memory of a dream, imperfectly understood but bleeding its colours into the rest of his life. The people he recalled in a series of vivid mental snapshots, frozen in their particular time and setting: Frank on his bunk, his nose in a book, Ajax curled in the crook of his arm . . . Si winding up to pitch, his eyes wicked with intent . . . Mo beaded with sweat in his Santa Claus suit . . . Davey hanging round the sentry box with his hands in his pockets, pretending not to give a damn. And then there was Janet, that first evening, holding his hand over her heart. 'Please . . . Please . . .'

And Rosemary – well, she was more than a snapshot. She lived in his head, flickered like a small pale flame that wouldn't go away. He knew now what people meant when they talked about carrying a torch. She'd seemed secretive, and yet she was in herself a secret. It was strange to realise that he knew something about her that she did not know herself. A hostage, perhaps, to fate.

In Moose Draw, things were pretty much the same; and those that weren't seemed changed only because he was. His mother looked a little older, but he saw in her face that he himself had altered profoundly. On his first night at home he caught her watching him with a kind of wary respect. That made him sad. They could none of them turn the clock back; he wanted to bring her with him, not to leave her behind. The proud and generous composure which she had displayed on his departure had temporarily deserted her. Then, she had maintained that composure to make him feel like a man. Now that he was one, he sensed she was thrown off balance.

It was slightly different with Mack, who perhaps felt that becoming a fully paid-up member of the great club of manhood was something they now had in common. Spencer was glad of this, but didn't want his mother, his old ally and confidante, the person for whom the water was wide, to be excluded by it.

To this end he saved telling her about his journey into the past until the next day when Mack had made an early start to go work on a pick-up at one of the hunting lodges, and the store wasn't yet open – Caroline said it was quiet these days, and anyway they had a young fellow who came in and helped.

It was like old times, with him sitting at the kitchen table with his mother, except that she didn't bustle as she used to do; she was quite happy to sit there and drink him in along with her second cup of coffee.

He said: 'There's something I haven't told you about.'

'You haven't told me anything – not really.' She smiled,

to show that it was not a criticism, but a pleasure yet to come.

'I found the house.'

'Oh! Did you—?' He could see in her eyes, along with delight, the anxiety that he himself might have been disappointed. 'It's just a very ordinary house.'

'Not really. The couple who live there run it as a rooming house now.'

'I can't imagine that.'

'They let three rooms on the first floor. They had a vacancy when I was there, so I stayed the night in one of them.'

'You didn't! You actually slept in the house?'

He nodded. 'Like a baby. The landlady was a good sort. When she found out why I was there she didn't even charge me.'

'Was it — oh, what am I saying?' She shook her head at her own foolishness. 'I was going to say, was it changed? But how would you know?'

'You forget, I feel I know it. I had it up here.' He tapped his head. 'And to begin with I couldn't make it out, I couldn't see what you'd told me about, because the neighbourhood's so different.'

'Tell me.'

'It's all built up these days — there are factories in back of your road, but there's a sports field in between them and the houses. And where you described the wood . . .'

'It wasn't much of a wood,' she put in apologetically. 'A sort of little island that had got forgotten. It seemed special to me because I was only little myself, but maybe I made too much of it.'

'No, I don't think so . . . But it isn't there now. They've made a park. I walked round it. As a matter of fact I was told to keep off the grass.'

'That's awful.'

'Grass is pretty much at a premium round there, they have to take care of it.' He smiled, jerked a thumb at the window. 'The opposite to here.'

She laughed. 'That's true. So — go on.'

'One thing, they had a whale's jawbone over one of the paths. You ever hear of that?'

'No!'

'Some old guy who lived nearby donated it to the park.'

'What about the pond?'

'There was a pond. Kind of formal, with fish in it. But the landlady remembered the one you talked about, she called it a dewpond.'

'That's right . . .'

'And there were one or two old trees that they'd kept from the original wood.'

'It was so pretty.' She was there now, in her mind's eye.

'I can imagine. She took me up to the top floor of the house, it's where she and her husband have their room now, because of the guests—'

'Cissy's room!'

'—and when you look out of the side window you can see the tops of the old trees, and not the rest of the park. So it was like when you were a kid. I could imagine being you looking out of the window.'

'We used to kneel up there for hours . . . Cissy used to tell me stories. I can remember always being happy up there.'

There were tears in her eyes. She started to say something, perhaps to thank him, and to stop her he held out his hand and she hesitated for a fraction of a second before placing hers in it. That was the difference, of course. Once, she had held out her hand, open-palmed to receive and enfold his smaller one. Now, it was the other way about. But they had always understood each other.

After the brief celebration of homecoming, the being hailed as a local hero with his picture on the front of the *Monitor*, the being described as a 'veteran' along with the other young men who'd come back, the rest of Spencer's life yawned before him. He'd forgotten, until now, just how slow was the pace of life in Moose Draw. The dream was over – he'd lived it, and come back safe, a new life had to be set in train.

Spencer discovered a new and healthy regard for the sloggers-on, the people who without fuss lived peacefully in small places and stuck faithfully to small tasks, and raised kids, and looked out for their folks. It took a certain kind of courage to do that, a grace and humility which he wasn't sure he possessed. As a boy, he had always somehow assumed that his mother would not end her days in Moose Draw, but be taken up, as in books, by some itinerant English aristocrat and carried away from an uncomplaining Mack to live out her days as the chatelaine of a big house. But though as he grew up he knew that no such thing would happen, he was still shocked to realise that Caroline really was going to see out her allotted span as wife of a small-town storekeeper and local jobbing mechanic.

Needing something to do in the short term, he went back to helping Mack, and soon discovered that business was down to a mere trickle, and a slow one at that.

'It's only outa kindness they ask me now,' Mack told him as they stripped down Judd Ellison's motorbike in the side lot one warm afternoon. It was companionable work – the warm, oily smell of the machinery, the feel of the metal parts, each distinct, some sleek some grooved and knubbly, their two pairs of blackened hands reviving old habits of co-operation.

'And because you do a good job.'

Mack pulled his mouth down. 'Pretty good, I'd say. Thorough. But slow. There's a big new filling station and works on the other side of town, they got three men working there, they can turn any job round in half the time I can.'

'The personal touch,' suggested Spencer. 'People know you, they trust you – and you charge a fair price.'

'A damn-fool price.'

'Then hike 'em up.'

Mack shook his head. 'I'd be pricing myself out of work. Same with the store. There's a self-service place in town now, right bang in the middle, and a five and dime . . . we can't compete.'

'Sure you can.' Spencer, unconvinced, described a banner in

425

the air with his hand: 'McColl's Convenience Store – Personal Service With a Smile.'

Mack, resolutely unsmiling, peered closely at the carburettor. 'Your mother and I are too old to start all that sort of thing.' He might have been referring to some bizarre perversion.

Spencer knew that this was his cue to step into the breach – to say that he would take on responsibility for the store and the repair business, and launch them into the brave new post-war world with the McColl colours flying proudly. He felt it, though there was no special tone in Mack's voice and he didn't look at Spencer in any particular way. This was the moment, all right. But he let it pass. A kind of panic stopped his throat. Later, he thought perhaps it hadn't been panic but simple common sense. If his parents' business needed turning round, there was someone out there in Moose Draw who would like nothing more, whose heart would be in it and whose head would be suited to it. But that person wasn't him.

Common sense or not, he burned with embarrassment during the long silence that followed. And it was left to him to end it, by saying lamely: 'Something'll come up. You could still sell it as a going concern.'

'We live here,' said Mack simply.

'You could get a little place out of town.'

Mack didn't reply to this. Spencer had the squirmy feeling he used to get as a boy when Mack disapproved not exactly of something he'd said or done, but of something he *was*, something he could do nothing about. They let it lie there among the motorbike parts, the bit that didn't fit.

Unloading a box of canned fruit on to the shelves that evening, when Mack was listening to the radio out back, he put out a few feelers on the subject to Caroline.

'Time must be coming you'll want to get away from all this.'

'Oh, I don't know.' She was running a soft polishing cloth over the counter. 'It's my life.' She dusted the till slowly, almost affectionately, as if wiping a child's face. 'The only one I know.'

'That's not true.' He'd said it before he meant to and instantly regretted it, but she didn't break rhythm.

'The only one I care to know. I'm quite content with it, Spencer.'

He could sort of see how it was with them – that to his mother this life was a safe haven after what had preceded it. While to Mack it was his pride, his identity, how he'd provided for his own.

He said, to get it out of the way: 'I don't think I could be content with it.'

'No.' Now she did stop, and looked at him levelly. 'No, you mustn't.'

'I know it's what Mack would like—'

'He'll understand.'

'I hope so.'

'He'll understand because I do, and I'll explain.'

'Thanks.'

She continued with her cleaning, her back to him now as she ran the cloth along the shelves behind the counter. 'So what will you do?'

'I don't know yet.'

'You should take your time, Spencer. We'll be glad of the help while you make up your mind.'

'And what will you do, Mom?'

She gave a little laugh. 'What other people do! Carry on as long as possible and then sell up.'

Something occurred to him. 'Mack could get work at the new garage. I bet they'd be glad to have him.'

'I don't know . . .' She folded the duster carefully and laid it on the counter, smoothing it with her hands. 'He might be too old. And he's awfully used to being his own boss.'

'It's worth thinking about. I couldn't suggest it, but you could.'

'Maybe.'

He sensed her divided loyalties – his commonsense suggestion against Mack's stubborn independence, her desire to be fair to both – and was filled with love and admiration. But he had lost his old childhood habit of intimacy and directness with her, and all he could say was, 'Mom, I really appreciate you being so understanding.'

To which she replied: 'It's what I'm here for.' And that, at least, was like old times.

There still remained the problem of what he was going to do, and it had become more urgent now that it was generally accepted he would be moving on. He continued to help Mack, but this was now seen by both of them as a mere token job. Spencer was asked to do less and less and felt his position to be an awkward one. He'd stated a wish to be independent, Mack seemed to be saying, now he must act on it.

There were other more tangible imperatives. Spencer took only a bare minimum from Mack, and money was running out. He bought himself a boneshaker whose only claim to glamour was that it was a convertible, so that if he chose he could inhale the clouds of dust as he clattered along the country roads. But at least he was free to come and go, and to think, in a way which he couldn't with Mack and his mother watching him.

He drove out to Buck's and was dismayed by how small and shabby it seemed. The cabins reminded him of a scaled down version of the Church Norton airbase, and the main house was dilapidated, with a sagging porch and scabby paintwork.

Boldly, because it all seemed so long ago, he rang the bell and was standing there waiting for an answer when a voice behind him said: 'You could wait till hell freezes over there, son.'

He turned round and saw that it was Abel Stone, the oldest of the team of labourers and handymen before the war.

'Abe – hi there.' He came down the steps, saw that he wasn't recognised, and added: 'Spencer McColl, remember me?'

'Spencer . . . Well, put it there boy. Well, I'll be . . . So you came back to us safe. Read about you in the paper.'

Spencer felt the hard, callused palm as they shook hands, and Abel gripped his elbow in a display of real emotion. Spencer was touched, but embarrassed. The conquering hero stuff seemed so undeserved and out of place when all he'd done was to escape, and do the one thing he'd always dreamed of.

'So what goes on, Abe?' He nodded at the house. 'All closed up?'

'Sold. New owners coming in any day.'

'You still got a job?'

'Sure, they kinda bought me up with the lot. Old timer like me, bit of local colour, I guess . . . But the place'll be closed till next spring, all kindsa improvements.' Abel spoke the last word with a disparaging emphasis. 'Swimming pool, movie theatre, new cabins. Customers'll never know they left town.'

Spencer shrugged despairingly. 'That's progress.'

'Maybe. I ain't complaining. So long as I got something to do.'

'They keep the horses?'

'Some – Charlie and Ross are looking after 'em and there'll be new stock coming in in the spring. And I forgot to say – there's going to be a plane doing joyrides out over the mountains. How about you flying that, Spencer? Give the dudes a bit of a thrill. I reckon the new owners'd be pleased as punch to have an air ace taking the customers up.'

'I don't think so, Abe. I'm not sure I could work here again – never go back, can you understand that?'

Abel cast him a wry look. 'Guess so. But then, what would I know? I never moved on. Never wanted to.'

'Mind if I take a walk around?'

'Liberty hall, no one's to stop you 'cept me.'

Spencer set off up the canyon. Away from the ranch itself the evidence of disuse was different, not deterioration but the opposite, a greedy reassertion of nature, so that the track was narrower, and the scrub and branches held out whiskery hands to drag at him as he passed. After a mile and a half or so he came to the first picnic lodge almost without realising it, for the neat wooden frame was netted with convolvulus and half-hidden by long grass and weeds, so that it looked like a cottage from some child's storybook in which he might find people in an enchanted sleep. But when he went to take a look it was all he could do to force the door open, and the only living thing was some animal that scuttled violently away, stirring the air with a strong, musky smell.

He pulled the door shut again – he wasn't sure why – and continued on his way. As the canyon sides got steeper and the path rose, so it became less overgrown. He climbed till he emerged on to the open hillside and now, suddenly, he was in a time warp, for here nothing had changed. He made his way to Lottie's stone and sat down next to it, feeling a sense of companionship. The famous writer had died a couple of years ago in sad and murky circumstances which hinted at alcoholism and suicide, or Spencer might have expected him to come riding up the slope out of the woods.

It was peaceful and Spencer's mind, which had felt cramped and restricted since his return, began to expand and examine the possibilities. Perhaps it was remembering the writer, or just being here, above the treeline and away from Moose Draw, but he began to sense a pattern of connections between past and present. He thought of his mother as a child, gazing out of the gable window and over the treetops of Victory Gardens. She had dreamed of boundless possibilities out there, beyond the water, and with the advent of his father realisation of the dream must have seemed within her grasp. There had followed disillusion, rescue, and reality, with all its limitations and compromises. He'd come up here as a boy to look out over the trees and speculate about Lottie, and think about what it might be like to escape Moose Draw – a small place in a vast landscape – with no idea what that escape might be. He remembered the writer's comment that the frightened little mare had not really wanted freedom. Spencer McColl had wanted freedom all right, but been scared of it. The barely contained ferocity of the captive bucking horse had showed him what was really meant by the need to be free. And then he'd seen that little plane, wheeling and swooping ecstatically in the blue, the closest thing to a bird that a man could be, a paradigm of freedom, and that had encapsulated the dream. That was a perspective which would put Moose Draw in its place and turn Wyoming from a prison into a map, softening into haze at its edges, full of endless possibilities.

He lay down on his back and stared into the sky. Right on cue an eagle appeared and did its stuff – a long, slow glide followed by a watchful turn, pinions spread like fingers. He could see only that elegant black silhouette, but way up there the eagle's opaque yellow eyes would be making out every hair on his head, the buttons on his shirt, his own eyes, slitted againt the light . . .

He closed them. He'd lived his dream – had flown up there like the eagle, had seen not just towns but whole countries reduced to a map, had experienced the heady combination of breathtaking freedom and stifling enclosure that was man-made flying. And with it the awesome complexity of half-understood relationships that had opened up dark and untravelled spaces in his own head. One dream had been fulfilled, but the effect of its fulfilment had been to leave more questions unresolved than answered. There was another dream out there, he could almost feel it at his shoulder, hovering near, close but not showing itself. Yet.

He was possessed by a sudden surge of happy certainty, a release from the tension and frustration that had been building up since his return. He was suddenly sure that this other dream would reveal itself, that some inspiration would be vouchsafed him. He only had to wait.

Nonetheless, he was prompted that evening to look along the bookshelves in his room and revisit the work of the famous writer. Spencer had three books of his: the novel they had studied at high school; an autobiographical volume dealing with the writer's experiences in the Dardanelles in the first world war; and another of twenty collected columns and articles spanning the writer's career, on topics ranging from cookery to cattle-driving. This last had belonged to Frank, it was a little legacy that Spencer had willed to himself, and now it was the one he chose, and went to lie down on the bed with his ankles crossed to browse through it.

He left the window open and the sounds of the main drag floated in: kids playing, the sound of cars slowing down after the rollercoaster of the country road, and that of less-tuned engines ticking over while their owners gazed under the hood; a dog barking; a distant telephone bell, still unusual enough in Moose Draw to be noticeable; a woman calling that supper was ready . . . And the smells, the small local ones of cooking and gasolene and cut grass, scattered randomly over that big, pervasive scent of prairie and mountain – the smell, as Spencer thought of it, of space. In a moment there was the pungent whiff of weather-proofing fluid, and he heard the rasp of Mack's brush as he began painting the store front, an annual ritual associated with this time of year.

Caroline's soft quick tread on the stair, and then she appeared in the doorway.

'Spencer?'

He lowered the book. 'Hey.'

She came in and stood, arms folded. 'What are you read-ing?'

He showed her. 'I went up to Buck's this afternoon.'

'It's a little bit sad up there at the moment.'

'Sure, but that'll change soon enough.'

'Is it good? The book?'

'Haven't read it yet.' He was aware of wanting her to go, and ashamed of himself for wanting it. 'I brought it back from England.'

She came in and sat on the end of the bed. It reminded him of when he was sick as a child. Then, she used to massage his feet through the bedclothes.

She nodded towards the book. 'He died not so long ago.'

'I know.'

She smiled. 'Am I in the way?'

'No. No, of course not.'

'Yes, I am.' She pressed her hands down on her knees and smoothed them away from her. She'd always managed to keep her hands pretty, no matter what, but he noticed with a pang that there were one or two brown spots on the backs. Suddenly embarrassed by the potential intimacy of the situation he closed the book with a snap and sat up.

'You are not.'

'I'm not complaining,' she said. 'It's just that you're not sure where you are at the moment.'

There was no comment he could make on this, so he

remained silent and she added: 'And I don't know where you are, either.'

'Right here.' He was deliberately misinterpreting her, and they both knew it.

'You miss the Airforce.'

'Not really . . .' He considered this. 'Maybe. I wouldn't want to go back to it, but I don't know what to replace it with either.'

'You have to take your time,' she said.

'Sure. But I need to get on with something.'

'And you don't need to stay here, Spencer. We shall be all right, you know.' She smiled. 'We may be dunces, but we got this far after all.'

He knew what she was doing, relieving him of responsibility, telling him not to worry, but it was having the opposite effect, unsettling him. Just now he wanted her to leave, but in his way he needed her and Mack, more than they needed him.

'What do you mean, dunces?' He gave her a nudge, lightening the atmosphere.

'We haven't been very adventurous with our lives.'

'They've been good lives, Mom. I had a war, that's all.'

Suddenly and wholly unexpectedly she put her arms round him, and laid her head in the crook of his neck and shoulder. It was the first time he was fully aware of how much smaller she was these days. His head used to rest on her shoulder like that: he had outgrown her.

'Mom?' Not sure of her mood he touched her back awkwardly with short light stroking movements. 'You okay?'

She nodded against him, but meant no. He was apalled, thrown off balance, prayed she wouldn't cry. He had never seen her cry, didn't know how he'd cope with it. But luckily for him the moment was interrupted first by a loud 'Damn!' from outside, and then Mack's voice at the door calling, 'Cairlahn! Cairlahn, you got a Band Aid?'

She straightened up and rose in one quick, smooth movement. 'Coming!'

Spencer didn't see her face, but then he didn't try that hard.

For a few minutes he listened absently to her dealing with Mack's splinter, the familiar tinny sound of the kitchen first-aid box, the splash of tap water, their combined murmurings, Mack explaining what had happened, her saying gently he should be more careful, something like that . . . Spencer hoped she wouldn't come back up.

But of course she didn't. The spell was broken, they would both pretend their separate moments of weakness had never happened. In a while he heard the boisterous sounds of Vic Lander's City Variety on the radio, and from outside the sibilant rasp of Mack's brush working once more on the fence. Cautiously, he lay back down and picked up the book.

He read several pieces rapidly. He was taken with them, not so much by the style, with which he was familiar, but by the content. What struck him was that the writer had done many things, and also that many of them were quite ordinary. Sure, he'd been a short-order cook and a crack shot, and ridden the white water on the Colorado. But some of the articles were about everyday stuff, the sort of thing anyone might experience, like having to bathe a cat when it got fleas – it made Spencer laugh out loud – and getting nervous over a date with a pretty woman (having met the writer in person Spencer found this last hard to imagine, but it was still entertaining). There was a kind of note that was struck, it said everything better than you could have done but it also said this guy was on your side, he saw things the same way you did – it was all part of life.

There was one chapter about riding a freight train right across the centre of America. Or at least riding several, hopping on and off, being part of a hobo community, trundling, walking, talking, moving on, striking up friendships and leaving them behind, easy come, easy go . . . Spencer was enchanted. The evening began to darken and he had to switch on the light. It was only when a flittering cloud of moths and bugs had gathered round the light, pattering on the shade and meeting sticky, hissing deaths on the bulb, that he tore himself away from the pages and went to pull down the blind. There was an enormous moon like a Hallowe'en lantern in the sky and Moose Draw was reduced to a little huddle of dim lights beneath it. The sky was not quite dark and the great craggy shoulders of the mountains stood out black against it.

Not bothering with the blind he turned out the light and went downstairs. Caroline was in the parlour, Mack was washing his hands at the kitchen sink. He had a way of holding his big hands under the running water when he was rinsing the soap off, just holding them there, first palm up, then backs up, like hands in a Bible picture, but for the Band-aid. He turned the tap off, gave them a shake and wiped them on the towel. He still carried a faint smell of weather-proofing.

'What you been doing?' It was a companionable enquiry, not a nosy one, and Spencer took it as such.

'Upstairs reading.'

'Any good?'

'Yes.' Spencer weighed up how much to elaborate. 'By that writer I met years ago up at Buck's, remember?'

'I do,' Mack nodded, adding disapprovingly: 'Did away with himself a year or two ago.'

'He was okay. He can really write.' There was a pause. Mack took a mug from the shelf and the coffee pot from the range.

'Want one?'

'No, thanks. I think I might go walk for a while.'

'You do that. Moon's a sight to see.'

Mack went through to join Caroline, and Spencer left him to tell his mother where he'd gone. He let himself out of the back door and walked quickly across the yard and up the out-of-town road until the surface grew rough and he was out of range of the lights.

Now he slowed down, and breathed deep. His footsteps were like a steady whispered heartbeat. The moon seemed even bigger and brighter as he left the town behind, a giant benign face gazing down on him. The spaces opened out on either side, a pale night-time sea of grey grass. Here and there in the middle distance he could make out the dark shapes of longhorn cattle like ships becalmed on its surface. Further on a startled horse stood near a fence, its ears acutely pricked, watching him. Half a mile beyond that two deer crossed the road in front of him side by side, quite leisurely, seeming to float, their slender legs wavering beneath them in the moonlight like waterweed. Once or twice a brisk trundle of movement at the side of the road advertised a racoon or a skunk, its snuffly business interrupted.

He was reminded again of the littleness of Moose Draw, set down at the foot of the mountains as if the doughty pioneers had looked up, marvelled, and gasped: 'That'll do'. He remembered how in England, even in the blackout, you could cycle from one village to the next and be able to see the one you'd left and the one you were going to, even if it was only the church spire. Here, one mile from town, you could smell the forest, and the rock, and the icy tumbling rivers of the mountain fastness to the west, and sense the awesome empty roll of the open country to the east. Miles and miles of miles, distances that were both terrifying and protective. It may have been called America, but it was just land, brute nature, massive and enduring. No wonder they saluted the flag and declared their Oath of Allegiance over and over – what lay between sea and shining sea was way beyond what any puny human colonists could call theirs. It was impossible to imagine it threatened and beleaguered like England. Surely it would just twitch its huge hide and shake off intruders like a fly . . .

These thoughts drifted around in his head at first randomly and then starting to form a pattern. It pleased him, he began to make more deliberate comparisons and to search his brain for clearer ways of expressing them. He walked steadily for more than an hour, and only turned back when he felt the bite of cold on his face and hands.

By the time his footsteps were once more silenced by tarmac, and the little lights of Moose Draw turned the shadows a sullen and secretive black, he was almost lightheaded, buoyed up by a balloon of happiness and hope.

It was more difficult than he thought, but not for the reasons he'd imagined. Spencer knew what he wanted to say and pretty much how he wanted to say it, but when he sat down to write he felt slightly foolish. What gave him the right to attempt this?

436

Did the desire to put something down on paper in itself make one a writer? And if not, when exactly did one become one? He kept catching a mental glimpse of himself and it made him wince with selfconsciousness – who did he think he was?

For this reason he kept his new ambition a secret. He continued to work for Mack and, it must be said, with a rather better grace for having his own small project in the background. The seasons were on his side, for with the turn of the year there were even fewer mechanics' jobs. His lack of sociability outside of work and mealtimes seemed not to arouse any curiosity in Mack, but he was aware of his mother watching him, she knew him too well. The last thing he wanted was for her to ask him about it. Perversely, the fact that she would understand, approve and be interested, was what put him off. If this thing wasn't exclusively his then it was nothing. Once he talked about it to someone else, especially someone like his mother who might with the very best of intentions give advice or encouragement or have suggestions to make, he'd be lost. He was wary of her English sensibility, her imagination and her strangely secretive heart. He didn't want a repeat of that emotional encounter in his room, didn't want her feelings, whatever they were, to spill over and cloud his own.

He decided that the only way to do this was to be absolutely firm and clear. However curious Caroline was he knew she would never breach his privacy if it was obvious that was what he wanted. So there would be no doors left ajar, no half-truths, no invitations for interruption. When dinner was cleared away he said goodnight to them both and went upstairs, closing the door firmly and audibly behind him.

Then came the infinitely harder challenge of getting the thing written. Whenever he made a start and read it over it seemed to him pompous and sententious. How did a writer get to sound so authoritative, so aware of an audience, and yet remain himself? How could he write as he wanted to and still be Spencer McColl? His thoughts and ideas seemed to be diminished rather than burnished by the process of writing, to lose their buoyancy and become clunking and pedestrian. He knew it wasn't their fault, they were good ideas: it was his, because he couldn't write.

Inspiration, when it came, was from an unlikely source. After a week of evenings that began in a ferment of hope and ended in a dry rustle of disappointment he took off on the Saturday for a drink in town.

He went to O'Connell's Bar, off the main street on the corner of Oaksey and Davenport. The identity of the eponymous Irishman was lost to memory, if he'd ever existed, but the bar was big and cheery and since the war was no longer a solidly male preserve. As well as Dec the barman there were now Sandy and Lucille, coiffed and corseted to kill, who served drinks with ferocious speed and dexterity and who (it was rumoured, and Spencer wouldn't have cared to test the proposition) could deal equally effectively with any trouble.

He bought a beer and a chaser and sat at the end of the bar furthest from the door. The juke box was playing something twangy and sentimental and one or two couples were dancing. The way they danced reminded him again how far he was from England. In Church Norton the band on the base had played Glen Miller and the local girls had quickstepped and jived and jitterbugged like New Yorkers. Here in O'Connell's the couples swung and swivelled to a different beat, cowboy dancing, something that no matter what the rhythm seemed to combine the lilt of a waltz with the stamp of a square dance. It was as distinctive as a native language, something out of the ground and in the blood, a western vocabulary that the dancers had learned without trying. Spencer liked it a lot. He had never been a great dancer, had always been glad of the crowded dance floors in London that meant everything was reduced to a rhythmic shuffle. These men clasped their partners tight with a brawny confidence, and the women scarcely needed to be led anyway, even the biggest of them stepped and twirled like soubrettes. He envied the dancers their easy self-assurance.

'Spencer? Spencer McColl?'

A big, heavy, dark guy stood there, grinning expectantly. Spencer didn't for a moment recognise him, but the red-haired woman with him was familiar. He slipped off his stool and extended his hand, praying for a clue.

'Hey . . . How you doin'?'

'Remember Minna?'

'Sure I do, who could forget?'

'Spencer. Good to see you again.'

'We're married now.'

'Well, congratulations.'

She was less changed, still pretty and sassy. He shook her hand and that reminded him that of course this was Bobby Forrest. Bobby the jock, the stud, the most envied boy in Moose Draw, now grown solid and unremarkable.

Keen to show he remembered, Spencer said heartily: 'Bobby, Minna – buy you a drink?'

'Uh-uh!' Bobby held up his hands. 'I saw you first, what's yours?'

The bar was filling up. Minna hoisted herself on to the spare stool next to Spencer, flashing trim little legs in peep-toe shoes, and Bobby rested his bulk on the bar in between. Spencer had to lean round him to offer her a cigarette, and then again to light it, but she didn't seem put out at being sidelined. While Bobby filled in Spencer about the refrigerator business, she simply smiled and struck up a conversation with the guy on the other side, who must have reckoned his luck was in. Minna was a prom-queen kind of girl, confident, in command, not motherly like Trudel. Even before she was Mrs Forrest you just kind of knew that she didn't spread it about: her bouncy little body was hers to do as she liked with and she might or might not bestow its favours on other people. She saw sex, he sensed, as a currency not, as Trudel did, as a shared benison. He was sure that in spite of Bobby's amiable small-town boorishness it was his wife who ran the show. She was – he stole another look at her sleek ankles and carmine-tipped toes – a nose-art kind of girl.

'. . . came through without a scratch then crunched my pelvis fooling around off duty.' Bobby was telling him about his war, with the infantry in North Africa. 'There's a moral in there somewhere, Christ knows what it is.'

'Forget it,' said Spencer. He entertained a fleeting image of *Fast 'n' Loose* hitting the ground, cartwheeling crazily, slamming to a moment's halt before pouring its life upward in a torrent of smoke and flame . . . 'There isn't one. You okay now?'

Bobby slapped his hip, a rueful expression. ''Bye-bye football.' Slapped his midriff. 'Hallo, rocking chair.'

Old rocking chair'll get me . . . Spencer was shocked. 'Nonsense. You've got a beautiful wife, a good job, your whole life in front of you.' It sounded pretty lame. He added: 'A whole lot more than me, I'm telling you.'

'So what are your plans, Spence? You're a flier, there's all kinds of doors open to you.'

'I guess so. But I've done with flying.'

'Boy!' Bobby clicked his teeth admiringly. 'You must have some stories. We used to envy you guys whizzing around up there, but one little sneeze and you could be dead, right? I read that piece about you in the *Monitor*.'

Spencer pulled a face. 'Don't believe everything you read in the paper, Bobby. It took all sorts to win the war.'

'Sure, but what an experience. Only thing was they made you sound kinda serious. I mean, I know you're a serious guy, but I kept thinking if you'd been telling all about it face to face there'd have been those stories, that stuff the paper thinks isn't worth bothering with?'

'Like what?' Spencer smiled at Bobby to show he wasn't being argumentative but was genuinely interested. To his surprise it was Minna who answered.

'He means the girls.'

'I do not!'

''Course you do, honey.' The endearment put Bobby in his place worse than a slap on the cheek. She adjusted her position slightly, her right arm resting on the bar, cigarette in hand, telling the other guy that she was part of this group now. She took a dainty drag, narrowing her eyes at Spencer as she did so. 'That's what guys want to know.'

Spencer opted for gallantry as being also expedient. 'The best girls were the ones you left behind.'

'Sure, sure . . .' She blew smoke, tapped the cigarette on an ashtray. 'But how did you know?'

Bobby jerked his head at his wife, gave Spencer a grin that was both of pride and apology. 'You don't have to answer that.'

'Well, naturally we had fun.'

They were both looking at him now, Bobby with salacious expectancy, his wife with a small droll smile, one eyebrow raised. Spencer's mouth was suddenly all stopped up with memories the power of which he could not possibly convey.

'But things are different in war, I don't have to tell you,' he muttered.

'You were the conquering heroes in that little English town,' declared Bobby. 'Bet the local ladies couldn't wait to show their gratitude.'

'It wasn't like that.' He sounded prim and humourless, even to himself, but they were trampling all unknowing on ground that even he could scarcely bring himself to tread.

'It's always like that!'

Suddenly Minna, as if calling a halt, pushed her glass in front of Bobby. 'Mine's another, honey.' Spencer thanked God for her tough tact.

A little later when she'd gone to the powder room, Bobby said: 'I hate to sound like a guy with only one thing on his mind, but you seen anything of Apples?'

It was so long since he'd heard the nickname that Spencer didn't react right away, and Bobby added: 'Apples Flaherty?'

He shook his head. 'We wrote one another when I first went overseas, but somehow or other we stopped . . .' He'd stopped, was the truth. The sweet, seductive spell of Craft Cottages had overtaken him body and soul and Trudel's last three letters had gone unanswered.

Bobby jerked his head and clicked his teeth, pleased to be the bearer of local news. 'Incredible.'

'Yeah?' Spencer waited.

'She's back right now, staying with her mother.' Bobby shook his head again. 'You ought to go call, bet she'd like that.'

'So what's so different?'

'You'll see.' He grinned as Minna returned. 'Hi, hon. Incredible.'

So that was two ideas Spencer brought away from O'Connell's that night. When he got home he picked up his sheets of paper off the chest and scribbled 'Bobby' at the top, and then wrote a few sentences. He'd put Bobby's name as a reminder of their conversation, but having it there made him feel he was still talking to him, and that in turn tweaked an end of the knot in his mind. The sentences looked fresh and bright, they started to say what he wanted them to say. By some process he scarcely understood, a psychological alchemy, he'd found his voice.

A couple of days later he'd almost finished and there was nothing much doing for Mack so when he'd written his quota Spencer drove into town and parked a little way down from the Flahertys' place. He sat in the car for a moment, not wanting to get out. He hadn't been this end of town since his return, only driven through. He'd kind of avoided stopping, partly through guilt, partly through the avoidance of old memories. Though he told himself it was crazy, he felt that he had betrayed Trudel in some way. It was true that she had finished with him rather than the other way round, but she had still been truer, more faithful. She it was who had written three unanswered letters. The last of these, he recalled, had ended with the words: 'So, Spencer, I'll leave this with you. If I hear from you that'll be great, if I don't I'll try not to think the worst, and hope to see you after the fat lady sings. Love always, Trudel.'

Love always.

He got out of the car and walked towards the house with his head down, sort of hoping that no one would look out of a window and recognise him as he approached. It was awkward enough without Trudel or her mother having the advantage over him.

But when he rang the bell there was a long interval before the door was answered, and then it was a woman he'd never seen before, young and brisk in a unifom.

'Yes?'

'I wonder if Trudel Flaherty's at home? Or her mother? I'm an old friend, Spencer McColl.' He returned the young woman's combative gaze.

'Mrs Flaherty's taking a nap. Mrs Samuelson's out right now.'

He thought he'd misheard. 'It was actually Trudel I wanted to see, Mrs Flaherty's daughter?'

'That's right.' She was loving it. 'Mrs Samuelson.'

He was felled. 'I see . . . Well, it seems a lot's happened since I went away.'

She didn't flicker. 'Shall I say you called?'

'Um – yes, why not? Sure.' He backed off, feeling an idiot. 'Thanks. 'Bye.'

Back in the car he thought, Bastard! The least Bobby could have done was tell him this the most obvious piece of information, the kind of thing any old friend wanted – needed, for Chrissakes – to know. It was nothing more nor less than a dirty trick designed to embarrass and humiliate him.

Smarting, he drove out to the creek and parked, pushing the door open and lighting a cigarette. Gradually, very gradually, he calmed down, the hot flustered feelings fell away one by one and he was left with a bleak sadness: Trudel was married. Apart from the manner of its discovery it could be no surprise. She was young, smart, sexy, and had by all accounts had a tough time. She needed and deserved a good man to look after her. But he realised now that the possibility of something with Trudel had always been there. Even now, after events in England, he had supposed they would pick up where they'd left off because he'd be able to tell her about the English sisters, and she would understand and not judge. They had something going. Or did have – now she was a married woman that easy intimacy would be over.

Another thought occurred to him. Perhaps Samuelson himself was there too? A duty visit to the ailing mother-in-law, what could be more appropriate? Spencer experienced a twist of jealousy. He wished he hadn't left his name.

But it was too late. That evening when he was in his

443

room the telephone jangled imperiously – it was Mack's big indulgence, invested in on business grounds – and Mack called up to him.

'Spence – for you!'

Coming down the stairs he asked, 'Who is it?'

'Woman . . . Search me.'

He picked up the receiver warily. 'Spencer McColl.'

'Spence, it's – Trudel.' There was a minute hesitation before the name.

'Oh, hi there.'

'I'm sorry I wasn't in when you called.'

'It doesn't matter.' What was he saying? Of course it didn't matter, she was allowed to go out.

'I'd really like to see you though. Could we meet?'

'Sure.'

She must have read his mind. 'I'm here on my own.'

'Okay.'

'Can you get away during the day?' She was being tactful, implying that his life was busy and productive.

'I'm only helping Mack. Things are quiet at the moment.'

'Perhaps we could, I don't know, go for a walk or something?'

'Fine.'

'Spencer . . . ?'

'Yeah?'

'Are you all right?'

'Yeah.'

'We have a lot of catching up to do.'

'Seems like it.' He knew he sounded boorish and blunt, but he couldn't help it, and typically she didn't comment.

'Mother has a nap in the afternoons, why not come over after lunch?'

'Fine.'

'I'll look forward to that.'

When he replaced the receiver and looked up he could see, across the hall, his mother sitting at the kitchen table doing accounts. She looked up briefly and smiled as if seeing him for the first time. Discretion seemed to be the order of the day. He went into the kitchen and took a cookie out of the barrel on the side.

'You want a glass of milk with that?' she asked, smiling again but not looking up.

'No, thanks.' He sat down opposite her and watched as she moved one piece of paper to the side, studied another, wrote neatly in the ledger that seemed always to have been the same ledger . . . Words and figures and columns and pages that chronicled a modest livelihood, quietly and industriously earned.

Still not looking at him she asked: 'How's it going?'

This was an open-ended question that covered just about everything, she was leaving it to him to decide what it referred to.

'Not bad.'

Now she put down her pencil and sat back. 'Tell me something.'

'If I can.'

'When you were in England – did you have a girl? I mean a special girlfriend?'

'There was somebody, yes. But it was over before I left.'

'Do you miss her?'

'I told you, it was over.'

He made to get up but she laid her hand quickly over his. 'It's never really over though, is it?'

He didn't answer.

The following afternoon he went back to the Flahertys' place and this time the door opened as he got out of the car and Trudel appeared, in a black coat, and closed the door behind her. To his relief she took the initiative, holding out both her hands to grasp his and kissing him on both cheeks before standing back to look at him.

'You look great, Spence.'

'You're not so dusty yourself.' She was thinner again, but was pretty and elegant with her hair caught back in two combs and a dark blue silky scarf setting off the creamy skin of her neck. Her smile was pure time-capsule, the old Trudel, the

445

smile that said it would all turn out just fine because the two of them were together. He felt himself unbend a little but he still couldn't bring himself to ask the important questions.

'Where would you like to go?'

She was decisive, she'd thought about it. 'Let's go to Battle Park. We can walk there.'

'You got it.'

Battle Park was on the edge of town, a green area surrounded by one of the loops in the creek. To get to it you crossed a wooden bridge. In the middle was a big old stone with a plaque commemorating the brave stand of General William A. McKinley's small scouting troop in defence of a waggon train against a raiding party of Sioux several hundred strong. 'And in death they were not divided' declared the plaque, above an engraving of the layout of the battle from which it was pretty clear that the engagement had been a massacre. It was easy to imagine the waggon train pulled up in this tranquil spot with the water all round, the shady trees . . . Equally easy to imagine the terrifying charge of Indian horsemen out of nowhere, storming through the creek with the water flying up around them . . .

In the ten minutes it took them to reach Battle Park they talked about changes to the town, Mrs Flaherty's health, the fluctuating fortunes of McColl's Mercantile. Once they were over the bridge and walking slowly along the path that followed the creek, Spencer bit the bullet.

'So, you got married.'

'I did.' She turned up her collar. 'The biggest mistake I ever made.'

'Oh?'

'We're divorced now.'

'I'm sorry.' He found that in spite of his relief he was sorry, for her anyway, because she sounded so sad.

'It wasn't anyone's fault,' she went on. 'We just weren't suited.'

'You were—' he skirted round the phrase 'in love' '—suited to begin with.'

'Oh, yes, mad about each other.' She gave a little ironic jerk of the head. 'Or plain mad.'

'So how long did it last?'

'A year. A whole year. A triumph, all things considered.'

He stopped, and took her left hand firmly in both of his. 'That's a real shame.'

'It was.' She let her hand lie there, looked down at it as if it didn't belong to her. 'But it's history now. By the way,' she linked her arm through his and began to walk again, 'I've dropped the Trudel.'

'Really? Why?'

'I never liked it. It's sort of cute. Milkmaidy.'

'But it's your name.'

'I have another one. Hannah.' She pronounced the first 'a' long, so it came out 'Harnah'. 'That's what I'm called now.'

He shook his head. So many changes. 'So it's goodbye, Apples Flaherty. Hallo, Hannah Samuelson.'

'Apples, hmm.' She half-laughed. 'I'd forgotten that.'

'You knew about it though?'

'Of course! I look back sometimes and think, Was that really me?'

She left his side and walked over to the rock with its commemorative plaque. He thought she was reading it, but when he joined her she said: 'I was so desperate for love.'

He was taken aback. 'Everybody loved you.'

She shook her head. 'No one.'

'Your parents.'

'No. Them least of all. They didn't love each other so how could they love their fat stupid daughter who glued them together?'

'Tru— you weren't . . .'

'It doesn't matter if I was or I wasn't, that was how I felt.'

She turned away and he went with her.

Desperate both to comfort her and to be truthful, he said: 'I loved you. You didn't want me.'

'No, I didn't believe you.'

'And you were so different when you came back from Chicago, so full of plans, so serious and grown-up—'

'Grown-up!' She threw her head back in a silent laugh that was almost bitter. 'I'm working on it.'

447

'Me too.'

'Yes. Let's talk about *that*.' They reached a seat made out of a big old tree trunk with a lengthwise section carved out. She sat down and made a little gesture with her coat as if making room for him. 'Tell me about *you*, Spencer.'

He did. Slowly and stumblingly at first, apologising for not having written, and then more rapidly, rediscovering his old ease with her and what a great listener she was, attentive and sympathetic. He told her the truth but not the whole truth about Janet and Rosemary – that he had been 'involved' with Janet and subsequently discovered the relationship between her and the girl, and it had ended. At this point she did say quietly: 'Was it so shocking?'

'It was for me. You have to understand I'd got used to seeing things in one way—'

'—and none of it was as you thought.' She nodded. 'Yes. I do see that. Go on.'

He told her about his writing, and his hopes for it. With her he felt not embarrassed or secretive but almost proud to be attempting something difficult and risky.

'That's wonderful,' she said when he'd finished. 'It's exactly what you should be doing. Promise to let me know what happens.'

'Of course.'

In turn she told him, as they walked on, that she was going to have 'another shot' as she put it at a medical training, no matter how long it took her.

'I was on my way once,' she said, 'when we last met before the war. Or I thought I was on my way, but I was still running. When I met Tom I just fell into his arms – like a great big apple! – and thought, This is it, I've got away. I put myself back to square one. He was such a lovely man, but he couldn't love me enough, no one could. I so regret what I did to him.'

'It takes two,' said Spencer sturdily.

'Yes, I know. We didn't know each other well enough, but we were so full of hope. In my case so full of false expectation, more than any man could live up to.'

Spencer wanted to say, Me, I could, but stopped himself in

448

time. He didn't know this new person, this Hannah, any more than her husband had.

When they got back to her house she asked if he wanted to come in, but he declined.

'How long are you here for?' he asked.

'Another week. Then it's back east to my little flat and my dull job and my studies.'

'Will you let me have your address?'

'Of course. Let's see each other before I go, and keep in touch. I want to know everything that happens.'

'You will.'

They touched cheeks, her hands on his shoulders, his on her waist, but he seemed to feel every bone and curve of her beneath the coat.

'Friends?' she asked.

'Friends,' he replied.

Ten days later, after she'd gone, he received a letter from the editorial office of the *Moose Draw Monitor*.

> *Dear Mr McColl,*
>
> *I was pleased to receive your piece entitled 'Over There', and think that it is just the sort of thing that would entertain our readers. I should therefore like to offer you the sum of $10 for the piece, and if you have anything in a similar vein on the stocks I would be interested to see it.*
>
> *Yours sincerely,*
> *P.J. Clarence, Editor*

CHAPTER SIXTEEN

'Is that all there is?
Is it over, have we done?
Is this the famous feeling when the bloody war is won?'
—Stella Carlyle, 'Is That All?'

Harry – 1854

If Harry had thought to be spared the sight of the battlefield south of the Alma, it wasn't to be, though he added nothing to the letter he sent Rachel. Not long after the appearance of the walking wounded through the miasma of smoke the Lights were ordered up the flank of the Kigourny Heights. By the time they reached their vantage point, they had picked their way through many hundreds of dead and dying of both sides, and had seen enough to convince the most hotblooded among them that even a famous victory had its price. It was not solely concern for Rachel's feelings that prevented Harry from describing these scenes, but a horror of reliving them.

Beyond the heights to the south an even more extraordinary, and this time welcome, sight greeted them: that of the Russian Army streaming away in full flight, shedding everything in order to hasten their progress – arms, packs, caps, coats, belts, flasks – leaving a trail of potential booty in their wake.

Now, thought Harry, now, surely, they would attack – ferocious pursuit would turn this retreat into a rout. It was the role of the Lights to launch just such a harrying charge across open country, to spread chaos and confusion, and turn a defeated army into a scattering rabble.

Leonard Palliser, to his left, spoke for them all. 'This is it, lads! This is what we came for, now we can show them!'

Even the weary horses seemed to catch their mood, shaking their heads and moving restlessly. When the order came down the line on no account to attack, they could scarcely believe it.

'They must be bringing others up,' ventured Harry.

'Let's hope so, there can be no other sense in it.'

For interminable minutes they sat there, watching their defeated foe stumble away from them in disarray. At last an ADC cantered down the line, bristling with importance and excitement.

'Order to advance and take prisoners! Do not attack! Only take prisoners.'

It was impossible, though, not to feel that it was an attack as they poured down the slope, giving the horses their heads, keeping perfect formation, knee to knee in all their pride. The agonised frustration of the last twenty-four hours fell away, there seemed to be nothing but this moment, this speed and purpose and élan. Harry raised his sabre, he shouted, he didn't know what, his blood was up and boiling.

Within two minutes they were upon the Russian stragglers.

'Get them!' yelled Palliser, red-faced, standing in his stirrups. 'Get them, lads, they're ours!'

But there was a difference, Harry discovered, between the enemy en masse and at a distance, the mighty foe who had inflicted so much damage; and the reality of terrified individuals, many of them already wounded, some begging for mercy and weeping, others running like stags, a few turning and preparing to fight bravely and madly, with nothing but their bare hands.

They must have rounded up a few dozen and a number of those were roughly handled without cause. One of Harry's captives was painfully young; the golden fur on his chin was soft as chicken-down. He maintained a brittle, exaggerated dignity. One could imagine the advice he had been given by some well-meaning mentor. Around him older and more experienced soldiers cursed and wept and spat and swore, but this boy walked with his head up. He appeared clean and unmarked, it was hard to imagine that he had seen fighting at all. Hero or coward, this was without doubt his finest hour.

They had accompanied their charges no more than halfway back up the slope when the ADC reappeared, this time skidding to a stop and then trotting fussily to the brigade commander several hundred yards to the left. They were ordered to halt. There was a heated exchange of the sort with which they'd become familiar, gestures, raised voices. Harry glanced at the Russian boy. He was impassive as a statue.

The order came down to release the prisoners. Incredulous, they did not at once do so but when Lucan himself bellowed at them they let them go with a poor grace. As they rode back up the hill, humiliated and frustrated once again, Palliser cast a scornful look over his shoulder.

'Look at them. One decent charge and we could have seen to the whole pack of them.'

Harry looked. Most of their former prisoners were running away, tripping and stumbling as if they could not believe their luck and expected to be fired on at any moment. Some were kneeling, perhaps praying, perhaps simply exhausted. The boy was still standing quiet and straight, apparently staring after them. Harry could almost believe that their eyes met, that some small bond of silent understanding had formed between them. But as he looked the boy's knees buckled, his head sagged to one side, and he pitched forward to lie motionless. No one came to his aid.

This Harry did mention in his letter to Rachel. '*It may sound fanciful, but he became for me a symbol of what was happening to us all. Of this mess and confusion which brings out both the worst and the best in us – his dignity was meaningless, his death (for I am sure he died) even more so, and he would certainly have killed me without a second thought. As for our pursuit of the Russians, there was I admit the thrill of the chase, but when the prey is close it is hard not to feel a sense of comradeship, which would not have prevented me, or anyone, from killing if that had been our order.*'

The night was long. At least the vanquished had left the field while they, the victors, must make what they could of the territory they'd won. As dusk fell, the grim housekeeping of the battlefield had to be done. The French casualties were taken by covered hospital wagon to their medical station. The British who were able to walk, or to crawl, made their way to the black flag that marked the hospital tent. The rest, British and Russian alike, lay in trenches and on the open ground with scarcely credible patience and stoicism until such time as they received attention. The lucky ones were carried to the hard-pressed surgeons working by moonlight, or to be conveyed by jolting *arabas* and open litters the three miles to the coast, to lie unattended below decks on a hospital ship bound for Scutari. And still there remained hundreds, mostly Russians, out there in the cold and dark.

Harry wrote: '*You would have been moved to tears, Rachel, by the gentleness and goodness of ordinary English fighting men doing what they could for their wounded enemy, taking them their own hard-won water, saying a few words, seeing to their comfort . . . And not only that, but bearing their own suffering with real nobility. No matter what their agony, or how much they groan and blaspheme, they are always ready to acknowledge that the medical men have more urgent matters to attend to, and that their turn will come . . . When the battle is over, every man is a casualty. And our nerves are continually plucked by the sound of random shots as horses – and, I fear, men – are mercifully dispatched, and firearms are discharged into the air as a warning by these improbable and practical angels of mercy . . . If only we cavalrymen did not feel so untried and unused. If only we could hold our heads up and know that we had shared the glory and the suffering. It is mortifying to be the objects of general scorn and derision and does nothing, either, to improve the already incendiary mood of our commanders who continue to chafe and bicker, often quite openly in front of us. The men, like Cardigan, fulminate against Lucan who once again pulled us back from the brink for no good reason that could be seen, and yet it is clear from his demeanour that he was subject to commands from on high. There is not a man among us, I think, who is, as some infantrymen are heard to comment, more enamoured of our uniforms and horses* than of fighting, but what can we do? It seems we are always to be held back.'

Reading back over what he'd written he was compelled to add: 'I see what you must think, my dearest Rachel – that with one breath I say that I wish to embrace the heat of battle and with another that I feel pity and admiration for a Russian prisoner. Let me assure you that it makes no more sense to me than it must to you. But we are all part of this infernal game now, nolens volens, and at least to participate fully would be to hasten the end of the thing whatever that may be.'

He and Palliser went out and set pickets, guards and vedettes, as much to restore a sense of stability as to defend against an enemy in such thorough disarray. Also, there was a sense among the Lights that they should, however late in the day, be seen to be useful, and so it was night when they finally sat round the fire. Sporadic explosions that at first had them leaping to their feet in alarm turned out, following investigations by their own cook, to be the result of Russian gun-barrels used by the men as cooking-grates. As these became red-hot, they exploded and some discharged their load. Awful screams and shouts in a distant part of camp told of at least one grim accident caused in this way.

The cook, a stone-faced Scot, was unsympathetic. 'No brains,' was his comment. 'What little they've got deserves to be blown out.'

Harry's night was not entirely sleepless, but sleep and consciousness merged into a confused restlessness. The shouts and moans from the hillside mingled with those in his dreams. When he awoke at four a.m. he flung his arm out to find himself touching the outstretched hand of a body on the ground next to him. It was that of a Russian soldier, already stiffening, one half of his chest blown away. Harry could scarcely imagine by what tortuous, agonising means he must have found his way here, or with what intention. To kill? To beg for help? Or had he, poor chap, been too far gone to know where he was? He crouched next to the man, gazing into his dark, bearded face and clouded half-closed eyes, trying to read something there. Unlike the boy prisoner, this was a mature man, coarse-featured, his skin pock-marked and webbed with broken veins. The hand that had reached for Harry's had a forefinger truncated by some earlier accident at the first joint so that it was no more than a smooth stub.

Harry detailed a couple of men to restore the Russian to his fellows. In the clammy grey light the piles of bodies on the hillside resembled clumps of manure on a field with the burial parties digging mass graves like farm workers.

They were assigned the rearguard for the day's march, but the likelihood of that beginning soon seemed remote. The regiment was saddled up by five and still standing by their mounts at ten, as the heat intensified. Tiredness and tedium hummed round them like the clouds of flies and midges which the horses barely had the energy to shake off.

Stories rippled through all ranks as the previous night's pickets returned. They had found the spot where the Russian spectators had sat, and there was every sign that a famous victory had been anticipated: parasols, champagne bottles and glasses, opera glasses, gloves and hats had been scattered on the grass as the fine company took flight, a prosperous civilian echo of the kit left in the valley below.

Harry wondered to himself whether Rachel would have been in such a company in similar circumstances, and found that he could not imagine it. Yet the image of Rachel herself, he found, grew stronger and more vivid the longer their separation lasted. Her face with its calm, steady look hung in his mind like a lantern. She had become the focus of his longing to return, the very embodiment of the idea of home, though he knew all too well that he had no right to think of her in this way. She was his sister-in-law, still in mourning, expecting his brother's child. When – if – he went back to Bells, what could he say or do that would not in some way betray the strength and duration of his feelings and so in some way harm Hugo's memory and her reputation? He was certain that he sensed, in every line of her letters, a reciprocal feeling, an empathy and understanding beyond what was appropriate in the circumstances. But whether this extended to the overwhelming strength of his own passion he dared not speculate, and could never presume to ask.

Betts, by some means or another, had come by a memento of the Russian ladies so rudely put to flight. It was a single black plume from a fan, the shaft beaded with jet.

'Pretty bit of nonsense, sir.'

'May I see?'

'All yours, sir, if you like.'

'Don't you want to take it back with you – as a souvenir?'

Betts pulled a wry face. 'If I get back I shan't want to remember, I'll want to forget. Besides, there's no woman waiting for me.'

Harry did not say that there was none waiting for him, either. As Betts did his quiet, concentrated work around Clemmie, he himself stood at Derry's side and turned the plume over in his hands. It was poignant not just for its feminine frivolity, but for the reminder it brought of Hugo's last journey to the church on the hill: the flutter of Piper's tossing mane, the soft sweep of black veiling, the dark heavy suits and the fragile country roses . . . He tucked the feather into his pack.

The first meet of the season had always been at Bells, by usage and invitation. Maria made no secret of the fact that she considered hunting barbaric, but first Percy's, then Hugo's, fondness for it, and her own liking for spectacle, meant that she acceded to the event taking place there. Sensible of her position as newcomer, Rachel too was content to let the tradition continue, and it was agreed that if Percy were well enough he and Maria would come up in the gig, well wrapped up, to watch the proceedings either outside if it were fine, or from a vantage point at the study window.

What chiefly attracted Rachel to the idea, apart from Percy's pleasure in it, was that it was one of those occasions when the gates of Bells stood open and any who wanted could come in. Most of the time she was solitary by nature as well as through circumstance, and she liked her own company well enough. The largely silent companionship of Ben, Cato, and the baby inside her was all she required. But she was well aware that Hugo in particular had been a popular and expansive landlord without any 'side' or airs and graces, and that whatever her natural inclination she must show herself willing to be a worthy successor. Her connection with the Bartlemas family had gone some way towards demonstrating this, but was also she knew taken to be a sign of her slight peculiarity. So it was a source of satisfaction to her to be able to stand at the door of Bells, big with Hugo's child, on this brilliant early October day, and welcome not just the hunt but all those who came to watch.

Happily, Percy was having a good day, and the gig carrying him and Maria was able to draw up at the front of the house as the hunt began to convene. Rachel went over to them and saw from the warning look on Maria's face that she must not react to or comment upon Percy's appearance, which was almost transparently fragile. Perhaps it was seeing him in the light of day and the bright, unforgiving out-of-doors, but he seemed a mere whisper of a man, his bones pushing at the glistening taut skin of his face and hands, his eyes sunk beneath lids frail and veined as butterfly wings.

'It's so good that you could come, Percy,' she said. 'It means so much to everyone that you both are here.'

'A perfect day for it.' His voice was firm, but his gaunt cheeks were pink, and she noticed a little intake of breath before and after he spoke, as if this short utterance had taken a great effort.

'And how are you, Rachel?' Maria asked, checking both her own and her husband's agitation by changing the subject.

'Well. Enormous.'

'Longing for it to be over?'

'Wishing for it to begin.' Rachel wondered as she often did if she had sounded unintentionally sharp, and added: 'I mean that I'm looking forward to holding Hugo's child in my arms.'

Percy said: 'Hope it's less trouble than its father.'

'Nonsense,' said Maria, 'Hugo could charm the birds from the trees.'

'And more obedient than his damn' dog . . .'

Rachel smiled. 'Charm and trouble so often go together, don't they?'

Percy reached out his hand to cover his wife's. 'I know.'

Maria twitched her head in mock offence, but Rachel saw how her eyes shone.

By the time the hunt moved off there were fifty or sixty people from the village there to watch. Rachel had arranged for punch to be served to the onlookers in lieu of the stirrup cup and Jeavons and Little passed round with trays and prevented small children from getting beneath the horses' feet. They made a proud sight, the heavy hunters with their well-turned out riders, the officials in their pink, hounds nosing and milling in amiable anticipation within the ambit of the huntsman's whip, their tails waving like long grasses in a meadow. Cato, shut in the stables for the morning, bayed mournfully.

Rachel found the Bartlemas family, or at least Ben found her and she asked him where his parents were. Dan Bartlemas removed his cap. His wife was as usual slightly on the defensive.

'Is he being a nuisance?'

'No. We're friends, aren't we?'

He nodded, caught between his mother's suspicion and Rachel's approval. 'Can I go and see Cato?'

'You may, he'd like that.' Ben began to run off and she called after him: 'But don't let him out whatever you do!'

He waved a hand to show that the message was received and understood. Dan Bartlemas, colouring, asked: 'Did I see old Mr Latimer over there?'

'You did. He was well enough to come up and see the hunt move off.'

'He used to like a day out with the hunt. How is he?'

'Very frail. But cheerful.'

'Our Colin thought the world of him,' said Mrs Bartlemas. 'He never gives much away, not a great talker, not free with his smiles like Mrs Latimer, but a really good man.'

'He is.'

'And Mr Harry's just like him.'

Her husband nudged her and she frowned. 'I didn't mean anything by that – about Mr Hugo—'

'I know that.' Rachel touched her arm briefly. 'I understand.'

The horn sounded and the clamour and jingle of the hunt moved away up the drive to the north, in the direction of the first covert. The spectators began to disperse, some in the same direction, most towards the village, saying their goodbyes and thanks to the Latimers though Percy's head had fallen back and his eyelids drooped.

Jeavons collected such glasses as remained, and Oliver brought a rake and levelled the gravel. Rachel went to release Cato from his imprisonment. When she entered the stable she was amused to find boy and dog lying side by side in the straw, not touching, but apparently in perfect soundless communication with one another. Ben lay on his back, hands behind his head, with one ankle resting on his upturned knee: Cato faced the door, front paws together, head held upright with a ponderous sphinx-like composure.

'You can come out now, you two.'

Cato rose slowly and came to her and Ben followed.

'Has the hunt gone?'

'Yes.'

'Good,' he said. 'Can I stay for a while?'

'As far as I'm concerned you can, Ben, but I think you should ask your parents.'

'They'll say no.'

'You don't know that.'

'Can I tell them you said yes?'

'Of course. But you must always do what your parents want you to no matter what I say. You'd better hurry, they were all leaving.'

He disappeared. She expected Cato to follow him but he did not. The dog remained at her side, padding along with his hide, looser in old age, rippling and jouncing on his shoulders like a heavy cloak. She knew that he was instinctively keeping

459

her company, adjusting his pace to hers now that she was heavy and slow and her time was near.

Around the side of the house two small tableaux had formed. On the far, south side of the park, near to where the wicket gate opened on to the path to the village, she could see Ben bargaining with his mother while Dan towered over them in silence. In the gig, Percy slept while Maria leaned forward with her hand on its side, talking to the driver, Edgar, and Oliver, leaning on his rake. Something urgent in her mother-in-law's attitude struck a warning chord with Rachel. She quickened her pace.

'Maria . . . Won't you both come in now and have some lunch with me?'

'Thank you. I was just asking Edgar if my husband could be carried into the house.'

Rachel turned to the groom. 'Oliver, will you help to bring Mr Latimer into the study?'

Both men said that it was no trouble and indeed it wasn't, for Percy weighed no more than a child. He did not stir as they lifted him down and carried him, making a seat of their arms, through the hall and to a chair in the sunlit window. Maria removed her hat and gloves and laid them on the window seat. Still in her short red plaid cape she sat down by him and took his hand in both of hers. Percy's nails were bluish, she chafed the hand gently. There was the fierce, frowning look on her face which her former employees knew only too well. Edgar retired to take the gig round to the yard and Oliver returned to his raking. Beyond him on the grass stood Ben, hands in pockets, uncertain of his territory. Rachel went to the door and shook her head at him and he went at once, in the direction of the stables.

She closed the front door. Now it seemed dark in the hall except for where long fingers of dusty light rested on the foot of the stairs. Seeking the warmth Cato plodded into this patch of sunshine and flopped down, rolling his eyes up at Rachel.

'Stay,' she ordered him and he laid his head on his paws.

She went into the study. 'Is he waking? Do you think he would like a glass of something? Madeira? Or a whisky?'

Maria shook her head. 'No, I think not.'

'For you?'

'Thank you, no.'

During this short exchange Maria had not taken her eyes off Percy's face, and she still sat on the footstool with his hand in both of hers. Rachel went over to them.

It was odd, but when Hugo had died, swiftly and suddenly, she had felt death's approach. One moment she had seen him on Piper careering between the trees towards his brother: the next she had been out on the lawn, perfectly aware of what had happened, the knowledge whole and crystal-clear as if the script and her part in it were already written.

Percy's death was expected, long-awaited even, an event for which they had had ample time to prepare, and yet now that it stood as it were at his shoulder she could not accept it. That it was just about to happen, that they were going to sit here and watch it steal over him, was almost too much to bear.

'No,' she said. 'No. Surely . . .'

Maria put up a hand, without looking at her, and grasped hers, so that she now held both of them, the link between them. Rachel recognised in her already the stoical serenity of widowhood. With her husband gone, nothing and no one could take him away from her again.

Rachel withdrew her hand and sat down on the windowseat next to Maria's hat and gloves. The low autumn sun meant that she cast a shadow on Percy and she moved so that the warm light was on his face again. He was still there, just, his eyelids fluttered and his breathing scarcely perceptible, a dwindling trace of life.

Maria said: 'He has been my great love, all these years.'

'I know.'

'I could never love my boys as I loved their father. Is that a dreadful thing to say?'

'No.' Rachel could believe that. Even expected it to be true. That she would love her child less for itself than because it was Hugo's.

Maria gave her a quick, tormented look as though she'd read her thoughts. 'So I was glad that Hugo had you, if only

461

for so short a while. And I hope that if Harry comes back he will find such love, for he deserves it.'

'I hope for that too.'

Maria lifted Percy's hand to her lips. Said, firmly and with feeling: 'It is the only thing worth living for. And the only thing to make death bearable.'

They sat in silence for another few minutes. It was tranquil in the sunlight. At one point Cato pushed open the door, looked in cautiously and when no reprimand was forthcoming padded in and lay at Rachel's feet.

She herself could not have pinpointed the moment when Percy died. It was a gentle drift from one peace into another. Even when Maria had laid his hands quietly together on his lap, and kissed first his brow, then each eyelid, then his mouth, the women did not move but sat bearing him and each other company. Rachel suspected, and was sure that Maria did too, that once Percy's death became known a great wave would break over them and they would all, for a while, be tossed about by it, separated, unable to focus on their own mourning or on the one taken from them.

The balance of authority, always delicately poised between the two women, had shifted for a while, almost imperceptibly, to Maria. At some point not long after Percy's death Rachel felt it return to her. Maria was widowed. Her life had changed for ever. She had suffered, a second time, one of the greatest losses that a woman can sustain. This house which had once been hers was Rachel's now and she must assume responsibility.

She got up and touched Maria's shoulder.

'I shall go and tell Jeavons, and send Oliver for the doctor. Stay with him.'

She left the room. Cato laid down his head and slept in the sun.

Due to the French having to reclaim their packs – seven thousand of them littered over the fields north of the Alma – it was another thirty-six hours before they moved off. To begin with the spirits of most of them were high: no matter what the missed opportunities it had still been a great victory and they could not yet guess at how inconclusive it would prove to be.

All too soon they were overtaken by the heat, flies, and a chronic shortage of water, the thirst of the troops made worse by the injudicious amounts of looted vodka consumed since the battle. And though allied losses at the Alma had been relatively small – a few hundred as opposed to the thousands of Russian dead – they were still at the mercy of cholera. As their exultant early-morning pace slowed, so they saw clearly, for the first time since reaching the Crimea, the vultures soaring overhead. It was impossible not to imagine these creatures gorging themselves on the abandoned battlefield, and though none mentioned it the picture haunted many of them. A single English army doctor and his servant had been left behind to tend the Russian wounded, with only his own courage and the promises of his grateful charges to protect him.

Between the rolling hills were long stretches of harsh grassland, pitilessly open, and there were frequent halts to allow the baggage and supply trains to catch up in the beating sun. The horses had had no oats in days and the forage was so sparse that many of them were stumbling with weakness. The moment a halt was called the poor things' heads hung and their sides sucked in and out like bellows over staring ribs. Once, among the detritus of the Russian retreat – which the men were permitted to loot – they came across a little Cossack pony with an injured leg, its saddle slewed round and trailing on the ground. Attempts to put it out of its misery with several shots to the head proved unsuccessful: it tottered but remained standing, dazed but still upright as the British troops marched past. Perhaps, thought Harry, it would die on its feet in the way that horses sometimes slept, and its skeleton, picked clean by the vultures, would still be there in weeks to come like a strange leafless tree in this barren plain.

It was during one of the sweltering pauses that Harry experienced something strange, and quite inexplicable. The sun was at its height, a time when morale, even following a famous victory, was always proportionately low. Near to him were at least two men doubled up in their saddles, their overalls bearing testament to the violent effects of cholera. Suddenly, without reason or warning, he felt a moment of coolness . . . a caress on his face, a brief and blessed eclipse, like a small cloud passing between him and the sun. For the few seconds that the sensation lasted his surroundings faded. The soft light and scent of England washed through him. He was transported.

Then as suddenly as it had come it was gone. The heat returned like a blow. He looked up. The sky was pale and fierce: not a cloud was in sight. One of the sick men had fallen from his saddle and Palliser was calling for assistance.

'Another gone,' he remarked to Harry. 'Let's for God's sake hope that the litter gets to him before the infernal buzzards.'

Maria did not go into a decline. On the contrary, she flared up like a funeral pyre, awesome in her grief but never more magnificent. Her theatricality came to her aid. She wore dramatic, elaborate black, Spanish lace and taffeta. A lightning-flash of pure white had appeared in her black hair in the days after Percy's death. She was if anything more beautiful and exotic than when he had brought her home as a young bride, to the astonishment of all. Everything about her was a declaration, not of acquiescent bereavement but of continuing passion. It was as if without her husband she was free to show what the love between them had meant – that it was not a pact, nor a mere accommodation between opposites, but an all-consuming fire from which she now removed the guard and would allow to burn itself out in a public glory.

So many people came to the funeral that they could not all be accommodated in the parish church, and a large number had to stand outside, in the rain. The funeral carriage was drawn by the heavy horses, Flower and Fury, huge and gentle, their shining tack dressed with purple and black ribbons for the day, Oliver at their heads. It was a big occasion, with the village street lined with mourners and Maria, tall and splendid, the focus of all eyes. Because of the weather the burial itself was a perilous business, the earth turned to mud and the ropes that supported the coffin on its descent were slick and wet. Shoes, boots and hems became sodden, hat brims dripped and the hair on the men's bare heads was plastered down. But no one flinched. Maria herself had scorned an umbrella, and now those that had brought them lowered them in respect. It was a token of the affection in which Percy Latimer had been held that not a man, woman or child sought shelter or complained, and free-flowing tears mixed with the rain.

Having helped her mother-in-law to make the arrangements Rachel stepped back and moved through the day softly as a shadow, content to be drab and inconspicuous The new life of which she was custodian seemed doubly precious, and now that her time was so near a stillness had overtaken her. The baby, grown to fill its watery cell, scarcely moved, but was quiet and heavy, biding its time.

When they had left the graveside the umbrellas went back up. While people were offering their condolences to Maria, Rachel withdrew to one side and leaned against the trunk of one of the great yew trees, its shaggy black branches creating a natural canopy through which the rain scarcely penetrated. Ben joined her – a strangely tidy Ben with parted hair and a too-tight jacket.

'Can I come in?'

'Please do, though I can't offer you anything. I didn't expect you to be here.'

'Mother said I had to.'

The candour of this answer made her smile. 'And are you glad you did?'

He gazed over his shoulder at the black gathering, the rain, the umbrellas. 'I don't know really.'

He meant no, but was being tactful. Appreciative of this she said gently: 'There has to be a funeral, a proper public ending to someone's life. It's a sad thing, but it has to be endured.'

He turned back to her with a bold look, not disrespectful but direct. 'You've been to two.'

'That's right. In fact more than that, in my lifetime.'

He seemed to consider this, before adding: 'Do you think my brother had a funeral?'

'Of course,' she said quickly, not giving herself time to think. 'Just because he died in another country in a war doesn't mean that he wasn't treated with proper respect. Captain Latimer will have seen to that. It will have been different from this, of course, but there will have been a ceremony.'

'We couldn't go, though.'

'No.'

He glanced back into the churchyard. Now that the mourners were dispersing they could see the glistening heap of newly turned soil, and Maria's spray of defiantly red roses. 'The only thing is . . .'

She waited. 'Yes?'

'Will people know where he is?'

'You mean, will there be a stone?'

He shrugged. She sensed tears perilously close and wished to save him from what he would see as their humiliation.

'There doesn't need to be, Ben. There doesn't have to be. Where brave men have died in a good cause people always remember.' She added something which she herself felt but was not sure he would understand. 'The ground remembers. There'll be a sort of – a grass memorial.'

There was a short silence during which, with head still averted, he swiped his jacket cuff over his upper lip. Then he said: 'Better go.' And was off.

God help me, she thought, by making it true.

When they came to the next river, where they were to bivouac for the night, it appeared like the promised land after the long day's arid route-march.

It was no more than a vigorous stream, smaller than the Alma but surrounded by rich soil supporting orchards groaning with the season's harvest of apples, plums, apricots and pears. And beyond the single post-bridge, miraculously left intact by the retreating Russians, was a straggling village of such fruitful and inviting beauty – all of it empty – that one might almost have suspected it of being a trap. Pretty cottages, deliciously coloured as sweets, sat among shady trees, and further up the slopes were ample villas hung with vines and set in snug, well-cultivated gardens bright with flowers. In the softening sunshine of evening it seemed nothing less than paradise.

But it was, as they found, a spoiled paradise. The Cossacks had been here before them and every last dwelling and outhouse had been ransacked with brutal thoroughness. It was now swarmed over greedily a second time by the hungry, thirsty British troops. Palliser remonstrated with one man emerging from a house carrying a handsome fur rug under one arm and a half-full carafe in the other hand, and was coarsely informed (courtesy no doubt of the local wine) that since he had seen at least one officer doing the same thing, he naturally assumed it was 'all right to take a few trophies'. Palliser ordered him furiously to return the items which the man did with a poor grace, scornfully upending the carafe and allowing its contents to splatter on the path as he went back into the house. It was only with difficulty that Harry prevented the choleric Palliser from dismounting and taking the matter further.

'Leonard – let it be, for God's sake.'

'The fellow's damnably insolent!'

'He's drunk.'

'And that is supposed to excuse him?'

'Look around you – if you take issue with him where do you intend to stop?'

It was true. On every side there were similar small transgressions taking place. The same men who had tended their defeated and wounded enemy with the utmost honour and gentleness only two nights before now exulted in an orgy of despoliation, whatever pangs of conscience they might have had on the matter stifled by the plentiful evidence that they were not the first.

The house where Harry, Leonard, Hector and Philip Gough billeted themselves was a shocking example of what had taken place. Once they had handed over the horses to the grooms and gone inside they were confronted by a scene of devastation all the more shocking because of the pleasant situation and what had clearly been the comfortable and civilised existence of the former occupants. Furniture was broken, glass and china smashed, clothes, curtains and rugs slashed and cushions and quilts ripped apart: downy feathers still drifted across the floor and floated, spiralling like snowflakes in the air.

Particular gleeful attention had been paid to pictures, which had been torn from their frames and savagely cut. A mirror above the fireplace had been smashed with a single blow to its centre, so that the cracks spread from the ugly black hole like a spider's web, and the fireplace itself was choked with charred and burnt paper, the remains of diaries, letters and ledgers, all the contents of an upturned bureau. The pen and inkwell had been used to write some words on the wall but Harry was glad that the daubs meant nothing to him. He could only wonder what damage might have been done to the houses of an enemy.

In the garden at the back, which was in the form of a shady arbour with an ornamental pond, statuary had been broken, and a stone nymph jutted from the water as if drowning, surrounded by pathetic domestic jetsam – a wooden spoon, paintbrushes, a doll, a lampshade. Worse, still emitting tendrils of smoke and an acrid smell, was a pile of burned books.

They were silent, aware that they constituted a second invasion, and that each crunching footstep was a further insult to the family who had lived here and had fled from their path only to have this havoc visited on their home and possessions.

There was one sign of life. Beneath the verandah at the front of the house, not two yards from where the cook had made a fire of splintered furniture, Harry found a skinny black and white cat. He reached his hand towards her and she flattened her ears and drew her lips back in a ferocious silent warning: she had six kittens with her, so small they were like furry insects, their tiny blind heads nudging for milk that wasn't there, protected but starving.

A shadow fell over Harry and he looked up to see Hector standing behind him, mopping his brow.

'What the devil have you found down there?'

'A cat with her kittens.'

Hector peered. 'Shooting her would be the kindest thing.'

'I don't know . . .' Harry stood up. 'Cats can fend for themselves.'

'Not with a litter.'

'It doesn't matter.'

'That's certainly true.' Losing interest, Hector clapped his hands together and turned to the fire. 'What delights have we tonight?'

After supper Harry walked to where the horses were picketed in a little scrubby field at the bend of the road. There was some tolerable grass in the field and the horses were cropping contentedly. As he'd half hoped he stumbled upon Betts in one corner, playing cards with a couple of others. They scrambled to their feet but he indicated to them to stand easy.

'Betts – a word?' He drew him aside. 'You have a way with animals.'

'Horses, sir,' said Betts warily.

'Well, give me your advice anyway.'

'If I can.'

'There's a cat under the house where we're staying.'

'No, sir. Really, sir?'

Harry ignored the gentle mockery. 'She has kittens. Naturally she can't feed them. What would you advise?'

Betts shrugged, poker-faced. 'What do you want to do, sir?'

'It seems a pity to kill all of them.'

'If you show me where they are, sir, I'll deal with it.'

Harry could never be sure, even with hindsight, whether Betts thought him mad or ridiculous or both, but at the time it seemed that some unspoken understanding was reached between them – that this mission was not about a fleabitten cat and her starving litter, but a matter of life and death no matter how inconsequential. Betts did everything that was required, straightfaced and with admirable speed and sureness. He grabbed the cat and stuffed her unceremoniously into a kit bag, to bellows of laughter from the other officers; scooped up all the kittens but one, wrapped them tight (with permission) in one of Harry's discarded shirts and dunked them firmly in the pond for a count of thirty seconds. He then returned the furious cat to her one kitten, with some biscuit and meat soaked in water, and announced it was the best he could do.

'At least two stand a better chance than seven. Leave her a bit more food when we move on, sir.'

'I will, thank you, Betts.'

'My pleasure.'

The others were rocking with mirth as he returned to the fire,

'What a gem that man of yours is!'

'A fearsome killing machine!'

'So one pest we shan't suffer from is mice, eh, Latimer?'

'Thank God for that, it would be too much to bear!'

But Harry felt sufficiently calmed to smile good-naturedly and didn't bother arguing. There was no point in pretending there was sense or logic to it, for there was neither. He didn't care for cats in general, and especially this one which was ugly, hostile and verminous. But as they stood to before dawn next day he took a tiny personal comfort from the notion that if the child who owned the doll were ever to return to the house she might be happy to find her cat and its kitten alive amidst the destruction.

The men had eaten too many unripe grapes, and both stand-to and march were marked by the after-effects of their foolishness. It was impossible for the untrained eye to tell the difference between this painful colic and the early stages of cholera, and several sufferers were noisily berated and jeered at, who subsequently died.

The letter had to be written, and two days after the funeral Rachel called on Maria at the dower house to ask about it in terms that were general and therefore diplomatic.

'Please – you will let me know if there is any correspondence that you would like me to deal with?'

Maria, seated at her desk, continued to look down at the letter she was reading. A pair of despised spectacles sat on the end of her long nose with an effect something like an insect on the face of a tiger.

'You mean Harry, don't you?'

'Any that I can help with.'

Maria pulled off the spectacles and looked at her. 'Please write to him for me, Rachel. I know how fond you are of him and how well you will manage it. Whereas I—' she swept a long beringed hand back and forth over the sea of letters '—I have enough to be going on with.'

'I shall say, shall I, that you will write yourself in due course?'

'Naturally. Thank you.' Maria was peremptory but Rachel knew and understood her by now. As she turned to leave Maria said: 'Have you seen the newspaper report?'

'Yes.'

'Do you think . . .' Maria placed the fingers of both hands momentarily over her mouth, eyes closed. 'Do you think that it is right to send this news at this time?'

Rachel was astonished. 'Of course. We must!'

'We have no idea what Harry's condition may be.'

'Whatever it is, he has a right to know that his father has died.' Maria flinched and Rachel regretted her bluntness, adding more gently: 'We have to write, whatever the reports in the papers. It would be unforgivable to leave him in ignorance.'

'Unless,' murmured Maria, the merest breath of sound, 'unless . . .'

'Unforgivable,' repeated Rachel firmly, not allowing either of them to entertain the thought.

It was a far from easy letter to write, and it was true that the first reports from the Crimea had not been encouraging. There was no alternative to simplicity.

'My dearest Harry,' she wrote, and almost immediately discarded the paper and began again.

My dear Harry,

It is with the greatest sadness that I have to tell you of the death of your father only four days ago. Though this news will not, I know, be wholly unexpected, it will be particularly hard to bear while you are so far away. I know how much you cared for him, and he for you. Your mother has been a tower of strength but has generously permitted me to write on her behalf at this time because she herself is still somewhat overcome with the shock, and the many tasks that follow bereavement. She is also, as we both are, desperately worried about you, and concerned that this dreadful news will necessarily add to your sufferings, but we both believe you would prefer to know as soon as the delays of the post allow.

Nothing I can say can alleviate your distress. But I must tell you that Percy died at Bells, peacefully in the sunshine with your mother at his side, and the sights and sounds of the first meet of the season still freshly remembered. If a man could be said to have a good death, then his was a good one. And Maria, as I have said, is quite wonderful – her beauty and courage are commented on by everyone.

Please take care of yourself insofar as it is possible where you are and with the task you must undertake. Accept my deepest sympathy, dearest Harry (she did not change it this time), *and I hope soon to be writing to you again with happier news.*

Believe me your loving sister-in-law,
Rachel

They had no idea where they were heading, or what plan or strategy there was – if, indeed, any such thing existed. They assumed that an assault would be made on Sevastopol – their original objective since leaving England – from the north, since that was the direction in which they were travelling. But each night brought no further news, and each morning delay and frustration before they moved off. They had no idea where the enemy might be, and as the elation of victory wore off so uncertainty took hold. On the third night the cavalry were led into a narrow defile with steep, wooded sides, and spent the night there in a state of uneasy alert, aware that if the enemy had knowledge and opportunity they would attack with almost certain success. But nothing of the kind transpired and they emerged next morning to rejoin the main column, none the wiser as to why such a demonstrably dangerous bivouac had been chosen.

That they had barely clapped eyes on any Russians since freeing the prisoners of the Alma did nothing to reassure them.

After all, the enemy had at his disposal a well-fortified city to which he had now had ample time to withdraw no matter what the condition of his troops and morale. The sighting of occasional small groups of Cossacks on the skyline was unsettling. The allies and the handful of distant horsemen would survey each other suspiciously but take no action, for it was impossible to tell whether the Cossacks were a scouting party, or merely the vanguard of a horde of hostile cavalry. The shallow hills and declivities of the area were deceptive and might conceal large numbers of troops.

So the army continued on its way, steadily but blindly, with no sense of an objective. They reached another river and another ransacked, empty village, equally fruitful, but this time there was no excited pillaging and gorging among the troops.

This was where Leonard Palliser died of cholera. It was very far from the first time Harry had witnessed such a death, but it was only the second that he had witnessed from first to last, of a man in whose company he had been constantly and whom, in spite of a certain bombast and pepperiness in this case, he had come to like.

Its onset was sudden. Not even then did Leonard complain of feeling unwell. As they dismounted near farm buildings he put his hand to his belly and commented that he, too, must have overindulged in the fruit. Such was his character that the rest of them laughed with him. But within half an hour the cramps and pain were so intense that he was obliged to lie down. An hour after that he could no longer stand, and his face already had the characteristic fish-belly pallor and dampness, the eyes sinking back into their sockets and the lips grey. Harry and Hector made him as clean and comfortable as they could, scarcely able to prevent themselves from retching as they did so, and laid him on the verandah of the farmhouse, rigging up a rough screen of blankets to protect him from the flies. They knew there was nothing to be done. Only rarely did a man recover from cholera, but it did happen, and that was a matter for the Almighty. To begin with, when he shouted in agony, one of them would go to him and sit for a while, but after another two hours had passed he was delirious and then barely conscious, the contents of his stomach long since voided, his flesh melting off him in a sour, noisome sweat.

Six hours after the first pain he was, thankfully, dead. It was one a.m. The ground was dry and hard but they dug a grave under a tree behind the pond and buried him, Hector saying a few appropriate words and agreeing to write to Leonard's parents who lived not far from his own in Leicestershire.

They none of them slept that night and the next morning after a stand-to of four hours they began the day's march with energies depleted by tiredness, depression and the fact that they still had no idea of the ultimate aim of their advance.

In the middle of that day they came to a small, isolated farmhouse which to their astonishment was still occupied. A woman, neat in a grey-and-white-striped dress and white apron, came out of the door and stood there waiting for them, with three wide-eyed little girls aged between perhaps three and eight (Harry was no judge of these things) clustered round her skirts.

Hector, who had some Russian, dismounted, handed his reins to Harry and walked over to her. The little girls shrank back, two of them into the house, and the little one bursting into wails of fright so that her mother picked her up and held her face into her shoulder. Harry saw that Hector – not noted for his fine feelings, and first among the tormentors over the cat episode – removed his glove and reached out to touch the child's hair as if to reassure her. It was a deliberate rather than a spontaneous gesture, and had the opposite effect from that which was intended, but the mother acknowledged it with a washed-out smile.

Hector returned, his usual caustic self. 'No language problem. She's married to an Englishman, but the Cossacks took him four days ago and she fears the worst. She's terrified naturally but has nowhere to go. She had a cart, but with their customary generosity they've taken that as well. The children are hungry and she's effectively cut off from both sides and safe with none.'

They found the woman a cart and horse and helped her load on to it as many of her possessions as it would carry. She spoke reasonable, heavily accented English, and her children none at all, though she instructed them to repeat 'thank you' after her, which they did charmingly.

Harry asked her where she intended to go, and she pointed north, adding with a glint of gallows humour: 'It would not be good to go to Sevastopol, I suppose.'

Harry conceded this. 'And your husband?'

She shrugged. 'We shall hope to find each other, God willing.'

'We wish you the very best of luck. You and your daughters.'

She relayed this to the children, already seated on the cart, and with a sharp nod cued another round of thank yous. All of them, like their mother, were the very image of respectability – their hair brushed, their clothes, hands and faces clean. The house itself, as they'd helped remove its contents, had been spotless. Harry could well imagine that this woman, left alone with her family, had been waging her own private war in the only way open to her, with a refusal to let domestic standards slide. His admiration for her was boundless.

As the cart rattled away with its toppling load, the oldest girl, peering round at them, lifted a hand and waved to Harry, who saluted in return.

The landscape was changing as they went south, becoming steeper, the areas of steppe smaller and less frequent. Information at last filtered through. They would not be launching any sort of attack on Sevastopol from the north, but circumventing it to the east, and laying siege to it both from there and from the south, by sea.

A troop of cavalry, accompanied by one of infantry, was sent forward through a wooded area to reconnoitre the main Sevastopol road beyond. The path, which began as a broad and promising one, soon dwindled to something scarcely more than a deer-track along which in places it was only possible for the cavalry to ride in single file. This being the most dangerous deployment possible they could only pray that the enemy had not placed any snipers in the undergrowth, for which they would have provided a virtually unmissable target. They had been assured that Lord Lucan was supplied with a knowledgeable guide for this exercise and that the route that seemed so unpropitious would lead them to the road, and had no alternative but to place their trust in this assurance.

If they had often cursed the baking treeless wastes of the open plain, they now thought of them almost fondly. Here there might be some shade but the air amongst the dense and thorny scrub was suffocating and the atmosphere forbidding. Had it not been for the piercing attack of legions of insects they might have been the only living creatures there. There was no birdsong, not the scurry of a rabbit or the slither of a grass snake. The horses fretted and laboured, their flanks covered in scratches, but theirs was nothing to the discomfort of the infantrymen, who were obliged to carry their rifles above their heads, whose faces and hands were cut to ribbons by the thorns and whose voluble fulminations and swearing punctuated their progress. Eventually any semblance of a path petered out altogether and they were forced to hack and plunge through unbroken coverts of needle-sharp branches that seemed to knit tight at their approach and to close after them.

When a halt was called the relief was shortlived – at least while they moved there was some possibility of emerging from what increasingly felt like a nightmare maze. Standing stock still in the airless heat, with every cut, abrasion and insect-bite smarting with sweat, was still more disorientating, and Harry felt an unfamiliar panic rise in his chest and constrict his lungs.

The delay lasted some twenty minutes. When at last they moved off they discovered that they had been not a quarter of a mile from the road, but that due to some miscalculation of Lucan's guide they had succeeded in arriving there after Lord Raglan himself – who more by luck than judgement had taken the correct route – thereby exposing him to a considerable force of Russians heading north with the intention of an outflanking movement. Only Raglan's composure, it was said, and the consequent uncertainty of the Russians as to what might be behind him, prevented a catastrophe. The two sides had outstared each other, the Russians had blinked first and backed off. Lucan had been publicly reprimanded by the Commander-in-Chief for an error which by any calculation was not his fault, and the result was a still greater blow to the cavalry's pride and morale.

'I am beginning to think,' observed Hector to Harry as they descended the road toward the coast, 'that your treatment of that mangy cat may turn out to be the most heroic act of the cavalry war.'

The port of Balaklava was greeted with acclaim. Steep slopes embraced a harbour of perfect safety, its narrow entrance shielded from the open sea by overlapping bluffs. The still water was so deep that great ships were anchored only yards from the cobbled quay. Pleasant houses, small shops, gardens, churches and secluded lanes spread upward from the harbour on the eastern side, and seabirds wheeled over the cliffs and masts.

The British Army swarmed over it as though this had been the sole objective of the past three months. To be near the great unoccupied expanse of the ocean, to know that once again they were united with the maritime might of England, and to have once more at their disposal the amenities of a populated town, no matter how small and ill-prepared, went to their heads like strong drink. Something like a festive atmosphere prevailed.

But it was a mood which Harry could not share. That night he rode Clemmie out of the town and up to the ruined Genoese fort that stood on the cliff overlooking the harbour entrance. Notwithstanding the lights and fires, the sound of tin whistles and singing, the soaring beauty of the early autumn sky, he could feel no satisfaction.

Behind them was the Crimea. Ahead, the sea. To the west, their enemy, reassembled and well fortified. There could be no turning back now. To Harry, it felt like the end of the road.

CHAPTER SEVENTEEN

'Blue, me?'
—Stella Carlyle, 'Joking Apart'

Stella – 1997

This made the third time in as many weeks that, like a naughty child, Stella had run away.

She knew that it was running away and not simply going out, because she did not tell anyone. Not where, or why, or when she would be back, nor even that she was going at all. If she happened to pass anyone on her way out she might smile but she did not say goodbye. She simply walked out of the villa, silent as a Sioux in her thick sandals, and made her escape.

Once or twice she had walked, but the heat and the steepness of the incline in both directions deterred her. Mostly, she got into the hired Uno and sped away down the pale road towards the village, or up to where it snaked over the lion-coloured Tuscan hills to Siena, thirty miles away. But she seldom had any specific design or plan – her destination was escape itself.

It was the only problem, she decided, in being the hostess. Or if that wasn't too grand a word, the resident, the householder – the chatelaine. She liked that. If the house where people were staying was temporarily yours, then you were the fixed point. It was others who came and went. They brought presents, they mucked in, they shopped and cooked and organised outings, they were assiduous about shared costs and responsibilities (almost too assiduous when Stella wished to retain the whip

478

hand), they 'got out of your hair'. But Stella had discovered in herself an urgent requirement, a need, an imperative, to get out of theirs. And the trouble was that if she told her guests she was going out they wanted to know where, in case they could just hop in and scrounge a lift to wherever it might be. Or they imagined that she must want company, and though she was quite prepared to say that she wished to be alone, that in itself set up a situation in which they were waiting, with cheery grins and barbecue lit, for her return, sure that she needed cheering up and taking out of herself.

Which was the last thing Stella wanted. She was used to herself. She and her self – her various selves – had reached an accommodation over many years of shared living. No matter how diverting and comforting the company of others she needed to get *into*, not out of herself, to dig deep and reflect, to touch base with what was going on in her head and her heart, to discover what it was she thought and felt, and gain a perspective on those thoughts and feelings.

That, after all, was where the songs came from. Not that she intended to write while she was in Italy, but part of the mind-game that she was playing was to allow the subconscious process to begin. She understood that process well enough by now to know that no matter how bad things got they were in the end, as the old journalistic adage went, all good copy. She no longer castigated herself as cold-blooded for this, it was simply how it was with her. It was not too much to say that it was her living in both the emotional and the material sense. And a process that saved her from both despair and insolvency couldn't be bad.

She was fleeing Robert, too. No matter what the professed changes in his life, in the wake of the miscarriage she trusted neither him nor herself. The brief picture that she had entertained of telling him about the baby, of his likely reaction, of how it might be – that was all academic now, just so much old fantasy. She had been in shock. But curiously her mother's suggestion of 'going away with friends', a suggestion dismissed at the time, now commended itself to her. She might not want to go away with people, but perhaps she could go away alone and allow people to come to her . . .

Once she had decided to take a villa she had made her choice and the necessary arrangements quickly and without thought for the cost. After all, she reasoned, her lifestyle was modest by many people's standards, not because she was deliberately economical but because her requirements were few and inexpensive. But if ever there was a moment for not spoiling the ship for a ha'porth of tar, this was it. She wanted a beautiful house in a beautiful place, for six weeks. She wanted a pool and a terrace and a garden big enough to get lost in. She wanted plenty of bedrooms, and she wanted old stones and tiles, with modern plumbing and cooking facilities. She wanted a view. She wanted a motherly soul to help around the place. And she wanted a rural location with amenities that were far enough away to be invisible from the terrace, but close enough to reach in five minutes when supplies ran out. There must be shops, a weekly farmer's market, cafés and a winery. Perhaps something vaguely artistic – a pottery, a local painter, country opera – which she didn't promise to visit but which it would be nice to know was there.

She got all of it, at a price. The Villa Paresi lounged like a jewel on the breast of a sun-kissed courtesan on a southfacing hill overlooking the village of Paresi itself. It was garlanded with vines and bougainvillaea and its skirts of golden-green grass, barred by the long shadows of cypresses, were sparked with wild flowers and flittering with bees and butterflies. Paths meandered through the grass and olive trees sculpted by time reached their knotty hands to the sun. The pool had been created in such a way that it might have been there for two hundred years, with a vine-covered arbour on one side and a curving *terrazza* on the other on which rough urns spouted torrents of crimson trailing geraniums like small volcanoes. There were two bathrooms each the size of a library, and several lavatories ranging from the mediaeval to the turn of the century, all in perfect working order. The kitchen was huge and dim and smelt of herbs, with a table big enough for human sacrifice and a range of pots, pans and cooking equipment second to none. There was help in the unmotherly form of Claudia, a woman minute and sinewy as a lizard and who functioned like one – she could remain inert for hours with a magazine or the works of Danielle Steele, only to explode into a whirlwind of activity when required, cleaning and cooking like some maddened dervish. She almost never smiled, and she rode back and forth from Paresi on a Miss Marple-ish bicycle without breaking sweat. But what she lacked in charm she made up for in efficiency, which was all Stella required.

Best of all was the view: a rolling sea of slumbrous, tawny hills from which a sense of rich ease and wellbeing seemed to rise like a vapour into the shimmering heat. Stella had not, until now, known Italy, but it was love at first sight. Here was a place where beauty and plenty, art and nature, were so constant and abundant that they engendered in people a natural moderation. They lived in perfect harmony with the good things of life because the good things were on tap. Theirs was a sybaritic life, calmed by custom.

Stella herself was by nature not a sybarite. Indulgence for its own sake did not come naturally to her. She saw pleasure as something to be earned, and which she derived mainly from her work. Even the planning of this trip had been deliberate, a means to an end, not something she had undertaken with a long sigh of relief but a project with a purpose. She recognised something feverish and driven in her nature which did not allow for the slow savouring of good things. She was nervy and impatient, anxious always to move on, never living in the moment unless that moment were on stage, its intensity a removal from real life. There was a quieter satisfaction in song-writing, but even that involved the inevitable contradictions of creativity. She was a poor taker of holidays – the notion of going away for a period of enforced leisure was foreign and incomprehensible to her, a quite unnecessary interruption to the hand-to-hand struggle with life.

Italy showed her another way of doing things. She was wise enough to know that it could never be her way to life, but to witness it was to learn more about herself, and to know it was there had a calming effect on her. An aspect of it about which she had had reservations – the warmly flirtatious attentions of the men – she found that she liked. Men, she knew. She'd always understood that with no claim whatever to beauty she nevertheless had a certain sexual power and in Italy she experienced something unusual – the charming admiration of men who recognised her quirky sex appeal as a quality to be acknowledged for its own sake. Their looks, their comments, their gentle advances she took as they were intended, as a compliment. Sitting on a rickety chair outside Paresi's premier café-bar, the Paradiso, with her blowsy early-morning face and hair, wearing her glasses and reading her novel, with a double espresso and a sticky bun, she was made to feel alluring and desirable. There was no tension in the feeling, she was relaxed, soothed by the men's sophistication. The proprietor of the Paradiso took to bringing her little presents – a chocolate, a flower, a postcard – and leaving them alongside the coffee, and men at other tables would chuckle or smile, as if they knew she was someone who needed to be cherished.

All of this was as unlike her past experience as it was possible to be. These men liked women, and they liked her intuitively – without knowing her – for what she was. Their lack of awkwardness or boastfulness charmed her and did not tally with the stories she had heard of outrageous and persistent pestering. She did not doubt that unwelcome bottom-pinching took place in the high summer 'hunting season' in big cities and resorts, but the attention she received was perceptive, kindly and restrained. And the Italian women, she observed, bloomed securely in its warmth and light. There was one ravishing girl who dropped in to the Paradiso on her way to work in the morning – a long, tall, undulating lily of a girl with golden skin and nut-brown hair. This girl received all the admiration she undoubtedly deserved, and received it with queenly calm, but Stella felt in no way diminished by the other's beauty and youth. Here was a liking for women that was like an embrace, and which included each for her own sake.

She had e-mailed selected friends, giving the address of the Villa Paresi and indicating that it would be open house for five weeks – she kept the first week free for herself. She suggested that they give her some idea of their intended arrival and departure dates to avoid any likelihood of a log jam, otherwise she made it clear that she was providing the accommodation and that was all – everyone could treat the place as their own. Those whom she contacted were George and the family, Roger and Fran; Derek and his wife; and Bill and Helen Rowlandson, Jamie's parents.

George and Brian were the first to arrive, somewhat care-worn having hacked door to door in the people-carrier. By far the grumpiest, but also the quickest to recover, was Brian who within an hour of arrival was heard to declare (as he floated on a lilo in the pool with a bottle of Grolsch resting on his midriff) that he intended to stay for ever and never go back – a remark which Stella sincerely hoped was a joke. The children also unwound under the influence of sun, water and a freezer full of *gelati*, and settled into a kind of not-unpleasant boredom, the older two getting up at lunchtime, sun worshipping to music in the heat of the afternoon (mad dogs and teenagers as Brian put it) and larking in the pool till one a.m. Under this dispensation Zoe became a sort of small honorary adult. They were also, Stella considered, rather sweet when taken out, with Zoe and Kirsty overwhelmed by the attentions of waiters, which Zoe accepted with aplomb and Kirsty with a delighted, scowling embarrassment. Mark, at the age when such things discomfited him without his really knowing why, resorted to taunts of the 'Ooh-hoo, Kirsty's got a boyfriend!' variety, while Brian rolled his eyes, pretending despair yet inwardly bursting with paternal pride, and declared that he supposed he'd got years of this to come and it boded nothing but ill.

George was preoccupied. One morning when Brian had taken the children to Siena for a 'spot of culture and a fat lunch' as he put it, she confided in Stella. They were lying on loungers beneath an olive tree a hundred yards from the house, but where they might have been a hundred miles from anywhere. The hill beneath them seemed to give off the warmth of centuries of good living. The tiny insect drone of some lone vehicle on the road only enhanced their sense of seclusion. On the grass between the loungers was a cold bag containing iced coffee, peaches, a bottle of water and another of wine, and a tube of factor 15. Both of them had books; neither was reading.

'I'm up the duff,' said George.

Stella absorbed the blow. 'Congratulations.'

'Brian's going to go ballistic.'

'Ah.'

'Zoe was bad enough – I don't mean Zoe herself, I mean the idea of Zoe when it first happened—'

'I understand.'

'—but this is going to look like deliberate sabotage.'

Stella, glad she was wearing dark glasses, opened the cold bag. 'Want an early one?'

'Oh, go on.'

She poured two glasses of white wine and handed one to George; closed the bag; asked: 'Forget Brian for a moment, how do you feel about it?'

'Queasy. I mean literally. There's a limit to how much longer I can go on pretending I'm spitting out toothpaste in the early morning.'

'Apart from that?'

'God, I don't know, it's all part of the great river of life, I suppose. I'm philosophical. I knew when I married the Army that I was never going to do anything much with my life—'

'*George!*'

'Well, it's true, and don't get me wrong, I have no regrets, I like my life. In an ideal world I wouldn't have wanted this, but once the baby's born I'll be right as rain. Dog-tired, run ragged and looking like hell, but otherwise . . .'

'You make it sound pretty resistible.'

George pulled an agonised face. 'I just want Brian not to be too furious. It's bad enough getting used to the idea myself and chucking up on a regular basis, without him sulking as well.'

'Two things.' Stella glanced at her sister. 'May I?'

'Go ahead.'

'Firstly, don't wait a second. Tell him while you're here, as soon as possible.'

'Good grief, do you know what you're saying?'

'It's a big house, I don't have to listen. Better yet I

484

can take the kids out for the day and show them a good time.'

'Right.' George sighed. 'And second?'

'When you tell him, at least try and sound pleased. Don't start with the assumption that it's the end of life as we know it.'

'No . . .'

'Hmm?'

'I know you're right.'

'Yeah, yeah – I know that tone of voice.'

'No,' protested George, 'I do know it. It's just that when two people know each other as well as Brian and me it's awfully difficult to behave out of character. I mean, he'll know that I'm not exactly over the moon, and he'll also know that I know how *he*'s going to feel. And I know that—'

'George.'

'Sorry. I'm sorry.'

'I won't presume to say I understand but I do see what you're getting at.'

'Do you?'

'I think so.' Stella felt for the wine bottle and dealt another splash into each glass.

'Cheers.'

'How did it happen anyway? Silly question.'

George lifted a shoulder. 'One got through. Nothing but the pill's foolproof and I've not been on that for yonks. I suppose I imagined the old juices were beginning to dry up . . . But no, I'm still at the mercy of it all.'

'You know you're alive, though.'

'In nine months' time at three in the morning it'll be the night of the living dead, I tell you. God, sometimes I envy you.'

Stella had almost subconsciously anticipated this turn in the conversation and prepared herself for it but not, she found, quite well enough. She didn't have to ask why, she knew George would tell her anyway.

'You've got real independence, Stella. You're in charge of your life. I'm not saying we could swap lives, each to

485

her own, but I do sometimes wish I had the freedom-to-choose gene.'

'I'm no different,' Stella reminded her. 'It wasn't so long ago you were telling me not to let myself be pushed around by a man.'

'God!' George slapped a hand to her brow. 'How could I have been so fucking condescending? Me of all people?'

'You weren't being condescending, it was sound sisterly advice. I only mention it to show that I am not the in-control ice maiden of your fantasies.'

'So, anyway, how is the chap?'

'Search me. I haven't seen him in months.'

'Choice or circumstance?'

Stella hoped that her hesitation was too slight to be noticed. 'Choice.'

'There you are, you see. Anyway, you're okay about it.'

'Not delirious. Resigned. Cool, I think your children would say. Cool about it.'

'Cool? Oh!' George rolled her head from side to side in torment. 'Cool is what I long to be!'

Two days later Stella pointedly organised a trip to Fiesole, with a picnic. She even included Zoe, as a sort of lightning conductor to absorb any possible friction between herself and the other two. In fact the day was one of almost unparalleled sweetness and light, and one which she subsequently recognised as being a key point in her rehabilitation. This, she saw, was what she was cut out for and was good at – what was more it actually served a useful function in other people's lives. She was ideally suited to the role of appropriate – or even when required inappropriate – adult without portfolio. Mark and Kirsty were coming into the age zone at which she and Jamie had first started to enjoy one another's company. She was never anything but completely loyal to her sister and discreet about her own life, but still the children were beginning to see not just that she was different – which they had always known – but why she was. They were themselves on the edge, balancing on that sharp and

486

uncomfortable cusp of teenagehood while at the same time assembling their view of others. There would be a spell, not quite yet, when her star would be in the ascendancy, when they would see her as the fount of all worldly wisdom, and that presented the most difficult line to tread – to retain their trust and affection while ensuring that their parents' position remained unshaken.

Kirsty, with more than her share of a girl's natural precocity, was ahead of the game. Mark was in turmoil, sometimes ill at ease, sometimes overdoing it, never quite getting it right. It came as no surprise to Stella that before lunch, when having walked up a steep hill to a vantage point below the church she declared herself ready to sit and drink a glass of wine in peace, it was Mark who took Zoe to explore and Kirsty who lay next to her with her sleek midriff exposed to the sun.

'Stella – may I have some wine?'

'Yes, if you like. But it'll make you thirsty.'

'I don't care.'

Stella poured her a glass.

'Thanks.' She reared up on her elbow and took a sip. 'I'll have a Coke as well.'

'Sure.'

'Don't you like the sun?'

'I do, but it doesn't like me.'

'You mean, you don't go brown?'

'No. And I don't want to be burnt, so I stay cool and pale.'

'Mum doesn't tan either, but Dad goes an amazing colour. He looks quite sexy on holiday.'

'Yes, he does.'

'Do you think?' Kirsty squinted at her as if she'd walked into a trap. 'Honestly?'

'Of course. Your dad's a good-looking man.'

This was going a bit far and Kirsty snorted with laughter. 'Do you fancy him?'

Stella weighed this one up. 'I could do. He's fanciable. But he's your dad, and your mum's husband. So I don't.'

'He fancies you.'

'He flirts with me, that's not the same thing.'

'He goes on about you. He calls you the sultry temptress.'

'That's a joke,' Stella pointed out, but Kirsty was on a roll.

'He does, he goes, "Is the sultry temptress going to be there, do I need more aftershave?"'

'And what does your mother say?'

'Mum says, "Dream on, big boy."' Kirsty sniggered. 'She does. She doesn't mind, she thinks it's funny.'

'She's dead right.'

Stella laughed and Kirsty, gratified at the success of this sally, joined in and knocked over her wine.

'Want some more?'

'No, thanks.'

They were silent for a moment. They could hear the soft wooden 'clop' of goat bells in the middle distance, and Zoe's small voice, its higher frequency carrying to them on the still air, though they couldn't make out what she was saying.

'Mark's being such a good brother,' remarked Stella.

'He is with Zoe, she's a pushover.'

'Don't knock it, it leaves you and me with our hands free.'

Kirsty rolled on to her stomach and lay with her cheek on her arms, facing away from Stella.

'Do you think my parents sleep together?'

'Yes.' It was one of those speak-first-think-later moments. 'I do.'

'Lots of married people don't.'

'What makes you say that?'

'I've read it. In novels. In magazines. They get sick of each other.'

'Probably some do. Having never tried marriage, I wouldn't know. But it doesn't strike me as true of your parents.'

'Why not?' This, Stella sensed, was not a trick or a trap, but a genuine enquiry.

'Because your father wouldn't flirt with me if he wasn't happy. And your mum wouldn't call him big boy if she wasn't.'

There was a silence.

'How does that grab you?' asked Stella.

'Okay.'

'Kirsty.'

'Yup.'

'Do us a favour and go and find the others. It's time we ate and Zoe must be cooking out there.'

'Do I have to . . .'

'No.'

'Oh, okay.'

Kirsty scrambled up. Her cheek, forearms and chest bore a pink lattice-pattern of grass stalks. Watching her trudge off, slapping the debris off her shorts and crop-top, Stella experienced a sudden pang of love for her niece, and a passionate empathy with her confused feelings now and for all the more confused ones that would follow – all the love and hate and hurt and emotional horsetrading that went on in the name of grown-up relationships

After lunch they dozed and fired grassheads at one another and eventually collected up their stuff and found a cool dark bar in which to eat ice lollies. Three men were sitting at the back watching soccer on the television. Zoe went to join them and the youngest of them – a godlike being with slick, black hair and a grubby singlet – took her on to his knee and sat there with his arm round her, pointing out the star players with his half-smoked cigarette.

'Is she all right?' asked Mark.

Stella glanced. 'She looks all right to me.'

Kirsty smirked. 'He's cute.'

'Oooh!'

Stella said to Mark, 'Go and watch if you'd like to.'

'No, thanks. I wouldn't half like a swim, though.'

'You're right. Home time.'

She paid the bill at the counter and retrieved Zoe from her admirers. They could hardly bear to let her go, pinching her cheeks, patting her legs, and ruffling her hair. When she primly flattened her hair and her sundress they laughed, enchanted. The young man who had held her on his knee asked: 'Your daughter?'

Stella shook her head. 'My niece. *La mia niece.*'

'Aah!' More smiles and laughter. The young man nodded towards Kirsty. '*E questa signorina?*'

'Also my niece.'

He spread his hands in a gesture that conveyed wonder, desolation, acceptance. 'So much beauty.'

When they got back the villa was silent. Mark and Kirsty were into the pool like a flash and Stella helped Zoe with her swimming costume and armbands and then sat on the side with her feet in the water to watch. She was almost certain that the silence boded well, it was part of a scenario that embraced declaration, confrontation, separation and reconciliation. This, she was sure, was the reconciliation bit – the big old bedroom cool and dark behind closed shutters, the bodies slithering and whispering on the cotton sheets, sucking and smacking with sweat where they touched . . .

But when an hour later she heard the light slap of footsteps on the stone floor no one appeared, and the next sound was that of the Volvo starting up and going away down the hill at speed. The kids, involved in a noisy infantile game involving the lilo and a lot of shouting, seemed not to have noticed. Stella sat tight.

Ten minutes later George emerged from the house with her arms folded, as if she were cold. She waggled a hand briefly at the children and walked round to join Stella who shone as broad a smile as she could manage.

'How you doing?'

'Hallo, I heard you were back. Sorry I didn't come out sooner.'

'That's okay. We're fine, as you see.'

'Good day?'

'I certainly enjoyed it.'

'It was so kind of you.'

'Not really. You must be doing something right, you have amazingly nice kids. I enjoyed their company.'

George burst into tears. There was no attempt at discretion, these were huge, heaving sobs of the end-of-tether variety. Stella took her by the elbow and pulled her to her feet.

'Mark!'

'Yeah – what's the matter with Mum?'

'She's a bit under the weather, too much sun. Can you two keep an eye on Zoe for a moment?'

'Yeah, sure.'

'They won't . . .' muttered George wetly.

'Then I'll send Claudia out here.'

'She won't like it.'

'Who's paying?'

Stella sat her sister down in the drawing room and went in search of Claudia, who was reading *Ciao!* in the kitchen.

'Claudia, Mrs Travis isn't well. Could you possibly sit out by the pool for a while, just while Zoe's in the water?'

Claudia made a gesture to indicate that such a responsibility was less than a gnat's arse to one who had so many, and withdrew, taking a slab of cooking chocolate from the fridge before doing so. Stella, who suspected that beneath the maid's steely exterior there beat a heart of purest granite, reflected that it was probably national pride which ensured that no matter how misanthropic by nature, Claudia must force herself to be good to children.

She returned to Geroge who was tearstained but composed.

'Drink?'

'No, thanks – oh, go on.'

Stella poured them both a more than medicinal shot of Calvados.

'So?'

'So he's pissed off.'

Stella refrained from making any sarcastic comment along 'poor baby' lines. 'He'll get over it.'

'I know. I just wish it could be yesterday.'

With a pang, Stella recalled that cry of their childhood years when things went wrong, or doom seemed imminent. Yesterday! Paradise – when everything was all right.

'If it was yesterday you'd still have it all to come. Tonight, it's over.'

George laughed feebly, sniffing. 'I suppose.'

'Of course. And this time tomorrow the sunny uplands of your family future will open up before you once again.'

'Uplands is right. I never lost all the weight after Zoe – God knows what I'll be like this time. The largest mammal to walk the south of England.'

'With the greatest cleavage. Buy plenty of tents with plunging necklines, he'll be eating out of your hand.'

'I wish.' George gulped at her drink. 'I sometimes wonder if he fancies me at all, or whether I'm just the nearest available repository.'

Stella thought of the afternoon's conversation with Kirsty. 'You're never going to know that without asking the sort of questions you'll wish you hadn't. My advice is, behave as if you have no doubts. Flaunt that stomach, flash those knockers, massage his machismo and anything else you can lay your hands on. Make him feel like a sex god for getting you up the stick again.'

George sent her a watery smile. 'What's all this? This doesn't sound like the old Stella.'

'What was that?'

'You know. Choose 'em, use 'em, lose 'em.'

'Well,' she replied, 'maybe I'm a changed woman.'

And the next day was the first of her escapes.

It was nothing dramatic, she simply drove to the next village and walked about. She went into the small, perfect church, she found a forge where a silent man made creatures out of black iron, she bought tomatoes and a round, flat, floury loaf, and she found the local equivalent of the Paradiso and sat inside with her book, with the soft click and murmuring of pool being played in the dim recesses at the back.

When she returned in the early afternoon and went upstairs for a siesta, Mark was bobbing in the pool while Kirsty lay face down on a lounger in her pink bikini, her arms dangling over the sides.

'Hallo. Where is everyone?'

'Resting.'

'What, Zoe too?' Kirsty nodded.

'I think I'll do the same.'

Upstairs she passed the door of Zoe's room and saw her niece spark out on the rumpled sheets. She went in to admire for a moment the extraordinary perfection of the very young which was only enhanced by grubby soles of the feet, a felt-tip bracelet drawn on the wrist, and a smear of chocolate at the corner of the mouth.

The villa lay silent, tranced in siesta. Stella's own room – selected on her arrival by *droit de chatelaine* – was on the top floor, the converted half of a loft space, its heat kept bearable by an electric fan, but more than compensated for by its seclusion and the view on three sides from its deep-set windows.

Her foot was already on the first of the wooden stairs when she heard a sound from the direction of George and Brian's room: the steady, quickening, urgent pulse of sex – familiar and unmistakable. She couldn't help listening for a moment, wistfully. But as she continued up the stairs she consoled herself with the knowledge that all was well.

Four days later, with the people-carrier packed up, they stood out on the drive while the kids made a final trawl of the bedrooms. Brian slapped the roof of the car as though it were a horse's rump.

'I thought it was pure affectation when George persuaded me to buy this thing, but now I know it was part of her evil scheme.'

'Really?' said Stella. George was rummaging in her le Sac, and now withdrew, muttering about sunglasses. Brian nodded at her retreating backview.

'Turns out she's expecting.'

Stella reacted on cue. 'Fantastically well done! Found out what's causing it yet?'

'Ha bloody ha.'

'Go on, you're thrilled to bits.' She kissed him and he gave her a more than fraternal squeeze.

'I am actually. God knows why. More bloody expense.' The children emerged from the house. 'Haven't told them yet.'

'They'll be disgusted.'

Brian laughed fruitily. 'Probably! The old aren't supposed to have goatish habits. Come on, you rabble, wheels turn in thirty seconds, where's your mother?'

'In the bog.'

He grimaced at Stella. 'That'll get worse before it gets better in my experience.' He leaned towards her confidingly. 'Tell you what, my darling, you've got it right.'

This being rhetorical she didn't reply, but as she waved them off she reflected that he had meant just the opposite.

After George and Brian left, there was a two–day interval before Roger and Fran arrived for a week, and a two–day period when they overlapped with their successors, Helen and Bill Rowlandson. In the wake of the Travises the villa was eerily quiet. Stella missed the children

Roger and Fran were very nearly the perfect guests. The 'old hippydom' to which Jamie had once glancingly referred stood them in good stead when it came to sharing other people's houses. They were serene, adaptable, happily self-sufficient or appreciatively convivial as required, and enjoyed a partnership of unparalleled amiability. That was the only word Stella could think of to describe it. She suspected that passion did not feature largely in their relationship but if so they were a wonderful advertisement for the deep, deep peace of the double bed. She was starting to form the impression that if marriage were to be tolerable it must either be fraught and fecund like her sister's, or tranquil and complacent as this one was.

Five days passed. Five days of calm, filled in the Turners' case with blameless sightseeing and postcard-sending. Stella accompanied them on only one trip, to Florence but even there they went their separate ways, Fran and Roger to OD on culture, Stella to meander less purposefully. The meanderings took her first to a jewellery shop of such ineffable elegance and modernity that she hesitated on the threshold and had to remind herself quite forcibly that it *was* only a shop and that her plastic was as good as the next person's.

The shop contained nothing as prosaic as a counter, though there was a circular glass table in the centre from which protruded a revolving glass cylinder that rose to the ceiling. The cylinder contained a pale swirl of thicker glass, so that the effect created was that of smoke rising in a transparent chimney. A woman in an aerodynamically tailored cream shantung shift and pearls stood at the back of the room and murmured *'Buongiorno'* with the languor born of a seller's market. The last time Stella had encountered such glacial elegance and condescension was at the Elmhurst Clinic, and the memory stiffened her sinews.

There were perhaps a dozen pieces at most displayed in the shop, but Stella craved one of only three in the window. She pointed and the woman glided to her side on a wave of *Giò*.

'That necklace – may I see it?'

'The collar?'

'Yes.'

The woman lifted it out and presented it to Stella on her upturned palms. It was a paper-thin circlet of beaten silver with a single asymmetric leaf hanging from it. It wasn't often Stella craved such a thing, but she craved this.

'Can I try it on?'

'Of course.' The woman indicated a mirror.

Stella put it on, fumbling with the minute clasp. The woman's cool fingers came to her assistance.

'Thank you.'

'Molto bella.'

The necklace was so fine it seemed like silk rather than metal, and so perfectly designed that it moulded itself to her thin collarbones as if it had been made for her. The woman stood with folded arms. Stella sensed a softening of her attitude, not attributable to a likely sale but to a shared appreciation of the piece.

'I'll take it.'

The woman waited for a second until she had undone the necklace and then withdrew to her lair behind an arras at the back of the room. Stella realised that the price had not been mentioned by either of them – the woman presumably from a discreet assumption of wealth in her customers, she through sheer pigheadedness.

It was stupendous. More than she had paid for any single item in her life, besides her car, her London flat and the Villa Paresi. She hoped that the woman would think it was insouciance rather than shock which kept her numb-faced as her card was swiped

But the moment she emerged into the beat and bustle of the sunlit street she forgot the money. To have bought beauty, for its own sake, was a pleasure she scarcely ever permitted herself. Now she knew why people did it.

She entered a web of twisting back streets and turned into the narrow door of a church. Inside it was dark; and so cool that her skin shrank into goose pimples. As her eyes grew accustomed to the twilight she took in the pale, circular dome with its gorgeous bucolic fresco of a shepherd and his sheep . . . a lush, doe-eyed Mary behind the altar, her blue robe swept in an involuntary and wholly Italian flourish around her legs . . . the Bible in a glass case . . . drooping fresh flowers and strident artificial ones . . . white walls and gilt candelabra . . . the austere and the exotic, the sacred and the sexy.

Stella was an unbeliever but she liked the sequestered anonymity of these Italian churches. There was an assumption of faith, or perhaps an acceptance of humanity, that she found absent in any church she'd been into in England. She bought a candle, lit it and added it to the half dozen or so already in the rack. Thought of her lost baby. Then placed another next to it, gently, for Robert.

She sat down on one of the hard chairs and took her necklace out of its bag, then its box. She held it in her hands, wondering if this constituted the worship of Mammon. It didn't feel like that. As she smoothed the ripples of silver between her fingers she could imagine that this was how it would feel to tell the rosary – a way of concentrating, of focusing the mind.

As she sat there she heard the door open and footsteps clicked on the stone floor. There was a pause – for holy water, a genuflection, the sign of the cross – and the footsteps came up the aisle. A smart matron in a leather coat and spike heels went to a chair at the front and knelt down, bowing her head on to a hand heavy with rings. After a couple of minutes she sat back and performed a few swift repair rituals, patting her hair, dabbing her eyes and cheeks with a tissue, smoothing her collar, before sweeping out with magnificent composure.

Stella allowed the silence to lap round her again for a while, and then returned the necklace to its bag and left. With her hand on the door she turned and made a swift mental obeisance to the kindly building – a genuflection of the heart.

Brimming over with a kind of benign melancholy, she treated Fran and Roger to a historic lunch, and became slightly drunk.

'So,' she said over the *linguini*, 'are you all Pitti-ed out? Got the t-shirt and the blisters to go with it?'

'It's all quite wonderful,' declared Fran. 'Such a comfort, somehow, to know there is another plane of existence.'

'Was,' Roger corrected her.

'Not at all, the great stream of human creative endeavour goes on. Look at Stella.'

'Steady on,' she said.

Roger looked embarrassed. 'How have you spent the morning?'

'I bought a necklace and sat in a church.'

'An excellent balance by the sound of it.'

'Come on then,' said Fran, 'let's see.'

They exclaimed over the necklace, and over the lunch. 'It's all so beautiful,' said Fran. 'So unnecessarily troubled over.'

Roger agreed. 'It's the unnecessary bits that make the difference.'

'It was so lovely of you to invite us.'

'My pleasure. It was the least I could do.'

'If you mean Ailmay, all those years ago – please! It's hardly the same.'

'No, you're right,' said Stella. 'Ailmay changed my life.'

★　　★　　★

497

It was not Helen and Bill Rowlandson's fault that their arrival threw out the balance at the Villa Paresi. It was simply that the balance depended on Stella, who now found herself perched precariously on the tightrope between two sets of old friends who no longer had anything in common. It was unwise, as the last in, to assume greater intimacy with either side; at the same time, if only for selfish reasons, she wished the forty-eight hours that they were together to run smoothly.

Jamie's mother Helen was a creamy Home Counties beauty who neither swam nor sunbathed and whose personal style resembled, in Stella's opinion, that of a model in her mother's back numbers of *Vogue*, known as Mrs Exeter. Only with the greatest effort could Stella accept that Helen was just five years older than her. On the other hand, since Helen had looked much the same for as long as Stella could remember, it seemed likely that this state of affairs would continue into the future, to Helen's probable advantage. They had nothing in common except Jamie and Bill, with whom Stella had had a brief and unmemorable liaison some fifteen years ago. She was painfully aware that in Bill's case a second pounce was a distinct possibility. Just as she knew Brian's robust flirtatiousness to be entirely safe, so she sensed Bill's lustfulness in every small avoidance of her eye and touch, his breezy, cowardly, feigned indifference.

She was sure that Fran and Roger were not aware of this, and just as sure that Helen was. Over dinner on the Rowlandsons' first night she enquired after Jamie.

'And how is the boy whose spiritual guidance I've so assiduously undertaken?'

Bill snorted. 'You did a good job. He's godless, like they all are.'

'He's doing very well,' protested Helen. 'Expanding his horizons as we speak.'

'In what way?'

'We liked Ingrid,' remarked Roger, as if reading Stella's thoughts. 'I suppose she's no longer around?'

'Good heavens, no,' laughed Helen, dismissing this youthful aberration with silvery lightness. 'That was years ago. We do need to bring you up to speed.'

'So what is he doing?' repeated Stella.

'Bumming round Europe,' replied Bill, 'with that waste of space Jonno and two females.'

'And is one of those a special female?' asked Fran.

'Yes,' said Helen. 'His current girlfriend, Nina. She's very nice. We like her, don't we, darling?'

Stella detected a glint of steel in this enquiry, which had the desired effect, because Bill agreed that, yes, they did.

'Actually,' went on Helen, 'we wondered if we could ask you a small favour?'

'Hang on, hang on!' Bill raised a hand like a policeman stopping traffic. 'Less of the "we". *You* wondered. And the favour you want to ask is not by even the most magnanimous standards small.'

'Anyway,' said Stella, 'ask away.'

'The thing is,' said Helen, 'they're swanning around the Black Sea ports at the moment, as far as we know. He's been keeping in touch by e-mail, I don't know if there's an internet café round here?' Bill spluttered. 'There might be, they're everywhere these days . . . Anyway, the last we heard he was in that neck of the woods, but they're rapidly running out of cash and we simply wondered—'

'Simply!'

'Do shut up, Bill, we simply wondered if we could let him have this address if he desperately needed a staging post.'

'Of course. I can't think of anything nicer.'

'Really? You must lead a sadder life than I thought,' said Bill.

Stella ignored this. 'I may not have taught him the Good Book, but I can provide him with food, drink and loose talk any time. And his pals as well.'

'There's absolutely no need for that. I mean, the contingency will probably not arise anyway, but if it does it goes without saying that no one's expecting you to—'

'For crying out loud, Hel,' said Bill loudly, 'if they're potless and starving she can hardly say, "I'll take that one and not those." It's love me, love my dogs. That's what I object to.'

'But I don't,' said Stella firmly. 'And there's a cybercafé in

Florence in the Plaza Medici. I'm not going anywhere for a while. Simple.'

After dinner, with coffee, *Strega*, and Dean Martin warbling on the stereo, Stella wandered off, thinking like a discreet matchmaker to leave the two couples to it, so she was put out to discover Bill hot on her heels. Or not so much hot as following at an elaborately unconcerned distance, positioned between her and the soft lights of the villa.

'You're right,' he said, as though she had spoken. 'A walk seems like a good idea.' And when she didn't reply, added: 'This is an incredible place, how did you find it?'

'In the newspaper, as one does.'

'It's sensational. A person could get used to this sort of thing.'

She continued to walk and he, to her annoyance, to follow, not drawing level but remaining about three paces behind her.

'Joking apart, it is extraordinarily decent of you to let us give your address to the Eurotrash.'

'That's not what they are, and I'd like to see them.'

'Whatever you say. Thanks anyway.'

'Don't mention it.'

'I say, Stella.' She heard from his voice that he had stopped – a way of stopping her without touching, or asking her to. She did stop, but didn't look at him. Gazed, instead, at the sky.

'Stella, you know what I'm going to say.'

She sighed. Said woundingly: 'Gimme a break.'

'If a bloke can't say it in this setting, where the hell can he? You know I've always cared about you. You still do it for me, you know.'

'Thank God. It's been preying on my mind: What if Bill's lost interest?'

'I love it when you're sarcastic.'

'Do you?' She turned to face him. 'Then I won't be. Don't kid yourself, Bill. You never cared about me, any more than I cared about you. We had a heartless little fuckfest – how many years ago? And if you entertained even the smallest notion of reviving it here, then think again. I'm paying. I reserve the

500

right to chuck out.' She took a couple of steps towards him. 'Just think of that long drive home, nine hundred miles in the car with Helen wanting to know why it all ended in tears.'

'Stella . . .' He adopted a wheedling, would-I? tone, spread his arms in supplication. 'What's all the fuss about? Can't a chap wax romantic with an old flame in Tuscany in July? Since when was that a hanging offence?'

'Since right now.' She stabbed a finger towards the ground. 'Excuse me, I'm going back to the others.'

What happened next shocked her. He stood back to let her pass, but as she did so he caught her chin in his hand, wrenched her face round and kissed her, open-mouthed, on the lips, his head shooting forward, tongue darting, like a snake's. It was over in a second and then he was walking in the opposite direction.

The next day was the second of her escapes.

An instant, and her period of fragile peace was over. She didn't concern herself overmuch with the Bill incident, which though disgusting had not been repeated. But when he'd turned her face to his and forced his slippery tongue between her teeth it was as if he had thrust before her a picture of herself. Like a blackmailer he had gloatingly confronted her with her past. She couldn't shake it off – who she was, what she had done, how she had behaved. It looked as if all that would stain and infect her life for ever.

After the Turners had gone, she told Bill and Helen she was going to try and do some work, and so left them to their own devices and fled. She drove towards Florence and stopped to visit a *palazzo* where it was rumoured that various international litterati had indulged in high jinks of the dope-and-doubling-up-variety between the wars. The house was huge and grand and the tiered gardens formal. She found it a gloomy, haunted place, in keeping with her mood. In some of the rooms, amongst the eighteenth-century magnificence, there were displays of photograhs of the dissolute English writer and his guests, their grinning faces mad and wild, so that Stella seemed to hear a shimmer of sound like gibbering ghosts in the stately rooms. Upstairs the writer's own bedroom had been kept as it was, furnished in black and white like a thirties ocean liner, except for a single portrait of a *contessa*, heavy-eyed and swan-necked, who gazed disdainfully down towards the bed.

In spite of its strange and threatening atmosphere she spent all day at the *palazzo*, retreating to the gardens and sitting beneath a tree when a coach party arrived. Was she like those people in the photographs? And if she was, did it matter? They had not been wicked, surely, only venal and amoral, and was that so terrible? Whence, she asked herself fiercely, all this conscience? It had scarcely troubled her for years, why now, when she least needed it?

The coach party began to trickle out of the long gallery, through the double doors and down the broad, shallow flight of steps. They paused dutifully while the guide directed their attention back to the building's stately façade. They were a group elderly yet sprightly, all neatly and appropriately dressed in pale drip-dry fabrics, trainers, baseball caps. The guide was speaking in English, but they might have been Scandinavian. The couple nearest to her were white-haired. The woman wore baggy beige trousers with a drawstring waist. As Stella watched, the man put out his hand and caressed his wife's bottom. The attention of neither of them wavered as he stroked and kneaded, his middle finger occasionally probing the furrow between her ample haunches. When the group turned to continue their tour, the couple's faces were perfectly collected and proper, the woman reading something out to her husband from the guide book.

Stella let them go by and then returned to the car, moving like a sleepwalker in the afternoon heat. She knew why the stupid, gross liberties of a man like Bill had so dashed her spirits, and why she could not bear to be reminded of her past. It was because love had come into her life. No matter how imperfect, how shabby and vexatious and compromised, it was love nonetheless. And that had changed her.

★　　★　　★

The Rowlandsons, to her intense relief, departed. Derek and Miriam Jackman arrived. They were a tonic. On holiday, Derek wanted nothing more than to do as he was told, to go, as he explained, where he was put, so long as it didn't entail too much effort. His was an enviably steady, sanguine nature and here, as on stage, Stella felt herself temporarily anchored by him.

Miriam was a bustling sprauncy blonde, never less than immaculate, fearsomely organised, born to shop and flirt with waiters. When you went out with Miriam, as Derek pointed out, you just let her get on with it. She was a force of nature.

'Now what I really *need*,' she would declare musingly as she painted her toenails by the pool, 'is a pair of tarty shoes.'

This would cause Derek to roll his eyes at Stella. 'What can she mean?'

'You know, darlin', the sort you come to Italy to buy. Red crocodile, six-inch heel and ankle strap.'

'Perfect for the superstore, Bexley Heath.'

'No, it's gotta be done!' This was her catch phrase, relating to everything from shoes and earrings to restaurants and Renaissance churches.

With the Jackmans, Stella had fun. Fun was what Miriam was good at, and Derek went along with her. Unsurprisingly, for his wife was a woman without a mean bone in her body. Because marriage was, to Stella, a foreign and uncharted land, she never ceased to be amazed by its peculiarities – that some devoted unions could be sundered by a puff of wind while others, on the face of it far less propitious, could withstand any number of storms. Not that she suspected the Jackmans of weathering storms, exactly, but given Derek's genial nature and his line of work the conditions could not have been entirely calm. Even her own professional relationship with him might for another woman have been a cause for jealousy, but on every occasion that she and Derek's wife had met Miriam had treated it as a reason not for resentment but for friendship.

Another of her lines, spoken in a spirit of warm sisterly collusion, was: 'Stella, he's only a bloke, but I love him – someone has to.'

For his part Derek, because he knew Stella first and foremost through her work, knew her better than anyone. He was the only one among her visitors who in a quiet moment was moved to ask: 'Everything okay, kiddo?'

They were sitting over coffee outside the Paradiso one morning when Miriam had elected to shop for dinner at the farmers' market.

There was no point in trying to deceive him. He was direct but also wholly discreet.

'I've been better.'

'Thought so.' He passed her a cigarette and lit hers, then his. 'That what all this is in aid of?'

'Yes.'

'And is it working?'

She considered this carefully. 'In a way. It is God's little acre. And it's given me time to think.'

'Not too much, I hope.'

'I've had plenty of company.'

Derek's eyes followed a pretty girl in a blue sundress. 'Any romance?'

'Hardly.'

'Rubbish! You never looked better, girl.'

'Thanks. Maybe that's why.'

'Don't go getting all bitter and twisted.'

'I'll try not to, but I don't see why not. Bitter and twisted's been my stock in trade and my living for the past twenty years.'

Unexpectedly, he stroked her forearm briefly with his blunt pianist's fingers. 'You like to think that but it ain't so.'

'Derek . . . Who writes the damn' songs?'

'You do, and full respect to you. But the thing is they're good songs, and good songs say all kinds of things you don't mean them to.'

It was perhaps the nicest, truest and most loving thing that had been said to her in months. Stella had to turn her head away to hide her face.

'Yeah?' said Derek. 'Yeah.'

★   ★   ★

The Jackmans left and Stella was alone at the Villa Paresi. With the end of her Italian idyll in sight she became restless, but resisted the urge to cut short her stay, for two reasons. One was because in spite of the restlessness she was reluctant to confront the uncertainties of her other 'real' life at home. The second more immediate and practical one was that Jamie and his friends might yet turn up.

By two days before her flight she had convinced herself that they were probably not going to, and was therefore astonished when one afternoon a sharp summons from Claudia recalled her from the shade of the olive tree to find four dusty figures on the far side of the pool.

'Jamie!'

'Any chance of a beer and a bed for the night, lady?'

She ran round and hugged him. No transgression of his father's could tarnish her pleasure in seeing him. She kissed the beaming, blushing Jonno, too, and was introduced to the two girls. Jenny was freckled and Junoesque with her brown hair clipped so that it stuck up in a spiky fan. Nina was slender and black, inscrutable in wraparound shades. Claudia brought a tray of frosted stubbies and a bottle opener and they stripped off and took the beer into the pool with them, shrieking and larking about like children with the drop-dead gorgeousness of it all.

They were gorgeous, too. Stella sat on the side and thought this should have happened earlier, this boisterous physical happiness, this exuberance. What Manley Hopkins called 'all this juice and all this joy'.

Nina stopped being inscrutable and came to the side with Jamie.

'This is so, so great. It's unbelievable.'

'Glad you like it,' said Stella. 'I don't always live like this.'

'Jamie said you were cool, but this is outrageous . . .'

'How were the olds?' asked Jamie.

Stella did not break stride. 'In good form, it was nice to see them.'

'It's really good of you to put us up, especially when you're so pushed for space . . .'

'That'll do.'

Jenny, it turned out, was a legal secretary, Nina was a publishing PR whom Jamie had met via the breakfast show. Over dinner, they told their travellers' tales. Amongst the usual stories of lost wallets, exotic rip-offs, historic nights and wicked beaches were those other ones: those places and experiences that you could tell were even now forming the way they thought. Prague, where they'd stopped on the bridge before dawn and heard a lone violin playing . . . a ruined castle miles off the beaten track in Cyprus . . . a jungle village in Thailand . . . a horrific zoo in Malaysia . . . a whale that nuzzled the boat off Queensland and caused Jonno to lose his camera . . . and a valley in the Ukraine where they'd lost each other in the maze of vines.

'That was creepy,' said Jenny. 'It was like they were actually growing while we were there. *The Day of the Vines. Vines III, The Nightmare Continues.*'

Jonno said: 'It wasn't that big an area, we were just disorientated. It only took us, what, half an hour?'

'It was bloody miles from anywhere,' said Jamie. 'Three hours on a Coca-Cola lorry from Simferopol with the missing link at the wheel . . . Christ!' They laughed ruefully, remembering. 'It was Nina who dragged us there.'

'It was brilliant.' She turned defiantly to Stella. 'It was the North Valley – where the Charge of the Light Brigade happened?'

'Yes, of course.'

'Crawler,' said Jamie.

Stella ignored him. 'And was it worth it?'

'Yes, it was amazing. Unchanged. Haunted, you know?' She batted Jamie's hand away good-naturedly. 'It was good being lost. The others were all out of sight, right, shouting and mucking around. I kind of stood there with these vines whispering all round and I was, like, all those men and horses died here. Their bones are probably right underneath where I'm standing. It was weird . . .' She shook her head. 'Brilliant.'

'No, fair play, it was all right,' agreed Jamie. 'Hey, Jonno, show Stella what you found.'

'She won't be interested . . .'

'Yes, I will.'

'Hang on, I've got it,' said Jenny. She went over to her rucksack and thrust her fingers into the outer pocket. Coming back, she handed a small object to Stella. 'There you go.'

'Cop that,' said Jamie.

It was a brass uniform button, cleaned up but with some greyish soil still clinging to the engraving. She held it to the lamp, turning it in her fingers.

'It's wonderful . . . I've got a picture at home of a soldier from the Crimean War – a photograph actually. I should think it's posed – sort of propaganda.'

'I've seen that,' said Jamie. 'It's called "Golden Slumbers" or something.'

'"Only Sleeping".'

'Go on,' said Jonno, 'you keep it.'

'Oh, no,' she held it out, 'I couldn't, it's precious.'

'All the more reason to do what the man says.' Jamie engulfed her hand in both of his, curling her fingers round the button. 'Take it. Peppercorn rent.'

And the next morning was the third escape.

On this occasion it was an escape only in the sense that the others didn't know she had gone. They'd all sat up until two a.m. and she knew they wouldn't surface before one. She went into Florence early enough to have her breakfast there, and to buy a couple of two-day-old English newspapers to keep her company over the cappuccino.

She didn't even glance at the papers for a while because it was so pleasant to sit there and feel at home, and watch the natives on their way to work. When she did do so she read the broadsheet first, and then did some of the cross-word – to sit at a table and not feel compelled to look up, that was a sign of accustomedness – before flipping through the tabloid.

The headline caught her eye: MOTHER CALLED 'NEUROTIC AND INTERFERING' BY DOCTOR WHO FAILED HER SON.

An enquiry has been called into the behaviour of a top ophthalmic consultant who hurled insults at the mother of a patient when she questioned his professional judgement. Mr Robert Vitelio, senior consultant in ophthalmics at St Xavier's Hospital in north London, allegedly called Mrs Eleanor Stuart, 34, 'neurotic and interfering' and 'a danger to shipping' when she asked why she had not been kept fully informed about the condition of her son Conor, 10, whose eyesight was damaged in a cycling accident. Mrs Stuart claims that not only was she 'treated like an idiot' for voicing normal parental concerns, but that following the failure of a course of laser treatment Mr Vitelio implied that her attitude had been unhelpful and positively detrimental to Conor's progress. Mr Vitelio has so far made no comment but one of his colleagues described him as a brilliant clinician not noted for his bedside manner. He and his wife, Dr Sian Vitelio, a GP, have recently separated. At her home in Ealing Dr Vitelio also refrained from commenting.

The incident is only the latest in a string of unfavourable publicity for the NHS which will do nothing to cheer the government . . .

Stella folded the paper and left it on the table with her payment.

That night they all got very drunk. They ate at the café in the village and then visited both bars before catching the local taxi back to the villa. Stella was at her best, the way she had been on the night – how long ago – when she'd taken Jamie and Jonno with Gordon to the Criterion after the London show. She was flying, she could do no wrong, and she had the perfect audience. They were under her spell.

At the villa they put on a salsa CD and danced wildly on the terrace, periodically jumping, or falling, into the pool. They drank several bottles of wine and smoked dope.

Stella couldn't remember going to bed. When she woke in the night, desperate to go to the lavatory, there was a warm, smooth body next to hers. Jonno. She wrapped herself in her swimming towel and went first to relieve herself, then to what had been Zoe's little room, lying on the unmade bed with her head throbbing, and sick to her stomach.

It was late afternoon next day before she saw any of them, and it was Jamie who came down first, sliding into the pool and leaning against the wall alongside her.

'Jonno wants you to know he's sorry.'

'Oh!' She groaned and covered her eyes with her hands. 'It takes two.'

'He was trolleyed.'

'We all were. No harm done.' He began to swim away. 'Jamie—'

'Yup?'

'You know Jonno . . . He's not going to make some sort of big deal of this, is he?'

'Hardly. It wasn't the biggest success ever.'

She frowned. She couldn't remember. 'No?'

'Uh-uh.' Jamie tapped his head. 'You were with someone else.' He crossed in three long strokes to the other side of the pool. 'Does nothing for a guy to be called by the wrong name.'

'Poor Jonno.'

'Poor you,' said Jamie. 'Poor bloody Robert.'

CHAPTER EIGHTEEN

———◦◦◦———

'Life seems more sweet that thou didst live
And men more true that thou wert one;
Nothing is lost that thou didst give,
Nothing destroyed that thou hast done'
—Anne Bronte, 'Farewell'

Spencer 1961

Not for the first time in Spencer's life, it was the small plane that made the big difference: the spunky little turbo-prop that droned and bounced from Wyoming to Denver. Once Spencer arrived in the mile-high city he felt he'd made the quantum leap – that was when the boy was taken out of Moose Draw, and Moose Draw had been taken out of the boy long since.

Or that was what he believed, and he hoped it was true. If he'd ever needed proof that it was the geography of the mind, not of the map, that mattered, the last fifteen years had supplied it. He was married, he had a lovely wife, a house, a big back yard and a dog named Thumper who played in it. No kids, but that aside his was the very model of the all-American good life.

Except for one thing – he wrote about it. And to write about it he had to be that little bit detached, to be always aware of his life's quirks and contradictions, its simple truths and its messy corners, its universalities and its idiosyncrasies. When it was a bitch, and when it was good. He had to chew on life and extract the juice, not swallow it whole.

One thing was for sure, he'd never have considered going

510

back to England for a reunion if it hadn't been for the syndicated column and the radio series, and the Rotarian meetings and ex-servicemen's dinners. He had let the sleeping dogs of the past lie for fifteen years now: Church Norton was a long way off in every respect. When at functions and fundraisers he spoke to other veterans of the war in Europe, he would always wind up inwardly thanking God he didn't have to live on the bygone glory days. There was no denying that the war had been an extraordinary chapter, but for a man to let it define him was to deny the present with all its possibilities.

So, no, he wouldn't have accepted the reunion invitation had it not represented grist to his mill, and having done so, he was wary. The writer in him warned against entering into the thing wholeheartedly: it was vital to maintain a distance, watch, observe, monitor his own reactions. But it was impossible not to feel some excitement, and he told himself this was only natural. There was no shame in making this one journey. He would surely never make it again.

Hannah, surprisingly, had been all for it.

'You should go, whatever. It's right that you should – it'll be a rite of passage.'

He smiled. It still amused him when she came out with these technical terms. 'In what way?'

'It'll close the door on the past.'

'I already closed it. What if this opens it again?'

'Then that'll be interesting as well.'

'Oh, it'll be interesting all right . . .'

She'd swiped at him affectionately and he'd caught her wrist and cuddled her, thanking his lucky stars as always that things had turned out the way they had. He was unashamedly uxorious, still in love after thirteen years of marriage, scarcely able to believe his good fortune. He knew now that he had been right all those years ago when, as a red-faced boy overcome by passion, he'd told Apples that he loved her, and it was as if some benign fate had been listening then and, giving him the benefit of the doubt, had granted him a second chance in spite of everything.

There had been no clearcut decision not to have kids, they had simply not come along, but he was glad of it – the truth was kids would have got in the way. Hannah and Spence were a great team, they knew it themselves and everyone said so: they had nothing to prove.

Though he couldn't help teasing her sometimes, he was terrifically proud of her. His wife, the doctor – and a psychiatrist at that! He even liked it that she used her maiden name professionally. It was a token of his love that he wanted her to soar and fly, he could only be enhanced, never diminished, by her success. And – what was a source of wonder to him – in spite of all she'd achieved there was still beneath it, warm and strong, the girl who had love to give away, more love than she knew what to do with, love to spare, only now it was all his. He felt as though he had been given the key of a beautiful garden and told: It's yours; enjoy.

Once Hannah qualified she'd come back and started a practice in Salutation, which was now a big modern town with a population that had tripled since the war. He'd remained in Moose Draw after Mack died, to be near Caroline, but after he and Hannah got married they built a beautiful wooden house about ten miles this side of Salutation, and bought his mother a neat retirement home in the suburbs. She'd acceded to this more than enthused. If there was one tiny problem nibbling at the edge of his marriage it was that it had distanced him slightly from his mother. This was not due to any change in his attitude, and certainly not to any behaviour of Hannah's, but Caroline herself seemed to have withdrawn, as though she felt she must leave them to it.

Together he and Hannah had rediscovered the mountains. They'd bought a four-wheel-drive and gone miles up the canyons, and over the top of the range, way, way up to the Medicine Ring, the two-thousand-year-old Indian monument. Standing gasping at ten thousand feet on that sharp ridge of rock, in a wind that was pure vaporised ice, they'd wondered at the spirit of the people who'd put the monument there, and the sheer tenacity of those who still came, regularly, to leave the votive offerings that streamed and snapped in the bitter air.

He took Hannah back to see the wild horses, now on a protected range, and tried to explain how they'd affected him as a boy. He described the mustang at the rodeo, something he hadn't thought about for years.

'He scared the living daylights out of me, I can tell you. That was one crazy horse.'

'Poor thing.' She was always so tenderhearted.

'Well . . . kinda. He was the champ, remember, he'd seen off just about everyone that tried to ride him.'

'Let's hope they pensioned him off on some beautiful slopes, with a harem.'

'A stallion has to fight for a harem.'

She'd chuckled. 'A dirty job but someone has to do it!'

He had once attempted to work Hannah into a column, thereby provoking the closest they'd ever come to a row. She had been absolutely white with fury, slapping the paper down on the table in front of him.

'What's this?'

'Honey – you don't mind?'

'Of course I mind.'

'But you're such an important part of my life, and it's my life I write about, I can't go on pretending you don't exist—'

'Not writing about me is not the same as pretending I don't exist. And I'm not just part of your life, I am all of my own.'

He was hurt. 'Naturally, I realise that, if I'd had any idea—'

She rounded on him. 'What I don't understand is *why* you had no idea? I'm a doctor, Spencer, I have patients whose confidentiality I have to respect.'

'I never mentioned your patients.'

'But how do you think they're going to feel, seeing me used as some kind of funny-ha-ha material in the local paper?'

The number of implied belittlings in this question took his breath away, and sent ice water through his veins.

'I am so sorry.'

'Me too.' He could hear that she didn't mean the same thing.

'Hannah? Honey?'

'It's okay.' She sat down and put her hands to her face; drew a long, deep breath. 'Forget it.'

But he knew he couldn't, and that he must not, either. It had blown over, but the incident had shown just how thin was the layer of experience and maturity they'd each of them laid down. It was all still there, waiting to ambush them – the confused and vulnerable past.

He'd asked her if she wanted to come to the reunion with him – wives were included in the invitation – but she'd declined. 'That's your history,' is what she said.

The pretext for the reunion was the creation of a memorial on what used to be the airbase. The chairman of the Church Norton branch of the British Legion had written to Spencer before Christmas explaining that such a memorial was long overdue, that it was something the Legion and the Parish Council wished to put in train, and to that end they were contacting as many people as possible who had served on the base for a reunion over a long weekend at the end of May 1961. At this stage they were simply trying to find out whether there would be enough people interested to make such a project viable, so if he'd be kind enough to let them know, etcetera, etcetera.

Now he had in his hand luggage the finalised programme of events: an introductory cocktail party, buffet and official welcome at Church Norton village hall; a tour of the airfield and proposed memorial site on the Saturday morning, followed by free drinks at the pub, lunch and a sightseeing trip to Cambridge in the afternoon; a dance at the village hall that evening, open to all, but at which veterans would be the guests of honour; and a service in the church on Sunday morning, with traditional Sunday lunch in various private homes afterwards.

There was an organised group going from the States, but he'd elected to be independent, reasoning that that way he could more easily dip in and out of the proceedings, and find time to make notes and collect his thoughts. Wanting to remain clearheaded, not fuddled with nostalgia, he booked into a roadhouse ten miles down the main London road from Church Norton, the nearest thing to an American motel in the neighbourhood.

On the Thursday night after he arrived he ate a limp, pale apology for a ham sandwich in the bar, accompanied by a Scotch in which a few tiny lozenges of ice floated like frogspawn. But the barman asked him if he was on holiday, and when he explained, gave him one on the house. He also told Spencer that coming from America he might be interested in a Roman villa which had been excavated beneath the main road.

'You'd never guess it was there,' he said proudly. 'Traffic buzzing to and fro right overhead.'

'You've seen it yourself?'

'Not as such,' admitted the barman. 'But I've sent quite a few of our guests there and they say it's well worth a visit.'

At nine o'clock Spencer went to his room, watched an hour's TV – he'd forgotten the spiky, shrugging quality of British humour – and set the alarm for six a.m., when he could call Hannah just as she was going to bed. At hotel prices they didn't talk for long and the call left him feeling dissatisfied and edgy as though he'd have been better off not making it at all.

Later on after breakfast he drove up to Church Norton. He figured that if he wanted to walk around quietly and look up a few old haunts, this was the time to do it, before reunion fever set in and every American was a marked man. It was then his plan to return to the hotel in the afternoon and rest up – perhaps even take in the Roman ruin – before attending the welcome party that night.

He parked on the outskirts of the village where, he noted, the old red bus request stop had been replaced by a proper shelter with a seat and a timetable. Then he walked, following a circular route that would take him past the places he remembered. He'd given some thought to what to wear on this anonymous visit, and hoped he didn't look too much like a Yank, though knowing the Brits' sensitivity to nuance, there were probably a hundred little details of his appearance that gave him away. He had on light trousers, brogues, a plain shirt and sports jacket. He didn't carry a camera or wear a hat. The weather was bright but he kept his sunglasses in his breast pocket for the time being – no Brit would be optimistic enough to carry a pair just in case.

Things weren't that much changed. Generally speaking the place seemed a little more spruce and tidy than he remembered, a fact which Spencer attributed to gentrification. There was a flat-roofed extension to the brick school building, and, most notably, a brand-new village hall. The pub had tubs of flowers outside and had been renamed the Haymakers' Arms, with a sign depicting a bucolic idyll peopled by apple-cheeked goliaths with pitchforks. At this time in the morning it was closed, but he resisted the temptation to peer in at the windows.

The church was the same – having withstood the vicissitudes of several centuries it was hardly likely to have altered in a mere sixteen years – but the grass in the churchyard had been cut, and there were fresh flower arrangements in the porch. Of course, he told himself, this was a big weekend for the village – it was playing host to the war veterans. Hence the scrubbed-up appearance, the flowers, the mown grass, the flag.

He opened the door of the church, but there were a couple of ladies in there doing their stuff with flowers, and he withdrew hastily before they had time to engage him in conversation.

He could no longer avoid it – the last leg of his circuit must take him past Craft Cottages. He had also to face the fact that whatever justification he'd made to himself for the trip this was an aspect of the past which exerted the mysterious, magnetic pull of unfinished business. So it was a shock to discover that the business had been finished for him: the cottages were no longer there. The whole row of five had disappeared, and in their place was a horseshoe-shaped development of small bungalows around a central lot: Craft Close. Shaken, he walked around the path that circled the lot, and saw in a couple of windows that these were old folks' houses, more modest versions of the one his mother lived in outside Salutation. Some of the postage-stamp front yards were art-fully laid out with grass and borders and winding stone paths flanked by cheery gnomes; others had been put to work as mini-allotments, with conical frameworks for beans and peas like tepee-poles, and neat rows of new season's vegetables. It was disorientating, he could not equate this trim development with what had been here before. Taking it from the road side, the Ransoms' end cottage must have corresponded to the lefthand bungalow, but there was no sense of it, not a trace. It had been wiped out.

'Can I help you?'

It was an elderly lady wearing a waterproof coat buttoned to the chin against the onslaught of the sun, and carrying a tartan bag from which greenery protruded.

'Er – no, thanks. Just looking.'

He at once felt stupid on two counts, for having answered as though she were a shop assistant and for blowing his cover.

'Would you be one of our American visitors?'

'I guess I would.'

'How do you do?' She held out a hand. 'This is a big day for Church Norton, you know.'

'And for me – for us. You bet.'

'I'm Dorothy Cornforth.'

She smiled expectantly, he had no option but to return the compliment. 'Ma'am. Spencer McColl.'

'I know.'

'I beg your pardon?'

'We've met before – at the children's Christmas party in 'forty-four? At the old hall?'

Now he saw that she was familiar – one of the good women of the village, always there, doing their bit. 'I remember. You'll have to forgive me, it's been quite a while.'

'You haven't changed,' she said.

He ran his hand over his hair. 'I wouldn't know about that . . .'

'No. You were a particular friend of the Ransoms', if my memory serves me.'

He felt a shimmer of apprehension, but her face was bland and cheerful.

'Yes, how are they? They still live around here?' He indicated the bungalows. 'All this is new.'

'And very nice too, I'm lucky enough to live in one myself. The Ransoms left Church Norton oh, ten years ago. Would you like a cup of tea, by the way?'

'No, thanks – but here, let me take that for you.'

He relieved her of the shopping bag and walked with her to her gate.

'Yes,' she went on, 'Janet Ransom got married again, we were all so pleased, and they moved to Bedford. And I believe her sister got married too, not so long ago.'

'Really?' It came out a little too abruptly, and he added: 'I forget her name.'

'Rosemary.'

'Didn't she used to sing in the choir?'

'Oh, yes. Like an angel.' Mrs Cornforth gave him a merry, conspiratorial look. 'A bit of a handful, but she came up trumps as handfuls often do.'

This seemed to pose more questions than it answered but he didn't want to seem too interested. 'Okay . . . What about—' he nearly said 'the other kids' but checked himself in time '—the kids? Davey, was it? And the little one?'

'Davey and Ellen. I'm afraid he went off the rails after the war, the lad was never out of trouble. And I've heard, though it's only hearsay, that he didn't care for the new husband so that didn't help. Ellen I don't know about.'

She opened the gate and he followed her to the front door and waited while she fiddled with the key.

'Well,' she said, turning once the door was open and taking the bag from him, 'I do feel honoured.'

'Honour's all mine ma'am.'

'Has life been good to you since the war, Mr McColl?'

'Yes, it has.' It was one of those all or nothing situations and he opted for nothing. She looked into his face with a little smile and a nod.

'That's good.'

He felt a touch awkward as if she had the advantage over him. 'Will you be attending any of these events they've got planned for us?'

'Oh, I'm helping with the food for the reception, and I shall be at the church on Sunday.' She nodded at the bag. 'I've been on flower fatigues.'

'I'll see you there, Mrs Cornforth.'

'You will indeed.'

Mrs Cornforth's return from the church indicated that it would probably be empty now, so Spencer went back and opened the smaller, north door gingerly. There was no one there and he went in. The scent of the fresh flowers filled the air and there were spatters of water on the stone flags and threadbare strips of carpet, where the ladies had slopped watering cans.

He was about to duck out again when his eye was caught by a sheet of lined paper on top of a pile of hymnbooks, open but still holding its folds. He glanced at it and saw that it was a rough seating plan written in biro. The block of pews on either side of the aisle at the front were marked 'Dignitaries and American visitors'; the blocks behind that were for 'Invited guests'; and from there to the back simply 'Village and friends'. Church Norton was going to a lot of trouble.

He skipped lunch – his stomach was still all at sixes and sevens from the flight – and took a rest in his room at the hotel. He lay on the bed but couldn't sleep, his brain teeming with questions and suppositions. It was not the glory days that reclaimed him, but the quiet spaces in between.

In the middle of the afternoon he roused himself and followed the receptionist's directions to the Roman villa. It was only a quarter of a mile away, so he walked. The barman was right, the entrance was right into the embankment beneath the main road, and was still no more than a kind of rickety wooden gangplank over the chalky mud. A well-spoken man in a shirt and tie sat in a portacabin taking a modest contribution towards further work, and handed out a single sheet showing a plan of the rooms.

Spencer was the only person there. Not knowing what

to expect, he had imagined entering a house, and the reality surprised him. The gangplank entrance turned into a wooden walkway that ran around the reinforced earth walls of the site, then doubled back on itself to return as a bridge across its centre, some twelve feet above the excavated remains. This meant that the plan was easy to follow, and also that the floors which were the chief wonder of the villa were displayed to best advantage. He strolled and paused, gazing down in awe at strange spiny fish, elaborate swags of flowers and swirling abstract designs that would not have been out of place in an *art nouveau* drawing room, all made up of an incalculable number of tiny coloured stones. The perfection of the mosaics and the brilliance of the colours made their age even more astonishing.

But it was – he checked the plan – the dining room that really stopped him in his tracks. This was the best-preserved part of the villa, and as well as the floor a six-foot section of one wall had been exposed. The decorations on both floor and wall were pornographic. The floor showed what looked at first like a round, stylised flower with overlapping concentric petals like those of a half-open rose. But on closer inspection Spencer saw that it was a couple entwined end-to-end in mutual gratification. The bodies were all sinuous curves and voluptuousness, the faces – when he could find them – curiously placid. On the wall there were several similar images, paintings rather than mosaics, each accurately and gracefully depicting a different act of love. Once again the bodies were vibrantly sensuous but the expressions of the participants impassive. He wondered whether this was because of some spurious Roman idea of decency – that if they didn't seem to be enjoying it that made it okay to have porn in your dining room – or because the people in the paintings were models and that was how they'd looked at the time: another job, another day, another dollar . . .

He spent some time gazing at the pictures and then went round the whole thing again to try and regain a less feverish perspective. But he still emerged feeling self-conscious, as if the respectable gent in the portacabin must know which area had absorbed most of his attention.

If he'd thought the Roman villa would take his mind off

things he was wrong. Back in his room, with an hour to spare before he had to get ready, he did finally fall asleep and was plagued by the sort of dreams he hadn't had since he was a kid. Dreams in which sex was both a temptation and a threat, but the only thing you could think about, and there were those goddam' calm, angelic faces watching him sweat . . . He woke up with a start, excited and ashamed and with a splitting headache, to find he was going to be late.

It was a nice enough evening, but it made him glad he hadn't opted for the organised trip. He could never have stood the enforced camaraderie, the relentless rehashing of old times because there was nothing else in common. Apart from a couple of senior officers, Mo di Angeli was the only one there he instantly recognised and was genuinely pleased to see. During the welcome drinks they washed up next to one another in the crush.

'Spencer, son of a gun! Why aren't you travelling with the rest of us?'

He didn't want to hurt Mo's feelings. 'Couldn't manage it – a long story.'

'Not your style either, huh?' He made a face, and swilled the punch around in his glass as though it were medicine. 'What is this stuff, cherryade?'

Mo had retrained as a graphic designer after the war and had a little business in his home town, doing layouts for business publications and leaflets, and occasionally indulging himself with a bit of sign-writing.

'You see that new sign at the pub? No offence but, Jeez, what a bummer! Haymakers? I tell you, they look like goddam' Nazis.'

Along with his Italian accent Mo had lost the soft edges of youth, where shared experience had enabled them to meld together, and acquired a shiny, grown-up post-war veneer – a bit more settled, a bit hardened, still a nice man but getting fixed in his Midwest ways. Spencer was disinclined to raise the past, preferring to let Mo make the running on that one, which he did only obliquely.

'Not many of us here, considering. Makes you realise how many got lost.'

'Yes. And how many preferred not to come.'

'Reckon so? You always were a cynical bastard.'

Spencer was oddly flattered by this retrospective distinction. 'I was not.'

'Sure you were. You and that guy who did away with himself—'

'Frank.'

'Frank, right, you and he were the watchful ones. Always got stuff going on in your heads.'

Spencer decided to broach a sensitive question, not because he needed the answer, but because the writer in him wanted to hear what Mo would say.

'Why do you reckon he did that?'

'Killed himself?' Mo made an extravagant gesture of ignorance and disbelief, saying at the same time: 'Because Si Santucci did.'

'That was an accident, surely?'

'An accident waiting to happen. He was crazy, that one. Dangerous. He hadn't been in a P-51, he'd'a been in gaol.'

'That's true. So Frank – your theory is he just cracked up under the strain? Si's death was the straw that broke the camel's back?'

Mo narrowed his eyes. 'Say, what is this, Spence? An interrogation?'

'I'm interested in what you think.'

'I think they were a couple of queers, okay?'

Spencer smiled blandly. 'I guess so.'

They were made a big fuss of by the locals, the Legion and the Parish Council, speeches of welcome were made and only at the very last was the delicate matter raised of funds for the planned memorial. The chairman of the Parish Council said that there were leaflets available explaining the costs involved, and that anyone who felt able to make a contribution, or better still a covenant, should fill in the slip at the bottom and leave it in the box which would be provided for the purpose this evening, at the dance tomorrow, and in the church porch on Sunday.

Mo grunted and grumbled. 'Might have known hard cash would come into it.'

'We don't have to contribute,' Spencer pointed out. 'We can vote with our wallets. No bucks, no memorial.'

'You going to ante up?'

'Yes. Just to show I'm not a cynic.'

'All right, all right, since I came I guess I may as well chip in . . . Say, when the speeches are finished shall we hit the Haymakers' and have ourselves a decent drink?'

As the proceedings were winding up, and Mo was making his excuses to the coach party, Spencer sought out Mrs Cornforth among her fellow workers in the kitchen.

'That was great food, ladies, thank you.' They declared that it was their pleasure and they were glad he'd enjoyed it. He approached Mrs Cornforth.

'There was something I meant to ask you this morning.'

'Ask away.'

'You said Davey had been in trouble – what sort of trouble?'

'With the police, so I hear. He was a proper tearaway. It's such a shame because he was a lovely little lad.'

Spencer could hardly believe it. It was impossible to link the Davey he remembered – so eager to please, so straightforward and affectionate – with the delinquent 'tearaway' of Mrs Cornforth's description.

In the saloon bar of the Haymakers' he'd have ordered a Scotch, but that they were obliged for politeness' sake to accept a round on the house so he amended it to a beer.

Mo chugged down half a pint before smacking his lips and saying: 'Don't get me wrong back there, I got nothing against queers. They want to play for the other team, that's their business.'

Spencer agreed that it was.

'So anyway, Spence, you married?'

'Ten years.'

'Childhood sweetheart?'

'Matter of fact, yes.'

'Me too, me too . . .' Mo shook his head with a reflective, salacious chuckle. 'Jeez, but we had some good times.'

'You were the expert,' said Spencer. 'I never knew anyone who could get the girls like you.'

'Did I ever . . . I tell you, I saw one or two at that bunfight tonight. There with their husbands, you know? Butter wouldn't melt in their mouths all of a sudden, but they weren't talking to me.'

'Does that bother you?'

'Hell, no, I'm a happily married man. Same again?'

Mo got in a couple of Scotches this time, and then asked: 'What happened to that lady you were seeing so much of back then? The widow with the kids?'

'I understand she got married and moved away.'

'You going to look her up?'

'Certainly not.'

'Yup,' sighed Mo, who was now mellowing by the second. 'Yup, that's right, it was all a long time ago . . . But I intend to enjoy myself at the dance tomorrow night!'

The next day dawned perfect, and Spencer drove up to Church Norton in brilliant sunshine. The early summer light had that pristine quality that he remembered from before. His schedule had the meeting time for veterans and officials as eleven o'clock, but he arrived a few minutes early and there was no one there as he parked on the edge of the airfield and got out.

His first instinct was: They don't need a memorial. This was it. The fields of bright new corn, and the hedges full of dog roses and blackthorn. Around the few remaining Quonsett huts, now used as barns, the long grass was bright with willowherb and campion and buttercups and cow parsley – names he remembered from Janet telling them to Ellen as they picked straggly bunches. Some of the runways were still there, roughened and narrowed by time but still running straight and true between the crops. Someone was walking a dog along one of them. It barked joyously. In the resonant silence that followed he could hear the birds singing.

The locals began to arrive, and then the coach. There was another round of handshaking and shoulder slapping and then they were led off on a circuit of the airfield. Remember this, remember that, this was where such and such was . . . Mo was in the thick of it this time, and in his element, full of stories and wisecracks, playing the cheery Yank for all he was worth. Spencer preferred to keep to the edge of the group, at the back. From time to time on the tour he paused to let the others get ahead, and turned to gaze around. Each time he felt the ground like a presence, it seemed to breathe, the grass and the corn stirred softly in the sun. These English fields, placid yet secretive, had grown back over the past and would keep it as it should be – hidden and safe.

The tour finished where it had begun, on the apex of the gentle hill between Church Norton and the next village, from where you could see the Norman tower of one church and the pointed steeple of the other. The president of the British Legion outlined what they had in mind, there was some discussion of the plans. Then they observed two minutes' silence in memory of those who had died. During the silence a little breeze got up and eddied round them as they stood there with their heads bowed, carrying the warm scent and whisper of the fields.

Spencer attended the dance that evening more from a sense of duty and a spirit of journalistic enquiry than from inclination. Mo was yet again the man of the moment and did not disguise his disappointment in his friend's dullness.

'Come on, Spence, shake a leg! There's a room full of great-looking women here just dying to show their appreciation for what we did in the war.'

Spencer held up his hands. 'Count me out, Mo, you're doing it for both of us.'

This much was true. Mo jived, jitterbugged, rocked, rolled and reeled tirelessly, jacket and tie soon discarded, his face gleaming with perspiration, his rotund frame pivoting and swaying on his implausibly trim and mobile legs. Spencer watched as mature matrons and giggling girls alike were subjected to the di Angeli effect and, as always, fell under its spell. Local husbands and boyfriends, amiable but envious, stood aside as Mo whirled from one partner to the next. Former top brass, steering their partners round the perimeter of the hall in a more stately measure, tried to ignore this impromptu floor show but it was hard when the band encouraged it by upping the ante, hurtling mercilessly from 'In the Mood' to 'Rock Around the Clock'.

At ten o'clock Spencer left them all to it. The perfect day had given way to a clear, still night, but at the end of May it was as yet not completely dark. He walked round the hall to where there had always been an iron kissing gate that led to a footpath over the fields. The gate, happily, was still there, and he went through it and walked a couple of hundred yards down the path with the music fading behind him. The grey light, the fledgling stars, the distant music – he seemed poised between several worlds, belonging in none.

As he went back to the car he resolved to set the alarm early again in the morning and speak to Hannah whose face already he could no longer picture in detail.

'Hallo,' she said drowsily. 'How's it going?'

'Pretty well. This morning's the church service, and then we're detailed off for lunch in various houses. I can't remember where I'm supposed to be going, but I shan't starve – the fatted calf's been killed around here.'

'It sounds fun. I almost wish I was there with you instead of watching *The Lucy Show*.'

'It's okay.'

'You sound a bit flat. Are you all right?'

'Sorry, sugar, it's early, I'm not properly awake yet.'

'But you are glad you went?'

'I guess so. Plenty of good material.'

'Well, that's the main thing.'

He thought he detected the merest edge in her tone. 'You

know me, I don't believe there's any purpose to be served in going back just for the sake of it.'

'No.'

'Tell you what,' he changed the subject, 'there's a terrific Roman ruin right near where I'm staying. Fantastic mosaics and wall paintings, half of them porn.'

'Did you say porn?'

'That's right, like a manual of positions, in the dining room. You'd love it.'

'Think we should try it here?'

'What, the pictures or the positions?'

'Both, tiger . . .' She growled. By the time he hung up he felt they'd got back in touch with each other. The trouble with the phone was it implied an intimacy that couldn't be properly realised so half the time hearing the other person's voice wound up doing more harm than good.

He'd managed to stay on the sidelines till now, but in church they made it clear that no backsliding would be tolerated. The churchwardens pretty well frogmarched him to the front, where Mo raised a hand and indicated he'd kept him a seat.

Mo leaned against him and stage whispered: 'Where'd you get to last night, you missed all the fun!'

'That was the general idea.'

'It was a riot, I tell ya.'

'I'll take your word for it.'

There had been more activity in the church since he'd been here on Friday – the English and American flags and the standards of the men's and women's branches of the British Legion hung above the chancel, the altar had some kind of prettified embroidered cloth draped over it, and on the shelf in front of each pew there were order of service sheets. Partly to dissuade Mo from communicating any further indiscretions, Spencer picked the sheet up and studied it. If it was to be believed there was a lot to be got through. Both National Anthems, four hymns, prayers, thanks and addresses by this person and that, a presentation by the school, a sermon . . .

His face must have showed something, for Mo leaned towards him again. 'Yeah,' he muttered throatily. 'My sentiments exactly.'

The vicar announced the first hymn from the back of the church and they all rose, bellowing out 'All People That on Earth Do Dwell' as the choir entered. Pretty much the same mix of people, Spencer noticed, apart from a couple of younger men, but they'd smartened their outfits up a bit since the war: dark blue gowns that fitted properly, with little white frilly jabots at the neck for the women. As they processed by they beefed up the congregation's singing appreciably, but there was no one whose voice or appearance could have held a candle to Rosemary's.

The service wore on. In spite of his misgivings it held Spencer's attention. The sense of occasion, the music, the experience held in common and individually remembered – even Mo blew his nose loudly at one point. These were good, kind people. Spencer was moved.

The stirring of emotion may have made him more receptive, but round about the third hymn he heard it. The hymn was one that in common with most of his compatriots he didn't know, so like them he was standing in silence, following the words on the service sheet with a suitably attentive expression. And because he wasn't singing, he heard her. Somewhere in amongst the swell of voices there was hers – rich, melodious, unmistakable, a tad more *chanteuse* than chorister.

He looked over his shoulder, briefly, but there were rows and rows of people, the church was packed and he spotted no one he knew except for a couple of peaky-looking ladies from last night, and Mrs Cornforth, trilling lustily away.

During the sermon he tried again, looking round under the pretence of smothering a cough, but only succeeded in attracting the attention of the nearest church warden who crept forward and asked if he'd like a glass of water. Horribly embarrassed, he declined. After the sermon came an invitation to stay behind for coffee, then the National Anthems, another hymn, more prayers and the blessing, and a final hymn during which the choir processed out.

When it was finally over Spencer told Mo he'd see him later, and slipped out of the pew and down the aisle, keeping his head down and a purposeful expression on his face as though he had some important objective in mind. At the back of the church there was a milling throng, and he was worried sick that even if she were here he might not recognise her. It had been a long time, she had only been a girl, she was bound to have changed. Then he realised that the north door was blocked off by a massive red, white and blue flower arrangement on a pedestal, so that the whole congregation had to leave, when it did, by the south porch. He edged and excuse-me'd his way there, and went out into the churchyard. Apart from a few kids released from boredom and larking around among the gravestones he seemed to be first out. If he waited here, everyone who had been at the service would have to pass him sooner or later, and if she was here he'd see her.

Not that escape was easy. He hadn't been there two minutes before one of the tea ladies bustled out with a cup and saucer, and a colonel and his wife came to join him, saying what a pity it was to waste the fine weather when in England . . . He had to talk to them, but as people began to filter out his attention wandered and he became tense and agitated. When the colonel and his lady left his side he had the distinct impression that his distracted manner might have given offence, but what the hell? The war was over.

He hung around for another half an hour. The Legion chairman introduced him to the couple with whom he was supposed to be having lunch, and he made some feeble excuse about not feeling well, and coming on in a while. He knew they didn't believe him and thought he was rude, but he couldn't help himself.

Mo appeared, dabbing his brow.

'I swear . . . I take it all back about the English weather. You going to lunch?'

'Probably. I'm just looking out for someone I know.'

'Is that so? Mighta known it − not a peep out of you at the hop, but an hour in church and you're eying up the girls. There's my charming hostess, gotta go.'

As Mo trundled off it half occurred to Spencer that he might never see his friend again, and was letting him go without so much as a fare thee well. But the thought was only the merest tap, well short of his conscience.

The church was pretty well empty now, and still he hadn't seen her. The vicar and the padre from the neighbouring barracks emerged, in conversation and carrying their surpluses. The vicar raised a cheery hand.

'Everything all right? You look a bit lost!'

'No, no, I'm doing fine. Just waiting for someone.'

'No one much left, I'm afraid, only the cooks and bottle-washers!'

'I'll go take a look.'

'If you're sure . . .'

They went on their way. He hardly wanted to look in the church in case she wasn't there, but it would be stupid to have waited this long and not to check. He strolled back into the porch and hung around there for a moment. He could see a couple of ladies packing crockery into boxes and another removing her plastic apron and folding it up, a scene that was definitely the Anglican Church's equivalent of putting chairs on tables. Surely there couldn't be anyone else there. He hesitated but one of the women spotted him.

'Anything we can do?'

'I think I may have left something . . .'

'Come on, come on in and take a look, we'll be a few minutes yet. What was it anyway? We may already have found it.'

'Er – a small book. My diary.'

Even to him it sounded supremely unlikely but they clucked and conferred and said they hadn't come across it. He entered and walked up the aisle to where he'd been sitting, glancing to right and left, checking the corners with his peripheral vision. No one there. Bathed in disappointment he sat down in the pew and made a show of looking under the seat, and under the shelf, along one way, then the other. It went quiet, the women were carrying stuff down the path to their car.

'Afternoon, lootenant.'

He still couldn't see her, or tell where her voice was coming from.

'Spencer? Over here.'

She was sitting in the box-seat at the end of the choir stalls, masked by the carved wooden wing, though now she was leaning forward, smiling at him, and as soon as he'd spotted her she rose and came down the steps.

'I wasn't playing hide and seek, honest, I just couldn't resist getting a view from my old seat. Hallo.' She held out her hand.

'Rosemary . . . This is extraordinary – I never expected—'

'Didn't you? I did. Or at least I hoped. That was why I came.'

Her directness had always made him feel that his brain was all thumbs. 'Really?'

'Yes, really.'

'I'm flattered.'

The women came back in, and the one he'd spoken to first bustled up.

'Did you find what you were looking for?'

'Yes, thank you.'

'Oh, splendid!' She told the others: 'This gentleman found it – his diary.'

He felt Rosemary's bright, quizzical look among the exclamations of delight.

The woman turned back to him. 'Now there's absolutely no rush, but we have to lock up in due course—'

'That's all right,' said Spencer, 'we're going.'

They walked down the church path to the road. He was tongue-tied. At the lychgate he said: 'Do you have a car?'

'Yes. Do you?' She was teasing him.

'I meant—'

'I know. I got a cab here.' Still that bright, perspicacious gaze, looking right into his head, laying him bare. 'So would you allow me to buy you a drink, lootenant?'

He was losing not just his presence of mind but his manners. 'Certainly not. But I'd like to buy you one – or perhaps some lunch, if you have time?'

'I do. If you're quite sure you don't have to be anywhere else?'

She was testing his conscience rather than his arrangements. He knew at once that his contingency excuse was going to have to do.

'No.'

'Then lovely, thank you.'

At her suggestion they drove to where she was staying, a coaching inn in the nearby market town. In the car they confined themselves to comments on the service, the route, changes in the neighbourhood . . . Neither of them elicited nor proffered the smallest personal detail, though he did notice that she wore a wedding ring. It was as if their meeting were taking place in a kind of bubble which neither of them wanted to burst.

At the hotel he glanced around involuntarily and she said, reading his mind: 'Don't worry, your lot aren't staying here.'

'Was it so obvious? They're great guys but I've had about as much reminiscing as I can stand over the past couple of days.'

'I can imagine.'

The hotel was busy on a Sunday lunchtime but because Rosemary was a guest there was no problem with a table in the restaurant. They went into the bar and while she studied the menu, Spencer studied her.

She was pretty and sassy as ever, but elegant these days in a tan skirt and high heels with a cream silk blouse and a light three-quarter coat that swung from the shoulders like a cape. When she removed the coat her figure was still great, but she was slimmer than he remembered, and he caught a provocative glimpse of white lace between the reveres of the blouse as she leaned forward. Her hair was paler, more of a strawberry blonde, and she had it cut in a face-framing urchin style like Kim Novak's. There were the cat's eyes and the humorous mouth that he remembered so well, and even now, delightfully, a few freckles.

'You look terrific,' he said.

'Thank you.' She glanced down at herself, tweaked a button, smiled. 'I won't pretend I didn't make an effort.'

His heart turned over. She was not being bold, nor even flirtatious. It was more that she seemed to take certain things as read between them.

'You're married.' The moment he'd said it he hoped it didn't sound prim or accusing, but here again she seemed to understand perfectly the weight of his remark.

'Yes, a couple of years. Very happily, more than I ever hoped for or deserve. You?'

'The same. But for longer.'

'Do you have a family?'

'No.'

'I don't either, but we hope to. My husband's a schoolmaster at a prep school – a private boarding school for quite young boys – so much of the time we have a tribe of surrogate sons.'

He thought, then said: 'Lucky guys.'

Over lunch he told her, at her instigation, about the work he did, the writing and the broadcasting.

She said: 'You really love it, don't you? It's in your face and in your voice.'

'I'm very lucky,' he conceded. 'It wasn't the kind of thing I'd ever considered, it just kind of came out of left field and ambushed me.'

'Have you done any flying since the war?'

He shook his head. 'Only as a passenger.'

'But what a thing to have done . . .' Her eyes rested on him with a reflective smile. 'Do you have any idea how much we all idolised you boys?'

It was his turn now to tease. 'I'm afraid we did. And we weren't slow to make the most of it either.'

'Would you like to capitalise on it now?'

He wasn't sure at first if he'd heard her correctly, or if he had whether he'd interpreted her right.

'I'm sorry?'

'Shall we go upstairs? If you've had enough, that is.'

'Why not?'

Even as they went up the stairs he still didn't allow himself to believe what her invitation meant. Even when she hung the sign on the door before closing it, and dropped her key on the dressing table and her coat on the chair. Even when she slipped out of her shoes and pulled her silk blouse from her waistband . . .

Only when she held out her arms and said his name did he dare to believe it. And realised, as they folded round one another, how often he had imagined this embrace.

It was not only love they made, but a pact. With their passion that afternoon they set the seal on what might have been, and now never would be. Though they had spoken so little they communicated through their lips and hands and skins. On her part there was none of the deep reserve which had characterised Janet's lovemaking: she made herself known to Spencer completely, her openness was a gift and a revelation. And for him there was a sense of coming home, of finding at last the magnetic north which had eluded him. This, they both knew, was something that had to happen, if only once.

And afterwards, peace.

As usual, she was the first to articulate it.

'We had to do this, didn't we?'

'Yes.'

'I loved you so much I almost hated you, did you know that?'

'I thought I annoyed the hell out of you.'

She shook with laughter against his shoulder. 'That too . . . I was fifteen when you came on the scene with your pilot's wings and your tin of ham. Fifteen!'

'You were jail-bait.'

'But I didn't know that. I didn't know what I was. Only that I was eaten up with jealousy. Did you love my mother?'

'I was attracted to her, she was a beautiful woman, but—' Suddenly he realised what she'd said. 'Rosemary – you know?'

She nodded. 'I guessed. It was the jealousy that did it. I think my blood must have been green. After I got married, and she married for the second time, I asked her, and she told me. It wasn't a big dramatic scene, we'd already done all the acting and pretending, it was very calm and easy. And a huge relief.'

Moved, he kissed her temple. 'You didn't feel cheated?'

'No. Or at least, only of you. But we didn't discuss that.'

'Is she happy now?'

She thought for a second. 'She's content. He's a nice man.'

'What about Davey? And Ellen?'

'Davey's drifting. Ellen's at university. I ought to tell you that I don't see any of them these days.'

'Why is that? You had a fight?'

'No. I just wanted to start all over again. To make a clean break, leave all the mess behind.'

'But they are your family.'

'They were. Now I want my own family.' She tilted her head back and looked up at him. 'That's given you something to disapprove of.'

'Why should I want to do that?'

'To make saying goodbye easier.'

It wasn't easy, but it was peaceful. Once he was ready to go they stood with their arms round one another for a full minute, and then she came down and saw him to his car. Her composure never faltered and he loved her for that. She looked great, a woman with a mind and a life of her own.

She waved him off, but when he glanced in his mirror, expecting to see her still there, she had gone.

CHAPTER NINETEEN

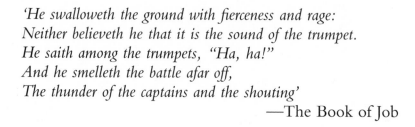

'He swalloweth the ground with fierceness and rage:
Neither believeth he that it is the sound of the trumpet.
He saith among the trumpets, "Ha, ha!"
And he smelleth the battle afar off,
The thunder of the captains and the shouting'
—The Book of Job

Harry – 1854

For a warlike scene, it was peaceful.

Not true peace, but the focused calm of order and purpose: of the coming together of training, expectation and opportunity after so long. After the freezing night, the broad gentle valley with its garlands of vines spread invitingly before them like a prospect of hope in the mid-morning sunshine. It drew the eye of every officer and man towards the horizon, and their unseen objective. All were united in that objective; each was wrapped in his own private concentration. Memories, hopes and thoughts of home were set aside, the future was circumscribed by this sunlit trough of fertile land.

Even the shabby horses, thin and knocked up in their patchy autumn coats, had regained their spirit. They tossed their ragged manes and snorted, their ears flicked back and forth expectantly. Harry could feel how Clemmie was bunched beneath him, nervous and eager as she hadn't been in months.

Beyond the valley's natural amphitheatre and the watchers, friend and foe, on the heights behind and on either side of them, was the squalid hinterland of war of which, for this magnificent moment, they were no longer a part: the tattered and depleted camps, the scarred fields and vineyards, and the human detritus of this day's earlier encounters – the heroes, the storytellers, the scapegoats, the wounded and the dead.

Here, all was disciplined symmetry as the cavalry drew up in three lines, six hundred and seventy-five of the finest horsemen and swordsmen in Britain. Between the first and second line was a distance of some four hundred yards; between second and third rather less; the Heavies were assembled far behind that; no infantry were in support, there was nothing to draw the eye from the parade-ground splendour of the Lights. The spectators on the Sapoune Heights to the north – the TGs and officers' ladies accompanying Raglan and his staff – were breathless with patriotic anticipation. The Russians would not be permitted to take the guns from the redoubts beneath the Causeway Ridge – honour would be saved by the swift and strong.

From their vantage point these same spectators, saving their wine and luncheon hampers for a timely celebration, could not see the condition of the horses or the torn jackets and patched and threadbare overalls of the men, the missing epaulettes and shoulder-scales, the few and draggled plumes. They could not see, as Harry could, the scattering of motley late arrivals – the butcher still in his bloodstained white smock, with his canvas trousers tucked in his boots, or the escapee from the guard tent preparing to charge unarmed, his weapons having been taken for smoking a pipe against orders; cooks, shirkers, invalids and drunks had scurried to join the ranks, many without equipment or headgear and with jackets unbuttoned. Young Philip Gough had borrowed Harry's handkerchief to wrap round his wrist and sword-hilt to strengthen his grip, brushing aside Harry's misplaced apology that it was not very clean . . .

The spectators saw only the distant splendour of the concourse on the plain. And the Lights in their turn fixed their eyes on Cardigan who sat his horse before them like a statue, his stature rigidly upright, his pelisse fastened over his rheumy chest to display a splash of gold.

On their right flank, the rough-coated terrier Jemmy,

mascot of the 8th, dug furiously for some buried prize, her tail wagging with excitement.

Not for long had Balaklava remained the welcoming, tranquil haven of their first impressions. Within hours the British Army had placed their unmistakable stamp upon it. Gardens were laid waste as they were stripped, roads and alleyways were choked with human and equine trafic and their litter, the cobbled docks were thick with carts, packs, arms and ammunition, and the waters of the harbour bobbed with every kind of rubbish. The little town itself was soon dwarfed by the sprawl of the huge encampment which barnacled the surrounding slopes to the north and east.

The spurious sense of achievement, of having gained an important objective, kept the troops tolerably cheerful. But then Harry was continually humbled by their stoicism. In undergoing far worse privations than their superiors, and with even less expectation of a possible reward, they maintained a dogged courage and a gallows humour that drew the sting of a situation by painting it even worse than it was.

These characteristics found their apotheosis in Betts. Almost since landing at Calamita Bay Harry had expected daily to find that his groom had succumbed to infection, injury, sickness or simple exhaustion, and every night he found this hobbling wisp of a man not merely alive but apparently unaffected by whatever horrors had gone before.

This was at least in part because Betts at his very best was hardly a picture of health. Runtish and limping, with his sallow complexion and silted lungs (his approach was always heralded by a hacking cough and tremendous hawking and spitting), there was quite simply less margin for change in him than in most other men. But aside from and more important than this was his devotion to the horses. His commitment to their welfare was selfless and unwavering. Though he and Harry had as good a relationship as could be between master and man, Harry did not flatter himself that Betts's loyalty and perseverance were for him. The horses were Betts's *raison d'être*. Even had he been given to the luxury of introspection he would not have indulged in it, for his every waking moment was taken up with doing what he could to improve the animals' lot.

And it was a parlous one. Betts was not the only man to complain of the apparent misconception that cavalry horses could function without food. Within a week of their arrival at Balaklava hay rations were restricted to six pounds per animal per day, and oats were a near-forgotten luxury. The effects of relentless marching, scarce and poor feed and extremes of temperature were plain to see. Once proud and pampered chargers looked dull and scraggy as donkeys. It was, as Betts said, 'Enough to make a saint swear,' and he was no saint.

He was no great rider and certainly no swordsman, but this did not prevent him from joining foraging parties to the cultivated area along the Tchernaya River some seven miles away, where in early October there was baled hay for the taking. Unarmed astride a pack-pony he set off with the troopers to return on more than one occasion with hair-raising stories of Cossack ambush and headlong flight.

Undernourished as he was he seemed to be able to subsist on less than other men, getting through days at a time on tobacco, rum and coffee and sharing his hard rations with the horses. When Harry upbraided him for this he had a plain answer.

'You can do without me, sir, but you can't do without them.'

'It's not a question of what I can or can't do without, Betts, but of your own health and strength. You force me to say it – your life.'

'Them's my life.'

This Harry had to concede was probably the truth. Betts had no family and his future if he returned to England was at best uncertain. While the horses lived and he could be of service to them, he too had a reason to live. He it was who still could not reconcile himself to the loss of Piper.

'I hate to think of it,' he would remark, shaking his head dourly. 'That one was superior horseflesh whichever way you look at it.'

'He'd never have survived all this.'

'Maybe not, sir, but we'd have seen him right,' was Betts's bizarre logic. 'How those bloody natives will have treated him don't bear thinking about.'

'He may have been rounded up by our men. The Heavies were there.'

'He weren't no heavy, sir, they'll have had no use for him.'

This too was correct, but when the Heavies did arrive both Harry and Betts could only hope that Piper wasn't among them, for their delayed voyage from Varna had been a terrible one. Betts went down to the docks to witness the arrival of the first contingent of Heavies and came back chalky white and tight-lipped about what he had seen. With the onset of autumn the storms had been many times worse than anything they'd encountered and on one ship alone the overcrowding below decks had been so bad that two-thirds of the horses had either died or had to be destroyed. On another an entire deck had collapsed, sending the officers' chargers plunging down on top of the troopers' horses in the hold below and causing terrible confusion and carnage.

'You got horses at home, sir?' Betts asked, and when Harry replied that there were carriage and work horses, he commented dourly: 'Best place for 'em.'

The 11th Hussars formed the second line. Before them, to right and left, were the 13th Light Dragoons and the 17th Lancers, and behind them the 8th Hussars and 4th Light Dragoons, with each regiment's two squadrons in line. Out in front their brigade commander on his big, white-socked chestnut sat haughty and motionless. The excitable Captain Nolan, who not long ago had hurtled down the Sapoune cliff-face bearing the order to attack, was in the front line to the left of Cardigan, his horse fretting and fussing like its rider in what was otherwise a curious pocket of quiet.

Harry glanced at Fyefield next to him. His profile was inscrutable, but a film of perspiration shone on his forehead.

On the neck of his horse, Constant, the rough coat showed several small scars.

Sensing Harry's eyes on him, Fyefield muttered: 'We've waited a long time for this. Let's hope we put up a good show.'

And live to hear the applause, thought Harry. He felt the rustle of the precious letters between his tunic and his heart: the black feather was tucked into his sabretache. And live.

It was twenty-past eleven when the trumpet sounded 'Walk'.

It was thought right and proper to celebrate harvest home in the usual way, because it was what Mr Latimer would have liked. And both his widow and the young Mrs Latimer confirmed this view. Not that in private they didn't have their differences on the matter.

'You're surely not thinking of going?' Maria's eyebrows shot up.

'I most certainly am,' replied Rachel. 'I'd take part in the Mickelmas Charge if I thought it would make a differ-ence.'

'The baby will come when it's ready.' Maria preached patience admirably for a woman who was herself congenitally impatient. 'There is nothing you can do.'

Though Rachel knew this to be true, and tried to make light of the situation, she was terribly afraid there might be something wrong. She was over thirty and had never had a child before, nor did she have a close female relative to confide in, so she didn't know what to think. She was a full two weeks beyond her predicted time, and the inert weight inside her was beginning to seem ominous.

'All's well,' the doctor had told her – the same Dr Jaynes Maria had characterised as an idiot during Percy's illness but whom she now commended to Rachel as an omniscient pro-fessional – 'there's nothing whatever to worry about.'

'But it never moves any more.'

'That's because it's a fine big child and there is no longer any room for it to move. The head is engaged. We must simply wait for nature to take its course.'

His avuncular plural infuriated Rachel. 'We?'

'I used the word sympathetically.'

'There's no need.'

'Then I stand corrected. But please be reassured.'

She was not, and when she encountered Ben's mother helping to prepare the tithe barn for harvest home, Rachel drew her aside and asked: 'Mrs Bartlemas – may I ask you something of a rather personal nature?'

Mrs Bartlemas glanced around warily. 'Please do, mum.'

'You have a large and healthy family. Is it normal for a pregnancy to go so long past its time as mine has?'

'Oh, is that all!' This was an area where Mrs Bartlemas had all the breezy confidence of experience. 'There isn't any "normal" as you put it, they're all as different before they're born as they are afterwards. Some are in a rush, some dawdle, some are nothing but trouble. Looks like you got a dreamer in there.'

'I hope so. Do you think—' She hesitated and Mrs Bartlemas cocked her head to one side, prompting her. 'Do you think this means I shall have a bad time of it?'

'Heavens above, no! On the contrary, the readier it is, the quicker it'll happen when it does.'

Another thing which experience had taught Corrie Bartlemas was the necessity and value of the great lie.

They moved forward at the walk, over heavy ploughed ground. The pocket of silence which had seemed to enclose them was now full of the creak of leather, the jingle of bits and spurs and the soft rumble of hooves. One or two of the horses sidestepped and broke stride, excited by the sounds. The terrier scampered back and forth alongside the 8th, full of exuberant energy on this fine morning.

On the slopes and ridges on either side the dense masses of armed men, still eerily holding their fire, were like patches of trees or scrub, a part of the landscape. Here and there the sun glinted off a rifle barrel as if the enemy were signalling a warning. Still at the walk they left the ploughed surface and were now on cultivated land, sometimes treading on crumpled vines, already crushed by the first line. Clemmie caught her foot and stumbled and Harry's whole body was instantly bathed in a sweat of shock.

Until that moment he had not realised how afraid he was.

By the second week in October the camp of the Light Brigade had been moved north and west to a position right of Raglan's HQ on Sapoune Heights. But if the Commander in Chief had thought to flatter his disgruntled cavalry by making them conspicuous, he was disappointed. The compliment was a poisoned chalice. Conspicuous they might be but in camp, and therefore dismounted, they were also painfully vulnerable and all agreed they should not have been placed in such an exposed position.

Also, the soubriquet 'Look-ons' which was now generally used of the Lights appeared doubly unjust when they were in many respects the most hard-worked division in the army. The tasks of foraging, picketing, scouting and patrolling all seemed to fall to them and as the nights grew longer and less friendly they were subjected by the enemy to what amounted to a war of nerves.

The Russians were now massed along the Tchernaya River at the north-eastern end of the broad basin divided in two by the ridge of the Causeway heights, so close in fact that a night patrol at an equidistant point could clearly see the cooking fires of both armies. Sentries and vedettes were understandably jumpy and there were numerous nocturnal alarms, all of which necessitated a cavalry stand-to. More often than not the last of these would be in the small hours only to be succeeded, an hour before dawn, by the regular stand-to which could last for a further two hours or more with only the most paltry breakfast to look forward to.

Cholera was still with them and men debilitated by the

cold, the poor diet and all manner of minor infections were increasingly susceptible to it. There was a constant traffic between the camps and the harbour of sick men being taken to the hospital ships, and the regimental bands were dispensed with in order that the bandsmen could be employed as ambulance men and makeshift medical orderlies. Without them the camps became sombre, cheerless places without so much as a bugle call to raise the spirits. As if to rub salt in this particular wound the Turkish encampments sprawled around the redoubts above the Woronzov highway rang night and day with wild pipe music, suggesting all kinds of abandoned activities not vouchsafed to the British.

Harry wrote to Rachel: '*You can imagine how we feel when we hear the cheerful din from the* bashi-bazouks – *it is terribly galling! But I must say that we also have a certain respect for these fellows who have in the main fought fiercely and well when required, who are treated contemptuously by the majority of our officers (who should know better), and who have precious little to be cheerful about in the way of material comforts. They must have an especially sanguine disposition as well as tremendous fighting spirit. We miss our music and realise just how inspiring and heartening it is now that we no longer have it. As I miss England, and Bells, and those that I love* . . .'

Here Harry refrained as always from saying more clearly and personally what his feelings were, but with the letter still uncompleted he received Rachel's with the news of his father's death.

It left him in turmoil. He was felled by sadness for his father for whom he had felt an unspoken kinship not only of blood but of the soul, who had died with so much unexpressed between them, and tortured also by remorse that, God forgive him, he had thought so little of him in recent weeks.

And through all the wretchedness, like a tenacious English wild flower, there was his love for Rachel who had been with Percy and Maria and performed the services that he, their son, should have performed. And who had written to him with such simple understanding and sincerity that he seemed to hear her quiet voice. He had wept – for his father, and his mother, and for Rachel. For Hugo, gone before. But mostly, he knew, for himself.

Rachel would always remember the music. Paget and his cronies played up a storm, the tithe barn had been bursting with it, the galloping rhythms of jigs, reels and polkas and the sweet, haunting lilt of waltzes and twosteps, and it followed her and Corrie Bartlemas as they walked through the crisp night the few hundred yards to Bells.

Now and again the two women paused, and stood arm in arm, the vapour of their breath melting together.

'Plenty of time . . .' said Corrie once. And the next time, 'Lean on me.' There was no longer the need for any spoken formality between them.

When they left the lee of the farm buildings and came round the corner of the house with the full glory of the sky overarching them, Corrie stopped of her own accord.

'Look at those stars.'

Rachel looked up, and there was a comfort in the stars' calm, bright distance as there was in her companion's sturdy closeness. Both, she felt, had seen so much of this experience that was so common and so unique.

'They talk about the music of the stars, don't they?' murmured Corrie. 'I wonder what sort of music that is . . . sad, I should think.'

As they opened the door, Cato was there waiting for them. He rose stiffly and plodded to greet Rachel with his big head hanging and his tail waving slowly.

'He knows,' said Corrie as she patted him. 'He knows all right. They're wonderful, are animals.'

Another pain surged, gripped, receded, and Rachel sank down on the high-backed chair. Now that she was back in the house she was afraid as she hadn't been out of doors. Here was the weight of expectation and of a tribal history not her own. The young Hugo grinned carelessly down at her from the family portrait she'd so often admired. She felt alone and alienated.

'Corrie . . . What must I do?'

'Nothing, my love, nothing at all. Do what you want to do.'

'The doctor is coming?'

'He is, Little's gone for him. But you're not sick. You're having a baby.'

'But it hurts.'

'Yes, it does.'

'How much worse will it get?'

The great lie must now be modified. Corrie chose her words carefully. 'It's going to get stronger, but that's because all the time your baby's getting closer.'

Rachel gripped her hand. 'You won't go?'

'You may depend on it.'

'What about your own family?'

'Dan's at the dance, he'll take them home. And Mercy's there too, even Ben won't dare give her any trouble.'

They stayed in the hall for a while, with the door standing open, the music drifting in. Rachel sat in the high-backed wing chair and Corrie perched next to her on the chest, clasping her hand, tapping on the back of it with her fingers in time to the tunes. Cato lay before them, gazing with heavy-lidded patience. When his mistress gasped he thumped his tail encouragingly.

It began to feel cold and Corrie got up to close the front door. As she did so the fiddlers in the barn struck up with something fast and furious and they could hear the whoops and cheers of the dancers taking the floor with renewed vigour.

The next two pains were closer together and they made their way upstairs with Cato following at a respectful distance, stopping when they did, waiting, moving on. Corrie lit the fire in the bedroom while Rachel took off her clothes, and the dog stretched out before the pale new flames with a contented sigh.

Rachel asked for the window to be opened but Corrie demurred.

'You'll let the warmth out.'

'I'm hot. And I want to hear the music.'

That was at eight o'clock. The doctor didn't arrive, but they managed together.

Just before midnight Paget on his own began playing a last, wistful waltz: a dance for lovers. And Rachel's baby was born, and laid on the pillow next to her. Round and pink with wide, opaque eyes and thick black hair which as it dried sprang into elfin curls.

'But she's beautiful!'

'What did you expect?' Corrie laughed as she set about the clearing up. 'A monster?'

'She has hair like Hugo's . . .'

'She does, a good head of hair. And I tell you why she's the belle of the ball.' Corrie rolled a sheet briskly around her two forearms. 'The longer they wait, the prettier they are.'

'And why is that?'

'Because they're properly cooked, that's why.'

'Just think, Corrie, no one knows she's here except you and me. Isn't that nice?'

'A secret for a little while, then.'

'Then we must let Maria know . . .' Rachel touched her daughter's cheek, where the skin was fine as air. 'And you must tell Ben – and ask him to come and see me.'

'All in good time.' Corrie came to the head of the bed and stood looking down at them. 'And what are you going to call her?'

Harvest home was over. The doctor came as the last revellers left the barn and began the walk home down the long, starlit hill, beneath the pale horse that leapt for the moon. Belle Latimer slept, while her mother bled.

After two hundred yards they broke into a trot, and the Russian artillery on either side of the valley opened fire. To maintain their steady pace beneath the fusillade became an act of collective pride. The parade ground could not inspire courage, but it had instilled the discipline which made courage possible.

The first volley of shells exploded around the front line. A minute later a white-eyed horse came plunging furiously back through the ranks, terrified of its lolling, bleeding burden. Harry retained a swift and terrible impression of the officer still upright in the saddle, staring wildly, chest slit to the heart and jacket scorched, empty sword arm raised in a gruesome parody of leadership.

'Nolan!' shouted Hector. 'Got what he wanted at last!'

Granted this glimpse of the glory to come, they trotted on.

Harry had written at once to his mother, and found himself curiously lost for words. His heartfelt expressions of grief and sympathy appeared stilted and inadequate, and he only hoped that she would read into them the genuine feeling that was there. After all, whatever the shortcomings of his own relationship with his father, Maria's had been a full, complete flowering. Her grief would not be stained, like his, by remorse.

By contrast, when he picked up his letter to Rachel, he could scarcely write fast enough.

We have more death than life here, so much that it has become almost meaningless, and yet your letter brought home to me the meaning of death. The plain, irreversible fact that I shall now never see my father again, nor have the opportunity to say those things which perhaps should be said between father and son is almost more than I can bear, and it reminds me of all those parents and wives of men who have died here. It shames me to say it and I can only do so to you, who I know will understand and not think the worse of me, but for us, in these circumstances, a dead man is just one more gone to what must *be a better place, and we almost envy him. But for those at home he is their unique beloved son, brother or husband, whose picture stands on the shelf, whose childhood transgressions they punished and whose triumphs they praised, whose joys they shared in . . .*

You say that you hope to be writing a happier letter very soon, and so I am going to keep this of my own letter till then.

You have been so much in my thoughts, more than you can ever know, and I want more than anything to hear that all is well with you. I wish that I could say that these feelings are simply those of gratitude for your kindness to my parents, and of natural affection for the wife of my dear brother. But, Rachel, they are not. We are here at what sometimes feels like the end of the earth, from which we may not ever return, and if my father's death has brought one blessing it is the knowledge that if I do not say or write these things you will never know them. I love you, and have always loved you. Your face, your voice, the way that you think and how you express those thoughts, the workings of your heart — I feel that I know them as I know my own. This may be presumptuous, but do not think me arrogant. I say these things in all humility and out of love. I long for you. I feel, for Hugo's sake, that it is wrong to do so, and yet I cannot help myself, and if it were not for Hugo whom we both loved, I should never have known you.

I am going to put this letter somewhere safe and hope that when next I take it out, to respond as I pray to joyful news, it will seem not too foolish, for it is the most in earnest that I have ever written.

He placed the unfinished letter, along with others from home, in his trunk, first wrapping it carefully to protect it from the other contents — dirty clothing, cracked boots, and biscuit, chocolate and rum husbanded against hard times.

With all the false alarms, the pickets were jumpy at night, and dawn often revealed the odd hapless dead cow whose resemblance to a Russian marksman had proved its undoing. And it was becoming colder, especially at night, dawn and dusk. Men made use of whatever clothing they had or had managed to acquire, including sheepskin waistcoats purloined from the Turks and fur coats from discarded Russian packs, so that much of the time it was impossible to tell officer from man, nationality from nationality, or friend from foe.

★　　★　　★

549

The enemy fire was now of an unimaginable ferocity, blasting continuously on both unprotected flanks. And still they trotted. Fyefield was struck: Harry heard the dull, wet implosion and felt a fine drizzle of Hector's blood on his cheek. Behind him he heard a man shout, 'Bloody bastards!' and the reprimand, 'Watch your filthy tongue, boy, you'll be facing your maker soon enough!'

They were now moving across the broad shallow depression in the centre of the valley and the fire seemed to be coming from all sides along with the swirling smoke, the boom of guns and the crack of rifle fire, the shouts of men and the screams of horses, and the hammering of hooves as riderless chargers sought desperately to rejoin the security of the ranks, weaving and jostling for position in the herd. A panic-stricken grey, dappled with blood, was trampling on its own entrails until it collapsed and somersaulted, squealing in agony.

Harry felt, rather than saw, the upward incline of the ground. A great shout, resounding and clamorous, of exultation or terror, perhaps both, rose from way ahead of them. The front line had seen the guns.

Rachel did at last stop bleeding, but only just in time. Dr Jaynes, on his mettle, told Maria in no uncertain terms that her daughter-in-law might have died.

'She's had the narrowest possible escape, and that she escaped at all is a mystery to me. In fact, nothing short of a miracle.'

Maria, who had been scared half to death herself, was accordingly sharp. 'For an intelligent woman she was very stupid to leave it so late before she sent for you.'

'It would have made no difference.' The doctor was matter-of-fact, he was belatedly beginning to get the measure of Maria. 'Your new granddaughter was an exceptionally large baby—'

'Bigger than both my boys!' Maria sounded both admiring and outraged.

'—and Rachel is not a young girl. She didn't begin to

haemorrhage until an hour after the birth. The woman who was with her did an excellent job.'

'She should also not have gone to the harvest home,' huffed Maria.

'There really was no reason why not. She assured me that she didn't dance but only watched. You were there yourself for a while,' he reminded her gently, 'and I'm quite sure you wouldn't have allowed her to endanger the life of your grandchild, or her own.'

'No, of course not, but I left early. I love to dance,' she added as if an excuse were required, 'but widows are not allowed to enjoy themselves.'

'And I must go.' The doctor rose. 'In any event, she will make a full recovery but she must rest. Eat and sleep, sleep and eat, that's the ticket. I'll call tomorrow.'

When he'd gone, Maria went up to see Rachel. Her face was as white as the pillow case, like a pencil drawing on the pale linen with only her hair and the shadows around her eyes and mouth to give it definition. Belle lay in her cradle making small popping and grunting sounds, only lightly asleep after the best efforts of the wet nurse. Mrs Bartlemas left the room discreetly. But when Maria sat down next to the bed she was surprised at how fixed and determined a look Rachel gave her.

'How is Belle?'

'Attending to her digestion. How are you, my dear? You look better.'

'Please, Maria – I have looked in the mirror.'

'I didn't say that you looked well, but that you looked better.'

Rachel closed her eyes briefly in acknowledgement of this brisk response. 'Will you write to Harry, and tell him about his niece?'

'Of course.'

'I promised I would let him know at once. And everything takes so long . . .'

'Then I shall do so at once. Immediately! Now that I know you, at least, are not going to die.'

Rachel's pale mouth suggested a smile. 'I'm sorry to have caused such panic and alarm.'

'Don't mention it,' said Maria, getting up. Her long fingers brushed Rachel's as if by accident. 'And anyway, it was my granddaughter's fault.'

If the charge was sounded, they did not hear it. But they did not need to, for the Lancers in the front line had broken into a gallop, hurtling headlong for the iron mouths of the Russian battery to escape the tearing fusillade from either side. Cardigan was obliged to match their pace in order to remain in front and squadron upon squadron followed suit. The charge had begun, spurred on by the tribal shouts of regimental rivalry: 'Come on, boys! Come on, Deaths! Don't let the busby-bags get in front!'

The second line breasted the rise and the ground fell away slightly, then levelled out. The horses were flying now – like arrows fired from a bow they were going to hit their target at the peak of their speed and the height of their trajectory. And hit it blind, for the fire continued to come from all sides. Beneath him Harry could sense Clemmie beginning to struggle and strive, overcoming weakness to become a pounding piston-pulse – neck, body, legs grabbing and releasing the ground so fast they barely touched it. The glare and blast of the cannons in front of them knocked over two troopers in their path, hurling them backwards in a screaming tangle of limbs, leather, weaponry and flesh split with glistening scarlet. The front row was gone, annihilated as though it had never been.

Clemmie leapt the first casualty and jinked like a hare to avoid the second. In response to the cries of 'Close up! Close the line!' the ranks parted and came together around the fallen like a stream swirling around driftwood. Ahead of them the battery was a churning wall of smoke, spitting flame. With a bludgeoning impact they were among the guns as the last salvo exploded about them.

Whirling his sword, killing in order to live, Harry heard

through the din an eerie howl like a vixen's, and realised that the cry was his.

Early on the morning of 25 October there had already been two engagements with the enemy, resulting in two British victories. Victories, it had to be said, due more to courage and initiative than to any strategic brilliance, but which the Lights had once again endured the indignity of watching from the sidelines.

The heroic stand of the Highlanders, a display of steadfast bloody-mindedness amounting to sheer bluff, was universally cheered and admired. But then the Scots had a leader whose judgement they trusted, literally, with their lives and whom they would have followed to hell and back. Several of the younger cavalry officers, believing Campbell to be (rightly) of the old guard and (wrongly) a stick in the mud, had now and again ventured to give him the benefit of their opinions, and had returned with a high colour and a flea in their ear. And the small Scots contingent's disciplined repulse of thousands of Russian cavalry silenced criticism.

But barely an hour later the Lights had been forced to see another chance of glory come, and go. As the Heavies had charged valiantly uphill at enemy cavalry advancing from the northwest the brigade under Cardigan were drawn up at right angles to the action. As the two sides engaged there was the perfect opportunity for a swift, punitive flank attack of the kind the Light Cavalry was designed for. Once again, as at the Alma, Harry had felt that primitive surge of the blood, the leap of expectancy and anticipation that this time surely, *surely*, they would be given their heads.

But no order came. It appeared that Lord Cardigan had been told to hold his ground and his position, and even the most heaven-sent opportunity – what was universally agreed to be a textbook opening for cavalry – would not tempt him into using his initiative over his orders. The Heavies carried the day with no assistance from the Lights except that of a few undisciplined hotheads who could stand it no longer and broke ranks to join the mêlée.

There followed a regrouping amid an air of celebration. The enemy's attempt to cut off the army from their supply source at Balaklava had been thwarted. The few had routed the many. Élan and *esprit de corps* had won the day. The bulldog spirit had prevailed.

The Lights were stood down, and many of them dismounted and were standing chatting and smoking, swapping much-needed food and rum rations in the sun. The horses' heads swung low, blowing hopefully at the thin stubble of grass.

Harry had undone one button on his jacket and would have taken out the unopened letter from his mother, but at that moment they received a peremptory order – delivered more furiously as it passed down the chain of command from one smarting officer to another – to douse their smokes, abandon their breakfast, mount and fall in.

Their services, it seemed, were required.

Suddenly, they were through, exploding from the mêlée like living roundshot.

As they emerged from the guns he was still yelling, and now they were confronted by a swarming pitched battle, the vanguard of the brigade struggling hand to hand with a huge concourse of Russian cavalry. Gough, slightly ahead of him, thrust his sword into a Russian soldier's neck to the hilt, but could not withdraw it because his hand was lashed to the hilt by Harry's handkerchief. The weight of his victim dragged him from the saddle and the blood spouting from the carotid artery sprayed over him as he fell. His horse reared back into Harry's path and he was obliged to fend it off with his sword, opening its shoulder.

He kept slashing with the sword, round his head, back and forth, all skill and orthodoxy abandoned in an attempt to stay alive. At first he could see no one to rally to in the heaving forest of flesh and steel, but then from his left he heard '8th! Close up! To me!' and saw Colonel Shawcross, his cigar still clamped between his teeth, his face running with blood. Soon a knot of them had formed around Shawcross, facing outward into the maelstrom. Men of both sides snatched at the flying reins of loose horses and scrambled aboard. The butcher, conspicuous in his abattoir smock of white spattered with scarlet, decapitated a Cossack and, lifting the head on the point of his sword, smashed it into the face of an oncoming rider.

A mile and a half away the spectators, looking through their spyglasses and binoculars, witnessed what seemed to be another ghostly lull as the last of the cavalry disappeared into the boiling smoke, and with their disappearance the fusillade from the hills stuttered and ceased.

Mercy Bartlemas put her head round the door.

'It's our Ben to see you, mum.'

'Tell him to come in . . .'

Ben entered the bedroom and stood just inside, uncertain of his ground as Cato went to greet him. 'Thank you, Mercy.'

'I'll wait in the kitchen. All right Ben?'

He nodded, and his sister gave him a sharp warning look as she closed the door.

Rachel smiled at him. 'She's over here in her cradle. Come and have a look.'

He advanced and looked down. At first it seemed no more than a polite compliance, but then she could see his interest catch alight and he leaned forward, tilting his head to look into the baby's face.

'You calling her Belle?'

'Yes, do you like it?'

'I don't mind. But my dad doesn't.'

'Why not?'

'He says it sounds like a music hall name.'

'Well, he's right in a way. But then I've nothing against the halls. I called her Belle because it means beautiful, and she is.'

'And it makes it sound as if the house belongs to her,' suggested Ben.

'I hadn't thought of that,' said Rachel. 'It does.'

He peered again. 'Can I touch her?'

'You can hold her if you like.'

'I don't know . . .' He pursed his lips. 'All right.'

He sat on the edge of the bed, gingerly holding the bundle that was Belle, and lowered his head to kiss the tiny fingers of the pink starfish hand that poked from her shawl. Rachel felt tears spring to her eyes because the kiss was so unaffected, a simple, instinctive, animal response.

After a minute he wriggled off the bed and laid the baby back in her cradle.

'Will you be all right?' he asked, and she knew at once that it was a farewell.

'Definitely. I shall be up and about very soon and then you must help me take her for walks.'

'What could I do?'

'You could . . .' for a moment she was lost for words '. . . you could keep Cato company.'

This seemed to tell Ben what he wanted to know. He nodded and went to the door.

''Bye then.'

'Goodbye, Ben, see you soon.'

When he'd gone she sat up and gazed at Belle, whose life had so nearly taken hers. She knew now that it was not only for Hugo that she loved her daughter, not merely because she was his legacy. She loved Belle because she was her own person, the custodian, like Ben, of the future.

A terrible confusion reigned. Clemmie was flagging now, and fearful that she would collapse in the middle of the carnage Harry used his spurs and the flat of his sword to keep her upright and moving. The ground was treacherous with broken tack, gore, and the bodies and severed limbs of the wounded. Loose horses careered crazily about hampered by flapping reins and hanging saddles, or stood shuddering in their death throes, with broken limbs and torn bellies. One lunged in pitiful circles, its shattered back leg swinging round and round. A man on the ground who had lost both his own legs screamed, 'Don't ride over me! For the love of God, don't ride over me!' Another was trapped beneath his fallen charger, covering his head against the flying hooves, an easy target for the lancers.

A corporal whom Harry recognised rode alongside, his shattered left arm dangling at his side and shouted chirpily 'Warm work, sir – honour satisfied?' before falling from the saddle and being dragged into the belly of the fighting, his foot caught in the stirrup.

They were retreating now, he could hear the cries of 'Close up!' and 'Back, back!' and see the scattered men of the Lights as they separated from the throng. Harry pulled Clemmie's head round and spurred her into one last effort back towards the guns.

For a long time all that could be seen from camp was the smoke, drifting up like that of a distant autumn bonfire at the far end of the valley. Betts's hand, grasping a wisp of dry grass, moved back and forth, back and forth on Derry's neck as he gazed at the smoke. When the firing from the heights started up again the word got round that the Light Brigade was coming back.

They returned through the scudding smoke into a hail of fire, and the valley floor strewn with dead men and horses. For perhaps a hundred yards they stumbled and dodged their way between these horrific obstacles, no longer noticing the torn limbs, the cries for help and mercy, the outstretched hands and convulsing bodies. The barrage of roundshot, grape-shot, shells and musketry was even deadlier to them in their depleted condition, without the solid formations of the regiments around them.

Another hundred yards, and now Harry could see the zouaves, the French *Chasseurs d'Afrique*, engaging the enemy on his right flank. Safety and survival seemed suddenly within his grasp. Then from nowhere came a blow that rocked them both, so violent that he couldn't tell whether it was he or Clemmie who had been hit. The mare leapt forward like a cat, bolting uncontrollably towards the mouth of a narrow defile at the foot of the Woronzov escarpment, the gulley lined with a tangle of dark scrub. He couldn't control her but she baulked at the scrub and wheeled sharply, heading back the way they'd come. Harry leaned forward, clutching at her cheek strap, hoping to turn her head by main force. But now he could feel the unevenness of her stride, and at the same moment that her legs gave way beneath her he felt a hot, wet explosion of pain that propelled him into darkness.

CHAPTER TWENTY

———◦◦◦◦———

'You, the man I'm thinking of,
Yes, you, my missing other half.
You, the man I long to love—
Are you there?'
                    —Stella Carlyle, 'Are You There?'

Stella – 1996

The curator handed the button back to Stella.

'It's actually Russian,' he said. 'But a nice little find nonetheless.'

'Is there anything else about it?'

'It's from an artillery regiment. Which makes sense if your
friend found it in the North Valley. Cannons to the right of
them, cannons to the left of them . . . Magnificent but not
war . . . Poor chaps, a fine example of the cock-up theory.'

'It sounds like it.' She put the button in her bag and pointed
at the picture which lay on the desk between them. 'And what
about that? It's propaganda, surely.'

'Let's see.' The curator picked up the picture and held it at
arm's length. 'Yes and no. It's obviously titled for what we might
call propaganda purposes, but . . .' He pushed his spectacles into
his hair and peered closely at the photograph. 'It's certainly not
a set-up.'

'No? You mean these aren't models?'

'Oh, good lord, no, this is the genuine article, probably taken
in the Crimea. It was the first war to be widely photographed

559

but most of what found its way back here was broadly what you'd call portraiture. Action photography wasn't an option, and undoctored post-battle scenes weren't good for public morale. But this one must have fallen into the photographer's lap, so to speak. You can tell from the state of the horse that it's the real thing. And it's in surprisingly good nick. It may even have some value but you need a specialist for that, I wouldn't want to stick my neck out.' He put his glasses back on his nose and held the picture at arm's length to survey it more generally. 'An acquired taste, but right up the Victorians' alley, of course – hero and horse united in death, gone to a better place . . . All that kind of thing.'

'We don't know that he was a hero.'

'Indeed not, but the poor man's entitled to his secrets, and whatever his story he was put to good use after death.'

'As a matter of fact—' Stella turned the picture slightly towards her to refresh her memory '—there isn't a mark on either of them.'

'True,' said the curator. 'None that we can see, anyway. I imagine that was how they came to have their picture taken.'

When she got back she rang Jamie to tell him he'd been right. Because his working day started at five a.m. he was home and often asleep in the late-afternoon, so she'd been half expecting to talk to his machine and was surprised when he answered. She could hear televised sport in the background.

'Am I disturbing you?'

'No – hang on.' There was a brief pause and the rugger sound was stifled.

'I am.'

'You are not, we're getting creamed anyway. What can I do for you?'

She relayed the curator's comments. 'There you go,' he said. 'Respect! It's nice to be proved correct by the experts.'

'He said it might even be valuable.'

'Really? Don't forget your friends when you're loaded.'

'I'm not thinking of selling it.'

'Stella, you are such a sentimental old cow.'

'Less of the old. Right, well, I only—'

'How's Robert?'

Although, or perhaps because, she had been thinking of nothing else for days she answered stupidly: 'Who?'

'If you don't know I certainly bloody don't. Robert. The man you talk about when you're pissed.'

She noted that he had been kind enough not to say 'when you're shagging my friends'. 'I don't know.'

'I assume he's the one you were talking about about when we had that lunch last year?'

'That's right. But I haven't seen him.'

'And that's the problem, is it?'

'It's rather more complicated than that.'

'Sure, but the longest journey starts with a single – Shit! Try! Fucking brilliant, what a screamer! Equalised, and everything to play for!'

Whatever its status in the mind of the giver, the advice was sound. She knew that, because it was the same advice she gave herself. Don't write the whole script, don't pre-empt the plot, take one small step. Contact him.

The trouble was that while it may have been one small step to Jamie, it was a giant leap where she was concerned: a giant leap across a howling abyss. All that stuff on both sides that had to be gone through, unravelled, relived, explained. They couldn't just go back to where they were, too much had happened, and that scared her too. Even if she managed her side of things, how would he be? She had only ever known him as an unqualified professional success – smart, rich, confident, at the top of his form. With this hanging over him, and his marriage over, would he be a different person? The thought of a humbled Robert, chastened and self-justifying, apalled her. God knows she had slept with enough men she neither admired nor respected because they were by definition dispensable. She had fallen in love with Robert for all the things he was, and one of those was what she herself aspired to be – a class act.

She and Derek had started rehearsals for their cabaret at the Parade on the Park. It was partly a way of kick-starting her on the writing: they needed at least half a dozen new numbers. He came round to her place in the mornings, around ten-thirty, and they went through till whatever time they ran out of steam and broke off for a pub lunch. If she got an idea for a tune or a lyric they'd roll it around between them and see if it achieved any momentum of its own. Derek was a completely unselfish performer, he recognised her as the creative engine and patiently followed her whims and flights and dead-ends, never chivvying, always exuding the unspoken assumption that they'd get there in the end.

The morning after her conversation with Jamie, the process was temporarily stalled and they were having an early beer to buy time. Derek was sitting on the piano stool at right angles to the keyboard, his hands on his knees, bottle in one hand, cigarette in the other.

'Jackman,' she said, 'why couldn't I have fallen in love with you?'

'Because you're an honourable lady and I'm a happily married man.'

'Leaving that aside.'

'Which I have been known to do myself from time to time . . . No, so what brought this on?'

'We're such a terrific team.'

'Because we're not having a thing, that's why.'

There was a silence while she acknowledged the truth of this, before saying: 'This man – this man I used to care about—' Derek pulled a wry face at her through his smoke '—anyway, this man. He's in trouble and I'd like to see him. But for one thing that's breaking all the rules, and for another it could be a total disaster, and for another – forget it, the nightmare continues.'

'Pick up the phone, girl.'

'I don't know where he is.'

'He works, doesn't he?'

'Yes, but he may not be there . . .' Some foolish, protective instinct prevented her from saying why.

'But they'll know where he is. Do it now, while I'm here.'

'No.'

'But do it, yeah? For me.' He leaned forward. 'I want to have a show to go to.'

'Okay, okay!'

It was another three days before she called the hospital main switchboard and asked to be put through to the ophthalmology department.

'May I ask what it's in relation to?'

'I'm trying to get hold of someone.'

'Is it with regard to an appointment?'

'Not exactly.'

'Do you need advice?'

She considered this was broadly true. 'Yes.'

'What is your patient number?'

Shit. 'I don't have it with me.'

'Name?'

'Stella Carlyle.'

'Postcode?'

She realised she was being looked up on a computer, and rang off.

The following afternoon she drove to the hospital, presented herself at reception and asked for the eye clinic.

'It's Clinic C, along here up the stairs or lift to Level One, turn left and through the double doors.'

'Thanks.

'But there's no clinic this afternoon.'

'Right – so will there be no one there?'

'No,' said the woman patiently. 'Can I help at all?'

Stella, sorely tried, bit back a smart answer. 'I'm trying to contact Dr Vitelio.'

'Mr Vitelio's not here at present, he's taking some time off.'

'I see. Will he be in tomorrow?'

'No, he may take a few weeks.'

'Is this to do with the enquiry?'

The receptionist's voice took on a hint of frost. 'Pending the outcome of an enquiry, that's right.'

563

'Does he come in at all? I mean, if I were to leave a message—'

'Are you the press?'

'Certainly not. I'm an acquaintance.'

The receptionist put a notepad and biro on the desk in front of her. 'If you want to leave your name, I'll give it to him if he should come in.' As Stella turned to leave, she added: 'But I wouldn't hold my breath if I were you.'

The weird thing was, she felt as though she was holding her breath. Every day was a long winching up of tension and expectation through which she struggled, only to collapse with a great exhalation into bed, and sleep, sometimes weeping with frustration but hanging on to the hope that tomorrow might be the day . . .

She had almost forgotten what it was like, the open-ended waiting. The feeling that every empty post and un-rung minute, every junk-fax and fatuous e-mail was an affront, and more than an affront: a blow, a cut. A slamming of the door.

The rehearsals helped, but she wasn't writing. Neither she nor Derek raised the subject of Robert again.

The weekend after her fruitless visit to the hospital she went to visit her parents. When she called her mother, Mary was touchingly delighted.

'Of course! You must! George has been telling me all about the wonderful time they had in Italy, we were so sorry we couldn't . . . Will you be able to spend the night?'

'Are you sure that won't be too much?'

'Darling – not enough, if anything.'

'How's Dad?'

'Doolally a lot of the time now. Be prepared.'

She thought she was, but it was still a shock. In some ways it was easier now that he had crossed the invisible line between everyone else's world and his own unique, out-of-sync one. There were no longer those agonised reachings-out, the mental fumblings, the half-understood exchanges. No twilight. Where Andrew was now was bright as day to him, and there was no point in trying to reclaim him. Like a sleepwalker you could only bear him company and direct his footsteps.

When she arrived on Friday night he was already in bed and Mary explained that this was the usual pattern.

'He gets sleepy in the evening and he's usually up there between seven and eight, but the small hours tend to be eventful.'

'Can't you keep him up so that he sleeps when you do?'

'I've thought of it, but how? We don't have conversations any more, I can't engage his mind or his attention, so short of poking him with a stick . . . And anyway, this is my quiet time. It means you and I can have supper together in peace. It cuts both ways.'

This was another difference, thought Stella: her mother, too, had crossed the line. She was as loving and attentive to Andrew as she'd always been, but between her and Stella there was no longer any pretence that the matter couldn't be discussed frankly. There had come a point where Mary had been left behind in the world her husband no longer inhabited. It was horribly sad, but it meant that for almost the first time in her adult life Stella found that she and her mother were talking to one another as friends and equals, without the invisible barrier of the perfectly happy marriage. Mary's strength as a mother was that she had always been primarily a wife. But now the emphasis had shifted.

After supper they sat with the last of the New Zealand Sauvignon in the conservatory. Mary had invested in an inter-com, and they could hear Andrew's breathing. Occasionally the pace and volume of the breathing altered, as if he were dreaming.

'Do you have any help?' asked Stella.

'Yes, I have big strong girls from Social Services who come and give him a bath once a week. And there's a nice woman, I forget her official title, who calls me every morning to check that I'm still holding up. I can unburden myself to her, which is useful.'

Stella said humbly: 'You could unburden yourself to me.'

'Darling, I know I could, but neither of us would be any

further forward. I'd feel I was being a bore, and you'd be upset not knowing what to do—'

Stella put her head in her hands. 'I should do more. I feel terrible.'

'Don't! Don't, or I shall feel I can't tell you anything. If there was something that only you could do, believe me I'd ask for it. Other than that, the best thing you can do is to be the star that we're both so proud of.'

'Scarcely a star. I can't even write at the moment.'

'How many times have I heard that before? You will.'

'I wish I had your confidence.'

'Come on.' Mary upended the last of the bottle into Stella's glass. 'It's not exactly confidence, but remember I've been watching you for a long time. Your songs are you, aren't they? You sing your life, or your feelings about life. And I suppose the feelings have to cook for a bit before you can turn them into songs.'

'You're absolutely right.' Stella didn't know why she should be surprised at the accuracy of this assessment. 'But it doesn't make the waiting any easier.' She looked directly at her mother. 'Did I ever tell you you're my hero?'

'No, thank heavens.'

'Well, tough, because I am now. You and Dad. I thrash about and pretend to be modern, but I envy what you have. What you've made.'

'You mean, our marriage?'

'Sort of.' With difficulty she made herself say the big words she could so easily have sung: 'More, your love. It's how love ought to be. In an ideal world.'

Mary turned aside so that her face was in profile to Stella's, vulnerable to inspection, displaying the softening tissues and creased skin of old age. 'Put Andrew on a pedestal if you must, but be so kind as to leave me my feet of clay.'

Stella said teasingly: 'Don't tell me you're about to confess to something shocking?'

'No – but Andrew's not the only man I've loved. Nor the man I've loved the most.'

Stella caught her breath. 'You think that's not shocking?'

'I'm sorry.'

'No – no – Mum, I'm not being critical, Jesus Christ would I . . . ? I'm just saying that at this moment I'm your selfish little girl and I'm shocked.'

'It was an awfully long time ago. In another lifetime.' Mary looked back at her and smiled. 'History, as they say.'

'Well, good for you. But let me put it on record that I'm awfully glad you picked Dad to have babies with.'

Mary didn't reply, but Stella thought she detected a sheen of tears on her smile. The air ached with things waiting to be said. There was a sudden flurry of sound over the intercom, and Mary got up and went through to the bedroom.

Stella sat, still, absorbing the blow as she listened to the intimate sounds of soothing, pillow-plumping, tucking-in, the soft 'tick' of a kiss: the sounds of childhood.

Her mother returned, brisk and practical. 'False alarm. It's not waking up time yet.'

Stella fell in step with her. 'Seriously, Mum, would you like me to come and stay for a bit? Share the burden?'

'Not to share the burden, no. You know that if you ever want to come for all the usual reasons, there's nothing I'd like more.' Stella noticed she did not say 'we'. 'But we have a system and a routine, and there is more professional help I can call on if I really need to. For goodness' sake, Andrew's not an invalid, he can still do all the basic things for himself, it's just a case of getting him to do them at the right time and place!'

At half-past ten they went to bed. Stella wondered what it must be like to share a double bed with a man whom one loved but who had become a stranger. She'd heard people say that when a marriage went wrong it was like that. But at least the other person would still speak the same language, have the same frame of reference and the recollection of a shared history. From her parents' room, with the intercom now switched off, there was silence.

It didn't last for long. After half an hour, it began – the mutterings and creakings, the click of light switches and running of taps, the perambulations, her mother's muted voice and her father's, alternately querulous and strident. Concerned that her mother might think she was asleep and be trying not to disturb her, Stella got out of bed and opened the door.

Her parents were standing in the passage, hand in hand, Andrew in his paisley pyjamas, Mary in her oversized pale blue t-shirt, both barefoot. They looked like a couple of children about to leave on some quixotic fairytale quest.

'There's no need to be quiet,' Stella said, 'I wasn't asleep.' She walked over and kissed her father. 'Hallo, Dad.'

'Can you tell me what time it is?'

She glanced at her watch. 'Five-past eleven?'

'Have we told the boys when to come?'

'Yes.' Mary was firm. 'Later.'

'I want to be dressed when they get here.'

'You will be, don't worry.'

'What am I wearing now?' He pulled at his pyjama jacket between finger and thumb and gazed down at it. 'What's this?'

'Your pyjamas.'

'I don't want to be wearing pyjamas when the boys arrive.'

'Of course not.' Mary lifted his hand and gave it a little encouraging tug. 'Let's go back to our room and then we can decide.'

Stella said: 'Can I help? What can I do?'

Andrew gave her a worried look. 'Will you tell the boys when to come?'

'Yes.'

'I don't want them here till I've dressed.'

'I understand.'

Mary mouthed 'thank you' and led him away. The bedroom door closed after them. But that was only the beginning of a long night of alarms and excursions. Stella knew from her watch that she herself was getting some rest, however interrupted, but when the first birds twittered beyond the grey window her last thought before falling into a final few hours of dead sleep was that her mother must have been up for most of the night.

And yet in the morning there was Mary in the kitchen, dressed, coiffed and made up, with bread standing to attention in the toaster and the cafetière ready by the kettle. Stella, still in her dressing gown, felt put to shame.

'Mum – how on earth do you do it?'

'With difficulty.' Mary kissed her. 'And practice.'

'Where is Dad anyway?'

'I give him breakfast in bed and then he has a bit of a zizz before we start again.'

'You didn't get up just for me?'

'I'd like to say yes, but no.' Mary put the cafetière on the table. 'I really do have to make the effort, it's the only thing that keeps me going.' She smiled to show this was a joke when it was plainly true.

Stella sat down at the table and pushed down the plunger in the coffee pot. 'So do you get any rest at all?'

'Not much, but then we don't need much at our age. Not so much proper sleep anyway. I've perfected the art of the casual doze. Like a horse standing under a tree, an indeterminate state.'

'Well, at least have a nap today at some point, and let me look after Dad.'

'Let's see.'

'And let me take you both out to lunch.'

'That would be absolutely lovely – but I warn you, it can be wearing.'

'At least there'll be the two of us.'

The pub lunch was wearing, though perhaps not for Stella in quite the way her mother had meant. There were the misunderstandings and wanderings and spillings, the odd, unconnected questions and remarks addressed to complete strangers. No, it wasn't coping with the practicalities that discomfited her so much as a kind of childish embarrassment. For the first time in years she caught herself asking what people would think, and realising that she minded. It wasn't that people weren't kind and tolerant – if anything that was the trouble. Once the situation had been resolved she found herself haunted by what she imagined to be their pity, their indulgence, their self-congratulation – their relief that the moment had passed, and it wasn't they who had to deal with it. The remarks they would make to one another *sotto voce*.

When Andrew wanted to go to the lavatory, she said she would take him and then realised there was a problem.

'Which one?' she asked her mother.

'Oh, the Gents.'

'Do I go in?'

'No, he can manage. Post him in at the door and if he's too long poke your head in. If some friendly male face is about you can deputise, it's no time for pride.'

'I can see that.'

'And, Stella – darling, check his flies when he comes out.'

Thankfully her father emerged with another nice elderly gentleman who confided 'All shipshape' as he went past.

Andrew frowned at her. 'It's not bath day.'

She decided it was time to bat the ball back. 'Isn't it?'

'Have I had a bath?'

'No. Which day is bath day?'

'I can't have one like this.'

She gave up.

When they got back to the bungalow she was therefore rather taken aback when Mary took her up on her earlier offer.

'Perhaps I will go and put my head down, for half an hour – are you sure that would be all right?'

'Of course! Is there anything I should know?'

'I don't think so . . . He loves musicals if there's one on.'

'I'll see.'

Stella joined her father in the living room, chastising herself for her slight reluctance and anxiety. He was sitting with his hands on his knees, tapping his fingers to some rhythm in his head, but gazing at his hands as though they belonged to someone else.

'Dad . . .' She leaned down to try and catch his eye. 'Dad, can I get you anything?'

Still tapping, he replied cheerfully: 'I wouldn't mind some chocolate.'

'Good idea, me too. Where is it?'

'On the sideboard, on the sideboard, by the shining big-sea water.'

There was no sideboard, but out in the kitchen she found a large bar of Fruit and Nut in the cupboard, and took it through. She unwrapped it, broke off a strip of squares and held it out to him.

'There you are.'

'What's this?'

'Chocolate. Fruit and nut.'

'I don't care for it.'

'All right.' She laid the squares on the table next to him. 'But it's there if you change your mind.' She broke off a chunk for herself and thought, If I had to do this every day I'd be a twenty-stone, chain-smoking, bullying alcoholic. Her admiration for her mother's stamina and spirit was increasing by the minute.

The fingers tapped away, then stopped. 'How does it go, that one?'

'Which one?'

'This.' He tapped again, this time humming tunelessly.

'What are the words?'

This was a long shot, but he didn't seem to hear and continued to hum, more a series of sniffs and puffs in time with his fingers.

Something occurred to her, and she laid her own fingers on the table top and tapped as she intoned the words: '"By the shining big-sea water, Daughter of the moon Nacomis . . ."'

'Hang on, I'll find it, you've got it somewhere.'

Elated with this small success, fearful of losing the moment, she scanned the bookshelves and found Longfellow. Then she sat cross-legged on the floor in front of her father's chair and began. He tapped, she read. He stared at whatever it was he could see, and smiled.

When Mary came in, with many apologies, at four o'clock, they were still at it, except that Stella was lying down. Mary made no comment but withdrew to make tea, and her return with the tray provided Stella with an excuse to stop.

'Good kip?'

'Absolutely wonderful. Out like a light.'

'I'm so pleased. And we've had a nice time too.'

'I can see that.' She looked a little wistful. 'It makes me realise how selfish and unimaginative I've become.'

'Mum,' said Stella, 'for goodness' sake. This is a novelty to me. I don't know how you manage half what you do.'

Mary sighed. 'Revelations apart, I do love him, you know . . .'

'Of course you do!'

'That's the bugger of it.' She leant across and stroked the ridged, veiny back of his hand. 'And I almost wish I didn't — love's such a hard taskmaster.'

The next day they all went to lunch with George and Brian at Bells. Over g and t and Kettle Chips in the kitchen George quizzed her sister.

'How do you find them?'

'Amazing all things considered. I don't know how Mum manages, she's a bloody superwoman.'

'Awesome or what? But our view is that the time is fast approaching when something will have to be done.'

'What, you mean a home?'

'It sounds so awful when you put it baldly like that, but I suppose that is what I'm getting at. Otherwise she's going to burn herself out.'

'But if she'd rather do it, that's her prerogative surely?'

'That's a terribly grown-up thing to say.'

'I mean, she has to decide, not us. And reach the point where she decides in her own time and her own way. And in the meantime she needs to feel that she's doing the right and loving thing. She needs our support.'

'Blimey, Stella.' George sloshed *vin du pays* into the gravy pan and gave her sister a sidelong look. 'First Italy, now this . . . If I didn't know better I'd suspect you of becoming a good woman.'

On the drive back into town Stella reflected that she was very far, thank God, from being a good woman — she was a loose one who had unexpectedly felt the tug of love. And was finding that love was, as her mother had said, a hard taskmaster.

As the summer grew tired and crawled into August, Robert had still not been in touch, but she did write the songs. This was due mainly to the reliable, non-negotiable imperative of the deadline – their two weeks at the Parade on the Park ran for the second half of the month – but also because the pigheaded performer in her would not be beaten. It became a point of honour with her that this season should be a triumph. She wanted to wear her experiences lightly, dazzlingly, like jewellery, to mug her audience with high emotion and terrific tunes. To slay them where they sat.

Derek was chuffed with her output. 'You're working well, girl, it was worth waiting for. This lot'll make them choke on their dinners.'

'Let's hope so.'

'You're looking great, by the way.'

'Thanks.'

She wasn't sure about this. When she looked at herself in the mirror these days she thought that she looked discernibly older. She had never had any pretensions to beauty, and had done precious little to take care of herself. She had not exercised, nor watched her diet, nor pampered herself at health farms; she had smoked, drunk and slept around. She had dyed her hair so often she had almost forgotten its natural colour; she dressed to please herself, she preferred glasses to contact lenses and only wore make-up on stage.

What she saw in her reflection was not so much the physical signs of ageing, which anyway would not have bothered her. It was something much less palpable: a look in the eyes, a set of the lips. It was – and here she perceived the germ of a song – as though the iron had gone from her soul.

One evening she went so far as to ring Robert's home telephone number, the only time she had ever done so, taking care to enter the blocking code first. Her call was answered immediately, she guessed the phone might be on a desk.

'Yes?'

'May I speak to Mr Vitelio, please?'

'Who is that?'

She was taken aback not so much by the question as the

implication that Robert might be there. She plucked a name from the ether.

'Sarah Jones, I'm a colleague.'

'Just a moment.'

A hand was placed over the receiver for what felt like an eternity but was perhaps thirty seconds. At one point the hand must have slipped, for she heard the woman's voice say '. . . you only have to . . .' before it was stifled again.

Then: 'Hang on, I'm passing you over.'

She did hang on until she heard his voice. Then she hung up.

Of course, she told herself, he would still be there. With her. Even if he had left he would have returned, and she would have taken him back. Whatever their difficulties and differences, that strong, calm wife of his was the person who had shared the vicissitudes of his life, she would be there for him when needed. As she, Stella, had not.

'It was her, wasn't it?'

'I've no idea,' he replied. 'She hung up.' Sian raised an eyebrow. 'I really couldn't say.'

She was standing in the study doorway, fingers criss-crossed before her like a siege defence. 'Got everything?'

'I think so.'

He picked up the box of books and nodded at the case full of folders and papers. 'I'll come back in for those.'

'I'll bring them.'

'Don't worry.'

She picked them up. 'Come on.'

He had been in the house for perhaps half an hour, and she had not mentioned the enquiry. But as he took the case off her and stashed it in the boot, she said: 'I'm sorry you're having a bad time.'

'My own damn-fool fault.' What was he supposed to say? 'This too shall pass.'

She made no further comment. He closed the boot, and gave it a tap. 'Well.'

'Robert, would you sort out the calls? Put a diversion on or something? I don't want any more.'

'I'll do my best.'

'If you would. And the post.' She raised a hand and turned away without looking at him again. 'Good luck.'

As he drove away he thought, Of course it was her. Of course it was Stella. That was the sort of impulsive, quixotic, death-wish kind of thing she would do. He felt the clamp of heartache around his chest. For the first time in his life he felt utterly disorientated, all at sea. The enquiry, the end of his marriage, his separation from Stella – most of all Stella – had presented him with a terrible freedom which he had no idea how to employ. Catching a glimpse of his own face in the rearview mirror it frightened the hell out of him: it was the stressed, scared, angry face of a middle-aged man who was his own worst enemy.

He pulled over for a moment and sat with his arms braced on the wheel, breathing deeply. His breaths had a rasping quality, as though all the sharp edges and rough corners of his life were snagging at his lungs. Time, he thought, for an audit.

Stella didn't try again. A melancholy calm descended on her. Never had she been more grateful for the nature and demands of her work. As the date of the cabaret drew closer she did not allow herself to look beyond it. This must be wonderful – everything else must take care of itself.

She bought a dress that was so different from anything else she'd ever worn that she asked George up to town for lunch at the flat.

'You asked me all the way up here for my opinion on a dress?'

'Not your opinion, I've already bought it.'

'So what if I don't like it?'

'Lie.'

'Seems clear enough to me. Put it on then.'

'Okay, but you'll have to imagine—'

'Trust me.'

Stella made an 'as if' face and went to put on the dress. It was a skinny black sheath with a high neck and cut-away shoulders, the back slashed from nape to waist. In amongst the black was the faintest dusting of silver which caught the light. Above its spare, uncompromising glamour Stella's skin was parchment white, and her shock of electric-red hair surprising and exotic as a cactus flower.

'Sorry,' said George.

'What?'

'Call me old-fashioned, but I can't lie.'

Robert was suspended on full pay for the duration of the enquiry, which he found humiliating. Something Calvinist in him had prevented him from calling his work a vocation, but now he discovered that taking money for not doing it was distasteful to him. It seemed to demean the work itself, to reduce it to the level of a product.

At the same time he was able to rent a decent small service apartment near the British Museum in which to do cold turkey. Time for reflection, he found, was what he had spent most of his adult life avoiding. Realistically he knew the enquiry could go either way. On his side were his excellent clinical record, his experience, a career coloured by a certain maverick quality but hitherto unblemished by formal complaints. Ranged against him were – as he saw it – timidity, jobsworthism and political correctness. That he had been rude was a fact, but not in itself a hanging offence, and his competence was not in question so far as he knew. His colleagues, when you got down to the wire, would support him; the nurses might be more ambivalent, there was nothing he could do about that. The patient's mother would be feverishly excited about the whole thing, it would have taken on the nature of a crusade for her and her associates, it made him tired to think of it. All this, and for what? Could it possibly be worth it to anyone? Certainly not the patient himself, who was continuing to receive treatment and for whom the long-term prognosis was pretty good. The trouble was that whatever he had called the awful

Mrs Stuart at the time he had meant it then, and would still, given the chance, mean it now. He was not remorseful on that count.

He forced himself to contemplate the worst-case scenario: losing his job. Setting aside the financial implications, which were dire, the idea of being prevented from doing what he was trained and suited for was outrageous to him. He was faster, better, a safer pair of hands than anyone else he knew in his field, and to be sidelined would be not just galling but a criminal waste of resources.

He found himself wondering why Stella had called – to sympathise, to crow, to sound him out? To ask to see him? Or perhaps he was flattering himself and she didn't know about any of it. She wasn't the world's most assiduous student of current affairs and could go for days without looking at a newspaper. And why would she be interested? She'd been freezing him out for months . . . It probably hadn't been her on the phone at all, but some nosy junior reporter hoping to steal a march and getting cold feet at the last moment.

In any event, the thought of seeing her in his present state of uncertainty was intolerable. Whatever else she thought of him she knew him as a success. He felt himself heavily identified by his profession, his ability to change lives. Without that he was a pretty standard failure. Whatever the outcome of the enquiry, he had to regroup, to recover his balance and his self-esteem.

Jamie called. 'Something of mine coming up on the show on Wednesday, might amuse you.'

She watched, but it didn't. The item, as trumpeted by the youthful presenters, was 'How rude can you be and get away with it?' The starting point was the story about the consultant who'd called his patient's mother 'a danger to shipping'. A great deal of crude fun was made out of this, including sending one of the wilder girl presenters on to the street to pick arguments with people, interviews with the foul-mouthed band Antichrist and a writer on modern etiquette, and the extending of an invitation to viewers to send in especially choice insults.

Jamie called again. 'So what did you reckon?'

'It's not my bag. But then your programme's not directed at me.'

'No, but I was pretty pleased with it, it was a nice little package.'

It was clear he hadn't the least idea of her connection to the subject and she wasn't going to tell him.

'Congratulations,' she said. 'Case proven.'

'Er – which case was that?'

'Rudeness isn't clever and it isn't funny.'

'You're joking, right?'

'Deadly serious.'

'Sorry I spoke.'

The difference between theatre and cabaret audiences was one not only of scale but of character. With Sorority Stella had played to numbers far smaller than this, and in numerous places where food and drink were being consumed, but in those days the eating and drinking had been a sign of the band's lowly status. If you could coax people to look up from their chips for a second you might get asked back.

At the Parade on the Park the shining ones with their fifteen-quid hamburgers and five-star pitta wraps were in themselves an accolade, the outward and visible sign that Stella and Derek had arrived. The urbane burble of well-heeled dining, the swift glide of waiters, the sparkle of immaculate tableware, all caused Derek to murmur as they entered: 'Well, girl, this is where we came in.'

The difference was that Stella discovered the special delight of entertaining a smaller, mellower audience. In many respects this was less like the Loch Ailmay Hotel and more like her impromptu performance at the Harbour Light. She was singing to the converted. She could feel the warm wave of sophisticated appreciation that came across with the first round of applause: she had only to give these people what they wanted and expected, and that she could do.

The songs she'd written for this show were funny, wistful,

ironic. Like that indefinable expression in her eyes that she took to be ageing, a little of the caustic edge had gone from her wit, a little more uncertainty had taken its place, an inconclusiveness, a blurring of the outlines that made the last line of each song hang in the mind like a question. To begin with it had been an instinctive, unconsidered development. But the professional in her, hearing it, had deconstructed it and identified its components.

She could tell the songs worked by the way people's faces lost their assumed, social expressions and became introspective, their thoughts and feelings led by her and not by the people around them. In the large, low dining room of the Parade she didn't have to push her voice, and Derek was by now so perfectly attuned to her that his accompaniment, always faultless, now seemed artless as well, as though her voice simply trailed the strings of notes like a gossamer scarf floating in her wake.

She wore the black dress, with tight black ankle boots; dramatic eyes, no lips to speak of, no jewellery; hair fiery and farouche, with a single black feather like an Indian brave's.

Something happened that she couldn't account for, but it did her no harm. For the third and final encore they signed off with 'Are You There?' and on the last soft, yearning phrase her voice sank to a whisper, and then failed. Derek allowed the piano to fade away after her. It might even have passed for a calculated *coup de théâtre*.

Unusually for Derek he did not comment on this lapse.

On these sultry late summer evenings Robert had taken to going for walks. He'd set out at about six without much thought for what direction he was taking, stop after about an hour at a pub and have a whisky and (less often) a sandwich, and decide on the rest of his route according to weather, location and his own mood. He walked to Regent's Park, round the outer circle and back round the inner, skirting the fantastic outlines of the zoo at dusk; went up to Primrose Hill and watched the sun wallow down over the city as people and their dogs orbited the lower slope; tramped the streets as far as Islington and followed the canal, getting a boat's eye view of the New Labour terraces; penetrated Soho and thought it sad and changed; traversed the hinterland of the West End to Hyde Park and as far as Kensington Gardens where the rollerblading young swooped and twirled like urban swallows and the indigent bedded down on benches while the affluent jogged, puffing and sweating, round the perimeter.

After the stifling longueurs of the day with its pretence at routine and paperwork, its brain-numbing forays into daytime TV, its nervy obsession with broadcast and printed news and its peculiarly wearing mixture of boredom and anxiety, the toxic anonymous bustle of London was soothing. It was both a distraction and a concealment. When he began his walks he was quite overwhelmed by the brash vibrancy of the streets, but as time and distance went by there was a comfort to be derived from being part of it.

His own appearance before the board of enquiry had gone as well as could be expected. He knew that humility, plain and simple, was the best card to play on such an occasion, but it was not his strongest suit. Even more than coming across as an arrogant bastard he dreaded being seen as a hypocritical creep. He answered the questions as briefly as was consistent with being civil, and tried for a tone of pragmatic regret without undue remorse. When the fatherly figure from the GMC had asked him wheedlingly how his own behaviour appeared to him 'with the benefit of hindsight', he had been lured into replying that he regarded hindsight as an affliction rather than a benefit, which had caused one faint, wry smile, and most heads to dip discreetly towards their notepads. But in the main he felt that while he had not exactly won them over he had commanded their attention and respect and could do no more.

With two days to go before the outcome was due to be announced Seppi rang to say he was in town for a trade show and invited him to dinner. They went to an old-fashioned French restaurant near the V & A. Seppi was right back to his dapper, prosperous, sanguine self: Natalie was much recovered and the prognosis was encouraging, business was good, and the trade fair an amusing jaunt. But his natural inclination to celebrate was tempered by concern for his brother.

'Let's have champagne, my treat – you need cheering up.'

'I'm surprisingly cheerful,' said Robert. 'But bored out of my skull.' With this one unconsidered remark he realised how clearly and damningly he had indicated his priorities, and Seppi was quick to pick up on it, waving a hand way to the side above shoulder height.

'Forget this nonsense with your work. You're a good doctor, it's going to be okay. How's Sian? We simply can't believe this is happening.'

'Well, it is.' Robert couldn't keep the impatience out of his voice. 'And you had better believe it.'

'But why . . . ?' Seppi let the question hang as the champagne was popped and poured. 'But why, Roberto? Why throw away so many good years at this late stage of the game?'

The one thing Robert could not do was tell his own brother to mind his own business. Family was business in common.

'We weren't happy, shall we leave it at that?'

'Who's happy all the time? What happened to "for better, for worse"?'

'We were the cause of each other's unhappiness.'

'That's marriage. Get over it.'

'Seppi—' Robert looked away, eyes closed, then back at his brother '—spare me the homespun philosophy. Please.'

'You don't seem all that happy now if I may say so.'

'Can you wonder when I've got this bloody enquiry hanging over me? Some hysterical fool of a woman could wreck my entire career, I'm not exactly dancing on air!'

'Okay. And is there someone else?'

'Yes, but it appears to be over.'

'She was the cause?'

'Not really.'

'Sure! You're such a fool, Roberto.' It was an admonishment but Seppi's voice was gentle. 'Look at yourself.'

'I have been.' Suddenly tired, Robert rubbed his hands over his face. 'And if it makes you feel any better, I don't like what I see.'

Seppi picked up the menu. 'You're the same as you always were, a clever useless bastard. She's out there somewhere, getting on with her life while you sulk. Maybe she spares the occasional thought for you, who knows? Let's order.'

After that, dinner followed a predictable pattern, eased by alcohol into a mellow trough of fraternal wellbeing. On the pavement outside, with a cab thrumming patiently at the kerb, they embraced, rocking slightly like dancers.

Seppi slapped Robert's back. 'Come and visit us, will you? We're always there, we'd love to see you.'

'Thanks, I may do.'

'And good luck with everything.'

'Thanks.'

They drew back, hands still on each other's shoulders. Seppi gave his brother a little shake. 'I nag you because I love you.'

'I know.'

'Okay.'

Seppi got into the cab, sat down and leaned out with his hand on the door.

'If you can't go back, go forward. And pocket the pride, Roberto, it's not worth it!'

As Robert wandered up Kensington Gore towards the park, he considered the worth of pride. It seemed to him that recent events had stripped him of virtually all his. He'd heard it said, and possibly even said himself on occasion, that others placed on you the value that you placed on yourself. If that were the case, he thought grimly, he had better hang on to the last remnant or it was a poor look-out.

He crossed into the park. It was midnight, but away from the glare of the streets and with a full moon the spaces of this *rus in urbe* were luminous. It looked tranquil but seethed with the rustling secrecy of night. It was easy to imagine that time more than a hundred years ago when this place and others like it had been the biggest sexual market place in London, the air alive with the susurration of illicit liaisons both private and commercial, the paths teeming with the nocturnal traffic of prostitution. A huge open secret in the close fabric of Victorian society.

Now it was still here, the sex, but more in the form of couples using the park through choice or necessity. Less clandestine, he supposed, but more furtive. In a time of so-called individual morality and pick-and-mix principles, what was right? Despite, or because of, his Catholic upbringing Robert had a horror of organised religion whereas Sian had been a churchgoer of a bloodless Anglican kind. But now he could almost have wished for divine intervention, for a shaft of light to split the sky and a sonorous voice to tell him what to do: the atheist's simplistic way out. And, he reminded himself, not even a realistic one since it assumed he had a choice. The truth was he was finding out what it was to be in other people's hands, and it was a humbling experience.

He crossed the bridge and followed the western side of the Serpentine in the direction of the Bayswater Road. The water was silken smooth, though he could hear the occasional soft splash of animal goings-on near the bank. By the statue of Peter Pan he stopped and sat on the step at the foot of the statue. A host of small carved creatures, rabbits, butterflies, birds, fairies, clustered at his shoulder. He wondered how many tens of thousands of children's hands, touching and stroking, it would take before the statue's detail was worn away, and the boy who never grew up was standing on top of a bumpy bronze outcrop like a termites' nest . . .

He lit a small cigar and inhaled deeply, savouring it. Exhaled, long and slow. As the first haze of aromatic smoke evaporated he saw a woman on the far bank. She was standing on the path, flanked by the dark masses of trees and shrubs that lined the bank on either side, her silhouette clear against the pale moonlit grass.

Given his recent reflections on the park's history he could be forgiven for thinking he had seen a ghost. Robert peered at the woman's long, high-necked dark clothes and neat black boots . . . the extravagantly coiffed hair . . . the rakishly elegant feather . . . her still, white face. For a long moment, time blurred.

He stood up, crushing the cigar beneath his foot, and moved to the opposite side of the path, near the water. As he did so he was possessed by the absolute certainty that the woman was looking straight back at him – not just gazing across the water, but subjecting him to the same intense scrutiny. The air seemed to close around them, cutting them off in their dreamlike state. Because of the not great but unbridgeable distance between them Robert felt that to move would be to break the spell. He would have called, but his throat seemed to be silted up with the heavy, electric silence.

The woman moved, and he saw that she was wearing a black cobweb shawl, and to rearrange it she spread it wide, like wings, with her thin white arms, before folding it back around her. The arms, the gesture, an inclination of the head that revealed glossy fronds of spiked hair, made him catch his breath.

Stella, he thought – are you there?

Until the man moved she was only aware of the minute red pulse of his smoke in the darkness at the base of the statue. A tramp, she assumed. She often walked here if she had time to kill before the show, there was a sort of nocturnal fraternity of which she was a part.

But when he stepped forward to the water's edge she knew he was watching her. There was an urgency, a focus, an immediate shock of connection . . . She could tell from his stance that he could not only see her, but was gazing intently. She was rooted to the spot. His gaze was like a soft net thrown over her, holding her in place. She was suddenly cold. Taking a long, shivering breath she opened her shawl and wrapped it close around her heart.

Around the memory of Robert.

A second later a lone swan slid across the dark sheet of water between them, the spreading V of its gentle wake softening and melting until the point where it touched either bank, linking them together.

CHAPTER TWENTY ONE

'The water is wide,
I cannot get o'er,
And neither have I wings to fly . . .'
—English folk song

Spencer 1997

After the '61 reunion Spencer had said he wouldn't ever be back, but this was different. This time, it was a pilgrimage of an entirely personal kind, made on his mother's behalf.

No one apart from Caroline – not even Hannah – could have persuaded him to change his mind. And even she had influenced him from beyond the grave. He'd half promised that he would take her back to England for a holiday, but she'd never pushed the matter and when she became ill she deteriorated with such terrifying speed that it was clear no such trip was going to take place. After she died he tried to clear his mind of the whole thing. But his seventy-seventh birthday, when he could no longer avoid thinking of himself as old, caused him to take stock, and Caroline's wishes were right there in the debit column. He suggested to Hannah that they go together as part of a longer trip to Europe.

'Europe we should do,' she said. 'Some time. But the England bit's all yours.'

'Not really, I'd be going there for my mother.'

'Yours and hers then. Whatever.'

Spencer didn't press her. She was nobody's fool, she sensed a no-go area. She had always treated the past, and particularly the war, with a reserve that was part discretion part self-protection. He didn't kid himself that it was only he who had secrets: he still knew almost nothing about his wife's lost years, and the lost baby. They'd rebuilt themselves and there was nothing to be gained by digging up the foundations.

In the end he did go on his own, and it felt right.

He went to Church Norton for a day, but only to see what the locals had done with the money. Over the years he'd resisted all further attempts to get him back, responding first with many excuses and expressions of regret, and winding up more recently by dumping the invitations unread in the bin. All that was over, not just the war but the subsequent meeting with Rosemary. They had not exchanged so much as a letter since. What happened had been a good and fitting farewell.

It was a cool, playful English summer's day with high cloud, splashes of pale sunshine, occasional handfuls of rain on the breeze. But they'd done a good job with the memorial – a P-51 propellor mounted on a handsome stone triptych bearing the badges of the various flying groups, and flanked by flagstaffs – and he was touched to see that a small memorial garden by the gate on to the road was carefully tended and bright with flowers. The litter bin was overflowing, and he picked up a Coke can that had gone astray and stuffed it back in, wiping his hand on the grass afterwards. Inside the gate was a a small plinth with a *bas-relief* layout of the airfield as it had been during the war, and 'You are here' to help sightseers orientate themselves. All around, it was much the same as his last visit, the same runways still intact, the ready rooms full of straw and sugar beet, one smart new barn, and the munitions sheds at the bottom of the hill pretty well gone back to nature, their brick skeletons all tangled with bindweed and bright with willowherb, daisies and dandelions.

He heard the rumble of an engine and saw a tractor making its way up from the direction of the new barn, where there was road-traffic access. He felt conspicuous standing there in his baseball jacket and cap, such an obvious Yank in this rustic English scene, and sure enough the tractor pulled up at the intersection. The driver killed the engine and got out, walking slowly towards him looking at the ground as the English so often did, to show that although they were coming your way they were not going to embarrass anyone by too much early eye contact.

Spencer decided to make the running.

'Morning! I was taking a look at this fine memorial.'

'How do you do?' The driver, a man in his mid-forties, held out a hand and they shook. 'Don't mind my asking, but have you got a connection with all this?'

'I was here in the war, yes.'

The man nodded, not one to make a big song and dance, then repeated the nod in the direction of the propellor. 'You fly one of those?'

'That's right.'

'Lovely job.'

Spencer recognised this as some kind of British idiom encompassing the memorial, the plane, himself, the war, this chance meeting, but to him it seemed more specific than that and he responded accordingly.

'You bet it was.'

'Are you staying round here?'

'No, no – just passing through.'

The man looked past him at the brimming garbage bin, and sucked his teeth disapprovingly. 'Dear, oh, dear, that doesn't give a very good impression of the modern village, does it? I'm afraid this layby's a bit of a snog-spot, if you know what I mean.'

'What – like a lovers' lane?'

'That's right. Not quite the ticket but can't be helped.'

When they'd shaken hands again and the man had gone back to his tractor, Spencer realised that on the contrary he was quite pleased about the courting couples. Good luck to them. After all when the Yanks had been here there had been only two things on their mind: winning the war and getting the girls. It was appropriate that with one of those out of the way, the other should continue unabated in the shadow of the Mustang.

*   *   *

The other village, the real focus of his trip, presented particular problems. Not only did he not know it personally, but what he did know came only from Caroline's imagination. This was the perfect English village that her friend Cissy had told her about. The place where Cissy herself had been born and raised and several generations of her family before her. Spencer had prepared himself for a let-down. Where a place had so much hope, memory, and – to put it bluntly – fantasy attached to it the reality could only disappoint.

He'd made a few notes to himself based on what he could remember, and once he'd checked in at the pub he left the car in the carpark and set out to get his bearings before lunch.

It was eerie, like taking part in a film that he'd watched and enjoyed many times. There was plenty of new development, but the core, the old part of Fort Mayden which he'd heard talked of so often, was exactly as Caroline had described it. It was easy to imagine how Cissy, a country girl working in a drab city house, might have idealised the place, and talked it up to her rapt audience of one lonely little girl. Yet here, incredibly, it all was, the landmarks showing through the veneer of modernity like a hidden pattern in a child's puzzle book. He was enchanted to see the high street with its snaggle of uneven roofs and chimneys, the houses made of that particular bland mix of honey-grey stone that he recognised as typical of this area . . . the Flying Horse pub with its distinctive sign, a palfrey-like Pegasus with great feathered hooves and snorting nostrils . . . the row of terraced cottages set back from the stream, each doorway accessible by its own narrow bridge . . . the fine tower of the parish church of St Catherine, topped by a listing weathervane . . . At the church he was reminded of something and looked up towards the hill to the north of the village. To the west he could see the crown of trees that must mark the site of the big house, but to the east he could make out nothing of the tiny 'fairy church' that his mother had mentioned. He decided that after lunch he would walk up that way – or perhaps drive – and see what was there.

A tad selfconsciously – he was never especially at home in

places of organised worship – he went into St Catherine's and found it mercifully empty. He put a pound coin in the wooden plate near the font, and took a couple of postcards from the rack, slipping them into his breast pocket. Then he slowly patrolled the side aisles, studying the plaques and engraved scrolls on the walls.

He found what he was looking for on the wall of the chancel, behind the choir stalls – a whole flock of Latimers, each one with a fulsome encomium, some in verse and many stanzas long. He scanned them carefully and found 'Henry Felix Latimer, Captain 8th Hussars, killed in the heroic charge at the Battle of Balaklava, October 1854. A beloved son and a valiant officer of the Queen. May rest eternal be his, a good and faithful servant'. A little to one side and lower down was a simple stone tablet with the name 'Colin John Bartlemas, Pte, 8th Huzzars, groom to the above. Died in the service of his country, in Varna, Bulgaria, June 1854'.

Checking a little sheepishly that no one was about, Spencer took a photograph of the Latimer inscription with its two warlike angels, and of the humbler one below it. Then on an impulse he stepped back and took a second photo of the whole wall. Then he went out into the churchyard.

Here again it didn't take long to find the Latimer plot, notable among whom were the twin graves of a Maria and Percy, 'Joined in death as in life' just in case that might have escaped one's attention, and presided over by more angels, with trumpets, and some portly cherubim carrying garlands to preserve their modesty. The plot was mowed and weeded, but not attended in any personal way that he could see, chiefly he supposed because the most recent grave was the large double one, and there appeared to have been no Latimer issue after that point. The Bartlemas tribe on the other hand seemed still to be going strong, and the latest to shuffle off his mortal coil was Barry Bartlemas, 1921–1995, 'much loved and sadly missed', who could still boast a perforated urn full of brown-edged roses.

Spencer took a photo of that, too, and went to the saloon bar of the Flying Horse for lunch. He was pleasantly surprised by the extent and range of the menu, and the presence of Budweiser in the cooler, but in a when-in-Rome spirit he ordered steak and kidney pie and a pint of IPA. The place was weekday-quiet and he fell into conversation with the guy behind the bar as he sat waiting for his food.

'You're a long way from home.'

'Couldn't be much further,' agreed Spencer. 'Wyoming's where I come from.'

'That what they call cowboy country?'

'Sure is. The most beautiful country on earth. Have one with me?'

'Thank you, squire, I'll have a half.'

'Tell me . . .' Spencer watched the bartender fill his glass. 'Is there still a family called Latimer around here?'

'Latimer.' The man gulped, wiped his upper lip, narrowed his eyes. 'It rings a bell, but I couldn't say. I don't know anyone of that name.'

'There's a few mentioned at the church. Did they used to be up at the big house or something? Kind of squires?'

'Could be. You're right.' He pointed a finger. 'But not any more, for as long as anyone can remember. Bells is an arts centre these days – potting, painting, poetry. Packs 'em in all through the year, people who can't cope with a holiday unless there's a bit of self-improvement thrown in. Beats me, give me sun and sand any day, but there's a lot of it about.'

'Is it open? I mean, can a person go and look round?'

'Don't see why not. A couple of the outbuildings have been turned into private houses, but the main house is a business concern.'

'I might just do that . . .' Spencer decided to pursue the advantage. 'What about people called Bartlemas? Are there any of those around?'

The landlord chuckled and shook his head. 'I should say so. It's like they say about rats, you're never more than ten feet away from one in this village.'

'Still going strong, huh?'

'Yup. Parish Council, cricket club, *boules* out the back here. There's scads of the buggers, pardon my French.'

'Really, is that so? My mother – she was English – used to know someone called Cissy Bartlemas.'

'Cissy, yeah, round in the sheltered housing but still going strong.'

Spencer caught his breath. 'You're telling me she's still alive?'

'Very much so.'

'But surely – she must be a colossal age?'

'Got the telegram from Her Majesty in April.'

'And she still lives on her own?'

'With a little help from her friends, and a lot from her family and Social Services. No, she does bloody well does Cissy, got all her buttons on.'

'Do you think she'd mind if I called on her?'

The landlord gave a wry grin. 'You like sweet sherry . . .?'

If Spencer hadn't been told her age, he'd never have guessed it. Cissy Bartlemas was skinny and wrinkled and her snow-white hair was thinning, but her eyes were bright and her voice was firm. She wore a big old pleated skirt that seemed to begin under her armpits, and a flowery blouse. On her feet, in a concession to the fine weather, she wore short white socks and rather fearsome punched-leather sandals. The little chink of leg that he could see between skirt and sock was surprisingly smooth and comely. A cheerful girl in platform trainers and a blue uniform asked him if he'd like tea, and when he havered, Cissy said: 'Well, I would, so put the kettle on.'

He perched on the sofa. It was unusual at his age to feel so much the junior of someone else, he couldn't quite get the weight of the occasion, but Cissy was more than up to it.

'So what can I do for you, Mr American?'

'Spencer.'

'Mr Spencer.'

'No, it's rather confusing, it's Spencer McColl.'

'Mr McColl then.'

He gave up. 'Okay, I'll jump right in. Cissy – my mother used to know you.'

'And what was your mother's name?'

'Caroline Wells.' He didn't add any more clues for the moment, he wanted to see what reaction the name caused.

'Little Carolina, yes.'

He could scarcely believe it. 'You remember her?'

'Carolina, of course I do.'

It all seemed too easy, but maybe this was the famed ability of the very old to recall the distant past. He leaned forward, smiling and frowning, wanting to be polite but to pin her down, too.

'So when was it that you knew her?'

'When I was in domestic service in Oxford before the war.'

'That would be the First World War.'

'The Great War,' she agreed, as if there were only one worth mentioning.

Incredibly, she was for real. Over one hundred years old and sharp as a tack. He could feel the frown dissolving as the smile spread.

'Tell me about it. My mother used to talk about you such a lot, your friendship meant a great deal to her.'

'We were both lonely, you see, both lonely. There was lots of love in my home but I was a long way away from it. She was in her own home but there was no love in it at all.'

This observation made Spencer's eyes sting. He realised that while his mother had never said as much, he had always known it.

'How old were you then?' he asked, no longer trying to soften the question for her benefit.

'Quite young, let me see . . .'

At this point the care attendant had arrived with the tea tray and said: 'Cissy, remember when your nephew was round that day and you were talking? He said you were sixteen when you went into service.'

'Sixteen? Yes, that would be right.'

'Good lord, you were just a child.' Spencer was shocked.

'I was not, I was a hard-working girl making my way.'

The care attendant smiled indulgently towards Spencer. 'That's telling you. Milk and sugar?'

As the tea was poured he realised that there hadn't been such a very great difference in the ages of the two girls – his mother had been about nine or ten during that time when she'd escaped and run up the ever-narrowing stairs to the attic floor and sat gazing out across Barton Wood and the dewpond towards a happy home she didn't even know. And now she was dead, having faded away in a nursing home while Cissy, the tough little parlourmaid, was still living under her own roof. He felt as if the whole pattern of his life had been grabbed and violently shaken, the past nudging the present and threatening to blunder right through.

The attendant put Cissy's mug, and a plate with two chocolate biscuits, on the table next to her, and did the same for him, though he raised his hand to ward off the biscuits.

'Well then,' said the girl, 'as you've got company, I'm going to pop and see Mr Murchy and I'll look in on you again on my way through. Della will be over at half-past five to give you your tea, okay?'

'Yes, you run along. This gentleman will look after me.'

Spencer must have looked alarmed, for the girl said: 'She's got a wicked sense of humour, haven't you, Cissy?' and winked at him as she left.

He watched with some trepidation as Cissy lifted the mug and stretched long, trembling lips towards it to sip. When she'd put it down and was dunking a biscuit, he remarked: 'There are lots of your family still in this neighbourhood, I believe.'

'Oh, there are . . .' She took a mouthful of tea-soaked biscuit and swallowed it down. 'In the village and in the churchyard.'

'Yes, I had a look around the church. I see one of your ancestors was killed in the Crimea.'

'That was my uncle. My father's brother, Colin. He and my brother worked with the horses at Bells.'

'So your father's name was . . . ?'

'Ben Bartlemas.'

'I've not heard of him.'

'He was the naughty one, the bad boy. The one who ran off with Belle Latimer.'

'Did he now? Ideas above his station, huh?'

593

'Depends which way you look at it,' said Cissy sharply, not to be patronised.

He let it pass. 'So what happened?'

'She got tired of him, double-quick. Tired of him, tired of everything, went off to Italy. It broke her mother's heart and my father's spirit. He came back to Fort Mayden with his tail between his legs, they say, married my mother – did as he was told from then on.'

'Great story,' said Spencer. Cissy grunted. 'So what about the mother?'

'Rachel Latimer. She was a window so that left her with nothing.' She pursed her lips disapprovingly. 'Grew old and cold up there on her own, but I hear she was a cold fish anyway.'

'You can hardly blame her.'

'Did I say that?'

He took this as rhetorical. 'And Bells is the big house on the hill?'

'A beautiful house. Beautiful. But there are no Latimers now, you see . . . Lots of us Bartlemice, but not a single Latimer left.'

'You're sturdy stock, you –' he tried it '—Bartlemice.'

She didn't react to this, but said: 'You want to go up and take a look.'

It might have been a question, a statement or a suggestion.

'Yes,' he said, 'I do. I will.'

He drove the two miles up to the main road, turned off in due course into the lane, and then down the long drive. He parked in front of the big house. The open front door revealed a reception area with a desk, noticeboards and a table covered in leaflets. He could hear the muted murmur of voices in other rooms, a soft burst of laughter. He went over to the desk and explained to the receptionist that he wasn't a prospective customer, but would like to look round the gardens.

'Certainly you may,' she replied heartily. 'Would you care to see the house? We have a group here this weekend but they're all in workshops at the moment.'

'No – no, thank you. I'd just been told it was pretty up here and I have a distant family connection, so—'

'You're not some long-lost transatlantic *Latimer*, surely?'

'No, far more tenuous than that. A long story.'

'Please.' She waved a large, commanding hand. 'Feel free. The barn and the stables are private houses, but they're a very tolerant lot.'

'Thank you.' He turned to go and then remembered something. 'Say, would you happen to know – is there some kind of little church up around this way?'

'There was. It's tumbledown now, but well worth a visit. A numinous place.'

'Numinous . . . is that right?'

'I should warn you there's no road access and it's quite a climb. But if you leave Bells by the stableyard gate—' she gestured firmly with her right arm '—you'll see the bridleway sign and you just keep following it. The view is quite wonderful.'

'Thanks, I might give it a try.'

He walked a slow circuit of the grounds, not wanting to overstretch himself if he was going to attempt the hill-climb afterwards. He crossed the wide lawn, where a badminton-net and some croquet hoops had been erected, and entered the woods. In amongst the trees he fetched his foot a painful crack on a random lump of stone sticking out of the ground. It was so unexpected that he parted the long grass for a closer look, thinking it might be the last vestige of some tied cottage or other, but it turned out to be a single rock like a milestone, covered in moss and lichen.

He hit a footpath and turned left. When he came out on the brow of the hill he found he was looking right over the valley and the village to the White Horse on the other side. It was a fine sight, with the cloud shadow rippling over it, and he paused to catch his breath and drink it in. Then he set off along the crest, returning to the house through a small gate at the side and going round the back through a more formal garden with gravel walks. At the far side of the house was a parking area, bounded by the house itself, a post-and-rail fence and the blind back wall of a barn. He rounded the side of the barn and came to a five-bar gate at the intersection of the driveway with a sign reading FOOTPATH TO OLD CHURCH HILL. At the side of the gate was a stile, and remembering the words of the woman on reception he climbed over.

The development of the outbuildings was nicely done, with the old pump and mounting block left in place, and two horse troughs filled with trailing geraniums. The barn seemed closed and quiet, but the door of the stable-house stood open and a large chocolate-coloured labrador trotted out and wagged round him, followed by a small girl of about four.

Spencer liked kids about the same as he liked adults – some more than others.

'Hallo there,' he said. 'Okay if I cross your front yard?'

'It's allowed,' she replied, and was joined by a nice, bluff-looking heavily pregnant woman whom he took to be her mother.

'Morning!' he said to the mother. 'Is that right, I'm allowed to come through here?'

'Absolutely. You'll see the footpath signs on the other side.'

'Thanks.'

'It's lovely up there, quite magical.'

'So I hear.'

'Good luck!'

He thought for a moment that the dog was going to follow him as Tallulah used to do at Buck's, but when he reached the stile on the other side it returned to the sunny doorway.

The receptionist had been right, it was a long climb, and a tough one for a man of his age, but he took it in easy stages, pausing every hundred yards or so but trying not to look back, saving the view till he reached the top.

The church was a ruin, its squat outline and scattering of graves like a partridge with her chicks amongst the long grass and high-summer wild flowers. Up here there was a wind, its long breaths combing the hill, shivering through the arches and between the standing stones. Spencer sat down and leaned his back against one of the tilting graves, its surface warmed by the afternoon sun. Seen from this angle the village was a tiny huddle of ancient roofs and the White Horse leapt away from him. He recalled a hymn they used to sing during the war. He hadn't thought of it once till now, didn't even realise it had lodged in his memory. *Before the hills in order stood, or earth received her frame . . .* It seemed to him that these small English hills, and the valley between them, represented that order, created by divine will or the buckling of the earth's crust, and now bearing the hallmarks of man's endeavours, old and new. Tomorrow, with the long tedium of the transatlantic flight ahead, he'd walk up the other side to see the horse close to.

He dozed for a little while and was woken by a drop in temperature. The sky had clouded over and the wind had become cool and blustery. It was hell getting to his feet, he was glad there was no one about to see him. He got on to his knees and used the grave stone to haul himself upright, noticing as he did so that it was another Latimer, 'Hugo, beloved husband of Rachel, 1830–1854' – another Victorian life cut cruelly short by something or other. Poor Rachel. All the same Spencer found himself thinking of the funeral cortège winding its way up the hill – how in hell had they done it? She must have loved him.

He began to retrace his steps, descending slowly, chary of his knees. At the first bend, taking a breather, he glanced back and saw to his surprise the silhouette of a woman in the churchyard, a youthful, hippyish figure with long strands of hair and a billowing skirt whipped by the wind. He hoped to God she hadn't witnessed his undignified struggle a few minutes ago.

He continued on his way and when he next looked back, she was gone.

WAKING

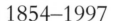

1854–1997

The photographer had taken care till now. He wished faithfully to record the people and places of this strange war, but not in such a way as to cause undue distress at home. So where a place had been the scene of a famous victory or a heroic defeat he was careful to wait until the dead and wounded had been removed. The text could describe what had happened, the numbers and scale of casualties: for them to be seen would be altogether too brutal a shock.

Yet the events of today were so extraordinary that they defied belief even in those, like him, who had witnessed them. He could not be sure whether what had taken place was heroism, or sheer folly, or both, nor how the news of it would be received in England. The glory, the élan, the stupidity, the carnage – they were still warring in his head.

That was why he wanted to take this photograph – to still those terrible mental pictures. The bareheaded young officer was lying alongside his horse for all the world as if the two of them were asleep in an English meadow: an image of war's waste, and of the peace of those it snatched from the midst of life. A symbol of trust, devotion – tranquillity even – after the shocking madness of the day.

He did not even go round the still figures to the other side, to study another angle. He did not wish to see the hideous wounds from which they'd died. From here they appeared unmarked. Quietly and deliberately, with a sort of reverence, he climbed down from the waggon and set up his camera.

When he had finished he left them as he found them, just as if they really were asleep. In the distance, the bells of Sevastopol were pealing, sounding a great victory.

First the mare struggled to her feet, then the foal.

They watched as it tottered and stumbled, its pipe-cleaner legs threatening to buckle, its small wild head scything and questing for its mother's nourishment. As it locked on, the mare tenderly licked the gummy fluid off its hide. Strands of the stuff hung from the foal's stumpy tuft of tail. A crow settled about ten metres off, its cold black eye on the smoking afterbirth.

Robert took Stella's stained hands in both of his.

'Look at us.'

'Bloody but unbowed.'

'I'll say.'

She felt washed through by a pristine, exhausted bliss. The sun was warm on their backs. Her hands were enfolded in his, lost to her. Slowly she allowed her head to droop on to his shoulder. As she did so, the crow took off and flew away. They could hear the soft, urgent suckling of the foal.

One at a time the bells of seven parishes began to peal, and the White Horse leapt in jubilation towards the sun.